Frederick Forsyth

THE DEVIL'S ALTERNATIVE

THE FOURTH PROTOCOL

CRESSET EDITIONS

This edition published in 1998 by Cresset Editions,
an imprint of Random House UK Ltd,
20 Vauxhall Bridge Road, London SW1V 2SA

The Devil's Alternative first published in 1979 by Hutchinson
The Fourth Protocol first published in 1984 by Hutchinson

Printed and bound in Australia by Griffin Press

ISBN 0 0918 6683 9

THE DEVIL'S ALTERNATIVE

For Frederick Stuart,
who does not know yet

Prologue

The castaway would have been dead before sundown but for the sharp eyes of an Italian seaman called Mario. Even when he was spotted he had lapsed into unconsciousness, the exposed parts of his near-naked body grilled to second-degree burns by the relentless sun, and those parts submerged in sea water soft and white between the salt-sores like the limbs of a rotting goose.

Mario Curcio was the cook/steward on the *Garibaldi*, an amiable old rust-bucket out of Brindisi, thumping her way eastward towards Cape Ince and on to Trabzon in the far eastern corner of the north shore of Turkey. She was on her way to pick up a cargo of almonds from Anatolia.

Just why Mario decided that morning in the last ten days of April 1982 to empty his bucket of potato peelings over the weather rail instead of through the rubbish chute at the poop he could never explain, nor was he ever asked to. But perhaps to take a breath of fresh Black Sea air and break the monotony of the steam-heat in the cramped galley, he stepped out on to deck, strolled to the starboard rail, and hurled his rubbish to an indifferent but patient ocean. He turned away and started to lumber back to his duties. After two steps he stopped, frowned, turned and walked back to the rail, puzzled and uncertain.

The ship was heading east-northeast to clear Cape Ince, so that as he shielded his eyes and gazed abaft the beam the noon sun was almost straight in his face. But he was sure he had seen something out there on the blue-green rolling swell between the ship and the coast of Turkey twenty miles to the south. Unable to see it again, he trotted up the after deck, mounted the outside ladders to the wing of the bridge and peered again. Then he saw it, quite clearly, for half a second between the softly moving hills of water. He turned to the open door behind him, leading into the wheelhouse, and shouted, '*Capitano*.'

Captain Vittorio Ingrao took some persuading, for Mario was a simple lad, but he was enough of a sailor to know that if a man might be out there on the water he was duty-bound to turn his ship around and have a closer look, and his radar had indeed revealed an echo. It took the captain half an hour to bring the *Garibaldi* around and back to the spot Mario had pointed at, and then he too saw it.

The skiff was barely twelve feet long, and not very wide. A light craft, of the type that could have been a ship's jolly boat. Forward of amidships there was a single thwart across the boat with a hole in it for the stepping of a mast. But either there had never been a mast, or it had been ill-secured and had gone overboard. With the *Garibaldi* stopped and wallowing in the swell, Captain Ingrao leaned on the bridge wing rail and watched Mario and the bo'sun Paolo Longhi set off in the motor lifeboat to bring the skiff alongside. From his elevation he could look down into the skiff as it was towed closer.

The man in it was lying on his back in several inches of sea water. He was gaunt and emaciated, bearded and unconscious, his head to one side, breathing in short gasps. He moaned a few times as he was lifted aboard and the sailors' hands touched his flayed shoulders and chest.

There was one permanently spare cabin in the *Garibaldi*, kept free as a sort of sick-bay, and the castaway was taken to it. Mario, at his own request, was given time off to tend the man, whom he soon came to regard as his personal property, as a boy will take especial care of a puppy he has personally rescued from death. Longhi, the bo'sun, gave the man a shot of morphine from the first-aid chest to spare him the pain, and the pair of them set to work on the sunburn.

Being Calabrians they knew a bit about sunburn and prepared the best sunburn salve in the world. Mario brought from his galley a fifty-fifty mixture of fresh lemon juice and wine vinegar in a basin, a light cotton cloth torn from his pillow case and a bowl of ice cubes. Soaking the cloth in the mixture and wrapping it round a dozen ice cubes, he gently pressed the pad to the worst areas, where the ultra-violet rays had bitten through almost to the bone. Plumes of steam rose from the unconscious man as the freezing astringent drew the heat out of the scorched flesh. The man shuddered.

'Better a fever than death by burn-shock,' Mario told him in Italian. The man could not hear, and if he had he could not have understood.

Longhi joined his skipper on the after deck where the skiff had been stowed.

'Anything?' he asked.

Captain Ingrao shook his head.

'Nothing on the man either. No watch, no name tag. A pair of cheap underpants with no label. And his beard looks about ten days old.'

'There's nothing here either,' said Ingrao. 'No mast, no sail, no oars. No food and no water container. No name on the boat even. But it could have peeled off.'

'A tourist from a beach resort, blown out to sea?' asked Longhi.

Ingrao shrugged. 'Or a survivor from a small freighter,' he said. 'We'll be at Trabzon in two days. The Turkish authorities can solve that one when he wakes up and talks. Meanwhile let's get under way. Oh, and we must cable our agent there and tell him what's happened. We'll need an ambulance on the quay when we dock.'

Two days later the castaway, still barely conscious and unable to speak, was tucked up between white sheets in a sick ward, in the small municipal hospital of Trabzon.

Mario the sailor had accompanied his castaway in the ambulance from the quay to the hospital, along with the ship's agent and the port's medical officer of health who had insisted on checking the delirious man for communicable diseases. After waiting an hour by the bedside, he had bade his unconscious friend farewell and returned to the *Garibaldi* to prepare the crew's lunch. That had been the previous day, and the old Italian tramp steamer had sailed during the evening.

Now another man stood by the bedside, accompanied by a police officer and the short-coated doctor. All three were Turkish, but the short, broad man in the civilian suit spoke passable English.

'He'll pull through,' said the doctor, 'but he's very sick for the moment. Heat-stroke, second-degree sunburns, exposure, and by the look of it he hasn't eaten for days. Generally weak.'

'What are these?' asked the civilian, gesturing at the drip-feed tubes that entered both the man's arms.

'Concentrated glucose drip for nourishment, saline drip to offset the shock,' said the doctor. 'The sailors probably saved his life by taking the heat out of the burns, but we've bathed him in calomine to help the healing process. Now it's between him and Allah.'

Umit Erdal, partner in the shipping and trading company of Erdal and Sermit, was the Lloyd's sub-agent for the port of Trabzon, and the *Garibaldi*'s agent had thankfully passed the matter of the castaway over to him. The sick man's eyelids fluttered in the nut-brown, bearded face. Mr Erdal cleared his throat, bent over the figure and spoke in his best English.

'What ... is ... you ... name?' he asked slowly and clearly.

The man groaned and moved his head from side to side several times. The Lloyd's man bent his head closer to listen. '*Zradzhenyi*,' the sick man murmured. '*Zradzhenyi*.'

Erdal straightened up. 'He's not Turkish,' he said with finality, 'but he seems to be called Zradzhenyi. What kind of country would that name come from?'

Both his companions shrugged. 'I'll inform Lloyd's in London,' said Erdal. 'Maybe they'll have news of a missing vessel somewhere in the Black Sea.'

The daily bible of the world's merchant marine fraternity is *Lloyd's List*, which is published Monday to Saturday and contains editorials, features and news on one topic only – shipping. Its partner in harness, *Lloyd's Shipping Index*, gives the movements of the world's 30,000 active merchant vessels: name of ship, owner, flag of registry, year of build, tonnage, where last reported coming from, and where bound.

Both organs are published out of a building complex at Sheepen Place, Colchester, in Essex. It was to this building that Umit Erdal telexed the shipping movements into and out of the port of Trabzon, and added a small extra for the attention of the Lloyd's Shipping Intelligence unit in the same building.

The SI unit checked their maritime casualty records to confirm that there were no recent reports of missing, sunk or simply overdue vessels in the Black Sea, and passed the paragraph over to the editorial desk of the list. Here a sub-editor gave it a mention as a news brief on the front page, including the name the castaway had given as his own. It appeared the following morning.

Most of those who read the *Lloyd's List* that day in late April flipped past the paragraph about the unidentified man in Trabzon.

But the piece caught and held the sharp eyes and the attention of a man in his early thirties who worked as senior clerk and trusted employee in a firm of chartered shipbrokers situated in a small street called Crutched Friars in the centre of the City of London. His colleagues in the firm knew him as Andrew Drake.

Having absorbed the content of the paragraph, Drake left his desk and went to the company boardroom where he consulted a framed chart of the world which showed prevailing wind and ocean current circulation. The winds in the Black Sea during spring and summer are predominantly from the north, and the currents screw anti-clockwise round this small ocean from the southern coast of the Ukraine in the far northwest of the sea, down past the coasts of Romania and Bulgaria, then swing eastwards again into the shipping lanes between Istanbul and Cape Ince.

Drake did some calculations on a scratch pad. A small skiff, setting off from the marshes of the delta of the River Dniester just south of Odessa could make four to five knots with a following wind and favourable current, southwards past Romania and Bulgaria towards Turkey. But after three days it would tend to be carried eastwards, away from the Bosphorus towards the eastern end of the Black Sea.

The 'Weather and Navigation' section of *Lloyd's List* confirmed there had been bad weather nine days earlier in that area. The sort, Drake mused, that could cause a skiff in the hands of an unskilled seaman to capsize, lose its mast and all its contents and leave its occupant, even if he could climb back into it again, at the mercy of the sun and the wind.

Two hours later Andrew Drake asked for a week of his owed holidays, and it was agreed that he could take it, but only starting the following Monday, 3rd May.

He was mildly excited as he waited out the week and bought himself from a nearby agency a return ticket from London to Istanbul. He decided to buy the connecting ticket from Istanbul to Trabzon for cash in Istanbul. He also checked to confirm that a British passport holder needs no visa for Turkey, but after work he secured for himself the needed smallpox vaccination certificate at the British Airways medical centre at Victoria.

He was excited because he thought there just might be a chance that, after years of waiting, he had found the man he was looking for. Unlike the three men by the castaway's bedside two days earlier, he *did* know what country the word *zradzhenyi* came from. He also knew it was not the man's name. The man in the bed had been muttering the word 'betrayed' in his native tongue, and that language was Ukrainian. Which could mean that the man was a refugee Ukrainian partisan.

Andrew Drake, despite his anglicized name, was also a Ukrainian, and a fanatic.

Drake's first call after arriving in Trabzon was at the office of Mr Erdal, whose name he had obtained from a friend at Lloyd's on the grounds that he was taking a holiday on the Turkish coast and, speaking not a word of Turkish, might need some assistance. Umit Erdal, seeing the letter of introduction that Drake was able to produce, was happily unquestioning as to why his visitor should want to see the castaway in the local hospital. He wrote a personal letter of introduction to the hospital administrator, and shortly after lunch Drake was shown into the small one-bed ward where the man lay.

The local Lloyd's agent had already told him that the man, while conscious again, spent much of the time sleeping, and during his periods of wakefulness had so far said absolutely nothing. When Drake entered the room the invalid was lying on his back, eyes closed. Drake drew up a chair and sat by the bedside. For a time he stared at the man's haggard face. After several minutes the man's eyelids flickered, half opened and closed again. Whether he had seen the visitor staring at him intently, Drake did not know. But he knew the man was on the fringe of wakefulness.

Slowly he leaned forward and said clearly in the sick man's ear: '*Shche ne vmerla Ukraina*.'

The words mean, literally, 'Ukraine is not dead', but a looser translation would be, 'Ukraine lives on'. They are the first words of the Ukrainian national anthem, banned by the Russian masters, and would be instantly recognizable by a nationally conscious Ukrainian.

The sick man's eyes flicked open and he regarded Drake intently. After several seconds he asked in Ukrainian, 'Who are you?'

'A Ukrainian, like yourself,' said Drake.

The other man's eyes clouded with suspicion. 'Quisling,' he said.

Drake shook his head. 'No,' he said calmly. 'I am British by nationality, born and bred there, son of a Ukrainian father and an English mother. But in my heart I'm as Ukrainian as you are.'

The man in the bed stared stubbornly at the ceiling.

'I could show you my passport, issued in London, but that would prove nothing. A Chekisti could produce one if he wanted, to try and trick you.' Drake had used the slang term for a Soviet secret policeman and KGB member.

'But you are not in the Ukraine any more, and there are no Chekisti here,' Drake went on. 'You were not washed up on the shores of the Crimea, nor of South Russia or Georgia. You did not land in Romania or Bulgaria either. You were picked up by an Italian ship and landed here at Trabzon. You are in Turkey. You are in the West. You made it.'

The man's eyes were on his face now, alert, lucid, wanting to believe.

'Can you move?' asked Drake.

'I don't know,' said the man.

Drake nodded across the small room to the window, beyond which the sounds of traffic could be heard. 'The KGB can dress up hospital staff to look like Turks,' he said, 'but they cannot change a whole city for one man whom they could torture for a confession if they wanted. Can you make the window?'

Helped by Drake, the castaway hobbled painfully to the window and looked out at the street scene.

'The cars are Austins and Morrises, imported from England,' said Drake. 'Peugeots from France and Volkswagens from West Germany. The words on the billboards are in Turkish. That advertisement over there is for Coca-Cola.'

The man put the back of one hand against his mouth and chewed at the knuckles. He blinked rapidly several times.

'I made it,' he said.

'Yes,' said Drake, 'by a miracle you made it.'

'My name,' said the castaway when he was back in bed, 'is Miroslav Kaminsky. I come from Ternopol. I was the leader of a group of seven Ukrainian partisans.'

Over the next hour the story came out. Kaminsky and six others like him, all from the Ternopol area, once a hotbed of Ukrainian nationalism and where some of the embers still glow, had decided to strike back at the programme of ruthless Russification of their land that had intensified in the sixties and become a 'final solution' in the seventies and early eighties for the whole area of Ukrainian national art, poetry, literature, language and consciousness. In six months of operations they had ambushed and killed two low-level Party secretaries – Russians imposed by Moscow on Ternopol – and a plain-clothes KGB agent. Then had come the betrayal.

Whoever had talked, he too had died in the hail of fire as the green insignia of the KGB special troops had closed in on the country cottage where the group was meeting to plan its next operation. Only Kaminsky had escaped, running like an animal through the undergrowth, hiding by day in barns and woodland, moving by night, heading south towards the coast with a vague idea of jumping a Western ship.

It had been impossible to get near the docks of Odessa. Living off potatoes and swedes from the fields, he had sought refuge in the swampy country of the Dniester estuary south-west of Odessa, towards the Romanian border. Finally, coming by night on a small fishing hamlet on a creek, he had stolen a skiff with a stepped mast and a small sail. He had never been in a sailing boat before, and knew nothing of the sea. Trying to manage the sail and the rudder, just holding on and praying, he had let the skiff run before the wind, southwards by the stars and the sun.

By pure luck he had avoided the patrol boats that cruise the offshore waters of the Soviet Union, and the fishing fleets. The tiny sliver of wood which contained him had slipped past the coastal radar sweeps until he was out of range. Then he was lost, somewhere between Romania and Crimea, heading south but far from the nearest shipping lanes, if he did but know where they were anyway. The storm caught him unawares. Not knowing how to shorten sail in time, he had capsized, spending the night using his last reserves of strength clinging to the upturned hull. By morning he had righted the skiff and crawled inside. His clothes, which he had taken off to let the night wind cool his skin, were gone. So also were his few raw potatoes, the open lemonade bottle of fresh water, the sail and the rudder. The pain came shortly after sunrise as the heat of the day increased. Oblivion came on the third day after the storm. When he regained consciousness he was in a bed, taking the pain of the burns in silence, listening to the voices he thought were Bulgarian. For six days he had kept his eyes closed and his mouth shut.

Andrew Drake heard him out with a song in his heart. He had found the man he had waited years for.

'I'll go and see the Swiss consul in Istanbul and try to obtain temporary travel documents for you from the Red Cross,' he said when Kaminsky showed signs of tiring. 'If I do, I can probably get you to England, at least on a temporary visa. Then we can try for asylum. I'll return in a few days.'

By the door he paused.

'You can't go back, you know,' he told Kaminsky. 'But with your help, I can. It's what I want. It's what I've always wanted.'

Andrew Drake took longer than he had thought in Istanbul, and it was not until 16th May that he was able to fly back to Trabzon with travel papers for Kaminsky. He had extended his leave after a long telephone call to London and a row with the broking firm's junior partner, but it was worth it. For through Kaminsky he was certain he could fulfil the single burning ambition of his life.

The tsarist and later Soviet empire, despite its monolithic appearance from outside, has two Achilles heels. One is the problem of feeding its 250 millions. The other is euphemistically called 'the nationalities question'. In the fourteen republics ruled by the Russian Republic are several score identifiable non-Russian nations, and the biggest and perhaps the most nationally conscious is the Ukraine. By 1982 the Great Russian state numbered only 120 millions out of the 250; the next most populous and richest with 70 millions was

Ukraine, which was one reason why under tsars and Politburo the Ukraine had always been singled out for special attention and particularly ruthless Russification.

The second reason lay in its history. Ukraine has always traditionally been divided into two, which has been its downfall: Western and Eastern Ukraine. Western Ukraine stretches from Kiev westwards to the Polish border. The eastern part is more Russified, having dwelt under the tsars for centuries; during those same centuries Western Ukraine was part of the old Austro-Hungarian empire. Its spiritual and cultural orientation was and remains more western than the rest, except possibly the three Baltic states which are too small to resist. Ukrainians read and write with Roman letters, not Cyrillic script; they are overwhelmingly Uniate Catholics, not Russian Orthodox Christians. Their language, poetry, literature, arts and traditions pre-date the rise of the Rus conquerors who swept down from the north.

In 1918 with the break-up of Austro-Hungary, Western Ukrainians tried desperately for a separate republic out of the empire's ruins; unlike the Czechs, Slovaks and Magyars, they failed and were annexed in 1919 by Poland as the province of Galicia. When Hitler swept into western Poland in 1939, Stalin came in from the east with the Red Army and took Galicia. In 1941 the Germans took it. What followed was a violent and vicious confusion of hopes, fears and loyalties. Some hoped for concessions from Moscow if they fought the Germans; others mistakenly thought Free Ukraine lay through the defeat of Moscow by Berlin and joined the Ukrainian Division, which fought against the Red Army, in German uniform. Others, like Kaminsky's father, took to the Carpathian Mountains as guerrillas and fought first one invader then the next, then the first again. They all lost; Stalin won and pushed his empire westwards to the Bug River, the new border for Poland. West Ukraine came under the new tsars, the Politburo, but the old dreams lived on. Apart from one glimmer in the last days of Khrushchev, the programme to crush them once and for all had steadily intensified.

Stepan Drach, a student from Rovno, joined up with the

Ukrainian Division. He was one of the lucky ones; he survived the war and was captured by the British in Austria in 1945. Sent to work as a farm labourer in Norfolk, he would certainly have been sent back for execution by the NKVD in 1946 as the British Foreign Office and American State Department quietly conspired to return the two million 'victims of Yalta' to the mercies of Stalin. But he was lucky again. Behind a Norfolk haystack he tumbled a Land Army girl and she became pregnant. Marriage was the answer, and six months later, on compassionate grounds, he was excused repatriation and allowed to stay. Freed from farm labour, he used the knowledge he had gained as a radio operator to set up a small repair shop in Bradford, a centre for Britain's 30,000 Ukrainians. The first baby died in infancy; a second son, christened Andriy, was born in 1950.

Andriy learned Ukrainian at his father's knee, and that was not all. He learned too of his father's land, of the great sweeping vistas of the Carpathians and Ruthenia. He imbibed his father's loathing of Russians. But the father died in a road crash when the boy was twelve; his mother, tired of her husband's endless evenings with fellow exiles round the sitting room fire, talking of the past in a language she could never understand, anglicized both their names to Drake, and Andriy's given name to Andrew. It was as Andrew Drake that the boy went to grammar school and university; as Andrew Drake that he received his first passport.

The re-birth came in his late teens at university. There were other Ukrainians there, and he became fluent again in his father's language. This was the late sixties, and the brief renaissance of Ukrainian literature and poetry back in the Ukraine had come and gone, its leading lights mostly by then doing slave labour in the camps of Gulag. So he absorbed these events with hindsight and knowledge of what had befallen the writers. He read everything he could get his hands on as the first years of the seventh decade dawned: the classics of Taras Shevchenko and those who wrote in the brief flowering under Lenin, suppressed and liquidated under Stalin. But most of all he read the works of those called 'the

Sixtiers', because they flourished for a brief few years until Brezhnev struck yet again to stamp out the national pride they called for. He read and grieved for Osdachy, Chornovil, Moroz and Dzyuba; and when he read the poems and secret diary of Pavel Symonenko, the young firebrand dead of cancer at twenty-eight, the cult figure of the Ukrainian students inside the USSR, his heart broke for a land he had never even seen.

With his love for this land of his dead father came a matching loathing of those he saw as its persecutors; avidly he devoured the underground pamphlets that came out, smuggled from the resistance movement inside: the *Ukrainian Herald*, with its accounts of what befell the hundreds of unknowns who did not receive the publicity accorded to the great Moscow trials of Daniel, Sinyavsky, Orlov, Scharansky, the miserable, forgotten ones. With each detail his hatred grew until for Andrew Drake, once Andriy Drach, the personification of all evil in the world was simply called KGB.

He had enough sense of reality to eschew the crude, raw nationalism of the older exiles, and their divisions between West and East Ukrainians. He rejected too their implanted anti-Semitism, preferring to accept the works of Gluzman, both a Zionist and a Ukrainian nationalist, as the words of a fellow-Ukrainian. He analysed the exile community in Britain and Europe and perceived there were four levels: the language nationalists for whom simply speaking and writing in the tongue of their fathers was enough; the debating nationalists who would talk for ever and a day, but do nothing; the slogan-daubers who irritated their adopted countrymen but left the Soviet behemoth untouched; and the activists who demonstrated before visiting Moscow dignitaries, were carefully photographed and filed by the Special Branch and achieved a passing publicity.

Drake rejected them all. He remained quiet, well-behaved and aloof. He came south to London and took a clerking job. There are many in such work who have one secret passion, unknown to all their colleagues, which absorbs all their savings, their spare time and their annual holidays. Drake was such a man. He quietly put together a small group of men who felt just as he did; he traced them, met them, befriended them, swore a common oath with them, and bade them be patient. For Andriy Drach had a secret dream and, as T. E. Lawrence said, he was dangerous because 'he dreamed with his eyes open'. His dream was that one day he would strike one single gigantic blow against the men of Moscow that would shake them as they had never been shaken before. He would penetrate the walls of their power and hurt them right inside the fortress.

His dream was alive and one step nearer fulfilment for the finding of Kaminsky, and he was a determined and excited man as his plane slipped once more out of a warm blue sky towards Trabzon.

Miroslav Kaminsky looked across at Drake with indecision on his face.

'I don't know, Andriy,' he said, 'I just don't know. Despite everything you have done, I just don't know if I can trust you that much. I'm sorry, it's the way I've had to live all my life.'

'Miroslav, you could know me for the next twenty years and not know more about me than you do already. Everything I've told you about me is the truth. If you cannot go back then let me go in your place. But I must have contacts there. If you know of any, anybody at all. . . .'

Kaminsky finally agreed.

'There are two men,' he said at last. 'They were not blown away when my group was destroyed, and no one knew of them. I had met them only a few months earlier.'

'But they are Ukrainians, and partisans?' asked Drake eagerly.

'Yes, they are Ukrainians. But that is not their primary motivation. Their people too have suffered. Their fathers, like mine, have been for ten years in the labour camps, but for a different reason. They are Jews.'

'But do they hate Moscow?' asked Drake. 'Do they too want to strike against the Kremlin?'

'Yes, they hate Moscow,' replied Kaminsky. 'As much as you or I. Their inspiration seems to be a thing called the Jewish Defence League. They heard about it on the radio. It seems their philosophy, like ours, is to begin to strike back; not to take any more persecution lying down.'

'Then let me make contact with them,' urged Drake.

The following morning Drake flew back to London with the names and addresses in Lvov of the two young Jewish partisans. Within a fortnight he had subscribed to a package tour run by Intourist for early July, visiting Kiev, Ternopol and Lvov. He also quit his job and withdrew his life savings in cash.

Unnoticed by anyone, Andrew Drake, alias Andriy Drach, was going to his private war – against the Kremlin.

1

A gently warming sun shone down on Washington that middle of May, bringing the first shirtsleeves to the streets and the first rich, red roses to the garden outside the french windows of the Oval Office in the White House. But though the windows were open and the fresh smells of grass and flowers wafted into the private sanctum of the most powerful ruler in the world, the attention of the four men present was focused upon other plants in a far and foreign country.

President William Matthews sat where American presidents have always sat: back to the south wall of the room, facing northward across a wide antique desk towards the classical marble fireplace that dominates the north wall. His chair, unlike that of most of his predecessors who had favoured personalized, made-to-measure seating, was a factory-made, high-backed swivel chair of the kind any senior corporate executive might have. For 'Bill' Matthews, as he insisted his publicity posters call him, had always through his successive and successful election campaigns stressed his ordinary, old-folks-at-home personal tastes in clothing, food and creature comforts. The chair, therefore, which could be seen by the scores of delegates he liked to welcome personally into the Oval Office, was not luxurious. The fine antique desk, he was at pains to point out, he had inherited and it had become part of the precious tradition of the White House. That went down well.

But there Bill Matthews drew the line. When he was in conclave with his senior advisers, the 'Bill' which his humblest constituent could call him to his face was out of court. He also dropped the nice-guy tones of voice and the rumpled bird-dog grin that had originally gulled the voters into putting the boy next door into the White House. He was not the boy next door, and his advisers knew it; he was the man at the top.

Seated in upright armchairs across the desk from the President were the three men who had asked to see him alone that morning. Closest to him in personal terms was the chairman of the National Security Council, his own adviser on security matters and confidant on foreign affairs. Variously referred to in the environs of the West Wing and the Executive Office Building as 'the doc' or 'that damned Polack', the sharp-faced Stanislav Poklewski was sometimes disliked but never underestimated.

They made a strange pair, to be so close; the blond, white, Anglo-Saxon Protestant from the deep South, and the dark, taciturn devout Roman Catholic who had come over from Cracow as a small boy. But what Bill Matthews lacked in understanding of the tortuous psychologies of Europeans in general and Slavs in particular could be made up by the Jesuit-educated calculating machine who always had his ear. There were two other reasons why Poklewski appealed to him: he was ferociously loyal and had no political ambitions outside the shadow of Bill Matthews. But there was one reservation: Matthews always had to balance the doctor's suspicious dislike of the men of Moscow with the more urbane assessments of his Bostonian secretary of state.

The secretary was not present that morning at the meeting asked for personally by Poklewski. The other two men on the chairs in front of the desk were Robert Benson, director of the Central Intelligence Agency, and Carl Taylor.

It has frequently been written that America's National Security Agency is the body responsible for all electronic espionage. It is a popular idea but not true. The NSA is responsible for that portion of electronic surveillance and espionage conducted outside the United States on her behalf that has to do with listening: wire-tapping, radio-monitoring and above all the plucking out of the ether of literally billions of words a day in hundreds of dialects and languages, for recording, de-coding, translating and analysing. But not spy satellites. The *visual* surveillance of the globe by cameras mounted in aeroplanes and, more importantly, in space satellites has always been the preserve of the National Reconnaissance Office, a joint US Air Force/CIA operation. Carl Taylor was its director and he was a two-star general of Air Force Intelligence.

The President shuffled together the pile of high-definition photographs on his desk and handed them back to Taylor, who rose to accept them and placed them back in his briefcase.

'All right, gentlemen,' he said slowly, 'so you have shown me that the wheat crop in a small portion of the Soviet Union, maybe even only in the few acres shown in these pictures, is coming up defective. What does it prove?'

Poklewski glanced across at Taylor and nodded. Taylor cleared his throat.

'Mr President, I've taken the liberty of setting up a screening of what is coming in right now from one of our Condor satellites. Would you care to see it?'

Matthews nodded and watched Taylor cross to one of the bank of television sets placed in the curving west wall below the bookcases, which had been specially shortened to accept the console of TV sets. When civilian deputations were in the room, the new row of TV screens was covered by sliding teak doors. Taylor turned on the extreme left-hand set and returned to the President's desk. He detached one of the six telephones from its cradle, dialled a number and said simply, 'Screen it.'

President Matthews knew about the Condor range of satellites. Flying higher than anything before, using cameras of a sophistication that could show close-up a human fingernail from two hundred miles, through fog, rain, hail, snow, cloud and night, the Condors were the latest and the best.

Back in the 1970s photographic surveillance though good had been slow, mainly because each cartridge of exposed film had to be ejected from the satellite at specific positions, free-fall to Earth in protective coverings, be retrieved with the aid of bleepers and tracing devices, air-freighted to the NRO's central laboratories, developed and screened. Only when the satellite was within that arc of flight which permitted a direct line from it to the USA or one of the American-controlled tracking stations, could simultaneous TV transmissions take place. But when the satellite passed close over the Soviet Union the curve of the Earth's surface baffled direct reception, so the watchers had to wait until it came round again.

Then in the summer of 1978 the scientists cracked the problem with the 'Parabola Game'. Their computers devised a cat's cradle of infinite complexity for the flight tracks of half a dozen space cameras around the globe's surface to this end: whichever spy-in-the-sky the White House wanted to tap into could be ordered by signal to begin transmitting what it was seeing, and throw the images in a low parabola arc to another satellite which was not out of vision. The second bird would throw the image on again, to a third satellite, and so on, like basketball players tossing the ball from fingertip to fingertip while they ran. When the needed images were fielded by a satellite over the USA they could be beamed back down to the NRO headquarters, and from there by patch-through to the Oval Office.

The satellites were travelling at over 40,000 land miles per hour; the globe was spinning with the hours, tilting with the seasons. The computations and permutations were astronomical, but the computers solved them. By 1980 the US President had twenty-four-hour access to every square inch of the world's surface at the touch of a button by simultaneous transmission. Sometimes it bothered him. It never bothered Poklewski: he had been brought up to the idea of the exposition of all private thoughts and actions in the confessional. The Condors were like confessionals, with himself as the priest he had once nearly become.

As the screen flickered into life, General Taylor spread a map of the Soviet Union on the President's desk and pointed with a forefinger.

'What you are seeing, Mr President, is coming to you from

Condor Five, tracking here, northeast, between Saratov and Perm, across the Virgin Lands and the Black Earth country.'

Matthews raised his gaze to the screen. Great tracts of land were unrolling slowly down the screen from top to bottom, a swathe about twenty miles broad. The land looked bare, as in autumn after the harvest. Taylor muttered a few instructions into the telephone. Seconds later the view concentrated, closing to a band barely five miles wide. A small group of peasant shacks, wooden plank *izbas* no doubt, lost in the infinity of the steppe, drifted past on the left of the screen. The line of a road entered the picture, stayed centre for a few uncertain moments, then drifted off screen. Taylor muttered again; the picture closed to a track a hundred yards wide. Definition was better. A man leading a horse across the vast expanse of steppe came and went.

'Slow it down,' instructed Taylor into the telephone. The ground beneath the cameras passed less quickly. High in space the satellite Condor was still on track at the same height and speed; inside the NRO's laboratories the images were being narrowed and slowed. The picture came closer, slower. Against the bole of a lone tree a Russian peasant slowly unbuttoned his fly. President Matthews was not a technical man and never ceased to be amazed. He was, he reminded himself, sitting in a warm office on an early summer morning in Washington, watching a man urinate somewhere in the shadow of the Urals mountain range. The peasant passed slowly out of vision towards the bottom of the screen. The image coming up was of a wheat field many hundreds of acres broad.

'And freeze,' instructed Taylor into the telephone. The picture slowly stopped moving and held.

'Close up,' said Taylor.

The picture came closer and closer until the entire square-yard screen was filled with twenty separate stalks of young wheat. Each looked frail, listless, bedraggled. Matthews had seen them like this in the dustbowls of the Middle West he had known in his boyhood fifty years before.

'Stan,' said the President. Poklewski, who had asked for the meeting and the screening, chose his words carefully.

'Mr President, the Soviet Union has a total grain target this year of two hundred and forty million metric tons. Now this breaks down into goal targets of one hundred and twenty million tons of wheat, sixty million of barley, and fourteen of oats, fourteen of maize or corn, twelve of rye and the remaining twenty of a mixture of rice, millet, buckwheat and leguminous grains. The giants of the crop are wheat and barley.'

He rose and came round the desk to where the map of the Soviet Union was still spread. Taylor flicked off the television and resumed his seat.

'About forty per cent of the annual Soviet grain crop or approximately one hundred million tons comes from here in the Ukraine and the Kuban area of southern Russian Republic,' Poklewski continued, indicating the areas on the map. 'And it is all winter wheat. That is, it's planted in September and October. It has reached the stage of young shoots by November when the first snows come. The snows cover the shoots and protect them from the bitter frosts of December and January.'

Poklewski turned and paced away from the desk to the curved ceiling-to-floor windows behind the presidential chair. He had this habit of pacing when he talked.

The Pennsylvania Avenue observer cannot actually see the Oval Office tucked away at the back of the tiny West Wing building, but because the tops of these south-facing tall windows to the office can just be observed from the Washington Monument a thousand yards away they have long been fitted with six-inch-thick, green-tinted bullet-proof glass just in case a sniper near the monument might care to try a long shot. As Poklewski reached the windows the aquamarine tinted light coming through them cast a deeper pallor across his already pale face.

He turned and walked back, just as Matthews was preparing to swing his chair round to keep him in vision.

'Last December the whole of Ukraine and Kuban was covered by a freak thaw during the early days. They've had them before, but never as warm. A great wave of warm southern air swept in off the Black Sea and the Bosphorus and rolled northeastward over Ukraine and Kuban. It lasted a week and melted the first coverings of snow, about six inches deep, to water. The young wheat and barley stems were exposed. Ten days later, as if to make up, the same freak weather patterns hammered the whole area with frosts going fifteen, even twenty degrees, below zero.'

'Which did the wheat a power of no good,' suggested the President.

'Mr President,' interjected Robert Benson of the CIA, 'our best agricultural experts have estimated the Soviets will be lucky if they salvage fifty per cent of that Ukrainian and Kuban crop. The damage was massive and irreparable.'

'So that is what you have been showing me?' asked Matthews.

'No, sir,' said Poklewski, 'that is the point of this meeting. The other sixty per cent of the Soviet crop, nigh on one hundred and forty million tons, comes from the great tracts of the Virgin Lands, first put under the plough by Khrushchev in the early sixties, and the Black Earth country, butting up against the Urals. A small portion comes from across the mountains in Siberia. That is what we have been showing you.'

'What is happening there?' asked Matthews.

'Something odd, sir. Something strange is happening to the Soviet grain crop. All this remaining sixty per cent is spring wheat, put down as seed in March/April after the thaw. It should be coming up sweet and green by now. It's coming up stunted, sparse, sporadic, like it was hit by some kind of blight.'

'Weather again?' asked Matthews.

'No. They had a damp winter and spring over this area, but nothing serious. Now the sun has come out, the weather is perfect, warm and dry.'

'How widespread is this . . . blight?'

Benson came in again. 'We don't know, Mr President. We have maybe fifty samples of film of this particular problem.

We tend to concentrate on military concentrations, of course: troop movements, new rocket bases, arms factories. But what we have indicates it must be pretty widespread.'

'So what are you after?'

'What we'd like,' resumed Poklewski, 'is your go-ahead to spend a lot more on this problem, find out just how big it is for the Soviets. It will mean trying to send in delegations, businessmen. Diverting a lot of space surveillance from non-priority tasks. We believe it is in America's vital interest to find out just exactly what it is that Moscow is going to have to handle here.'

Matthews considered and glanced at his watch. He had a troop of ecologists due to greet him and present him with yet another plaque in ten minutes. Then there was the attorney general before lunch about the new labour legislation. He rose.

'Very well, gentlemen, you have it. By my authority. This is one I think we need to know. But I want an answer within thirty days.'

General Carl Taylor sat in the seventh-floor office of Robert Benson, the director of central intelligence, or DCI, ten days later and gazed down at his own report, clipped to a large sheaf of photo stills, that lay on the low coffee table in front of him.

'It's a funny one, Bob. I can't figure it out,' he said.

Benson turned away from the great sweeping picture windows that form one entire wall of the DCI's office at Langley and face out north by northwest across vistas of trees towards the invisible Potomac River. Like his predecessors, he loved that view, particularly in late spring and early summer, when the woodlands were a wash of tender green. He took his seat on the low settee across the coffee table from Taylor.

'Neither can my grain experts, Carl. And I don't want to go to the Department of Agriculture. Whatever is going on over there in Russia, publicity is the last thing we need, and if I bring in outsiders it'll be in the press within a week. So what have you got?'

'Well, the photos show the blight, or whatever it is, is not pandemic,' said Taylor. 'It's not even regional. That's the twister. If the cause was climatic, there'd be weather phenomena to explain it. There are none. If it was a straight disease of the crop, it would be at least regional. If it was parasite-caused, same applies. But it's haphazard. There are stands of strong, healthy, growing wheat right alongside the affected acreage. The Condor reconnaissance shows no logical pattern at all. How about you?'

Benson nodded in agreement.

'It's illogical all right. I've put a couple of assets in on the ground, but they haven't reported back yet. The Soviet press has said nothing. My own agronomy boys have been over your photos backwards and forwards. All they can come up with is some blight of the seed or in the earth. But they too cannot figure the haphazard nature of it all. It fits no known pattern. But the important thing is I have to produce some kind of estimate for the President for the total probable Soviet grain harvest next September/October. And I have to produce it soon.'

'There's no way I can photograph every damn stand of wheat and barley in the Soviet Union, even with Condor,' said Taylor. 'It would take months. Can you give me that?'

'Not a chance,' said Benson. 'I need information about the troop movements along the China border, the build-up opposite Turkey and Iran. I need a constant watch on the Red Army deployments in East Germany and the locations of the new SS Twenties behind the Urals.'

'Then I can only come up with a percentage figure based on what we have photographed to date, and extrapolate for a Soviet-wide figure,' said Taylor.

'It's got to be accurate,' said Benson. 'I don't want a repeat of 1977.'

Taylor winced at the memory, even though he had not been director of the NRO in that year. In 1977 the American intelligence machine had been fooled by a gigantic Soviet confidence trick. Throughout the summer all the experts of the CIA and Department of Agriculture had been telling the

President the Soviet grain crop would reach around 215 million metric tons. Agriculture delegates visiting Russia had been shown fields of fine healthy wheat; in fact these had been the exceptions. Photo-reconnaissance analysis had been faulty. In the autumn the then Soviet President, Leonid Brezhnev, had calmly announced the Soviet crop would be only 194 million tons.

As a result the price of US wheat surplus to domestic requirements had shot up, in the certainty the Russians would after all have to buy in close on 20,000,000 tons. Too late. Through the summer, acting through French-based front companies, Moscow had already bought up futures for enough wheat to cover the deficit – and at the old, low price. They had even chartered dry-cargo shipping space through front-men, then re-directed the ships, which were en route for Western Europe, into Soviet ports. The affair was known in Langley as 'the Sting'.

Carl Taylor rose. 'OK, Bob, I'll go on taking happy snapshots.'

'Carl.' The DCI's voice stopped him in the doorway. 'Nice pictures are not enough. By 1st July I want the Condors back on military deployment. Give me the best grain figure estimates you have by the end of the month. Err, if you must, on the side of caution. And if there's *anything* your boys spot that could explain the phenomenon, go back and re-shoot it. Somehow we have to find out what the hell is happening to the Soviet wheat.'

President Matthews' Condor satellites could see most things in the Soviet Union but they could not observe Harold Lessing, one of the three first secretaries in the Commercial Section of the British embassy in Moscow, at his desk the following morning. It was probably just as well, for he would have been the first to agree he was not an edifying sight. He was pale as a sheet and feeling extremely sick.

The main embassy building of the British mission in the Soviet capital is a fine old, pre-Revolution mansion facing north on Maurice Thorez Embankment, staring straight across the Moscow River at the south façade of the Kremlin wall. It once belonged to a millionaire sugar merchant in tsarist days, and was snapped up by the British soon after the revolution. The Soviet government has been trying to get the British out of there ever since. Stalin hated the place; every morning as he rose he had to see, across the river from his private apartments, the Union Jack fluttering in the morning breeze, and it made him very angry.

But the Commercial Section does not have the fortune to dwell in this elegant cream and gold mansion. It functions in a drab complex of post-war jerry-built office blocks two miles away on Kutuzovsky Prospekt, almost opposite the wedding-cake-styled Ukraina Hotel. The same compound, guarded at its single gate by several watchful militia men, contains more drab apartment buildings set aside for the flats of diplomatic personnel from a score or more of foreign embassies, and called collectively the 'Korpus Diplomatik' or Diplomats' Compound.

Harold Lessing's office was on the top floor of the commercial office block. When he finally fainted at ten-thirty that bright May morning it was the sound of the telephone he brought crashing to the carpet with him that alerted his secretary in the neighbouring office. Quietly and efficiently she summoned the commercial counsellor, who had two young attachés assist Lessing, by this time groggily conscious again, out of the building, across the parking lot and up to his own sixth-floor apartment in Korpus 6, a hundred yards away.

Simultaneously the counsellor telephoned the main embassy on Maurice Thorez Embankment, informed the head of chancery and asked for the embassy doctor to be sent over. By noon, having examined Lessing in his own bed in his own flat, the doctor was conferring with the commercial counsellor. To his surprise the senior man cut him short and suggested they drive over to the main embassy to consult jointly with the head of chancery. Only later did the doctor, an ordinary British general practitioner doing a three-year stint on attachment to the embassy with the rank of first secretary, realize why the move was necessary. The head of chancery took them all to a special room in the embassy building which is secure from wire-tapping; something the Commercial Section was definitely not.

'It's a bleeding ulcer,' the medico told the two diplomats. 'He seemingly has been suffering from what he thought was an excess of acid indigestion for some weeks, even months. Put it down to strain of work and bunged down loads of antacid tablets. Foolish, really; he should have come to me.'

'Will it require hospitalization?' asked the head of chancery, gazing at the ceiling.

'Oh, yes indeed,' said the doctor. 'I think I can get him admitted here within a few hours. The local Soviet medical men are quite up to that sort of treatment.'

There was a brief silence as the two diplomats exchanged glances. The commercial counsellor shook his head. Both men had the same thought; because of their need to know, both of them were aware of Lessing's real function in the embassy. The doctor was not. The counsellor deferred to Chancery.

'That will not be possible,' said Chancery smoothly. 'Not in Lessing's case. He'll have to be flown to Helsinki on the afternoon shuttle. Will you ensure that he can make it?'

'But surely...' began the doctor. Then he stopped. He realized why they had had to drive two miles to have this conversation. Lessing must be the head of the Secret Intelligence Service operation in Moscow. 'Ah, yes. Well, now. He's shocked and has lost probably a pint of blood. I've given him a hundred milligrams of pethidine as a tranquillizer. I could give him another shot at three this afternoon. If he's chauffeur-driven to the airport and escorted all the way, yes, he can make Helsinki. But he'll need immediate entry into hospital when he gets there. I'd prefer to go with him myself just to be sure. I could be back tomorrow.'

The head of chancery rose. 'Splendid,' he pronounced. 'Give yourself two days. And my wife has a list of little items she's run short of, if you'd be so kind. Yes? Thank you so much. I'll make all the arrangements from here.'

For years it has been customary in newspapers, magazines and books to refer to the headquarters of Britain's Secret Intelligence Service, or the SIS, or MI6, as being at a certain office block in the Borough of Lambeth in London. It is a custom that causes quiet amusement to the staff members of the firm for the Lambeth address is a sedulously maintained front.

In much the same way a front is maintained at Leconfield House in Curzon Street, still supposed to be the home of the counter-intelligence arm, MI5, to decoy the unneeded enquirer. In reality those indefatigable spy-catchers have not dwelt near the Playboy Club for years.

The real home of the world's most secret Secret Intelligence Service is a modern-design, steel and concrete block allocated by the Department of the Environment a stone's throw from one of the capital's principal Southern Region railway stations, and it was taken over in the early 1970s.

It was in his top-floor suite with its tinted windows looking out towards the spire of Big Ben and the Houses of Parliament across the river that the director-general of the SIS received the news of Lessing's illness just after lunch. The call came on one of the internal lines from the head of personnel who had received the message from the basement cipher room. He listened carefully.

'How long will he be off?' he asked at length.

'Several months at least,' said Personnel. 'There'll be a couple of weeks in hospital in Helsinki, then home for a bit more. Probably several more weeks' convalescence.'

'Pity,' mused the director-general. 'We shall have to replace him rather fast.' His capacious memory recalled that Lessing had been running two Russian agents, low-level staffers in the Red Army and the Soviet Foreign Ministry respectively, not world-beating, but useful. Finally he said, 'Let me know when Lessing is safely tucked up in Helsinki. And get me a short list of possibles for his replacement. By close of play tonight, please.'

Sir Nigel Irvine was the third successive professional intelligence man to rise to the post of director-general of the SIS, or 'the firm' as it is more colloquially known in the community of such organizations.

The vastly bigger American CIA, which had been founded and brought to the peak of its powers by Allen Dulles, had as a result of abusing its strength with go-it-alone antics in the early seventies finally been brought under the control of an outsider, Admiral Stansfield Turner. It was ironic that, at exactly the same period, a British government had finally done the opposite, breaking the tradition of putting the firm under a senior diplomat from the Foreign Office and letting a professional take over.

The risk had worked well. The firm had paid a long penance for the Burgess, MacLean and Philby affairs, and Sir Nigel Irvine was determined that the tradition of a professional at the head of the firm would continue after him. That was why he intended to be as strict as any of his immediate predecessors in preventing the emergence of any Lone Rangers.

'This is a service, not a trapeze act,' he used to tell the novices at Beaconsfield. 'We're not here for the applause.'

It was already dark by the time the three files arrived on Sir Nigel Irvine's desk, but he wanted to get the selection finished and was prepared to stay on. He spent an hour poring over the files, but the selection seemed fairly obvious. Finally he used the telephone to ask the head of personnel, who was still in the building, to stop by. His secretary showed the staffer in two minutes later.

Sir Nigel hospitably poured the man a whisky and soda to match his own. He saw no reason not to permit himself a few of the gracious things of life, and he had arranged a well-appointed office, perhaps to compensate for the stink of combat in 1944 and 1945, and the dingy hotels of Vienna in the late forties when he was a junior agent in the firm suborning Soviet personnel in the Russian-occupied areas of Austria. Two of his recruits of that period, sleepers for years, were still being run, he was able to congratulate himself.

Although the building housing the SIS was of modern steel, concrete and chrome, the top-floor office of its director-general was decorated to an older and more elegant motif. The wallpaper was a restful *café au lait*, the wall-to-wall carpet a burnt orange. The desk, the high chair behind it, the two uprights in front of it and the button-back leather Chesterfield were all genuine antiques.

From the Department of the Environment store of pictures, to which the mandarins of Britain's Civil Service have access for the decoration of their office walls, Sir Nigel had collared a Dufy, a Vlaminck and a slightly suspect Breughel. He had had his eye on a small but exquisite Fragonard, but a shifty grandee in Treasury had got there first.

Unlike the Foreign and Commonwealth Office whose walls were hung with oils of past foreign ministers like Canning and Grey, the firm had always eschewed ancestral portraits. In any case, who ever heard of such self-effacing men as Britain's successive spymasters enjoying having their likeness put on record in the first place? Nor were portraits of the Queen in full regalia much in favour, as the White House and Langley were plastered with signed photos of the latest president.

'One's commitment to service of Queen and country in this building needs no further advertisement,' a dumbfounded visitor from the CIA at Langley had once been told. 'If it did, one wouldn't be working here anyway.'

Sir Nigel turned from the window and his study of the lights of the West End across the water.

'It looks like Munro, wouldn't you say?' he asked.

'I would have thought so,' answered Personnel.

'What's he like? I've read the file, I know him slightly. Give me the personal touch.'

'Secretive.'

'Good.'

'A bit of a loner.'

'Blast.'

'It's a question of his Russian,' said Personnel. 'The other two have good, working Russian. Munro can pass for one. He doesn't normally. Speaks to them in strongly accented moderate Russian. When he drops that he can blend right in. It's just that, well, to run Mallard and Merganser at such short notice, brilliant Russian would be an asset.'

Mallard and Merganser were the code-names for the two low-level agents recruited and run by Lessing. Russians being run inside the Soviet Union by the firm tend to have bird names, in alphabetical order according to the date of recruitment. The two Ms were recent acquisitions. Sir Nigel grunted.

'Very well. Munro it is. Where is he now?'

'On training. At Beaconsfield. Tradecraft.'

'Have him here tomorrow afternoon. Since he's not married, he can probably leave quite quickly. No need to hang about. I'll have the Foreign Office agree the appointment in the morning as Lessing's replacement in the Commercial Section.'

Beaconsfield, being within easy reach of central London, was years ago a favoured area for the elegant country homes of those who enjoyed high and wealthy status in the capital. By the early 1970s most of them played host to seminars, retreats, executive courses in management and marketing or even religious observation. One of them housed the Joint Services School of Russian and was quite open about it; another smaller house contained the training school of the SIS and was not open about it at all.

Adam Munro's course in tradecraft was popular, not the least because it broke the wearisome routine of enciphering and deciphering. He had his class's attention and he knew it.

'Right,' said Munro that morning in the last week of the month. 'Now for some snags, and how to get out of them.'

The class was still with expectancy. Routine procedures were one thing; a sniff of some real opposition was more interesting.

'You have to pick up a package from a contact,' said

Munro, 'but you are being tailed by the local fuzz. You have diplomatic cover in case of arrest, but your contact does not. He's right out in the cold, a local man. He's coming to a meet and you can't stop him. He knows that if he hangs about too long he could attract attention, so he'll wait ten minutes. What do you do?'

'Shake the tail,' suggested someone. Munro shook his head.

'For one thing you're supposed to be an innocent diplomat, not a Houdini. Lose the tail and you give yourself away as a trained agent. Secondly, you might not succeed. If it's the KGB and they're using the first team, you won't do it, short of dodging back into the embassy. Try again.'

'Abort,' said another trainee. 'Don't show. The safety of the unprotected contributor is paramount.'

'Right,' said Munro. 'But that leaves your man with a package he can't hold on to for ever, and no procedure for an alternative meet.' He paused for several seconds. 'Or does he . . . ?'

'There's a second procedure established in the event of an abort,' suggested a third student.

'Good,' said Munro. 'When you had him alone in the good old days before the routine surveillance was switched to yourself, you briefed him on a whole range of alternative meets in the event of an abort. So he waits ten minutes, you don't show up, he goes off nice and innocently to the second meeting point. What is this procedure called?'

'Fall-back,' ventured the bright spark who wanted to shake off the tail.

'First fall-back,' corrected Munro. 'We'll be doing all this on the streets of London in a couple of months, so get it right.' They scribbled hard. 'OK. You have a second location in the city, but you're still tailed. You haven't got anywhere. What happens at the first fall-back location?'

There was a general silence. Munro gave them thirty seconds.

'You don't meet at this location,' he instructed. 'Under the procedures you have taught your contact, the second location is always a place where he can observe you but you can stay well away from him. When you know he is watching you from a terrace perhaps, from a café, but always well away from you, you give him a signal. Can be anything: scratch an ear, blow your nose, drop a newspaper and pick it up again. What does that mean to the contact?'

'That you're setting up the third meet, according to your pre-arranged procedures,' said Bright Spark.

'Precisely. But you're *still* being tailed. Where does the third meet happen? What kind of place?'

This time there were no takers.

'It's any building – a bar, club, restaurant or what you like – that has a closed front so that once the door is closed no one can see through any plate-glass windows from the street inside the ground floor. Now, why is that the place for the exchange?'

There was a brief knock on the door and the head of student programme put his face round the door. He beckoned to Munro, who left his desk and went across to the door. His superior officer drew him outside into the corridor.

'You've been summoned,' he said quietly. 'The Master wants to see you. In his office at three. Leave here at the lunchbreak. Bailey will take over afternoon classes.'

Munro returned to his desk somewhat puzzled. The Master was the half affectionate and half respectful nickname for any holder of the post of director-general of the firm.

One of the class had a suggestion to make. 'So that you can walk to the contact's table and pick up the package unobserved?'

Munro shook his head. 'Not quite. When you leave the place the tailing opposition might leave one man behind to question the waiters. If you approached your man directly the face of the contact could be observed and the contributor identified, even by description. Anyone else?'

'Use a drop [dead-letter box] inside the restaurant,' proposed Bright Spark. Another shake from Munro.

'You won't have time,' he advised. 'The tails will be tumbling into the place a few seconds after you. Maybe the contact, who by arrangement was there before you, will not have found the right toilet cubicle free. Or the right table unoccupied. It's too hit-or-miss. No, this time we'll use the brush-pass. Note it; it goes like this.

'When your contact received your signal at the first fall-back location that you were under surveillance, he moved into the agreed procedure. He synchronized his watch to the nearest second with a reliable public clock, or, better still, the speaking clock operated by the telephone service. In another place, you did exactly the same.

'At an agreed hour he is already sitting in the agreed bar, or whatever. Outside the door, you are approaching at exactly the same time, to the nearest second. If you're ahead of time, delay a bit by adjusting your shoelace, pausing at a shop window. Do not consult your watch in an obvious manner.

'To the second, you enter the bar and the door closes behind you. At the same second, the contact is on his feet, bill paid, moving towards the door. At a minimum, five seconds will elapse before the door opens again and the fuzz come in. You brush past your contact a couple of feet inside the door, making sure it is closed to block off vision. As you brush past, you pass the package, or collect it, then part company and proceed to a vacant table or bar stool. The opposition will come in seconds later. As they move past him, the contact steps out and vanishes. Later the bar staff will confirm you spoke to nobody, contacted nobody. You paused at nobody's table, nor anyone at yours. You have the package in an inside pocket and you finish your drink and go back to the embassy. The opposition will hopefully report that you contacted nobody throughout the entire stroll.

'That is the brush-pass ... and *that* is the lunch bell. All right, we'll scrub it for now.'

By mid-afternoon Adam Munro was closeted in the secure library beneath the firm's HQ building beginning to bore through a pile of buff folders. He had just five days to master and commit to memory enough background material to enable him to take over from Harold Lessing as the firm's 'legal resident' in Moscow.

On 31st May he flew from London to Moscow to take up his new appointment.

Munro spent the first week settling in. To all the embassy staff but an informed few he was just a professional diplomat and the hurried replacement for Harold Lessing. The ambassador, head of chancery, chief cipher clerk and commercial counsellor knew what his real job was. The fact of his relatively advanced age at forty-six years to be only a first secretary in the Commercial Section was explained by his late entrance into the diplomatic corps.

The commercial counsellor ensured that the commercial files placed before him were as unburdensome as possible. Munro had a brief and formal reception by the ambassador in the latter's private office, and a more informal drink with the head of chancery. He met most of the staff and was taken to a round of diplomatic parties to meet many of the other diplomats from Western embassies. He also had a face-to-face and more businesslike conference with his opposite number at the American embassy. 'Business', as the CIA man confirmed to him, was quiet.

Though it would have made any staffer at the British embassy in Moscow stand out like a sore thumb to speak no Russian, Munro kept his use of the language to a formal and accented version both in front of his colleagues and when talking to official Russians during the introduction process. At one party two Soviet foreign ministry personnel had had a brief exchange in rapid, colloquial Russian a few feet away. He had understood it completely, and as it was mildly interesting he had filed it to London.

On his tenth day he sat alone on a park bench in the sprawling Soviet Exhibition of Economic Achievements in the extreme northern outskirts of the Russian capital. He was waiting to make first contact with the agent from the Red Army whom he had taken over from Lessing.

Munro had been born in 1936, the son of an Edinburgh doctor, and his boyhood through the war years had been conventional, middle class, untroubled and happy. He had attended a local school up to the age of thirteen years and then spent five at Fettes College, one of Scotland's best schools. It was during his period here that his senior languages master had detected in the lad an unusually acute ear for foreign languages.

In 1954, with national service then obligatory, he had gone into the army and after basic training secured a posting to his father's old regiment, the First Gordon Highlanders. Transferred to Cyprus, he had been on operations against EOKA partisans in the Troodos Mountains that late summer.

Sitting in a park in Moscow he could see the farmhouse still, in his mind's eye. They had spent half the night crawling through the heather to surround the place, following a tip-off from an informant. When dawn came, Munro was posted alone at the bottom of a steep escarpment behind the hill-top house. The main body of his platoon stormed the front of the farm just as dawn broke, coming up the shallower slope with the sun behind them.

From above him, on the other side of the hill, he could hear the chattering of the Stens in the quiet dawn. By the first rays of the sun he could see the two figures that came tumbling out of the rear windows, in shadow until their headlong flight down the escarpment took them clear of the lee of the house. They came straight at him, crouched behind his fallen olive tree in the shadow of the grove, their legs flying as they sought to keep their balance on the shale. They came nearer and one of them had what looked like a short, black stick in his right hand. Even if he had shouted, he told himself later, they could not have stopped their momentum. But he did not say that to himself at the time. Training took over; he just stood up as they reached a point fifty feet from him and loosed off two short, lethal bursts.

The force of the bullets lifted them both, one after the other, stopped their momentum and slammed them on to the shale at the foot of the slope. As a blue plume of cordite smoke drifted away from the muzzle of his Sten, he moved forward to look down at them. He thought he might feel sick, or faint. There was nothing; just a dead curiosity. He looked at the faces. They were boys, younger than himself, and he was eighteen.

His sergeant came crashing through the olive grove.

'Well done, laddie,' he shouted. 'You got 'em.'

Munro looked down at the bodies of the boys who would never marry or have children, never dance to a bouzouki or feel the warmth of sun and wine again. One of them was still clutching the black stick; it was a sausage. A piece of it hung out of the body's mouth. He had been having breakfast. Munro turned on the sergeant.

'You don't own me,' he shouted, 'you don't bloody own me. Nobody owns me but me.'

The sergeant put the outburst down to first-kill nerves and failed to report it. Perhaps that was a mistake. For authority failed to notice that Adam Munro was not completely, not one hundred per cent, obedient. Not ever again.

Six months later he was urged to consider himself as potential officer material and extend his time in the army to three years so as to qualify for a short-service commission. Tired of Cyprus, he did so and was posted back to England, to the Officer Cadet Training Unit at Eaton Hall. Three months later he got his 'pip' as a second lieutenant.

While form-filling at Eaton Hall, he had mentioned that he was fluent in French and German. One day he was casually tested in both languages and his claim proved to be correct. Just after his commissioning it was suggested he might like to apply for the Joint Services Russian language course, which in those days was situated at a camp called Little Russia at Bodmin in Cornwall. The alternative was regimental duties at the barracks in Scotland, so he agreed. Within six months he emerged not merely fluent in Russian but virtually able to pass for a Russian.

In 1957, despite considerable pressure from the regiment to stay on, he left the army, for he had decided he wanted to be a foreign correspondent. He had seen a few of them in Cyprus and thought he would prefer the job to office work. At the age of twenty-one he joined the *Scotsman* in his native Edinburgh as a cub reporter, and two years later he moved to London where he was taken on by Reuters, the international news agency with its headquarters at 85 Fleet Street. In the summer of 1960 his languages again came to his rescue: at twenty-four he was posted to the Reuters office in West Berlin as second man to the bureau chief, the late Alfred Kluehs. That was the summer before the Wall went up, and within three months he had met Valentina, the woman who he now realized was the only one he had ever really loved in his life.

A man sat down beside him and coughed. Munro jerked himself out of his reverie. Teaching tradecraft to sprogs one week, he told himself, and forgetting the basic rules a fortnight later. Never slacken attention before a meet.

The Russian looked at him uncomprehendingly, but Munro wore the necessary polka-dot tie. Slowly the Russian put a cigarette in his mouth, eyes on Munro. Corny, but it still worked; Munro took out his lighter and held the flame to the cigarette tip.

'Ronald collapsed at his desk two weeks ago,' he said softly and calmly. 'Ulcers, I'm afraid. I am Michael. I've been asked to take over from him. Oh, and perhaps you can help me; is it true that the Ostankino TV tower is the highest structure in Moscow?'

The Russian officer in plain clothes exhaled smoke and relaxed. The words were exactly the ones established by Lessing, whom he had known only as Ronald.

'Yes,' he replied. 'It is five hundred and forty metres high.'

He had a folded newspaper in his hand, which he laid on the seat between them. Munro's folded raincoat slipped off his knees to the ground. He retrieved it, re-folded it and placed it on top of the newspaper. The two men ignored each other for ten minutes, while the Russian smoked. Finally he rose and stubbed the butt into the ground, bending as he did so.

'A fortnight's time,' muttered Munro. 'The men's toilet under G block at the New State Circus. During the clown Popov's act. The show starts at seven-thirty.'

The Russian moved away and continued strolling. Munro

surveyed the scene calmly for ten minutes. No one showed interest. He scooped up the mackintosh, newspaper and buff envelope inside it and returned by metro to Kutuzovsky Prospekt. The envelope contained an up-to-date list of Red Army officer postings.

2

While Adam Munro was changing trains at Revolution Square shortly before 11 a.m. that morning of 10th June, a convoy of a dozen sleek, black, Zil limousines was sweeping through the Borovitsky Gate in the Kremlin wall a hundred feet above his head and one thousand three hundred feet southwest of him. The Soviet Politburo was about to begin a meeting that would change history.

The Kremlin is a triangular compound with its apex, dominated by the Sobakin Tower, pointing due north. On all sides it is protected by a fifty-foot wall studded by eighteen towers and penetrated by four gates.

The southern two-thirds of this triangle is the tourist area where docile parties troop along to admire the cathedrals, halls and palaces of the long-dead tsars. At the mid-section is a cleared swathe of tarmacadam, patrolled by guards, an invisible dividing line across which tourists may not step. But the cavalcade of hand-built limousines that morning purred across this open space towards the three buildings in the northern part of the Kremlin.

The smallest of these is the Kremlin Theatre to the east. Half exposed and half hidden behind the theatre stands the building of the Council of Ministers, seemingly the home of the government, in as much as the ministers meet here. But the real government of the USSR lies not in the Cabinet of Ministers, but in the Politburo, the tiny, exclusive group who constitute the pinnacle of the Central Committee of the Communist Party of the Soviet Union, or CPSU.

The third building is the biggest. It lies along the western façade, just behind the wall's crenellations, overlooking the Alexandrovsky Gardens down below. In shape it is a long, slim rectangle running north. The southern end is the old Arsenal, a museum for antique weaponry. But just behind the Arsenal the interior walls are blocked off. To reach the upper section, one must arrive from outside and penetrate a high, wrought-iron barrier that spans the gap between the ministers' building and the Arsenal. The limousines that morning swept through the wrought-iron gates and came to rest beside the upper entrance to the secret building.

In shape the upper Arsenal is a hollow rectangle; inside is a narrow courtyard running north/south and dividing the complex into two even narrower blocks of apartments and offices. There are four storeys including the attics. Halfway up the inner, eastern office block, on the third floor, overlooking the courtyard only and screened from prying eyes, is the room where the Politburo meets every Thursday morning to hold sway over 250 million Soviet citizens and scores of millions more who like to think they dwell outside the boundaries of the Russian empire.

For an empire it is. Although in theory the Russian Republic is one of fifteen republics that make up the Soviet Union, in effect the Russia of the tsars, ancient or modern, rules the other fourteen non-Russian republics with a rod of iron. The three arms Russia uses and needs to implement this rule are: the Red Army, including as it always does the navy and air force; the Committee of State Security, or KGB, with its 100,000 staffers, 300,000 armed troops and 600,000 informers; and the Party Organizations Section of the General Secretariat of the Central Committee, controlling the Party cadres in every place of work, thought, abode, study and leisure from the Arctic to the hills of Persia, from the fringes of Brunswick to the shores of the Sea of Japan. And that is just inside the empire.

The room in which the Politburo meets in the Arsenal of the Kremlin is about fifty feet long and twenty-five feet wide, not enormous for the power enclosed in it. It is decorated in the heavy, marbled decor favoured by the Party bosses, but dominated by a long, T-shaped table topped in green baize.

That 10th of June morning, 1982, was unusual, for they had received no agenda, just a summons. And the men who grouped at the table to take their places sensed with the perceptive collective nose for danger that had brought them all to this pinnacle that something of importance was afoot.

Seated in his usual chair at the centre point of the head of the T was the chief of them all, Maxim Rudin. Ostensibly his superiority lay in his title of president of the USSR. But nothing except the weather is ever quite what it appears in Russia. His real power came to him through his title of general secretary of the Communist Party of the USSR. As such, he was also chairman of the Central Committee, and chairman of the Politburo.

At the age of seventy-one he was craggy, brooding and immensely cunning; had he not been the latter he would never have occupied the chair that had once supported Stalin (who rarely called Politburo meetings), Malenkov, Khrushchev and Brezhnev. To his left and right he was flanked by four secretaries from his own personal secretariat, men loyal to him personally above all else. Behind him, at each corner of the north wall of the chamber, was a small table. At one sat two stenographers, a man and a woman, taking down every word in shorthand. At the other, as a counter-check, two men hunched over the slowly turning spools of a tape recorder. There was a spare recorder to take over during spool changes.

The other twelve members of the Politburo ranged themselves, six a side, down the stem of the T-shaped table, facing jotting pads, carafes of water, ashtrays. At the far end of this arm of the table was one single chair. The Politburo men checked numbers to make sure no one was missing. For the empty seat was the penal chair, sat in only by a man on his last appearance in that room, a man forced to listen to his own denunciation by his former colleagues, a man facing disgrace, ruin, and once, not long ago, death at the Black Wall of the Lubyanka. The custom has always been to delay the condemned man until, on entering, he finds all seats taken and only the penal chair free. Then he knows. But this morning it was empty. And all were present.

Rudin leaned back and surveyed the twelve through half-closed eyes, the smoke from his inevitable cigarette drifting past his face. He still favoured the old-style Russian papyross, half tobacco and half thin cardboard tube, the tube nipped twice between finger and thumb to filter the smoke. His aides had been taught to pass them to him one after the other, and his doctors to shut up.

To his left on the stem of the table was Vassili Petrov, aged forty-nine, Rudin's own protégé and young for the job he held, head of the Party Organizations Section of the General Secretariat of the Central Committee. Rudin could count on Petrov in the trouble that lay ahead. Beside Petrov was the veteran foreign minister, Dmitri Rykov, who would side with Rudin because he had nowhere else to go. Beyond him was Yuri Ivanenko, slim and ruthless at fifty-three, standing out like a sore thumb in his elegant London-tailored suit as if flaunting his sophistication to a group of men who hated all forms of Western-ness. Picked personally by Rudin to be chairman of the KGB, Ivanenko would side with him simply because the opposition would come from quarters who hated Ivanenko and wanted him destroyed.

On the other side of the table sat Yefrem Vishnayev, also young for the job, like half the post-Brezhnev Politburo. At fifty-five he was the Party theoretician, spare, ascetic, disapproving, the scourge of dissidents and deviationists, guardian of the Marxist purity and consumed by a pathological loathing of the capitalist West. The opposition would come here, Rudin knew. By his side was Marshal Nikolai Kerensky, aged sixty-three, defence minister and chief of the Red Army. He would go where the interests of the Red Army led him.

That left seven, including Komarov, responsible for agriculture. He was sitting white-faced because he, like Rudin and Ivanenko alone, knew roughly what was to come. The KGB chief betrayed no emotion, the rest did not know.

'It' came when Rudin gestured to one of the Kremlin praetorian guards at the door at the far end of the room to admit the person waiting in fear and trembling outside.

'Let me present Professor Ivan Ivanovich Yakovlev, comrades,' Rudin growled as the man advanced timorously to the end of the table and stood waiting, his sweat-damp report in his hands. 'The professor is our senior agronomist and grain specialist from the Ministry of Agriculture and member of the Academy of Sciences. He has a report for our attention. Proceed, professor.'

Rudin, who had read the report several days earlier in the privacy of his study, leaned back and gazed above the man's head at the far ceiling. Ivanenko carefully lit a Western filter kingsize. Komarov wiped his brow and studied his hands. The professor cleared his throat.

'Comrades,' he began hesitantly. No one disagreed that they were comrades. With a deep breath the scientist stared down at his papers and plunged straight into his report. 'Last December and January our long-range weather forecast satellites predicted an unusually damp winter and early spring. As a result and in accordance with habitual scientific practice it was decided at the Ministry of Agriculture that our seed grain for the spring planting should be dressed with a prophylactic dressing to inhibit fungoid infections that would probably be prevalent as a result of the dampness. This has been done many times before.

'The dressing selected was a dual-purpose seed dressing: an organo-mercury compound to inhibit fungoid attack on the germinating grain and a pesticide and bird-repellant called Lindane. It was agreed in scientific committee that because the USSR, following the unfortunate damage through frost to the winter wheat crop, would need at least a hundred and forty million tons of crop from the spring wheat plantings, it would be necessary to sow six and a quarter million tons of seed grain.'

All eyes were on him now, the fidgeting stilled. The Politburo members could smell danger a mile off. Only Komarov, the one responsible for agriculture, stared at the table in misery. Several eyes swivelled to him, sensing blood.

The professor swallowed hard and went on. 'At the rate of

two ounces of organo-mercury seed dressing per ton of grain, the requirement was for three hundred and fifty tons of dressing. There were only seventy tons in stock. An immediate order was sent to the manufacturing plant for this dressing at Kuibyshev to go into immediate production to make up the required two hundred and eighty tons.'

'Is there only one such factory?' asked Petrov.

'Yes, comrade. The tonnages required do not justify more factories. The Kuibyshev factory is a major chemical plant, making many insecticides, weed-killers, fertilizers and so forth. The production of the two hundred and eighty tons of this chemical would take less than forty hours.'

'Continue,' ordered Rudin.

'Due to a confusion in communication, the factory was undergoing annual maintenance, and time was running short if the dressing was to be distributed to the one hundred and twenty-seven dressing stations for seed grain scattered across the union, the grain treated, and then taken back to the thousands of state and collective farms in time for planting. So an energetic young official and Party cadre was sent from Moscow to hurry things along. It appears he ordered the workmen to terminate what they were doing, restore the plant to operating order and start it functioning again.'

'He failed to do it in time?' rasped Marshal Kerensky.

'No, comrade marshal, the factory started work again, although the maintenance engineers had not quite finished. But something malfunctioned. A hopper valve. Lindane is a very powerful chemical, and the dosage of the Lindane to the remainder of the organo-mercury compound has to be strictly regulated.

'The valve on the Lindane hopper, although registering one-third open on the control panel, was in fact stuck at full-open. The whole two hundred and eighty tons of dressing was affected.'

'What about quality control?' asked one of the members who had been born on a farm. The professor swallowed again, and wished he could quietly go into exile in Siberia without any more of this torture.

'There was a conjunction of coincidence and error,' he confessed. 'The chief analytical and quality-control chemist was away on holiday at Sochi during the plant close-down. He was summoned back by cable. But because of fog in the Kuibyshev area, he had to divert and continue his return by train. When he arrived, production was complete.'

'The dressing was not tested?' asked Petrov in incredulity. The professor looked more sick than ever.

'The chemist insisted on making quality-control tests. The young functionary from Moscow wanted the entire production shipped at once. An argument ensued. In the event a compromise was reached. The chemist wanted to test every tenth bag of dressing, twenty-eight in all. The functionary insisted he could only have one. That was when the third error occurred.

'The new bags had been stacked along with the reserve of seventy tons left over from last year. In the warehouse one of the loaders, receiving a report to send one single bag to the laboratory for testing, selected one of the old bags. Tests proved it was perfectly in order and the entire consignment was shipped.'

He ended his report. There was nothing more to say. He could have tried to explain that a conjunction of three mistakes – a mechanical malfunction, an error of judgement between two men under pressure and a piece of carelessness by a warehouseman – had combined to produce the catastrophe. But that was not his job, and he did not intend to make lame excuses for other men. The silence in the room was murderous.

Vishnayev came in with icy clarity.

'What exactly is the effect of an excessive component of Lindane in this organo-mercury compound?' he asked.

'Comrade, it causes a toxic effect against the germinating seed in the ground, rather than a protective effect. The seedlings come up, if at all, stunted, sparse and mottled brown. There is virtually no grain yield from such affected stems.'

'And how much of the spring planting has been affected?' asked Vishnayev coldly.

'Just about four-fifths, comrade. The seventy tons of reserve compound was perfectly all right. The two hundred and eighty tons of new compound was all affected by the jammed hopper valve.'

'And the toxic dressing was all mixed in with seed grain and planted?'

'Yes, comrade.'

Two minutes later the professor was dismissed, to his privacy and his oblivion. Vishnayev turned to Komarov.

'Forgive my ignorance, comrade, but it would appear you had some foreknowledge of this affair. What has happened to the functionary who produced this ... cock-up?' He used a crude Russian expression that refers to a pile of dog-mess on the pavement.

Ivanenko cut in. 'He is in our hands,' he said, 'along with the analytical chemist who deserted his function, the warehouseman, who is simply of exceptionally low intelligence, and the maintenance team of engineers who claim they demanded and received written instructions to wind up their work before they had finished.'

'This functionary; has he talked?' asked Vishnayev.

Ivanenko considered a mental image of the broken man in the cellars beneath the Lubyanka.

'Extensively,' he said.

'Is he a saboteur, a fascist agent?'

'No,' said Ivanenko with a sigh. 'Just an idiot; an ambitious apparatchik trying to over-fulfil his orders. You can believe me on that one. We do know by now the inside of that man's skull.'

'Then one last question, just so that we can all be sure of the dimensions of this affair.' Vishnayev swung back to the unhappy Komarov. 'We already know we will only save fifty million tons of the expected hundred million from the winter wheat. How much will we now get from the spring wheat this coming October?'

Komarov glanced at Rudin who nodded imperceptibly.

'Out of the hundred-and-forty-million-ton target for the spring-sown wheat and other grains, we cannot reasonably expect more than fifty million tons,' he said quietly.

The meeting sat in stunned horror.

'That means a total yield over both crops of one hundred million tons,' breathed Petrov. 'A national shortfall of a hundred and forty million tons. We could have taken a shortfall of fifty, even seventy million tons. We've done it before, endured the shortages and bought what we could from elsewhere. But this. . . .'

Rudin closed the meeting.

'We have as big a problem here as we have ever confronted, Chinese and American imperialism included. I propose we adjourn and separately seek some suggestions. It goes without saying that this news does not pass outside those present in this room. Our next meeting will be today week.'

As the thirteen men and the four aides at the top table came to their feet, Petrov turned to the impassive Ivanenko.

'This doesn't mean shortages,' he muttered. 'This means famine.'

The Soviet Politburo descended to their chauffeur-driven Zil limousines still absorbing the knowledge that a weedy professor of agronomy had just placed a time-bomb under one of the world's two super-powers.

Adam Munro's thoughts a week later as he sat in the circle at the Bolshoi Theatre on Karl Marx Prospekt were not on crops, but on love; and not for the excited embassy secretary beside him who had prevailed on him to take her to the ballet.

He was not a great fan of ballet, though he conceded he liked some of the music. But the grace of the *entrechats* and *fouettés*, or, as he called it, the jumping-about, left him cold. By the second act of 'Giselle', the evening's offering, his thoughts were straying back again to Berlin.

It had been a beautiful affair, a once-in-a-lifetime love. He was twenty-four, turning twenty-five, and she nineteen, dark and lovely. Because of her job they had had to conduct their affair in secret, furtively meeting in darkened streets so that he could pick her up in his car and take her back to his small flat at the western end of Charlottenburg without anyone seeing. They had loved and talked, she had made him suppers and they had loved again.

At first the clandestine nature of their affair, like married people slipping away from the world and each other's partners, had added spice, piquancy to the loving. But by the summer of '61 when the forests of Berlin were ablaze with leaves and flowers, when there was boating on the lakes and swimming from the shores, it had become cramped, frustrating. That was when he had asked her to marry him, and she had almost agreed. She might still have agreed, but then came the Wall. It was completed on 14th August 1961, but it was obvious for a week that it was going up.

That was when she made her decision, and they loved for the last time. She could not, she told him, abandon her parents to what would happen to them; to the disgrace, the loss of her father's trusted job, her mother's beloved apartment for which she had waited so many years through the dark times. She could not destroy her young brother's chances of a good education and prospects; and finally she could not bear to know that she would never see her beloved homeland again.

So she left, and he watched from the shadows as she slipped back into the East through the last uncompleted section in the Wall, sad and lonely and heart-broken – and very, very beautiful.

He had never seen her again, and he had never mentioned her to anyone, guarding her memory with his quiet Scottish secretiveness. He never let on that he had loved and still loved a Russian girl called Valentina who had been a secretary/stenographer with the Soviet delegation to the Four-Power Conference in Berlin. And that, as he well knew, was far out against the rules.

After Valentina, Berlin had palled. A year later he was transferred by Reuters to Paris, and it was two years after that, when he was back in London, kicking his heels in head office in Fleet Street, that a civilian he had known in Berlin, a man who had worked at the British headquarters there – Hitler's old Olympic stadium – had made a point of looking him up and renewing acquaintance. There had been a dinner and another man had joined them. The acquaintance from the stadium had excused himself and left during coffee. The newcomer was friendly and non-committal. But by the second brandy he made his point.

'Some of my associates in the firm,' he said with disarming diffidence, 'were wondering if you could do us a little favour.'

That was the first time Munro had heard the term 'the firm'. Later he would learn the terminology. To those in the Anglo-American alliance of intelligence services, a strange and guarded, but ultimately vital, alliance, the SIS was always called 'the firm'. To its employees those in the counter-intelligence arm, the MI5, were 'the colleagues'. The CIA at Langley, Virginia, was 'the company' and its staff 'the cousins'. On the opposite side worked 'the opposition' whose headquarters was at Number 2, Dzerzhinsky Square, Moscow, named after the founder of the old Cheka, Feliks Dzerzhinsky, Lenin's secret police boss. This building would always be known as 'the centre' and the territory east of the Iron Curtain as 'the bloc'.

The meeting in the London restaurant was in December 1964, and the proposal, confirmed later in a small flat in Chelsea, was for a 'little run into the bloc'. He made it in the spring of 1965 while ostensibly covering the Leipzig Fair in East Germany. It was a pig of a run.

He left Leipzig at the right time and drove to the meet in Dresden, close by the Albertinium Museum. The package in his inner pocket felt like five Bibles, and everyone seemed to be looking at him. The East German army officer who knew where the Russians were locating their tactical rockets in the Saxon hillsides showed up half an hour late, by which time two People's Policemen undoubtedly *were* watching him. The swap of packages went off all right, somewhere in the bushes of the nearby park. Then he returned to his car and set off southwest for the Gera crossroads and the Bavarian border checkpoint. On the outskirts of Dresden a local driver rammed him from the front offside, although Munro had right of way. He had not even had time to transfer the package to the hiding place between the boot and the back seat: it was still in the breast pocket of his blazer.

There were two gut-wrenching hours in a local police station, every moment dreading the command, 'Turn out your pockets, please, *mein herr*.' There was enough up against his breastbone to collect him twenty-five years in Pótma labour camp. Eventually he was allowed to go. Then the battery went flat and four People's Policemen had to push-start him.

The front offside wheel was screaming from a fractured roller-bearing inside the hub, and it was suggested he might like to stay overnight and get it mended. He pleaded that his visa time expired at midnight – which it did – and set off again. He made the checkpoint on the Saale River between Plauen in East Germany and Hof in the West ten minutes before midnight, having driven at twenty miles per hour all the way, rending the night air with the screaming of the front wheel. When he chugged past the Bavarian guards on the other side, he was wet with sweat.

A year later he left Reuters and accepted a suggestion to sit for the Civil Service entrance examination as a late entrant. He was twenty-nine.

The CSE examinations are unavoidable for anyone trying to join the Civil Service. Based on the results, the Treasury has first choice of the cream, which enables that department to foul up the British economy with impeccable academic references. The Foreign and Commonwealth Office gets next choice, and as Munro had a first-class pass he had no trouble entering the foreign service, usually the cover for staffers of the firm.

In the next sixteen years he had specialized in economic intelligence matters and the Soviet Union, though he had never been there before. He had foreign postings in Turkey, Austria and Mexico. In 1967 he had married, just turned thirty-one. But after the honeymoon it had been an increasingly loveless union, a mistake, and it was quietly ended six years later. Since then there had been affairs, of course, and they were all known to the firm, but he had stayed single.

There was one affair he had never mentioned to the firm,

and had the fact of it, and his covering up of it, leaked out he would have been fired on the spot. On joining the service, like everyone else, he had to write a complete life story of himself, followed by a *viva voce* examination by a senior officer.

This procedure is repeated every five years of service. Among the matters of interest are inevitably any emotional or social involvement with personnel from behind the Iron Curtain – or anywhere else, for that matter.

The first time he was asked, something inside him rebelled, as it had in the olive grove in Cyprus. He knew he was loyal, that he would never be suborned over the matter of Valentina, even if the opposition knew about it, which he was certain they did not. If an attempt were ever made to blackmail him over it, he would admit it and resign, but never accede. He just did not want the fingers of other men, not to mention filing clerks, rummaging through a part of the most private inside of him. Nobody owns me but me. So he said no to the question, and broke the rules. Once trapped by the lie, he had to stick with it. He repeated it three times in sixteen years. Nothing had ever happened because of it, and nothing ever would happen. He was certain of it. The affair was a secret, dead and buried. It would always be so.

Had he been less deep in his reverie, and not spellbound by the ballet like the girl beside him, he might have noticed something. From a private box high in the left-hand wall of the theatre, he was being observed. Before the lights went up for the *entr'acte*, the watcher had vanished.

The thirteen men who grouped around the Politburo table in the Kremlin the following day were subdued and watchful, sensing that the report of the professor of agronomy could trigger a faction fight such as there had not been since Khrushchev fell.

Rudin as usual surveyed them all through his drifting spire of cigarette smoke. Petrov of Party Organizations was in his customary seat to his left, with Ivanenko of the KGB beyond him. Rykov of Foreign Affairs shuffled his papers, Vishnayev the theoretician and Kerensky of the Red Army sat in stony silence. Rudin surveyed the other seven, calculating which way they would jump if it came to a fight.

There were the three non-Russians: Vitautas the Balt, from Vilnius, Lithuania; Chavadze the Georgian from Tbilisi; and Mukhamed the Tadjik, an oriental and born a Moslem. The presence of each was a sop to the minorities, but in fact each had paid the price to be there. Each, Rudin knew, was completely Russified; the price had been high, higher than a Great Russian would have to pay. Each had been first party secretary for his republic, and two still were. Each had overlorded programmes of vigorous repression against their fellow nationals, crushing dissidents, nationalists, poets, writers, artists, intelligentsia and workers who had even hinted at a less than one hundred per cent acceptance of the rule of Great Russia over them. Each could not go back without the protection of Moscow, and each would side, if it came to it, with the faction which would ensure their survival; that is, the winning one. Rudin did not relish the prospect of a faction fight, but he had held it in mind since he had first read Professor Yakovlev's report in the privacy of his study.

That left four, all Russians. There was Komarov of agriculture, still extremely ill at ease; Stepanov, head of the trade unions; Shushkin, responsible for liaison with foreign Communist parties worldwide; and Petryanov with special responsibilities for economics and the industrial plan.

'Comrades,' began Rudin slowly, 'you have all studied the Yakovlev report at your leisure. You have all observed Comrade Komarov's separate report to the effect that next September/October our aggregate grain yield will fall short of target by close to one hundred and forty million tons. Let us consider first questions first. Can the Soviet Union survive for one year on no more than one hundred million tons of grain?'

The discussion lasted an hour. It was bitter, acrimonious but virtually unanimous. Such a shortage of grain would lead to privations that had not been seen since the Second World War. If the state bought in even an irreducible minimum to make bread for the cities, the countryside would be left with almost nothing. The slaughter of livestock, as the winter snows covered the grazing lands and the beasts were left without forage or feed grains, would strip the Soviet Union of every four-footed animal. It would take a generation to recover the livestock herds. To leave even the minimum of grain on the land would starve the cities.

At last Rudin cut them short.

'Very well. If we insist on accepting the famine, both in grains and, as a consequence, in meat several months later, what will be the outcome in terms of national discipline?'

Petrov broke the ensuing silence. He admitted that there existed a groundswell of restiveness already among the broad masses of the people, evidenced by a recent rash of small outbreaks of disorder and resignations from the Party, all reported back to him in the Central Committee through the million tendrils of the Party machine. In the face of a true famine, many Party cadres could side with the proletariat.

The non-Russians nodded in agreement. In their republics the grip of the centre was always likely to be less total than inside Russia itself.

'We could strip the six East European satellites,' suggested Petryanov, not even bothering to refer to the East Europeans as fraternal comrades.

'Poland and Romania would burst into flame for a start,' countered Shushkin, the liaison man with Eastern Europe. 'Probably Hungary to follow suit.'

'The Red Army could deal with them,' snarled Marshal Kerensky.

'Not three at a time, not nowadays,' said Rudin.

'We are still only talking of a total acquisition of ten million tons,' said Komarov. 'It's not enough.'

'Comrade Stepanov?' asked Rudin.

The head of the state-controlled trade unions chose his words carefully.

'In the event of genuine famine this winter and next spring through summer,' he said, studying his pencil, 'it would not be possible to guarantee the absence of the outbreak of acts of disorder, perhaps on a wide scale.'

Ivanenko, sitting quietly gazing at the Western kingsize filter between his right forefinger and thumb, smelled more than smoke in his nostrils. He had smelled fear many times; in the arrest procedure, in the interrogation rooms, in the corridors of his craft. He smelled it now. He and the men around him were powerful, privileged, protected. But he knew them all well; he had the files. And he, who knew no fear for himself as the soul-dead know no fear, knew also that they all feared one thing more than war itself. If the Soviet proletariat, long-suffering, patient, ox-like in the face of deprivation, ever went berserk. . . .

All eyes were on him. Public 'acts of disorder', and the repression of them, were his country.

'I could,' he said evenly, 'cope with one Novocherkassk.' There was a hiss of indrawn breath down the table. 'I could cope with ten, or even twenty. But the combined resources of the KGB could not cope with fifty.'

The mention of Novocherkassk brought the spectre right out of the wallpaper as he knew it would. On the 2nd June 1962, almost exactly twenty years earlier, the great industrial city of Novocherkassk erupted in worker riots. But twenty years had not dimmed the memory.

It had started when by a stupid coincidence one ministry raised the price of meat and butter, while another cut wages at the giant NEVZ locomotive works by thirty per cent. In the resulting riots the shouting workers took over the city for three days, an unheard of phenomenon in the Soviet Union. Equally unheard of, they booed the local Party leaders into trembling self-imprisonment in their own headquarters, shouted down a full Soviet general, charged ranks of armed soldiers and pelted the tanks with mud until the vision-slits clogged up and the tanks ground to a halt.

The response of Moscow was massive. Every single line, every road, every telephone, every track in and out of Novocherkassk was sealed. The city became a vacuum, so the news should not leak out. Two divisions of KGB special troops had to be drafted to finish off the affair and mop up the rioters. There were eighty-six civilians shot down in the streets, over three hundred wounded. None ever returned home, none were buried locally. Not only the wounded, but every single member of every family of a dead or wounded man, woman or child, was deported to the camps of Gulag, lest they persist in asking after their relatives and thus keeping memory of the affair alive. Every trace was wiped out, but two decades later it was still well-remembered inside the Kremlin.

When Ivanenko dropped his bombshell there was silence again round the table. Rudin broke it.

'Very well then, the conclusion seems unescapable. We will have to buy in from abroad as never before. Comrade Komarov, what is the minimum we would need to buy abroad to avoid disaster?'

'Secretary-General, if we leave the irreducible minimum on the countryside, and use every scrap of our thirty million tons of national reserve, we will need fifty-five million tons of grain from outside. That would mean the entire surplus, in a year of bumper crops, from both the USA and Canada,' Komarov answered.

'They'll never sell it to us,' shouted Kerensky.

'They are not fools, Comrade Marshal,' Ivanenko cut in quietly. 'Their Condor satellites must have warned them already that something is wrong with our spring wheat. But they cannot know what, or how much. Not yet, but by the autumn they will have a pretty fair idea. And they are greedy, endlessly greedy for more money. I can raise the production levels in the gold mines of Siberia and Kolyma, ship more labour there from the camps of Mordovia. The money for such a purchase we can raise.'

'I agree with you on one point,' said Rudin, 'but not on the other, Comrade Ivanenko. They may have the wheat, we may have the gold, but there is a chance, just a chance, that this time they will require concessions.'

At the word 'concession' everyone stiffened.

'What kind of concession?' asked Marshal Kerensky suspiciously.

'One never knows until one negotiates,' said Rudin, 'but

it's a possibility we have to face. They might require concessions in military areas. . . .'

'Never,' shouted Kerensky, on his feet and red-faced.

'Our options are somewhat closed,' countered Rudin. 'We appear to have agreed that a severe and nationwide famine is not tolerable. It would set back the progress of the Soviet Union and thence the global rule of Marxist-Leninism by a decade, maybe more. We need the grain; there are no more options. If the imperialists exact concessions in the military field, we may have to accept a drawback lasting two or three years; but only in order all the better to advance after the recovery.'

There was a general murmur of assent. Rudin was on the threshold of carrying his meeting.

Then Vishnayev struck. He rose slowly as the buzz subsided.

'The issues before us, comrades,' he began with silky reasonableness, 'are massive, with incalculable consequences. I propose that this is too early to reach any binding conclusion. I propose an adjournment until this day fortnight while we all think over what has been said and suggested.'

His ploy worked. He had bought his time, as Rudin privately feared he would. The meeting agreed, ten against three, to adjourn without a resolution.

Yuri Ivanenko had reached the ground floor and was about to step into his waiting limousine when he felt a touch at his elbow. Standing beside him was a tall, beautifully tailored major of the Kremlin Guard.

'The Comrade Secretary-General would like a word with you in his private suite, Comrade Chairman,' he said quietly. Without another word he turned and headed down a corridor leading along the building away from the main doorway. Ivanenko followed. As he tailed the major's perfectly fitting barathea jacket, fawn whipcord trousers and gleaming boots, it occurred to him that if any one of the men of the Politburo came to sit one day in the penal chair, the subsequent arrest would be carried out by his own KGB special troops, called border guards, with their bright green cap bands and shoulder-flashes, the sword-and-shield insignia of the KGB above their peaks.

But if he, Ivanenko alone, were to be arrested, the KGB would not be given the job, as they could not be trusted almost thirty years earlier to arrest Lavrenti Beria. It would be these elegant, disdainful Kremlin elite guards, the praetorians round the seat of ultimate power, who would do the job. Perhaps the self-assured major walking before him, and he would have no qualms at all.

They reached a private lift, ascended to the third floor again, and Ivanenko was shown into the private apartment of Maxim Rudin.

Stalin had used to live in seclusion right in the heart of the Kremlin, but Malenkov and Khrushchev had ended the practice, preferring to establish themselves and most of their cronies in luxury apartments in a nondescript (from the outside) complex of apartment blocks at the far end of Kutuzovsky Prospekt. But when Rudin's wife had died two years earlier, he had moved back to the Kremlin.

It was a comparatively modest apartment for this most powerful of men: six rooms including a fitted kitchen, marbled bathroom, private study, sitting room, dining room and bedroom. Rudin lived alone, ate sparingly, dispensed with most luxuries and was cared for by an elderly cleaning woman and the ever-present Misha, a hulking but silent-moving ex-soldier, who never spoke but was never far away. When Ivanenko entered the study at Misha's silent gesture, he found Maxim Rudin and Vassili Petrov already there.

Rudin waved him to a vacant chair and began without preamble. 'I've asked you both here because there is trouble brewing and we all know it,' he rumbled. 'I'm old and I smoke too much. Two weeks ago I went out to see the quacks at Kuntsevo. They took some tests. Now they want me back again.'

Petrov shot Ivanenko a sharp look. The KGB chief was still impassive. He knew about the visit to the super-exclusive clinic in the woods southwest of Moscow; one of the doctors there reported back to him.

'The question of the succession hangs in the air, and we all know it,' Rudin continued. 'We all also know, or should, that Vishnayev wants it.'

Rudin turned to Ivanenko.

'If he gets it, Yuri Aleksandrovich, and he's young enough, that will be the end of you. He never approved of a professional taking over the KGB. He'll put his own man, Krivoi, in your place.'

Ivanenko steepled his hands and gazed back at Rudin. Three years earlier Rudin had broken a long tradition in Soviet Russia of imposing a political Party luminary as chairman and chief of the KGB. Shelepin, Semichastny, Andropov – they had all been Party men placed over the KGB from outside the service. Only the professional Ivan Serov had nearly made it to the top through a tide of blood. Then Rudin had plucked Ivanenko from among the senior deputies to Andropov and favoured him as the new chief.

That was not the only break with tradition. Ivanenko was young for the job of the world's most powerful policeman and spymaster. Then again, he had served as an agent in Washington twenty years earlier, always a base for suspicion among the xenophobes of the Politburo. He had a taste for Western elegance in his private life. And he was reputed, though none dared mention it, to have certain private reservations about dogma. That, for Vishnayev at least, was absolutely unforgivable.

'If he takes over, now or ever, that will also mark your cards, Vassili Alexeivitch,' Rudin told Petrov. In private he was prepared to call both his protégés by their familiar patronymics; never in public session.

Petrov nodded that he understood. He and Anatoly Krivoi had worked together in the Party Organizations section of the General Secretariat of the Central Committee. Krivoi had been older and senior. He had expected the top job, but when it fell vacant Rudin had preferred Petrov for the post that sooner or later carried the ultimate accolade, a seat on the all-powerful Politburo. Krivoi, embittered, had accepted the courtship of Vishnayev and had taken a post as the Party theoretician's chief of staff and right-hand man. But Krivoi still wanted Petrov's job.

Neither Ivanenko nor Petrov had forgotten that it was Vishnayev's predecessor as Party theoretician, Mikhail Suslov, who had put together the majority that toppled Khrushchev in 1963.

Rudin let his words sink in. 'Yuri, you know my successor cannot be you, not with your background.' Ivanenko inclined his head; he had no illusions on that score. 'But,' Rudin resumed, 'you and Vassili together can keep this country on a steady course, if you stick together and behind me. Next year, I'm going, one way or the other. And when I go, I want you, Vassili, in this chair.'

The silence between the two younger men was electric. Neither could recall any predecessor of Rudin ever having been so forthcoming. Stalin had suffered a heart attack and been finished off by his own Politburo as he prepared to liquidate them all; Beria had tried for power and been arrested and shot by his fearful colleagues; Malenkov had fallen in disgrace, likewise Khrushchev; Brezhnev had kept them all guessing till the last minute.

Rudin stood up to signal the reception was at an end.

'One last thing,' he said. 'Vishnayev is up to something. He's going to try and do a Suslov on me over this wheat foul-up. If he succeeds, we're all finished, perhaps Russia, too. Because he's an extremist; he's impeccable on theory but impossible on practicalities. Now I have to know what he's doing, what he's going to spring, who he's trying to enlist. Find out for me. Find out in fourteen days.'

The headquarters of the KGB, the Centre, is a huge stone complex of office blocks taking up the whole northeastern façade of Dzerzhinsky Square at the top end of Karl Marx Prospekt. The complex is actually a hollow square, the front and both wings being devoted to the KGB, the rear block being Lubyanka interrogation centre and prison. The proximity of the one to the other, with only the inner courtyard separating them, enables the interrogators to stay well on top of their work.

The chairman's office is on the third floor, left of the main doorway. But he always comes by limousine with chauffeur and bodyguard through the side gateway. The office is a big, ornate room with mahogany-panelled walls and luxurious oriental carpets. One wall carries the required portrait of Lenin, another a picture of Feliks Dzerzhinsky himself. Through the four, tall, draped, bulletproof windows overlooking the square, the observer must look at yet another representation of the Cheka's founder, standing twenty feet tall in bronze in the centre of the square, sightless eyes staring down Marx Prospekt to Revolution Square.

Ivanenko disliked the heavy, fustian, over-stuffed and brocaded decor of Soviet officialdom, but there was little he could do about the office. The desk alone, of the decor inherited from his predecessor Andropov, he appreciated. It was immense and adorned with seven telephones. The most important was the Kremlevka, linking him directly with the Kremlin and Rudin. Next was the Vertushka, in KGB green, which linked him with other Politburo members and the Central Committee. Others linked him through high-frequency circuits to the principal KGB representatives throughout the Soviet Union and the East European satellites. Still others went direct to Ministry of Defence and its intelligence arm, the GRU. All through separate exchanges. It was on this last one that he took the call for which he had been waiting ten days, that afternoon three days before the end of June.

It was a brief call, from a man who called himself Arkady. Ivanenko had instructed the exchange to accept Arkady and put him straight through. The conversation was short.

'Better face to face,' said Ivanenko shortly. 'Not now, not here. At my house this evening.' He put the phone down.

Most senior Soviet leaders never take their work home with them. In fact almost all Russians have two distinct personae: they have their official life and their private life, and never if possible shall the twain meet. The higher one gets, the greater the divide. As with the Mafia dons, whom the Politburo chiefs remarkably resemble, wives and families are simply not to be involved, even by listening to business talk, in the usually less-than-noble affairs that make up official life.

Ivanenko was different, the main reason why he was distrusted by the risen apparatchiks of the Politburo. For the oldest reason in the world he had no wife and family. Nor did he choose to live near the others, most of them content to dwell cheek by jowl with each other in the apartments on the western end of Kutuzovsky Prospekt on weekdays, and in neighbouring villas grouped around Zhukovka and Usovo at weekends. Members of the Soviet elite never like to be too far from each other.

Soon after taking over the KGB Yuri Ivanenko had found a handsome old house in the Arbat, the once fine residential town quarter of central Moscow favoured before the revolution by merchants. Within six months teams of KGB builders, painters and decorators had restored it – an impossible feat in Soviet Russia save for a Politburo member.

Having restored the building to its former elegance, albeit with the most modern security and alarm devices, Ivanenko had no trouble either in furnishing it with the ultimate in Soviet status symbols – Western furniture. The kitchen was the last cry in California-convenience, the entire room flown to Moscow from Sears Roebuck in packing crates. The living room and bedroom were panelled in Swedish pine via Finland, and the bathroom was sleek in marble and tile. Ivanenko himself occupied only the upper floor, which was a self-contained suite of rooms and also included his study/music room with its wall-to-wall stereo deck by Phillips, and a library of foreign and forbidden books, in English, French and German, all of which he spoke. There was a dining room off the living room, and a sauna off the bedroom to complete the floor area of the upper storey.

The staff of chauffeur, bodyguard and personal valet, all KGB men, lived on the ground floor which also housed the drive-in garage. Such was the house to which he returned after work and awaited his caller.

Arkady, when he came, was a thick-set, ruddy-faced man

in civilian clothes, though he would have felt more at home in his usual uniform of a brigadier on the Red Army staff. He was one of Ivanenko's agents inside the army. He hunched forward on his chair in Ivanenko's sitting room, perched on the edge as he talked. The spare KGB chief leaned back at ease, asking a few questions, making the occasional note on a jotting pad. When the brigadier had finished, Ivanenko thanked him and rose to press a wall-button. In seconds the door opened as the valet, a young blond guard of startling good looks, arrived to show the visitor out by the door in the side wall.

Ivanenko considered the news for a long time, feeling increasingly tired and dispirited. So that was what Vishnayev was up to. He would tell Maxim Rudin in the morning.

He had a lengthy bath, redolent with an expensive London bath oil, wrapped himself in a silk robe and sipped an old French brandy. Finally he returned to the bedroom, turned out the lights barring only a small lamp in the corner and stretched himself on the wide coverlet. Picking up the telephone by the bedside he pressed one of the call buttons. It was answered instantly.

'Valodya,' he said quietly, using the affectionate diminutive of Vladimir, 'come up here, will you, please.'

3

The Polish Airlines twin-jet dipped a wing over the wide sweep of the Dnieper River and settled into its final approach to Borispil Airport outside Kiev, capital of the Ukraine. From his window seat Andrew Drake looked down eagerly at the sprawling city beneath him. He was tense with excitement.

Along with the other hundred-plus package tourists from London who had staged through Warsaw earlier in the day, he queued nearly an hour for passport control and customs. At the immigration control he passed his passport under the plate-glass window and waited. The man in the booth was in uniform, border guard uniform, with the green band around his cap and the sword-and-shield emblem of the KGB above its peak.

He looked at the photo in the passport, then stared hard at Drake. 'An-Drev ... Drak?' he asked.

Drake smiled and bobbed his head. 'Andrew Drake,' he corrected gently.

The immigration man glowered back. He examined the visa, issued in London, tore off the incoming half and clipped the exit visa to the passport. Then he handed it back. Drake was in.

On the Intourist coach from the airport to the seventeen-storey Lybid Hotel he took stock again of his fellow travellers. About half were of Ukrainian extraction, visiting the land of their fathers, excited and innocent. The other half were of British stock, just curious tourists. All seemed to have British passports. Drake with his English name was among the second group. He had given no indication he spoke Ukrainian fluently and passable Russian.

During the coach ride they met Ludmilla, their Intourist guide for the tour. She was a Russian, and spoke Russian to the driver who, though a Ukrainian, replied in Russian. As the coach left the airport she smiled brightly and in reasonable English began to describe the tour ahead of them.

Drake glanced at his itinerary: two days in Kiev, trotting round St Sophia's Cathedral ('A wonderful example of Kievan-Rus architecture where Prince Yaroslav the Wise is buried,' warbled Ludmilla from up front); the tenth-century Golden Gate and Vladimir Hill, not to mention the state university, the Academy of Sciences and the Botanical Gardens. No doubt, thought Drake bitterly, no mention would be made of the 1964 fire at the academy library in which priceless manuscripts, books and archives devoted to Ukrainian national literature, poetry and culture had been destroyed; no mention of the fire brigade failing to arrive for three hours; no mention of the fire-setting by the KGB itself as their answer to the nationalistic writings of the Sixtiers.

After Kiev, there would be a day-trip by hydrofoil to Kaniv, then a day in Ternopol where a man called Miroslav Kaminsky would certainly not be a subject for discussion, and finally on to Lvov. As he had expected, he heard only Russian on the streets of the intensively Russified capital city of Kiev. It was not until Kaniv and Ternopol that he heard Ukrainian spoken extensively. His heart sang to hear it spoken so widely by so many people, and his only regret was that he had to keep saying, 'I'm sorry, do you speak English?' But he would wait, until he could visit the two addresses that he had memorized so well he could say them backwards.

Five thousand miles away the United States President was in conclave with his security adviser Poklewski, Robert Benson of the CIA, and a third man, Myron Fletcher, chief analyst of Soviet grain affairs in the Department of Agriculture.

'Bob, are you sure beyond any reasonable doubt that General Taylor's Condor reconnaissance and your ground reports point to these figures?' he asked, his eye running once again down the columns of numbers in front of him.

The report that his intelligence chief had presented to him via Stanislaw Poklewski five days earlier consisted of a breakdown of the entire Soviet Union into one hundred grain-producing zones. From each zone a sample square, ten miles by ten, had been seen in close-up and its grain problems analysed. From the hundred portraits, his experts had drawn up the nationwide grain forecast.

'Mr President, if we err, it is on the side of caution, of giving the Soviets a better grain crop than they have any right to expect,' replied Benson.

The President looked across at the man from Agriculture.

'Dr Fletcher, how does this break down in layman's terms?'

'Well, sir, Mr President, for a start one has to deduct at a very minimum ten per cent of the gross harvest to produce a figure of usable grain. Some would say we should deduct twenty per cent. This modest, ten per cent figure is to account for moisture content, foreign matter like stones and grit, dust and earth, losses in transport and wastage through inadequate storage facilities, from which we know they badly suffer.

'Starting from there, one then has to deduct the tonnages the Soviets have to keep on the land itself, right in the countryside, before any state procurements can be made to feed the industrial masses. You will find my table for this on the second page of my separate report.'

President Matthews flicked over the sheets before him and examined the table. It read:

1. *Seed grain*. The tonnage the Soviets must put by for re-planting next year, both for winter wheat and spring-sown wheat .... 10 million tons
2. *Human feeding*. The tonnage that must be set aside to feed the masses who inhabit the rural areas, the state and collective farms and all sub-urban units from hamlets through villages up to townlets of population less than 5000 head . . 28 million tons

3. *Animal feedstuffs*. The tonnage that must be set aside for the feeding of the livestock through the winter months until the spring thaw .... 52 million tons

4. *Irreducible total* .... 90 million tons

5. Representing a gross total, prior to a ten per cent unavoidable wastage deduction, of .... 100 million tons

'I would point out, Mr President,' went on Fletcher, 'that these are not generous figures. They are the absolute minima required before they start feeding the cities. If they cut down on the human rations, the peasants will simply consume the livestock, with or without permission. If they cut back on the animal feedstuff the livestock slaughter will be wholesale; they'll have a meat glut in the winter, then a meat famine for three to four years.'

'Okay, doctor, I'll buy that. Now what about their reserves?'

'We estimate they have a national reserve of thirty million tons. It is unheard of to use up the whole of it, but if they did, that would give them an extra thirty million tons. And they *should* have twenty million tons left over from this year's crop available for the cities – a grand total for their cities of fifty million.'

The President swung back to Benson.

'Bob, what do they have to have by way of state procurements to feed the urban millions?'

'Mr President, 1977 was their worst year for a long time, the year they perpetrated "the Sting" on us. They had a total crop of a hundred and ninety-four million tons. They bought from their own farms sixty-eight million. They *still* needed to buy twenty million from us by subterfuge. Even in 1975, their worst year for a decade and a half, they needed seventy million tons for the cities. And that led to savage shortages. They cannot do nowadays, with a greater population than at that time, with less than eighty-five million tons of state buy-in.'

'Then,' concluded the President, 'by your figures even if they use the total of their national reserve, they are going to need thirty to thirty-five million tons of foreign grain?'

'Right, Mr President,' cut in Poklewski. 'Maybe even more. And we and the Canadians are the only people who are going to have it. Dr Fletcher?'

The man from Agriculture nodded. 'It appears North America is going to have a bumper crop this year. Maybe fifty million tons over domestic requirements for both us and Canada considered together.'

Minutes later Dr Fletcher was escorted out. The debate resumed. Poklewski pressed his point.

'Mr President, this time we have to act. We have to require a *quid pro quo* from them this time around.'

'Linkage?' asked the President suspiciously. 'I know your thoughts on that, Stan. Last time it didn't work; it made things worse. I will not have another repeat of the Jackson Amendment.'

All three men recalled the fate of that piece of legislation with little joy. At the end of 1974 the Americans had introduced the Jackson Amendment which specified in effect that unless the Soviets went easier on the question of Russian–Jewish emigration to Israel, there would be no US trade credits for the purchase of technology and industrial goods. The Politburo under Brezhnev contemptuously rejected the pressure, launched a series of predominantly anti-Jewish show trials, and bought their requirements, with trade credits, from Britain, Germany and Japan.

'The point about a nice little spot of blackmail,' Sir Nigel Irvine, who was in Washington in 1975, had remarked to Bob Benson, 'is that you must be sure the victim simply cannot do without something that you have, and cannot acquire it anywhere else.'

Poklewski had learned this remark from Benson and repeated it to President Matthews, avoiding the word blackmail.

'Mr President, this time around they cannot get their wheat elsewhere. Our wheat surplus is no longer a trading matter. It is a strategic weapon. It is worth ten squadrons of nuclear bombers. There is no way we would sell nuclear technology to Moscow for money. I urge you to invoke the Shannon Act.'

In the wake of 'the Sting' of 1977, the US administration had finally and belatedly in 1980 passed the Shannon Act. This said simply that in any year the Federal Government had the right to buy the option for the US grain surplus at the going rate per ton at the time of the announcement that Washington wished to exercise its option.

The grain speculators had hated it, but the farmers went along. The act smoothed out some of the wilder fluctuations in the world grain prices. In years of glut the farmers had got a too-low price for their grain; in years of shortage the prices had been exceptionally high. The Shannon Act ensured that, if operated, the farmers would get a fair price, but the speculators would be out of business. The act also gave the administration a gigantic new weapon in dealing with customer countries, both the aggressive and the humble and poor.

'Very well,' said President Matthews, 'I will activate the Shannon Act. I will authorize the use of Federal funds to buy the futures for the expected surplus of fifty million tons of grain.'

Poklewski was jubilant.

'You won't regret it, Mr President. This time the Soviets will have to deal direct with your presidency, not with middlemen. We have them over a barrel. There is nothing else they can do.'

Yefrem Vishnayev thought differently. At the outset of the Politburo meeting he asked for the floor and got it.

'No one here, comrades, denies that the famine that faces us is not acceptable. No one denies that the surplus foods lie in the decadent capitalist West. It has been suggested that the only thing we can do is to humble ourselves, possibly accept concessions in our military might and therefore in the onward march of Marxism-Leninism in order to buy these surpluses to tide us over.

'Comrades, I disagree and I ask you to join me in rejection of the course of yielding to blackmail and betraying our great inspirator, Lenin. There is one other way; one other way in which we can secure acceptance by the entire Soviet people of rigid rationing at the minimum level, a nationwide upsurge of patriotism and self-sacrifice, and an imposition of that discipline without which we cannot get through the hunger that has to come.

'There is a way in which we can use what little harvest grain we shall cull this autumn, spin out the national reserve until the spring next year, use the meat from our herds and flocks in place of grain, and then, when all is used, turn to Western Europe where the milk lakes are, where the beef and butter mountains are, where the national reserves of ten wealthy nations are.'

'And buy them?' asked Foreign Minister Rykov ironically.

'No, comrade,' replied Vishnayev softly, 'take them. I yield the floor to Comrade Marshal Kerensky. He has a file he would wish each of us to examine.'

Twelve thick files were passed round. Kerensky kept his own and began reading from it. Rudin left his unopened in front of him and smoked steadily. Ivanenko also left his on the table and contemplated Kerensky. He and Rudin had known for four days what the file would be. In collaboration with Vishnayev, Kerensky had brought out of the general staff safe the Plan Boris file, named after Boris Goudonov, the great Russian conqueror. Now it had been brought right up to date.

And it was impressive, as Kerensky spent the next two hours reading it. During the following May the usual massive spring manoeuvres of the Red Army in East Germany would be bigger than ever, but with a difference. These would be no manoeuvres, but the real thing. On the command, all 30,000 tanks and armoured personnel carriers, mobile guns and amphibious craft would swing westwards, hammer across the Elbe and plough into West Germany, heading for France and the Channel ports.

Ahead of them, 50,000 paratroops would drop in over fifty locations to take out the principal tactical nuclear airfields of the French inside France and the Americans and British on

German soil. Another 100,000 would drop on the four countries of Scandinavia to possess the capital cities and main arteries, with massive naval back-up from offshore.

The military thrust would avoid the Italian and Iberian peninsulas, whose governments, all partners with the Euro-Communists in office, would be ordered by the Soviet ambassador to stay out of the fight or perish by joining in. Within half a decade later, they would fall like ripe plums anyway. Likewise Greece, Turkey and Yugoslavia. Switzerland would be avoided, Austria used only as a through-route. Both would later be islands in a Soviet sea, and would not last long.

The primary zone of attack and occupation would be the three Benelux countries, France and West Germany. Britain, as a prelude, would be crippled by strikes and confused by the extreme Left which, on instructions, would mount an immediate clamour for non-intervention. London would be informed that if the nuclear Strike Command was used east of the Elbe, Britain would be wiped off the face of the map.

Throughout the entire operation the Soviet Union would be stridently demanding an immediate ceasefire in every capital in the world and the United Nations, claiming the hostilities were local to West Germany, temporary and caused entirely by a West German pre-emptive strike towards Berlin, a claim that most of the non-German European Left would believe and support.

'And the United States, all this time?' Petrov interrupted. Kerensky looked irritated at being stopped in full flow after ninety minutes.

'The use of tactical nuclear weapons right across the face of Germany cannot be excluded,' pursued Kerensky, 'but the overwhelming majority of them will destroy West Germany, East Germany and Poland, no loss of course for the Soviet Union. Thanks to the weakness of Washington there is no deployment of either Cruise missiles or neutron bombs. Soviet military casualties are estimated at between one hundred and two hundred thousand, at the maximum. But as two million men in all three services will be involved, such percentages will be acceptable.'

'Duration?' asked Ivanenko.

'The point units of the forward mechanized armies will enter the French Channel ports one hundred hours after crossing the Elbe. At that point the ceasefire may be allowed to operate. The mopping up can take place under the ceasefire.'

'Is that time-scale feasible?' asked Petryanov.

This time Rudin cut in.

'Oh, yes, it's feasible,' he said mildly. Vishnayev shot him a suspicious look.

'I still have not had an answer to my question,' Petrov pointed out. 'What about the USA? What about their nuclear strike forces – not tactical nukes, strategic nukes? The hydrogen-bomb warheads in their intercontinental ballistic missile force, their bombers and their submarines.'

The eyes of the table riveted on Vishnayev. He rose again.

'The American President must, at the outset, be given three solemn assurances in absolutely credible form,' he said. 'One, that for her part the USSR will never be the first to use thermo-nuclear weapons. Two, that if the three hundred thousand American troops in Western Europe are committed to the fight, they must take their chances in conventional or tactical nuclear warfare with ours. Three, that in the event the USA resorts to ballistic missiles aimed at the Soviet Union, the top hundred cities of the USA will cease to exist.

'President Matthews, comrades, will not trade New York for the decadence of Paris, nor Los Angeles for Frankfurt. There will be *no* American thermo-nuclear riposte.'

The silence was heavy as the perspectives sank in. The vast storehouse of food, including grain, of consumer goods, and of technology that was contained in Western Europe. The fall within a few years of Italy, Spain, Portugal, Austria, Greece and Yugoslavia. The treasure trove of gold beneath the streets of Switzerland. The utter isolation of Britain and Ireland off the new Soviet coast. The domination without a shot fired of the entire Arab and Third World. It was a heady mixture.

'It's a fine scenario,' said Rudin at last, 'but it all seems to be based on one assumption. That the USA will not rain her nuclear warheads on the Soviet Union if we promise not to let ours loose on her. I would be grateful to hear if Comrade Vishnayev has any corroboration for that confident declaration. In short, is it a proven fact, or a fond hope?'

'More than a hope,' snapped Vishnayev. 'A realistic calculation. As capitalists and bourgeois nationalists, the Americans will always think of themselves first. They are paper tigers, weak and indecisive. Above all, when the prospect of losing their own lives faces them, they are cowards.'

'Are they indeed?' mused Rudin. 'Well, now, comrades, let me attempt to sum up. Comrade Vishnayev's scenario is realistic in every sense, but it all hangs on his hope – I beg his pardon – on his calculation that the Americans will not respond with their heavy thermo-nuclear weapons. Had we ever believed this before, we would surely already have completed the process of liberating the captive masses of Western Europe from Fascism-Capitalism to Marxism-Leninism. Personally, I perceive no new element to justify the calculation of Comrade Vishnayev.

'However, neither he nor the Comrade Marshal have ever had any dealings with the Americans, or ever been in the West. Personally, I have, and I disagree. Let us hear from Comrade Rykov.'

The elderly and veteran foreign minister was white-faced.

'All this smacks of Khrushchevism, as in the case of Cuba. I have spent thirty years in foreign affairs. Ambassadors around the world report to me, not Comrade Vishnayev. None of them, not one; not one single analyst in my department, nor I, have a single doubt that the US president would use the thermo-nuclear response on the Soviet Union. It is not a question of exchanging cities. He too can see that the outcome of such a war would be domination by the Soviet Union of almost the whole world. It would be the end of America as a super-power, as a power, as anything other than a nonentity. They will devastate the Soviet Union before they yield Western Europe and thence the world.'

'I would point out that if they do,' said Rudin, 'we cannot as yet stop them. Our high-energy-particle laser beams from space satellites are not fully functional yet. One day we will no doubt be able to vaporize incoming rockets in inner space before they can reach us. But not yet. The latest assessments of our experts – our experts, Comrade Vishnayev, not our optimists – suggest a full-blown Anglo-American thermonuclear strike would take out one hundred million of our citizens, mostly Great Russians, and devastate sixty per cent of the union from Poland to the Urals. But, to continue, Comrade Ivanenko, you have experience of the West. What do you say?'

'Unlike Comrades Vishnayev and Kerensky,' observed Ivanenko, 'I control hundreds of agents throughout the capitalist West. Their reports are constant. I too have no doubt at all the Americans would respond.'

'Then let me put it in a nutshell,' said Rudin brusquely. The time for sparring was over. 'If we negotiate with the Americans for wheat, we may have to accede to demands that could set us back by five years. If we tolerate the famine, we would probably be set back by ten years. If we launch a European war, we could be wiped out, certainly set back by twenty to forty years.

'I am not the theoretician that Comrade Vishnayev undoubtedly is. But I seem to recall the teachings of Marx and Lenin are very firm on one point; that while the triumph of the world rule of Marxism must be pursued at every stage by every means, the progress should not be endangered by the incurring of foolish risks. I estimate this plan as being based on a foolish risk. Therefore I propose that we –'

'I propose a vote,' said Vishnayev softly.

So that was it. Not a vote of no confidence in him, thought Rudin; that would come later, if he lost this round. The faction fight was out in the open now. He had not had the feeling so clearly in years that he was now fighting for his life. If he lost there would be no graceful retirement, no retaining the villas and the privileges like Mikoyan had done. It would be ruin, exile, perhaps the bullet in the nape of the neck. But he kept his composure. He put his own motion first. One by one the hands went up.

Rykov, Ivanenko, Petrov, all voted for him and the negotiation policy. There was hesitancy down the table. Who had Vishnayev got to? What had he promised them?

Stepanov and Shushkin raised their hands. Last, slowly, came Chavadze the Georgian. Rudin put the counter-motion, for war in the spring. Vishnayev and Kerensky of course were for it. Komarov of Agriculture joined them. Bastard, thought Rudin, it was your bloody ministry that got us into this mess. Vishnayev must have persuaded the man that Rudin was going to ruin him in any case, so he thought he had nothing to lose. You're wrong, my friend, thought Rudin, face impassive; I'm going to have your entrails for this. Petryanov raised his hand. He's been promised the prime ministership, thought Rudin. Vitautas the Balt and Mukhamed the Tadjik also went with Vishnayev for war. The Tadjik would know that if nuclear war came, the orientals would rule over the ruins. The Lithuanian had been bought.

'Six for each proposal,' he said quietly. 'And my own vote for the negotiations.'

'Too close,' he thought, 'much too close.'

It was sundown when the meeting dissolved. But the faction fight, all knew, would now go on until it was resolved; no one could back away now, no one could stay neutral any more.

It was not until the fifth day of the tour that the party arrived in Lvov and stayed at the Intourist hotel. Up to this point Drake had gone with all the guided tours on the agenda, but this time he made an excuse that he had a headache and wished to stay in his room. As soon as the party left by coach for St Nicholas Church, he changed into more casual clothes and slipped out of the hotel.

Kaminsky had told him the sort of clothes that would pass without attracting attention: socks with sandals, light trousers, not too smart, and an open-necked shirt of the cheaper variety. With a street map he set off on foot for the seedy, poor, working-class suburb of Levandivka. He had not the slightest doubt that the two men he sought would treat him with the profoundest suspicion, once he found them. And this was hardly surprising when one considered the family backgrounds and circumstances that had forged them. He recalled what Miroslav Kaminsky in his Turkish hospital bed had told him.

On the 29th September 1966 near Kiev, at the gorge of Babi Yar where over 50,000 Jews were slaughtered by the SS in Nazi-occupied Ukraine in 1941/42, the Ukraine's foremost contemporary poet, Ivan Dzuba, gave an address which was remarkable in as much as a Ukrainian Catholic was speaking out powerfully against anti-Semitism. Anti-Semitism has always flourished in the Ukraine, and successive rulers – tsars, Stalinists, Nazis, Stalinists again, and their successors – have vigorously encouraged it to flourish.

Dzuba's long speech began as a seeming plea for remembrance of the slaughtered Jews of Babi Yar, a straight condemnation of Nazism and Fascism. But as it developed, his theme began to encompass all those despotisms which, despite their technological triumphs, brutalize the human spirit and seek to persuade even the brutalized that this is normal.

'We should therefore judge each society,' he said, 'not by its external technical achievements but by the position and meaning it gives to man, by the value it puts on human dignity and human conscience.'

By the time he had reached this point the Chekisti who had infiltrated the silent crowd realized the poet was not talking about Hitler's Germany at all; he was talking about the Politburo's Soviet Union. Shortly after the speech he was arrested.

In the cellars of the local KGB barracks the chief interrogator, the man who had at his beck and call the two hulks in the corners of the room, the ones gripping the metre-long heavy hosepipes, was a fast-rising young colonel of the Second Chief Directorate, sent in from Moscow. His name was Yuri Ivanenko.

But at the address at Babi Yar there had been, in the front row, standing next to their fathers, two small ten-year-old boys. They did not know each other then, and would only meet and become firm friends six years later on a building site. One was called Lev Mishkin, the other was David Lazareff.

The presence of both the fathers of Mishkin and Lazareff at the meeting had also been noted, and when years later they had applied for permission to emigrate to Israel, both had been accused of anti-Soviet activities and drawn long sentences in labour camps.

Their families had lost their apartments, the sons any hope of university. Though highly intelligent, they were destined for pick-and-shovel work. Now both aged twenty-six, these were the young men Drake sought among the hot and dusty byways of Levandivka.

It was at the second address that he found David Lazareff who, after the introductions, treated him with extreme suspicion. But he agreed to bring his friend Mishkin to a rendezvous, since Drake knew both their names anyway.

That evening he met Lev Mishkin, and the pair regarded him with something close to hostility. He told them the whole story of the escape and rescue of Miroslav Kaminsky, and the background to himself. The only proof he could produce was the photograph of himself and Kaminsky together, taken in the hospital room at Trabzon on a Polaroid instant camera by a nursing orderly. Held up in front of them was that day's edition of the local Turkish newspaper. Drake had brought the same newspaper as suitcase-lining and showed it to them as proof of his story.

'Look,' he said finally, 'if Miroslav had been washed up in Soviet territory and been taken by the KGB, if he had talked and revealed your names, and if I was from the KGB, I'd hardly be asking for your help.'

The two Jewish workers agreed to consider his request overnight. Unknown to Drake, both Mishkin and Lazareff had long shared an ideal close to his own – that of striking one single powerful blow of revenge against the Kremlin hierarchy in their midst. But they were near to giving up, weighed down by the hopelessness of trying to do anything without outside help.

Impelled by their desire for an ally beyond the borders of the USSR, the two shook hands in the small hours of the morning and agreed to take the Anglo-Ukrainian into their confidence. The second meeting was that afternoon, Drake having skipped another guided tour. For safety they strolled through wide, unpaved lanes near the outskirts of the city, talking quietly in Ukrainian. They told Drake of their desire also to strike at Moscow in a single, deadly act.

'The question is, what?' said Drake. Lazareff, who was the more silent and more dominant of the pair, spoke.

'Ivanenko,' he said, 'the most hated man in the Ukraine.'

'What about him?' asked Drake.

'Kill him.'

Drake stopped in his tracks and stared at the dark, intense young man.

'You'd never get near him,' he said finally.

'Last year,' said Lazareff, 'I was working on a job here in Lvov. I'm a house painter, right? We were redecorating the apartment of a party big-wig. There was a little old woman staying with them. From Kiev. After she'd gone, the Party man's wife mentioned who she was. Later I saw a letter postmarked Kiev in the letter box. I took it, and it was from the old bird. It had her address on it.'

'So who was she?' asked Drake.

'His mother.'

Drake considered the information. 'You wouldn't think people like that have mothers,' he said. 'But you'd have to watch her flat for a long time before he might come to visit her.'

Lazareff shook his head. 'She's the bait,' he said, and outlined his idea. Drake considered the enormity of it.

Before coming to the Ukraine, he had envisaged the great single blow he had dreamed of delivering against the might of the Kremlin in many terms, but never this. To assassinate the head of the KGB would be to strike into the very centre of the

Politburo, to send hairline cracks running through every corner of the power structure.

'It might work,' he conceded.

If it did, he thought, it would be hushed up at once. But if the news ever got out, the effect on popular opinion, especially in the Ukraine, would be traumatic.

'It could trigger the biggest uprising there has ever been here,' he said.

Lazareff nodded. Alone with his partner Mishkin, far away from outside help, he had evidently given the project a lot of thought.

'True,' he said.

'What equipment would you need?' asked Drake.

Lazareff told him.

Drake nodded. 'It can all be acquired in the West,' he said, 'but how to get it in?'

'Odessa,' cut in Mishkin. 'I was on the docks there for a while. The place is completely corrupt. The black market is thriving. Every Western ship brings seamen who do a vigorous trade with the local spivs in Turkish leather jackets, suede coats and denim jeans. We would meet you there. It is inside the Ukraine; we would not need inter-state passports.'

Before they parted the plan was agreed. Drake would acquire the equipment and bring it to Odessa by sea. He would alert Mishkin and Lazareff by a letter, posted inside the Soviet Union, well in advance of his own arrival. The wording would be innocent. The rendezvous in Odessa was to be a café that Mishkin knew from his days as a teenage labourer there.

'Two more things,' said Drake. 'When it is over, the publicity for it, the worldwide announcement that it has been done, is vital; almost as important as the act itself. And that means that you personally must tell the world. Only you will have the details to convince the world of the truth. But that means you must escape from here to the West.'

'It goes without saying,' murmured Lazareff. 'We are both Refuseniks. We have tried to emigrate to Israel like our fathers before us, and have been refused. This time we will go, with or without permission. When this is over, we have to get to Israel. It is the only place we will ever be safe, ever again. Once there, we will tell the world what we have done and leave those bastards in the Kremlin and the KGB discredited in the eyes of their own people.'

'The other point follows from the first,' said Drake. 'When it is done, you must let me know by coded letter or postcard – in case anything goes wrong with the escape. So that I can try to help get the news to the world.'

They agreed that an innocently worded postcard would be sent from Lvov to a *poste restante* address in London. With the last details memorized, they parted, and Drake rejoined his tour group.

Two days later Drake was back in London. The first thing he did was to buy the most comprehensive book he could find on small arms. The second was to send a telegram to a friend in Canada, one of the best of that elite private list he had built up over the years of emigrés who thought as he did of carrying their hatred to the enemy. The third was to begin preparations for a long-dormant plan to raise the needed funds by robbing a bank.

At the far end of Kutuzovsky Prospekt on the southeastern outskirts of Moscow, a driver pulling to the right off the main boulevard on the Rublevo Road will arrive twenty kilometres later at the little village of Uspenskoye, in the heart of the weekend-villa country. In the great pine and birch forests around Uspenskoye lie the hamlets like Usovo and Zhukovka where stand the country mansions of the Soviet elite. Just beyond Uspenskoye bridge over the Moscow River is a beach where in summer the lesser-privileged but nevertheless very well-off (they have their own cars) come from Moscow to bathe from the sandy shore.

The Western diplomats come here too, and it is one of the rare places where a Westerner can be cheek by jowl with ordinary Muscovite families. Even the routine KGB tailing of Western diplomats seems to let up on Sunday afternoons in high summer.

Adam Munro came here with a party of British embassy staffers that Sunday afternoon, 11th July 1982. Some of them were married couples, some single and younger than he. Shortly before three the whole party of them left their towels and picnic baskets among the trees, ran down the low bluff towards the sandy beach and swam. When he came back, Munro picked up his rolled towel and began to dry himself. Something fell out of it.

He stopped to pick it up. It was a small pasteboard card, half the size of a postcard, white on both sides. On one side was typed, in Russian, the words: 'Three kilometres north of here is an abandoned chapel in the woods. Meet me there in thirty minutes. Please. It is urgent.'

He maintained his smile as one of the embassy secretaries came over, laughing, to ask for a cigarette. While he lit it for her, his mind was working out all the angles he could think of. A dissident wanting to pass over the underground literature? A load of trouble, that. A religious group wanting asylum in the embassy? The Americans had that in 1978, and it had caused untold problems. A trap, set by the KGB to identify the SIS man inside the embassy? Always possible. No ordinary commercial secretary would accept such an invitation, slipped into a rolled towel by someone who had evidently tailed him and watched from the surrounding woods. And yet it was too crude for the KGB. They would have set up a pretended defector in central Moscow with information to pass, arranged for secret photographs at the handover point. So who was the secret writer?

He dressed quickly, still undecided. Finally, he pulled on his shoes and made up his mind. If it was a trap, then he had received no message and was simply walking in the forest. To the disappointment of his hopeful secretary he set off alone. After ninety metres he paused, took out his lighter and burnt the card, grinding the ash into the carpet of pine needles.

The sun and his watch gave him due north, away from the river bank which faced south. After ten minutes he emerged on the side of a slope and saw the onion-shaped dome of a chapel two kilometres further on across the valley. Seconds later he was back in the trees.

The forests around Moscow have dozens of such small chapels, once the worshipping places of the villagers, now mainly derelict, boarded up, deserted. The one he was approaching stood in its own clearing among the trees. At the edge of the clearing he stopped and surveyed the tiny church. He could see no one. Carefully he advanced into the open. He was a few metres from the sealed front door when he saw the figure standing in deep shadow under an archway. He stopped, and for minutes on end the two stared at each other.

There was really nothing to say, so he just said her name, 'Valentina.'

She moved out of the shadow and replied, 'Adam.'

'Twenty-one years,' he thought in wonderment. 'She must be turned forty.' She looked like thirty, still raven-haired, beautiful and ineffably sad.

They sat on one of the tombstones and talked quietly of the old times. She told him she had returned from Berlin to Moscow a few months after their parting, and had continued to be a stenographer for the Party machine. At twenty-three she had married a young army officer with good prospects. After seven years there had been a baby, and they had been happy, all three of them. Her husband's career had flourished, for he had an uncle high in the Red Army, and patronage is no different in the Soviet Union than anywhere else. The boy was now ten.

Five years ago her husband, having reached the rank of colonel at a young age, had been killed in a helicopter crash while surveying Red Chinese troop deployments along the Ussuri River in the Far East. To kill the grief she had gone back to work. Her husband's uncle had used his influence to secure her good, highly placed work, bringing with it privileges in the form of special food shops, special restaurants, better apartments, a private car – all the things that go with high rank in the Party machine.

Finally, two years ago, after special clearance, she had been offered a post in the tiny, closed group of stenographers and typists, a sub-section of the General Secretariat of the Central Committee, that is called the Politburo Secretariat.

Munro breathed deeply. That was high, very high, and very trusted.

'Who,' he asked, 'is the uncle of your late husband?'

'Kerensky,' she murmured.

'Marshal Kerensky?' he asked. She nodded. Munro exhaled slowly. Kerensky, the ultra-hawk. When he looked again at her face, the eyes were wet. She was blinking rapidly, on the verge of tears. On an impulse he put his arm round her shoulders and she leaned against him. He smelt her hair, the same sweet odour that had made him feel both tender and excited two decades ago in his youth.

'What's the matter?' he asked gently.

'Oh, Adam, I'm so unhappy.'

'In God's name, why? In your society you have everything.'

She shook her head, slowly, then pulled away from him. She avoided his eyes, gazing across the clearing into the woods.

'Adam, all my life, since I was a small girl, I believed. I truly believed. Even when we loved, I believed in the goodness, the rightness, of socialism. Even in the hard times, the times of deprivation in my country, when the West had all the consumer riches and we had none, I believed in the justice of the Communist ideal that we in Russia would one day bring to the world. It was an ideal that would give us all a world without Fascism, without money-lust, without exploitation, without war.

'I was taught it, and I really believed it. It was more important than you, than our love, than my husband and child. As much at least as this country, Russia, which is part of my soul.'

Munro knew about the patriotism of the Russians towards their country, a fierce flame that would make them endure any suffering, any privation, make any sacrifice and which, when manipulated, would make them obey their Kremlin overlords without demur.

'What happened?' he asked quietly.

'They have betrayed it. Are betraying it. My ideal, my people and my country.'

'They?' he asked. She was twisting her fingers till they looked as if they would come off.

'The Party chiefs,' she said bitterly. She spat out the Russian slang word meaning 'the fat cats'. 'The *nachalstvo*.'

Munro had twice witnessed a recantation. When a true believer loses the faith, the reversed fanaticism goes to strange extremes.

'I worshipped them, Adam. I respected them. I revered them. Now, for years, I have lived close to them all. I have lived in their shadow, taken their gifts, been showered with their privileges. I have seen them close up, in private, heard them talk, about the people, whom they despise. They are rotten, Adam, corrupt and cruel. Everything they touch they turn to ashes.'

Munro swung one leg across the tombstone so he could face her, took her in his arms. She was crying softly. 'I can't go on, Adam, I can't go on,' she murmured into his shoulder.

'All right, my darling, do you want me to try to get you out?'

He knew it would cost him his career, but this time he was not going to let her go. It would be worth it, everything would be worth it.

She pulled away, her face tear-streaked. 'I cannot leave. I have Sasha to think about.'

He held her quietly for a while longer. His mind was racing.

'How did you know I was in Moscow?' he asked carefully.

She gave no hint of surprise at the question. It was in any case natural enough for him to ask it.

'Last month,' she said between sniffs, 'I was taken to the ballet by a colleague from the office. We were in a box. When the lights were low, I thought I must be mistaken. But when they went up in the interval, I knew it was really you. I could not stay after then. I pleaded a headache and left quickly.'

She dabbed her eyes, the crying spell over.

'Adam,' she asked eventually, 'did you marry?'

'Yes,' he said. 'Long after Berlin. It didn't work. We were divorced years ago.'

She managed a little smile. 'I'm glad,' she said. 'I'm glad there is no one else. That is not very logical, is it?'

He grinned back at her.

'No,' he said, 'it is not. But it is nice to hear. Can we see each other? In the future.'

Her smile faded; there was a hunted look in her eyes. She shook her dark head.

'No, not very often, Adam,' she said. 'I am trusted, privileged, but if a foreigner came to my apartment, it would soon be noticed and reported. The same applies to your apartment. Diplomats are watched – you know that. Hotels are watched also; no apartments are for rent here, without any formalities. It is not possible, Adam, it is just not possible.'

'Valentina, you started this meeting. You took the initiative. Was it just for old times' sake? If you do not like your life, here, if you do not like the men you work for. . . . But if you cannot leave because of Sasha, then what is it you want?'

She composed herself and thought for a while. When she spoke it was quite calmly.

'Adam, I want to try and stop them. I want to try and stop what they are doing. I suppose I have for several years now, but since I saw you at the Bolshoi, and remembered all the freedoms we had in Berlin, I began thinking about it more and more. Now I am certain. Tell me if you can; is there an intelligence officer in your embassy?'

Munro was shaken. He had handled two defectors-in-place, one from the Soviet embassy in Mexico City, the other in Vienna. One had been motivated by a conversion from respect to hatred for his own regime, like Valentina; the other by bitterness at lack of promotion. The former had been the trickier to handle.

'I suppose so,' he said slowly. 'I suppose there must be.'

Valentina rummaged in the shoulder-bag on the pine needles by her feet. Having made up her mind she was apparently determined to go through with her betrayal. She withdrew a thick padded envelope.

'I want you to give this to him, Adam. Promise me you will never tell him who it came from. Please, Adam, I am frightened by what I am doing. I cannot trust anyone, not anyone but you.'

'I promise,' he said. 'But I have to see you again. I can't just see you walk away through the gap in the wall as I did last time.'

'No, I cannot do that again either. But do not try to contact me at my apartment. It is in a walled compound for senior functionaries, with a single gate in the wall and a policeman on it. Do not try to telephone me. The calls are monitored. And I will never meet anyone else from your embassy, not even the intelligence chief.'

'I agree,' said Munro. 'But when can we meet again?'

She considered for a moment. 'It is not always easy for me to get away. Sasha takes up most of my spare time. But I have my own car and I am not followed. Tomorrow I must go away for two weeks, but we can meet here, four Sundays from today.' She looked at her watch. 'I must go, Adam. I am one of a house party at a *dacha* a few miles from here.'

He kissed her, on the lips, the way it used to be. And it was as sweet as it had ever been. She rose and walked away across the clearing. At the fringe of the trees he called after her.

'Valentina, what is in this?' He held up the package.

She paused and turned. 'My job,' she said, 'is to prepare the verbatim transcripts of the Politburo meetings, one for each member. And the digests for the candidate members. From the tape recordings. That is a copy of the recording of the meeting of 10th June.'

Then she was gone into the trees. Munro sat on the tombstone and looked down at the package.

'Bloody hell,' he said.

4

Adam Munro sat in a locked room in the main building of the British embassy on Maurice Thorez Embankment and listened to the last sentences of the tape recording on the machine in front of him. The room was safe from any chance of electronic surveillance by the Russians, which was why he had borrowed it for a few hours from head of chancery.

'... goes without saying that this news does not pass outside those present in this room. Our next meeting will be today week.'

The voice of Maxim Rudin died away and the tape hissed on the machine, then stopped. Munro switched off. He leaned back and let out a long, low whistle.

If it was true, it was bigger than anything Oleg Penkovsky had brought over, twenty years before. The story of Penkovsky was folklore in the SIS, the CIA and most of all in the bitterest memories of the KGB. He was the full brigadier-general of the GRU, with access to the highest information, who, disenchanted with the Kremlin hierarchy, had approached first the Americans and then the British with an offer to provide information.

The Americans had turned him down, suspecting a trap. The British had accepted him, and for two and a half years 'run' him until he was trapped by the KGB, exposed, tried and shot. In his time he had brought over a golden harvest of secret information, but most important of all it was at the time of the October 1962 Cuban missile crisis. In that month the world had applauded the exceptionally skilful handling by President Kennedy of the eyeball-to-eyeball confrontation with Nikita Khrushchev over the matter of the planting of Soviet missiles in Cuba. What the world had not known was that the exact strengths and weaknesses of the Russian leader were already in the Americans' hands, thanks to Penkovsky.

When it was finally over, the Soviet missiles were out of Cuba, Khrushchev was humbled, Kennedy was a hero, and Penkovsky was under suspicion. He was arrested in November. Within a year, after a show trial, he was dead. Within a year also, Khrushchev had fallen, toppled by his own colleagues; ostensibly because of his failure in the grain policy, in fact because his adventurism had scared the daylights out of them. And that same winter of 1963 Kennedy too had died, just thirteen months after his triumph. The democrat, the despot and the spy had all left the stage. But even Penkovsky had never got right inside the Politburo.

Munro took the spool off the machine and carefully rewrapped it. The voice of Professor Yakovlev was of course unknown to him, and most of the tape was of him reading his report. But in the discussion following the professor there were ten voices and three at least were identifiable. The low growl of Rudin was well enough known, the high tones of Vishnayev he had heard before, when watching televised speeches by the man to Party congresses; and the bark of Marshal Kerensky he had heard at May Day celebrations, also on film and tape.

His problem, when he took the tape back to London for voice-print analysis, as he knew he must, was how to cover his source. He knew if he admitted to the secret rendezvous in the forest, following the typed note in the bathing towel, the question would be asked: 'Why you, Munro? How did she know you?' It would be impossible to avoid that question, and equally impossible to answer it. The only solution was to devise an alternative source, credible and uncheckable.

He had only been in Moscow six weeks, but his unsuspected mastery of even slang Russian had paid a couple of dividends. At a diplomatic reception in the Czech embassy a fortnight earlier he had been in conversation with an Indian attaché when he heard two Russians in muttered conversation behind him. One of them had said: 'He's a bitter bastard. Thinks he should have had the top slot.'

He had followed the gaze of the two who had spoken and noted they were observing and presumably talking about a Russian across the room. The guest list later confirmed the man was Anatoly Krivoi, personal aide and right-hand man to the Party theoretician, Vishnayev. So what had he got to be bitter about? Munro checked his files and came up with Krivoi's history. He had worked in the Party Organizations section of the Central Committee; shortly after the nomination of Petrov to the top job, Krivoi had appeared on Vishnayev's staff. Quit in disgust? Personality conflict with Petrov? Bitter at being passed over? They were all perfectly possible, and all interesting to an intelligence chief in a foreign capital.

Krivoi, he mused. Maybe. Just maybe. He too would have access, at least to Vishnayev's copy of the transcript, maybe even of the tape. And he was probably in Moscow; certainly his boss was. Vishnayev had been present when the East German premier had arrived a week before.

'Sorry, Anatoly, you've just changed sides,' he said as he slipped the fat envelope into an inside pocket and took the stairs to see the head of chancery.

'I'm afraid I have to go back to London with the Wednesday bag,' he told the diplomat. 'It's unavoidable, and it can't wait.'

Chancery asked no questions. He knew Munro's job and promised to arrange it. The diplomatic bag, which actually *is* a bag or at least a series of canvas sacks, goes from Moscow to London every Wednesday and always on the British Airways flight, never Aeroflot. A Queen's messenger, one of that team of men who constantly fly around the world from London picking up embassy bags and protected by the insignia of the crown and greyhound, comes out from London for it. The very secret material is carried in a hard-frame despatch box chained to the man's left wrist; the more routine stuff in the canvas sacks, the messenger personally checks into the aircraft hold. Once there it is on British territory. But in the case of Moscow the messenger is accompanied by an embassy staffer.

The escort job is sought after, since it permits a quick trip home to London, a bit of shopping and a chance of a good night out. The second secretary who lost his place in the rota that week was annoyed, but asked no questions.

The following Wednesday the British Airways airbus-300B lifted out of the new, post-1980-Olympics Sheremetyevo Airport and turned its nose towards London. By Munro's side the messenger, a short, dapper ex-army major, withdrew straight into his hobby, composing crossword puzzles for a major newspaper.

'You have to do something to while away these endless aeroplane flights,' he told Munro. 'We all have our in-flight hobbies.'

Munro grunted and looked back over the wingtip at the receding city of Moscow. Somewhere down there in the sun-drenched streets the woman he loved was working and moving among people she was going to betray. She was on her own and right out in the cold.

The country of Norway, seen in isolation from its eastern neighbour Sweden, looks like a great, pre-historic, fossilized human hand stretching down from the Arctic towards Denmark and Britain. It is a right hand, palm downwards to the ocean, a stubby thumb towards the east clenched into the forefinger. Up the crack between thumb and forefinger lies Oslo, its capital.

To the north the fractured forearm bones stretch up to Tromso and Hammerfest, deep in the Arctic, so narrow that in places there are only forty miles from the sea to the Swedish border. On a relief map the hand looks as if it has been smashed by some gigantic hammer of the gods, splintering bones and knuckles into thousands of particles. Nowhere is this breakage more marked than along the west coast, where the chopping edge of the hand would be.

Here the land is shattered into a thousand fragments and

between the shards the sea has flowed in to form a million creeks, gullies, bays and gorges; winding narrow defiles where the mountains fall sheer to glittering water. These are the fjords, and it was from the headwaters of these that a race of men came out 1500 years ago who were the best sailors ever to set keel to the water or sail to the wind. Before their age was over they had sailed to Greenland and America, conquered Ireland, settled Britain and Normandy, hunted to Spain and Morocco and navigated from the Mediterranean to Iceland. They were the Vikings, and their descendants still live and fish along the fjords of Norway.

Such a man was Thor Larsen, sea captain and ship's master, who strode that mid-July afternoon past the royal palace in the Swedish capital of Stockholm from his company's head office back to his hotel. People tended to step aside for him; he was six feet three inches tall, wide as the pavements of the old quarter of the city, blue-eyed and bearded. Being shorebound, he was in civilian clothes, but he was happy because he had reason to think, after visiting the head office of the Nordia Line, that now lay behind him along the Ship Quay, that he might soon have a new command.

After six months attending a course at the company's expense in the intricacies of radar, computer navigation and supertanker technology, he was dying to get back to sea again. The summons to head office had been to receive from the hands of the personal secretary to the proprietor, chairman and managing director of Nordia Line his invitation to dinner that evening. The invitation also included Larsen's wife, who had been informed by telephone and was flying in from Norway on a company ticket. The Old Man was splashing out a bit, thought Larsen. There must be something in the wind.

He took his rented car from the hotel car park across the bridge on Nybroviken and drove the thirty-seven kilometres to the airport. When Lisa Larsen arrived in the concourse with her overnight bag, he greeted her with the delicacy of an excited St Bernard, swinging her off her feet like a girl. She was small and petite, with dark bright eyes, soft chestnut curls and a trim figure that belied her thirty-eight years. And he adored her.

Twenty years earlier, when he had been a gangling second mate of twenty-five, he had met her one freezing winter day in Oslo. She had slipped on the ice, he had picked her up like a doll and set her back on her feet. She was wearing a fur-trimmed hood that almost hid her tiny, red-nosed face, and when she thanked him he could only see her eyes, looking out of the mass of snow and fur like the bright eyes of a snow-mouse in the forests of winter. Ever since, through their courtship and marriage and the years in between, he had called her snow-mouse.

He drove her back into central Stockholm, asking all the way about their home in Alesund far away on Norway's western coast, and of the progress of their two teenage children. To the south a British Airways airbus passed by on its great circle route from Moscow to London. Thor Larsen neither knew nor cared.

The dinner that evening was to be in the famous Aurora Cellar, built below ground in the cellar-storerooms of an old palace in the city's medieval quarter. When Thor and Lisa Larsen arrived and were shown down the narrow steps to the cellar, the proprietor Leonard was waiting for them at the bottom.

'Mr Wennerstrom is already here,' he said, and showed them into one of the private rooms, a small, intimate cavern, arched in 500-year-old brick, spanned by a thick table of glittering ancient timber and lit by candles in cast-iron holders. As they entered, Larsen's employer, Harald Wennerstrom, lumbered to his feet, embraced Lisa and shook hands with her husband.

Harald 'Harry' Wennerstrom was something of a legend in his own lifetime among the seafaring people of Scandinavia. He was now seventy-five, grizzled and craggy with bristling eyebrows. Just after the Second World War, returning to his native Stockholm, he had inherited from his father half a dozen small cargo ships. In thirty-five years he had built up the biggest independently owned fleet of tankers outside the hands of the Greeks and the Hong Kong Chinese. The Nordia Line was his creation, diversifying from dry-cargo ships to tankers in the mid-fifties, laying out the money, building the ships for the oil boom of the sixties, backing his own judgement, often going against the grain.

They sat and ate, and Wennerstrom talked only of small things, asking after the family. His own forty-year marriage had ended with the death of his wife four years earlier; they had had no children. But if he had had a son, he would have liked him to be like the big Norwegian across the table from him, a sailor's sailor, and he was particularly fond of Lisa.

The salmon, cured in brine and dill, Scandinavian way, was delicious, the tender duck from the Stockholm salt marshes excellent. It was only when they sat finishing their wine – Wennerstrom unhappily sipping at his balloon glass of water, 'all the bloody doctors will allow me nowadays' – that he came to business.

'Three years ago, Thor, back in 1979, I made three forecasts to myself. One was that by the end of 1982 the solidarity of the Organization of Petroleum Exporting Countries, OPEC, would have broken down. The second was that the American president's policy to curb the United States' consumption of oil energy and by-products would have failed. The third was that the Soviet Union would have changed from a net oil exporter to a net oil importer. I was told I was crazy, but I was right.'

Thor Larsen nodded. The formation of OPEC and its quadrupling of oil prices in the winter of 1973 had produced a world slump that had nearly broken the economies of the Western world. It had also sent the oil tanker business into a seven-year decline, with millions of tons of partially built tankers laid up, useless, uneconomic, loss-making. It was a bold spirit who could have seen three years earlier the events between 1979 and 1982: the break-up of OPEC as the Arab world split into feuding factions, the second revolution in Iran, the disintegration of Nigeria, the rush by the radical oil-producing nations to sell oil at any price to finance arms-buying sprees; the spiralling increase in US oil consumption based on the ordinary American's conviction of his God-given right to rape the globe's resources for his own comforts; and the Soviet native oil industry peaking at such a low production figure through poor technology and forcing Russia to become once again an oil importer. The three factors had produced the tanker boom into which they were now, in the summer of 1982, beginning to move.

'As you know,' Wennerstrom resumed, 'last September I signed a contract with the Japanese for a new supertanker. Down in the market place they all said I was mad; half my fleet laid up in Stromstad Sound, and I order a new one. But I'm not mad. You know the story of the East Shore Oil Company?'

Larsen nodded again. A small, Louisiana-based oil company in America ten years ago, it had passed into the hands of the dynamic Clint Blake. In ten years it had grown and expanded until it was on the verge of joining the Seven Sisters, the mastodons of the world oil cartels.

'Well, in the summer of next year, 1983, Clint Blake is invading Europe. It's a tough, crowded market, but he thinks he can crack it. He's putting several thousand service stations across the motorways of Europe, marketing his own brand of gasoline and oil. And for that he'll need tanker tonnage. And I've got it: a seven-year contract to bring crude from the Middle East to Western Europe. He's already building his own refinery at Rotterdam, alongside Esso, Mobil and Chevron. That is what the new tanker is for. She's big and she's ultra-modern and she's expensive, but she'll pay. She'll make five or six runs a year from the Arabian Gulf to Rotterdam, and in five years she'll amortize the investment. But that's not the reason I'm building her. She's going to be the biggest and the best; my flagship, my memorial. And you're going to be her skipper.'

Thor Larsen sat in silence. Lisa's hand stole across the table and laid itself on top of his, squeezing gently. Two years ago, Larsen knew, he could never have skippered a Swedish-flag vessel, being himself a Norwegian. But since the Gothenburg Agreement of the previous year, which Wennerstrom had helped to push through, a Swedish shipowner could apply for honorary citizenship of Sweden for exceptional Scandinavian but non-Swedish officers in his employ so that they could be offered a captaincy. He had applied successfully on behalf of Larsen.

The coffee came and they sipped in appreciation.

'I'm having her built at the Ishikawajima-Harima yard in Japan,' said Wennerstrom. 'It's the only yard in the world that can take her. They have the dry dock.'

Both men knew the days of ships being built on slipways and then allowed to slide into the water were long past. The size and weight factors were too great. The giants were now built in enormous dry docks, so that when ready for launching the sea was let in through dock sluices and the ship simply floated off her blocks and rode water inside the dock.

'Work began on her last 4th November,' Wennerstrom told them. 'The keel was laid 30th January. She's taking shape now. She'll float on 1st November next, and after three months at the fitting-out berth and sea trials, she'll sail on 2nd February. And you'll be on her bridge, Thor.'

'Thank you,' said Larsen. 'What are you calling her?'

'Ah, yes. I've thought of that. Do you remember the Sagas? We'll name her to please Niorn, the god of the sea,' said Wennerstrom quietly. He was gripping his glass of water, staring at the flame of the candle in its cast-iron holder before him. 'For Niorn controls the fire and the water, the twin enemies of a tanker captain; the explosion and the sea herself.'

The water in his glass and the flame of the candle reflected in the old man's eyes, as once fire and water had reflected in his eyes as he sat helpless in a lifeboat in the mid-Atlantic in 1942 four cables from his blazing tanker, his first command, watching his crew fry in the sea around him.

Thor Larsen stared at his patron, doubting that the old man could really believe this mythology; Lisa, being a woman, knew he meant every word of it. At last Wennerstrom sat back, pushed the glass aside with an impatient gesture, and filled his spare glass with red wine.

'So we will call her after the daughter of Niorn, Freya, the most beautiful of all the goddesses. We will call her the *Freya*.' He raised his glass. 'To the *Freya*.'

They all drank.

'When she sails,' said Wennerstrom, 'the world will never have seen the like of her. And when she is past sailing, the world will never see the like of her again.'

Larsen was aware that the two biggest tankers in the world were the French Shell tankers *Bellamya* and *Batillus*, both just over 500,000 tons.

'What will be her deadweight, the *Freya*?' asked Larsen. 'How much crude will she carry?'

'Ah, yes, I forgot to mention that,' said the old shipowner mischievously. 'She'll be carrying one million tons of crude oil.'

Thor Larsen heard a hiss of indrawn breath from his wife beside him.

'That's big,' he said at last. 'That's very big.'

'The biggest the world has ever seen,' said Wennerstrom.

Two days later a jumbo jet arrived at Heathrow Airport from Toronto. Amongst its passengers it carried one Azamat Krim, Canadian-born son of an emigré, who like Andrew Drake had anglicized his name to Arthur Crimmins. He was one of those whom Drake had noted years before as a man who shared his beliefs completely.

Drake was waiting to meet him as he came out of the customs area, and together they drove to Drake's flat off the Bayswater Road.

Azamat Krim was a Crimean Tatar, short, dark and wiry. His father, unlike Drake's, had fought in the Second World War *with* the Red Army rather than against it. His loyalty to Russia had availed him nothing. Captured by the Germans in combat, he and all his race had been accused by Stalin of collaboration with the Germans, a patently unfounded charge, but one which sufficed to allow Stalin to deport the entire Tatar nation to the wilds of the orient. Tens of thousands had died in the unheated cattle trucks, thousands more in the frozen wastes of Kazakhstan and Siberia without food or clothing.

In a German forced labour camp Chinghis Krim had heard of the death of his entire family. Liberated by the Canadians in 1945, he had been lucky not to be sent back to Stalin for execution or the slave camps. He had been befriended by a Canadian officer, a former rodeo rider from Calgary, who one day on an Austrian horse farm had admired the Tatar soldier's mastery of horses and brilliant riding. The Canadian had secured Krim's authorized emigration to Canada, where he had married and borne a son. Azamat was the boy, now aged thirty and like Drake bitter against the Kremlin for the sufferings of his father's people.

In his flat Andrew Drake explained his plan and the Tatar agreed to join him in it. Together they put the final touches to the scheme for securing the needed funds by taking out a bank in Northern England.

The man Adam Munro reported to at head office was his controller, Barry Ferndale, the head of the Soviet section. Years before, Ferndale had done his time in the field, and assisted in the exhaustive de-briefings of Oleg Penkovsky when the Russian defector had visited Britain while accompanying Soviet trade delegations.

He was short and rotund, pink-cheeked and jolly. He hid his keen brain and a profound knowledge of Soviet affairs behind mannerisms of great cheerfulness and seeming naïveté.

In his office on the fourth floor of the firm's headquarters, he listened to the tape from Moscow from end to end. When it was over he began furiously polishing his glasses, hopping with excitement.

'Good gracious me, my dear fellow. My dear Adam. What an extraordinary affair. This really is quite priceless.'

'If it's true,' said Munro carefully. Ferndale started, as if the thought had not occurred to him.

'Ah, yes, of course. If it's true. Now, you simply must tell me how you got hold of it.'

Munro told his story carefully. It was true in every detail, save that he claimed the source of the tape had been Anatoly Krivoi.

'Krivoi, yes, yes, know of him, of course,' said Ferndale. 'Well, now, I shall have to get this translated into English and show it to the Master. This could be very big indeed. You won't be able to return to Moscow tomorrow, you know. Do you have a place to stay? Your club? Excellent. First class. Well, now, you pop along and have a decent dinner and stay at the club for a couple of days.'

Ferndale called his wife to tell her he would not be home to their modest house at Pinner that evening, but he would be spending the night in town. She knew his job and was accustomed to such absences.

Then he spent the night working on the translation of the tape, alone in his office. He was fluent in Russian, without the ultra-keen ear for tone and pitch that Munro had which denotes the truly bilingual speaker. But it was good enough. He missed nothing of the Yakovlev report, or the brief but stunned reaction that had followed it among the thirteen Politburo members.

At ten o'clock the following morning, sleepless but shaved and breakfasted, looking as pink and fresh as he always did, Ferndale called Sir Nigel Irvine's secretary on the private line and asked to see him. He was with the director-general in ten minutes.

Sir Nigel Irvine read the transcript in silence, put it down and regarded the tape lying on the desk before him.

'Is this genuine?' he asked.

Barry Ferndale had dropped his bonhomie. He had known Nigel Irvine for years as a colleague and the elevation of his friend to the supreme post and a knighthood had changed nothing between them.

'Don't know,' he said thoughtfully. 'It's going to take a lot of checking out. It's possible. Adam told me he met this Krivoi briefly at a reception at the Czech embassy just over two weeks ago. If Krivoi was thinking of coming over, that would have been his chance. Penkovsky did exactly the same; met a diplomat on neutral ground and established a secret meeting later. Of course he was regarded with intense suspicion until his information checked out. That's what I want to do here.'

'Spell it out,' said Sir Nigel.

Ferndale began polishing his glasses again. The speed of his circular movements with handkerchief on the lenses, so went the folklore, was in direct proportion to the pace of his thinking, and he polished furiously.

'Firstly, Munro,' he said. 'Just in case it is a trap and the second meeting is to spring the trap, I would like him to take furlough here until we have finished with the tape. The opposition might, just might, be trying to create an incident between governments.'

'Is he owed leave?' asked Sir Nigel.

'Yes, he is, actually. He was shifted to Moscow so fast at the end of May he is owed a fortnight's summer holiday.'

'Then let him take it now. But he should keep in touch. And inside Britain, Barry. No wandering abroad until this is sorted out.'

'Then there's the tape itself,' said Ferndale. 'It breaks down into two parts. The Yakovlev report and the voices of the Politburo. So far as I know we have never heard Yakovlev speak. So no voice print tests will be possible with him. But what he says is highly technical. I'd like to check that out with some experts in chemical seed-dressing techniques. There's an excellent section in the Ministry of Agriculture who deal with that sort of thing. No need for anyone to know why we want to know, but I'll have to be convinced this accident with the Lindane hopper valve is feasible.'

'You recall that file the cousins lent us a month ago?' asked Sir Nigel. 'The photos taken by the Condor satellites?'

'Of course.'

'Check the symptoms against the apparent explanation. What else?'

'The second section comes down to voice print analysis,' said Ferndale. 'I'd like to chop that section up into bits, so no one need know what is being talked about. The language laboratory at Beaconsfield could check out phraseology, syntax, vernacular expressions, regional dialects and so forth. But the clincher will be the comparison of voice prints.'

Sir Nigel nodded. Both men knew that human voices, reduced to a series of electronically registered blips and pulses, are as individual as fingerprints. No two are ever quite alike.

'Very well,' he said, 'but Barry, I insist on two things. For the moment no one knows about this outside of you, me and Munro. If it's a phoney we don't want to raise false hopes; if it's not, it's high-explosive. None of the technical side must know the whole. Secondly, I don't want to hear the name of Anatoly Krivoi again. Devise a cover name for this asset and use it in future.'

Two hours later Barry Ferndale called Munro over lunch at his club. The telephone line being open, they used the commercial parlance that was habitual.

'The managing director's terribly happy with the sales report,' Ferndale told Munro. 'He's very keen that you take a fortnight's leave to enable us to break it right down and see where we go from here. Have you any ideas for a spot of leave?'

Munro hadn't, but he made up his mind. This was not a request, it was an order.

'I'd like to go back to Scotland for a while,' he said. 'I've always wanted to walk during the summer from Lochaber up the coast to Sutherland.'

Ferndale was ecstatic. 'The Highlands, the glens of Bonnie Scotland. So pretty at this time of year. Never could stand physical exercise myself, but I'm sure you'll enjoy it. Stay in touch with me, say, every second day. You have my home number, don't you?'

A week later Miroslav Kaminsky arrived in England on his Red Cross travel papers. He had come across Europe by train, the ticket paid for by Drake who was nearing the end of his financial resources.

Kaminsky and Krim were introduced and Kaminsky given his orders.

'You learn English,' Drake told him. 'Morning, noon and night. Books and gramophone records, faster than you've ever learned anything before. Meanwhile, I'm going to get you some decent papers. You can't travel on Red Cross documents for ever. Until I do, and until you can make yourself understood in English, don't leave the flat.'

Adam Munro had walked for ten days through the Highlands of Inverness, Ross and Cromarty and finally into Sutherland County. He had arrived at the small town of Lochinver, where the waters of the North Minch stretch away westwards to the Isle of Lewis, when he made his sixth call to Barry Ferndale's home on the outskirts of London.

'Glad you called,' said Ferndale down the line. 'Could you come back to the office? The managing director would like a word.'

Munro promised to leave within the hour and make his way as fast as possible to Inverness. There he could pick up a flight for London.

At his home on the outskirts of Sheffield, the great steel town of Yorkshire, Mr Norman Pickering kissed his wife and daughter farewell that brilliant late-July morning and drove off to the bank of which he was manager.

Twenty minutes later a small van bearing the name of an electrical appliance company drove up to the house and disgorged two men in white coats. One carried a large cardboard carton up to the front door, preceded by his companion bearing a clipboard. Mrs Pickering answered the door and the two men went inside. None of the neighbours took any notice.

Ten minutes later the man with the clipboard came out and drove away. His companion apparently stayed to fix and test the appliance they had delivered.

Thirty minutes after that the van was parked round two corners from the bank and the driver, without his white coat and wearing a charcoal-grey business suit, carrying not a clipboard but a large attaché case, entered the bank. He proffered an envelope to one of the girl clerks who looked at it, saw that it was addressed personally to Mr Pickering and took it in to him. The businessman waited patiently.

Two minutes later the manager opened his office door and looked out. His eye caught the waiting businessman.

'Mr Partington?' he asked. 'Do come in.'

Andrew Drake did not speak until the door had closed behind him. When he did, his voice had no trace of his native Yorkshire, but a guttural edge as if it came from Europe. His hair was carrot red, and heavy-rimmed, tinted glasses masked his eyes to some extent.

'I wish to open an account,' he said, 'and to make a withdrawal in cash.'

Pickering was perplexed; his chief clerk could have handled this transaction.

'A large account, and a large transaction,' said Drake. He slid a cheque across the desk. It was a bank cheque, the sort that can be obtained across the counter. It was issued by the Holborn, London, branch of Pickering's own bank, and was drawn to £30,000.

'I see,' said Pickering. That kind of money was definitely the manager's business. 'And the withdrawal?'

'Twenty thousand pounds in cash.'

'Twenty thousand pounds in cash?' asked Pickering. He reached for the phone. 'Well, of course I shall have to call the Holborn branch and –'

'I don't think that will be necessary,' said Drake and pushed a copy of that morning's London *Times* over the desk. Pickering stared at it. What Drake handed him next caused him to stare even more. It was a photograph, taken with a Polaroid camera. He recognized his wife, whom he had left ninety minutes earlier, sitting round-eyed with fear in his own fireside chair. He could make out a portion of his own sitting room. His wife held their child close to her with one arm. Across her knees was the same issue of *The Times*.

'Taken sixty minutes ago,' said Drake.

Pickering's stomach tightened. The photo would win no prizes for photographic quality, but the shape of the man's shoulder in the foreground and the sawn-off shotgun pointing at his family was quite clear enough.

'If you raise the alarm,' said Drake quietly, 'the police will come here, not to your home. Before they break in, you will be dead. In exactly sixty minutes, unless I make a phone call to say I am safely away with the money, that man is going to pull that trigger. Please don't think we are joking; we are quite prepared to die if we have to. We are the Red Army Faction.'

Pickering swallowed hard. Under his desk, a foot from his knee, was a button linked to a silent alarm. He looked at the photograph again and moved his knee away.

'Call your chief clerk,' said Drake, 'and instruct him to open the account, credit the cheque to it, and provide the cheque for the twenty-thousand-pound withdrawal. Tell him you have telephoned London and all is in order. If he expresses surprise, tell him the sum is for a very big commercial promotion campaign in which prize money will be given away in cash. Pull yourself together and make it good.'

The chief clerk *was* surprised, but his manager seemed calm enough, a little subdued perhaps, but otherwise normal. And the dark-suited man before him looked relaxed and friendly. There was even a glass of the manager's sherry before each of them, though the businessman had kept his light gloves on, odd for such warm weather. Thirty minutes later the chief clerk brought the money from the vault, deposited it on the manager's desk and left.

Drake packed it calmly into the attaché case.

'There are thirty minutes left,' he told Pickering. 'In twenty-five I shall make my phone call. My colleague will leave your wife and child perfectly unharmed. If you raise the alarm before that, he will shoot first and take his chances with the police later.'

When he had gone, Mr Pickering sat frozen for half an hour. In fact Drake phoned the house five minutes later from a call box. Krim took the call, smiled briefly at the woman on the floor with her hands and ankles taped, and left. Neither used the van, which had been stolen the previous day. Krim used a motorcycle parked further down the road in readiness. Drake took a motorcycle helmet from the van to cover his flaming red hair, and used the second motorcycle parked near the van. Both were out of Sheffield within thirty minutes. They abandoned the vehicles north of London and met again in Drake's flat where he washed the red dye out of his hair and crushed the eyeglasses to fragments.

Munro caught the following morning's breakfast flight south from Inverness. When the plastic trays were cleared away the hostess offered round newspapers fresh up from London. Being at the back of the aircraft, Munro missed *The Times* and the *Telegraph*, but secured a copy of the *Daily Express*. The headline story concerned two unidentified men, believed to be Germans from the Red Army Faction, who had robbed a Sheffield bank of £20,000.

'Bloody bastards,' said the English oilman from the North Sea rigs who was in the seat next to Munro. He tapped the *Express* headline. 'Bloody Commies. I'd string them all up.'

Munro conceded that upstringing would definitely have to be considered in future.

At Heathrow he took a taxi to a point near the office and was shown straight into Barry Ferndale's room.

'Adam, my dear chap, you're looking a new man.'

He sat Munro down and proffered coffee.

'Well, now, the tape. You must be dying to know. Fact is, m'dear chap, it's genuine. No doubt about it. Everything checks. There's been a fearful blow-up in the Soviet Agriculture Ministry. Six or seven senior functionaries ousted, including one we think must be that unfortunate fellow in the Lubyanka.

'That helps corroborate it. But the voices are genuine. No doubt, according to the lab boys. Now for the big one; one of our assets working out of Leningrad managed to take a drive out of town. There's not much wheat grown up there in the north, but there is a little. He stopped his car for a pee, and swiped a stalk of the afflicted wheat. It came home in the bag three days ago. I got the report from the lab last night. They confirm there is an excess of this Lindane stuff present in the root of the seedling.

'So, there we are. You've hit what our American cousins so charmingly call pay-dirt. In fact, twenty-four carat gold. By the way, the Master wants to see you. You're going back to Moscow tonight.'

Munro's meeting with Sir Nigel Irvine was friendly but brief.

'Well done,' said the Master. 'Now I understand your next meeting will be in a fortnight.'

Munro nodded.

'This might be a long-term operation,' Sir Nigel resumed, 'which makes it a good thing you are new to Moscow. There will be no raised eyebrows if you stay on for a couple of years. But just in case this fellow changes his mind, I want you to press for more; everything we can squeeze out. Do you want any help, any back-up?'

'No, thank you,' said Munro. 'Now that he's taken the plunge, the asset has insisted he'll talk only to me. I don't think I want to scare him off at this stage by bringing others in. Nor do I think he can travel, as Penkovsky could. Vishnayev never travels, so there's no cause for Krivoi to, either. I'll have to handle it alone.'

Sir Nigel nodded. 'Very well, you've got it.'

When Munro had gone, Sir Nigel Irvine turned over the file on his desk, which was Munro's personal record. He had his misgivings. The man was a loner, ill at ease working in a team. A man who walked alone in the mountains of Scotland for relaxation.

There was an adage in the firm: there are old agents and there are bold agents, but there are no old, bold agents. Sir Nigel was an old agent, and he appreciated caution. This one had come swinging in from the outfield, unexpected, unprepared for. And it was moving fast. But then, the tape was genuine, no doubt of it. So was the summons on his desk to see the Prime Minister that evening at Downing Street. He had of course informed the foreign secretary when the tape had passed muster, and this was the outcome.

The black door of Number 10, Downing Street, residence of the British prime minister, is perhaps one of the best-known doors in the world. It stands on the right, two-thirds down a small cul-de-sac off Whitehall, an alley almost, sandwiched between the imposing piles of the Cabinet Office and the Foreign Office.

In front of this door, with its simple white figures 10, and the brass knocker, attended by a single, unarmed police constable, the tourists gather to take each other's photograph and watch the comings and goings of the messengers and the well known.

In fact it is the men of words who go in through the front door; the men of influence tend to use the side. The house called Number 10 stands at ninety degrees to the Cabinet Office block and the rear corners almost touch each other, enclosing a small lawn behind black railings. Where the corners almost meet, the gap is covered by a passageway leading to a small side door, and it was through this that the director-general of the SIS, accompanied by Sir Julian Flannery, the Cabinet secretary, passed that last evening of July. The pair were shown straight to the second floor, past the Cabinet room, to the Prime Minister's private study.

The Prime Minister had read the transcript of the Politburo tape, passed to her by the foreign secretary.

'Have you informed the Americans of this matter?' she asked directly.

'Not yet, ma'am,' Sir Nigel answered. 'Our final confirmation of its authenticity is only three days old.'

'I would like you to do it personally,' said the Prime Minister. Sir Nigel inclined his head. 'The political perspectives of this pending wheat famine in the Soviet Union are immeasurable, of course, and as the world's biggest surplus wheat producer, the USA should be involved from the outset.'

'I would not wish the cousins to move in on this agent of ours,' said Sir Nigel. 'The running of this asset may be extremely delicate. I think we should handle it ourselves, alone.'

'Will they try to move in?' asked the Prime Minister.

'They may, ma'am. They may. We ran Penkovsky jointly, even though it was we who recruited him. But there were reasons why. This time I think we should go it alone.'

The Prime Minister was not slow to see the value in political terms of controlling such an agent as one who had access to the Politburo transcripts.

'If pressure is brought,' she said, 'refer back to me and I will speak to President Matthews personally about it. In the meantime I would like you to fly to Washington tomorrow and give them the tape, or at least a verbatim copy of it. I intend to speak to President Matthews tonight in any case.'

Sir Nigel and Sir Julian rose to leave.

'One last thing,' said the Prime Minister. 'I fully understand that I am not allowed to know the identity of this agent. Will you be telling Robert Benson who it is?'

'Certainly not, ma'am.' Not only would the director-general of the SIS refuse point blank to inform his own Prime Minister, or the foreign secretary of the identity of the Russian, but he would not tell them even of Munro who was running that agent. The Americans would know who Munro was, but never who he was running. Nor would there be any tailing of Munro by the cousins in Moscow; he would see to that as well.

'Then presumably this Russian defector has a code name. May I know it?' asked the Prime Minister.

'Certainly, ma'am. The defector is now known in every file simply as the Nightingale.'

It just happened that Nightingale was the first songbird in the N section of the list of birds after which all Soviet agents were code named, but the Prime Minister did not know this. She smiled for the first time.

'How very appropriate.'

5

Just after ten in the morning of a wet and rainy 1st August an ageing but comfortable four-jet VC-10 of the Royal Air Force Strike Command lifted out of Lyneham base in Wiltshire and headed west for Ireland and the Atlantic. It carried a small enough passenger complement: one air chief marshal who had been informed the night before that this of all days was the best for him to visit the Pentagon in Washington to discuss the forthcoming USAF-RAF tactical bomber exercises, and a civilian in a shabby mackintosh.

The air chief marshal had introduced himself to the unexpected civilian, and learned in reply that his companion was Mr Barrett of the Foreign Office who had business with the British embassy on Massachusetts Avenue and had been instructed to take advantage of the VC-10 flight to save the taxpayer the cost of a two-way air ticket. The air force officer never learned that the purpose of the RAF plane's flight was in fact the other way around.

On another track south of the VC-10 a Boeing jumbo jet of British Airways left Heathrow bound for New York. Among its 300-plus passengers it bore Azamat Krim, alias Arthur Crimmins, Canadian citizen, heading west with a back-pocket full of money on a buying mission.

Eight hours later the VC-10 landed perfectly at Andrews air force base in Maryland, ten miles southeast of Washington. As it closed down its engines on the apron, a Pentagon staff car swept up to the foot of the steps and disgorged a two-star general of the USAF. Two air force police snapped to attention as the air chief marshal came down the steps to his welcoming committee. Within five minutes it was all over; the Pentagon limousine drove away to Washington, the police 'snowdrops' marched off, and the idle and curious of the air base went back to their duties.

No one noticed the modest-priced sedan with non-official number plates that drove to the parked VC-10 ten minutes later – no one, that is, with enough observation to note the odd-shaped aerial on the roof that betrayed a CIA car. No one bothered with the rumpled civilian who trotted down the steps and straight into the car moments later, and no one saw the car leave the air base.

The company man in the US embassy in Grosvenor Square, London, had been alerted the night before, and his coded signal to Langley had laid on the car. The driver was in civilian clothes, a low-level staffer, but the man in the back who welcomed the guest from London was the chief of the Western European division, one of the regional subordinates of the deputy director of operations. He had been chosen to meet the Englishman because, having once headed the CIA operation in London, he knew him well. No one likes substitutions.

'Nigel, good to see you again,' he said after confirming to himself that the arrival was indeed the man they expected.

'How good of you to come to meet me, Lance,' responded Sir Nigel Irvine, well aware there was nothing good about it; it was a duty. The talk in the car was of London, family, the weather. No question of 'what are you doing here'. The car swept along the Capital Beltway to the Woodrow Wilson Memorial Bridge over the Potomac and headed west into Virginia.

On the outskirts of Alexandria the driver pulled right into the George Washington Memorial Parkway which fringes the whole western bank of the river. As they cruised past the National Airport and Arlington Cemetery, Sir Nigel Irvine glanced out to his right at the skyline of Washington where years before he had been the SIS liaison man with the CIA, based in the British embassy. Those had been tough days, in the wake of the Philby affair, when even the state of the weather was classified information so far as the English were concerned. He thought of what he carried in his briefcase and permitted himself a small smile.

After thirty minutes' cruising they pulled off the main highway, swung over it again and headed into the forest. He remembered the small notice saying simply BPR-CIA and wondered again why they had to signpost the place. You either knew where it was or you didn't, and if you didn't you weren't invited anyway.

At the security gate in the great seven-foot-high, chain-link fence that surrounds Langley, they halted while Lance showed his pass, then drove on and turned left past the awful conference centre known as the Igloo, because that is just what it resembles.

The company's headquarters consists of five blocks, one in the centre and one at each corner of the centre block, like a rough St Andrew's cross. The Igloo is stuck on to the corner block nearest the main gate. Passing the recessed centre block, Sir Nigel noticed the imposing main doorway and the great seal of the United States paved in terrazza into the ground in front of it. But he knew this front entrance was for congressmen, senators and other undesirables. The car swept on, past the complex, then pulled to the right and drove round the back.

Here there is a short ramp, protected by a steel portcullis, running down one floor to the first basement level. At the bottom is a select car park for no more than ten cars. The black sedan came to a halt, and the man called Lance handed Sir Nigel over to his superior, Charles 'Chip' Allen, the deputy director of operations. They too knew each other well.

Set in the back wall of the car park is a small lift, guarded by steel doors and two armed men. Chip Allen identified his guest, signed for him and used a plastic card to open the lift doors. The lift hummed its way quietly seven floors up to the director's suite. Another magnetized plastic card got them both out of the lift, into a lobby faced by three doors. Chip Allen knocked on the centre one, and it was Bob Benson himself who, alerted from below, welcomed the British visitor into his suite.

Benson led him past the big desk to the lounge area in front of the beige marble fireplace. In winter Benson liked a crackling log fire to burn here, but Washington in August is no place for fires and the air conditioning was working overtime. Benson pulled the rice-paper screen across the room to separate the lounge from the office and sat back opposite his guest. Coffee was ordered, and when they were alone Benson finally asked, 'What brings you to Langley, Nigel?'

Sir Nigel sipped and sat back.

'We have,' he said undramatically, 'obtained the services of a new asset.'

He spoke for almost ten minutes, before the director of central intelligence interrupted him.

'Inside the Politburo?' he queried. 'You mean, right inside?'

'Let us just say, with access to Politburo meeting transcripts,' said Sir Nigel.

'Would you mind if I called Chip Allen and Ben Kahn in on this?'

'Not at all, Bob. They'll have to know within an hour or so anyway. Prevents repetition.'

Bob Benson rose, crossed to a telephone on a coffee table and made a call to his private secretary. When he had finished he stared out of the picture window at the great green forest. 'Jesus H. Christ,' he breathed.

Sir Nigel Irvine was not displeased that his two old contacts in the CIA should be in on the ground floor of his briefing. All pure intelligence agencies, as opposed to intelligence/secret police forces like the KGB, have two main arms. One is Operations, covering the business of actually obtaining information; the other is Intelligence, covering the business of collating, cross-referencing, interpreting and analysing the great mass of raw, unprocessed information that is gathered in.

Both have to be good. If the information is faulty the best analysis in the world will only come up with nonsense; if the analysis is inept all the efforts of the information gatherers are wasted. Statesmen need to know what other nations, friend or potential foe, are doing and if possible what they intend to do. What they are doing is nowadays often observable; what they intend to do is not. Which is why all the space cameras in the world will never supplant a brilliant analyst working with material from inside the other's secret councils.

In the CIA the two men who hold sway under the director of central intelligence, who may be a political appointee, are the deputy director (Operations) and the deputy director (Intelligence). It is Operations that inspire the thriller-writers; Intelligence is back-room work, tedious, slow, methodical, often boring but always invaluable.

Like Tweedledum and Tweedledee, the DDO and the DDI have to work hand in hand; they have to trust each other. Benson, as a political appointee, was lucky. His DDO was Chip Allen, WASP and former football player; his DDI was Ben Kahn, Jewish former chess master; they fitted together like a pair of gloves. In five minutes both were sitting with Benson and Irvine in the lounge area. Coffee was forgotten.

The British spymaster talked for almost an hour. He was uninterrupted. Then the three Americans read the Nightingale transcript and watched the tape recording in its polythene bag with something like hunger. When Irvine had finished there was a short silence. Chip Allen broke it.

'Roll over, Penkovsky,' he said.

'You'll want to check it all,' said Sir Nigel evenly. No one dissented. Friends are friends, but.... 'It took us ten days, but we can't fault it. The voice prints check out, every one. We've already exchanged cables about the bust-up in the Soviet Agriculture Ministry. And of course, you have your Condor photographs. Oh, one last thing....'

From his bag he produced a small polythene sack with a sprig of young wheat inside it.

'One of our chaps swiped this from a field outside Leningrad.'

'I'll have our Agriculture Department check it out as well,' said Benson. 'Anything else, Nigel?'

'Oh, not really,' said Sir Nigel. 'Well, perhaps a couple of small points. . . .'

'Spit it out.' Sir Nigel drew a breath.

'The Russian build-up in Afghanistan. We think they may be mounting a move towards Pakistan and India through the passes. That we regard as our patch. Now if you could ask Condor to have a look. . . .'

'You've got it,' said Benson without hesitation.

'And then,' resumed Sir Nigel, 'that Soviet defector you brought out of Geneva two weeks ago. He seems to know quite a bit about Soviet assets in our trade union movement.'

'We sent you transcripts of that,' said Allen hastily.

'We'd like direct access,' said Sir Nigel.

Allen looked at Kahn. Kahn shrugged.

'OK,' said Benson. 'Can we have access to Nightingale?'

'Sorry, no,' said Sir Nigel. 'That's different. The Nightingale's too damn delicate, right out in the cold. I don't want to disturb the fish just yet in case of a change of heart. You'll get everything we get, as soon as we get it. But no moving in. I'm trying to speed up the delivery and volume, but it's going to take time, and a lot of care.'

'When's your next delivery slated for?' asked Allen.

'Today week. At least, that's the meet. I'll hope there'll be a handover.'

Sir Nigel Irvine spent the night at a CIA safe house in the Virginia countryside, and the next day 'Mr Barrett' flew back to London with his air chief marshal.

It was three days later than Azamat Krim sailed from Pier 49 in New York harbour aboard the elderly *Queen Elizabeth II* for Southampton. He had decided to sail rather than fly because he felt he had a better chance of his main luggage escaping X-ray examination by sea.

His purchases were complete. One of his pieces of luggage was a standard aluminium shoulder-case such as professional photographers use to protect their cameras and lenses. As such it could not be X-rayed, but would have to be hand examined. The moulded plastic sponge inside that held the cameras and lenses from banging against each other was glued to the bottom of the case, but ended two inches short of the real bottom. In the cavity were two handguns with ammunition clips.

Another piece of luggage, deep in the heart of a small cabin trunk full of clothes, was an aluminium tube with a screw-top, containing what looked like a long, cylindrical camera lens, some four inches in diameter. He calculated that if it was examined it would pass in the eyes of all but the most suspicious of customs officers as the sort of lens that camera freaks use for very long range photography, and a collection of books of bird photographs and wildlife pictures lying next to the lens inside the trunk were designed to corroborate the explanation.

In fact the lens was an image-intensifier, also called a night-sight, of the kind that may be commercially bought without a permit in the United States but not in Britain.

It was boiling hot that Sunday, 8th August, in Moscow and those who could not get to the beaches crowded instead to the numerous swimming baths of the city, especially the new complex built for the 1980 Olympics. But the British embassy staff, along with those of a dozen other legations, were at the beach on the Moscow River upstream from Uspenskoye Bridge. Adam Munro was among them.

He tried to appear as carefree as the others, but it was hard. He checked his watch too many times, and finally got dressed.

'Oh, Adam, you're not going back already? There's ages of daylight left,' one of the secretaries called to him.

He forced a rueful grin. 'Duty calls, or rather the plans for the Manchester Chamber of Commerce visit call,' he shouted back to her.

He walked through the woods to his car, dropped his bathing things inside, had a covert look to see if anyone was interested, and locked the car. There were too many men in sandals, slacks and open shirts for one extra to be of notice, and he thanked his stars the KGB never seem to take their jackets off. There was no one looking remotely like the opposition within sight of him. He set off through the trees to the north.

Valentina was waiting for him, standing back in the shade of the trees. His stomach was tight, knotted, for all that he was pleased to see her. She was no expert at spotting a tail and might have been followed. If she had, his diplomatic cover would save him from worse than expulsion, but the repercussions would be enormous. Even that was not his main worry; it was what they would do to her if she were ever caught. Whatever the motives, the word for what she was doing was high treason.

He took her in his arms and kissed her. She kissed him back, and trembled in his arms.

'Are you frightened?' he asked her.

'A bit,' she nodded. 'You listened to the tape recording?'

'Yes, I did. Before I handed it over. I suppose I should not have done, but I did.'

'Then you know about the famine that faces us. Adam, when I was a girl I saw the famine in this country, just after the war. It was bad, but it was caused by the war, by Germans. We could take it. Our leaders were on our side, they would make things get better.'

'Perhaps they can sort things out this time,' said Munro lamely.

Valentina shook her head angrily. 'They're not even trying,' she burst out. 'I sit there listening to their voices, typing the transcripts. They are just bickering, trying to save their own skins.'

'And your husband's uncle, Marshal Kerensky?' he asked gently.

'He's as bad as the rest. When I married my husband, Uncle Nikolai was at the wedding. I thought he was so jolly, so kindly. Of course, that was his private life. Now I listen to him in his public life; he's like all of them, ruthless and cynical. They just jockey for advantage among each other, for power, and to hell with the people. I suppose I should be one of them, but I can't be. Not now, not any more.'

Munro looked across the clearing at the pines but saw olive trees and heard a boy in uniform shouting, 'You don't own me.' Strange, he mused, how establishments with all their power sometimes went too far and lost control of their own servants through sheer excess. Not always, not often, but sometimes.

'I could get you out of here, Valentina,' he said. 'It would mean my leaving the diplomatic corps, but it's been done before. Sasha is young enough to grow up somewhere else.'

'No, Adam, no, it's tempting but I can't. Whatever the outcome, I am part of Russia, I have to stay. Perhaps, one day ... I don't know.'

They sat in silence for a while, holding hands. She broke the quiet at last.

'Did your ... intelligence people pass the tape recording on to London?'

'I think so. I handed it to the man I believe represents the Secret Service in the embassy. He asked me if there would be another one.'

She nodded at her shoulder-bag.

'It's just the transcript. I can't get the tape recordings any more. They're kept in a safe after the transcriptions, and I don't have the key. The papers in there are of the following Politburo meeting.'

'How do you get them out, Valentina?' he asked.

'After the meetings,' she told him, 'the tapes and the stenographic notes are brought under guard to the Central Committee building. There is a locked department there where we work, me and five other women. With one man in charge. When the transcripts are finished the tapes are locked away.'

'Then how did you get the first one?'

She shrugged.

'The man in charge is new, since last month. The other one, before him, was more lax. There is a tape studio next door where the tapes are copied once before being locked in the safe. I was alone in there last month, long enough to steal the second tape and substitute a dummy.'

'A dummy?' exclaimed Munro. 'They'll spot the substitution if ever they play them back.'

'It's unlikely,' she said. 'The transcripts form the archives once they have been checked against the tapes for accuracy. I was lucky with that tape; I brought it out in a shopping bag under the groceries I had bought in the Central Committee commissary.'

'Aren't you searched?'

'Hardly ever. We are trusted, Adam, the elite of the New Russia. The papers are easier. At work I wear an old-fashioned girdle. I copied the last meeting of June on the machine, but ran off one extra copy, then switched the number-control back by one figure. The extra copy I stuck inside my girdle. It made no noticeable bulge.'

Munro's stomach turned at the risk she was taking.

'What do they talk about in this meeting?' he asked, gesturing towards the shoulder-bag.

'The consequences,' she said. 'What will happen when the famine breaks. What the people of Russia will do to them. But Adam ... there's been one since. Early in July. I couldn't copy it, I was on leave. I couldn't refuse my leave, it would have been too obvious. But when I got back I met one of the girls who had transcribed it. She was white-faced, and wouldn't describe it.'

'Can you get it?' asked Munro.

'I can try. I'll have to wait until the office is empty and use the copying machine. I can reset it afterwards so it will not show it has been used. But not until early next month; I shall not be on the late shift when I can work alone until then.'

'We shouldn't meet here again,' Munro told her. 'Patterns are dangerous.'

He spent another hour describing the sort of tradecraft she would need to know if they were to go on meeting. Finally he gave her a pad of close-typed sheets he had tucked in his waistband under his loose shirt.

'It's all in there, my darling. Memorize it and burn it. Flush the ashes down the toilet.'

Five minutes later she gave him a wad of flimsy paper sheets covered with neat, typed Cyrillic script from her bag and slipped away through the forest to her car on a sandy track half a mile away.

Munro retreated into the darkness of the main arch above the church's recessed side door. He produced a roll of tape from his pocket, slipped his trousers to his knees and taped the batch of sheets to his thigh. With the trousers back up again and belted he could feel the paper snug against his thigh as he walked, but under the baggy, Russian-made trousers they did not show.

By midnight, in the silence of his flat, he had read them all a dozen times. The next Wednesday they went in the messenger's wrist-chained briefcase to London, wax-sealed in a stout envelope and coded for the SIS liaison man at the Foreign Office only.

The glass doors leading to the rose garden were tight shut and only the whir of the air conditioner broke the silence in the Oval Office of the White House. The balmy days of June were long gone and the steam heat of a Washington August forbade open doors and windows.

Round the building on the Pennsylvania Avenue façade the tourists, damp and hot, admired the familiar aspect of the White House front entrance, with its pillars, flag and curved driveway; or queued for the guided tour of this most holy of American holies. None of them would penetrate to the tiny West Wing building where President Matthews sat in conclave with his advisers.

In front of his desk were Stanislaw Poklewski and Robert Benson. They had been joined by Secretary of State David Lawrence, a Boston lawyer and pillar of the East Coast establishment.

President Matthews flicked the file in front of him closed. He had long since devoured the first Politburo transcript, translated into English; what he had just finished reading was his experts' evaluation of it.

'Bob, you were remarkably close with your estimate of a shortfall of thirty million tons,' he said. 'Now it appears they are going to be fifty to fifty-five million tons short this fall. And you have no doubts this transcript comes right from inside the Politburo?'

'Mr President, we've checked it out in every way. The voices are real; the traces of excessive Lindane in the root of the wheat plant are real; the hatchet job inside the Soviet Agriculture Ministry is real. We don't believe there is room for any substantive doubt that tape recording was of the Politburo in session.'

'We have to handle this right,' mused the President. 'There must be no way we make a miscalculation on this one. There has never been an opportunity like it.'

'Mr President,' said Poklewski, 'this means the Soviets are not facing severe shortages as we supposed when you invoked the Shannon Act last month. They are facing a famine.'

Unknowingly he was echoing the words of Petrov in the Kremlin two months earlier, in his aside to Ivanenko, which had not been on the tape. President Matthews nodded slowly.

'We can't disagree with that, Stan. The question is, what do we do about it?'

'Let them have their famine,' said Poklewski. 'This is the biggest mistake they have made since Stalin refused to believe Western warnings about the Nazi build-up on his frontier in spring 1941. This time the enemy is within. So let them sort it out in their own way.'

'David?' asked the President of his secretary of state.

Secretary Lawrence shook his head. The differences of opinion between the arch-hawk Poklewski and the cautious Bostonian were legendary.

'I disagree, Mr President,' he said at length. 'Firstly, I don't think we have examined deeply enough the possible permutations of what might happen if the Soviet Union is plunged into chaos next spring. As I see it, it is more than simply a question of letting the Soviets stew in their own juice. There are massive implications on a worldwide basis consequent on such a phenomenon.'

'Bob?' asked President Matthews. His director of central intelligence was lost in thought.

'We have the time, Mr President,' he said. 'They know you invoked the Shannon Act last month. They know if they want the grain, they have to come to you. As Secretary Lawrence says, we really should examine the perspectives consequent upon a famine across the Soviet Union. We can do that as of now. Sooner or later the Kremlin has to make a play. When they do, we have all the cards. We know how bad their predicament is; they don't know we know. We have the wheat, we have the Condors, we have the Nightingale and we have the time in hand. We hold all the aces this time. No need to decide yet which way to play them.'

Lawrence nodded and regarded Benson with new respect. Poklewski shrugged. President Matthews made up his mind.

'Stan, as of now I want you to put together an *ad hoc* group within the National Security Council. I want it small, and absolutely secret. You, Bob and David here. Chairman joint chiefs of staff, secretaries of defense, treasury and agriculture. I want to know what will happen, worldwide, if the Soviet Union starves. I need to know, and soon.'

One of the telephones on his desk rang. It was the direct line from the State Department. President Matthews looked enquiringly at David Lawrence.

'Are you calling me, David?' he asked with a smile.

The secretary of state rose and took the machine off its rest. He listened for several minutes, then replaced the receiver.

'Mr President, the pace is speeding up. Two hours ago in Moscow Foreign Minister Rykov summoned Ambassador Donaldson to the Foreign Ministry. On behalf of the Soviet Government he has proposed the sale by the United States to the Soviet Union by next spring of fifty-five million tons of mixed cereal grains.'

For several moments only the ormolu carriage clock above the marble fireplace could be heard in the Oval Office.

'What did Ambassador Donaldson reply?' asked the President.

'Of course, that the request would be passed on to Washington for consideration,' said Lawrence, 'and that no doubt your answer would be forthcoming in due course.'

'Gentlemen,' said the President, 'I need those answers, and I need them fast. I can hold my answer for four weeks at the outside, but by 15th September at the latest I shall have to reply. When I do, I shall want to know what we are handling here. Every possibility.'

'Mr President, within a few days we may be receiving a second package of information from the Nightingale. That could give an indication of the way the Kremlin sees the same problem.'

President Matthews nodded. 'Bob, if and when it comes, I would like it translated into English and on my desk immediately.'

As the presidential meeting broke up in the dusk of Washington, it was already long after dark in Britain. Police records later showed that scores of burglaries and break-ins had taken place during the night of 11–12 August, but the one that most disturbed the police of the county of Somerset was the theft from a sporting gunshop in the pleasant country town of Taunton.

The thieves had evidently visited the shop in daylight hours during the previous day or so, for the alarm had been neatly cut by someone who had spotted where the cable ran. With the alarm system out of commission, the thieves had used powerful bolt-cutters on the window grill in the back alley that ran behind the shop.

The place had not been ransacked, and the usual haul, shotguns for the holding up of banks, had not been taken. What was missing, the proprietor confirmed, was a single hunting rifle, one of his finest, a Finnish-made Sako Hornet .22, a highly accurate precision piece. Also gone were two boxes of shells for the rifle, soft-nosed 45 grain, hollow-point

Remingtons, capable of high velocity, great penetration and considerable distortion on impact.

In his flat in Bayswater, Andrew Drake sat with Miroslav Kaminsky and Azamat Krim and gazed at their haul laid out on the sitting room table; it consisted of two hand guns, each with two magazines fully loaded; the rifle with two boxes of shells, and the image-intensifier.

There are two basic types of night-sight: the infra-red scope and the intensifier. Men who shoot by night tend to prefer the latter, and Krim, with his Western Canadian hunting background and three years with the Canadian paratroopers, had chosen well.

The infra-red sight is based on the principle of sending a beam of infra-red light down the line of fire to illuminate the target, which appears in the sight like a greenish outline. But because it emits light, even a light invisible to the naked eye, the infra-red sight requires a power source. The image-intensifier works on the principle of gathering all those tiny elements of light that are present in a 'dark' environment, and concentrating them, as the gigantic retina of a barn owl's eye can concentrate what little light there is and see a moving mouse where a human eye would detect nothing. It needs no power source.

Originally developed for military purposes, the small, hand-held image-intensifiers had by the late seventies come to interest the vast American security industry and were of use to factory guards and others. Soon they were on commercial sale. By the early eighties the larger versions, capable of being mounted on a rifle barrel were also purchasable in America for cash across the counter. It was one of these that Azamat Krim had bought.

The rifle already had grooves along the upper side of its barrel to take a telescopic sight for target practice. Working with a file and a vice screwed to the edge of the kitchen table, Krim began to convert the clips of the image-intensifier to fit into these grooves.

While Krim was working, a mile away in Grosvenor Square, Barry Ferndale paid a visit to the United States embassy. By pre-arrangement he was visiting the head of the CIA operation in London, who was apparently a diplomat attached to his country's embassy staff.

The meeting was brief and cordial. Ferndale removed from his briefcase a wad of papers and handed them over.

'Fresh from the presses, my dear fellow,' he told the American. 'Rather a lot, I'm afraid. These Russians do tend to talk, don't they? Anyway, best of luck.'

The papers were the Nightingale's second delivery, and already in translation into English. The American knew he would have to encode them himself, and send them himself. No one else would see them. He thanked Ferndale and settled down to a long night of hard work.

He was not the only man who slept little that night. Far away in the city of Ternopol in the Ukraine a plain-clothes agent of the KGB left the non-commissioned officers club and commissary beside the KGB barracks and began to walk home. He was not of the rank to rate a staff car and his own private vehicle was parked near his house. He did not mind; it was a warm and pleasant night and he had had a convivial evening with his colleagues in the club.

Which was probably why he failed to notice the two figures in the doorway across the street who seemed to be watching the club entrance and who nodded to each other.

It was after midnight and Ternopol, even on a warm August night, has no life to speak of. The secret policeman's path took him away from the main streets and into the sprawl of Shevchenko Park where the trees in full leaf almost covered the narrow pathways. It was the longest shortcut he ever made. Halfway across the park there was a scuttling of feet behind him; he half turned, took the blow from the cosh that had been aimed at the back of his head on the temple and went down in a heap.

It was nearly dawn before he recovered. He had been dragged into a tangle of bushes and robbed of his wallet, money, keys, ration card and ID card. Police and KGB enquiries continued for several weeks into this most unaccustomed mugging, but no culprits were discovered. In fact both had been on the first dawn train out of Ternopol and were back in their homes in Lvov.

President Matthews personally chaired the meeting of the *ad hoc* committee that considered the Nightingale's second package, and it was a subdued meeting.

'My analysts have already come up with some possibilities consequent upon a famine in the Soviet Union next winter/spring,' Benson told the eight men in the Oval Office, 'but I don't think any one of them would have dared go as far as the Politburo themselves have done in predicting a pandemic breakdown of law and order. It's unheard of in the Soviet Union.'

'That's true of my people, too,' agreed David Lawrence of the State Department. 'The Politburo are talking here about the KGB not being able to hold the line. I don't think we could have gone that far in our prognosis.'

'So what answer do I give Maxim Rudin to his request to purchase fifty-five million tons of grain?' asked the President.

'Mr President, tell him no,' urged Poklewski. 'We have here an opportunity that has never occurred before and may never occur again. You have Maxim Rudin and the whole Politburo in the palm of your hand. For two decades successive US administrations have bailed the Soviets out every time they have gotten into problems with their economy. Every time, they have come back more aggressive than ever. Every time, they have responded by pushing further with their involvement in Africa, Asia, Latin America. Every time, the Third World has been encouraged to believe the Soviets have recovered from their setbacks through their own efforts, that the Marxist economic system works.

'This time the world can be shown beyond a doubt that the Marxist economic system does not work and never will. This time I urge you to screw the lid down tight, real tight. You can demand a concession for every ton of wheat. You can require them to get out of Asia, Africa and America. And if he won't, you can bring Rudin down.'

'Would this,' President Matthews tapped the Nightingale report in front of him, 'bring Rudin down?'

David Lawrence answered, and no one disagreed with him.

'If what is described in here by the members of the Politburo themselves actually happened inside the Soviet Union, yes, Rudin would fall in disgrace, as Khrushchev fell,' he said.

'Then use the power,' urged Poklewski. 'Use it. Rudin has run flush out of options. He has no alternative but to agree to your terms. If he won't, topple him.'

'And the successor –' began the President.

'Will have seen what happened to Rudin, and will learn his lesson from that. Any successor will have to agree to the terms we lay down.'

President Matthews sought the views of the rest of the meeting. All but Lawrence and Benson agreed with Poklewski. President Matthews made his decision; the hawks had won.

The Soviet Foreign Ministry is one of seven near-identical buildings of the wedding-cake architectural style that Stalin favoured; neo-Gothic as put together by a mad patissier, in brown sandstone and standing on Smolensky Boulevard, corner of Arbat.

On the penultimate day of the month the Fleetwood Brougham Cadillac of the American ambassador to Moscow hissed into the parking bay before the main doors, and Mr Morton Donaldson was escorted to the plush fourth-floor office of Dmitri Rykov, the veteran Soviet foreign minister. They knew each other well; before coming to Moscow, Ambassador Donaldson had done a spell at United Nations where Dmitri Rykov was a well-known figure. Frequently they had drunk friendly toasts there together, and here in Moscow also. But today's meeting was formal. Donaldson was attended by his head of chancery and Rykov by five senior officials.

Donaldson read his message, carefully, word for word, in its original English. Rykov understood and spoke English well, but an aide did a rapid running translation into his right ear.

President Matthews' message made no reference to his knowledge of the disaster that had struck the Soviet wheat crop, and it expressed no surprise at the Soviet request earlier in the month for the staggering purchase of 55,000,000 tons of grain. In measured terms it expressed regret that the United States of America would not be in a position to make a sale to the Union of Soviet Socialist Republics of the requested tonnage of wheat.

With hardly a pause, Ambassador Donaldson read on, into the second part of the message. This, seemingly unconnected with the first, though following without a break, regretted the lack of success of the Strategic Arms Limitation Talks known as SALT Three, concluded in the winter of 1980, in lessening world tension, and expressed the hope that SALT Four, scheduled for preliminary discussion this coming autumn and winter, would achieve more, and enable the world to make genuine steps along the road to a just and lasting peace. That was all.

Ambassador Donaldson laid the full text of the message on Rykov's desk, received the formal, straight-faced thanks of the grey-haired, grey-visaged Soviet foreign minister, and left.

Andrew Drake spent most of that day poring over books. Azamat Krim, he knew, was somewhere in the hills of Wales fine-testing the hunting rifle with its new sight mounted above the barrel. Miroslav Kaminsky was still working at his steadily improving English. For Drake the problems centred on the South Ukrainian port of Odessa.

His first work of reference was the red-covered *Lloyd's Loading List*, a weekly guide to ships loading in European ports for destinations all over the world. From this he learned that there was no regular service from Northern Europe to Odessa, but there was a small, independent, inter-Mediterranean service which also called at several Black Sea ports. It was named the Salonika Line, and listed two vessels.

From here he went to the blue-covered *Lloyd's Shipping Index* and scoured the columns until he came to the vessels in question. He smiled. The supposed owners of each vessel trading in the Salonika Line were one-ship companies registered in Panama, which meant beyond much of a doubt that the owning 'company' in each case was a single brass plate attached to the wall of a lawyer's office in Panama City, and no more.

From his third work of reference, a brown-covered book called the *Greek Owner's Directory*, he ascertained that the managing agents were listed as a Greek firm and that their offices were in Piraeus, the port of Athens. He knew what that meant. In ninety-nine cases out of a hundred, when one talks to the managing agents of a Panama-flag ship, and they are Greek, one is in effect talking to the ship's owners. They masquerade as 'agents only' in order to take advantage of the fact that agents cannot be held legally responsibile for the peccadilloes of their principals. Some of these peccadilloes include inferior rates of pay and conditions for the crew, unseaworthy vessels and ill-defined safety standards but well-defined valuations for 'total loss' insurance, and occasionally some very careless habits with crude oil spillages.

For all that, Drake began to like the Salonika Line for one reason; a Greek-registered vessel would inevitably be allowed to employ only Greek senior officers, but could employ a cosmopolitan crew with or without official discharge books; passports alone would be sufficient. And her ships visited Odessa regularly.

Maxim Rudin leaned forward, lay the Russian translation of President Matthews' negative message as delivered by Ambassador Donaldson on his coffee table, and surveyed his three guests. It was dark outside, and he liked to keep the lights low in his private study at the north end of the arsenal building in the Kremlin.

'Blackmail,' said Petrov angrily. 'Bloody blackmail.'

'Of course,' said Rudin. 'What were you expecting? Sympathy?'

'That damned Poklewski is behind this,' said Rykov. 'But this cannot be Matthews' final answer. Their own Condors and our offer to buy fifty-five million tons of grain must have told them what position we are in.'

'Will they talk eventually, will they negotiate after all?' asked Ivanenko.

'Oh, yes, they'll talk eventually,' said Rykov. 'But they'll delay as long as they can, spin things out, wait until the famine begins to bite, then trade the grain against humiliating concessions.'

'Not too humiliating, I hope,' murmured Ivanenko. 'We only have a seven to six majority in the Politburo, and I for one would like to hold on to it.'

'That is precisely my problem,' growled Rudin. 'Sooner or later I have to send Dmitri Rykov into the negotiating chamber to fight for us, and I don't have a single damned weapon to give him.'

On the last day of the month Andrew Drake flew from London to Athens to begin his search for a ship heading towards Odessa.

The same day a small van, converted into a two-bunk mobile home such as students like to use for a roving continental holiday, left London for Dover on the Channel coast, and thence to France and Athens by road. Concealed beneath the floors were the guns, ammunition and image-intensifier. Fortunately most drug consignments head the other way, from the Balkans towards France and Britain. Customs checks were perfunctory at Dover and Calais.

At the wheel was Azamat Krim with his Canadian passport and international driving licence. Beside him, with new, albeit not quite regular, British papers, was Miroslav Kaminsky.

6

Close by the bridge across the Moscow River at Uspenskoye is a restaurant called the Russian Izba. It is built in the style of the timber cottages in which Russian peasants dwell, and which are called *izbas*. Both interior and exterior are of split pine tree trunks, nailed to timber uprights. The gap between is traditionally filled with river clay, not unlike the Canadian log cabin.

These *izbas* may look primitive, and from the point of sanitation often are, but they are much warmer than brick or concrete structures through the freezing Russian winters. The Izba restaurant is snug and warm inside, divided into a dozen small private dining rooms, many of which will only seat one dinner party. Unlike the restaurants of central Moscow, it is permitted a profit incentive linked to staff pay, and as a result and in even more stark contrast to the usual run of Russian eateries it has tasty food and fast and willing service.

It was here that Adam Munro had set up his next meeting with Valentina, scheduled for Saturday, 4th September. She had secured a dinner date with a male friend and had persuaded him to take her to this particular restaurant. Munro had invited one of the embassy secretaries to dinner and had booked the table in her, not his, name. The written reservations record would therefore not show that either Munro or Valentina were present that evening.

They dined in separate rooms, and on the dot of nine o'clock each made the excuse of going to the toilet and left the table. They met in the car park and Munro, whose own car would be too noticeable with its embassy plates, followed

Valentina to her own private Zhiguli saloon. She was subdued and puffed nervously at a cigarette.

Munro, as a result of handling the previous Russian defectors-in-place, knew the incessant strain that begins to wear at the nerves after a few weeks of subterfuge and secrecy.

'I got my chance,' she said at length. 'Three days ago. The meeting of early July. I was nearly caught.'

Munro was tense. Whatever she might think about her being trusted within the Party machine, no one, no one at all, is ever really trusted in Moscow politics. She was walking a high-wire, they both were. The difference was, he had a net: his diplomatic status.

'What happened?' he asked.

'Someone came in. A guard. I had just switched off the copying machine and was back at my typewriter. He was perfectly friendly. But he leant against the machine. It was still warm. I don't think he noticed anything, but it frightened me. That's not all that frightened me. I couldn't read the transcript until I got home. I was too busy feeding it into the copier. Adam, it's awful.'

She took her car keys, unlocked the glove compartment and extracted a fat envelope which she handed to Munro. The moment of handover is usually the moment when the watchers pounce, if they are there; the moment when the feet pound on the gravel, the doors are torn open, the occupants dragged out. Nothing happened.

Munro glanced at his watch. Nearly ten minutes. Too long. He put the envelope in his inside breast pocket.

'I'm going to try for permission to bring you out,' he said. 'You can't go on like this forever, even for much longer. Nor can you simply settle back to the old life, not now. Not knowing what you know. Nor can I carry on, knowing you are out in the city, knowing that we love each other. I have a leave break next month. I'm going to ask them in London then.'

This time she made no demur, a sign that her nerve was showing the first signs of breaking.

'All right,' she said. Seconds later she was gone into the darkness of the car park. He watched her enter the pool of light by the open restaurant door and disappear inside. He gave her two minutes then returned to his own impatient escort.

It was three in the morning before Munro had finished reading the Plan Boris, Marshal Nikolai Kerensky's scenario for the conquest of Western Europe. He poured himself a double brandy and sat staring at the papers on his sitting room table. Valentina's jolly, kindly Uncle Nikolai, he mused, had certainly laid it on the line. He spent two hours staring at a map of Europe, and by sunrise was as certain as Kerensky himself that in terms of conventional warfare the plan would work. Secondly, he was sure that Rykov too was right; thermonuclear war would ensue. And thirdly he was convinced there was no way of convincing the dissident members of the Politburo of this, short of the holocaust actually happening.

He rose and went to the window. Daylight was breaking in the east, out over the Kremlin spires; an ordinary Sunday was beginning for the citizens of Moscow, as it would in two hours for the Londoners and five hours later for the New Yorkers.

All his adult life the guarantee that summer Sundays would remain just plain ordinary had been dependent on a fine balance: a balance of belief in the might and willpower of the opponent super-powers, a balance of credibility, a balance of fear, but a balance for all that. He shivered, partly from the chill of morning, more from the realization that the papers behind him proved that at last the old nightmare was coming out of the shadows; the balance was breaking down.

The Sunday sunrise found Andrew Drake in far better humour, for his Saturday night had brought information of a different kind.

Every area of human knowledge, however small, however

arcane, has its experts and its devotees. And every group of these appear to have one place where they congregate to talk, discuss, exchange their information and impart the newest gossip.

Shipping movements in the eastern Mediterranean hardly form a subject on which doctorates are earned, but in that area they do form a subject of great interest to out-of-work seamen, such as Andrew Drake was pretending to be. The information centre about such movements is a small hotel called the Cavo d'Oro, standing above a yacht basin in the port of Piraeus.

Drake had already observed the offices of the agents, and probable owners, of the Salonika Line, but the last thing he knew he should do was to visit them. Instead he checked into the Cavo d'Oro Hotel and spent his time at the bar, where captains, mates, bo'suns, agents, dockland gossips and job-seekers sat over drinks to exchange what titbits of information they had. On Saturday night Drake found his man, a bo'sun who had once worked for the Salonika Line. It took half a bottle of retsina to extract the information.

'The one that visits Odessa most frequently is the MV *Sanadria*,' he was told. 'She is an old tub. Captain is Nikos Thanos. I think she's in harbour now.'

She *was* in harbour, and Drake found her by mid-morning. She was a 5000-ton deadweight, 'tween-deck Mediterranean trader, rusty and none too clean, but if she was heading into the Black Sea and up to Odessa on her next voyage, Drake would not have minded if she was full of holes.

By sundown he had found her captain, having learned that Thanos and all his officers were from the Greek island of Chios. Most of these Greek-run traders are almost family affairs, the master and his senior officers usually being from the same island, and often inter-related. Drake spoke no Greek, but English was fortunately the *lingua franca* of the international maritime community even in Piraeus, and just before sundown he found Captain Thanos.

North Europeans when they finish work head for home, wife and family. East Mediterraneans head for the coffee shop, friends and gossip. The Mecca of the coffee shop community in Piraeus is a street alongside the waterfront called Akti Miaouli; its vicinity contains little else but shipping offices and coffee shops.

Each frequenter has his favourite shop, and they are always crammed. Captain Thanos hung out when he was ashore at an open-fronted affair called Miki's, and here Drake found him, sitting over the inevitable thick black coffee, glass of cold water and shot tumbler of ouzo. He was short, broad and nut-brown, with black curly hair and several days of stubble.

'Captain Thanos?' asked Drake. The man looked up in suspicion at the Englishman and nodded.

'Nicos Thanos, of the *Sanadria*?' The seaman nodded again. His three companions had fallen silent, watching.

Drake smiled. 'My name is Andrew Drake. Can I offer you a drink?'

Captain Thanos used one forefinger to indicate his own glass and those of his companions. Drake, still standing, summoned a waiter and ordered five of everything. Thanos nodded to a vacant chair, the invitation to join them. Drake knew it would be slow, and might take days. But he was not going to hurry. He had found his ship.

The meeting in the Oval Office five days later was far less relaxed. All seven members of the *ad hoc* committee of the National Security Council were present, with President Matthews in the chair. All had spent half the night reading the transcript of the Politburo meeting in which Marshal Kerensky had laid out his plan for war and Vishnayev had made his bid for power. All eight men were shaken. The focus was on the chairman of the joint chiefs of staff, General Martin Craig.

'The question is, general,' President Matthews asked, 'is it feasible?'

'In terms of a conventional war across the face of Western Europe from the Iron Curtain to the Channel ports, even involving the use of tactical nuclear shells and rockets, yes, Mr President, it's feasible.'

'Could the West, before next spring, increase her defences to the point of making it completely unworkable?'

'That's a harder one, Mr President. Certainly we in the US could ship more men, more hardware, over to Europe. That would give the Soviets ample excuse to beef up their own levels, if they ever needed such an excuse. But as to our European allies, they don't have the reserves we have; for over a decade they have run down their manning levels, arms levels and preparation levels to a point where the imbalance in conventional manning and hardware between the NATO forces and the Warsaw Pact forces is at a stage that cannot be recouped in a mere nine months. The training that the personnel would need, even if recruited now; the production of new weapons of the necessary sophistication; these cannot be achieved in nine months.'

'So they're back to 1939 again,' said the secretary of the treasury gloomily.

'What about the nuclear option?' asked Bill Matthews quietly.

General Craig shrugged.

'If the Soviets attack in full force, it's inescapable. Forewarned may be forearmed, but nowadays armament programmes and training programmes take too long. Forewarned as we are, we could slow up a Soviet advance westwards, spoil Kerensky's time-scale of a hundred hours. But whether we could stop him dead – the whole damn Soviet army, navy and air force – that's another matter. By the time we knew the answer, it would probably be too late anyway. Which makes our use of the nuclear option inescapable. Unless of course, sir, we abandon Europe and our three hundred thousand men there.'

'David?' asked the President.

Secretary of State David Lawrence tapped the file in front of him.

'For about the first time in my life I agree with Dmitri Rykov. It's not just a question of Western Europe. If Europe goes, the Balkans, the eastern Mediterranean, Turkey, Iran and the Arabian states cannot hold. Ten years ago five per cent of our oil was imported; five years ago it had risen to fifty per cent. Now it's running at sixty-two per cent and rising. Even the whole of continental America, north and south, cannot fulfil more than fifty-five per cent of our needs at maximum production. We need the Arabian oil. Without it we are as finished as Europe, without a shot fired.'

'Suggestions, gentlemen?' asked the President.

'The Nightingale is valuable, but not indispensable, not now,' said Stanislaw Poklewski. 'Why not meet with Rudin and lay it on the table? We now know about the Plan Boris, we know the intent. And we will take steps to head off that intent, to make it unworkable. When he informs his Politburo of that, they'll realize the element of surprise is lost, that the war option won't work any more. It'll be the end of the Nightingale, but it will also be the end of Plan Boris.'

Bob Benson of the CIA shook his head vigorously.

'I don't think it's that simple, Mr President. As I read it, it's not a question of convincing Rudin or Rykov. There's a vicious faction fight now going on inside the Politburo, as we know. At stake is the succession to Rudin. And the famine is hanging over them.

'Vishnayev and Kerensky have proposed a limited war as a means of both obtaining the food surpluses of Western Europe, and of imposing war discipline on the Soviet peoples. Reveal what we know to Rudin – it changes nothing. It might even cause him to fall. Vishnayev and his group would take over; they are completely ignorant of the West and the way we Americans react to being attacked. Even with the element of surprise gone, with the grain famine pending they could still try the war option.'

'I agree with Bob,' said David Lawrence. 'There is a parallel here with the Japanese position forty years ago. The oil embargo caused the fall of the moderate Konoya faction. Instead we got General Tojo and that led to Pearl Harbour. If Maxim Rudin is toppled now, we could get Yefrem Vishnayev in his place. And on the basis of these papers, that could lead to war.'

'Then Maxim Rudin must not fall,' said President Matthews.

'Mr President, I protest,' said Poklewski heatedly. 'Am I to understand that the efforts of the United States are now to be bent towards saving the skin of Maxim Rudin? Have any of us forgotten what he did, the people liquidated under his regime, to get him to the pinnacle of power in Soviet Russia?'

'Stan, I'm sorry,' said President Matthews with finality. 'Last month I authorized a refusal by the United States to supply the Soviet Union with the grain it needs to head off a famine. At least until I knew what the perspectives of that famine would be. I can no longer pursue that policy of rejection, because I think we now know what those perspectives entail.

'Gentlemen, I am going this night to draft a personal letter to President Rudin proposing that David Lawrence and Dmitri Rykov meet on neutral territory to confer together. And that they confer on the subject of the new SALT Four arms limitation treaty, and *any other matters of interest*.'

When Andrew Drake returned to the Cavo d'Oro after his second meeting with Captain Thanos, there was a message waiting for him. It was from Azamat Krim, to say he and Kaminsky had just checked in to their agreed hotel.

An hour later Drake was with them. The van had come through unscathed. During the night Drake had the guns and ammunition transferred piece by piece to his own room at the Cavo d'Oro in separate visits from Kaminsky and Krim. When all was safely locked away he took them both out to dinner. The following morning Krim flew back to London, to live in Drake's apartment and await his phone call. Kaminsky stayed on in a small pension in the back streets of Piraeus. It was not comfortable, but it was anonymous.

While they were dining, the US secretary of state was locked in private conference with the Irish ambassador to Washington.

'If my meeting with Foreign Minister Rykov is to succeed,' said David Lawrence, 'we must have privacy. The discretion must be absolute. Reykjavik in Iceland is too obvious; our base at Keflavik there is like US territory. The meeting has to be on neutral territory. Geneva is full of watching eyes; ditto Stockholm and Vienna. Helsinki, like Iceland, would be too obvious. Ireland is halfway between Moscow and Washington, and you still foster the cult of privacy there.'

That night coded messages passed between Washington and Dublin. Within twenty-four hours the government in Dublin had agreed to host the meeting and proposed flight plans for both parties. Within hours President Matthews' personal and private letter to President Maxim Rudin was on its way to Ambassador Donaldson in Moscow.

Andrew Drake at his third attempt secured a private conversation with Captain Nikos Thanos. There was by then little doubt in the old Greek's mind that the young Englishman wanted something from him, but he gave no hint of curiosity. As usual Drake bought the coffee and ouzo.

'Captain,' said Drake, 'I have a problem, and I think you may be able to help me.'

Thanos raised an eyebrow but studied his coffee.

'Sometime near the end of the month the *Sanadria* will sail from Piraeus for Istanbul and the Black Sea. I believe you will be calling at Odessa.'

Thanos nodded. 'We are due to sail on the 30th,' he said, 'and, yes, we will be discharging cargo at Odessa.'

'I want to go to Odessa,' said Drake. 'I must reach Odessa.'

'You are an Englishman,' said Thanos. 'There are package tours of Odessa. You could fly there. There are cruises by Soviet liners out of Odessa, you could join one.'

Drake shook his head.

'It's not as easy as that,' he said. 'Captain Thanos, I would not receive a visa for Odessa. My application would be dealt with in Moscow, and I would not be allowed in.'

'And why do you want to go?' asked Thanos with suspicion.

'I have a girl in Odessa,' said Drake. 'My fiancée. I want to get her out.'

Captain Thanos shook his head with finality. He and his ancestors from Chios had been smuggling the odd package around the eastern Mediterranean since Homer was learning to talk, and he knew that a brisk smuggling trade went into and out of Odessa, and that his own crew made a tidy living on the side from bringing such luxury items as nylons, perfume and leather coats to the black market of the Ukrainian port. But smuggling people was quite different, and he had no intention of getting involved in that.

'I don't think you understand,' said Drake. 'There's no question of bringing her out on the *Sanadria*. Let me explain.'

He produced a photograph of himself and a remarkably pretty girl, sitting on the balustrade of the Potemkin Stairway that links the city with the port. Thanos' interest revived at once for the girl was definitely worth looking at.

'I am a graduate in Russian studies of the University of Bradford,' said Drake. 'Last year I was an exchange student for six months and spent those six months at Odessa University. That was where I met Larissa. We fell in love. We wanted to get married.'

Like most Greeks, Nikos Thanos prided himself on his romantic nature. Drake was talking his own language.

'Why didn't you?' he asked.

'The Soviet authorities would not let us,' said Drake. 'Of course, I wanted to bring Larissa back to England and marry her and settle down. She applied for permission to leave and was turned down. I kept reapplying on her behalf from the London end. No luck. Then last July I did as you just suggested; I went on a package tour to the Ukraine, through Kiev, Ternopol and Lvov.'

He flicked open his passport and showed Thanos the date stamps at Kiev Airport.

'She came up to Kiev to see me. We made love. Now she has written to me to say she is having our baby. So now I have to marry her more than ever.'

Captain Thanos also knew the rules. They had applied to

his society since time began. He looked again at the photograph. He was not to know that the girl was a Londoner who had posed in a studio not far from King's Cross station, nor that the background of the Potemkin Stairway was an enlarged detail from a tourist poster obtained at the London office of Intourist.

'So how are you going to get her out?' he asked.

'Next month,' said Drake, 'there is a Soviet liner, the *Litva*, leaving Odessa with a large party from the Soviet Youth movement, the Komsomol, for an off-season educational tour of the Mediterranean.'

Thanos nodded, he knew the *Litva* well.

'Because I made too many scenes over the matter of Larissa, the authorities will not let me back in. Larissa would not normally be allowed to go on this tour. But there is an official in the local branch of the Interior Ministry who likes to live well above his income. He will get her on to that cruise with all her papers in order, and when the ship docks at Venice, I will be waiting for her. But the official wants ten thousand American dollars. I have them, but I have to get the package to her.'

It made perfect sense to Captain Thanos. He knew the level of bureaucratic corruption that was endemic to the southern shore of Ukraine, Crimea, and Georgia, communism or no communism. That an official should 'arrange' a few documents for enough Western currency to improve his lifestyle substantially was quite normal.

An hour later the deal was concluded. For a further $5000 Thanos would take Drake on as a temporary deckhand for the duration of the voyage.

'We sail on the 30th,' he said, 'and we should be in Odessa on the 9th or 10th. Be at the quay where the *Sanadria* is berthed by six p.m. on the 30th. Wait until the agent's waterclerk has left, then come aboard just before the immigration people.'

Four hours later in Drake's flat in London, Azamat Krim took Drake's call from Piraeus giving him the date that Mishkin and Lazareff needed to know.

It was on the 20th that President Matthews received Maxim Rudin's reply. It was a personal letter, as his had been to the Soviet leader. In it Rudin agreed to the secret meeting between David Lawrence and Dmitri Rykov in Ireland, scheduled for the 24th.

President Matthews pushed the letter across his desk to Lawrence.

'He's not wasting time,' he remarked.

'He has no time to waste,' returned the secretary of state. 'Everything is being prepared. I have two men in Dublin now, checking out the arrangements. Our ambassador to Dublin will be meeting the Soviet ambassador tomorrow, as a result of this letter, to finalize details.'

'Well, David, you know what to do,' said the American President.

Azamat Krim's problem was to be able to post a letter or card to Mishkin from inside the Soviet Union, complete with Russian stamps and written in Russian, without going through the necessary delay in waiting for a visa to be granted to him by the Soviet consulate in London, which could take up to four weeks. With the help of Drake he had solved it relatively simply.

Prior to 1980 the main airport of Moscow, Sheremetyevo, had been a small, drab and shabby affair. But for the Olympics the Soviet government had commissioned a grand new airport terminal there, and Drake had done some research on it.

The facilities in the new terminal, which handled all long-distance flights out of Moscow, were excellent. There were numerous plaques praising the achievements of Soviet technology all over the airport; conspicuous by its absence was any mention that Moscow had had to commission a West German firm to build the place, because no Soviet construction company could have achieved the standard or the completion date. The West Germans had been handsomely paid in hard currency, but their contract had had rigorous penalty clauses in the case of non-completion by the start of the 1980 Olympics. For this reason, the Germans had used only two local Russian ingredients – sand and water. Everything else had been trucked in from West Germany in order to be certain of delivery on time.

In the great transit lounge and departure lounges, they had built letter boxes to handle the mail of anyone forgetting to post his last picture postcards from inside Moscow before leaving. The KGB vets every single letter, postcard, cable or phone call coming into or leaving the Soviet Union. Massive though the task may be, it gets done. But the new departure lounges at Sheremetyevo were used both for international flights and long-distance internal Soviet Union flights.

Krim's postcard therefore had been acquired at the Aeroflot offices in London. Modern Soviet stamps sufficient for a postcard at the internal rate had been openly bought from the London stamp emporium, Stanley Gibbons. On the card, which showed a picture of the Tupolev 144 supersonic passenger jet, was written in Russian the message: 'Just leaving with our factory's Party group for the expedition to Khabarovsk. Great excitement. Almost forgot to write you. Many happy returns for your birthday on the tenth. Your cousin, Ivan.'

Khabarovsk being in the extreme orient of Siberia, close to the Sea of Japan, a group leaving by Aeroflot for that city would leave from the same terminal building as a flight leaving for Japan. The letter was addressed to David Mishkin at his address in Lvov.

Azamat Krim took the Aeroflot flight from London to Moscow and changed planes there for the Aeroflot flight from Moscow to Narita Airport, Tokyo. He had an open-dated return. He also had a two-hour wait in the transit lounge in Moscow. Here he dropped the card in the letter box and went on to Tokyo. Once there he changed to Japan Air Lines, and flew back to London.

The card was examined by the KGB postal detail at Moscow's airport, assumed to be from a Russian to a Ukrainian cousin, both living and working inside the USSR, and sent on. It arrived in Lvov three days later.

While the tired and very jet-lagged Crimean Tatar was flying back from Japan, a small jet of the Norwegian internal airline Braathens-SAFE banked high over the fishing town of Alesund and began to let down to the municipal airport on the flat island across the bay. From one of its passenger windows Thor Larsen looked down with a thrill of excitement that never left him whenever he returned to the small community that had raised him and which would always be home.

He had arrived in the world in 1935, in a fisherman's cottage in the old Buholmen quarter, long since demolished to make way for the new highroad. Buholmen before the war had been the fishing quarter, a maze of wooden cottages in grey, blue and ochre. From his father's cottage a yard had run down, like all the others along the row, from the back stoop to the sound. Here were the rickety wooden jetties where the independent fishermen like his father had tied their small vessels when they came home from the sea; here the smells of his childhood had been of pitch, resin, paint, salt and fish.

As a child he had sat on his father's jetty, watching the big ships moving slowly up to berth at the Storneskaia, and he had dreamed of the places they must visit, far away across the western ocean. By the age of seven he could manage his own small skiff several hundred yards off the Buholmen shore to where old Sula Mountain cast her shadow from across the fjord on the shining water.

'He'll be a seaman,' said his father, watching with satisfaction from his jetty, 'not a fisherman, staying close to these waters, but a seaman.'

He was five when the Germans came to Alesund, big, grey-coated men who tramped around in heavy boots. It was not until he was seven that he saw the war. It was the summer and his father had let him come fishing with him during the holidays from Norvoy School. With the rest of the Alesund fishing fleet his father's boat was far out at sea under the guard of a German E-Boat. During the night he awoke because men were moving about. Away to the west were twinkling lights, the mastheads of the Orkneys fleet.

There was a small rowing boat bobbing beside his father's vessel, and the crew were shifting herring boxes. Before the child's astounded gaze a young man, pale and exhausted, emerged from beneath the boxes in the hold and was helped into the rowboat. Minutes later it was lost in the darkness, heading for the Orkneys men. Another radio operator from the Resistance was on his way to England for training. His father made him promise never to mention what he had seen. A week later in Alesund there was a rattle of rifle fire one evening, and his mother told him he should say his prayers extra hard, because the schoolmaster was dead.

By the time he was in his early teens, growing out of clothes faster than his mother could make them, he too had become obsessed with radio and in two years had built his own transmitter/receiver. His father gazed at the apparatus in wonderment; it was beyond his comprehension. Thor was sixteen when, the day after Christmas of 1951, he picked up an SOS message from a ship in distress in the mid-Atlantic. She was the *Flying Enterprise*. Her cargo had shifted and she was listing badly in heavy seas.

For sixteen days the world and a teenage Norwegian boy watched and listened with baited breath as the Danish-born American captain, Kurt Carlsen, refused to leave his sinking ship and nursed her painfully eastwards through the gales towards the south of England. Sitting in his attic hour after hour with his headphones over his ears, looking out through the dormer window at the wild ocean beyond the mouth of the fjord, Thor Larsen had willed the old freighter to make it home to port. On 10th January 1952 she finally sank, just fifty-seven miles off Falmouth harbour.

Larsen heard her go down, listened to the shadowing tugs tell of her death, and the rescue of her indomitable captain. He took off his headphones, laid them down and descended to his parents who were at table.

'I have decided,' he told them, 'what I am going to be. I am going to be a sea captain.'

A month later he entered the merchant marine.

The plane touched down and rolled to a stop outside the small, neat terminal with its goose pond by the car park. His wife Lisa was waiting for him with Kristina, his sixteen-year-old daughter and Kurt, his fourteen-year-old son. The pair chattered like magpies on the short drive across the island to the ferry, and across the sound to Alesund, and all the way home to their comfortable ranch-style house in the secluded suburb of Bogneset.

It was good to be home. He would go fishing with Kurt out on the Borgund Fjord as his father had taken him fishing there in his youth; they would picnic in the last days of the summer on their little cabin cruiser or on the knobby green islands that dotted the sound. He had three weeks of leave; then Japan, and in February the captaincy of the biggest ship the world had ever seen. He had come a long way from the wooden cottage in Buholmen, but Alesund was still his home and for this descendant of Vikings there was nowhere in the world quite like it.

On the night of the 23rd September a Grumman Gulfstream in the livery of a well-known commercial corporation lifted off from Andrews air force base and headed east across the Atlantic with long-distance tanks for Shannon Airport. It was phased into the Irish air traffic control network as a private charter flight. When it landed at Shannon it was shepherded in darkness to the side of the airfield away from the international terminal and surrounded by five black and curtained limousines.

Secretary of State David Lawrence and his party of six were greeted by the US ambassador and the head of chancery, and all five limousines swept out of the airport perimeter fence by a side gate. They headed northeast through the sleeping countryside towards County Meath.

That same night a Tupolev 134 twin-jet of Aeroflot refuelled at East Berlin's Schönefeld Airport and headed west over Germany and the Low Countries towards Britain and Ireland. It was slated as a special Aeroflot flight bringing a trade delegation to Dublin. As such the British air traffic controllers passed it over to their Irish colleagues as it left the coast of Wales. The Irish had their military air traffic network take it over, and it landed two hours before dawn at the Irish Air Corps base at Baldonnel, outside Dublin.

Here the Tupolev was parked between two hangars out of vision of the main airfield buildings, and it was greeted by the Soviet ambassador, the Irish deputy foreign minister, and six limousines. Foreign Minister Rykov and his party entered the vehicles, were screened by the interior curtains, and left the air base.

High above the banks of the River Boyne, in an environment of great natural beauty and not far from the market town of Slane in County Meath, stands Slane Castle, ancestral home of the family Conyngham, Earls of Mount Charles. The youthful earl had been quietly asked by the Irish government to accept a week's holiday in a luxury hotel in the west with his pretty countess, and to lend the castle to the government for a few days. He had agreed. The restaurant attached to the castle was marked as closed for repairs, the staff were given a week's leave, government caterers moved in and Irish police in plain clothes discreetly posted themselves at all points of the compass round the castle. When the two cavalcades of limousines had entered the grounds the main gates were shut. If the local people noticed anything they were courteous enough to make no mention of it.

In the Georgian private dining room before the marble fireplace by Adam, the two statesmen met for a sustaining breakfast.

'Dmitri, good to see you again,' said David Lawrence extending his hand.

Rykov shook it warmly. He glanced around him at the silver gifts from George the Fourth and the Conyngham portraits on the walls. 'So this is how you decadent bourgeois capitalists live,' he said.

Lawrence roared with laughter. 'I wish it were, Dmitri, I wish it were.'

At eleven o'clock, surrounded by their aides in Johnston's magnificent Gothic circular library, the two men settled down to negotiate. The bantering was over.

'Mr Foreign Minister,' said Lawrence, 'it seems we both have problems. Ours concern the continuing arms race between our two nations, which nothing seems able to halt or even slow down, and which worries us deeply. Yours seems to concern the forthcoming grain harvest in the Soviet Union. I hope we can find a means between us to lessen these, our mutual problems.'

'I hope so too, Mr Secretary of State,' said Rykov cautiously. 'What have you in mind?'

There is only one direct flight a week between Athens and Istanbul, the Tuesday Sabena connection, leaving Athens' Hellenikon Airport at 14.00 and landing at Istanbul at 16.45. On Tuesday, September 28th, Miroslav Kaminsky was on it, instructed to secure for Andrew Drake a consignment of sheepskin and suede jackets for trading in Odessa.

The same afternoon Secretary of State Lawrence finished reporting to the *ad hoc* committee of the National Security Council in the Oval Office.

'Mr President, gentlemen, I think we have it. Providing Maxim Rudin can keep his hold on the Politburo and secure their agreement.

'The proposal is that we and the Soviets each send two teams of negotiators to a resumed strategic arms limitation conference. The suggested venue is Ireland again. The Irish government has agreed and will prepare a suitable conference hall and living accommodation, providing we and the Soviets signal our assent.

'One team from each side will face the other across the table to discuss a broad range of arms limitations. This is the big one; I secured a concession from Dmitri Rykov that the ambit of the discussion need not exclude thermo-nuclear weapons, strategic weapons, inner space, international inspection, tactical nuclear weapons, conventional weapons and manning levels, or disengagement of forces along the Iron Curtain line.'

There was a murmur of approval and surprise from the other seven men present. No previous American-Soviet arms conference had ever had such widely drawn terms of reference. If all areas showed a move towards genuine and monitored détente, it would add up to a peace treaty.

'These talks will be what the conference is supposedly about, so far as the world is concerned, and the usual press bulletins will be necessary,' resumed Secretary Lawrence. 'Now, in back of the main conference, the secondary conference of technical experts will negotiate the sale to the Soviets at financial costs still to be worked out, but probably lower than world prices, of up to fifty-five million tons of grain, consumer-product technology, computers and oil-extraction technology.

'At every stage there will be liaison between the up-front and the in-back teams of negotiators, on each side. They make a concession on arms, we make a concession on low-cost goodies.'

'When is this slated for?' asked Poklewski.

'That's the surprise element,' said Lawrence. 'Normally the Russians like to work very slowly. Now it seems they are in a hurry. They want to start in two weeks.'

'Good God, we can't be ready for "go" in two weeks!' exclaimed the secretary of defense, whose department was intimately involved.

'We have to be,' said President Matthews. 'There will never be another chance like this again. Besides, we have our SALT team ready and briefed. They have been ready for months. We have to bring in Agriculture, Trade and Technology on this, and fast. We have to get together the team who can talk on the other, the trade/technology, side of the deal. Gentlemen, please see to it. At once.'

Maxim Rudin did not put it to his Politburo quite like that the following day.

'They have bitten to the bait,' he said from his chair at the head of the table. 'When they make a concession on wheat or technology in one of the conference rooms, we make the absolute minimum concession in the other conference room. We will get our grain, comrades; we will feed our people, we will head off the famine, and at the minimum price. Americans, after all, have never been able to out-negotiate the Russians.'

There was a general buzz of agreement.

'What concessions?' snapped Vishnayev. 'How far back will these concessions set the Soviet Union and the triumph of world Marxism-Leninism?'

'As to your first question,' replied Rykov, 'we cannot know until we are negotiating. As to your second, the answer must be substantially less than a famine would set us back.'

'There are two points we should be clear on before we decide whether to talk or not,' said Rudin. 'One is that the Politburo will be kept fully informed at every stage, so if the moment comes when the price is too high, this council will have the right to abort the conference, and I will defer to Comrade Vishnayev and his plan for a war in the spring. The second is that no concession we may make to secure the wheat need necessarily remain valid for very long after the deliveries have taken place.'

There were several grins round the table. This was the sort of realpolitik the Politburo was much more accustomed to, as they had shown in transforming the old Helsinki agreement on détente into a farce.

'Very well,' said Vishnayev, 'but I think we should lay down the exact parameters of our negotiating teams' authority to concede points.'

'I have no objection to that,' said Rudin.

The meeting continued on this theme for an hour and a half. Rudin got his vote to proceed, by the same margin as before, seven against six.

On the last day of the month Andrew Drake stood in the shade of a crane and watched the *Sanadria* battening down her hatches. Conspicuous on deck were Vacuvators for Odessa, powerful suction machines like vacuum cleaners for sucking wheat out of the hold of a ship and straight into a grain silo. The Soviet Union must be trying to improve her grain unloading capacity, he mused, though he did not know why. Below the weather-deck were fork-lift trucks for Istanbul and agricultural machinery for Varna in Bulgaria, part of a transhipment cargo that had come in from America as far as Piraeus.

He watched the agent's waterclerk leave the ship, giving Captain Thanos a last shake of the hand. Thanos scanned the pier and made out the figure of Drake loping towards him, his kitbag over one shoulder and suitcase in the other hand.

In the captain's day cabin Drake handed over his passport and vaccination certificates. He signed the ship's articles and became a member of the deck crew. While he was down below stowing his gear Captain Thanos entered his name in the ship's crew list, just before the Greek immigration officer came on board. The two men had the usual drink together.

'There's an extra crew man,' said Thanos as if in passing. The immigration officer scanned the list and the pile of discharge books and passports in front of him. Most were Greek, but there were six non-Greeks. Drake's British passport stood out. The immigration officer selected it and rifled through the pages. A fifty-dollar bill fell out.

'An out-of-work,' said Thanos, 'trying to get to Turkey and head for the East. Thought you'd be glad to be shot of him.'

Five minutes later the crew's identity documents had been returned to their wooden tray and the vessel's papers stamped for outward clearance. Daylight was fading as her ropes were cast off and *Sanadria* slipped away from her berth and headed south before turning northeast for the Dardanelles.

Below decks the crew were grouping round the greasy mess-room table. One of them was hoping no one would look under his mattress where the Sako Hornet rifle was stored. In Moscow his target was sitting down to an excellent supper.

7

While high-ranking and secret men launched themselves into a flurry of activity in Washington and Moscow, the old *Sanadria* thumped her way impassively northeast towards the Dardanelles and Istanbul.

On the second day Drake watched the bare brown hills of Gallipoli slide by and the sea dividing European and Asian Turkey widened into the Sea of Marmara. Captain Thanos, who knew these waters like his own back yard on Chios, was doing his own pilotage.

Two Soviet cruisers steamed past them, heading from Sebastopol out to the Mediterranean to shadow the US Sixth Fleet manoeuvres. Just after sundown the twinkling lights of Istanbul and the Galatea Bridge spanning the Bosphorus came into view. The *Sanadria* anchored for the night and entered port at Istanbul the following morning.

While the fork-lift trucks were being discharged, Andrew Drake secured his passport from Captain Thanos and slipped ashore. He met Miroslav Kaminsky at an agreed rendezvous in central Istanbul and took delivery of a large bundle of sheepskin and suede coats and jackets. When he returned to the ship Captain Thanos raised an eyebrow.

'You aiming to keep your girlfriend warm?' he asked.

Drake shook his head and smiled. 'The crew tell me half the seamen bring these ashore in Odessa,' he said. 'I thought it would be the best way to bring my own package.'

The Greek captain was not surprised. He knew half a dozen of his own seamen would be bringing such luggage back to the ship with them, to trade the fashionable coats and jeans for five times their buying price to the black market spivs of Odessa.

Thirty hours later the *Sanadria* cleared the Bosphorus, watched the Golden Horn drop away astern and chugged north for Bulgaria with her tractors.

Due west of Dublin lies County Kildare, site of the Irish horse-racing centre at the Curragh and of the sleepy market town of Celbridge. On the outskirts of Celbridge stands the largest and finest Palladian stately home in the land, Castletown House. With the agreement of the American and Soviet ambassadors, the Irish government had proposed Castletown as the venue for the disarmament conference.

For a week teams of painters, plasterers, electricians and gardeners had been at work night and day putting the final touches to the two rooms that would hold the twin conferences, though no one knew the reason for the second conference.

The façade of the main house alone is 142 feet wide, and from each corner covered and pillared corridors lead away to further quarters. One of these wing blocks contains the kitchens and staff apartments, and it was here the American security force would be quartered; the other block contained the stables, with more apartments above them, and here the Russian bodyguards would live.

The main house would act as both conference centre and home for the subordinate diplomats who would inhabit the numerous guest rooms and suites on the top floor. Only the two principal negotiators and their immediate aides would return each night to their respective embassies, equipped as they were with facilities for coded communications with Washington and Moscow.

This time there was to be no secrecy, save in the matter of the secondary conference. Before a blaze of world publicity the two foreign ministers, David Lawrence and Dmitri Rykov, arrived in Dublin and were greeted by the Irish President and premier. After the habitual televised handshaking and toasting, they left Dublin in two cavalcades for Castletown.

At midday on 8th October the two statesmen and their twenty advisers entered the vast Long Gallery, decorated in Wedgwood Blue in the Pompeian manner and 140 feet long. Most of the centre of the hall was taken up with the gleaming Georgian table, down each side of which the delegations seated themselves. Flanking each foreign minister were experts in defence, weapons systems, nuclear technology, inner space and armoured warfare.

The two statesmen knew they were only there formally to open the conference. After the opening and the agreement of agenda, each would fly home to leave the talks in the hands of the delegation leaders, Professor Ivan I. Sokolov for the Soviets and former Assistant Secretary of Defense Edwin J. Campbell for the Americans.

The remaining rooms on this floor were given over to the stenographers, typists and researchers.

One floor below, at ground level, in the great dining room of Castletown, with drapes drawn to mute the autumn sunshine pouring on to the southeastern face of the mansion, the secondary conference quietly filed in to take their places. These were mainly technologists, experts in grain, oil, computers and industrial plant.

Upstairs, Dmitri Rykov and David Lawrence each made a short address of welcome to the opposing delegation and expressed the hope and the confidence that the conference would succeed in diminishing the problems of a beleaguered and frightened world. Then they adjourned for lunch.

After lunch Professor Sokolov had a private conference with Rykov before the latter's departure for Moscow.

'You know our position, comrade professor,' said Rykov. 'Frankly, it is not a good one. The Americans will go for everything they can get. Your job is to fight every step of the way to minimize our concessions. But we must have that grain. Nevertheless, every concession on arms levels and deployment patterns in Eastern Europe must be referred back to Moscow. This is because the Politburo insists on being involved in the approval or rejection in the sensitive areas.'

He forbore to say that the sensitive areas were those that might impede a future Soviet strike into Western Europe, or that Maxim Rudin's political career hung by a thread.

In another drawing room at the opposite end of Castletown, a room which, like Rykov's, had been swept by his own electronics experts for possible 'bugs', David Lawrence was conferring with Edwin Campbell.

'It's all yours, Ed. This won't be like Geneva. The Soviet problems won't permit endless delays, adjournments and referring-back to Moscow for weeks on end. I estimate they have to have an agreement with us within six months. Either that or they don't get the grain.

'On the other hand, Sokolov will fight every inch of the way. We know each concession on arms will have to be referred to Moscow, but Moscow will have to decide fast one way or the other, else the time will run out.

'One last thing. We know Maxim Rudin cannot be pushed too far. If he is, he could fall. But if he doesn't get the wheat he could fall, too. The trick will be to find the balance; to get the maximum concessions without provoking a revolt in the Politburo.'

Campbell removed his glasses and pinched the bridge of his nose. He had spent four years commuting from Washington to Geneva on the so-far abortive SALT talks and he was no newcomer to the problems of trying to negotiate with Russians.

'Hell, David, that sounds fine. But you know how they give nothing of their own inner position away. It would be a hell of a help to know just how far they can be pushed, and where the stop-line lies.'

David Lawrence opened his attaché case and withdrew a sheaf of papers. He proffered them to Campbell.

'What are these?' asked Campbell.

Lawrence chose his words carefully.

'Eleven days ago in Moscow the full Politburo authorized Maxim Rudin and Dmitri Rykov to begin these talks. But only by a vote of seven against six. There's a dissident faction inside the Politburo that wishes to abort the talks and bring Rudin down. After the agreement the Politburo laid out the exact parameters of what Professor Sokolov could or could not concede, what the Politburo would or would not allow Rudin to grant. Go beyond the parameters and Rudin could be toppled. If that happened we would have bad, very bad, problems.'

'So what are the papers?' asked Campbell, holding the sheaf in his hands.

'They came in from London last night,' said Lawrence. 'They are the verbatim transcript of that Politburo meeting.'

Campbell stared at them in amazement.

'Jesus,' he breathed, 'we can dictate our own terms.'

'Not quite,' corrected Lawrence. 'We can require the maximum that the moderate faction inside the Politburo can get away with. Insist on more and we could be eating ashes.'

The visit of the British Prime Minister and her foreign secretary to Washington two days later was described in the press as being informal. Ostensibly Britain's first woman premier was to address a major meeting of the English-Speaking Union and take the opportunity of paying a courtesy call on the United States President.

But the crux of the latter came in the Oval Office where President Bill Matthews, flanked by his special security adviser, Stanislaw Poklewski, and his secretary of state, David Lawrence, gave the British visitors an exhaustive briefing on the hopeful start of the Castletown conference. The agenda, reported President Matthews, had been agreed with unusual alacrity. At least three main areas for future discussion had been defined between the two teams with a minimal presence of the usual Soviet objections to every dot and comma.

President Matthews expressed the hope that after years of frustration a comprehensive limitation of arms levels and troop deployments along the Iron Curtain from the Baltic to the Aegean Seas could well emerge from Castletown.

The crunch came as the meeting between the two heads of government closed.

'We regard it as vital, ma'am, that the inside information of which we are in possession and without which the conference could well fail, continues to reach us.'

'You mean, the Nightingale,' said the British premier crisply.

'Yes, ma'am, I do,' said Matthews. 'We regard it as indispensable that the Nightingale continues to operate.'

'I understand your point, Mr President,' she answered calmly. 'But I believe that the hazard levels of that operation are very high. I do not dictate to Sir Nigel Irvine what he shall or shall not do in the running of his service. I have too much respect for his judgement for that. But I will do what I can.'

It was not until the traditional ceremony in front of the principal façade of the White House of seeing the British visitors into their limousines and smiling for the cameras was complete that Stanislaw Poklewski could give vent to his feelings.

'There's no hazard to a Russian agent in the world that compares with the success or failure of the Castletown talks,' he said.

'I agree,' said Bill Matthews, 'but I understand from Bob Benson the hazard lies in the exposure of the Nightingale at this point. If that happened, and he were caught, the Politburo would learn what had been passed over. If that happened, they would shut off at Castletown. So the Nightingale either has to be silenced or brought out, but neither until we have a treaty sewn up and signed. And that could be six months yet.'

That same evening while the sun was still shining on Washington it was setting over the port of Odessa as the *Sanadria* dropped anchor in the roads. When the clatter of the anchor cable had ceased, silence fell on the freighter, broken only by the low humming of the generators in the engine room and the hiss of escaping steam on deck. Andrew

Drake leaned on the fo'c's'le rail, watching the lights of the port and city twinkle into life.

West of the ship, at the northern extremity of the port, lay the oil harbour and refinery, circled by chain-link fencing. To the south the port was bounded by the protective arm of the great seaward mole. Ten miles beyond the mole the River Dniester flowed into the sea through the swampy marshes where five months before Miroslav Kaminsky had stolen his skiff and made a desperate bid for freedom. Now, thanks to him, Andrew Drake, Andriy Drach, had come home to the land of his ancestors. But this time he had come armed.

That evening Captain Thanos was informed that he would be brought into port and moored alongside the following morning. Port health and customs visited the *Sanadria* but they spent the hour on board closeted with Captain Thanos in his cabin, sampling his top-grade Scotch whisky, kept for the occasion. There was no rummage search of the ship. Watching the launch leave the ship's side, Drake wondered if Thanos had betrayed him. It would have been easy enough; Drake would be arrested ashore, and Thanos would sail with his $5000.

It all depended, he thought, on Thanos accepting his story of bringing money to his fiancée. If he had, there was no motive to betray him, for the offence was routine enough; his own sailors brought contraband goods into Odessa on every voyage, and dollar bills were only another form of contraband. And if the rifle and pistols had been discovered the simple thing would have been to throw the lot into the sea and sling Drake off the ship once back in Piraeus. Still, he could neither eat nor sleep that night.

Just after dawn the pilot boarded. The *Sanadria* weighed anchor, took a tug in attendance and moved slowly between the breakwaters and into her berth. Often, Drake had learned, there was a berthing delay in this, the most congested of the Soviet Union's warm-sea ports. They must want their Vacuvators badly. He had no idea how badly. Once the shore cranes had started to discharge the freighter, the watchkeepers among the crew were allowed to go ashore.

During the voyage Drake had become friendly with the *Sanadria*'s carpenter, a middle-aged Greek seaman who had visited Liverpool and was keen to practise his twenty words of English. He had repeated them continuously to his intense delight whenever he met Drake during the voyage, and each time Drake had nodded furious encouragement and approval. He had explained to Constantine in English and sign language that he had a girlfriend in Odessa and was bringing her presents. Constantine approved. With a dozen others, they trooped down the gangway and headed for the dock gates. Drake was wearing one of his best suede sheepskin coats, although the day was reasonably warm. Constantine carried a duffel shoulder-bag with a brace of bottles of export-proof Scotch whisky.

The whole port area of Odessa is cordoned off from the city and its citizens by a high chain fence, topped with barbed wire and arc lights. The main dock gates habitually stand open in the daytime, the entrance being blocked only by a balanced red-and-white striped pole. This marks the passageway for lorries and trucks, with a customs official and two armed militiamen attending it.

Astride the entrance gate is a long, narrow shed, with one door inside the port area and one on the outside. The party from the *Sanadria* entered the first door with Constantine in charge. There was a long counter, attended by one customs man, and a passport desk attended by an immigration officer and a militiaman. All three looked scruffy and exceptionally bored. Constantine approached the customs man and dumped his shoulder-bag on the counter. The official opened it and extracted a bottle of whisky. Constantine gestured that it was a present from one to the other. The customs man managed a friendly nod and placed the bottle beneath his table.

Constantine clasped a brawny arm round Drake and pointed to him.

'*Droog*,' he said and beamed widely. The customs man nodded that he understood the newcomer was the Greek carpenter's friend and should be recognized as such. Drake smiled broadly. He stood back, eyeing the customs man as an outfitter eyes a customer. Then he stepped forward, slipped off the sheepskin coat and held it out, indicating that he and the customs man were about the same size. The official did not bother to try it on; it was a fine coat, worth a month's salary at least. He smiled his acknowledgement, placed the coat under the table and waved the entire party through.

The immigration officer and militiaman showed no surprise. The second bottle of whisky was for the pair of them. The *Sanadria* crew members surrendered their discharge books and, in the case of Drake, his passport with the immigration officer, and each received in return a shore pass from a leather satchel the officer wore over his shoulder. Within a few minutes the *Sanadria* party emerged into the sunshine beyond the shed.

Drake's rendezvous was in a small café in the dockland area of old, cobbled streets, not far from the Pushkin Memorial where the ground rises from the docks to the main city. He found it after thirty minutes of wandering, having separated himself from his fellow seamen on the grounds that he wanted to meet his mythical girlfriend. Constantine did not object; he had to contact his underworld friends to set up the delivery of his sack full of denim jeans.

It was Lev Mishkin who came, just after noon. He was wary, cautious, and sat alone, making no sign of recognition. When he had finished his coffee he rose and left the café. Drake followed him. Only when the pair had reached the wide, seafront highway of Primorsky Boulevard did he allow Drake to catch up. They spoke as they walked.

Drake agreed that he would make his first run, with the handguns stuck in his waistband and the image-intensifier in a duffel bag with two clinking bottles of whisky, that evening. There would be plenty of western ships' crew coming through for an evening in the dockland bars at the same time. He would be wearing another sheepskin coat to cover the handguns in his belt, and the chill of the evening air would justify his keeping the coat buttoned at the front. Mishkin and his friend David Lazareff would meet Drake in the darkness by the Pushkin Monument and take over the hardware.

Just after eight that evening Drake came through with his first consignment. He saluted jovially at the customs man, who waved him on and called to his colleague at the passport desk. The immigration man handed out a shore pass in exchange for his passport, jerked his chin towards the open door to the city of Odessa and Drake was through. He was almost at the foot of the Pushkin Monument, seeing the writer's head raised against the stars above, when two figures joined him out of the darkness between the plane trees that crowd Odessa's open spaces.

'Any problems?' asked Lazareff.

'None,' said Drake.

'Let's get it over with,' said Mishkin. Both men were carrying the briefcases that everyone seems to carry in the Soviet Union. These cases, far from carrying documents, are the male version of the string bags the women carry, called 'perhaps bags'. They get their name from the hope that each person carried with them that perhaps they may spot a worthwhile consumer article on sale and snap it up before it is sold out or the queues form. Mishkin took the image-intensifier and stuffed it into his larger briefcase; Lazareff took both the handguns, the spare ammunition clips and the box of rifle shells and put them in his own.

'We're sailing tomorrow evening,' said Drake. 'I'll have to bring the rifle in the morning.'

'Damn,' said Mishkin, 'daylight is bad. David, you know the port area best. Where is it to be?'

Lazareff considered. 'There is an alley,' he said, 'between two crane maintenance workshops.'

He described the mud-coloured workshops, not far from the docks.

'The alley is short, narrow. One end looks towards the sea, the other to a third blank wall. Enter the seaward end of the alley on the dot of eleven a.m. I will enter the other end. If there is anyone else in the alley, walk on, go round the block and try again. If the alley is empty, we'll take delivery.'

'How will you be carrying it?' asked Mishkin.

‘Sheepskin coats wrapped around it,’ said Drake, ‘and stuffed in a kitbag, about three feet long.’

‘Let’s scarper,’ said Lazareff, ‘someone is coming.’

When Drake returned to the *Sanadria* the customs men had changed shifts and he was frisked. He was clean. The next morning he asked Captain Thanos for an extra spell ashore on the grounds that he wanted to spend the maximum time with his fiancée. Thanos excused him deck duties and let him go. There was a nasty moment in the customs shed when Drake was asked to turn out his pockets. Placing his kitbag on the ground he obeyed and revealed a wad of four ten-dollar bills. The customs man, who seemed to be in a bad mood, wagged an admonishing finger at Drake and confiscated the dollars. He ignored the kitbag. Sheepskin coats, it seemed, were respectable contraband; dollars were not.

The alley was empty, save for Mishkin and Lazareff walking down from one end and Drake walking up from the other. Mishkin gazed beyond Drake to the seaward end of the alley; when they were abreast he said, ‘Go’, and Drake hefted the kitbag on to Lazareff’s shoulder. ‘Good luck,’ he said as he walked on. ‘See you in Israel.’

Sir Nigel Irvine retained membership of three clubs in the West End of London, but selected Brooks’s for his dinner with Barry Ferndale and Adam Munro. By custom the serious business of the evening was left until they had quit the dining room and retired to the subscription room where the coffee, port and cigars were served.

Sir Nigel had asked the chief steward, called the dispense waiter, to reserve his favourite corner near the windows looking down into St James’s Street, and the group of four deep, leather club chairs was waiting for him when he arrived. Munro selected brandy and water, and Ferndale and Sir Nigel took a decanter of the club’s vintage port and had it set on the table between them. Silence reigned while the cigars were lit, the coffee sipped. From the walls the Dilettantes, the eighteenth-century group of men-about-town, gazed down at them.

'Now my dear Adam, what seems to be the problem?' asked Sir Nigel at last. Munro glanced to a nearby table where two senior civil servants conversed. For keen ears, they were within eavesdropping distance. Sir Nigel noticed the look.

'Unless we shout,' he observed equably, 'no one is going to hear us. Gentlemen do not listen to other gentlemen's conversations.'

Munro thought this over.

'We do,' he said simply.

'That's different,' said Ferndale, 'it's our job.'

'All right,' said Munro, 'I want to bring the Nightingale out.'

Sir Nigel studied the tip of his cigar.

'Ah, yes,' he said. 'Any particular reason?'

'Partly strain,' said Munro. 'The original tape recording in July had to be stolen and a blank substituted in its place. That could be discovered, and it's preying on Nightingale's mind. Secondly, the chances of discovery. Every abstraction of Politburo minutes heightens this. We now know Maxim Rudin is fighting for his political life, and the succession when he goes. If Nightingale gets careless, or is even unlucky, he could get caught.'

'Adam, that's one of the risks of defecting,' said Ferndale. 'It goes with the job. Penkovsky was caught.'

'That's the point,' pursued Munro. 'Penkovsky had provided just about all he could. The Cuban missile crisis was over. There was nothing the Russians could do to undo the damage that Penkovsky had done to them.'

'I would have thought that was a good reason for keeping Nightingale in place,' observed Sir Nigel. 'There is still an awful lot more he can do for us.'

'Or the reverse,' said Munro. 'If Nightingale comes out, the Kremlin can never know what has been passed. If he is caught, they'll make him talk. What he can reveal now will be enough to bring Rudin down. This would seem to be the moment the West precisely would not wish Rudin to fall.'

'Indeed it is,' said Sir Nigel. 'Your point is taken. It's a question of a balance of chances. If we bring Nightingale out, the KGB will check back for months. The missing tape will presumably be discovered and the supposition will be that even more was passed over before he left. If he is caught, it's even worse; a complete record of what he has passed over will be abstracted from him. Rudin could well fall as a result. Even though Vishnayev would probably be disgraced also, the Castletown talks would abort. Thirdly, we keep Nightingale in place until the Castletown talks are over and the arms limitation agreement signed. By then there will be nothing the war faction in the Politburo can do. It's a teasing choice.'

'I'd like to bring him out,' said Munro. 'Failing that, let him lie low, cease transmitting.'

'I'd like him to go on,' said Ferndale, 'at least until the end of Castletown.'

Sir Nigel reflected on the alternative arguments.

'I spent the afternoon with the Prime Minister,' he said at length. 'The PM made a request, a very strong request, on behalf of herself and the President of the USA. I cannot at this moment turn that request down, unless it could be shown the Nightingale was on the very threshold of exposure. The Americans regard it as vital to their chances of securing an all-embracing treaty at Castletown that Nightingale keep them abreast of the Soviet negotiating position. At least until the New Year.

'So I'll tell you what I'll do. Barry, prepare a plan to bring the Nightingale out. Something that can be activated at short notice. Adam, if the fuse begins to burn under the Nightingale's tail, we'll bring him out. Fast. But for the moment the Castletown talks and the frustration of the Vishnayev clique have to take first priority. Three or four more transmissions should see the Castletown talks in their final stages. The Soviets cannot delay some sort of a wheat agreement beyond February or March at the latest. After that, Adam, Nightingale can come to the West, and I'm sure the Americans will show their gratitude in the habitual manner.'

The dinner in Maxim Rudin's private suite in the Kremlin's inner sanctum was far more private than that at Brooks's Club in London. No confidence concerning the integrity of gentlemen where other gentlemen's conversations are concerned has ever marred the acute caution of the men of the Kremlin. There was no one within earshot but the silent Misha when Rudin took his place in his favourite chair of the study and gestured Ivanenko and Petrov to other seats.

'What did you make of today's meeting?' Rudin asked Petrov without preamble.

The controller of Party Organizations of the Soviet Union shrugged. 'We got away with it,' he said. 'Rykov's report was masterly. But we still have to make some pretty sweeping concessions if we want that wheat. And Vishnayev is still after his war.'

Rudin grunted.

'Vishnayev is after my job,' he said bluntly. 'That's his ambition. It's Kerensky who wants the war. He wants to use his armed forces before he's too old.'

'Surely it amounts to the same thing,' said Ivanenko. 'If Vishnayev can topple you, he will be so beholden to Kerensky he will neither be able, nor particularly wish, to oppose Kerensky's recipe for a solution to all the Soviet Union's problems. He will let Kerensky have his war next spring or early summer. Between them they'll devastate everything it has taken two generations to achieve.'

'What is the news from your de-briefing yesterday?' asked Rudin. He knew Ivanenko had recalled two of his most senior men from the Third World for consultations face to face. One was the controller of all subversive operations throughout Africa; the other his counterpart for the Middle East.

'Optimistic,' said Ivanenko. 'The capitalists have screwed up their Africa policies for so long now their position is virtually irrecoverable. The liberals rule still in Washington and London, at least in foreign affairs. They are so totally absorbed with South Africa, they don't seem to notice Nigeria and Kenya at all. Both are on the verge of falling to us. The French in Senegal are proving more difficult. In the Middle East, I think we can count on Saudi Arabia falling within three years. They're almost encircled.'

'Time scale?' asked Rudin.

'Within a few years, say by 1990 at the outside, we shall effectively control the oil and the sea routes. The euphoria campaign in Washington and London is being steadily increased, and it is working.'

Rudin exhaled his smoke and stubbed the tube of his cigarette into an ashtray proffered by Misha.

'I won't see it,' he said, 'but you two will. Inside a decade the West will die of malnutrition, and we won't have to fire a shot. All the more reason why Vishnayev must be stopped while there is still time.'

Four kilometres southwest of the Kremlin, inside a tight loop in the Moscow River and not far from the Lenin Stadium, stands the ancient monastery of Novodevichi. Its main entrance is right across the street from the principal Beriozka shop where the rich and privileged, or foreigners, may buy for hard currency luxuries unobtainable by the common people.

The monastery grounds contain three lakes and a cemetery, and access to the cemetery is available to pedestrians. The gatekeeper will seldom bother to stop those bearing bunches of flowers.

Adam Munro parked his car in the Beriozka car park among others whose number plates revealed them to belong to the privileged.

'Where do you hide a tree?' his instructor used to ask the class. 'In a forest. And where do you hide a pebble? On the beach. Always keep it natural.'

Munro crossed the road, traversed the cemetery with his bunch of carnations, and found Valentina waiting for him by one of the smaller lakes. Late October had brought the first bitter winds off the steppes to the east, and grey, scudding clouds across the sky. The surface of the water rippled and shivered in the wind.

'I asked them in London,' he said gently. 'They told me it is too risky at the moment. Their answer was that to bring you out now would reveal the missing tape, and thus the fact of the transcripts having been passed over. They feel if that happened the Politburo would withdraw from the talks in Ireland and revert to the Vishnayev plan.'

She shivered slightly, whether from the chill of the lakeside or from fear of her own masters he could not tell. He put an arm round her and held her to him.

'They may be right,' she said quietly. 'At least the Politburo is negotiating for food and peace, not preparing for war.'

'Rudin and his group seem to be sincere in that,' he suggested.

She snorted. 'They are as bad as the others,' she said. 'Without the pressure they would not be there at all.'

'Well, the pressure is on,' said Munro. 'The grain is coming in. They know the alternatives now. I think the world will get its peace treaty.'

'If it does, what I have done will have been worthwhile,' said Valentina. 'I don't want Sasha to grow up among the rubble as I did, nor live with a gun in his hand. That is what they would have for him, up there in the Kremlin.'

'He won't,' said Munro. 'Believe me, my darling, he'll grow up in freedom, in the West, with you as his mother and me as his stepfather. My principals have agreed to bring you out in the spring.'

She looked up at him with hope shining in her eyes.

'In the spring? Oh, Adam, when in the spring?'

'The talks cannot go on for too long. The Kremlin needs its grain by April at the latest. The last of the supplies and all the reserves will have run out by then. When the treaty is agreed, perhaps even before it is signed, you and Sasha will be brought out. Meanwhile, I want you to cut down on the risks you are taking. Only bring out the most vital material concerning the peace talks at Castletown.'

'There's one in here,' she said, nudging the bag over her

shoulder. 'It's from ten days ago. Most of it is so technical I can't understand it. It refers to permissible reductions of mobile SS Twenties.'

Munro nodded grimly.

'Tactical rockets with nuclear warheads, highly accurate and highly mobile, borne on the backs of tracked vehicles and parked in groves of trees and under netting all across Eastern Europe.'

Twenty-four hours later the package was on its way to London.

Three days before the end of the month an old lady was heading down Sverdlov Street in central Kiev towards her apartment block. Though she was entitled to a car and a chauffeur, she had been born and brought up in the country, of strong peasant stock. Even in her mid-seventies she preferred to walk rather than drive for short distances. Her visit to spend the evening with a friend two blocks away was so short she had dismissed the car and chauffeur for the night. It was just after ten when she crossed the road in the direction of her own front door.

She didn't see the car, it came so fast. One minute she was in the middle of the road with no one about but two pedestrians a hundred yards away, the next the vehicle was on her, lights blazing, tyres squealing. She froze. The driver seemed to steer right at her, then swerved away. The wing of the vehicle crashed into her hip, bowling her over in the gutter. It failed to stop, roaring away towards Kreshchatik Boulevard at the end of Sverdlov. She vaguely heard the crunch of feet running towards her as passers-by came to her aid.

That evening Edwin J. Campbell, the chief US negotiator at the Castletown talks, arrived back tired and frustrated at the ambassadorial residence in Phoenix Park. It was an elegant mansion that America provided for its envoy in Dublin, and fully modernized, with handsome guest suites, the finest of which Edwin Campbell had taken over. He was looking forward to a long, hot bath and a rest.

When he had dropped his coat and responded to his host's greeting, one of the messengers from the embassy handed him a fat manilla envelope. As a result his sleep was curtailed that night, but it was worth it.

The next day, he took his place in the Long Gallery at Castletown and gazed impassively across the table at Professor Ivan I. Sokolov.

All right, professor, he thought, I know what you can concede and what you cannot. So let's get on with it.

It took forty-eight hours for the Soviet delegate to agree to cut the Warsaw Pact presence of tracked tactical nuclear rockets in Eastern Europe by half. Six hours later, in the dining room, a protocol was agreed whereby the USA would sell the USSR $200,000,000 worth of oil drilling and extraction technology at bargain-basement prices.

The old lady was unconscious when the ambulance brought her to the general hospital of Kiev, the October Hospital at 39 Karl Liebknecht Street. She remained so until the following morning. When she was able to explain who she was, panicked officials had her wheeled out of the general ward and into a private room, which rapidly filled with flowers. During that day the finest orthopaedic surgeon in Kiev operated to set her broken femur.

In Moscow Ivanenko took a call from his personal aide and listened intently.

'I understand,' he said without hesitation. 'Inform the authorities that I shall come at once. What? Well, then, when she has come out of the anaesthetic. Tomorrow night? Very well, arrange it.'

It was bitter cold on the evening of the last night of October. There was no one moving in Rosa Luxembourg Street, on to which the October Hospital backs. The two long black limousines stood unobserved on the kerbside by this back entrance which the KGB chief had chosen to use rather than the grand portico at the front.

The whole area stands on a slight rise of ground, amid trees, and further down the street on the opposite side an annexe to the hospital was under construction, its unfinished upper levels jutting above the greenery. The watchers among the frozen cement sacks rubbed their hands to keep the circulation going, and stared at the two cars by the door, dimly illuminated by a single bulb above the archway.

When he came down the stairs the man with seven seconds to live was wearing a long, fur-collared overcoat and thick gloves, even for the short walk across the pavement to the warmth of the waiting car. He had spent two hours with his mother, comforting her and assuring her the culprits would be found, as the abandoned car had been found.

He was preceded by an aide who ran ahead and flicked off the doorway light. The door and the pavement were plunged in darkness. Only then did Ivanenko advance to the door, held open by one of his six bodyguards, and pass through it. The knot of four others outside parted as his fur-coated figure emerged, merely a shadow among shadows.

He advanced quickly to the Zil, engine running, across the pavement. He paused for a second as the passenger door was swung open, and died, the bullet from the hunting rifle skewering through his forehead, splintering the parietal bone and exiting through the rear of the cranium to lodge in an aide's shoulder.

The crack of the rifle, the whack of the impacting bullet and the first cry from Colonel Yevgeni Kukushkin, his senior bodyguard, took less than a second. Before the slumping man had hit the pavement, the plain-clothes colonel had him under the armpits, dragging him physically into the recess of the rear seat of the Zil. Before the door was closed the colonel was screaming, 'Drive, drive', to the shocked driver.

Colonel Kukushkin pillowed the bleeding head in his lap as the Zil screeched away from the kerbside. He thought fast. It was not merely a question of a hospital, but of which hospital for a man like this. As the Zil cleared the end of Rosa Luxembourg Street, the colonel flicked on the interior light. What he saw, and had seen much in his career, was enough to tell him his master was beyond hospitals. His second reaction was programmed into his mind and his job: no one must know. The unthinkable had happened, and no one must know, save only those entitled to know. He had secured his promotion and his job by his presence of mind. Watching the second limousine, the bodyguards' Chaika, swing out of Rosa Luxembourg Street behind him, he ordered the driver to choose a quiet and darkened street not less than two miles away, and park.

Leaving the curtained and motionless Zil by the kerbside, with the bodyguards scattered in a screen around it, he took off his blood-soaked coat and set off on foot. He finally made his phone call from a militia barracks, where his ID card and rank secured him instant access to the commandant's private office and phone. It also secured him a direct line. He was patched through in fifteen minutes.

'I must speak to Comrade Secretary-General Rudin urgently,' he told the Kremlin switchboard operator. The woman knew from the line on which the call was coming that this was neither joke nor impertinence. She put it through to an aide inside the armoury building, who held the call and spoke to Maxim Rudin on the internal phone. Rudin authorized the pass-through of the call.

'Yes,' he grunted down the line, 'Rudin here.'

Colonel Kukushkin had never spoken to him before, though he had seen him and heard him at close quarters many times. He knew it was Rudin. He swallowed hard, took a deep breath and spoke.

At the other end Rudin listened, asked two brief questions, rapped out a string of orders, and put the phone down. He turned to Vassili Petrov who was with him, leaning forward alert and worried.

'He's dead,' said Rudin in disbelief. 'Not a heart attack. Shot. Yuri Ivanenko. Someone has just assassinated the chairman of the KGB.'

Beyond the windows the clock in the tower above Saviour's Gate chimed midnight, and a sleeping world began to move slowly towards war.

8

The KGB has always ostensibly been answerable to the Soviet Council of Ministers. In practice it answers to the Politburo.

The everyday working of the KGB, the appointment of every officer within it, every promotion and the rigorous indoctrination of every staffer – all are supervised by the Politburo through the Party Organizations Section of the Central Committee. At every stage of the career of every KGB man he is watched, informed on and reported on; even the watchdogs of the Soviet Union are never themselves free of watching. Thus it is unlikely that this most pervasive and powerful of control machines can ever run out of control.

In the wake of the assassination of Yuri Ivanenko, it was Vassili Petrov who took command of the cover-up operation that Maxim Rudin directly and personally ordered.

Over the telephone Rudin had ordered Colonel Kukushkin to bring the two-car cavalcade straight back to Moscow by road, stopping neither for food, drink nor sleep, driving through the night, refuelling the Zil bearing Ivanenko's corpse with jerry-cans, brought to the car by the Chaika and always out of sight of passersby.

On arrival on the outskirts of Moscow the two cars were directed straight to the Politburo's own private clinic at Kuntsevo, where the corpse with the shattered head was quietly buried amid the pine forest within the clinic perimeter, in an unmarked grave. The burial party was of Ivanenko's own bodyguards, all of whom were then placed under house arrest at one of the Kremlin's own villas in the forest. The guard detail on these men was drawn not from the KGB but from the Kremlin palace guard. Only Colonel Kukushkin was not held incommunicado. He was summoned to Petrov's private office in the Central Committee building.

The colonel was a frightened man, and when he left Petrov's office he was little less so. Petrov gave him one chance to save his career and his life: he was put in charge of the cover-up operation.

At the Kuntsevo clinic he organized the closure of one entire ward and brought KGB men from Dzerzhinsky Square to mount guard on it. Two KGB doctors were transferred to Kuntsevo and put in charge of the patient in the closed ward, a patient who was in fact an empty bed. No one else was allowed in, but the two doctors, knowing only enough to be badly frightened, ferried all the equipment and medicaments into the closed ward as would be needed for the treatment of a heart attack. Within twenty-four hours, save for the closed ward in the secret clinic off the road from Moscow to Minsk, Yuri Ivanenko had ceased to exist.

At this early stage only one other man was let into the secret. Among Ivanenko's six deputies, all with their offices close to his on the third floor of the KGB centre, one was his official deputy as chairman of the KGB. Petrov summoned General Konstantin Abrassov to his office and informed him of what had happened, a piece of information that shook the general as nothing in a thirty-year career in secret police work had done. Inevitably he agreed to continue the masquerade.

In the October Hospital in Kiev, the dead man's mother was surrounded by local KGB men and continued to receive daily written messages of comfort from her son.

Finally, the three workmen on the annexe to the October Hospital who had discovered a hunting rifle and night-sight when they came to work the morning after the shooting were removed with their families to one of the camps in Mordovia, and two criminal detectives were flown in from Moscow to investigate an act of hooliganism. Colonel Kukushkin was with them. The story they were given was that the shot had been fired at the moving car of a local Party official; it had passed through the windscreen and was recovered from the upholstery. The real bullet, recovered from the KGB guard's shoulder and well washed, was presented to them. They were told to trace and identify the hooligans in conditions of complete secrecy. Somewhat perplexed and much frustrated, they proceeded to try. Work on the annexe was stopped, the half-finished building sealed off, and all the forensic equipment they could ask for supplied. The only thing they did not get was a true explanation.

When the last piece of the jigsaw puzzle of deception was in place, Petrov reported personally to Rudin. To the old chief fell the worst task, that of informing the Politburo of what had really happened.

The private report of Dr Myron Fletcher of the Agriculture Department to President William Matthews two days later was all and more that the *ad hoc* committee formed under the personal auspices of the President could have wished for. Not only had the benign weather brought North America a bumper crop in all areas of grain and cereals, it had broken existing records. Even with probable requirements for domestic consumption taken care of, and even with existing aid levels to the poor countries of the world maintained, the surplus would nudge 60,000,000 tons for the combined harvest of the USA and Canada.

'Mr President, you've got it,' said Stanislaw Poklewski. 'You can buy that surplus any time you wish at July's price. Bearing in mind the progress at the Castletown talks, the House Appropriations Committee will not stand in your way.'

'I should hope not,' said the President. 'If we succeed at Castletown the reductions in defence expenditure will more than compensate for the commercial losses on the grains. What about the Soviet crop?'

'We're working on it,' said Bob Benson. 'The Condors are sweeping right across the Soviet Union, and our analysts are working out the yields of harvested grain region by region. We should have a report for you in a week. We can correlate that with reports from our people on the ground over there and give a pretty accurate figure, to within five per cent, anyway.'

'As soon as you can,' said President Matthews. 'I need to know the exact Soviet position in every area. That includes the Politburo reaction to their own grain harvest. I need to know their strengths and their weaknesses. Please get them for me, Bob.'

No one in the Ukraine that winter would be likely to forget the sweeps by the KGB and militia against those in whom the slightest hint of nationalist sentiment could be detected.

While Colonel Kukushkin's two detectives carefully interviewed the pedestrians in Sverdlov Street the night Ivanenko's mother had been run down, meticulously took to pieces the stolen car that had performed the hit-and-run job on the old lady, and pored over the rifle, the image-intensifier and the surrounds of the hospital annexe, General Abrassov went for the nationalists.

Hundreds were detained in Kiev, Ternopol, Lvov, Kanev, Rovno, Zhitomir and Vinnitsa. The local KGB, supported by teams from Moscow, carried out the interrogations, ostensibly concerned with sporadic outbreaks of hooliganism such as the mugging of the KGB plain-clothes man in August in Ternopol. Some of the senior interrogators were permitted to know their enquiries also concerned the firing of a shot in Kiev in late October, but no more.

In the seedy Lvov working-class district of Levandivka that November David Lazareff and Lev Mishkin strolled through the snowy streets during one of their rare meetings. Because the fathers of both had been taken away to the camps, they knew time would run out for them eventually also. The word 'Jew' was stamped on the identity card of each, as on those of every one of the Soviet Union's 3,000,000 Jews. Sooner or later the spotlight of the KGB must swing away from the nationalists to the Jews. Nothing ever changes that much in the Soviet Union.

'I posted the card to Andriy Drach yesterday, confirming the success of the first objective,' said Mishkin. 'How are things with you?'

'So far, so good,' said Lazareff. 'Perhaps things will ease off soon.'

'Not this time, I think,' said Mishkin. 'We have to make our break soon if we are going to at all. The ports are out. It has to be by air. Same place next week. I'll see what I can discover about the airport.'

Far away to the north of them an SAS jumbo jet thundered on its polar route from Stockholm to Tokyo. Among its first-class passengers it bore Captain Thor Larsen towards his new command.

Maxim Rudin's report to the Politburo was delivered in his gravelly voice, without frills. But no histrionics in the world could have kept his audience more absorbed, nor their reaction more stunned. Since an army officer had emptied a handgun at the limousine of Leonid Brezhnev as he passed through the Kremlin's Borovitsky Gate a decade before, the spectre of the lone man with a gun penetrating the walls of security around the hierarchs had persisted. Now it had come out of conjecture to sit and stare at them from their own green baize table.

This time the room was empty of secretaries. No tape recorders turned on the corner table. No aides, no stenographers were present. When he had finished, Rudin handed the floor to Petrov who described the elaborate measures taken to mask the outrage, and the secret steps then in progress to identify and eliminate the killers after they had revealed all their accomplices.

'But you have not found them yet?' snapped Stepanov.

'It is only five days since the attack,' said Petrov evenly. 'No, not yet. They will be caught, of course. They cannot escape, whoever they are. When they are caught, they will reveal every last one of those who helped them. General Abrassov will see to that. Then every last person who knows what happened that night in Rosa Luxembourg Street, wherever they may be hiding, will be eliminated. There will be no trace left.'

'And in the meantime?' asked Komarov.

'In the meantime,' said Rudin, 'it must be maintained with unbreakable solidarity that Comrade Yuri Ivanenko has sustained a massive heart attack and is under intensive care. Let us be clear on one thing. The Soviet Union cannot and will not tolerate the public humiliation of the world ever being allowed to know what happened in Rosa Luxembourg Street. There are no Lee Harvey Oswalds in Russia and never will be.'

There was a murmur of assent. No one was prepared to disagree with Rudin's assessment.

'With respect, Mr Secretary-General,' Petrov cut in, 'while the catastrophe of such news leaking abroad cannot be overestimated, there is another aspect, equally serious. If this news leaked out, the rumours would begin among our own population. Before long they would be more than rumours. The effect internally I leave to your imagination.'

They all knew how closely the maintenance of public order was linked to a belief in the impregnability and invincibility of the KGB.

'If this news leaked out,' said Chavadze, the Georgian, slowly, 'and even more so if the perpetrators escaped, the effect would be as bad as that of the grain famine.'

'They cannot escape,' said Petrov sharply. 'They must not. They will not.'

'Then who are they?' growled Kerensky.

'We do not yet know, Comrade Marshal,' replied Petrov, 'but we will.'

'But it was a Western gun?' insisted Shushkin. 'Could the West be behind this?'

'I think it almost impossible,' said Rykov of Foreign Affairs. 'No Western government, no Third-World government, would be crazy enough to support such an outrage, in the same way as we had nothing to do with the Kennedy assassination. Emigrés, possibly. Anti-Soviet fanatics, possibly. But not governments.'

'Emigré groups abroad are also being investigated,' said Petrov, 'but discreetly. We have most of them penetrated. So far nothing has come in. The rifle, ammunition and night-sight are all of Western make. They are all commercially purchasable in the West. That they were smuggled in is beyond doubt. Which means either the users brought them in, or they had outside help. General Abrassov agrees with me that the primary requirement is to find the users, who will reveal their suppliers. Department V will take over from there.'

Yefrem Vishnayev watched the proceedings with keen interest but took little part. Kerensky expressed the dissatisfaction of the dissident group instead. Neither sought a further vote on the choice of the Castletown talks or a war in 1983. Both knew that in the event of a tie, the chairman's vote would prevail. Rudin had come one step nearer to falling, but was not finished yet.

The meeting agreed that the announcement should be made, only within the KGB and the upper echelons of the Party machine, that Yuri Ivanenko had suffered a heart attack and was in hospital. When the killers had been identified and they and their aides eliminated, Ivanenko would quietly expire from his illness.

Rudin was about to summon the secretaries to the chamber for the resumption of the usual Politburo meeting when Stepanov, who had originally voted for Rudin and negotiations with the USA, raised his hand.

'Comrades, I would regard it as a major defeat for our country if the killers of Yuri Ivanenko were to escape and publish their action to the world. Should that happen, I would not be able to continue my support for the policy of negotiation and further concession in the matter of our armaments levels in exchange for American grain. I would switch my support to the proposal of Party Theoretician Vishnayev.'

There was dead silence.

'So would I,' said Shushkin.

Eight against four, thought Rudin as he gazed impassively down the table. Eight against four if these two shits change sides now.

'Your point is taken, comrades,' said Rudin without a flicker of emotion. 'There will be no publication of this deed. None at all.'

Ten minutes later the meeting reopened with a unanimous expression of regret at the sudden illness of Comrade Ivanenko. The subject then turned to the newly arrived figures of wheat and grain yields.

The Zil limousine of Yefrem Vishnayev erupted from the mouth of the Borovitsky Gate at the Kremlin's southwestern corner and straight across Manege Square. The policeman on duty in the square, forewarned by his bleeper that the Politburo cavalcade was leaving the Kremlin, had stopped all traffic. Within seconds the long, black, hand-tooled cars were scorching up Frunze Street past the Defence Ministry towards the homes of the privileged in Kutuzovsky Prospekt.

Marshal Kerensky sat beside Vishnayev in the latter's car, having accepted his invitation to drive together. The partition between the spacious rear area and the driver was closed and soundproof. The curtains shut out the gaze of the pedestrians.

'He's near to falling,' growled Kerensky.

'No,' said Vishnayev, 'he's one step nearer and a lot weaker without Ivanenko, but he's not near to falling yet. Don't underestimate Maxim Rudin. He'll fight like a cornered bear on the taiga before he goes, but go he will because go he must.'

'Well, there's not much time,' said Kerensky.

'Less than you think,' said Vishnayev. 'There were food riots in Vilnius last week. Our friend Vitautas who voted for our proposal in July is getting nervous. He was on the verge of switching sides despite the very attractive villa I have offered him next to my own at Sochi. Now he is back in the fold, and Shushkin and Stepanov may change sides in our favour.'

'But only if the killers escape, or the truth is published abroad,' said Kerensky.

'Precisely. And that is what must happen.'

Kerensky turned in the back seat, his florid face turning brick beneath his shock of white hair.

'Reveal the truth? To the whole world? We can't do that,' he exploded.

'No, we can't. There are far too few people who know the truth, and mere rumours cannot succeed. They can be too easily discounted. An actor looking precisely like Ivanenko could be found, rehearsed, seen in public. So others must do it for us. With absolute proof. The guards who were present that night are in the hands of the Kremlin elite. That only leaves the killers themselves.'

'But we don't have them,' said Kerensky, 'and are not likely to. The KGB will get them first.'

'Probably, but we have to try,' said Vishnayev. 'Let's be plain about this, Nikolai. We are not fighting for the control of the Soviet Union any more. We are fighting for our lives, like Rudin and Petrov. First the wheat, now Ivanenko. One more scandal, Nikolai, one more – whoever is responsible, let me make that clear, whoever is responsible – and Rudin will fall. There must be one more scandal. We must ensure that there is.'

Thor Larsen, dressed in overalls and a safety helmet, stood on a gantry crane high above the dry dock at the centre of the Ishikawajima-Harima shipyard and gazed down at the mass of the vessel that would one day be the *Freya*.

Even three days after his first sight, the size of her took his breath away. In his apprenticeship days tankers had never gone beyond 30,000 tons, and it was not until 1956 that the world's first over that tonnage took to the sea. A new class was created for such vessels, and they were called supertankers. When someone broke the 50,000-ton ceiling there was another new class, the VLCC, or very large crude carrier. As the 200,000-ton barrier was broken in the late sixties the new class of Ultra-Large Crude Carrier, or ULCC, came into being.

Once at sea Larsen had seen one of the French leviathans, weighing in at 550,000 tons, move past him. His crew had poured out on deck to watch her. What lay below him now was twice that size. As Wennerstrom had said, the world had never seen the like of her, nor ever would again.

She was 515 metres, or 1689 feet, long, like ten city blocks. She was 90 metres, or 295 feet, broad, from scupper to scupper, and her superstructure reared five stories into the air above her deck. Far below what he could see of her deck area, her keel plunged 36 metres, or 118 feet, towards the floor of the dry dock. Each of her sixty holds was bigger than a neighbourhood cinema. Deep in her bowels below the superstructure the four steam turbines mustering a total of 90,000 shaft horsepower were already installed, ready to drive her twin screws whose forty-foot-diameter bronze propellers could be vaguely seen glinting below her stern.

From end to end she teemed with ant-like figures, the workers preparing to leave her temporarily while the dock was filled. For twelve months, almost to the day, they had cut and burned, bolted, sawn, riveted, hacked, plated, and hammered her hull together. Great modules of high-tensile steel had swung in from the overhead gantries to drop into preassigned places and form her shape. As the men cleared away the ropes and chains, lines and cables that hung about her, she lay exposed at last, her sides clean of encumbrances, painted twenty coats of rustproof paint, waiting for the water.

At last only the blocks that cradled her remained. The men who had built this, the biggest dry dock in the world at Chita, near Nagoya on Ise Bay, had never thought to see their handiwork put to such use. It was the only dry dock that could take a million-tonner, and it was the first and last it would ever hold. Some of the veterans came to peer across the barriers to see the ceremony.

The religious ceremony took half an hour as the Shinto priest called down the blessings of the divine ones on those who had built her, those who would work on her yet and those who would sail her one day, that they should enjoy safe labour and safe sailing. Thor Larsen attended, barefoot, with his chief engineer and chief officer, the owner's chief superintendent (marine architect) who had been there from the start, and the yard's equivalent architect. These were the two men who had really designed and built her.

Shortly before noon the sluices were opened, and with a thundering roar the western Pacific began to flow in.

There was a formal lunch in the chairman's office, but when it was over Thor Larsen went back to the dock. He was joined by his first officer, Stig Lundquist, and his chief engineer, Bjorn Erikson, both from Sweden.

'She's something else,' said Lundquist as the water climbed her sides.

Shortly before sunset the *Freya* groaned like a waking giant, moved half an inch, groaned again, then came free of her underwater supports and rode the tide. Around the dock 4000 Japanese workers broke their studied silence and burst into cheering. Scores of white helmets were thrown into the air; the half dozen Europeans from Scandinavia joined in, pumping hands and thumping backs. Below them the giant waited patiently, seemingly aware her turn would come in time.

The next day she was towed out of the dock to the commissioning quay where for three months she would once again play host to thousands of small figures working like the demons to prepare her for the sea beyond the bay.

Sir Nigel Irvine read the last lines of the Nightingale transcript, closed the file and leaned back.

'Well, Barry, what do you make of it?'

Barry Ferndale had spent most of his working life studying the Soviet Union, its masters and power structure. He breathed once more on his glasses and gave them a final rub.

'It's one more blow that Maxim Rudin's going to have to survive,' he said. 'Ivanenko was one of his staunchest supporters. And an exceptionally clever one. With him in hospital Rudin has lost one of his ablest counsellors.'

'Will Ivanenko still retain his vote in the Politburo?' asked Sir Nigel.

'It's possible he can vote by proxy should another vote come,' said Ferndale, 'but that's not really the point. Even at a six-to-six tie on a major issue of policy at Politburo level, the chairman's vote swings the issue. The danger is that one or two of the waverers might change sides. Ivanenko upright inspired a lot of fear, even that high up. Ivanenko in an oxygen tent perhaps less so.'

Sir Nigel handed the folder across the desk to Ferndale.

'Barry, I want you to go over to Washington with this one. Just a courtesy call, of course. But try to have a private dinner with Ben Kahn and compare notes with him. This exercise is becoming too damn much of a close-run thing.'

'The way we see it, Ben,' said Ferndale, two days later after dinner in Kahn's Georgetown house, 'is that Maxim Rudin is holding on by a thread in the face of a fifty per cent hostile Politburo, and that thread is getting extremely thin.'

The deputy director (Intelligence) of the CIA stretched his feet towards the log fire in his red-brick grate and gazed at the brandy he twirled in his glass.

'I can't fault you on that, Barry,' he said carefully.

'We also are of the view that if Rudin cannot persuade the Politburo to continue conceding the things he is yielding to you at Castletown, he could fall. That would leave a fight for the succession, to be decided by the full Central Committee. In which, alas, Yefrem Vishnayev has a powerful amount of influence and friends.'

'True,' said Kahn. 'But then so does Vassili Petrov. Probably more than Vishnayev.'

'No doubt,' rejoined Ferndale, 'and Petrov would probably swing the succession towards himself; if he had the backing of Rudin who was retiring in his own time and on his own terms, and if he had the support of Ivanenko whose KGB clout could help offset Marshal Kerensky's influence through the Red Army.'

Kahn smiled across at his visitor.

'You're moving a lot of pawns forward, Barry. What's your gambit?'

'Just comparing notes,' said Ferndale.

'All right, just comparing notes. Actually our own views at Langley go along pretty much with yours. David Lawrence at the State Department agrees. Stan Poklewski wants to ride the Soviets hard at Castletown. The President's in the middle – as usual.'

'Castletown's pretty important to him, though?' suggested Ferndale.

'Very important. Next year is his last in office. In thirteen months there'll be a new president-designate. Bill Matthews would like to go out in style, leaving a comprehensive arms limitation treaty behind him.'

'We were just thinking. . . .'

'Ah,' said Kahn, 'I think you are contemplating bringing your knight forward.'

Ferndale smiled at the oblique reference to his 'knight', the director-general of his service.

'. . . Castletown would certainly abort if Rudin fell from control at this juncture. And that he could use something from Castletown, from your side, to convince any waverers among his faction that he was achieving things there and that he was the man to back.'

'Concessions?' asked Kahn. 'We got the final analysis of the Soviet grain harvest last week. They're over a barrel. At least that's the way Poklewski put it.'

'He's right,' said Ferndale. 'But the barrel's on the point of collapsing. And waiting inside it is dear Comrade Vishnayev, with his war plan. And we all know what that would entail.'

'Point taken,' said Kahn. 'Actually my own reading of the combined Nightingale file runs along very similar lines. I've got a paper in preparation for the President's eyes at the moment. He'll have it next week when he and Benson meet with Lawrence and Poklewski.'

'These figures,' asked President Matthews, 'they represent the final aggregate grain crop the Soviet Union brought home a month ago?'

He glanced across at the four men seated in front of his desk. At the far end of the room a log fire crackled in the marble fireplace, adding a touch of visual warmth to the already high temperature assured by the central heating system. Beyond the bulletproof south windows the sweeping lawns held their first dusting of November morning frost. Being from the South, William Matthews appreciated warmth.

Robert Benson and Dr Myron Fletcher nodded in unison. David Lawrence and Stanislaw Poklewski studied the figures.

'All our sources have been called on for these figures, Mr President, and all our information has been correlated extremely carefully,' said Benson. 'We could be out by five per cent either way, not more.'

'And according to the Nightingale even the Politburo agrees with us,' interposed the secretary of state.

'One hundred million tons, total,' mused the President. 'It will last them till the end of March, with a lot of belt tightening.'

'They'll be slaughtering the cattle by January,' said Poklewski. 'They will have to start making sweeping concessions at Castletown next month if they want to survive.'

The President laid down the Soviet grain report and picked up the presidential briefing prepared by Ben Kahn and presented by his director of central intelligence. It had been read by all four in the room as well as himself. Benson and Lawrence had agreed with it; Dr Fletcher was not called for an opinion; the hawkish Poklewski dissented.

'We know and they know they are in desperate straits,' said Matthews. 'The question is, how far do we push them?'

'As you said weeks ago, Mr President,' said Lawrence, 'if

we don't push hard enough we don't get the best deal we can for America and the free world. Push too hard and we force Rudin to abort the talks to save himself from his own hawks. It's a question of balance. At this point I feel we should make them a gesture.'

'Wheat?'

'Animal feedstuffs to help them keep some of their herds alive,' suggested Benson.

'Dr Fletcher?' asked the President.

The man from Agriculture shrugged.

'We have them available, Mr President,' he said. 'The Soviets have a large proportion of their own merchant fleet, Sovfracht, standing by. We know that because with their subsidized freight rates they could all be busy, but they're not. They're positioned all over the warm-water ports of the Black Sea and down the Soviet Pacific coast. They'll sail for the USA if they're given the word from Moscow.'

'What's the latest we need to give a decision on this one?' asked President Matthews.

'New Year's Day,' said Benson. 'If they know a respite is coming, they can hold off slaughtering the herds.'

'I urge you not to ease up on them,' pleaded Poklewski. 'By March they'll be desperate.'

'Desperate enough to concede enough disarmament to assure peace for a decade, or desperate enough to go to war?' asked Matthews rhetorically. 'Gentlemen, you'll have my decision by Christmas Day. Unlike you, I have to take five chairmen of Senate sub-committees with me on this one: defense, agriculture, foreign affairs, trade and appropriations. And I can't tell them about the Nightingale, can I, Bob?'

The chief of the CIA shook his head.

'No, Mr President. Not about the Nightingale. There are too many Senate aides, too many leaks. The effect of a leak of what we really know at this juncture could be disastrous.'

'Very well, then. Christmas Day it is.'

On 15th December Professor Ivan Sokolov rose to his feet at Castletown and began to read a prepared paper. The Soviet Union, he said, ever true to its traditions as a country devoted to the unswerving search for world peace, and mindful of its often-reiterated commitment to peaceful co-existence. . . .

Edwin J. Campbell sat across the table and watched his Soviet opposite number with some fellow feeling. Over two months, working until fatigue overcame both of them, he had developed a fairly warm relationship with the man from Moscow, as much at least as their positions and their duties would allow.

In breaks between the talks, each had visited the other in the opposing delegation's rest room. In the Soviet drawing room, with the Muscovite delegation present and its inevitable complement of KGB agents, the conversation had been agreeable but formal. In the American room where Sokolov had arrived alone, he relaxed to the point of showing Campbell pictures of his grandchildren on holiday on the Black Sea coast. As a leading member of the Academy of Sciences the professor was rewarded for his loyalty to Party and cause with a limousine, chauffeur, city apartment, country *dacha*, seaside chalet, and access to the Academy grocery store and commissary. Campbell had no illusions that Sokolov was paid for his loyalty, for his ability to devote his talents to the service of a regime that committed tens of thousands to the labour camps of Mordovia; that he was one of the fat cats, the *nachalstvo*. But even the *nachalstvo* have grandchildren.

He sat and listened to the Russian with growing surprise.

You poor old man, he thought. What this must be costing you.

When the peroration was over Edwin Campbell rose and gravely thanked the professor for his statement, which on behalf of the United States of America he had listened to with the utmost care and attention. He moved an adjournment while the US government considered its position. Within an hour he was in his Dublin embassy to begin transmitting Sokolov's extraordinary speech to David Lawrence.

Some hours later in Washington's State Department, David

Lawrence lifted one of his telephones and called President Matthews on his private line.

'I have to tell you, Mr President, that six hours ago in Ireland the Soviet Union conceded six major points at issue. They concern total numbers of intercontinental ballistic missiles with hydrogen-bomb warheads through conventional armour to disengagement to forces along the Elbe River.'

'Thanks, David,' said Matthews. 'That's great news. You were right. I think we should let them have something in return.'

The area of birch and larch forest lying southwest of Moscow where the Soviet elite have their country *dachas* covers little more than a hundred square miles. They like to stick together. The roads in this area are bordered mile after mile by green-painted steel railings, enclosing the private estates of the men at the very top. The fences and the driveway gates seem largely abandoned, but anyone trying to scale the first or drive through the second will be intercepted within moments by guards who materialize out of the trees.

Lying beyond Uspenskoye Bridge, the area centres on a small village called Zhukovka, usually known as Zhukovka village. This is because there are two other and newer settlements nearby: Sovmin Zhukovka where the Party hierarchs have their weekend villas, and Akademik Zhukovka which groups the writers, artists, musicians and scientists who have found favour in Party eyes.

But across the river lies the ultimate, the even more exclusive settlement of Usovo. Nearby the General Secretary of the Communist Party of the Soviet Union, the chairman of the Praesidium of the Supreme Soviet, the Politburo, retires to a sumptuous mansion set in hundreds of acres of rigorously guarded forest.

Here on the night before Christmas, a feast he had not recognized in fifty years, Maxim Rudin sat in his favourite button-back leather chair, feet towards the enormous fireplace in rough-cut granite blocks where metre-long logs of split pine crackled. It was the same fireplace that had warmed Leonid Brezhnev and Nikita Khrushchev before him.

The bright yellow glare of the flames flickered on the panelled walls of the study and illuminated the face of Vassili Petrov who faced him across the fire. By Rudin's chair arm a small coffee table held an ashtray and half a tumbler of Armenian brandy, which Petrov eyed askance. He knew his ageing protector was not supposed to drink. Rudin's inevitable cigarette was clipped between first finger and thumb.

'What news of the investigation?' asked Rudin.

'Slow,' said Petrov. 'That there was outside help is beyond doubt. We now know the night-sight was bought commercially in New York. The Finnish rifle was one of a consignment exported from Helsinki to Britain. We don't know which shop it came from, but the export order was for sporting rifles, therefore it was a private-sector commercial order, not an official one. The footprints at the building site have been checked out against the boots of all the workers at the place, and there are two sets of footprints that cannot be traced. There was damp in the air that night and a lot of cement dust lying around, so the prints are clear. We are reasonably certain there were two men.'

'Dissidents?' asked Rudin.

'Almost certainly. And quite mad.'

'No, Vassili, keep that for the Party meetings. Madmen take pot-shots, or sacrifice themselves. This was planned over months by someone: someone out there, inside or outside Russia, who has got to be silenced, once and for all, with his secret untold. Who are you concentrating on?'

'The Ukrainians,' said Petrov. 'We have all their groups in Germany, Britain and America completely penetrated. No one has heard a rumour of such a plan. Personally, I still think they are in the Ukraine. That Ivanenko's mother was used as a bait is undeniable. So who would have known she *was* Ivanenko's mother? Not some slogan-dauber in New York. Not some armchair nationalist in Frankfurt. Not some pamphleteer in London. Someone local, with contacts outside. We are concentrating on Kiev. Several hundred former detainees who were released and returned to the Kiev area are under interrogation.'

'Find them, Vassili, find them and silence them.' Maxim Rudin changed the subject as he had a habit of doing without a change of tone. 'Anything new from Ireland?'

'The Americans have resumed talking, but have not responded to our initiative,' said Petrov.

Rudin snorted. 'That Matthews is a fool. How much further does he think we can go before we have to pull back?'

'He has those Soviet-hating senators to contend with,' said Petrov, 'and that Catholic Fascist Poklewski. And of course he cannot know how close things are for us inside the Politburo.'

Rudin grunted. 'If he doesn't offer us something by the New Year, we won't carry the Politburo in the first week of January. . . .'

He reached out and took a draught of brandy, exhaling with a satisfied sigh.

'Are you sure you should be drinking?' asked Petrov. 'The doctors forbade you five years ago.'

'Screw the doctors,' said Rudin. 'That's what I really called you here for. I can inform you beyond any doubt that I am not going to die of alcoholism or liver failure.'

'I'm glad to hear it,' said Petrov.

'There's more. On 30th April I am going to retire. Does that surprise you?'

Petrov sat motionless, alert. He had twice seen the supremos go down. Khrushchev in flames, ousted and disgraced, to become a non-person. Brezhnev on his own terms. He had been close enough to feel the thunder when the most powerful tyrant in the world gives way to another. But never this close. This time he wore the mantle, unless others could snatch it from him.

'Yes,' he said carefully, 'it does.'

'In April I am calling a meeting of the full Central Committee,' said Rudin, 'to announce to them my decision to go on 30th April. On May Day there will be a new leader at the centre of the line on the Mausoleum. I want it to be you. In

June the plenary Party congress is due. The leader will outline the policy from then on. I want it to be you. I told you that weeks ago.'

Petrov knew he was Rudin's choice since that meeting in the old leader's private suite in the Kremlin, when the dead Ivanenko had been with them, cynical and watchful as ever. But he had not known it would be so fast.

'I won't get the Central Committee to accept your nomination unless I can give them something they want. Grain. They all know the position long since. If Castletown fails, Vishnayev will have it all.'

'Why so soon?' asked Petrov.

Rudin held up his glass. From the shadows the silent Misha appeared and poured brandy into it.

'I got the results of the tests from Kuntsevo yesterday,' said Rudin. 'They've been working on tests for months. Now they're certain. Not cigarettes and not Armenian brandy. Leukaemia. Six to twelve months. Let's just say I won't see a Christmas after this one. And if we have a nuclear war, neither will you.

'In the next hundred days we have to secure a grain agreement from the Americans and wipe out the Ivanenko affair once and for all time. The sands are running out and too damn fast. The cards are on the table, face up, and there are no more aces to play.'

On 28th December, the United States formally offered the Soviet Union a sale, for immediate delivery and at commercial rates, of ten million tons of animal feed grains, to be considered as being outside any terms still being negotiated at Castletown.

On New Year's Eve an Aeroflot twin-jet Tupolev 134 took off from Lvov Airport bound for Minsk on an internal flight. Just north of the border between the Ukraine and White Russia, high over the Pripet Marshes, a nervous-looking young man rose from his seat and approached the stewardess who was several rows back from the steel door leading to the flight deck, speaking with a passenger.

Knowing the toilets were at the other end of the cabin, she straightened as the young man approached her. As she did so the young man spun her round, clamped his left forearm across her throat, drew a handgun and jammed it into her ribs. She screamed. There was a chorus of shouts and yells from the passengers. The hijacker began to drag the girl backwards to the locked door to the flight deck. On the bulkhead next to the door was the intercom, enabling the stewardess to speak to the flight crew, who had orders to refuse to open the door in the event of a hijack.

From mid-way down the fuselage one of the passengers rose, automatic in hand. He crouched in the aisle, both hands clasped round his gun, pointing it straight at the stewardess and the hijacker behind her.

'Hold it,' he shouted. 'KGB. Hold it right there.'

'Tell them to open the door,' yelled the hijacker.

'Not a chance,' shouted the armed flight guard from the KGB to the hijacker.

'If they don't I'll kill the girl,' screamed the man holding the stewardess.

The girl had a lot of courage. She lunged backward with her heel, caught the gunman in the shin, broke his grip and made to run towards the police agent. The hijacker sprang after her, passing three rows of passengers. It was a mistake. From an aisle seat one of them rose, turned and slammed a fist into the nape of the hijacker's neck. The man pitched face downward; before he could move his assailant had snatched the man's gun and was pointing it at him. The hijacker turned, sat up, looked at the gun, put his face in his hands and began to moan softly.

From the rear the KGB agent stepped past the stewardess, gun still at the ready, and approached the rescuer.

'Who are you?' he asked. For answer the rescuer reached into an inside pocket, produced a card and flicked it open.

The agent looked at the KGB card.

'You're not from Lvov,' he said.

'Ternopol,' said the other. 'I was going home on leave in Minsk, so I had no sidearm. But I have a good right fist.' He grinned.

The agent from Lvov nodded.

'Thanks, comrade. Keep him covered.' He stepped to the speaker-phone and talked rapidly into it. He was relating what had happened and asking for a police reception at Minsk.

'Is it safe to have a look?' asked a metallic voice from behind the door.

'Sure,' said the KGB agent. 'He's safe enough now.'

There was a clicking behind the door, and it opened to show the head of the engineer, somewhat frightened and intensely curious.

The agent from Ternopol acted very strangely. He turned from the man on the floor, crashed his revolver into the base of his colleague's skull, shoved him aside and thrust his foot in the door before it could close. In a second he was through it, pushing the engineer backwards on to the flight deck. The man on the floor behind him rose, grabbed the flight guard's own automatic, a standard KGB Tokarev 9 mm, followed through the steel door and slammed it behind him. It locked automatically.

Two minutes later, under the guns of David Lazareff and Lev Mishkin, the Tupolev turned due west for Warsaw and Berlin, the latter being the ultimate limit of its fuel supply. At the controls Captain Rudenko sat white-faced with rage; beside him his co-pilot, Vatutin, slowly answered the hurried requests from Minsk control tower regarding the change of course.

By the time the airliner had crossed the border into Polish air space, Minsk tower and four other airliners on the same wavelength knew the Tupolev was in the hands of hijackers. When it bored clean through the centre of Warsaw's air traffic control zone, Moscow already knew. A hundred miles west of Warsaw a flight of six Polish-based but Soviet Mig-23 fighters swept in from starboard and formated on the

Tupolev. The flight leader was jabbering rapidly into his mask.

At his desk in the Defence Ministry in Frunze Street, Moscow, Marshal Nikolai Kerensky took an urgent call on the line linking him to Soviet air force headquarters.

'Where?' he barked.

'Passing overhead Poznan,' was the answer. 'Three hundred kilometres to Berlin. Fifty minutes' flying time.'

The marshal considered carefully. This could be the scandal which Vishnayev had demanded. There was no doubt what should be done. The Tupolev should be shot down, with its entire passenger and crew complement. Later the version given out would be that the hijackers had fired within the fuselage, hitting a main fuel tank. It had happened twice in the past decade.

He gave his orders. A hundred metres off the airliner's wingtip the commander of the Mig flight listened five minutes later.

'If you say so, comrade colonel,' he told his base commander. Twenty minutes later the airliner passed across the Oder–Neisse line and began its letdown into Berlin. As it did so the Migs peeled gracefully away and slipped down the sky towards their home base.

'I have to tell Berlin we're coming in,' Captain Rudenko appealed to Mishkin. 'If there's a plane on the runway, we'll end up as a ball of fire.'

Mishkin stared ahead at the banks of steel-grey winter clouds. He had never been in an airplane before, but what the captain said made sense.

'Very well,' he said, 'break silence and tell Tempelhof you are coming in. No requests, just a flat statement.'

Captain Rudenko was playing his last card. He leaned forward, adjusted the channel selection dial and began to speak.

'Tempelhof, West Berlin. Tempelhof, West Berlin. This is Aeroflot flight 351. . . .'

He was speaking in English, the international language of air traffic control. Mishkin and Lazareff knew almost none of it, apart from what they had picked up on broadcasts in

Ukrainian from the West. Mishkin jabbed his gun into Rudenko's neck.

'No tricks,' he said in Ukrainian.

In the control tower at East Berlin's Schönefeld Airport the two controllers looked at each other in amazement. They were being called on their own frequency, but addressed as Tempelhof. No Aeroflot plane would dream of landing in West Berlin, apart from which Tempelhof had not been West Berlin's civil airport for ten years. Tempelhof had reverted to a US Air Force base when Tegel took over as the civil airport.

One of the East Germans, faster than the other, snatched the microphone. 'Tempelhof to Aeroflot 351, you are clear to land. Straight run in,' he said.

In the airliner Captain Rudenko swallowed hard and lowered flap and under-carriage. The Tupolev let down rapidly to the main airport of Communist East Germany. They broke cloud at a thousand feet and saw the landing lights ahead of them. At five hundred feet Mishkin peered suspiciously through the streaming perspex. He had heard of West Berlin, of brilliant lights, packed streets, teeming crowds of shoppers up the Kurfurstendam, and Tempelhof Airport right in the heart of it all. This airport was right out in the countryside.

'It's a trick,' he yelled at Lazareff. 'It's the East.' He jabbed his gun into Captain Rudenko's neck. 'Pull out,' he screamed, 'pull out or I'll shoot.'

The Ukrainian captain gritted his teeth and held on course for the last hundred metres. Mishkin reached over his shoulder and tried to haul back on the control column. The twin booms, when they came, were so close together that it was impossible to tell which came first. Mishkin claimed the thump of the wheels hitting the tarmac caused the gun to go off; Co-pilot Vatutin maintained Mishkin had fired first. It was too confused for a final and definitive version ever to be established.

The bullet tore a gaping hole in the neck of Captain Rudenko and killed him instantly. There was blue smoke in the flight deck, Vatutin hauling back on the stick, yelling to his engineer for more power. The jet engines screamed a mite louder than the passengers as the Tupolev, heavy as a wet loaf, bounced twice more on the tarmac then lifted into the air, rolling, struggling for lift. Vatutin held her, nose high, wallowing, praying for more engine power, as the outer suburbs of East Berlin blurred past beneath them, followed by the Berlin Wall itself. When the Tupolev came over the perimeter of Tempelhof it cleared the nearest houses by six feet.

White-faced, the young co-pilot hammered the plane on to the main runway with Lazareff's gun in his back. Mishkin held the red-soaked body of Captain Rudenko from falling across the control column. The Tupolev finally came to rest three-quarters down the runway, still on all its wheels.

Staff-sergeant Leroy Coker was a patriotic man. He sat huddled against the cold at the wheel of his air police jeep, his fur-trimmed parka drawn tight round the edges of his face, and he thought longingly of the warmth of Alabama. But he was on guard duty and he took it seriously.

When the incoming airliner lurched over the houses beyond the perimeter fence, engines howling, under-carriage and flaps hanging, he let out a 'What the sheee-yit . . .' and sat bolt upright. He had never been to Russia, nor even across to the East, but he had read all about them over there. He did not know much about the Cold War, but he well knew that an attack by the Communists was always imminent unless men like Leroy Coker kept on their guard. He also knew a red star when he saw one, and a hammer and sickle.

When the airliner slithered to a stop he unslung his carbine, took a bead and blew the nosewheel tyres out.

Mishkin and Lazareff surrendered three hours later. The intent had been to keep the crew, release the passengers, take on board three notables from West Berlin and be flown to Tel Aviv. But a new nosewheel for a Tupolev was out of the question; the Russians would never supply one. And when the news of the killing of Rudenko was made known to the USAF base authorities, they refused to lay on a plane of their own. Marksmen ringed the Tupolev; there was no way two men could herd others, even at gunpoint, to an alternative aircraft. The sharpshooters would cut them down. After an hour's talk with the base commander, they walked out with their hands in the air.

That night they were formally handed over to the West Berlin authorities for imprisonment and trial.

9

The Soviet ambassador to Washington was coldly angry when he faced David Lawrence at the State Department on 2nd January.

The American secretary of state was receiving him at the Soviet request, though insistence would have been a better word.

The ambassador read his formal protest in a flat monotone. When he had finished he laid the text on the American's desk. Lawrence, who had known exactly what it would be, had an answer ready, prepared by his legal counsellors, three of whom stood flanking him behind his chair.

He conceded that West Berlin was indeed not sovereign territory, but a city under Four-Power occupation. Nevertheless the Western Allies had long conceded that in matters of jurisprudence the West Berlin authorities should handle all criminal and civil offences other than those falling within the ambit of the purely military laws of the Western Allies. The hijacking of the airliner, he continued, while a terrible offence, was not committed by US citizens against US citizens or within the US air base of Tempelhof. It was therefore an affair within civil jurisprudence. In consequence the United States government maintained it could not legally have held non-US nationals or non-US material witnesses within the territory of West Berlin, even though the airliner had come to rest on a USAF air base. He had no recourse, therefore, but to reject the Soviet protest.

The ambassador heard him out in stony silence. He rejoined that he could not accept the American explanation, and rejected it. He would report back to his government in that vein. On this note, he left to return to his embassy and report to Moscow.

In a small flat in Bayswater, London, three men sat that day and stared at the tangle of newspapers strewn on the floor around them.

'A disaster,' snapped Andrew Drake, 'a bloody disaster. By now they should have been in Israel. Within a month they'd have been released and could have given their press conference. What the hell did they have to shoot the captain for?'

'If he was landing at Schönefeld and refused to fly into West Berlin, they were finished anyway,' observed Azamat Krim.

'They could have clubbed him,' snorted Drake.

'Heat of the moment,' said Kaminsky. 'What do we do now?'

'Can those handguns be traced?' asked Drake of Krim.

The small Tatar shook his head. 'To the shop that sold them, perhaps,' he said. 'Not to me. I didn't have to identify myself.'

Drake paced the carpet, deep in thought.

'I don't think they'll be extradited back,' he said at length. 'The Soviets want them now for hijacking, shooting Rudenko, hitting the KGB man on board and of course the other one they took the identity card from. But the killing of the captain is the serious one. Still, I don't think a West German government will send two Jews back for execution. On the other hand, they'll be tried and convicted. Probably to life. Miroslav, will they open their mouths about Ivanenko?'

The Ukrainian refugee shook his head.

'Not if they've got any sense,' he said. 'Not in the heart of West Berlin. The Germans might have to change their minds and send them back after all. If they believed them, which they wouldn't because Moscow would deny Ivanenko is dead, and produce a look-alike as proof. But Moscow would believe them and have them liquidated. The Germans, not believing them, would offer no special protection. They wouldn't stand a chance. They'll keep silent.'

'That's no use to us,' pointed out Krim. 'The whole point of the exercise, of all we've gone through, was to deal a single massive humiliation to the whole Soviet state apparatus. *We* can't give that press conference; we don't have the tiny details that will convince the world. Only Mishkin and Lazareff can do that.'

'Then they have to be got out of there,' said Drake with finality. 'We have to mount a second operation to get them to Tel Aviv, with guarantees of their life and liberty. Otherwise it's all been for nothing.'

'What happens now?' repeated Kaminsky.

'We think,' said Drake. 'We work out a way, we plan it and we execute it. They are not going to sit and rot their lives away in Berlin, not with a secret like that in their heads. And we have little time; it won't take Moscow forever to put two and two together. They have their lead to follow now; they'll know who did the Kiev job pretty soon. Then they'll begin to plan the revenge. We have to beat them to it.'

The chilly anger of the Soviet ambassador to Washington paled into insignificance beside the outrage of his colleague in Bonn as the Russian diplomat faced the West German foreign minister two days later. The refusal of the Federal German government to hand the two criminals and murderers over to either the Soviet or East German authorities was a flagrant breach of their hitherto friendly relations and could only be construed as a hostile act, he insisted.

The West German foreign minister was deeply uncomfortable. Privately he wished the Tupolev had stayed on the runway in East Germany. He refrained from pointing out that as the Russians had always insisted West Berlin was not a part of West Germany, they ought to be addressing themselves to the Senate in West Berlin.

The ambassador repeated his case for the third time: the criminals were Soviet citizens, the victims were Soviet citizens, the airliner was Soviet territory, the outrage had taken place in Soviet airspace and the murder either on or a few feet above the runway of East Germany's principal airport. The crime should therefore be tried under Soviet or at the very least under East German law.

The foreign minister pointed out as courteously as he could that all precedent indicated that hijackers could be tried under the law of the land in which they arrived, if that country wished to exercise the right. This was in no way an imputation against the fairness of the Soviet judicial procedure. . . .

Was it hell, he thought privately. No one in West Germany from the government to the press to the public had the slightest doubt that handing Mishkin and Lazareff back would mean KGB interrogation, kangaroo court and the firing squad. And they were Jewish, that was another problem.

The first few days of January are slack for the press, and the West German press was making a big story out of this. The conservative and powerful Axel Springer newspapers were insisting that whatever they had done, the two hijackers should receive a fair trial, and that could only be guaranteed in West Germany. The Bavarian CSU party, on which the governing coalition depended, was taking the same line. Certain quarters were giving the press a large amount of precise information and lurid details about the latest KGB crackdown in the Lvov area from which the hijackers came, suggesting that escape from the terror was a justifiable reaction, albeit a deplorable way of doing it. And lastly the recent exposure of yet another Communist agent high in the Civil Service would not increase the popularity of a government taking a conciliatory line towards Moscow. And with the provincial elections pending. . . .

The minister had his orders from the Chancellor. Mishkin and Lazareff, he told the ambassador, would go on trial in West Berlin as soon as possible and if, or rather when, convicted, would receive salutary sentences.

The Politburo meeting at the end of the week was stormy.

Once again the tape recorders were off, the stenographers absent.

'This is an outrage,' snapped Vishnayev. 'Yet another scandal which diminishes the Soviet Union in the eyes of the world. It should never have happened.'

He implied that it had only happened due to the ever-weakening leadership of Maxim Rudin.

'It would not have happened,' retorted Petrov, 'if the comrade marshal's fighters had shot the plane down over Poland according to custom.'

'There was a communications breakdown between ground control and the fighter leader,' said Kerensky. 'A chance in a thousand.'

'Fortuitous, though,' observed Rykov coldly. Through his ambassadors he knew the Mishkin and Lazareff trial would be public and would reveal exactly how the hijackers had first mugged a KGB officer in a park for his identity papers, then masqueraded as him to penetrate to the flight deck.

'Is there any question,' asked Petryanov, a supporter of Vishnayev, 'that these two men could be the ones that killed Ivanenko?'

The atmosphere was electric.

'None at all,' said Petrov firmly. 'We know those two come from Lvov, not Kiev. They were Jews who had been refused permission to emigrate. We are investigating, of course, but so far there is no connection.'

'Should such a connection emerge, we will of course be informed?' asked Vishnayev.

'That goes without saying, comrade,' growled Rudin.

The stenographers were recalled and the meeting went on to discuss the progress at Castletown and the purchase of 10,000,000 tons of feed grain. Vishnayev did not press the issue. Rykov was at pains to show that the Soviet Union was gaining the quantities of wheat she would need to survive the winter and spring with minimal concessions of weapons levels, a point Marshal Kerensky disputed. But Komarov was forced to concede that the imminent arrival of 10,000,000 tons of animal winter feeds would enable him to release the same tonnage from hoarded stocks immediately, and prevent wholesale slaughter. The Maxim Rudin faction with its hair-breadth supremacy stayed intact.

As the meeting dispersed the old Soviet chief drew Vassili Petrov aside.

'*Is* there any connection between the two Jews and the Ivanenko killing?' he enquired.

'There may be,' conceded Petrov. 'We know they did the mugging in Ternopol, of course, so they were evidently prepared to travel outside Lvov to prepare their escape. We have their fingerprints from the aircraft, and they match those in their living quarters in Lvov. We have found no shoes that match the prints at the Kiev murder site, but we are still searching for those shoes. One last thing; we have an area of palm-print taken from the car that knocked down Ivanenko's mother. We are trying to get a complete palm-print of both from inside Berlin. If they check. . . .'

'Prepare a plan, a contingency plan, a feasibility study,' said Rudin, 'to have them liquidated inside their jail in West Berlin. Just in case. And another thing, if their identity is proved as the killers of Ivanenko, tell me, not the Politburo. We wipe them out first, then inform our comrades.'

Petrov swallowed hard. Cheating the Politburo was playing for the highest stakes in Soviet Russia. One slip, and there would be no safety net. He recalled what Rudin had told him by the fire out at Usovo a fortnight earlier. With the Politburo tied six against six, Ivanenko dead and two of their own six about to change sides, there were no aces left.

'Very well,' he said.

West German Chancellor Dietrich Busch received his justice minister in his private office in the chancellery building next to the old Palais Schaumberg just after the middle of the month. The government chief of West Germany was standing at his modern picture window gazing out at the frozen snow.

Inside the new modern government headquarters overlooking Federal Chancellor Square the temperature was warm enough for shirtsleeves, and nothing of the raw, bitter January of the riverside town penetrated.

'This Mishkin and Lazareff affair, how goes it?' asked Busch.

'It's strange,' admitted his justice minister, Ludwig Fischer. 'They are being more cooperative than one could hope for. They seem eager to achieve a quick trial with no delays.'

'Excellent,' said the chancellor. 'That's exactly what we want. A quick affair. Let's get it over with. In what way are they cooperating?'

'They were offered a star lawyer from the right wing. Paid for by subscribed funds, possibly German contributions, possibly Jewish Defense League from America. They turned him down. He wanted to make a major spectacle out of the trial, plenty of detail about the KGB terror against Jews in the Ukraine.'

'A *right*-wing lawyer wanted that?'

'All grist to their mill. Bash the Russians, etc.,' said Fischer. 'Anyway, Mishkin and Lazareff want to go for an admission of guilt and plead mitigating circumstances. They insist on it. If they do so, and claim the gun went off by accident when the plane hit the runway at Schönfeld, they have a partial defence. Their new lawyer is asking for murder to be reduced to culpable homicide if they do.'

'I think we can grant them that,' said the Chancellor. 'What would they get?'

'With the hijacking thrown in, fifteen to twenty years. Of course, they could be paroled after a third. They're young, mid-twenties. They could be out by thirty.'

'That's in five years,' growled Busch. 'I'm concerned about the next five months. Memories fade. In five years they'll be in the archives.'

'Well, they admit everything, but they insist that the gun went off by accident. They claim they just wanted to reach Israel the only way they knew how. They'll plead guilty right down the line – to culpable homicide.'

'Let them have it,' said the Chancellor. 'The Russians won't like it, but it's as broad as long. They'd draw life for murder, but that's effectively twenty years nowadays.'

'There's one other thing. They want to be transferred after the trial to jail in West Germany.'

'Why?'

'They seem terrified of revenge by the KGB. They think they'll be safer in West Germany than in West Berlin.'

'Rubbish,' snorted Busch, 'they'll be tried and jailed in West Berlin. The Russians would not dream of trying to settle accounts inside a Berlin jail. They wouldn't dare. Still, we could do an internal transfer in a year or so. But not yet. Go ahead, Ludwig. Make it quick and clean, if they wish to cooperate. But get the press off my back before the elections, and the Russian ambassador as well.'

At Chita the morning sun glittered along the deck of the *Freya*, lying as she had for two and a half months by the commissioning quay. In those seventy-five days she had been transformed. Day and night she had lain docile while the tiny creatures who had made her swarmed into and out of every part of her. Hundreds of miles of lines had been laid the length and breadth of her, cables, pipes, tubes and flexes. Her labyrinthine electrical networks had been connected and tested, her incredibly complex system of pumps installed and tried.

The computer-linked instruments that would fill her holds and empty them, thrust her forward or shut her down, hold her to any point of the compass for weeks on end without a hand on her helm and observe the stars above her and the sea-bed below had been set in their places.

The food lockers and deep-freezes to sustain her crew for months were fully installed; so too the furniture, door knobs, light bulbs, lavatories, galley stoves, central heating, air conditioning, cinema, sauna, three bars, two dining rooms, beds, bunks, carpets and clothes hangers.

Her five-storey superstructure had been converted from an

empty shell into a luxury hotel; her bridge, radio room and computer room from empty echoing galleries to a low-humming complex of data banks, calculators and control systems.

When the last of the workmen picked up their tools and left her alone, she was the ultimate in size, power, capacity, luxury and technical refinement that the technology of man could ever have set to float on water.

The rest of her crew of thirty had arrived by air fourteen days earlier to familiarize themselves with every inch of her. They were made up of her master, Captain Thor Larsen, a first officer, a second mate and a third mate; the chief engineer, first engineer, second engineer and electrical engineer, who ranked as a 'first'; her radio officer and chief steward also ranked as officers. Twenty others made up the full complement: first cook, four stewards, three firemen/engine room artificers, one repair man/engine room artificer; ten able seamen/deckhands and one pumpman.

Two weeks before she was due to sail, the tugs drew her away from the quay to the centre of Ise Bay. There her great twin propellers bit into the waters to bring her out to the western Pacific for sea trials. For officers and crew, as well as for the dozen Japanese technicians who went with her, it would mean a fortnight of gruelling hard work, testing every single system against every known or possible contingency.

There was a $170,000,000 worth of her moving out to the mouth of the bay that morning and the small ships standing off Nagoya watched her pass with awe.

Twenty kilometres outside Moscow lies the touristic village and estate of Archangelskoye, complete with museum and gastronomic restaurant, noted for its genuine bear steaks. In the last week of that freezing January Adam Munro had reserved a table there for himself and an escort from the secretarial pool at the British embassy.

He always varied his dinner dates so that no one girl should notice too much, and if the young hopeful of the evening wondered why he chose to drive the distance he did over icy roads in temperatures fifteen degrees below freezing, she made no comment on it.

The restaurant in any case was warm and snug, and when he excused himself to fetch extra cigarettes from his car she thought nothing of it. In the car park he shivered as the icy blast hit him, and hurried to where the twin headlights glowed briefly in the darkness.

He climbed into the car beside Valentina, put an arm round her, drew her close and kissed her.

'I hate the thought of you being in there with another woman, Adam,' she whispered as she nuzzled his throat beneath his chin.

'It's nothing,' he said, 'not important. An excuse for being able to drive out here to dine without being suspected. I have news for you.'

'About us?' she asked.

'About us. I have asked my own people if they would help you to come out, and they have agreed. There is a plan. Do you know the port of Constantza on the Romanian coast?'

She shook her head.

'I have heard of it, but never been there. I always holiday on the Soviet coast of the Black Sea.'

'Could you arrange to holiday there, with Sasha?'

'I suppose so,' she said. 'I can take my holidays virtually where I like. Romania is within the Socialist bloc. It should not raise eyebrows.'

'When does Sasha break up from school for the spring holidays?'

'The last few days of March, I think. Is that important?'

'It has to be in mid-April,' he told her. 'My people think you could be brought off the beach to a freighter offshore by speedboat. Can you make sure to arrange a spring holiday with Sasha at Constantza or the nearby Mamaia Beach in April?'

'I'll try,' she said. 'I'll try. April. Oh, Adam, it seems so close.'

'It is close, my love. Less than ninety days. Be patient a little longer as I have been, and we will make it. We'll start a whole new life.'

Five minutes later she had given him the transcription of the early January Politburo meeting and driven off into the night. He stuffed the sheaf of papers inside his waistband beneath his shirt and jacket and returned to the warmth of the Archangelskoye Restaurant.

This time, he vowed, as he made polite conversation with the secretary, there would be no mistakes, no drawing back, no letting her go, as there had been in 1961. This time it would be forever.

Edwin Campbell leaned back from the Georgian table in the Long Gallery at Castletown House and looked across at Professor Sokolov. The last point on the agenda had been covered, the last concession wrung. From the dining room below a courier had reported that the secondary conference had matched the concessions of the upper floor with trade bargains from the United States to the Soviet Union.

'I think that's it, Ivan my friend,' said Campbell. 'I don't think we can do any more at this stage.'

The Russian raised his eyes from the pages of Cyrillic handwriting in front of him, his own notes. For over a hundred days he had fought tooth and claw to secure for his country the grain tonnages that could save her from disaster and yet retain the maximum in weapons levels from inner space to Eastern Europe. He knew he had had to make concessions that would have been unheard of four years earlier at Geneva, but he had done the best he could in the time-scale allowed.

'I think you are right, Edwin,' he replied. 'Let us have the arms reduction treaty prepared in draft form for our respective governments.'

'And the trade protocol,' said Campbell. 'I imagine they will want that also.'

Sokolov permitted himself a wry smile.

'I am sure they will want it very much,' he said.

For the next week the twin teams of interpreters and stenographers prepared both the treaty and the trade protocol. Occasionally the two principal negotiators were needed to clarify a point at issue, but for the most part the transcription and translation work was left to the aides. When the two bulky documents, each in duplicate, were finally ready, the two chief negotiators departed to their separate capitals to present them to their masters.

Andrew Drake threw down his magazine and leaned back.

'I wonder,' he said.

'What?' asked Krim as he entered the small sitting room with three mugs of coffee. Drake tossed the magazine to the Tatar.

'Read the first article,' he said. Krim read in silence while Drake sipped his coffee. Kaminsky eyed them both.

'You're crazy,' said Krim with finality.

'No,' said Drake. 'Without some audacity we'll be sitting here for the next ten years. It could work. Look, Mishkin and Lazareff come up for trial in a fortnight. The outcome is a foregone conclusion. We might as well start planning now. We know we're going to have to do it anyway, if they are ever to come out of that jail. So let's start planning. Azamat, you were in the paratroopers in Canada?'

'Sure,' said Krim. 'Five years.'

'Did you ever do an explosives course?'

'Yep. Demolition and sabotage. On secondment to the engineers for three months.'

'And years ago I used to have a passion for electronics and radio,' said Drake. 'Probably because my dad had a radio repair shop before he died. We could do it. We'd need help but we could do it.'

'How many more men?' asked Krim.

'We'd need one on the outside, just to recognize Mishkin and Lazareff on their release. That would have to be Miroslav here. For the job, us two plus five to stand guard.'

'Such a thing has never been done before,' observed the Tatar doubtfully.

'All the more reason why it will be unexpected, therefore unprepared for.'

'We'd get caught at the end of it,' said Krim.

'Not necessarily. I'd cover the pull-out if I had to. And anyway the trial would be the sensation of the decade. With Mishkin and Lazareff free in Israel, half the Western world would applaud. The whole issue of a free Ukraine would be blazoned across every newspaper and magazine outside the Soviet bloc.'

'Do you know five more who would come in on it?'

'For years I've been collecting names,' said Drake. 'Men who are sick and tired of talking. If they knew what we'd done already, yes, I can get five before the end of the month.'

'All right,' said Krim, 'if we're into this thing, let's do it. Where do you want me to go?'

'Belgium,' said Drake. 'I want a large apartment in Brussels. We'll bring the men there and make the apartment the group's base.'

On the other side of the world while Drake was talking, the sun rose over Chita and the IHI shipyard. The *Freya* lay alongside her commissioning quay, her engines throbbing.

The previous evening had seen a lengthy conference in the office of the IHI chairman, attended by both the yard's and the company's chief superintendents, the accountants, Harry Wennerstrom and Thor Larsen. The two technical experts had agreed that every one of the giant tanker's systems was in perfect working order. Wennerstrom had signed the final release document, conceding that the *Freya* was all he had paid for.

In fact he had paid for five per cent of her on the signature of the original contract to build her, five per cent at the keel-laying ceremony, five per cent when she rode water and five per cent at official handover. The remaining eighty per cent plus interest was payable over the succeeding eight years. But to all intents and purposes, she was his. The yard's company flag had been ceremoniously hauled down, and the silver-on-blue winged Viking helmet emblem of the Nordia Line now fluttered in the dawn breeze.

High on the bridge, towering over the vast spread of her deck, Harry Wennerstrom drew Thor Larsen by the arm into the radio room and closed the door behind him. The room was completely soundproof with the door closed.

'She's all yours, Thor,' he said. 'By the way, there's been a slight change of plan regarding your arrival in Europe. I'm not lightening her offshore. Not for her maiden voyage. Just this once, you're going to bring her into Europort at Rotterdam fully laden.'

Larsen stared at his employer in disbelief. He knew as well as either of them that fully loaded ULCCs never entered ports; they stood well offshore and lightened themselves by disgorging most of their cargo into other, smaller tankers in order to reduce their draught for the shallow seas. Or, they berthed at 'sea islands', networks of pipes on stilts, well out to sea, from which their oil could be pumped ashore. The idea of a girl in every port was a hollow joke for the crews of the supertankers; they often never berthed anywhere near a city from year's end to year's end, being flown off their ship for periodical leave. That was why the crew quarters had to be a real home from home.

'The English Channel will never take her,' said Larsen.

'You're not going up the Channel,' said Wennerstrom. 'You're going west of Ireland, west of the Hebrides, north of the Pentland Firth, between the Orkneys and the Shetlands, then south down the North Sea, following the twenty-fathom line, to moor at the deep-water anchorage. From there the pilots will bring you down the main channel towards the Maas Estuary. The tugs will bring you in from the Hook of Holland to Europort.'

'The Inner Channel from KI Buoy to the Maas won't take her fully laden,' protested Larsen.

'Yes, it will,' said Wennerstrom calmly. 'They have dredged this channel to a hundred and fifteen feet over the past four years. You'll be drawing ninety-eight feet. Thor, if I was asked to name any mariner in the world who could bring a million-tonner into Europort, it would be you. It'll be tight as all hell, but let me have this one last triumph. I want the world to see her, Thor. My *Freya*. I'll have them all there waiting for her. The Dutch government, the world's press. They'll be my guests, and they'll be dumbfounded. Otherwise no one will ever see her; she'll spend her whole life out of sight of land.'

'All right,' said Larsen slowly. 'Just this once. I'll be ten years older when it's over.'

Wennerstrom grinned like a small boy.

'Just wait till they see her,' he said. 'First of April. See you in Rotterdam, Thor Larsen.'

Ten minutes later he was gone. At noon, with the Japanese workers lining the quayside to cheer her on her way, the mighty *Freya* eased away from the shore and headed for the mouth of the bay. At 2 p.m. on 2nd February she came out again into the Pacific and swung her bow south towards the Philippines, Borneo and Sumatra at the start of her maiden voyage.

On 10th February the Politburo in Moscow met to consider, approve or reject the draft treaty and accompanying trade protocol negotiated at Castletown. Rudin and those who supported him knew that if they could carry the terms of the treaty at this meeting, then barring accidents thereafter it could be ratified and signed. Yefrem Vishnayev and his faction of hawks were no less aware. The meeting was lengthy and exceptionally hard-fought.

It is often assumed that world statesmen, even in private conclave, use moderate language and courteous address to their colleagues and advisers. This is not true of several recent US presidents, and is completely untrue of the Politburo in closed session. The Russian equivalent of four-letter words flew thick and fast. Only the fastidious Vishnayev kept his language restrained though his tone was acid, as he and his allies fought every concession line by line.

It was Foreign Minister Dmitri Rykov who carried the others in the moderate faction.

'What we have gained,' he said, 'is the assured sale to us, at last July's reasonable prices, of fifty-five million tons of grains. Without them we faced disaster on a national scale. On top we have nearly three billion dollars' worth of the most modern technology, in consumer industries, computers and oil production. With these we can master the problems that have beset us for two decades and conquer them within five years.

'Against this we have to offset certain minimal concessions in arms levels and states of preparedness, which, I stress, will in no way at all hinder or retard our capacity to dominate the Third World and its raw material resources inside the same five years. From the disaster that faced us last May, we have emerged triumphant thanks to the inspired leadership of Comrade Maxim Rudin. To reject this treaty now would bring us back to last May, but worse: the last of our 1982 harvest grains will run out in sixty days.'

When the meeting voted on the treaty terms, which was in fact a vote on the continuing leadership of Maxim Rudin, the six-to-six tie remained intact. The chairman's vote therefore prevailed.

'There's only one thing that can bring him down now,' said Vishnayev with quiet finality to Marshal Kerensky in the former's limousine as they drove home that evening. 'If something serious happens to sway one or two of his faction before the treaty is ratified. If not, the Central Committee will approve the treaty on the Politburo's recommendation and it will go through. If only it could be proved that those two damned Jews in Berlin killed Ivanenko. . . .'

Kerensky was less than his blustering self. Privately he was beginning to wonder if he had chosen the wrong side. Three months ago it had looked so certain that Rudin would be pushed too far, too fast, by the Americans and would lose his crucial support at the green baize table. But Kerensky was committed to Vishnayev now; there would be no massive Soviet manoeuvres in East Germany in two months, and he had to swallow that.

'One other thing,' said Vishnayev. 'If it had appeared six months ago the power struggle would be over by now. I heard news from a contact out at the Kuntsevo clinic. Maxim Rudin is dying.'

'Dying?' repeated the defence minister. 'When?'

'Not soon enough,' said the theoretician. 'He'll live to carry the day over this treaty, my friend. Time is running out for us, and there is nothing we can do about it. Unless the Ivanenko affair can yet blow up in his face.'

As he was speaking the *Freya* was steaming through the Sunda Straits. To her port side lay Java Head and far to starboard the great mass of the volcano Krakatoa reared towards the night sky. On the darkened bridge a battery of dimly lit instruments told Thor Larsen, the senior officer of the watch and the junior officer all they needed to know. Three separate navigational systems correlated their findings into the computer, set in the small room aft of the bridge, and those findings were dead accurate. Constant compass readings, true to within half a second of a degree, cross-checked themselves with the stars above, unchanging and unchangeable. Man's artificial stars, the all-weather satellites, were also monitored and the resultant findings fed into the computer. Here the memory banks had absorbed tide, wind, undercurrents, temperatures, and humidity levels. From the computer endless messages were flashed automatically to the gigantic rudder which, far below the stern transom, flickered with the sensitivity of a sardine's tail.

High above the bridge the two radar scanners whirled unceasingly, picking up coasts and mountains, ships and buoys, feeding them all into the computer, which processed this information too, ready to throw its hazard alarm device at the first hint of danger. Beneath the water, the echo-sounders relayed a three-dimensional map of the sea-bed far below, while from the bulbous bow section the forward sonar scanner looked three miles forward and down into the black waters. For the *Freya*, from full-ahead to crash-stop, would take thirty minutes and she would cover two to two and a half miles. She was that big.

Before dawn she had cleared the narrows of Sunda and her computers had turned her northwest along the hundred-fathom line to cut south of Ceylon for the Arabian Sea.

Two days later on the 12th eight men grouped themselves in the apartment Azamat Krim had rented in a suburb of Brussels. The five newcomers had been summoned by Drake who long ago had noted them all, met and spoken with them at great length, before deciding that they too shared his dream of striking a blow against Moscow. Two of the five were German-born Ukrainians, scions of the large Ukrainian community in the Federal Republic. One was an American, from New York, also of a Ukrainian father, and the other two were Ukrainian-British.

When they heard what Mishkin and Lazareff had done to the head of the KGB, there was a babble of excited comment. When Drake proposed that the operation could not be completed until the two partisans were free and safe, no one dissented. They talked through the night, and by dawn they had split into four teams of two.

Drake and Kaminsky would return to England and buy the necessary electronic equipment that Drake estimated he required. One of the Germans would partner one of the Englishmen and return to Germany to seek out the explosives they needed. The other German, who had contacts in Paris, would take the other Englishman to find and buy, or steal, the weaponry. Azamat Krim took his fellow North American to seek the motor launch. The American, who had worked in a leisure-boat yard in upper New York State, reckoned he knew what he wanted.

Eight days later in the tightly guarded courtroom attached to Moabit Prison in West Berlin, the trial of Mishkin and Lazareff started. Both men were silent and subdued in the dock as, within concentric walls of security from the barbed-wire entanglements atop the perimeter walls to the armed guards scattered all over the courtroom, they listened to the charges. The list took ten minutes to read. There was an audible gasp from the packed press benches when both men pleaded guilty to all charges. The state prosecutor rose to begin his narration of the events of New Year's Eve to the panel of judges. When he had finished, the judges adjourned to discuss the sentence.

The *Freya* moved slowly and sedately through the Straits of Hormuz and into the Arabian Gulf. The breeze had freshened with the sunrise into the chilly shamal wind coming into her nose from the northeast, sand-laden, causing the horizon to be hazy and vague. Her crew all knew this landscape well enough, having passed many times on their way to collect crude oil from the Gulf. They were all experienced tanker-men.

To one side of the *Freya* the barren, arid Quoin Islands slid by barely two cables away; to the other the officers on the bridge could make out the bleak moonscape of the Musandam Peninsula, with its sheer rocky mountains. The *Freya* was riding high, and the depth in the channel presented no problems. On the return, laden with crude oil, it would be different. She would be almost shut down, moving slowly, eyes riveted on her depth sounder, watching the map of the sea-bed pass barely a few feet beneath her keel ninety-eight feet below the waterline.

She was still in ballast, as she had been all the way from Chita. She had sixty giant tanks, or holds, three abreast in lines of twenty fore-to-aft. One of these was the slop tank, to be used for nothing else but gathering the slops from her fifty crude-carrying cargo tanks. Nine were permanent ballast tanks, to be used for nothing but pure sea water to give her stability when she was empty of cargo.

But her remaining fifty crude oil tanks were sufficient. Each held 20,000 tons of crude oil. It was with complete confidence in the impossibility of her causing accidental oil pollution that she steamed on to Abu Dhabi to load her first cargo.

There is a modest bar in the rue Miollin in Paris where the small fry of the world of mercenaries and arms sellers are wont to foregather and take a drink together. It was here the German-Ukrainian and his English colleague were brought by the German's French contact man.

There were several hours of low-voiced negotiation between the Frenchman and another French friend of his. Eventually the contact man came across to the two Ukrainians.

'My friend says it is possible,' he told the Ukrainian from Germany. 'Five hundred dollars each, American dollars, cash. One magazine per unit included.'

'We'll take it, if he'll throw in one handgun with full magazine,' said the man from Germany.

Three hours later in the garage of a private house near Neuilly, six submachine carbines and one MAB automatic nine-millimetre handgun were wrapped in blankets and stowed in the boot of the Ukrainians' car. The money changed hands. In twelve hours, just before midnight of 24th February, the two men arrived at their apartment in Brussels and stored their equipment in the base of the wardrobe.

As the sun rose on 25th February the *Freya* eased her way back through the Strait of Hormuz, and on the bridge there was a sigh of relief as the officers gazing at the depth-sounder saw the sea-bed drop away from in front of their eyes to the deep of the ocean. On the digital display the figures ran rapidly from twenty to one hundred fathoms. The *Freya* moved steadily back to her full-load service speed of fifteen knots as she went southeast back down the Gulf of Oman.

She was heavy-laden now, doing what she had been designed and built for – carrying 1,000,000 tons of crude oil to the thirsty refineries of Europe and the millions of family saloons that would drink it. Her draught was now at her designed ninety-eight feet, and her hazard alarm devices had ingested the knowledge and knew what to do if the sea-bed ever approached too close.

Her nine ballast tanks were now empty, acting as buoyancy tanks. Far away in the fore part the first row of three tanks contained a full crude tank port and starboard, with the single slop tank in the centre. One row back were the first three empty ballast tanks. The second row of three was amidships, and the third row of three was at the foot of the superstructure on the fifth floor of which Captain Thor Larsen handed the *Freya* to the senior officer of the watch and went down to his handsome day cabin for breakfast and a short sleep.

On the morning of 26th February, after an adjournment of several days, the presiding judge in the Moabit courtroom in West Berlin began to read the judgement of himself and his two colleagues. It took several hours.

In their walled dock, Mishkin and Lazareff listened impassively. From time to time each sipped water from the glasses placed on the tables in front of them. From the packed booths reserved for the international press they were under scrutiny, as were the figures of the judges while the findings were read. But one magazine journalist representing a leftist German monthly magazine seemed more interested in the glasses they drank from than the prisoners themselves.

The court adjourned for lunch, and when it resumed the journalist was missing from his seat. He was phoning from one of the kiosks outside the hearing. Shortly after three the judge reached his conclusion. Both men were required to rise, to hear themselves sentenced to fifteen years' detention.

They were led away to begin their sentences at Tegel Jail in the northern part of the city, and within minutes the courthouse had emptied. The cleaners took over, removing the brimming waste-paper baskets, carafes and glasses. One of the middle-aged ladies occupied herself with cleaning the interior of the dock. Unobserved by her colleagues she quietly picked up the prisoners' two drinking glasses, wrapped each in dusters and placed them in her shopping bag beneath the empty wrappers of her sandwiches. No one noticed and no one cared.

On the last day of the month Vassili Petrov sought and received a private audience with Maxim Rudin in the latter's Kremlin suite.

'Mishkin and Lazareff,' he said without preamble.

'What about them? They got fifteen years. It should have been the firing squad.'

'One of our people in West Berlin abstracted the glasses they used for water during the trial. The palm-print on one matches that from the car used in the hit-and-run affair in Kiev in October.'

'So it was them,' said Rudin grimly. 'Damn them to hell. Vassili, wipe them out. Liquidate them, as fast as you can. Give it to "wet affairs".'

The KGB, vast and complex in its scope and organization, consists basically of four Chief Directorates, seven Independent Directorates and six Independent Departments.

But the four Chief Directorates comprise the bulk of the KGB. One of these, the First, concerns itself exclusively with clandestine activities outside the USSR.

Deep within the heart of it is a section known simply as Department V (as in Victor) or the Executive Action Department. This is the one the KGB would most like to keep hidden from the rest of the world, inside and outside the USSR. For its tasks include sabotage, extortion, kidnapping and assassination. Within the jargon of the KGB itself it usually has yet another name – the department of *mokrie dyela*, or 'wet affairs', so-called because its operations not infrequently involve someone getting wet with blood. It was to this Department V of the First Chief Directorate of the KGB that Maxim Rudin ordered Petrov to hand the elimination of Mishkin and Lazareff.

'I have already done as much,' said Petrov. 'I thought of giving the affair to Colonel Kukushkin, Ivanenko's head of security. He has a personal reason to wish to succeed – saving his own skin apart from avenging Ivanenko and his own humiliation. He already served his time in "wet affairs" ten years ago. Inevitably he is already aware of the secret of what happened in Rosa Luxembourg Street – he was there. And he speaks German. He would report back only to General Abrassov or to me.'

Rudin nodded grimly.

'All right, let him have the job. He can pick his own team. Abrassov will give him everything he needs. The apparent reason will be to avenge the death of Flight Captain Rudenko. And, Vassili, he had better succeed first time. If he tries and fails, Mishkin and Lazareff could open their mouths. After a failed attempt to kill them, someone might believe them. Certainly Vishnayev would, and you know what that would mean.'

'I know,' said Petrov quietly. 'He will not fail. He'll do it himself.'

10

'It's the best we'll get, Mr President,' said Secretary of State David Lawrence. 'Personally I believe Edwin Campbell has done us well at Castletown.'

Grouped before the President's desk in the Oval Office were the secretaries of state, defense and treasury, with Stanislaw Poklewski and Robert Benson of the CIA. Beyond the french windows the rose garden was whipped by a bitter wind. The snows had gone but 1st March was bleak and uninviting.

President William Matthews laid his hand on the bulky folder in front of him, the draft agreement wrung out of the Castletown talks.

'A deal of it is too technical for me,' he confessed, 'but the digest from the Defense Department impresses me. The way I see it is this: if we reject this now, after the Soviet Politburo has accepted it, there'll be no renegotiation anyway. The matter of grain deliveries will become academic to Russia in three months in any case. By then they'll be starving and Rudin will be gone. Yefrem Vishnayev will get his war. Right?'

'That seems to be the unavoidable conclusion,' said David Lawrence.

'How about the other side of it, the concessions we have made?' asked the President.

'The secret trade protocol in the separate document,' said the secretary of the treasury, 'requires us to deliver fifty-five million tons of mixed grains at production costs and nearly three billion dollars worth of oil, computer and consumer industry technology rather heavily subsidized. The total cost to the United States runs to almost three billion dollars. On the other hand, the sweeping arms reductions should enable us to claw back that much and more by reduced defence expenditure.'

'If the Soviets abide by their undertakings,' said the secretary of defense hastily.

'But if they do, and we have to believe they will,' countered Lawrence, 'by your own experts' calculations they could not launch a successful conventional or tactical nuclear war across the face of Europe for at least five years.'

'President Matthews knew that the presidential election of the coming November would not see his candidacy. But if he could step down leaving behind him peace for even half a decade with the burdensome arms race of the seventies halted in its tracks, he would take his place among the great US presidents. He wanted that more than anything else this spring of 1983.

'Gentlemen,' he said, 'we have to approve this treaty as it stands. David, inform Moscow we join them in agreeing the terms and propose that our negotiators reconvene at Castletown to draw up the formal treaty ready for signing. While this is going on we will permit the loading of the grain ships, ready to sail on the day of signature. That is all.'

On 3rd March Azamat Krim and his Ukrainian-American collaborator clinched the deal that acquired them a sturdy and powerful launch. She was the kind of craft much favoured by enthusiastic sea-anglers on both the British and European coasts of the North Sea, steel-hulled, forty feet long, tough and second-hand. She had Belgian registration and they had found her near Ostend.

Up front, she had a cabin whose roof extended the forward third of her length. A companionway led down to a cramped four-berth resting area, with a tiny toilet and a camping-gas cooker. Aft of the rear bulkhead she was open to the elements, and beneath the deck lay a powerful engine capable of taking her through the wild North Sea to the fishing grounds and back.

Krim and his companion brought her from Ostend to Blankenberge further up the Belgian coast, and when she was moored in the leisure-boat harbour she attracted no attention. Spring always brings its crop of hardy sea-anglers to the coasts with their boats and tackle. The American chose to live on board and work on the engine. Krim returned to Brussels to find that Andrew Drake had taken over the kitchen table as a workbench and was deeply engrossed in preparations of his own.

For the third time on her maiden voyage the *Freya* had crossed the equator and 7th March found her entering the Mozambique Channel heading south by southwest towards the Cape of Good Hope. She was still following her 100-fathom line, leaving 600 feet of clear ocean beneath her keel, a course which took her to seaward of the main shipping lanes. She had not seen land since coming out of the Gulf of Oman, but on the afternoon of the 7th she passed through the Comoro Islands at the north of the Mozambique Channel. To starboard her crew, taking advantage of the moderate winds and seas to stroll the quarter mile of forward deck or lounge beside the screened swimming pool up on 'C' deck, saw Grande Comore Island, the peak of its densely wooded mountain hidden in clouds, the smoke from the burning undergrowth on her flanks drifting across the green water. By nightfall the skies had overcast with grey cloud, the wind turned squally. Ahead lay the heaving seas of the Cape and the final northward run to Europe and her welcome.

The following day Moscow replied formally to the proposal of the United States President, welcoming his agreement to the terms of the draft treaty and agreeing that the chief negotiators of Castletown should reconvene jointly to draft the formal treaty while remaining in constant contact with their respective governments.

The bulk of the Soviet merchant marine fleet Sovfracht, along with the numerous other vessels already chartered by the Soviet Union, had already sailed at American invitation for the eastern seaboard of North America to load their grain. In Moscow the first reports were coming in of excessive quantities of meat appearing in the peasant markets, indicating livestock slaughter was taking place even on the state and collective farms where it was forbidden. The last reserves of feedstuffs for animals and humans alike were running out.

In a private message to President Matthews, Maxim Rudin regretted that for health reasons he would not personally be able to sign the treaty on behalf of the Soviet Union unless the ceremony was in Moscow; he therefore proposed a formal signature by foreign ministers in Dublin on 10th April.

The winds of the Cape were hellish; the South African summer was over and the autumn gales thundered up from the Antarctic to batter Table Mountain. The *Freya* by 12th March was in the heart of the Agulhas Current, pushing westwards through mountainous green seas, taking the gales from the southwest on her port beam.

It was bitter cold out on deck, but no one was there. Behind the double-glazing of the bridge Captain Thor Larsen and his two officers of the watch stood with the helmsman, radio officer and two others in shirtsleeves. Warm, safe, protected by the enshrouding aura of her invincible technology, they gazed forward to where forty-foot waves impelled by the force ten out of the southwest reared above the *Freya*'s port side, hovered for a moment, then crashed down to obscure her gigantic deck and its myriad pipes and valves in a swirling maelstrom of white foam. While the waves burst, only the fo'c's'le, far ahead, was discernible, like a separate entity. As the foam receded defeated through the scuppers, the *Freya* shook herself and buried her bulk in another oncoming mountain. A hundred feet beneath the men, 90,000 shaft horsepower pushed 1,000,000 tons of crude oil another few yards towards Rotterdam. High above, the Cape albatrosses wheeled and glided, their lost cries unheard behind the Plexiglass. Coffee was served by one of the stewards.

Two days later, on Monday the 14th, Adam Munro drove out of the courtyard of the Commercial Section of the British embassy and turned sharp right into Kutuzovsky Prospekt towards the city centre. His destination was the main embassy building where he had been summoned by the head of chancery. The telephone call, certainly tapped by the KGB, had referred to the clarification of minor details for the forthcoming trade delegation visit from London. In fact it meant that there was a message awaiting him in the cipher room.

The cipher room in the embassy building on Maurice Thorez Embankment is in the basement, a secure room regularly checked by the 'sweepers' who are not looking for dust but listening devices. The cipher clerks are diplomatic personnel and security-checked to the highest level. Nevertheless, sometimes messages come in which bear a coding to indicate they will not and cannot be decoded by the normal decoding machines. The tag on these messages will indicate they have to be passed to one particular cipher clerk, a man who has the right to know because he has a need to know. Occasionally a message for Adam Munro bore such a coding, as today. The clerk in question knew Munro's real job, because he needed to: if for nothing else, to protect him from those who did not.

Munro entered the cipher room and the clerk spotted him. They withdrew to a small annexe where the clerk, a precise, methodical man with bifocal glasses, used a key from his waistband to unlock a separate decoding machine. He passed the London message into it and the machine spat out the translation. The clerk took no notice, averting his gaze as Munro moved away.

Munro read the message and smiled. He memorized it within seconds and passed it straight into a shredder which reduced the thin paper to fragments hardly bigger than dust. He thanked the clerk and left, with a song in his heart. Barry Ferndale had informed him that with the Russian-American treaty on the threshold of signature, the Nightingale could be brought out to a discreet but extremely generous welcome, from the coast of Romania near Constantza, in the week of 16th to 23rd April. There were further details for the exact pick-up. He was asked to consult with the Nightingale and confirm acceptance and agreement.

After receiving Maxim Rudin's personal message, President Matthews had remarked to David Lawrence: 'Since this is more than a mere arms limitation agreement, I suppose we must call it a treaty. And since it seems destined to be signed in Dublin, no doubt history will call it the Treaty of Dublin.'

Lawrence had consulted with the government of the Republic of Ireland, who agreed with barely hidden delight that they would be pleased to host the formal signing ceremony between David Lawrence for the United States and Dmitri Rykov for the USSR in Saint Patrick's Hall, Dublin Castle, on 10th April.

On 16th March therefore President Matthews replied to Maxim Rudin agreeing to his place and date.

There are two fairly large rock quarries in the mountains outside Ingolstadt in Bavaria. During the night of 18th March the nightwatchman in one of these was attacked and tied up by four masked men, at least one of them armed with a handgun, he later told police. The men, who seemed to know what they were looking for, broke into the dynamite store using the nightwatchman's keys, and stole 250 kilograms of TNT rock-blasting explosives and a number of electric detonators. Long before morning they were gone and as the following day was Saturday the 19th, it was almost noon before the trussed nightwatchman was rescued and the theft discovered. Subsequent police investigations were intensive and, in view of the apparent knowledge of the layout of the quarry by the robbers, concentrated on the area of former employees. But the search was for extreme left-wingers, and the name of Klimchuk, employed three years earlier at the quarry, attracted no particular attention, being assumed to be of Polish extraction. Actually it is a Ukrainian name. By that Saturday evening the two cars bearing the explosives had arrived back in Brussels, penetrating the German/Belgian border on the Aachen/Liège motorway. They were not stopped, weekend traffic being especially heavy.

By the evening of the 20th the *Freya* was well past Senegal, having made good time from the Cape with the aid of the southeast trade winds and a helpful current. Though it was early in the year for Northern Europe, there were holidaymakers on the beaches of the Canary Islands.

The *Freya* was far to the west of the islands but just after dawn on the 21st her bridge officers could make out the volcanic peak of Monte Teide on Tenerife, their first landfall since they had glimpsed the rugged coastline of Cape Province. As the mountains of the Canaries dropped away, they knew that apart from the chance of seeing Madeira's summit they would next see the lights warning them to stay clear of the wild coasts of Mayo and Donegal.

Adam Munro had waited impatiently for a week to see the woman he loved, but there was no way he could get through to her before their pre-arranged meet on Monday the 21st. For the site he had returned to the Exhibition of Economic Achievements, whose 238 hectares of parks and grounds merged with the main Botanical Gardens of the USSR Academy of Sciences. Here, in a sheltered arboretum in the open air he found her waiting just before noon. Because of the chance of a casual glance from a passerby he could not take the risk of kissing her as he wanted to. Instead he told her with controlled excitement of the news from London. She was overjoyed.

'I have news for you,' she told him. 'There will be a Central Committee fraternal delegation to the Romanian Party Congress during the first half of April, and I have been asked to accompany it. Sasha breaks up from school on the 29th, and we will leave for Bucharest on the 5th. After ten days it will be perfectly normal for me to take a bored little boy to the resort beaches for a week.'

'Then I'll fix it for the night of Monday the 18th of April. That will give you several days in Constantza to find your way around. You must hire or borrow a car, and acquire a powerful torch. Now, Valentina my love, these are the details. Memorize them, for there can be no mistakes:

'North of Constantza lies the resort of Mamaia, where the Western package tourists go. Drive north from Constantza through Mamaia on the evening of the 18th. Exactly six miles north of Mamaia a track leads right from the coast highway to the beach. On the headland at the junction you will see a short stone tower with its lower half painted white. It is a coast-marker for fishermen. Leave the car well off the road and descend the bluff to the beach. At 2 a.m. you will see a light from the sea: three long dashes and three short ones. Take your own torch with its beam cut down by a tube of cardboard and point it straight at where the light came from. Flash back the reverse signal, three shorts and three longs. The speedboat will come out of the sea for you and Sasha.

'There will be one Russian-speaker and two marines. Identify yourself with the phrase "the Nightingale sings in Berkeley Square". Have you got that?'

'Yes. Adam, where is Berkeley Square?'

'In London. It is very beautiful, like you. It has many trees.'

'And do nightingales sing there?'

'According to the words of the song, one used to. Darling, it seems so short. Four weeks today. When we get to London I'll show you Berkeley Square.'

'Adam, tell me something. Have I betrayed my own people, the Russian people?'

'No,' he said with finality, 'you have not. The leaders nearly did. If you had not done what you did, Vishnayev and your uncle might have got their war. In it, Russia would have been destroyed, most of America, my country and Western Europe. You have not betrayed the people of your country.'

'But they would never understand, never forgive me,' she said. There was a hint of tears in her dark eyes. 'They will call me a traitor. I shall be an exile.'

'One day, perhaps, this madness will end. One day perhaps you could come back. Listen, my love, we cannot stay longer. It's too risky. There is one last thing. I need your private phone number. No, I know we agreed that I would never ring. But I will not see you again until you are in the West in safety. If there should by any remote chance be a change of plan, or date, I may have to contact you as a matter of emergency. If I do, I will pretend to be a friend called Gregor, explaining that I cannot attend your dinner party. If that happens, leave at once and meet me in the car park of the Mojarsky Hotel at the top of Kutuzovsky Prospekt.'

She nodded meekly and gave him her number. He kissed her on the cheek.

'I'll see you in London, my darling,' he told her, and was gone through the trees. Privately he knew he would have to resign and take the icy anger of Sir Nigel Irvine when it became plain the Nightingale was not Anatoly Krivoi but a woman, and his wife to be. But by then it would be too late for even the servicc to do anything about it.

Ludwig Jahn stared at the two men who occupied the available chairs of his tidy bachelor flat in the Wedding working-class district of West Berlin with growing fear. They bore the stamp of men he had seen once, long before, and whom he hoped never to see again.

The one who was talking was undoubtedly German, he had no doubt about that. What he did not know was that the man's name was Major Schulz, of the East German secret police, the dreaded Staatssicherheitsdienst, known simply as

SSD. He would never know the name, but he could guess the occupation.

He could also guess that the SSD had copious files on every East German who had ever quit to come to the West, and that was his problem. Thirty years earlier, as an eighteen-year-old, Jahn had taken part in the building workers' riots in East Berlin that had become the East German uprising. He had been lucky. Although he had been picked up in one of the sweeps by the Russian police and their East German Communist acolytes, he had not been held. But he recalled the smell of the detention cells, and the stamp of the men who ruled them. His visitors this 22nd of March three decades later bore the same stamp.

He had kept his head low for eight years after the 1953 riots, then in 1961 before the Wall was completed he quietly walked into the West. For the past fifteen years he had had a good job with the West Berlin Civil Service, starting as a warder in the prison service and rising to Oberwachmeister chief officer of Two Block, Tegel Jail.

The other man in his room that evening kept silent. Jahn would never know that he was a Soviet colonel called Kukushkin, present on behalf of the 'wet affairs' department of the KGB.

Jahn stared in horror at the photographs the German eased from a large envelope and placed before him, slowly, one by one. They showed his widowed mother, in a cell, terrified, aged nearly eighty, staring at the camera obediently, hopeful of release. There were his two younger brothers, handcuffs on wrists, in different cells, the masonry of the walls showing up clearly in the high-definition prints.

'Then there are your sisters-in-law and your three delightful little nieces. Oh yes, we know about the Christmas presents. What is it they call you? Uncle Ludo? How very charming. Tell me, have you ever seen places like these?'

There were more photographs, pictures that made the comfortably plump Jahn close his eyes for several seconds. Strange, zombie-like figures moved through the pictures, clad in rags, shaven, skull-like faces peering dully at the camera.

They huddled, they shuffled, they wrapped their withered feet in rags to keep out the Arctic cold. They were stubbled, shrivelled, sub-human. They were some of the inhabitants of the slave labour camps of the Kolyma complex, far away in the eastern end of Siberia north of the Kamchatka Peninsula, where the gold is mined deep in the Arctic Circle.

'Life sentences in these ... resorts ... are only for the worst enemies of the state, Herr Jahn. But my colleague here can ensure such life sentences for all your family; yes, even your dear old mother, with just one single telephone call. Now tell me, do you want him to make that call?'

Jahn gazed across into the eyes of the man who had not spoken. The eyes were as bleak as the Kolyma camps.

'*Nein*,' he whispered, 'no, please. What do you want?'

It was the German who answered.

'In Tegel Jail are two hijackers, Mishkin and Lazareff. Do you know them?'

Jahn nodded dumbly.

'Yes. They arrived four weeks ago. There was much publicity.'

'Where exactly are they?'

'Number Two block. Top floor, east wing. Solitary confinement, at their own request. They fear the other prisoners. Or so they say. There is no reason. For child rapists there is a reason, but not these two. Yet they insist.'

'But you can visit them, Herr Jahn? You have access?' Jahn remained silent. He began to fear what the visitors wanted with the hijackers. They came from the East; the hijackers had escaped from there. It could not be to bring them birthday gifts.

'Have another look at the pictures, Jahn. Have a good look, before you think of obstructing us.'

'Yes, I can visit them. On my rounds. But only at night. During the day-shift there are three warders in that corridor. One or two would always accompany me if I wished to visit them. But in the day-shift there would be no reason for me to visit them. Only to check on them during the night-shift.'

'Are you on the night-shift at the moment?'

'No. Day-shift.'

'What are the hours of the night-shift?'

'Midnight to eight a.m. Lights are out at ten p.m. Shift changes at midnight. Relief is at eight a.m. During the night-shift I would patrol the block three times, accompanied by the duty officer of each floor.'

The unnamed German thought for a while.

'My friend here wishes to visit them. When do you return to night-shift?'

'Monday, 4th April,' said Jahn.

'Very well,' said the East German. 'This is what you will do.'

Jahn was instructed to acquire from the locker of a vacationing colleague the necessary uniform and pass-card. At 2 a.m. on the morning of Monday, 4th April, he would descend to the ground floor and admit the Russian by the staff entrance from the street. He would accompany him to the top floor and hide him in the staff day room, to which he would acquire a duplicate key. He would cause the night duty officer on the top floor to absent himself on an errand and take over the watch from him while he was away. During the man's absence he would allow the Russian into the solitary-confinement corridor, lending him his pass-key to both cells. When the Russian had 'visited' Mishkin and Lazareff, the process would be reversed. The Russian would hide again until the duty officer returned to his post. Then Jahn would escort the Russian back to the staff entrance and let him out.

'It won't work,' whispered Jahn, well aware that it probably would.

The Russian spoke at last, in German.

'It had better,' he said. 'If it does not, I will personally ensure that your entire family begins a regime in Kolyma that will make the "extra-strict" regime operating there seem like the honeymoon suite at the Kempinski Hotel.'

Jahn felt as if his bowels were being sprayed with liquid ice. None of the hard men in special wing would compare with this man. He swallowed.

'I'll do it,' he whispered.

'My friend will return here at six in the evening of Sunday, 3rd April,' said the East German. 'No reception committees from the police, if you please. It will do no good. We both have diplomatic passes in false names. We will deny everything and walk away quite freely. Just have the uniform and pass-card awaiting him.'

Two minutes later they were gone. They took their photos with them. There was no evidence left. It did not matter. Jahn could see every detail in his nightmares.

By 23rd March over 250 ships, the first wave of the waiting merchant fleet, were docked in thirty ports from the St Lawrence Seaway in Canada down the eastern seaboard of North America to Carolina. There was still ice in the St Lawrence, but it was broken to mosaic by the ice-breakers, aware of its defeat as the grain ships moved through it to berth by the silos.

A fair proportion of these ships were of the Russian Sovfracht fleet, but the next largest numbers were flying the US flag, for one of the conditions of the sale had been that American carriers take the prime contracts to move the grain.

Within ten days they would begin moving east across the Atlantic, bound for Archangel and Murmansk in the Soviet Arctic, Leningrad at the end of the Baltic, and the warm-water ports of Odessa, Simferopol and Novorossisk in the Black Sea. Flags of ten other nations mingled with them to effect the biggest single dry-cargo movement since the Second World War. From a hundred silos from Winnipeg to Charleston the pumps spewed a golden tide of wheat, barley, oats, rye and maize into their bellies, all destined within a month for the hungry millions of Russia.

On the 26th Andrew Drake rose from his work at the kitchen table of an apartment in the suburbs of Brussels and pronounced that he was ready.

The explosives had been packed into ten fibre suitcases, the submachine guns rolled in towels and stuffed into haversacks. Azamat Krim kept the detonators bedded into cotton wool in a cigar box which never left him. When darkness fell the cargo was carried in relays down to the group's second-hand, Belgian-registered panel-van and they set off for Blankenburge.

The little seaside resort facing the North Sea was quiet, the harbour virtually deserted, when they transferred their equipment under cover of darkness to the bilges of the fishing launch. It was a Saturday, and though a man walking his dog along the quay noticed them at work, he thought no more of it. Parties of sea-anglers stocking up for a weekend's fishing were common enough, even though it was a mite early in the year and still chilly.

On Sunday the 27th Miroslav Kaminsky bade them goodbye, took the van and drove back to Brussels. His job was to clean the Brussels flat from top to bottom and end to end, to abandon it and drive the van to a pre-arranged rendezvous in the polders of Holland. There he would leave it, with its ignition key in an agreed place, then take the ferry from the Hook back to Harwich and London. He had his itinerary well rehearsed and was confident he could carry out his part of the plan.

The remaining seven men left port and cruised sedately up the coast to lose themselves in the islands of Walcheren and North Beveland, just across the border into Holland. There, with their fishing rods much in evidence, they hove-to and waited. On a powerful radio down in the cabin, Andrew Drake sat hunched, listening to the wavelength of Maas Estuary Control and the endless calls of the ships heading into or out of Europort and Rotterdam.

'Colonel Kukushkin is going into Tegel Jail to do the job on the night of 3rd to 4th April,' Vassili Petrov told Maxim Rudin in the Kremlin that same Sunday morning. 'There is a senior warder who will let him in, bring him to the cells of

Mishkin and Lazareff, and let him out of the jail by the staff doorway when it is over.'

'The warder is reliable, one of our people?' asked Rudin.

'No, but he has family in East Germany. He has been persuaded to do as he is told. Kukushkin reports that he will not contact the police. He is too frightened.'

'Then he knows already who he is working for. Which means he knows too much.'

'Kukushkin will silence him also, just as he steps out of the doorway. There will be no trace,' said Petrov.

'Eight days,' grunted Rudin. 'He had better get it right.'

'He will,' said Petrov, 'he too has family. By a week tomorrow Mishkin and Lazareff will be dead and their secret with them. Those who helped them will keep silent to save their own lives. Even if they talk, it will be disbelieved. Mere hysterical allegations. No one will believe them.'

When the sun rose on the morning of the 29th its first rays picked up the mass of the *Freya* twenty miles west of Ireland, cutting north by northeast through the eleven degree longitude on a course to skirt the Outer Hebrides.

Her powerful radar scanners had picked up the fishing fleet in the darkness an hour before and her officer of the watch noted them carefully. The nearest to her was well to the east or landward side of the tanker.

The sun glittered over the rocks of Donegal, a thin line on the eastward horizon to the men on the bridge with their advantage of eighty feet of altitude. It caught the small fishing smacks of the men from Killybegs, drifting out in the western seas for mackerel, herring and whiting. And it caught the bulk of *Freya* herself, like a moving landmass, steaming out of the south past the drifters and their gently bobbing nets.

Christy O'Byrne was in the tiny wheelhouse of the smack he and his brother owned, the *Bernadette*. He blinked several times, put down his cocoa mug and stepped the three feet from the wheelhouse to the rail. His vessel was the nearest to the passing tanker.

From behind him, when they saw the *Freya*, the fishermen tugged on the horn lanyards and a chorus of thin whoops disturbed the dawn. On the bridge of the *Freya* Thor Larsen nodded to his junior officer; seconds later the bellowing bull roar of the *Freya* answered the Killybegs fleet.

Christy O'Byrne leaned on the rail and watched the *Freya* fill the horizon, heard the throb of her power beneath the sea and felt the *Bernadette* begin to roll in the widening wake of the tanker.

'Holy Mary,' he whispered, 'would you look at the size of her.'

On the eastern shore of Ireland compatriots of Christy O'Byrne were at work that morning in Dublin Castle, for 700 years the seat of power of the British. As a tiny boy perched on his father's shoulder Martin Donahue had watched from outside as the last British troops marched out of the castle forever, following the signing of a peace treaty. Sixty-three years later on the verge of retirement from government service, he was a cleaner, pushing a Hoover back and forth over the electric blue carpet of Saint Patrick's Hall.

He had not been present when any of Ireland's successive presidents had been inaugurated beneath Vincent Waldré's magnificent 1778 painted ceiling, nor would he be present in twelve days when two super-powers signed the Treaty of Dublin below the motionless heraldic banners of the long-gone Knights of Saint Patrick. For forty years he had just kept the Hall dusted for them.

Rotterdam too was preparing, but for a different ceremony. Harry Wennerstrom arrived on the 30th and installed himself in the best suite at the Hotel Hilton.

He had come by his private executive jet now parked at Schiedam Airport just outside the city. Throughout the day four secretaries fussed around him, preparing for the Scandinavian and Dutch dignitaries, the tycoons from the worlds of oil and shipping, and the scores of press people who would attend his reception on the evening of 1st April for Captain Thor Larsen and his officers.

A select party of notables and press would be his guests on the flat roof of the modern Maas Control building, situated on the very tip of the sandy shore at the Hook of Holland. Well protected against the stiff spring breeze, they would watch from the north shore of the Maas Estuary as the six tugs pulled and pushed the *Freya* those last few miles from the estuary into the Caland Kanal, from there to the Beer Kanal and finally to rest by Clint Blake's new oil refinery in the heart of Europort.

While the *Freya* closed down her systems during the afternoon, the group would come back by cavalcade of limousines to central Rotterdam, twenty-five miles up the river, for an evening reception. A press conference would precede this, during which Wennerstrom would present Thor Larsen to the world's press.

Already, he knew, newspapers and television had leased helicopters to give the last few miles of the *Freya* and her berthing complete camera coverage.

Harry Wennerstrom was a contented old man.

By the early hours of 30th March the *Freya* was well through the channel between the Orkneys and the Shetlands. She had turned south, heading down the North Sea. As soon as she entered the crowded lanes of the North Sea, the *Freya* had reported in, contacting the first of the shore-based area traffic control officers at Wick on the coast of Caithness in the far north of Scotland.

Because of her size and draught, she was a 'hampered vessel'. She had reduced speed to ten knots and was following the instructions fed to her from Wick by VHF radiotelephone. All around her, unseen, the various control centres had her marked on their high-definition radars, manned by qualified pilot operators. These centres are equipped with computerized support systems capable of rapid assimilation of weather, tide and traffic density information.

Ahead of the *Freya* as she crawled down the southbound traffic lane, smaller ships were crisply informed to get out of her way. At midnight she passed Flamborough Head on the coast of Yorkshire, now moving further east, away from the British coast towards Holland. Throughout her passage she had followed the deep-water channel, a minimum of twenty fathoms. On her bridge, despite the constant instructions from ashore, her officers watched the echo-sounder readings, observing the banks and sand-bars that make up the floor of the North Sea slide past on either side of her.

Just before sundown of 31st March, at a point exactly fifteen sea miles due east of the Outer Gabbard Light, now down to her bare steerage speed of five knots, the giant swung gently eastwards and moved to her overnight position, the deep-draught anchorage located at 52 degrees north. She was twenty-seven sea miles due west of the Maas Estuary, twenty-seven miles from home and glory.

It was midnight in Moscow. Adam Munro had decided to walk home from the diplomatic reception at the embassy. He had been driven there by the commercial counsellor, so his own car was parked by his flat off Kutuzovsky Prospekt.

Halfway over the Serafimov Bridge he paused to gaze down at the Moscow River. To his right he could see the illuminated cream-and-white stucco façade of the embassy; to his left the dark red walls of the Kremlin loomed above him, and above them the upper floor and dome of the Great Tsar Palace.

It had been roughly ten months since he had flown from London to take up his new appointment. In that time he had pulled off the greatest espionage coup for decades, 'running' the only spy the West had ever operated inside the heart of the Kremlin. They would savage him for breaking training, for not telling them all along who she was, but they could not diminish the value of what he had brought out.

Three weeks more and she would be out of this place, safe

in London. He would be out, too, resigning from the service to start a new life somewhere else with the only person in the world he loved, ever had loved or ever would.

He would be glad to leave Moscow, with its secrecy, its endless furtiveness, its mind-numbing drabness. In ten days the Americans would have their arms reduction treaty, the Kremlin its grain and technology, the service its thanks and gratitude from Downing Street and the White House alike. A week more and he would have his wife to be, and she her freedom. He shrugged deeper into his thick, fur-collared coat and walked on across the bridge.

Midnight in Moscow is 10 p.m. in the North Sea. By 2200 hours the *Freya* was motionless at last. She had steamed 7085 miles from Chita to Abu Dhabi and a further 12,015 miles from there to where she now lay. She lay motionless along the line of the tide; from her stem a single anchor chain streamed out and down to the sea-bed with five shackles on deck. Each link of the chain needed to hold her was nearly a yard long, the steel thicker than a man's thigh.

Because of her hampered state Captain Larsen had brought her down from the Orkneys himself, with two navigating officers to assist him as well as the helmsman. Even at the overnight anchorage he left his First Officer Stig Lundquist, his Third Mate Tom Keller, one of the Danish-Americans, and an able seaman on the bridge through the night. The officers would maintain constant anchor watch, the seaman would carry out periodic deck-inspection.

Though the *Freya*'s engines were closed down, her turbines and generators hummed rhythmically, churning out the power to keep her systems functioning. Among these were the constant feed-in of tide and weather, of which the latest reports were heartening. He could have had March gales; instead an unseasonal area of high pressure almost stationary over the North Sea and the English Channel had brought a mild early spring to the coasts. The sea was almost a flat calm, a one-knot tide ran northeastwards from the vessel towards the Friesians. The sky had been a near cloudless blue all day and, despite a touch of frost that night, bade fair to be so again on the morrow.

Bidding his officers good night, Captain Larsen left the bridge and descended one floor to 'D' deck. Here, on the extreme starboard side, he had his suite. The spacious and well-appointed day cabin carried four windows looking forward down the length of the vessel, and two looking out to starboard. Aft of the day cabin was his bedroom, with bathroom en suite. The sleeping cabin also had two windows, both to starboard. All the windows were sealed, save one in the day cabin which was closed but with screw bolts which could be manually undone.

Outside his sealed windows to forward, the façade of the superstructure fell sheer to the deck; to starboard the windows gave on to ten feet of steel landing, beyond which was the starboard rail and beyond it the sea. Five flights of steel ladders ran from the lowest 'A' deck up five floors to the bridge wing above his head, each stage of the ladders debouching on to a steel landing. All these sets of ladders and landings were open to the sky, exposed to the elements, but they were seldom used, for the interior stairwells were heated and warm.

Thor Larsen lifted the napkin off the plate of chicken and salad the chief steward had left him, looked longingly at the bottle of Scotch in his drinks cabinet and settled for a coffee from the percolator. After eating he decided to work the night away on a final run-through of the channel charts for the morning's berthing. It was going to be tight, and he wanted to know that channel as well as the two Dutch pilots who would arrive by helicopter from Amsterdam's Schiphol Airport at 0730 to take her over. Prior to that, he knew, a gang of ten men from ashore, the extra hands needed for the berthing operation called riggers, would arrive by launch at 0700.

As midnight struck he settled at the broad table in his day cabin, spread his charts and began to study.

At ten minutes before three in the morning it was frosty but clear outside. A half-moon caused the rippling sea to glitter. Inside the bridge Stig Lundquist and Tom Keller shared a companionable coffee. The able seaman prowled the glowing screens along the bridge console.

'Sir,' he called, 'there's a launch approaching.'

Tom Keller rose and crossed to where the seaman pointed at the radar screen. There were a score of blips, some stationary, some moving, but all well away from the *Freya*. One tiny blip seemed to be approaching from the southeast.

'Probably a fishing boat making sure of being ready on the fishing grounds by sunrise,' said Keller.

Lundquist was looking over his shoulder. He flicked to a lower range.

'She's coming very close,' he said.

Out at sea the launch had to be aware of the mass of the *Freya*. The tanker carried anchor lights above the fo'c's'le and at the stern. Besides, her deck was floodlit and her superstructure was lit like a Christmas tree by the lights in the accommodation. The launch, instead of veering away, began to curve in towards the stern of the *Freya*.

'She looks as if she's going to come alongside,' said Keller.

'She can't be the berthing crew,' said Lundquist. 'They're not due till seven.'

'Perhaps they couldn't sleep, wanted to be well on time,' said Keller.

'Go down to the head of the ladder,' Lundquist told the seaman, 'and tell me what you see. Put on the headset when you get there, and stay in touch.'

The accommodation ladder on the ship was amidships. On a big vessel it is so heavy that steel cables powered by an electric motor either lower it from the ship's rail to the sea level, or raise it to lie parallel to the rail. On the *Freya*, even fully laden, the rail was thirty feet above the sea, an impossible jump, and the ladder was fully raised.

Seconds later the two officers saw the seaman leave the superstructure below them and begin to stroll down the deck. When he reached the ladder-head, he mounted a small platform that jutted over the sea and looked down. As he did so he took a headset from a weatherproof box and fitted the earphones over his head. From the bridge Lundquist pressed a switch and a powerful light came on, illuminating the seaman far away along the deck as he peered down to the black sea. The launch had vanished from the radar screen; she was too close to be observed.

'What do you see?' asked Lundquist into a stick microphone.

The seaman's voice came back into the bridge. 'Nothing, sir.'

Meanwhile the launch had passed round the rear of the *Freya*, under the very overhang of her stern. For seconds it was out of sight. Either side of the stern, the guard rail of 'A' deck was at its nearest point to the sea, just nineteen and a half feet above the water. The two men standing on the cabin roof of the launch had reduced this to ten feet. As the launch emerged from the transom shadow both men slung the three-point grapnels they held, the hooks sheathed in black rubber hose.

Each grapnel, trailing rope, rose twelve feet, dropped over the guard rail and caught fast. As the launch moved on, both men were swept off the cabin roof to hang by the ropes, ankles in the sea. Then each began to climb, rapidly, hand over hand, unheeding of the submachine carbines strapped to their backs. In two seconds the launch emerged into the light and began to run down the side of the *Freya* towards the courtesy ladder.

'I can see it now,' said the seamen high above. 'It looks like a fishing launch.'

'Keep the ladder up until they identify themselves,' ordered Lundquist from the bridge.

Far behind and below him the two boarders were over the rail. Each unhooked his grapnel and heaved it into the sea, where it sank trailing rope. The two men set off at a fast lope, round to the starboard side and straight for the steel ladders. Onsoundless rubber-soled shoes they began to race upwards.

The launch came to rest beneath the ladder, twenty-six feet

above the cramped cabin. Inside, four men crouched. At the wheel, the helmsman stared silently up at the seaman above him.

'Who are you?' called the seaman. 'Identify yourself.'

There was no answer. Far below, in the glare of the spotlight, the man in the black woollen helmet just stared back.

'He won't answer,' said the seaman into his mouthpiece.

'Keep the spotlight on them,' ordered Lundquist. 'I'm coming to have a look.'

Throughout the interchange the attention of both Lundquist and Keller had been to the port side and forward of the bridge. On the starboard side the door leading from the bridge wing into the bridge suddenly opened, bringing a gust of icy air. Both officers spun round. The door closed. Facing them were two men in black balaclava helmets, black roll-neck sweaters, black track-suit trousers and rubber deck-shoes. Each pointed a submachine carbine at the officers.

'Order your seamen to lower the ladder,' said one in English. The two officers stared at them unbelievingly. This was impossible.

The gunman raised his weapon and squinted down the sight at Keller. 'I'll give you three seconds,' he said to Lundquist, 'then I'm blowing the head off your colleague.'

Brick red with anger, Lundquist leaned to the stick-mike.

'Lower the ladder,' he told the seaman.

The disembodied voice came back into the bridge. 'But, sir. . . .'

'It's all right, lad,' said Lundquist. 'Do as I say.'

With a shrug the seaman pressed a button on the small console at the ladder-head. There was a hum of motors and the ladder slowly lowered to the sea. Two minutes later four other men, all in black, were herding the seaman back along the deck to the superstructure while the fifth man made the launch fast. Two more minutes and the six of them entered the bridge from the port side, the seaman's eyes wide with fright. When he entered the bridge he saw the other two gunmen holding his officers.

'How on earth . . . ?' asked the seaman.

'Take it easy,' ordered Lundquist. To the only gunman who had spoken so far he asked in English, 'What do you want?'

'We want to speak to your captain,' said the man behind the mask. 'Where is he?'

The door from the wheelhouse to the inner stairwell opened and Thor Larsen stepped on to the bridge. His gaze took in his three crewmen with their hands behind their heads, and seven black-clad terrorists. His eyes when he turned to the man who had asked the question were as blue and friendly as a cracking glacier.

'I am Captain Thor Larsen, master of the *Freya*,' he said slowly, 'and who the hell are you?'

'Never mind who we are,' said the terrorist leader. 'We have just taken over your ship. Unless your officers and men do as they are told, we shall start by making an example of your seaman. Which is it to be?'

Larsen looked slowly around him. Three of the submachine guns were pointing straight at the eighteen-year-old deckhand. He was as white as chalk.

'Mr Lundquist,' said Larsen formally, 'do as these men say.' Turning back to the leader he asked: 'What exactly is it you want with the *Freya*?'

'That is easy,' said the terrorist without hesitation. 'We wish you no harm personally, but unless our requirements are carried out, to the letter, we shall not hesitate to do what we have to in order to secure compliance.'

'And then?' asked Lundquist.

'Within thirty hours the West German government is going to release two of our friends from a West Berlin jail and fly them to safety. If they do not, I am going to blast you, your crew, your ship and one million tons of crude oil all over the North Sea.'

11

0300 to 0900

The leader of the seven masked terrorists set his men to work with a methodical precision that he had evidently rehearsed over many hours in his own mind. He issued a rapid stream of orders in a language Captain Larsen, his own officers and the young seaman could not understand.

Five of the masked men herded the two officers and seaman to the rear of the bridge, well away from the instrument panels, and surrounded them.

The leader jerked his handgun at Captain Larsen and said in English: 'Your cabin, if you please, captain.'

In single file, Larsen leading, the leader of the terrorists next and his henchman with a submachine carbine bringing up the rear, the three men descended the stairs from the bridge to 'D' deck one flight below. Halfway down the stairs, at the turn, Larsen turned to look back and up at his two captors, measuring the distances, calculating whether he could overcome them both.

'Don't even try it,' said the voice behind the mask at his shoulder. 'No one in his right mind argues with a submachine gun at a range of ten feet.'

Larsen led them onwards down the stairs. 'A' deck was the senior officers' living quarters. The captain's suite, as ever, was in the extreme starboard corner of the great sweep of superstructure. Moving to port, next came a small chart library, the door open to reveal locker after locker of high-quality sea charts, enough to take him into any ocean, any bay, any anchorage in the world. They were all copies of originals made by the British Admiralty, and the best in the world.

Next was the conference suite, a spacious cabin where the captain or owner could if he wished receive a sizeable number of visitors all at one time. Next to this were the owner's staterooms, closed and empty, reserved for the chairman should he ever wish to sail with his ship. At the port end was another suite of cabins identical but in reverse to the captain's quarters. Here the chief engineer lived.

Aft of the captain's cabins was the smaller suite for the chief officer, and aft of the engineer dwelt the chief steward. The whole complex formed a hollow square, whose centre was taken up by the flight of stairs, going round and round, and downwards to 'A' deck three floors below.

Thor Larsen led his captors to his own cabin and stepped into the day room. The terrorist leader followed him in and quickly ran through the other rooms, bedroom and bathroom. There was no one else present.

'Sit down, captain,' he said, the voice slightly muffled by the mask. 'You will remain here until I return. Please do not move. Place your hands on the table and keep them there, palms downwards.'

There was another stream of orders in a foreign language, and the machine-gunner took up position with his back to the far bulkhead of the cabin, facing Thor Larsen but twelve feet away, the barrel of his gun pointing straight at the roll-neck white sweater Thor Larsen wore. The leader checked to see that all the curtains were well drawn, then left, closing the door behind him. The other two inhabitants of the deck were asleep in their respective cabins and heard nothing.

Within minutes the leader was back on the bridge. 'You,' he pointed his gun at the boyish seaman, 'come with me.'

The lad looked imploringly at First Officer Stig Lundquist.

'You harm that boy and I'll personally hang you out to dry,' said Tom Keller in his American accent. Two submachine-gun barrels moved slightly in the hands of the ring of men round him.

'Your chivalry is admirable, your sense of reality deplorable,' said the voice behind the leader's mask. 'No one gets hurt unless they try anything stupid. Then there'll be a bloodbath, and you'll be right under the taps.'

Lundquist nodded to the seaman.

'Go with him,' he said, 'do what he wants.'

The seaman was escorted back down the stairs. At the 'D' deck level the terrorist stopped him.

'Apart from the captain, who lives on this deck?' he asked.

'The chief engineer, over there,' said the seaman. 'The chief officer, over there, but he's up on the bridge now. And the chief steward, there.'

There was no sign of life behind any of the doors.

'The paint locker, where is it?' asked the terrorist. Without a word the seaman turned and headed down the stairs. They went through 'C' deck and 'B' deck. Once a murmur of voices came to them, from behind the door of the seamen's messroom where four men who could not sleep were apparently playing cards over coffee.

At 'A' deck they had reached the level of the base of the superstructure. The seaman opened an exterior door and stepped outside. The terrorist followed him. The cold night air made them both shiver after the warmth of the interior. They found themselves aft of the superstructure on the poop. To one side of the door from which they emerged the bulk of the funnel towered a hundred feet up towards the stars.

The seaman led the way across the poop to where a small steel structure stood. It was six feet by six, and about the same in height. In one side of it there was a steel door, closed by two great screw bolts with butterfly nuts on the outside.

'Down there,' said the seaman.

'Go on down,' said the terrorist. The boy spun the twin butterfly handles, unscrewing the cleats, and pulled them back. Seizing the door handle he swung it open. There was a light inside, showing a tiny platform and a steel stairway running down to the bowels of the *Freya*. At a jerk from the gun, the seaman stepped inside and began to head downwards, the terrorist behind him.

Over seventy feet the stairs led down, past several galleries from which steel doors led off. When they reached the bottom they were well below the waterline, only the keel beneath the deck plating under their feet. They were in an enclosure with four steel doors. The terrorist nodded to the one facing aft.

'What's that lead to?'

'Steering gear housing.'

'Let's have a look.'

When the door was open it showed a great vaulted hall all in metal and painted pale green. It was well lit. Most of the centre of the deck space was taken up by a mountain of encased machinery, the device which, receiving its orders from the computers of the bridge, would move the rudder. The walls of the cavity were curved to the nethermost part of the ship's hull. Aft of the chamber, beyond the steel, the great rudder of the *Freya* would be hanging inert in the black waters of the North Sea. The terrorist ordered the door closed again and bolted shut.

Port and starboard of the steering gear chamber were respectively a chemical store and a paint store. The chemical store the terrorist ignored; he was not going to make men prisoners where there was acid to play with. The paint store was better. It was quite large, airy, well-ventilated and its outer wall was the hull of the ship.

'What's the fourth door?' asked the terrorist. The fourth was the only door with no handles.

'It leads to the rear of the engine room,' said the seaman. 'It is bolted on the other side.'

The terrorist pushed against the steel door. It was rock-solid. He seemed satisfied.

'How many men on this ship?' he asked. 'Or women. No tricks. If there is one more than the figure you give, we'll shoot them.'

The boy ran his tongue over dry lips.

'There are no women,' he said. 'There might be wives next trip, but not the maiden voyage. There are thirty men, including Captain Larsen.'

Knowing what he needed to know, the terrorist pushed the frightened young man into the paint locker, swung the door closed and threw one of the twin bolts into its socket. Then he returned back up the ladder.

Emerging on the poop deck, he avoided the interior stairs and raced back up the outside ladders to the bridge, stepping in from outside where they reached the bridge-wing.

He nodded to his five companions who still held the two officers at gunpoint and issued a stream of further orders. Minutes later the two bridge officers, joined by the chief steward and chief engineer, roused from their beds on 'D' deck below the bridge, were marched down to the paint locker. Most of the crew were asleep on 'B' deck where the bulk of the cabins were situated, much smaller than the officers' accommodation above their heads on 'C' and 'D'.

There were protests, exclamations, bitter language, as they were herded out and down. But at every stage the leader of the terrorists, the only one who spoke at all, informed them in English that their captain was held in his own cabin and would die in the event of any resistance. The officers and men obeyed their orders.

Down in the paint locker the crew was finally counted: twenty-nine. The first cook and two of the four stewards were allowed to return to the galley on 'A' deck and ferry down to the paint store trays of buns and rolls, along with crates of bottled lemonade and canned beer. Two buckets were provided for toilets.

'Make yourselves comfortable,' the terrorist leader told the twenty-nine angry men who stared back at him from inside the paint locker. 'You won't be here long. Thirty hours at most. One last thing: your captain wants the pumpman. Who is he?'

A Swede called Martinsson stepped forward.

'I'm the pumpman,' he said.

'Come with me.' It was four-thirty.

'A' deck, the ground floor of the superstructure, was entirely devoted to the rooms containing the services of the marine giant. There was the main galley, deep freeze chamber, cool room, other assorted food stores, liquor store, soiled linen store, automatic laundry, cargo control room including the inert gas control, and the fire-fighting control room, also called the foam room.

Above it was 'B' deck, with all non-officer accommodation, cinema, library, four recreation rooms and three bars.

'C' deck held the officer cabins apart from the four on the level above, plus the officers' dining saloon and smoke-room and the crew club with verandah, swimming pool, sauna and gymnasium.

It was the cargo-control room on 'A' deck that interested the terrorist, and he ordered the pumpman to bring him to it. There were no windows; it was centrally heated, air conditioned, silent and well-lit. Behind his mask the eyes of the terrorist chief flickered over the banks of switches and settled on the rear bulkhead. Here, behind the control console where the pumpman now sat, a visual display board nine feet wide and four feet tall occupied the wall. It showed in map form the crude-tank layout of the *Freya*'s cargo capacity.

'If you try to trick me,' he told the pumpman, 'it may cost me the life of one of my men, but I shall surely find out. If I do, I shall not shoot you, my friend. I shall shoot your Captain Larsen. Now, point out to me where the ballast holds are, and the cargo holds.'

Martinsson was not going to argue with his captain's life at stake. He was in his mid-twenties and Thor Larsen was a generation older. He had sailed with Larsen twice before, including his first-ever voyage as pumpman, and like all the crew he had enormous respect and liking for the towering Norwegian, who had a reputation for unflagging consideration for his crew and for being the best mariner in the Nordia fleet. He pointed at the diagram in front of him.

The sixty holds were laid out in sets of three across the beam of the *Freya*; twenty such sets.

'Up here in the forepart,' said Martinsson, 'the port and starboard tanks are full of crude. The centre is the slop tank, empty now like a buoyancy tank, because we have not discharged cargo yet. So there has been no need to scour the cargo tanks and pump the slops in here. One row back, all three are ballast tanks; they were full of sea-water from Japan to the Gulf, now full of air.'

'Open the valves,' said the terrorist, 'between all three ballast tanks and the slop tank.' Martinsson hesitated. 'Go on, do it.'

Martinsson pressed three square plastic controls on the console in front of him. There was a low humming from behind the console. A quarter of a mile in front of them, down below the steel deck, great valves the size of normal garage doors swung open, forming a single linked unit out of the four tanks, each capable of holding 20,000 tons of liquid. Not only air, but any liquid now entering one of the tanks would flow freely to the other three.

'Where are the next ballast tanks?' asked the terrorist. Martinsson pointed with his forefinger halfway down the ship.

'Here, amidships, there are three in a row, side by side,' he said.

'Leave them alone,' said the terrorist. 'Where are the others?'

'There are nine ballast tanks in all,' said Martinsson, 'the last three are here, side by side as usual, right up close to the superstructure.'

'Open the valves so they communicate with each other.'

Martinsson did as he was bid.

'Good,' said the terrorist. 'Now, can the ballast tanks be linked straight through to the cargo tanks?'

'No,' said Martinsson, 'it's not possible. The ballast tanks are permanent for ballast, that is, sea water or air, but never oil. The cargo tanks are the reverse. The two systems do not inter-connect.'

'Fine,' said the masked man. 'We can change all that. One last thing. Open all the valves between all the cargo tanks, laterally and longitudinally, so that all fifty communicate with each other.'

It took fifteen seconds for all the necessary control buttons to be pushed. Far down in the treacly blackness of the crude oil scores of gigantic valves swung open, forming one enormous single tank containing 1,000,000 tons of crude. Martinsson stared at his handiwork in horror.

'If she sinks with one tank ruptured,' he whispered, 'the whole million tons will flow out.'

'Then the authorities had better make sure she doesn't sink,' said the terrorist. 'Where is the master power source from this control panel to the hydraulic pumps that control the valves?'

Martinsson gestured to an electrical junction box on the wall near the ceiling. The terrorist reached up, opened the box and pulled the contact breaker downwards. With the box dead, he removed the ten fuses and pocketed them. The pumpman looked on with fear in his eyes. The valve-opening process had become irreversible. There were spare fuses, and he knew where they were stored. But he would be in the paint locker. No stranger entering his sanctum could find them in time to close those vital valves.

Bengt Martinsson knew, because it was his job to know, that a tanker cannot simply be loaded or unloaded haphazardly. If all the starboard cargo tanks are filled on their own, with the others left empty, the ship will roll over and sink. If the port tanks are filled alone, she will roll the other way. If the forward tanks are filled, but not balanced at the stern, she will dive by the nose, her stern high in the air; and the reverse if the stern half is full of liquid and the for'ard empty.

But if the stem and stern ballast tanks are allowed to flood with water while the centre section is buoyant with air, she will arch like an acrobat doing a backspring. Tankers are not designed for such strains; the *Freya*'s massive spine would break at the mid-section.

'One last thing,' said the terrorist. 'What would happen if we opened all the fifty inspection hatches to the cargo tanks?'

Martinsson was tempted, sorely tempted, to let them try it. He thought of Captain Larsen sitting high above him facing a submachine carbine. He swallowed.

'You'd die,' he said, 'unless you had breathing apparatus.'

He explained to the masked man beside him that when a tanker's holds are full, the liquid crude is never quite up to the ceilings of the holds. In the gap between the slopping surface of the oil and the ceiling of the hold gases form, given off by the crude oil. They are volatile gases, highly explosive. If they were not bled off, they would turn the ship into a bomb.

Years earlier the system for bleeding them off was by way of gas lines fitted with pressure valves so that the gases could escape to the atmosphere above deck where, being very light, they would go straight upwards. More recently a far safer system was devised; inert gases from the main engine exhaust flue were fed into the holds to expel oxygen and seal the surface of the crude oil; these inert gases were mainly carbon monoxide.

Creating as they did a completely oxygen-free atmosphere, fire or spark, which requires oxygen, was banished. But every tank had a one-yard circular inspection hatch let into to the main deck; if these were opened by an incautious visitor, he would immediately be enveloped in a carpet reaching to above his head of inert gas. He would die choking, asphyxiated in an atmosphere containing no oxygen.

'Thank you,' said the terrorist. 'Who handles the breathing apparatus?'

'The chief officer is in charge of it,' said Martinsson, 'but we are all trained to use it.'

Two minutes later he was back in the paint store with the rest of the crew. It was five o'clock.

While the leader of the masked men had been in the cargo control room with Martinsson, and another held Thor Larsen prisoner in his own cabin, the remaining five had unloaded their launch. The ten suitcases of explosives stood on the deck amidships at the top of the courtesy ladder, awaiting the leader's instructions for placing. These orders he gave with crisp precision. Far away on the foredeck the inspection hatches of the port and starboard ballast tanks were unscrewed and removed, revealing the single steel ladder descending eighty feet into the black depths of musty air.

Azamat Krim took off his mask, stuffed it in his pocket,

took his torch and descended into the first hatch. Two suitcases were lowered after him on long cords. Working in the base of the hold by lamplight, he placed one entire suitcase against the outer hull of the *Freya* and lashed it to one of the vertical ribs with cord. The other case he opened and extracted its contents in two halves. One half went against the forward bulkhead, beyond which lay 20,000 tons of oil; the other half went against the aft bulkhead, behind which was another 20,000 tons of crude. Sandbags, also brought from the launch, were packed around the charges to concentrate the blast. When Krim was satisfied that the detonators were in place and linked to the triggering device, he came back to the starlight on deck.

The same process was repeated on the other side of the *Freya*, and then twice again in the port and starboard ballast tanks close up to the superstructure. He had used eight of his suitcases in four ballast holds. The ninth he placed in the centre ballast tank amidships, not to blast a hole to the waiting sea, but to help crack the spine.

The tenth was brought down to the engine room. Here in the curvature of the *Freya*'s hull, close up against the bulkhead to the paint locker, strong enough to break both open simultaneously, it was laid and primed. If it went off, those men in the paint locker a half-inch of steel away who survived the blast would drown when the sea, under immense pressure at eighty feet below the waves, came pounding through.

It was six-fifteen and dawn was breaking over the *Freya*'s silent decks when he reported to Andrew Drake.

'The charges are laid and primed, Andriy,' he said. 'I pray to God we never set them off.'

'We won't have to,' said Drake. 'But I have to convince Captain Larsen. Only when he has seen and believed will he convince the authorities. Then they'll have to do as we want. They'll have no alternative.'

Two of the crew were brought from the paint locker, made to don protective clothing, face masks and oxygen bottles, and proceed down the deck from the fo'c's'le to the housing, opening every one of the fifty inspection hatches to the oil cargo tanks. When the job was done, the men were returned to the paint locker. The steel door was closed and the two bolts screwed shut on the outside, not to be opened again until two prisoners were safe in Israel.

At six-thirty Andrew Drake, still masked, returned to the captain's day cabin. Wearily he sat down, facing Thor Larsen, and told him from start to finish what had been done. The Norwegian stared back at him impassively, held in check by the submachine gun pointing at him from the corner of the room.

When he had finished, Drake held up a black plastic instrument and showed it to Larsen. It was no larger than two kingsize cigarette packs bound together; there was a single red button on the face of it, and a four-inch steel aerial sticking from the top.

'Do you know what this is, captain?' asked the masked Drake. Larsen shrugged. He knew enough about radio to recognize a small transistorized transmitter.

'It's an oscillator,' said Drake. 'If that red button is pressed, it will emit a single VHF note, rising steadily in tone and pitch to a scream that our ears could not begin to listen to. But attached to every single charge on this ship is a receiver that can and will listen. As the tonal pitch rises, a dial on the receivers will show the pitch, the needles moving round the dials until they can go no further. When that happens the devices will blow their fuses and a current will be cut. The cutting of that current in each receiver will convey its message to the detonators, which will then operate. You know what that would mean?'

Thor Larsen stared back at the masked face across the table from him. His ship, his beloved *Freya*, was being raped and there was nothing he could do about it. His crew was crowded into a steel coffin inches away through a steel bulkhead from a charge that would crush them all, and cover them in seconds in freezing sea water.

His mind's eye conjured a picture of hell. If the charges blew, great holes would be torn in the port and starboard sides of four of his ballast tanks. Roaring mountains of sea would rush in, filling both the outer and the centre ballast tanks in minutes. Being heavier than the crude oil, the sea water would have the greater pressure; it would push through the other gaping holes inside the tanks to the neighbouring cargo holds, spewing the crude oil upwards through the inspection hatches, so that six more holds would fill with water. This would happen right up in the forepeak, and right aft beneath his feet. In minutes the engine room would be flooded with tens of thousands of tons of green water. The stern and the bow would drop at least ten feet, but the buoyant mid-section would ride high, its ballast tanks untouched. The *Freya*, most beautiful of all the Norse goddesses, would arch her back once, in pain, and split in two. Both sections would drop straight, without rolling, twenty-five feet to the sea-bed beneath, to sit there with fifty inspection hatches open and facing upwards. A million tons of crude oil would gurgle out to the surface of the North Sea.

It might take an hour for the mighty goddess to sink completely, but the process would be irreversible. In such shallow water part of her bridge might still be above the tide, but she could never be re-floated. It might take three days for the last of her cargo to reach the surface, but no diver could work among fifty columns of vertically rising crude oil. No one would close the hatches again. The escape of the oil, like the destruction of his ship, would be irreversible.

He stared back at the masked face but made no reply. There was a deep, seething anger inside him, growing with each passing minute, but he gave no sign of it.

'What do you want?' he growled. The terrorist glanced at the digital display clock on the wall. It read a quarter to seven.

'We're going to the radio room,' he said. 'We talk to Rotterdam. Or rather, you talk to Rotterdam.'

Twenty-six miles to the east the rising sun had dimmed the great yellow flames that spout day and night from the oil refineries of Europort. Through the night, from the bridge of the *Freya*, it had been possible to see these flames in the dark sky above Chevron, Shell, BP and even, far beyond them, the cool blue glow of Rotterdam's street lighting.

The refineries and the labyrinthine complexity of Europort, the greatest oil terminal in the world, lie on the south shore of the Maas Estuary. On the north shore is the Hook of Holland, with its ferry terminal and the Maas Control building, squatting beneath its whirling radar antennae.

Here at 0645 hours on the morning of 1st April Duty Officer Bernhard Dijkstra yawned and stretched. He would be going home in fifteen minutes for a well-earned breakfast. Later, after a sleep, he would motor back from his home at Gravenzande in his spare time to see the new super-giant tanker pass through the estuary. It should be quite a day.

As if to answer his thoughts the speaker in front of him came to life. 'Pilot Maas, Pilot Maas, here is the *Freya*.'

The supertanker was on channel twenty, the usual channel for a tanker out at sea to call up Maas Control by radio-telephone. Dijkstra leaned forward and flicked a switch.

'*Freya*, this is Pilot Maas. Go ahead.'

'Pilot Maas, this is *Freya*. Captain Thor Larsen speaking. Where is the launch with my berthing crew?'

Dijkstra consulted a clipboard to the left of his console.

'*Freya*, this is Pilot Maas. They left the Hook over an hour ago. They should be with you in twenty minutes.'

What followed caused Dijkstra to shoot bolt upright in his chair.

'*Freya* to Pilot Maas. Contact the launch immediately and tell them to return to port. We cannot accept them on board. Inform the Maas pilots not to take off, repeat not to take off. We cannot accept them on board. We have an emergency, I repeat, we have an emergency.'

Dijkstra covered the speaker with his hand and yelled to his fellow duty officer to throw the switch on the tape recorder. When it was spinning to record the conversation, Dijkstra removed his hand and said carefully, 'Freya, this is Pilot Maas. Understand you do not wish the berthing crew to come alongside. Understand you do not wish the pilots to take off. Please confirm.'

'Pilot Maas, this is *Freya*. Confirm. Confirm.'

'*Freya*, please give details of your emergency.'

There was silence for ten seconds, as if a consultation were taking place on the *Freya*'s bridge far out at sea. Then Larsen's voice boomed out again in the control room.

'Pilot Maas, *Freya*. I cannot give the nature of the emergency. But if any attempt is made by anyone to approach the *Freya*, people will get killed. Please stay away. Do not make any further attempt to contact the *Freya* by radio or telephone. Finally, the *Freya* will contact you again at zero nine hundred hours exactly. Have the chairman of the Rotterdam Port Authority present in the control room. That is all.'

The voice ended and there was a loud click. Dijkstra tried to call back two or three times. Then he looked across at his colleague. 'What the hell did that mean?'

Officer Schipper shrugged. 'I didn't like the sound of it,' he said. 'Captain Larsen sounded as if he might be in danger.'

'He spoke of men getting killed,' said Dijkstra. 'How killed? What's he got, a mutiny? Someone run amok?'

'We'd better do what he says until this is sorted out,' said Schipper.

'Right,' said Dijkstra. 'You get on to the chairman, I'll contact the launch and the two pilots up at Schiphol.'

The launch bearing the berthing crew was chugging at a steady ten knots across the flat calm towards the *Freya*, with three miles still to go. It was developing into a beautiful spring morning, warm for the time of year. At three miles the bulk of the giant tanker was already looming large, and the ten Dutchmen who would help her berth, but who had never seen her before, were craning their necks as they came closer.

No one thought anything when the ship-to-shore radio by the helmsman's side crackled and squawked. He took the handset off its cradle and held it to his ear. With a frown he cut the engine to idling and asked for a repeat. When he got it, he put the helm hard a-starboard and brought the launch round in a semi-circle.

'We're going back,' he told the men who looked at him

with puzzlement. 'There's something wrong. Captain Larsen's not ready for you yet.'

Behind them the *Freya* receded again towards the horizon as they headed back to the Hook.

Up at Schiphol Airport south of Amsterdam the two estuary pilots were walking towards the Port Authority helicopter that would airlift them out to the deck of the tanker. It was routine procedure; they always went out to waiting ships by whirlybird.

The senior pilot, a grizzled veteran with twenty years at sea, a master's ticket and fifteen years a Maas pilot, carried his 'brown box', the instrument which would help him steer her to within a yard of sea water if he wished to be so precise. With the *Freya* clearing only twenty feet from the shoals and the Inner Channel barely fifty feet wider than the *Freya* itself, he would need it this morning.

As they ducked underneath the whirling blades, the pilot leaned out and wagged a warning finger at them.

'Something seems to be wrong,' he yelled above the roar of the engine. 'We have to wait. I'm closing her down.'

The engine cut, the blades swished to a stop.

'What the hell's all that about?' asked the second pilot.

The helicopter flier shrugged. 'Don't ask me,' he said, 'just came through from Maas Control. The ship isn't ready for you yet.'

At his handsome country house outside Vlaardingen Dirk van Gelder, chairman of the Port Authority, was at breakfast a few minutes before eight when the phone rang.

His wife answered it. 'It's for you,' she called, and went back to the kitchen where the coffee was perking. Van Gelder rose from the breakfast table, dropped his newspaper on the chair and shuffled in carpet slippers out to the hallway.

'Van Gelder,' he said down the telephone. As he listened he stiffened, his brow furrowed.

'What did he mean, killed?' he asked. There was another stream of words into his ear. 'Right,' said van Gelder, 'stay there. I'll be with you in fifteen minutes.'

He slammed the phone down, kicked off the slippers and

put on his shoes and jacket. Two minutes later he was at his garage doors. As he climbed into his Mercedes and backed out to the gravel driveway, he was fighting back thoughts of his personal and abiding nightmare.

'Dear God, not a hijack. Please, not a hijack.'

After replacing the VHF radio-telephone on the bridge of the *Freya*, Captain Thor Larsen had been taken at gunpoint on a tour of his own ship, peering with torch into the forward ballast holds to note the big packages strapped far down below the water-line.

Returning down the deck he had seen the launch with the berthing crew turn, three miles out, and head back for the shore. To seaward a small freighter had passed, heading south, and had greeted the leviathan at anchor with a cheery hoot. It was not returned.

He had seen the single charge in the centre ballast tank amidships, and the further charges in the after ballast tanks close by the superstructure. He did not need to see the paint locker. He knew where it was and could imagine how close the charges were placed.

At half-past eight, while Dirk van Gelder was striding into the Maas Control building to listen to the tape recording, Thor Larsen was escorted back to his day cabin. He had noted one of the terrorists, muffled against the chill, perched right up in the fo'c's'le apron of the *Freya*, watching the arc of sea out in front of the vessel. Another was high on the top of the funnel casing over a hundred feet up with a commanding view of the sea around him. A third was on the bridge, patrolling the radar screens, able thanks to the *Freya*'s own technology to see a forty-eight-mile radius circle of ocean around her, and most of the sea beneath her.

Of the remaining four, two, the leader and another, were with him; the other two must be below decks somewhere.

The terrorist leader forced him to sit at his own table in his own cabin. The man tapped the oscillator which was clipped to his belt.

'Captain, please don't force me to press this red button. And please don't think that I will not, either if there is any attempt at heroics on this ship, or if my demands are not met. Now, please read this.'

He handed Captain Larsen a sheaf of three sheets of foolscap paper covered with typed writing in English. Larsen went rapidly through it.

'At nine o'clock you are going to read that message over the ship-to-shore radio to the chairman of the Port Authority of Rotterdam. No more, and no less. No breaking into Dutch or Norwegian. No supplementary questions. Just the message. Understand?'

Larsen nodded grimly. The door opened and a masked terrorist came in. He had apparently been in the galley. He bore a tray with fried eggs, butter, jam and coffee, which he placed on the table between them.

'Breakfast,' said the terrorist leader. He gestured towards Larsen. 'You might as well eat.'

Larsen shook his head, but drank the coffee. He had been awake all night and had risen from his bed the previous morning at seven. Twenty-six hours awake, and many more to go. He needed to stay alert and guessed the black coffee might help. He calculated that the terrorist across the table from him had also been awake the same amount of time.

The terrorist signalled the remaining gunman to leave. As the door closed they were alone, but the broad expanse of table put the terrorist well out of Larsen's reach. The gun lay within inches of the man's right hand, the oscillator was at his waist.

'I don't think we shall have to abuse your hospitality for more than thirty hours, maybe forty,' said the masked man. 'But if I wear this mask during that time I shall suffocate. You have never seen me before and after tomorrow you will never see me again.'

With his left hand the man pulled the black balaclava helmet from his head. Larsen found himself staring at a man in his early thirties, with brown eyes and medium brown hair. He puzzled Larsen. The man spoke like an Englishman, behaved like one. But Englishmen do not hijack tankers, surely. Irish perhaps? IRA? But he had referred to friends of his in prison in Germany. Arab, perhaps? There were PLO terrorists in prison in Germany. And he spoke a strange language to his companions. Not Arabic by the sound of it, yet there were scores of different dialects in Arabic, and Larsen only knew the Gulf Arabs. Again, Irish perhaps.

'What do I call you?' he asked the man whom he would never know as Andriy Drach or Andrew Drake.

The man thought for a moment, as he ate. 'You can call me "Svoboda",' he said after a while. 'It is a common name in my language. But it is also a word. It means "freedom".'

That's not Arabic,' said Larsen. The man smiled for the first time.

'Certainly not. We are not Arabs. We are Ukrainian freedom fighters, and proud of it.'

'And you think the authorities will free your friends in prison?' asked Larsen.

'They will have to,' said Drake confidently. 'They have no alternative. Come, it is almost nine o'clock.'

12

0900 to 1300

'Pilot Maas, Pilot Maas, this is the *Freya*.'

Captain Thor Larsen's baritone voice echoed into the main control room at the squat building on the tip of the Hook of Holland. In the first-floor office with its sweeping picture windows gazing out over the North Sea, now curtained against the bright morning sun to give clarity to the radar screens, five men sat waiting.

Dijkstra and Schipper were still on duty, thoughts of breakfast forgotten. Dirk van Gelder stood behind Dijkstra, ready to take over when the call came through. At another console one of the day-shift men was taking care of the rest of estuary traffic, bringing ships in and out but keeping them away from the *Freya*, whose blip on the radar screen was at the limit of vision but still larger than all the others. The senior maritime safety officer to Maas Control was also present.

When the call came, Dijkstra slipped out of his chair before the speaker and van Gelder sat down. He gripped the stem of the table microphone, cleared his throat and threw the 'transmit' switch.

'*Freya*, this is Pilot Maas. Go ahead, please.'

Beyond the confines of the building, looking for all the world like a chopped-off air traffic control tower sitting on the sand, other ears were listening. During the earlier transmission two other ships had caught part of the conversation and there had been a deal of chit-chat between ships' radio officers in the intervening ninety minutes. Now a dozen were listening keenly.

On the *Freya*, Larsen knew he could switch to channel sixteen, speak to Scheveningen Radio and ask for a patch-through to Maas Control for greater privacy, but the listeners would soon join him on that channel. So he stayed with channel twenty.

'*Freya* to Pilot Maas, I wish to speak personally to the chairman of the Port Authority.'

'This is Pilot Maas. This is Dirk van Gelder speaking. I am the chairman of the Port Authority.'

'This is Captain Thor Larsen, master of the *Freya*.'

'Yes, Captain Larsen, your voice is recognized. What is your problem?'

At the other end, on the bridge of the *Freya*, Drake gestured with the tip of his gun to the written statement in Larsen's hand. Larsen nodded, flicked his 'transmit' switch and began to read into the telephone.

'I am reading a prepared statement. Please do not interrupt and do not pose questions.

' "At oh three hundred hours this morning the *Freya* was taken over by armed men. I have already been given ample reason to believe they are in deadly earnest and prepared to carry out all their threats unless their demands are met." '

In the control tower on the sand there was a hiss of indrawn breath from behind van Gelder. He closed his eyes wearily. For years he had been urging that some security measures be taken to protect these floating bombs from hijackings. He had been ignored, and now it had happened at last. The voice from the speaker went on, the tape recorder revolved impassively.

' "My entire crew is presently locked in the lowest portion of the ship, behind steel doors, and cannot escape. So far no harm has come to them. I myself am held at gunpoint on my own bridge.

' "During the night explosive charges have been placed at strategic positions at various points inside the *Freya*'s hull. I have examined these myself and can corroborate that if exploded they would blast the *Freya* apart, kill her crew instantly, and vent one million tons of crude oil into the North Sea." '

'Oh, my God,' said a voice behind van Gelder. He waved an impatient hand for the speaker to shut up.

' "These are the immediate demands of the men who hold the *Freya* prisoner. One, all sea traffic is to be cleared at once from the area inside the arc from a line forty-five degrees south of a bearing due east of the *Freya*, and forty-five degrees north of the same bearing; that is, inside a ninety-degree arc between the *Freya* and the Dutch coast. Two, no vessel, surface or submarine, is to attempt to approach the *Freya* on any other bearing to within five miles. Three, no aircraft is to pass overhead the *Freya* within a circle of five miles' radius of her, and below a height of ten thousand feet. Is that clear? You may answer." '

Van Gelder gripped the microphone hard.

'*Freya*, this is Pilot Maas. Dirk van Gelder speaking. Yes, that is clear. I will have all surface traffic cleared from the area enclosed by a ninety-degree arc between the *Freya* and the Dutch coast, and from an area five sea miles from the *Freya* on all other sides. I will instruct Schiphol Airport traffic control to ban all air movements within the five-mile radius area below ten thousand feet. Over.'

There was a pause, and Larsen's voice came back.

'I am informed that if there is any attempt to breach these orders, there will be an immediate riposte without further consultation. Either the *Freya* will vent twenty thousand tons of crude oil immediately, or one of my seamen will be . . . executed. Is that understood? You may answer.'

Dirk van Gelder turned to his traffic officers.

'Jesus, get the shipping out of that area, fast. Get on to Schiphol and tell them. No commercial flights, no private aircraft, no choppers taking pictures, nothing. Now move.'

To the microphone he said, 'Understood, Captain Larsen. Is there anything else?'

'Yes,' said the disembodied voice. ' "There will be no further radio contact with the *Freya* until twelve hundred hours. At that time the *Freya* will call you again. I will wish to speak directly and personally to the Prime Minister of the Netherlands and the West German ambassador. Both must be present. That is all." '

The microphone went dead. On the bridge of the *Freya* Drake removed the handset from Larsen's hand and replaced it. Then he gestured the Norwegian to return to the day cabin. When they were seated with the seven-foot table between them, Drake laid down his gun and leaned back. As his sweater rode up Larsen saw the lethal oscillator clipped at his waistband.

'What do we do now?' asked Larsen.

'We wait,' said Drake. 'While Europe goes quietly mad.'

'They'll kill you, you know,' said Larsen. "You've got on board, but you'll never get off. They may have to do what you say, but when they have done it they'll be waiting for you.'

'I know,' said Drake. 'But you see, I don't mind if I die. I'll fight to live, of course, but I'll die, and I'll kill, before I'll see them kill off my project.'

'You want these two men in Germany free that much?' asked Larsen.

'Yes, that much. I can't explain why, and if I did you wouldn't understand. But for years my land, my people, have been occupied, persecuted, imprisoned, killed. And no one cared a shit. Now I threaten to kill one single man, or hit Western Europe in the pocket, and you'll see what they do. Suddenly it's a disaster. But for me, the slavery of my land, that is the disaster.'

'This dream of yours, what is it exactly?' asked Larsen.

'A free Ukraine,' said Drake simply. 'Which cannot be achieved short of a popular uprising by millions of people.'

'In the Soviet Union?' said Larsen. 'That's impossible. That will never happen.'

'It could,' countered Drake. 'It could. It happened in East Germany, in Hungary, in Czechoslovakia. But first, the conviction by those millions that they could never win, that their oppressors are invincible, must be broken. If it once were, the floodgates could open wide.'

'No one will ever believe that,' said Larsen.

'Not in the West, no. But there's the strange thing. Here in the West people would say I cannot be right in that calculation. But in the Kremlin they know I am.'

'And for this ... popular uprising, you are prepared to die?' asked Larsen.

'If I must. That is my dream. That land, that people, I love more than life itself. That's my advantage; within a hundred-mile radius of us here there is no one else who loves something more than his life.'

A day earlier Thor Larsen might have agreed with the fanatic. But something was happening inside the big, slow-moving Norwegian that surprised him. For the first time in his life he hated a man enough to kill him. Inside his head a private voice said, 'I don't care about your Ukrainian dream, Mr Svoboda. You are not going to kill my crew and my ship.'

At Felixstowe on the coast of Suffolk, the English coastguard officer walked quickly away from his coastal radio set and picked up the telephone.

'Get me the Department of the Environment in London,' he told the operator.

'By God, those Dutchies have got themselves a problem this time,' said his deputy, who had heard the conversation between the *Freya* and Maas Control also.

'It's not just the Dutch,' said the senior coastguard. 'Look at the map.'

On the wall was a map of the entire southern portion of the North Sea and the northern end of the English Channel. It showed the coast of Suffolk right across to the Maas Estuary. In chinagraph pencil the coastguard had marked the *Freya* at her overnight position. It was exactly halfway between the two coasts.

'If she blows, lad, our coasts will also be under a foot of oil from Hull round to Southampton.'

Minutes later he was talking to a civil servant in London, one of the men in the department of the ministry specifically concerned with oil-slick hazards. What he said caused the morning's first cup of tea in London to go quite cold.

Dirk van Gelder managed to catch the Prime Minister at his residence, just as he was about to leave for his office. The urgency of the Port Authority chairman finally persuaded the young aide from the Cabinet Office to pass the phone to the premier.

'Jan Grayling,' he said down the speaker. As he listened to van Gelder his face tightened.

'Who are they?' he asked.

'We don't know,' said van Gelder. 'Captain Larsen was reading from a prepared statement. He was not allowed to deviate from it, or answer questions.'

'If he was under duress, perhaps he had no choice but to confirm the placing of the explosives. Perhaps that's a bluff,' said Grayling.

'I don't think so, sir,' said van Gelder. 'Would you like me to bring the tape to you?'

'Yes, at once, in your own car,' said the premier. 'Straight to the Cabinet Office.'

He put the phone down and walked to his limousine, his mind racing. If what was threatened was indeed true, the bright summer morning had brought the worst crisis of his term of office. As his car left the kerbside, followed by the inevitable police vehicle, he leaned back and tried to think out some of the first priorities. An immediate emergency Cabinet meeting, of course. The press, they would not be long. Many ears must have listened to the ship-to-shore conversation; someone would tell the press before noon.

He would have to inform a variety of foreign governments through their embassies. And authorize the setting up of an immediate crisis management committee of experts. Fortunately he had access to a number of such experts since the hijacks by the South Moluccans several years earlier. As he drew up in front of the prime ministerial office building he glanced at his watch. It was half past nine.

The phrase 'crisis management committee' was already being thought, albeit as yet unspoken, in London. Sir Rupert Mossbank, permanent under-secretary to the Department of the Environment was on the phone to the Cabinet secretary, Sir Julian Flannery.

'It's early days yet, of course,' said Sir Rupert. 'We don't know who they are, how many, if they're serious or whether there are really any bombs on board. But if that amount of crude oil did get spilt, it really would be rather messy.'

Sir Julian thought for a moment, gazing out through his first floor windows on to Whitehall.

'Good of you to call so promptly, Rupert,' he said. 'I think I'd better inform the PM at once. In the meantime, just as precaution, could you ask a couple of your best minds to put together a memo on the prospective consequences if she does blow up? Question of spillage, area of ocean covered, tide flow, speed, area of our coastline likely to be affected. That sort of thing. I'm pretty sure she'll ask for it.'

'I have it in hand already, old boy.'

'Good,' said Sir Julian, 'excellent. Fast as possible. I suspect she'll want to know. She always does.'

He had worked under three prime ministers, and the latest was far and away the toughest and most decisive. For years it had been a standing joke that the government party was full of old women of both sexes, but fortunately was led by a real man. The name was Mrs Joan Carpenter. The Cabinet secretary had his appointment within minutes and walked through the bright morning sunshine across the lawn to Number 10, with purpose but without hurry, as was his wont.

When he entered the Prime Minister's private office she was at her desk, where she had been since eight o'clock. A coffee set of bone china lay on a side table, and three red despatch boxes lay open on the floor. Sir Julian was admiring; the woman went through documentation like a paper shredder, and the papers were already finished by 10 a.m., either agreed, rejected or bearing a crisp request for further information, or a series of pertinent questions.

'Good morning, Prime Minister.'

'Good morning, Sir Julian, a beautiful day.'

'Indeed, ma'am. Unfortunately it has brought a piece of unpleasantness with it.'

He took a seat at her gesture, and accurately sketched in the details of the affair in the North Sea, as well as he knew them. She was alert, absorptive.

'If it is true, then this ship, the *Freya*, could cause an environmental disaster,' she said flatly.

'Indeed, though we do not know yet the exact feasibility of sinking such a gigantic vessel with what are presumably industrial explosives. There are men who would be able to give an assessment, of course.'

'In the event that it is true,' said the PM, 'I believe we should form a crisis management committee to consider the implications. If it is not, then we have the opportunity for a realistic exercise.'

Sir Julian raised an eyebrow. The idea of putting a thunderflash down the trousers of a dozen ministerial departments as an exercise had not occurred to him. He supposed it had a certain charm.

For thirty minutes the Prime Minister and her Cabinet secretary listed the areas in which they would need professional expertise if they were to be accurately informed of the options in a major tanker hijack in the North Sea.

In the matter of the supertanker herself, she was insured by Lloyd's, who would be in possession of a complete plan of her layout. Concerning the structure of tankers, British Petroleum marine division would have an expert in tanker construction who could study those plans and give a precise judgement on feasibility.

In spillage control, they agreed to call on the senior research analyst at the Warren Springs laboratory, run jointly by the Department of Trade and Industry and the Ministry of

Agriculture, Fisheries and Food, at Stevenage, close to London.

The Ministry of Defence would be called on for a serving officer in the Royal Engineers, an expert in explosives, to estimate that side of things, and the Department of the Environment itself had people who could calculate the scope of the catastrophe to the ecology of the North Sea. Trinity House, head authority of the pilotage services round Britain's coasts, would be asked to inform on tide flows and speeds. Relations and liaison with foreign governments would fall to the Foreign Office, who would send an observer. By ten-thirty the list seemed complete. Sir Julian prepared to leave.

'Do you think the Dutch government will handle this affair?' asked the Prime Minister.

'It's early days to say, ma'am. At the moment the terrorists wish to put their demands to Mr Grayling personally at noon, in ninety minutes. I have no doubt The Hague will feel able to handle the matter. But if the demands cannot be met, or if the ship blows up anyway, then as a coastal nation we are involved in any case.

'Furthermore, our capacity to cope with oil spillage is the most advanced in Europe, so we may be called on to help by our allies across the North Sea.'

'Then the sooner we are ready the better,' said the PM. 'One last thing, Sir Julian. It will probably never come to it, but if the demands cannot be met, the contingency may have to be considered of storming the vessel to liberate the crew and defuse the charges.'

For the first time Sir Julian was not comfortable. He had been a professional civil servant all his life, since leaving Oxford with a Double First. He believed the word, written and spoken, could solve most problems, given time. He abhorred violence.

'Ah, yes, Prime Minister. That would of course be a last resort. I understand it is called "the hard option".'

'The Israelis stormed the airliner at Entebbe,' mused the PM. 'The Germans stormed the one at Mogadishu. The Dutch stormed the train at Assen – when they were left with no alternative. Supposing it were to happen again.'

'Well, ma'am, perhaps they would.'

'Could the Dutch marines carry out such a mission?'

Sir Julian chose his words carefully. He had a vision of burly marines clumping all over Whitehall. Far better to keep those people playing their lethal games well out of the way on Exmoor.

'If it came to storming a vessel at sea,' he said, 'I believe a helicopter landing would not be feasible. It would be spotted by the deck-watch, and of course the ship has a radar scanner. Similarly, an approach by a surface vessel would also be observed. This is not an airliner on a concrete runway, nor a stationary train, ma'am. This is a ship over twenty-five miles from land.'

That, he hoped, would put a stop to it.

'What about an approach by armed divers or frogmen?' she asked.

Sir Julian closed his eyes. Armed frogmen indeed. He was convinced politicians read too many novels for their own good.

'Armed frogmen, Prime Minister?'

The blue eyes across the desk did not leave him. 'I understand,' she said clearly, 'that our capacity in this regard is among the most advanced in Europe.'

'I believe it may well be so, ma'am.'

'And who are these underwater experts?'

'The Special Boat Service, Prime Minister.'

'Who, in Whitehall, liaises with our special services?' she asked.

'There is a Royal Marine colonel in Defence,' he conceded, 'called Holmes.'

It was going to be bad, he could see it coming. They had used the land-based counterpart of the SBS, the better-known Special Air Service or SAS, to help the Germans at Mogadishu, and in the Balcombe Street siege. Harold Wilson had always wanted to hear all the details of the lethal games these roughnecks played with their opponents. Now they were going to start another James Bond-style fantasy.

'Ask Colonel Holmes to attend the crisis management committee, in a consultative capacity only, of course.'

'Of course, ma'am.'

'And prepare the UNICORNE. I shall expect you to take the chair at noon, when the terrorists' demands are known.'

Three hundred miles across the North Sea the activity in Holland was already by mid-morning becoming frenetic.

From his office in the seaside capital of The Hague, the premier Jan Grayling and his staff were putting together the same sort of crisis management committee that Mrs Carpenter in London had in mind. The first requirement was to know the exact perspectives of any conceivable human or environmental tragedy stemming from damage at sea to a ship like the *Freya*, and the various options the Dutch government faced.

To secure this information the same kinds of experts were being called upon for their specialized knowledge: in shipping, oil slicks, tides, speeds, directions, future weather prospects and even the military option.

Dirk van Gelder, having delivered the tape recording of the nine o'clock message from the *Freya*, drove back to Maas Control on the instructions of Jan Grayling to sit by the VHF radio-telephone set in case the *Freya* called up again before twelve noon.

It was he who at 10.30 took the call from Harry Wennerstrom. Having finished breakfast in his penthouse suite at the Rotterdam Hilton, the old shipping magnate was still in ignorance of the disaster to his ship. Quite simply, no one had thought to call him.

Wennerstrom was calling to enquire of the progress of the *Freya* which, by this time, he thought would be well into the Outer Channel, moving slowly and carefully towards the Inner Channel, several miles past Euro Buoy One and moving along a precise course of oh-eight-two and a half degrees. He expected to leave Rotterdam with his convoy of notables to witness the *Freya* coming into sight about lunchtime as the tide rose to peak.

Van Gelder apologized for not having called him at the Hilton, and carefully explained what had happened at 0730 and 0900 hours. There was silence from the Hilton end of the line. Wennerstrom's first reaction could have been to mention that there was $170,000,000 worth of ship being held prisoner out beyond the western horizon, carrying $140,000,000 worth of crude oil. It was a reflection on the man that he said at length:

'There are thirty of my seamen out there, Mr van Gelder. And starting right now let me tell you if anything happens to any one of them because the terrorists' demands are not met, I shall hold the Dutch authorities personally responsible.'

'Mr Wennerstrom,' said van Gelder, who had also commanded a ship in his career, 'we are doing everything we can. The requirements of the terrorists regarding the distance of clear water round the *Freya* are being met, to the letter. Their primary demands have not yet been stated. The Prime Minister is back in his office now in The Hague doing what he can, and he will be back here at noon for the next message from the *Freya*.'

Harry Wennerstrom replaced the handset and stared through the picture windows of the sitting room into the sky towards the west where his dream ship was lying at anchor on the open sea with armed terrorists aboard her.

'Cancel the convoy to Maas Control,' he said suddenly to one of his secretaries. 'Cancel the champagne lunch. Cancel the reception this evening. Cancel the press conference. I'm going.'

'Where, Mr Wennerstrom?' asked the amazed young woman.

'To Maas Control. Alone. Have my car waiting by the time I reach the garage.'

With that the old man stumped from the suite and headed for the lift.

Around the *Freya* the sea was emptying. Working closely with their British colleagues at Flamborough Head and Felixstowe, the Dutch marine traffic control officers diverted shipping into sea lanes west of the *Freya*, the nearest being over five miles west of her.

Eastwards of the stricken ship coastal traffic was ordered to stop or turn back, and movements into and out of Europort and Rotterdam were halted. Angry sea captains, whose voices poured into Maas Control demanding explanation, were simply told that an emergency had arisen and they were to avoid at all costs the sea area whose coordinates were read out to them.

It was impossible to keep the press in the dark. A group of several score journalists from technical and marine publications, as well as the shipping correspondents of the major daily papers from the neighbouring countries, were already in Rotterdam for the reception arranged for the *Freya*'s triumphal entry that afternoon. By 11 a.m. their curiosity was aroused partly by the cancellation of the journey to the Hook to witness the *Freya* come over the horizon into the Inner Channel, and partly by tips reaching their head offices from those numerous radio hams who like to listen to maritime radio talk.

Shortly after eleven calls began to flood in to the penthouse suite of their host, Harry Wennerstrom, but he was not there and his secretaries knew nothing. Other calls came to Maas Control, and were referred to The Hague. In the Dutch capital the switchboard operators put the calls through to the Prime Minister's private press secretary, on Mr Grayling's orders, and the harassed young man fended them off as best he could.

The lack of information simply intrigued the press corps more than ever, so they reported to their editors that something serious was afoot with the *Freya*. The editors despatched other reporters, who foregathered through the morning outside the Maas Control building at the Hook, where they were firmly kept outside the chain-link fence that surrounds the building. Others grouped in The Hague to pester the various ministries, but most of all the Prime Minister's office.

The editor of *De Telegraaf* received a tip from a radio ham that there were terrorists on board the *Freya*, and that they would issue their demands at noon. He at once ordered a radio monitor to be placed on channel twenty with a tape recorder to catch the whole message.

Jan Grayling personally telephoned the West German ambassador, Konrad Voss, and told him in confidence what had happened. Voss called Bonn at once. and within thirty minutes replied to the Dutch premier that he would of course accompany him to the Hook for twelve o'clock as the terrorists had demanded. The Federal German government, he assured the Dutchman, would do everything it could to help.

The Dutch Foreign Ministry as a matter of courtesy informed the ambassadors of all the nations remotely concerned: Sweden, whose flag the *Freya* flew and whose seamen were on board; Norway, Finland and Denmark, who also had seamen on board; the USA, because four of those seamen were Scandinavian-Americans with US passports and dual nationality; Britain, as a coastal nation and whose institution, Lloyd's, was insuring both ship and cargo; and Belgium, France and West Germany, all as coastal nations.

In nine European capitals the telephones rang between ministry and department, from call box to editorial room, in insurance offices, shipping agencies and private homes. For those in government, banking, shipping, insurance, the armed forces and the press, the prospect of a quiet weekend that Friday morning receded into the flat blue ocean where under a warm spring sun a 1,000,000-ton bomb called the *Freya* lay silent and still.

Harry Wennerstrom was halfway from Rotterdam to the Hook when an idea occurred to him. The limousine was passing out of Schiedam on the motorway towards Vlaardingen when he recalled that his private jet was at Schiedam Municipal Airport. He reached for the telephone and called his principal secretary still trying to fend off calls from the press in his suite at the Hilton. When he got through to her at the third attempt he gave her a string of orders for his pilot.

'One last thing,' he said. 'I want the name and office phone number of the police chief of Alesund. Yes, Alesund, in Norway. As soon as you have it, call him up and tell him to stay where he is and await my call back to him.'

Lloyd's Intelligence Unit had been informed shortly after ten o'clock. A British dry-cargo vessel had been preparing to enter the Maas Estuary for Rotterdam when the 0900 call was made from the *Freya* to Maas Control. The radio officer had heard the whole conversation, noted it verbatim in shorthand, and shown it to his captain. Minutes later he was dictating it to the ship's agent in Rotterdam, who passed it to head office in London. The office had called Colchester, Essex, and repeated the news to Lloyd's. One of the chairmen of twenty-five separate firms of underwriters had been contacted and informed. The consortium that had put together the $170,000,000 hull insurance on the *Freya* had to be big; so also was the group of firms covering the 1,000,000-ton cargo for Clint Blake in his office in Texas. But despite the size of the *Freya* and her cargo, the biggest single policy was the Protection and Indemnity insurance, for the persons of the crew and pollution compensation. The P. and I. policy would be the one to cost the biggest money if the *Freya* was blown apart.

Shortly before noon the chairman of Lloyd's, in his office high above the City, stared at a few calculations on his jotting pad.

'We're talking about a thousand million dollars' loss if the worst comes to the worst,' he remarked to his personal aide. 'Who the hell *are* these people?'

The leader of these people sat at the epicentre of the growing storm and faced a bearded Norwegian captain in the day cabin beneath the starboard wing of the *Freya*'s bridge. The curtains were drawn back and the sun shone warmly. From the windows a panoramic view was shown of the silent foredecks, running away a quarter of a mile to the tiny fo'c's'le.

The miniature, shrouded figure of a man sat high on the bow apron above the stem looking out and around him at the glittering blue sea. Either side of the vessel the same blue water lay flat and calm, a mild zephyr ruffling its surface. During the morning that breeze had gently blown away the invisible clouds of poisonous inert gases that had welled out from the holds when the inspection hatches were lifted; it was now safe to walk along the deck, or the man on the fo'c's'le would not be there.

The temperature in the cabin was still stabilized, the air conditioning having taken over from the central heating when the sun became hotter through the double-glazed windows.

Thor Larsen sat where he had sat all morning, at one end of his main table, with Andrew Drake at the other.

Since the argument between the 0900 radio call and 1000 there had been mainly silence between them. The tension of waiting was beginning to make itself felt. Each knew that across the water in both directions frantic preparations would be taking place; firstly to try and estimate exactly what had happened aboard the *Freya* during the night, and secondly to estimate what if anything could be done about it.

Larsen knew no one would do anything, take any initiative, until the noon broadcast of demands. In that sense the intense young man facing him was not stupid. He had elected to keep the authorities guessing. By forcing Larsen to speak in his stead, he had given no clue to his identity nor his origins. Even his motivations were unknown outside the cabin in which they sat. And the authorities would want to know more, to analyse the tapes of the broadcasts, identify the speech patterns and ethnic origins of the speaker, before taking action. The man who called himself Svoboda was denying them that information, undermining the self-confidence of the men he had challenged to defy him.

He was also giving the press ample time to learn of the disaster, but not the terms; letting them evaluate the scale of the catastrophe if the *Freya* blew up, so that their head of steam, their capacity to pressure the authorities, would be well-prepared ahead of the demands. When the demands came, they would appear mild compared to the alternative, thus subjecting the authorities to press pressure before they had considered the demands.

Larsen, who knew what the demands would be, could not see how the authorities would refuse. The alternative was too terrible for all of them. If Svoboda had simply kidnapped a politician, as the Baader-Meinhof people had kidnapped Hans-Martin Schleyer, or the Red Brigade's Aldo Moro, he might have been refused his friends' release. But he had elected to destroy five coasts, one sea, thirty lives and a thousand million dollars of money.

'Why are these two men so important to you?' asked Larsen suddenly.

The younger man stared back.

'They're friends,' he said.

'No,' said Larsen. 'I recall from last January reading that they were two Jews from Lvov who had been refused permission to emigrate, so they hijacked a Russian airliner and forced it to land in West Berlin. How does that produce your popular uprising?'

'Never mind,' said his captor. 'It is five to twelve. We return to the bridge.'

Nothing had changed on the bridge, except that there was an extra terrorist there, curled up asleep in the corner, his gun still clutched in his hand. He was masked, like the one who patrolled the radar and sonar screens. Svoboda asked the man something in the language Larsen now knew to be Ukrainian. The man shook his head and replied in the same language. At a word from Svoboda the masked man turned his gun on Larsen.

Svoboda walked over to the scanners and read them. There was a peripheral ring of clear water round the *Freya* at least to five miles on the western, southern and northern side. To the east the sea was clear to the Dutch coast. He strode out through the door leading to the bridge-wing, turned and called upwards. From high above, Larsen heard the man on top of the funnel assembly shout back.

Svoboda returned to the bridge. 'Come,' he said to the captain, 'your audience is waiting. One attempt at a trick, and I shoot one of your seamen, as promised.'

Larsen took the handset of the radio-telephone and pressed for transmit.

'Maas Control, Maas Control, this is the *Freya*.'

Though he could not know it, over fifty different offices received that call. Five major intelligence services were listening, plucking channel twenty out of the ether with their sophisticated listeners. The words were heard and relayed simultaneously to the National Security Agency in Washington, to the SIS, the French SDECE, the West German BND, the Soviet Union and the various services of Holland, Belgium and Sweden. There were ships' radio officers listening, radio hams and journalists.

A voice came back from the Hook of Holland. '*Freya*, this is Maas Control. Go ahead, please.'

Thor Larsen read from his sheet of paper. 'This is Captain Thor Larsen. I wish to speak personally to the Prime Minister of the Netherlands.'

A new voice, speaking English, came on the radio from the Hook.

'Captain Larsen, this is Jan Grayling. I am the Prime Minister of the Kingdom of the Netherlands. Are you all right?'

In the *Freya* Svoboda clapped his hand over the mouthpiece of the telephone.

'No questions,' he said to Larsen. 'Just ask if the West German ambassador is present, and get his name.'

'Please ask no questions, Prime Minister. I am not permitted to answer them. Is the West German ambassador with you?'

In Maas Control the microphone was passed to Konrad Voss.

'Here is the ambassador of the Federal Republic of Germany,' he said. 'My name is Konrad Voss.'

On the bridge of the *Freya* Svoboda nodded at Larsen.

'That's right,' he said, 'go ahead and read it out.'

The seven men grouped around the console in Maas Control listened in silence. One premier, one ambassador, one psychiatrist, a radio engineer in case of a transmission breakdown, van Gelder of the Port Authority and the duty officer. All other shipping traffic had now been diverted to a spare channel. The two tape recorders whirled silently. Volume was switched high; Thor Larsen's voice echoed in the room.

'I repeat what I told you at nine this morning. The *Freya* is in the hands of partisans. Explosive devices have been placed which would, if detonated, blow her apart. These devices can be detonated at the touch of a button. I repeat, at the touch of a button. No attempt whatever must be made to approach her, board her or attack her in any way. In such an event the detonator button will be pressed instantly. The men concerned have convinced me they are prepared to die rather than give in.

'I continue: if any approach at all is made, by surface craft or light aircraft, one of my seamen will be executed, or twenty thousand tons of crude oil vented, or both. Here are the demands of the partisans:

'The two prisoners of conscience, David Lazareff and Lev Mishkin, presently in jail at Tegel in West Berlin, are to be liberated. They are to be flown by a West German civilian jet from West Berlin to Israel. Prior to this, the premier of the State of Israel is to give a public guarantee that they will be neither repatriated to the Soviet Union, nor extradited back to West Germany, nor re-imprisoned in Israel.

'Their liberation must take place at dawn tomorrow. The Israeli guarantee of safe conduct and freedom must be given by midnight tonight. Failure to comply will place the entire responsibility for the outcome on the shoulders of West Germany and Israel. That is all. There will be no more contact until the demands have been met.'

The radio-telephone went dead with a click. The silence persisted inside the control building. Jan Grayling looked at Konrad Voss. The West German envoy shrugged.

'I must contact Bonn urgently,' he said.

'I can tell you that Captain Larsen is under some strain,' said the psychiatrist.

'Thank you very much,' said Grayling. 'So am I. Gentlemen, what has just been said cannot fail to be made public within the hour. I suggest we return to our offices. I shall prepare a statement for the one o'clock news. Mr Ambassador, I fear the pressure will now begin to swing towards Bonn.'

'Indeed it will,' said Voss. 'I must be back inside the embassy as soon as possible.'

'Then accompany me to The Hague,' said Grayling. 'I have police outriders, and we can talk in the car.'

Aides brought the two tapes, and the group left for The Hague, fifteen minutes up the coast. When they were gone Dirk van Gelder walked up to the flat roof where Harry Wennerstrom would have held his lunch by Gelder's permission, the other guests looking eagerly to seaward, as they supped champagne and salmon sandwiches, to catch the first glimpse of the leviathan.

Now perhaps she would never come, thought van Gelder, staring out at the blue water. He too had his master's ticket, a Dutch merchant navy captain until he was offered the shore job with the promise of a regular life with his wife and children. As a seaman he thought of the *Freya*'s crew, locked far beneath the waves, waiting helplessly for rescue or death. But as a seaman he would not be in charge of negotiations. It was out of his hands now. Smoother men, calculating in political rather than human terms, would take over.

He thought of the towering Norwegian skipper he had never met but whose picture he had seen, now facing madmen armed with guns and dynamite, and wondered how he would have reacted had it ever happened to him. He had warned that this could happen one day, that the supertankers were too unprotected and highly dangerous. But the money had spoken louder; the more powerful argument had been the extra cost of installing the necessary devices to make tankers like banks and explosive stores, both of which in a way they were. No one had listened, and no one ever would. People were concerned about airliners because they could crash on houses; but not about tankers which were out of sight. So the politicians had not insisted, and the merchants had not volunteered. Now, because supertankers could be taken like piggy-banks, a captain and his crew of twenty-nine might die like rats in a swirl of oil and water.

He ground a cigarette under his heel into the tar-felt of the roof, and looked again at the empty horizon.

'You poor bastards,' he said, 'you poor bloody bastards. If only they'd listened.'

13

1300 to 1900

If the reaction of the media to the 0900 transmission had been muted and speculative, due to the uncertainty of the reliability of their informants, the reaction to the 1200 broadcast was frantic.

From 1200 onwards there was no doubt whatever what had happened to the *Freya*, nor what had been said by Captain Larsen on his radio-telephone to Maas Control. Too many people had been listening.

Banner headlines that had been available for the noon editions of the evening papers, prepared at 1000 hours, were swept away. Those that went to press at 1230 were stronger in tone and size. There were no more question marks at the end of sentences. Editorial columns were hastily prepared, specialist correspondents in matters of shipping and the environment required to produce instant assessments within the hour.

Radio and television programmes were interrupted throughout Europe's Friday lunch-hour to beam the news to listeners and viewers.

On the dot of five past twelve a man in a motorcyclist's helmet, with goggles and scarf drawn round the lower part of the face, had walked calmly into the lobby of 85 Fleet Street, and deposited an envelope addressed to the news editor of the Press Association. No one later recalled the man; dozens of such messengers walk into that lobby every day.

By twelve-fifteen the news editor was opening the envelope.

It contained the transcript of the statement read by Captain Larsen fifteen minutes earlier, though it must have been prepared well before that. The news editor reported the delivery to his editor-in-chief who told the metropolitan police. That did not stop the text going straight on to the wires, both of the PA and their cousins downstairs, Reuters, who put the text across the world.

Leaving Fleet Street, Miroslav Kaminsky dumped his helmet, goggles and scarf in a dustbin, took a taxi to Heathrow Airport and boarded the 1415 plane for Tel Aviv.

By two o'clock the editorial pressure on both the Dutch and West German governments was beginning to build up. Neither had had any time to consider in peace and quiet the reactions they should make to the demands. Both governments began to receive a flood of phone calls urging them to agree to release Mishkin and Lazareff rather than face the disaster promised by the destruction of the *Freya* off their coasts.

By one o'clock the German ambassador to The Hague was speaking directly to his foreign minister in Bonn, Klaus Hagowitz, who interrupted the Chancellor at his desk-lunch. The text of the 1200 broadcast was already in Bonn, once from the BND intelligence service and once on the Reuters teleprinter. Every newspaper office in Germany also had the text from Reuters, and the telephone lines to the chancellery press office were jammed with calls.

At one forty-five the chancellery put out a statement to the effect that an emergency Cabinet meeting had been called for three o'clock to consider the entire situation. Ministers cancelled their plans to leave Bonn at the weekend for their constituencies. Lunches were ill-digested.

The governor of Tegel Jail put down his telephone at two minutes past two with a certain deference. It was not often the federal justice minister cut clean through the protocol of communicating with the governing mayor of West Berlin and called him personally.

He picked up the internal phone and gave an order to his secretary. Doubtless the Berlin senate would be in contact in due course with the same request, but so long as the governing mayor was out of touch at lunch somewhere, he would not refuse the minister from Bonn.

Three minutes later one of his senior prison officers entered the office.

'Have you heard the two o'clock news?' asked the governor.

It was only five past two. The officer pointed out that he had been on his rounds when the bleeper in his breast pocket buzzed, requiring him to go straight to a wall-phone and check in. No, he had not heard the news. The governor told him of the noon demand of the terrorists on board the *Freya*. The officer's jaw dropped open.

'One for the book, isn't it?' said the governor. 'It looks as if we shall be in the news within minutes. So, batten down hatches. I've given orders to main gate: no admissions by anyone other than staff. All press enquiries to the authorities at City Hall.

'Now, as regards Mishkin and Lazareff. I want the guard on that floor and particularly in that corridor trebled. Cancel free periods to raise enough staff. Transfer all other prisoners in that corridor to other cells or other levels. Seal the place. A group of intelligence people are flying in from Bonn to ask them who their friends in the North Sea are. Any questions?'

The prison officer swallowed and shook his head.

'Now,' resumed the governor, 'we don't know how long this emergency will last. When were you due off duty?'

'Six o'clock tonight, sir.'

'Returning on Monday morning at eight?'

'No, sir. On Sunday night at midnight. I go on night-shift next week.'

'I'll have to ask you to work right on through,' said the governor. 'Of course, we'll make up the free time to you later with a generous bonus. But I'd like you right on top of the job from here on. Agreed?'

'Yes, sir. Whatever you say. I'll get on with it now.'

The governor, who liked to adopt a comradely attitude with his staff, came around the desk and clapped the man on the shoulder.

'You're a good fellow, Jahn. I don't know what we'd do without you.'

Squadron Leader Mark Latham stared down the runway, heard his take-off clearance from the control tower and nodded to his co-pilot. The younger man's gloved hand eased the four throttles slowly open; in the wing-roots four Rolls-Royce Spey engines rose in pitch to push out 45,000 pounds of thrust and the Nimrod Mark Two climbed away from RAF station Kinloss and turned southeast from Scotland towards the North Sea and the Channel.

What the thirty-one-year-old squadron leader of Coastal Command was flying he knew to be about the best aircraft for submarine and shipping surveillance in the world. With its crew of twelve, improved power plants, performance and surveillance aids, the Nimrod could either skim the waves at low level, slow and steady, listening on electronic ears to the sounds of underwater movement, or cruise at altitude, hour after hour, two engines shut down for fuel economy, observing an enormous area of ocean beneath it.

Its radars would pick up the slightest movement of a metallic substance down there on the water's surface, its cameras could photograph by day and night; it was unaffected by storm or snow, hail or sleet, fog or wind, light or dark. Its Datalink computers could process the received information, identify what it saw for what it was, and transmit the whole picture, in visual or electronic terms, back to base or to a Royal Navy vessel tapped in to Datalink.

His orders, that sunny spring Friday, were to take up station 15,000 feet above the *Freya* and keep circling until relieved.

'She's coming on screen, skipper,' Latham's radar operator called down the intercom. Back in the hull of the Nimrod the operator was gazing at his scanner screen, picking out the area of traffic-free water round the *Freya* on its northern side, watching the large blip move from the periphery towards the centre of the screen as they approached.

'Cameras on,' said Latham calmly. In the belly of the Nimrod the F.126 daytime camera swivelled like a gun, spotted the *Freya* and locked on. Automatically it adjusted range and focus for maximum definition. Like moles in their blind hull, the crew behind him saw the *Freya* come on to their picture screen. From now on the aircraft could fly all over the sky, the cameras would stay locked on the *Freya*, adjusting for distance and light-changes, swivelling in their housings to compensate for the circling of the Nimrod. Even if the *Freya* began to move, they would still stay on her, like an unblinking eye, until given fresh orders.

'And transmit,' said Latham.

The Datalink began to send the pictures back to Britain, and thence to London. When the Nimrod was overhead the *Freya* she banked to port, and from his left-hand seat S/L Latham looked down visually. Behind and below him the camera zoomed closer, beating the human eye. It picked out the lone figure of the terrorist in the forepeak, masked face staring upwards at the silver swallow three miles above him. It picked out the second terrorist on top of the funnel, and zoomed until his black balaclava filled the screen. The man cradled a submachine carbine in his arms in the sunshine far below.

'There they are, the bastards,' called the camera operator. The Nimrod established a gentle, rate one turn above the *Freya*, went over the automatic pilot, closed down two engines, reduced power to maximum endurance setting on the other two and began to do its job. It circled, watched and waited, reporting everything back to base. Mark Latham ordered his co-pilot to take over, unbuckled and left the flight deck. He went aft to the four-man dining area, visited the toilet, washed his hands and sat down with a vacuum-heated lunch box. It was, he reflected, really rather a comfortable way to go to war.

The gleaming Volvo of the police chief of Alesund ground up the gravel drive of the timber-construction, ranch-style house at Bogneset, twenty minutes out from the town centre, and halted by the rough-stone porch.

Trygve Dahl was a contemporary of Thor Larsen. They had grown up together in Alesund, and Dahl had entered the force as a police cadet about the time Larsen had joined the merchant marine. He had known Lisa Larsen since his friend had brought the young bride back from Oslo after their marriage. His own children knew Kurt and Kristina, played with them at school, sailed with them in the long summer holidays.

Damn it, he thought as he climbed out of the Volvo, what the hell do I tell her?

There had been no reply on the telephone, which meant she must be out. The children would be at school. If she was shopping, perhaps she had met someone who had told her already. He rang the bell and, when it did not answer, walked round to the back.

Lisa Larsen liked to keep a large vegetable garden, and he found her feeding carrot tops to Kristina's pet rabbit. She looked up and smiled when she saw him coming round the house.

She doesn't know, he thought. She pushed the remainder of the carrots through the wire of the cage and came over to him, pulling off her garden gloves.

'Trygve, how nice to see you. What brings you out of town?'

'Lisa, have you listened to the news this morning on the radio?'

She considered the question.

'I listened to the eight o'clock over breakfast. I've been out here since then, in the garden.'

'You didn't answer the telephone?'

For the first time a shadow came into her bright brown eyes. The smile faded.

'No. I wouldn't hear it. Has it been ringing?'

'Look, Lisa, be calm. Something has happened. No, not to the children. To Thor.'

She went pale beneath the honey-coloured outdoor tan. Carefully, Trygve Dahl told her what had happened since the small hours of the morning, far to the south off Rotterdam.

'So far as we know, he's perfectly all right. Nothing has happened to him, and nothing will. The Germans are bound to release these two men, and all will be well.'

She did not cry. She stood quite calmly amid the spring lettuce and said, 'I want to go to him.'

The police chief was relieved. He could have expected it of her, but he was relieved. Now he could organize things. He was better at that.

'Harald Wennerstrom's private jet is due at the airport in twenty minutes,' he said. 'I'll run you there. He called me an hour ago. He thought you might want to go to Rotterdam, to be close. Now don't worry about the children. I'm having them picked up from school before they hear from the teachers. We'll look after them; they can stay with us, of course.'

Twenty minutes later she was in the rear seat of the car with Dahl, heading fast back towards Alesund. The police chief used his radio to hold the ferry across to the airfield. Just after one-thirty the Jetstream in the silver and ice-blue livery of the Nordia Line howled down the runway, swept out over the waters of the bay and climbed towards the south.

Since the sixties and particularly through the seventies the growing outbreaks of terrorism caused the formation of a routine procedure on the part of the British government to facilitate the handling of them. The principal procedure is called the crisis management committee.

When the crisis is serious enough to involve numerous departments and sections, the committee, grouping liaison officers from all these departments, meets at a central point close to the heart of government to pool information and correlate decisions and actions. This central point is a well-protected chamber two floors below the parquet of the Cabinet Office on Whitehall and a few steps across the lawn from 10 Downing Street. In this room meets the United Cabinet Office Review Group (National Emergency), or UNICORNE.

Surrounding the main meeting room are smaller offices; a separate telephone switchboard, linking the Unicorne with every department of state through direct lines that cannot be interfered with; a teleprinter room fitted with the printers of the main news agencies; a telex room and radio room; and a room for secretaries with typewriters and copiers. There is even a small kitchen where a trusty commissionaire prepares coffee and light snacks.

The men who grouped under the chairmanship of Cabinet Secretary Sir Julian Flannery just after noon that Friday represented all the departments he adjudged might conceivably be involved.

At this stage no cabinet ministers were present, though each had sent a representative of at least assistant undersecretary level. These included the Foreign Office, Home Office, Defence Ministry, Department of Trade and Industry, Departments of the Environment, and of Energy, and the Ministry of Agriculture and Fisheries.

Assisting them were a bevy of specialist experts, including three scientists in various disciplines, notably explosives, ships and pollution; the vice-chief of defence staff (a vice-admiral), someone from Defence Intelligence, from MI5, from the SIS, a Royal Air Force group captain, and a senior Royal Marine colonel called Tim Holmes.

'Well now, gentlemen,' Sir Julian Flannery began, 'we have all had time to read the transcript of the noon broadcast from Captain Larsen. First I think we ought to have a few indisputable facts. May we begin with this ship, the ... er ... *Freya*. What do we know about her?'

The shipping expert, coming under the Trade and Industry people, found all eyes on him.

'I've been to Lloyd's this morning and secured the plan of the *Freya*,' he said briefly. 'I have it here. It's detailed down to the last nut and bolt.'

He went on for ten minutes, the plan spread on the table,

describing the size, cargo capacity and construction of the *Freya* in clear, layman's language.

When he had finished the expert from the Department of Energy was called on. He had an aide bring to the table a five-foot-long model of a supertanker.

'I borrowed this, this morning,' he said, 'from British Petroleum. It's a model of their supertanker the British *Princess*, quarter of a million tons, but the design differences are few; the *Freya* is just bigger, really.'

With the aid of the model of the *Princess* he went on to point out where the bridge was, where the captain's cabin would be, where the cargo holds and ballast holds would probably be, adding that the exact locations of these holds would be known when the Nordia Line could pass them over to London.

The surrounding men watched the demonstration and listened with attention. None more than Colonel Holmes; of all those present he would be the one whose fellow marines might have to storm the vessel and wipe out her captors. He knew those men would want to know every nook and cranny of the real *Freya* before they went on board.

'There is one last thing,' said the scientist from Energy, 'she's full of Mubarraq.'

'God,' said one of the other men at the table. Sir Julian Flannery regarded the speaker benignly.

'Yes, Dr Henderson?'

The man who had spoken was the scientist from Warren Springs Laboratory who had accompanied the representative of Agriculture and Fisheries.

'What I mean,' said the doctor in his unrecycled Scottish accent, 'is that Mubarraq, which is a crude oil from Abu Dhabi, has some of the properties of diesel fuel.'

He went on to explain that when crude oil is spilled on the sea, it contains both the 'lighter fractions' which evaporate into the air, and the 'heavier fractions' which cannot evaporate and which are what viewers see washed on to the beaches as thick black gunge.

'What I mean is,' he concluded, 'it'll spread all over the

bloody place. It'll spread from coast to coast before the lighter fractions evaporate. It'll poison the whole North Sea for weeks denying the marine life the oxygen it needs to live.'

'I see,' said Sir Julian gravely. 'Thank you, doctor.'

There followed information from other experts. The explosives man from Royal Engineers explained that, placed in the right areas, industrial dynamite could destroy a ship this size.

'It's also a question of the sheer latent strength contained in the weight represented by a million tons, of oil or anything. If the holes are made in the right places, the unbalanced mass of her would pull her apart. There's one last thing; the message read out by Captain Larsen mentioned the phrase "at the touch of a button". He then repeated that phrase. It seems to me there must be nearly a dozen charges placed. That phrase "the touch of a button" seems to indicate triggering by radio impulse.'

'Is that possible?' asked Sir Julian.

'Perfectly possible,' said the sapper, and explained how an oscillator worked.

'Surely, they could have wires to each charge, linked to a plunger,' asked Sir Julian.

'It's a question of the weight again,' said the engineer. 'The wires would have to be waterproof, plastic-coated. The weight of that number of miles of flex would nearly sink the launch on which these terrorists arrived.'

There was more information about the destructive capacity of the oil by pollution, the few chances of rescuing the trapped crewmen, and SIS admitted they had no information that might help identify the terrorists from among foreign groups of such people.

The man from MI5 who was actually the deputy chief of C-4 department within that body, the section dealing exclusively with terrorism as it affected Britain, underlined the strange nature of the demands of the captors of the *Freya*.

'These men, Mishkin and Lazareff,' he pointed out, 'are Jewish. Hijackers who tried to escape from the USSR and ended up shooting a flight captain. One has to assume that those seeking to free them are their friends or admirers. That tends to indicate fellow-Jews. The only ones who fit into that category are those of the Jewish Defense League. But so far they just demonstrate and throw things. In our files we haven't had Jews threatening to blow people to pieces to free their friends since the Irgun and the Stern Gang.'

'Oh dear, one hopes they don't start that again,' observed Sir Julian. 'If not them, then who else?'

The man from C-4 shrugged.

'We don't know,' he admitted. 'We can notice no one on our files conspicuous by being missing, nor do we have a trace from what Captain Larsen has broadcast to indicate their origins. This morning I thought of Arabs, even Irish. But neither would lift a finger for imprisoned Jews. It's a blank wall.'

Still photographs were brought in, taken by the Nimrod an hour earlier, some showing the masked men on the lookout. They were keenly examined.

'MAT 49,' said Colonel Holmes briefly, studying the submachine gun one of the men cradled in his arms. 'It's French.'

'Ah,' said Sir Julian, 'now perhaps we have something. These blighters could be French?'

'Not necessarily,' said Holmes. 'You can buy these things in the underworld. The Paris underworld is famous for its taste for submachine guns.'

At three-thirty Sir Julian Flannery brought the meeting into recess. It was agreed to keep the Nimrod circling above the *Freya* until further notice. The vice-chief of defence staff put forward and had accepted his proposal to divert a naval warship to take up station just over five miles west of the *Freya* to watch her also in case of an attempt by the terrorists to leave under cover of darkness. The Nimrod would spot them, and pass their position to the navy. The warship would easily overhaul the fishing launch still tied by the *Freya*'s side.

The Foreign Office agreed to ask to be informed of any decision by West Germany and Israel on the terrorists' demands.

'There does not, after all, appear much that Her Majesty's government can do at the present moment,' Sir Julian pointed out. 'The decision is up to the Israeli Prime Minister and the West German Chancellor. Personally I cannot see what else they can do, except to let these wretched young men go to Israel, repugnant though the idea of yielding to blackmail must be.'

When the men left the room only Colonel Holmes of the marines stayed behind. He sat down again and stared at the model of the quarter-million ton British Petroleum tanker in front of him.

Supposing they don't; he said to himself.

Carefully he began to measure the distance in feet from the sea to the stern taffrail.

The Swedish pilot of the Jetstream was at 15,000 feet off the Friesian Islands, preparing to let down into Schiedam Airfield outside Rotterdam. He turned round and called something to the petite woman who was his passenger. She unbuckled and came forward to where he sat.

'I asked if you wanted to see the *Freya*,' the pilot repeated. The woman nodded.

The Jetstream banked away to the sea and five minutes later tilted gently on to one wing. From her seat, face pressed to the tiny porthole, Lisa Larsen looked down. Far below, in a blue sea, like a grey sardine nailed to the water, the *Freya* lay at anchor. There were no ships around her; she was quite alone in her captivity.

Even from 15,000 feet, through the clear spring air, Lisa Larsen could make out where the bridge would be, where the starboard side of that bridge was; below it she knew her husband was facing a man with a gun pointed straight at his chest, with dynamite beneath his feet. She did not know whether the man with the gun was mad, brutal or reckless. That he must be a fanatic she knew.

Two tears welled out of her eyes and ran down her cheeks. When she whispered her breath misted the perspex disc in front of her.

'Thor, my darling, please come out of there alive.'

The Jetstream banked again and began its long drop towards Schiedam. The Nimrod, miles away across the sky, watched it go.

'Who was that?' asked the radar operator of no one in particular.

'Who was what?' replied a sonar operator, having nothing to do.

'Small executive jet just banked over the *Freya*, had a look and went off to Rotterdam,' said the radar man.

'Probably the owner checking on his property,' said the crew's wit from the radio console.

On the *Freya* the two lookouts gazed through eye-slits after the tiny sliver of metal high above as it headed east towards the Dutch coast. They did not report it to their leader; it was well above 10,000 feet.

The West German Cabinet meeting began just after 3 p.m. in the Chancellery Office, with Dietrich Busch in the chair as usual. He went straight to the point as he had a habit of doing.

'Let's be clear of one thing: this is not Mogadishu all over again. This time we do not have a German plane with a German crew and mainly German passengers on an airstrip whose authorities were prepared to be collaborative towards us. This is a Swedish vessel with a Norwegian captain in international waters; she has crewmen from five countries including the US, an American-owned cargo insured by a British company, and her destruction would affect at least five coastal nations, including ourselves. Foreign minister?'

Hagowitz informed his colleagues he had already received polite queries from Finland, Norway, Sweden, Denmark, Holland, Belgium, France and Britain regarding the kind of decision the Federal government might come to. After all, they held Mishkin and Lazareff.

'They are being courteous enough not to exert any pressure

to influence our decision, but I have no doubt they would view a refusal on our part to send Mishkin and Lazareff to Israel with the deepest misgivings,' he said.

'Once you start giving in to this terrorist blackmail it never ends,' put in the defence minister.

'Dietrich, we gave in over the Peter Lorenz affair years ago and paid for it. The very terrorists we freed came back and operated again. We stood up to them over Mogadishu and won; we stood up again over Schleyer and had a corpse on our hands. But at least those were pretty well all-German affairs. This isn't. The lives at stake aren't German; the property isn't German. Moreover, the hijackers in Berlin aren't from a German terrorist group. They're Jews who tried to get away from Russia the only way they knew how. Frankly, it puts us in the devil of a spot,' Hagowitz concluded.

'Any chance that it's a bluff, a confidence trick; that they really can't destroy the *Freya* or kill her crew?' someone asked.

The interior minister shook his head.

'We can't bank on that. These pictures the British have just transmitted to us show the armed and masked men are real enough. I've sent them along to the leader of GSG 9 to see what he thinks. But the trouble is, approaching a ship with all-round, over-and-under radar and sonar cover is not their area of expertise. It would mean divers or frogmen.'

He was referring by GSG 9 to the ultra-tough unit of West German commandos drawn from the border troops who stormed the hijacked aircraft at Mogadishu five years earlier.

The argument continued for an hour: whether to concede the terrorists' demands in view of the internationality of the probable victims of a refusal, and accept the inevitable protests from Moscow; or whether to refuse and call their bluff; or whether to consult with the British allies about the idea of storming the *Freya*. A compromise view of adopting delaying tactics, stalling for time, testing the determination of the *Freya*'s captors, seemed to be gaining ground. At four-fifteen there was a quiet knock on the door. Chancellor Busch frowned; he did not like interruptions.

'*Herein*,' he called. An aide entered the room and whispered urgently in the chancellor's ear. The head of the Federal government paled.

'*Du lieber Gott*,' he breathed.

When the light aircraft, later traced as a privately owned Cessna on charter from Le Touquet Airfield on the northern French coast, began to approach, she was spotted by three different air traffic control zones, at Heathrow, Brussels and Amsterdam. She was flying due north, and the radars put her at 5000 feet, on track for the *Freya*. The ether began to crackle furiously.

'Unidentified light aircraft at position ... identify yourself and turn back. You are entering a prohibited area....'

French and English was used, later Dutch. It had no effect. Either the pilot had switched off his radio or was on the wrong channel. The operators on the ground began to sweep through the wave bands.

The circling Nimrod picked the aircraft up on radar and tried to contact her.

On board the Cessna the pilot turned to his passenger in despair.

'They'll have my licence,' he yelled. 'They're going mad down there.'

'Switch off,' the passenger shouted back. 'Don't worry, nothing will happen. You never heard them, OK?'

The passenger gripped his camera and adjusted the telephoto lens. He began to sight up on the approaching supertanker. In the forepeak, the masked lookout stiffened and squinted against the sun, now in the southwest. The plane was coming from due south. After watching for several seconds he took a walkie-talkie from his anorak and spoke sharply into it.

On the bridge one of his colleagues heard the message, peered forward through the panoramic screen, and walked hurriedly outside on to the wing. Here he too could hear the engine note. He re-entered the bridge and shook his sleeping colleague awake, snapping several orders in Ukrainian. The man ran downstairs to the door of the day cabin and knocked.

Inside the cabin, Thor Larsen and Andriy Drach, both looking unshaven and more haggard than twelve hours earlier, were still at the table, the gun by the Ukrainian's right hand. A foot away from him was his powerful transistor radio, picking up the latest news. The masked man entered on his command and spoke in Ukrainian. His leader scowled and ordered the man to take over in the cabin.

Drake left the cabin quickly, raced up to the bridge and out on to the wing. As he did so he pulled on his black mask. From the bridge he gazed up as the Cessna, banking at 1000 feet, performed one orbit of the *Freya* and flew back to the south, climbing steadily. While it turned he had seen the great zoom lens poking down at him.

Inside the aircraft, the freelance cameraman was exultant.

'Fantastic,' he shouted at the pilot. 'Completely exclusive. The magazines will pay their right arms for this.'

Andriy Drach returned to the bridge and issued a rapid stream of orders. Over the walkie-talkie he told the man up front to continue his watch. The bridge lookout was sent below to summon two men who were catching sleep. When all three returned he gave them further instructions. When he returned to the day cabin, he did not dismiss the extra guard.

'I think it's time I told those stupid bastards over there in Europe that I am not joking,' he told Thor Larsen.

Five minutes later the camera operator on the Nimrod called over the intercom to his captain.

'There's something happening down there, skipper.'

Squadron Leader Latham left the flight deck and walked back to the centre section of the hull where the visual image of what the cameras were photographing was on display. Two men were walking down the deck of the *Freya*, the great wall of superstructure behind them, the long lonely deck ahead. One of the men, the one at the rear, was in black from head to foot, with a submachine gun. The one ahead wore sneakers, casual slacks and a nylon-type anorak with three horizontal black stripes across its back. The hood was up against the chill afternoon breeze.

'Looks like a terrorist at the back, but a seaman in front,' said the camera operator. Latham nodded. He could not see the colours; his pictures were monochrome.

'Give me a closer look,' he said, 'and transmit.'

The camera zoomed down until the frame occupied forty feet of foredeck, both men walking in the centre of the picture.

Captain Thor Larsen could see the colours. He gazed through the wide forward windows of his cabin beneath the bridge in disbelief. Behind him the guard with the machine gun stood well back, muzzle trained in the middle of the Norwegian's white sweater.

Halfway down the foredeck, reduced by distance to matchstick figures, the second man, in black, stopped, raised his machine gun and aimed at the back in front of him. Even through the glazing the crackle of the one-second burst could be heard. The figure in the pillar-box red anorak arched as if kicked in the spine, threw up its arms, pitched forward, rolled once and came to rest half-obscured beneath the inspection catwalk.

Thor Larsen slowly closed his eyes. When the ship had been taken over, his third mate, Danish-American Tom Keller, had been wearing fawn slacks and a light nylon windbreaker in bright red with three black stripes across the back. Larsen leaned his forehead against the back of his hand on the glass. Then he straightened, turned to the man he knew as Svoboda, and stared at him.

Andriy Drach stared back.

'I warned them,' he said angrily. 'I told them exactly what would happen, and they thought they could play games. Now they know they can't.'

Twenty minutes later the still pictures showing the sequence of what had happened on the deck of the *Freya* were coming out of a machine in the heart of London. Twenty minutes after that, the details in verbal terms were rattling off a teleprinter in the Federal Chancellery in Bonn. It was 4.30 p.m.

Chancellor Busch looked at his cabinet.

'I regret to have to inform you,' he said, 'that one hour ago a private plane apparently sought to take pictures of the *Freya* from close range, about a thousand feet. Ten minutes later the terrorists walked one of the crew halfway down the deck and, under the cameras of the British Nimrod above them, executed him. His body now lies half under the catwalk, half under the sky.'

There was dead silence in the room.

'Can he be identified?' asked one of the ministers in a low voice.

'No, his face was mainly covered by the hood of his anorak.'

'Bastards,' said the defence minister. 'Now thirty families all over Scandinavia will be in anguish instead of one. They're really turning the knife.'

'In the wake of this, so will the four governments of Scandinavia, and I shall have to answer their ambassadors,' said Hagowitz. 'I really don't think we have any alternative.'

When the hands were raised, they were in majority for Hagowitz's proposal: that he instruct the German ambassador to Israel to seek an urgent interview with the Israeli premier and ask from him, at Germany's request, the guarantee the terrorists had demanded. Following which, if it was given, the Federal government would announce that with regret it had no alternative, in order to spare further misery to innocent men and women outside West Germany, but to release Mishkin and Lazareff to Israel.

'The terrorists have given the Israeli premier until midnight to offer that guarantee,' said Chancellor Busch. 'And ourselves until dawn to put these hijackers on a plane. We'll hold our announcement until Jerusalem agrees. Without that, there is nothing we can do anyway.'

At 5 p.m. the lookouts were changed. The men from the

fo'c's'le and funnel top, who had been there for ten hours, were allowed to return chilled and stiff to the accommodation for food, warmth and sleep. For the night-watch, they were replaced by others equipped with walkie-talkies and powerful torches.

By agreement between the NATO allies concerned, the RAF Nimrod remained the only aircraft in the sky above the *Freya*, circling endlessly, watching and noting, sending pictures back to base whenever there was anything to show; pictures which immediately went to London and to the capital of the relevant country.

The allied agreement on the Nimrod did not extend to surface ships. Each coastal nation wanted an on-site observer from its own navy. During the late afternoon the French light cruiser *Montcalm* stole quietly out of the south and hove-to just over five nautical miles from the *Freya*. Out of the north, where she had been cruising off the Friesians, came the Dutch missile frigate *Breda*, who stopped six nautical miles to the north of the helpless tanker. She was joined by the German missile frigate *Brunner*, and the frigates lay five cable lengths away from each other, both watching the dim shape on the southern horizon.

From the Scottish port of Leith where she had been on a courtesy visit the HMS *Argyll* put to sea, and as the first evening star appeared in the cloudless sky she took up her station due west of the *Freya*. She was a guided-missile light cruiser, known as a DLG, of just under 6000 tons, armed with batteries of Exocet missiles. Her modern gas turbine and steam engines had enabled her to put to sea at a moment's notice, and deep in her hull the Datalink computer she carried was tapped in to the Datalink of the Nimrod circling 15,000 feet above in the darkening sky. Towards her stern, one step up from the after deck, she carried her own Westland Wessex helicopter.

Beneath the water, the sonar ears of the warships surrounded the *Freya* on three sides; above the water the radar scanners swept the ocean constantly. With the Nimrod above, *Freya* was cocooned in an invisible shroud of electronic surveillance. She lay silent and inert as the sun prepared to fall over the English coast.

It was five o'clock in western Europe but seven in Israel when the West German ambassador asked for a personal audience with Premier Benyamin Golen. It was pointed out to him at once that the Sabbath had started one hour before and that, as a devout Jew, the premier was at rest in his own home. Nevertheless the message was relayed, because neither the Prime Minister's private office nor he himself was unaware of what was happening in the North Sea. Indeed, since the 0900 broadcast from Thor Larsen the Israeli intelligence service, Mossad, had been keeping Jerusalem informed, and following the demands made at noon concerning Israel the most copious position papers had been prepared. Before the official start of Sabbath at six o'clock, Premier Golen had read them all.

'I am not prepared to break *Shabbat* and drive to the office,' he told his aide, who telephoned him with the news, 'even though I am now answering this telephone. And it is rather a long way to walk. Ask the ambassador to call on me personally.'

Ten minutes later the German embassy car drew up outside the premier's ascetically modest house in the suburbs of Jerusalem. When the envoy was shown in, he was apologetic.

After the traditional greetings of '*Shabbat Shalom*', the ambassador said: 'Prime Minister, I would not have disturbed you for all the world during the hours of Sabbath, but I understand it is permitted to break Sabbath if human life is at stake.'

Premier Golen inclined his head.

'It is permitted, if human life is at stake or in danger,' he conceded.

'In this case, that is very much so,' said the ambassador. 'You will be aware, sir, of what has been happening on board the supertanker *Freya* in the North Sea these past twelve hours.'

The premier was more than aware; he was deeply concerned, for since the noon demands it had become plain that the terrorists, whoever they were, could not be Palestinian Arabs, and might even be Jewish fanatics. But his own agencies, the external Mossad and the internal Sherut Bitachon, called from its initials Shin Bet, had not been able to find trace of such fanatics being missing from their usual haunts.

'I am aware, ambassador, and I join in sorrow for the murdered seaman. What is it that the Federal Republic wants of Israel?'

'Prime Minister, my country's Cabinet has considered all the issues here for several hours. Though it regards the prospect of conceding to terrorist blackmail with utter repugnance, and though if the affair were a completely internal German matter it might be prepared to resist, in the present case it feels it must accede.

'My government's request is therefore that the State of Israel agree to accept Lev Mishkin and David Lazareff, with the guarantees of non-prosecution and non-extradition that the terrorists demand.'

Premier Golen had in fact been considering the reply he would make to such a request for several hours. It came as no surprise to him. He had prepared his position. His government was a finely balanced coalition, and privately he was aware that many if not most of his own people were so incensed by the continuing persecution of Jews and the Jewish religion inside the USSR that for them Mishkin and Lazareff were hardly to be considered terrorists in the same class as the Baader-Meinhof gang or the PLO. Indeed, some sympathized with them for seeking to escape by hijacking a Soviet airliner, and accepted that the gun in the cockpit had gone off by accident.

'You have to understand two things, ambassador. One is that although Mishkin and Lazareff may be Jews, the State of Israel has had nothing to do with their original offences, nor the demand for their freedom now made.'

If the terrorists themselves turn out to be Jewish, how many people are going to believe that, he thought.

'The second thing is that the State of Israel is not directly affected by the plight of the *Freya*'s crew, nor the effects of her possible destruction. It is not the State of Israel that is under pressure here, or being blackmailed.'

'That is understood, Prime Minister,' said the German.

'If, therefore, Israel agrees to receive these two men, it must be clearly and publicly understood that she does so at the express and earnest request of the Federal government.'

'That request is being made, sir, by me, now, on behalf of my government.'

Fifteen minutes later the format was agreed. West Germany would publicly announce that it had made the request to Israel on its own behalf. Immediately afterwards, Israel would announce that she had reluctantly agreed to the request. Following that, West Germany could announce the release of the prisoners at 0800 hours the following morning, European time. The announcements would come from Bonn and Jerusalem, and would be synchronized at ten-minute intervals, starting one hour hence. It was seven-thirty in Israel, five-thirty in Europe.

Across that continent the last editions of the afternoon newspapers whirled on to the streets to be snapped up by a public of 300,000,000 who had followed the drama since midmorning. The latest headlines gave details of the murder of the unidentified seaman and the arrest of a freelance French photographer and a pilot at Le Touquet.

Radio bulletins carried the news that the West German ambassador to Israel had visited Premier Golen in his private house during Sabbath, and left twenty minutes later. There was no news from the meeting, and speculation was rife. Television had pictures of anyone who would pose for them, and quite a few who preferred not to. The latter were the ones who knew what was going on. No pictures of the seaman's body, taken from the Nimrod, were released by the authorities.

The daily papers, preparing for issues starting at midnight, were holding front pages for the chance of a statement from Jerusalem or Bonn, or another transmission from the *Freya*. The learned articles on the inside pages about the *Freya* herself, her cargo, the effects of its spillage, speculation on the identity of the terrorists and editorials urging the release of the two hijackers, covered many columns of copy.

A mild and balmy dusk was ending a glorious spring day when Sir Julian Flannery completed his report to the Prime Minister in her office at 10 Downing Street. It was comprehensive and yet succinct, a masterpiece of draftsmanship.

'We have to assume then, Sir Julian,' she said at length, 'that they certainly exist, that they have undoubtedly taken complete possession of the *Freya*, that they could well be in a position to blow her apart and sink her, that they would not stop at doing so, and that the financial, environmental and human consequences would constitute a catastrophe of appalling dimensions.'

'That, ma'am, might seem to be the most pessimistic interpretation, yet the crisis management committee feels it would be rash to assume a more hopeful tone,' the secretary to the Cabinet replied.

'Only four have been seen, the two lookouts and their replacements. We feel we must assume another on the bridge, one watching the prisoners, and a leader; that makes a minimum of seven. They might be too few to stop an armed boarding party, but we cannot assume so. They might have no dynamite on board, or too little, or have placed it wrongly, but we cannot assume so. Their triggering device might fail, they might have no second device, but we cannot assume so. They might not be prepared to kill any more seamen, but we cannot assume so. Finally, they might not be prepared actually to blow the *Freya* apart and die with her, but we cannot assume so. Your committee feels it would be wrong to assume less than the possible, which is the worst.'

The telephone from her private staff tinkled and she answered it. When she replaced the receiver, she gave Sir Julian a fleeting smile.

'It looks as if we may not face the catastrophe after all,' she said. 'The West German government has just announced it has made the request to Israel. Israel has replied that she concedes the German request. Bonn countered by announcing the release of these two men at eight tomorrow morning.'

It was twenty to seven.

The same news came over the transistor radio in the day cabin of Captain Thor Larsen. Keeping him covered all the time, Drake had switched the cabin lights on an hour earlier and drawn the curtains. The cabin was well-lit, warm, almost cheery. The percolator of coffee had been exhausted and replenished five times. It was still bubbling. Both men, the mariner and the fanatic, were stubbled and tired. But one was filled with grief for the death of a friend, and anger; the other triumphant.

'They've agreed,' said Drake. 'I knew they would. The odds were too long, the consequences too bad.'

Thor Larsen might have been relieved at the news of the pending reprieve of his ship. But the controlled anger was burning too hot even for this comfort.

'It's not over yet,' he growled.

'It will be. Soon. If my friends are released at eight, they will be in Tel Aviv by one p.m. or two at the latest. With an hour for identification and the publication on the news by radio, we should know by three or four o'clock tomorrow. After dark, we will leave you, safe and sound.'

'Except Tom Keller out there,' snapped the Norwegian.

'I'm sorry about that. The demonstration of our seriousness was necessary. They left me no alternative.'

The Soviet ambassador's request was unusual, highly so, in that it was repeated, tough and insistent. Although representing a supposedly revolutionary country, Soviet ambassadors are usually meticulous in their observance of diplomatic procedures, originally devised by Western capitalist nations.

David Lawrence repeatedly asked over the telephone

whether Ambassador Konstantin Kirov could not talk to him, as US secretary of state. Kirov replied that his message was for President Matthews personally, extremely urgent, and finally that it concerned matters Chairman Maxim Rudin personally wished to bring to President Matthews' attention.

The President granted Kirov his face-to-face, and the long black limousine with the hammer-and-sickle emblem swept into the White House grounds during the lunch-hour.

It was a quarter to seven in Europe, but only quarter to two in Washington. The envoy was shown straight to the Oval Office to face a President who was puzzled, intrigued and curious. The formalities were observed, but neither party's mind was on them.

'Mr President,' said Kirov, 'I am instructed by a personal order from Chairman Maxim Rudin to seek this urgent interview with you. I am instructed to relay to you his personal message, without variation. It is: "In the event that the hijackers and murderers Lev Mishkin and David Lazareff are freed from jail and released from their just deserts, the USSR will not be able to sign the Treaty of Dublin in the week after next, or at any time at all. The Soviet Union will reject the treaty permanently." '

President Matthews stared at the Soviet envoy in stunned amazement. It was several seconds before he spoke.

'You mean, Maxim Rudin will just tear it up?'

Kirov was ramrod stiff, formal, unbending.

'Mr President, that is the first part of the message I have been instructed to deliver to you. It goes on to say that if the nature or contents of this message are revealed, the same reaction from the USSR will apply.'

When he was gone William Matthews turned helplessly to Lawrence.

'David, what the hell is going on? We can't just bully the German government into reversing its decision without explaining why.'

'Mr President, I think you are going to have to. With respect, Maxim Rudin has just left you no alternative.'

14

1900 to Midnight

President William Matthews sat stunned by the suddenness, the unexpectedness and the brutality of the Soviet reaction. He waited while his CIA director, Robert Benson, and his security adviser, Stanislaw Poklewski, were sent for.

When the pair joined the state secretary in the Oval Office, Matthews explained the burden of the visit from Ambassador Kirov.

'What the hell are they up to?' demanded the President.

None of his three principal advisers could come up with an answer. Various suggestions were put forward, notably that Maxim Rudin had suffered a reverse within his own Politburo and could not proceed with the Treaty of Dublin; the *Freya* affair was simply his excuse for getting out of signing.

This idea was rejected by mutual consent: without the treaty, the Soviet Union would receive no grain, and they were at their last few truckloads. It was suggested the dead Aeroflot pilot, Captain Rudenko, represented the sort of loss of face that the Kremlin could not stomach. This too was rejected: international treaties are not torn up because of dead pilots.

The director of central intelligence summed up the feelings of everybody after an hour.

'It just doesn't make sense, and yet it must. Maxim Rudin would not react like a madman unless he had a reason, a reason we don't know.'

'That still doesn't get us out from between two appalling alternatives,' said President Matthews. 'Either we let the release of Mishkin and Lazareff go through, losing the most important disarmament treaty of our generation, and witness war within a year, or we use our clout to block that release, and subject Western Europe to the biggest ecological disaster of this generation.'

'We have to find a third choice,' said David Lawrence. 'But in hell's name, where?'

'There is only one place to look,' replied Poklewski. 'Inside Moscow. The answer lies inside Moscow, somewhere. I do not believe we can formulate a policy aimed at avoiding both the alternative disasters unless we know why Maxim Rudin has reacted in this way.'

'I think you're referring to the Nightingale,' Benson cut in. 'There just isn't the time. We're not talking about weeks, or even days. We only have hours. I believe, Mr President, that you should seek to speak personally with Maxim Rudin on the direct line. Ask him, as President to President, why he is taking this attitude over two Jewish hijackers.'

'And if he declines to give his reason?' asked Lawrence. 'He could have given a reason through Kirov. Or sent a personal letter. . . .'

President Matthews made up his mind.

'I am calling Maxim Rudin,' he said. 'But if he will not take my call, or declines to give me an explanation, we will have to assume he is himself under intolerable pressures of some kind within his own circle. So while I am waiting for the call, I am going to entrust Mrs Carpenter with the secret of what has just happened here, and ask for her help, through Sir Nigel Irvine and the Nightingale. In the last resort I will call Chancellor Busch in Bonn and ask him to give me more time.'

When the caller asked for Ludwig Jahn personally, the switchboard operator at Tegel Jail was prepared to cut the caller off. There had been numerous press calls seeking to speak with specific officers on the staff in order to elicit details of Mishkin and Lazareff. The operator had her orders: no calls.

But when the caller explained he was Jahn's cousin and that Jahn was to have attended his daughter's wedding the following day at noon, the operator softened. Family was different. She put the call through; Jahn took it from his office.

'I think you remember me,' the voice told Jahn. The officer remembered him well, the Russian with the labour-camp eyes.

'You shouldn't call me here,' he whispered hoarsely. 'I can't help you. The guards have been trebled, the shifts changed. I am on shift permanently now, sleeping here in the office. Until further notice; those are the orders. They are unapproachable now, those two men.'

'You had better make an excuse to get out for an hour,' said the voice of Colonel Kukushkin. 'There's a bar four hundred metres from the staff gate.' He named the bar and gave its address. Jahn did not know it, but he knew the street. 'In one hour,' said the voice, 'or else. . . .' There was a click.

It was 8 p.m. in Berlin, and quite dark.

The British Prime Minister had been taking a quiet supper with her husband in the private apartments in 10 Downing Street when she was summoned to accept a personal call from President Matthews. She was back at her desk when the call came through. The two government leaders knew each other well and had met a dozen times since Britain's first woman premier came to office. Face to face they used Christian names, but even though the super-security-vetted call across the Atlantic could not be eavesdropped, there was an official record made, so they stayed with the formalities.

In careful, succinct terms, President Matthews explained the message he had received from Maxim Rudin via his ambassador in Washington.

Joan Carpenter was stunned. 'In heaven's name, why?' she asked.

'That's my problem, ma'am,' came the Southern drawl from across the Atlantic. 'There is no explanation. None at all. Two more things. Ambassador Kirov advised me that if the content of Rudin's message ever became public knowledge, the same consequences to the Treaty of Dublin would still apply. I may count on your discretion?'

'Implicitly,' she replied. 'The second thing?'

'I've tried to call Maxim Rudin on the hot line. He is unavailable. Now from that, I have to assume he has his own problems right in the heart of the Kremlin, and he can't talk about them. Frankly, that has put me in an impossible position. But of one thing I am absolutely determined. I cannot let that treaty be destroyed. It is far too important to the whole of the Western world. I have to fight for it. I cannot let two hijackers in a Berlin jail destroy it; I cannot let a bunch of terrorists on a tanker in the North Sea unleash an armed conflict between East and West such as would ensue.'

'I entirely agree with you, Mr President,' said the premier from her London desk. 'What do you want from me? I imagine you would have more influence with Chancellor Busch than I.'

'It's not that, ma'am. Two things. We have a certain amount of information about the consequences to Europe of the *Freya* blowing up, but I assume you have more. I need to know every conceivable possible consequence and option, in the event the terrorists aboard do their worst.'

'Yes,' said Mrs Carpenter, 'during the whole of today our people here have put together an in-depth study of the ship, her cargo, the chances of containing the spillage, and so forth. So far we haven't examined the idea of storming her; now we may have to. I will have all our information on those aspects on their way to you within the hour. What else?'

'This is the hard one, and I hardly know how to ask it,' said William Matthews. 'We believe there has to be an explanation of Rudin's behaviour, and until we know it we are groping in the dark. If I am to handle this crisis, I have to see some daylight. I have to have that explanation. I need to know if there is a third option. I would like you to ask your people to activate the Nightingale one last time and get that answer for me.'

Joan Carpenter was pensive. She had always made a policy never to interfere with the way Sir Nigel Irvine ran his service. Unlike several of her predecessors she had steadily declined to poke around in the intelligence services to satisfy her curiosity. Since coming to office she had doubled the budgets of both her directors, of SIS and MI5, had chosen hard-core professionals for the posts, and had been rewarded by their unswerving loyalty. Secure in that loyalty, she trusted them not to let her down. And neither had.

'I will do what I can,' she said at length. 'But we are talking about something in the very heart of the Kremlin, and a matter of hours. If it is possible, it will be done. You have my word on it.'

When the telephone was back in its cradle she called her husband to tell him not to wait for her; she would be at her desk all night. From the kitchen she ordered a pot of coffee. The practical side of things arranged, she called Sir Julian Flannery at his home, told him simply over the open line that a fresh crisis had arisen, and asked him to return at once to the Cabinet Office. Her last call was not on an open line; it was to the duty officer at the head office of the firm. She asked for Sir Nigel Irvine to be contacted wherever he was, and to be asked to come immediately to Number 10. While waiting, she switched on the office television and caught the start of the nine o'clock BBC news. The long night had begun.

Ludwig Jahn slipped into the booth and sat down, sweating gently. From across the table the Russian regarded him coldly. The plump warder could not know that the fearsome Russian was fighting for his own life; the man gave no hint.

He listened impassively as Jahn explained the new procedures, instituted since two that afternoon. In point of fact, he had no diplomatic cover; he was hiding out in an SSD safe house in West Berlin as a guest of his East German colleagues.

'So you see,' concluded Jahn, 'there is nothing I can do. I

could not possibly get you into that corridor. There are three on duty, as a minimum figure, night and day. Passes have to be shown every time one enters the corridor, even by me, and we all know each other. We have worked together for years. No new face would be admitted without a check call to the governor.'

Kukushkin nodded slowly. Jahn felt relief rising in his chest. They would let him go; they would leave him alone; they would not hurt his family. It was over.

'You enter the corridor, of course,' said the Russian. 'You may enter the cells.'

'Well, yes, I am the Oberwachtmeister. At periodic intervals I have to check that they are all right.'

'At night they sleep?'

'Maybe. They have heard about the matter in the North Sea. They lost their radios just after the noon broadcasts, but one of the other prisoners in solitary shouted the news across to them before the corridor was cleared of all other prisoners. Perhaps they will sleep, perhaps not.'

The Russian nodded sombrely.

'Then,' he said, 'you will do the job yourself.'

Jahn's jaw dropped.

'No, no,' he babbled. 'You don't understand. I couldn't use a gun. I couldn't kill anyone.'

For answer the Russian laid two slim tubes like fountain pens on the table between them.

'Not guns,' he said. 'These. Place the open end, here, a few centimetres from the mouth and nose of the sleeping man. Press the button on the side, here. Death is within three seconds. Inhalation of potassium cyanide gas causes instantaneous death. Within an hour the effects are identical to those of cardiac arrest. When it is done, close the cells, return to the staff area, wipe the tubes clean and place them in the locker of another warder with access to the same pair of cells. Very simple, very clean. And it leaves you in the clear.'

What Kukushkin had laid before the horrified gaze of the senior officer was an up-dated version of the same sort of poison-gas pistols with which the 'wet affairs' department of the KGB had assassinated the two Ukrainian nationalist leaders Stepan Bandera and Lev Rebet in Germany two decades earlier. The principle was still simple, the efficiency of the gas increased by further research. Inside the tubes glass globules of prussic acid rested. The trigger impelled a spring which worked on a hammer which crushed the glass. Simultaneously the acid was vapourized by a compressed air canister, activated in the same motion of pressing the trigger button. Impelled by the compressed air, the gas vapour shot out of the tube into the breathing passages in an invisible cloud. An hour later the tell-tale almond smell of prussic acid was gone, the muscles of the corpse relaxed again; the symptoms were of a heart attack.

No one would believe two simultaneous heart attacks in two young men; a search would be made. The gas-guns, found in the locker of a warder, would incriminate the man almost completely.

'I . . . I can't do that,' whispered Jahn.

'But I can, and will, see your entire family in an Arctic labour camp for the rest of their lives,' murmured the Russian. 'A simple choice, Herr Jahn. The overcoming of your scruples for a brief ten minutes, against all their lives. Think about it.'

Kukushkin took Jahn's hand, turned it over and placed the tubes in the palm.

'Think about it,' he said, 'but not for too long. Then walk into those cells and do it. That's all.'

He slid out of the booth and left. Minutes later Jahn closed his hand round the gas-guns, slipped them in his raincoat pocket, and went back to Tegel Jail. At midnight, in three hours, he would relieve the evening shift supervisor. At 1 a.m. he would enter the cells and do it. He knew he had no alternative.

As the last rays of the sun left the sky, the Nimrod over the *Freya* had switched from her daytime F.126 camera to her nighttime F.135 version. Otherwise nothing changed. The night-vision camera, peering downwards with its infra-red sights, could pick out most of what was happening 15,000 feet beneath. If the Nimrod's captain wanted, he could take still pictures with the aid of the F.135's electronic flash, or throw the switch on his aircraft's million-candlepower searchlight.

The night camera failed to notice the figure in the anorak, lying prostrate since the mid-afternoon, slowly begin to move, crawling under the inspection catwalk and from there inching its way back towards the superstructure. When the figure finally crawled over the sill of the half-open doorway and stood up in the interior, no one noticed. At dawn it was supposed the body had been thrown into the sea.

The man in the anorak went below to the gallery, rubbing hands and shivering repeatedly. In the galley he found one of his colleagues and helped himself to a piping hot coffee. When he had finished he returned to the bridge and sought out his own clothes, the black tracksuit and sweater he had come aboard with.

'Jeez,' he told the man on the bridge in his American accent, 'you sure didn't miss. I could feel the wadding from those blanks slapping into the back of the windbreaker.'

The bridge-watch grinned.

'Andriy said to make it good,' he replied. 'It worked. Mishkin and Lazareff are coming out at eight tomorrow morning. By afternoon they'll be in Tel Aviv.'

'Great,' said the Ukrainian-American. 'Let's just hope Andriy's plan to get us off this ship works as well as the rest.'

'It will,' said the other. 'You better get your mask on and give those clothes back to that Yankee in the paint locker. Then grab some sleep. You're on watch at six in the morning.'

Sir Julian Flannery re-convened the crisis management committee within an hour of his private talk with the Prime Minister. She had told him the reason why the situation had changed, but he and Sir Nigel Irvine would be the only ones to know, and they would not talk. The members of the committee would simply need to know that, for reasons of state, the release of Mishkin and Lazareff at dawn might be delayed or cancelled, depending on the reaction of the German chancellor.

Elsewhere in Whitehall, page after page of data about the *Freya*, her crew, cargo and hazard potential was being photographically transmitted direct to Washington.

Sir Julian had been lucky: most of the principal experts from the committee lived within a sixty-minute fast drive radius of Whitehall. Most were caught over dinner at home, none had left for the countryside; two were traced to restaurants, one to the theatre. By nine-thirty the bulk of them were seated once again in the Unicorne.

Sir Julian explained that their duty now was to assume that the whole affair had passed from the realm of a form of exercise and into major crisis category.

'We have to assume that Chancellor Busch will agree to delay the release, pending the clarification of certain other matters. If he does, we have to assume the chance that the terrorists will at least activate their first threat, to vent oil cargo from the *Freya*. Now we have to plan to contain and destroy a possible first slick of twenty thousand tons of crude oil; secondly, to envisage that figure being multiplied by fifty fold.'

The picture that emerged was gloomy. Public indifference over years had led to political neglect; nevertheless, the amounts of crude oil emulsifier in the hands of the British, and the vehicles for their delivery on to an oil slick were still greater than those of the rest of Europe combined.

'We have to assume that the main burden of containing the ecology damage will fall to us,' said the man from Warren Springs. 'In the *Amoco Cadiz* affair in 1978 the French refused to accept our help, even though we had better emulsifiers and better delivery systems than they did. Their fishermen paid bitterly for that particular stupidity. The old-fashioned detergent they used instead of our emulsifier-concentrates caused as much toxic damage as the oil itself.

And they had neither enough of it nor the right delivery systems. It was like trying to kill an octopus with a pea-shooter.'

'I have no doubt the Germans, Dutch and Belgians will not hesitate to ask for a joint allied operation in this matter,' said the man from Foreign Office.

'Then we must be ready,' said Sir Julian. 'How much have we got?'

Dr Henderson from Warren Springs continued. 'The best emulsifier, in concentrate form, will emulsify – that is, break down into minuscule globules which permit natural bacteria to complete the destruction – twenty times its own volume. One gallon of emulsifier for twenty gallons of crude oil. We have one thousand tons in stock.'

'Enough for one slick of twenty thousand tons of crude oil,' observed Sir Julian. 'What about a million tons?'

'Not a chance,' said Henderson grimly. 'Not a chance in hell. If we start to produce more now, we can manufacture a thousand tons every four days. For a million tons, we'd need fifty thousand tons of emulsifier. Frankly, those maniacs in the black helmets could wipe out most marine life in the North Sea and the English Channel, and foul up the beaches from Hull to Cornwall on our side, and Bremen to Ushant on the other.'

There was silence for a while.

'Let's assume the first slick,' said Sir Julian quietly. 'The other is beyond belief.'

The committee agreed to issue immediate orders for the procurement during the night of every ton of emulsifier from the store in Hampshire; to commandeer lorry tankers from the petroleum companies through the Energy Department; to bring the whole consignment to the esplanade car park at Lowestoft on the east coast; and to get under way and divert to Lowestoft every single marine tug with spray equipment, including the Port of London fire-fighting vessels and the Royal Navy equivalents. By late morning it was hoped to have the entire flotilla in Lowestoft port, tanking up with emulsifier.

'If the sea remains calm,' said Dr Henderson, 'the slick will drift gently northeast of the *Freya* on the tide, heading for North Holland, at about two knots. That gives us time. When the tide changes, it should drift back again. But if the wind rises, it might move faster in any direction, according to the wind, which will overcome the tide at surface level. We should be able to cope with a twenty-thousand-ton slick.'

'We can't move ships into the area five miles round the *Freya* on three sides, or anywhere between her and the Dutch coast,' the vice-chief of defence staff pointed out.

'But we can watch the slick from the Nimrod,' said the group captain from RAF. 'If it moves out of range of the *Freya*, your navy chaps can start squirting.'

'So far, so good, for the threatened twenty-thousand-ton spillage,' said the Foreign Office man. 'What happens after that?'

'Nothing,' said Dr Henderson. 'After that we're finished, expended.'

'Well, that's it then. An enormous administrative task awaits us,' said Sir Julian.

'There is one other option,' said Colonel Holmes of the Royal Marines. 'The hard option.'

There was an uncomfortable silence round the table. The vice-admiral and the group captain did not share the discomfort; they were interested. The scientists and bureaucrats were accustomed to technical and administrative problems, their counter-measures and solutions. Each suspected the raw-boned colonel in civilian clothes was talking about shooting holes in people.

'You may not like the option,' said Holmes reasonably, 'but these terrorists have killed one sailor in cold blood. They may well kill another twenty-nine. The ship costs one hundred and seventy million dollars, the cargo one hundred and forty million dollars, the clean-up operation treble that. If, for whatever reason, Chancellor Busch cannot or will not release the men in Berlin, we may be left with no alternative but to try to storm the ship and knock off the man with the detonator before he can use it.'

'What exactly do you propose, Colonel Holmes?' asked Sir Julian.

'I propose that we ask Major Fallon to drive up from Dorset and that we listen to him,' said Holmes.

It was agreed, and on that note the meeting adjourned until 3 a.m. It was 9.50 p.m.

During the meeting, not far away from the Cabinet Office, the Prime Minister had received Sir Nigel Irvine.

'That then, is the position, Sir Nigel,' she concluded. 'If we cannot come up with a third option, either the men go free and Maxim Rudin tears up the Treaty of Dublin; or they stay in jail and their friends tear up the *Freya*. In the case of the second, they might stay their hand and not do it, but we can entertain no hopes of that. It might be possible to storm it, but chances of success are slim. In order to have a chance of perceiving the third option, we have to know why Maxim Rudin is taking this course. Is he, for example, overplaying his hand? Is he trying to bluff the West into sustaining enormous economic damage in order to offset his own embarrassment over his grain problems? Will he really go through with his threat? We have to know.'

'How long have you got, Prime Minister? How long has President Matthews got?' asked the director-general of the SIS.

'One must assume, if the hijackers are not released at dawn, we will have to stall the terrorists, play for time. But I would hope to have something for the President by afternoon tomorrow.'

'As a rather long-serving officer, I would have thought that was impossible, ma'am. It is the middle of the night in Moscow. The Nightingale is virtually unapproachable, except at meetings planned well ahead. To attempt an instant rendezvous might well blow that agent sky-high.'

'I know your rules, Sir Nigel, and I understand them. The safety of the agent out in the cold is paramount. But so are matters of state. The destruction of the treaty, or the destruction of the *Freya*, are matters of state. The first could jeopardize peace for years, perhaps put Yefrem Vishnayev in power, with all its consequences. The financial losses alone sustained by Lloyd's and, through Lloyd's the British economy if the *Freya* destroyed herself and the North Sea would be disastrous, not to mention the loss of thirty seamen. I make no flat order, Sir Nigel; I ask you to put the certain options against the putative hazard to one single Russian agent.'

'Ma'am, I will do what I can. You have my word on it,' said Sir Nigel, and left to return to his headquarters.

From an office in the Defence Ministry Colonel Holmes was on the telephone to Poole, Dorset, headquarters of another service, the SBS. Major Simon Fallon was found befriending a pint of beer in the officers' mess and brought to the telephone. The two marines knew each other well.

'You've been following the *Freya* affair?' asked Holmes from London.

There was a chuckle from the other end. 'I thought you'd come shopping here eventually,' said Fallon. 'What do they want?'

'Things are turning sour,' said Holmes. 'The Germans may have to change their minds and keep those two jokers in Berlin after all. I've just spent an hour with the re-convened CMC. They don't like it, but they may have to consider our way. Got any ideas?'

'Sure,' said Fallon. 'Been thinking about it all day. Need a model, though, and a plan. And the gear.'

'Right,' said Holmes. 'I have the plan here, and a pretty good model of another similar ship. Get the boys together. Get all the gear out of stores: underwater, magnets, all the types of hardware, stun grenades, you name it. The lot. What you don't need can be returned. I'm asking the navy to come round from Portland and pick up the lot – the gear and the team. When you've left a good man in charge, jump into the car and get up to London. Report to my office as soon as you can.'

'Don't worry,' said Fallon, 'I've got the gear sorted and bagged already. Get the transport here as fast as you can. I'm on my way.'

When the hard, chunky major returned to the bar there was silence. His men knew he had taken a call from London. Within minutes they were rousing the NCOs and marines from their barracks, changing rapidly out of the plain clothes they had been wearing in the mess into the black webbing and green berets of their unit. Before midnight they were waiting on the stone jetty tucked away in their cordoned section of the marine base; waiting for the arrival of the navy to take their equipment to where it was needed.

There was a bright moon rising over Portland Bill to the west of them as the three fast patrol boats *Sabre*, *Cutlass* and *Scimitar* came out of the harbour, heading east for Poole. When the throttles were open the three prows rose, the sterns buried into the foaming water, and the thunder echoed across the bay.

The same moon illuminated the long track of the Hampshire motorway as Major Fallon's Rover saloon burned up the miles to London.

'Now, what the hell do I tell Chancellor Busch?' President Matthews asked his advisers.

It was five in the afternoon in Washington; though night had long settled on Europe, the late afternoon sun was still on the rose garden beyond the french windows where the first buds were responding to the spring warmth.

'I don't believe you can reveal to him the real message received from Kirov,' said Robert Benson.

'Why the devil not? I told Joan Carpenter, and no doubt she'll have had to tell Nigel Irvine.'

'There's a difference,' pointed out the CIA chief. 'The British can put in hand the necessary precautions to cope with an ecology problem in the sea off their coasts by calling on their technical experts. It's a technical problem; Joan Carpenter did not need to call a full Cabinet meeting. Dietrich Busch is going to be asked to hold on to Mishkin and Lazareff at the risk of provoking a catastrophe for his European neighbours. For that he'll almost certainly consult his Cabinet. . . .'

'He's an honourable man,' cut in Lawrence. 'If he knows that the price is the Treaty of Dublin, he'll feel bound to share that knowledge with his Cabinet.'

'And there's the problem,' concluded Benson. 'That a minimum of fifteen more people would learn of it. Some of them would confide in their wives, their aides. We still haven't forgotten the Guenther Guillaume affair. There are just too damn many leaks in Bonn. If it got out, the Dublin Treaty would be finished in any case, regardless of what happened in the North Sea.'

'His call will be through in a minute. What the hell do I tell him?' repeated Matthews.

'Tell him you have information that simply cannot be divulged on any telephone line, even a secure trans-Atlantic line,' suggested Poklewski. 'Tell him the release of Mishkin and Lazareff would provoke a greater disaster than even frustrating the terrorists on the *Freya* for a few more hours. Ask him at this stage simply to give you a little time.'

'How long?' asked the President.

'As long as possible,' said Benson.

'And when the time runs out?' asked the President.

The call to Bonn came through. Chancellor Busch had been contacted at his home. The security-vetted call was patched through to him there. There was no need of translators on the line; Dietrich Busch spoke fluent English. President Matthews spoke to him for ten minutes while the German government chief listened with growing amazement.

'But why?' he asked at length. 'Surely the matter hardly affects the United States?'

Matthews was tempted. At the Washington end Robert Benson wagged a warning finger.

'Dietrich, please. Believe me. I'm asking you to trust me. On this line, on any line across the Atlantic, I can't be as frank as I'd like to be. Something has cropped up, something of enormous dimension. Look, I'll be as plain as I can. Over here we have discovered something about these two men; their release would be disastrous at this stage, for the next few hours. I'm asking for time, Dietrich my friend, just time. A delay, until certain things can be taken care of.'

The German Chancellor was standing in his study with the strains of Beethoven drifting through the door from the sitting room where he had been enjoying a cigar and a concert on the stereo. To say that he was suspicious was putting it mildly. So far as he was concerned the trans-Atlantic line, established years before to link the NATO government heads and checked regularly, was perfectly safe. Moreover, he reasoned, the United States had perfectly good communications with their Bonn embassy and could send him a personal message on that route if desired. It did not occur to him that Washington would simply not trust his Cabinet with a secret of this magnitude after the repeated exposure of East German agents close to the seat of power on the Rhine.

On the other hand, the President of the United States was not given to making late-night calls or crazy appeals. He had to have his reasons, Busch knew. But what he was being asked was not something he could decide without consultation.

'It is just past ten p.m. over here,' he told Matthews. 'We have until dawn to decide. Nothing fresh ought to happen until then. I shall re-convene my Cabinet during the night and consult with them. I cannot promise you more.'

President William Matthews had to be satisfied with that.

When the phone was replaced, Dietrich Busch stayed for long minutes in thought. There was something going on, he reasoned, and it concerned Mishkin and Lazareff, sitting in their separate cells in Tegel Jail in West Berlin. If anything happened to them, there was no way in which the Federal government would escape a howl of censure from within Germany, by the combined media and the opposition. And with the regional elections coming up. . . .

His first call was to Ludwig Fischer, his minister of justice, also at home in the capital. None of his ministers would be weekending in the country, by prior agreement. His suggestion was met with immediate agreement by the justice minister – to transfer the pair from the old-fashioned prison of Tegel to the much newer and super-secure jail of Moabit was an obvious precaution. No CIA operatives would ever get at them inside Moabit. Fischer telephoned the instruction to Berlin immediately.

There are certain phrases, innocent enough, which used by the senior cipher clerk at the British embassy in Moscow to the man he knows to be the SIS resident on the embassy staff, mean in effect, 'Get the hell down here fast; something urgent is coming through from London.' Such was the phrase that brought Adam Munro from his bed at midnight (Moscow time), 10 p.m. London time, across town to Maurice Thorez Embankment.

Driving back from Downing Street to his office, Sir Nigel Irvine had realized the Prime Minister was absolutely right. Compared to the destruction of the Treaty of Dublin on the one hand or the destruction of the *Freya*, her crew and cargo on the other, putting a Russian agent at risk of exposure was the lesser evil. What he was going to ask Munro in Moscow to do, and the way he would have to demand it, gave him no pleasure. But before he arrived at the SIS building he knew it would have to be done.

Deep in the basement, the communications room was handling the usual routine traffic when he entered and startled the night duty staff. But the scrambler telex had raised Moscow in less than five minutes. No one queried the right of the Master to talk directly to his Moscow resident in the middle of the night. It was thirty minutes later that the telex from the Moscow cipher room chattered its message that Munro was there and waiting.

The operators at both ends, senior men of a lifetime's experience, could be trusted with the whereabouts of Christ's bones if necessary; they had to be, they handled as routine messages that could bring down governments. From London the telex would send its scrambled, uninterceptable, message down to a forest of aerials outside Cheltenham, better known for its horse-races and ladies' college. From there the words would be converted automatically into an unbreakable one-off code and beamed out over a sleeping Europe to an aerial on the embassy roof. Four seconds after they were typed in London they would emerge, in clear, on the telex in the basement of the old sugar-magnate's house in Moscow.

There, the cipher clerk turned to Munro standing by his side.

'It's the Master himself,' he said, reading the code-tag on the incoming message. 'There must be a flap on.'

Sir Nigel had to tell Munro the burden of Kirov's message to President Matthews of only three hours earlier. Without that knowledge, Munro could not ask the Nightingale for the answer to Matthews' question: why.

The telex rattled for several minutes. Munro read the message that spewed out with horror.

'I can't do that,' he told the impassive clerk, over whose shoulder he was reading. When the message from London was ended, he told the clerk: 'Reply as follows: "not repeat not possible obtain this sort of answer in time-scale". Send it.'

The interchange between Sir Nigel Irvine and Adam Munro went on for fifteen minutes. There is a method of contacting N at short notice, suggested London. Yes, but only in case of dire emergency, replied Munro. This qualifies one hundred times as emergency, chattered the machine from London. But N could not begin to enquire in less than several days, pointed out Munro. Next regular Politburo meeting not due until Thursday following. What about records of last Thursday's meeting? asked London. *Freya* was not hijacked last Thursday, retorted Munro. Finally Sir Nigel did what he hoped he would not have to do.

'Regret,' tapped the machine, 'prime ministerial order not refusable. Unless attempt made avert this disaster, operation to bring out N to West cannot proceed.'

Munro looked down at the stream of paper coming out of the telex in disbelief. For the first time he was caught in the net of his own attempts to keep his love for the agent he ran from his superiors in London. Sir Nigel Irvine thought the Nightingale was an embittered Russian turncoat called Anatoly Krivoi, right-hand man to the warmonger Vishnayev.

'Make to London,' he told the clerk dully, 'the following: "will try this night, stop, decline to accept responsibility if N refuses or is unmasked during attempt, stop".'

The reply from the Master was brief: 'Agree. Proceed.' It was half-past one in Moscow, and very cold.

Half-past six in Washington, and the dusk was settling over the sweep of lawns beyond the bulletproof windows behind the President's chair, causing the lamps to be switched on. The group in the Oval Office was waiting: waiting for Chancellor Busch, waiting for an unknown agent in Moscow, waiting for a masked terrorist of unknown origins sitting on a 1,000,000-ton bomb off Europe with a detonator in his belt. Waiting for the chance of a third option.

The phone rang, and it was for Stanislaw Poklewski. He listened, held a hand over the mouthpiece and told the President it was from the Navy Department in answer to his query of an hour earlier.

There was one US Navy vessel in the area of the *Freya*. She had been paying a courtesy visit to the Danish coastal city of Esbjerg, and was on her way back to join her squadron of the Standing Naval Force Atlantic, then cruising on patrol west of Norway. She was well off the Danish coast, steaming north by west to rejoin her NATO allies.

'Divert her,' said the President.

Poklewski passed the commander-in-chief's order back to the Navy Department, who soon began to make signals via STANFORLANT headquarters to the American warship.

Just after one in the morning the USS *Moran*, halfway between Denmark and the Orkney Islands, put her helm about, opened her engines to full power, and then began racing through the moonlight southwards for the English Channel. She was a guided missile ship of almost 8000 tons which, although heavier than the British light cruiser *Argyll*, was classified as a destroyer, or DD. Moving at full power in a calm sea, she was making close to thirty knots to bring her to her station five miles from the *Freya* at 8 a.m.

There were few cars in the car park of the Mojorsky Hotel, just off the roundabout at the far end of Kutuzovsky Prospekt. Those that were there were dark, uninhabited, save two.

Munro watched the lights of the other car flicker and dim, then climbed from his own vehicle and walked across. When he climbed into the passenger seat beside her, Valentina was alarmed and trembling.

'What is it, Adam? Why did you call me at the apartment? The call must have been listed.'

He put his arm round her, feeling the trembling through her coat.

'It was from a call box,' he said, 'and only concerned Gregor's inability to attend your dinner party. No one will suspect anything.'

'At two in the morning,' she remonstrated, 'no one makes calls like that at two in the morning. I was seen to leave the apartment compound by the nightwatchman. He will report it.'

'Darling, I'm sorry. Listen.'

He told her of the visit by Ambassador Kirov to President Matthews the previous evening; of the news being passed to London; of the demand to him that he try to find out why the Kremlin was taking such an attitude over Mishkin and Lazareff.

'I don't know,' she said simply. 'I haven't the faintest idea. Perhaps because those animals murdered Captain Rudenko, a man with a wife and children.'

'Valentina, we have listened to the Politburo these past nine months. The Treaty of Dublin is vital to your people. Why would Rudin put it in jeopardy over these two men?'

'He has not done so,' answered Valentina. 'It is possible for the West to control the oil slick if the ship blows up. The costs can be met. The West is rich.'

'Darling, there are thirty men aboard that ship. They too have wives and children. Thirty men's lives against the imprisonment of two. There has to be another and more serious reason.'

'I don't know,' she repeated. 'It has not been mentioned in Politburo meetings. You know that also.'

Munro stared miserably through the windscreen. He had hoped against hope she might have an answer for Washington, something she had heard inside the Central Committee building. Finally he decided he had to tell her.

When he had finished, she stared through the darkness with round eyes. He caught a hint of tears in the dying light of the moon.

'They promised,' she whispered, 'they promised they would bring me and Sasha out, in a fortnight, from Romania.'

'They've gone back on their word,' he confessed. 'They want this last favour.'

She placed her forehead on her gloved hands, supported by the steering wheel.

'They will catch me,' she mumbled. 'I am so frightened.'

'They won't catch you,' he tried to reassure her. 'The KGB acts much more slowly than people think, and the higher their suspect is placed the more slowly they act. If you can get this piece of information for President Matthews, I think I can persuade them to get you out in a few days, you and Sasha, instead of two weeks. Please try, my love. It's our only chance left of ever being together.'

Valentina stared through the glass.

'There was a Politburo meeting this evening,' she said finally. 'I was not there. It was a special meeting, out of sequence. Normally on Friday evenings they are all going to the country. Transcription begins tomorrow; that is, today, at ten in the morning. The staff have to give up their weekend to get it ready for Monday. Perhaps they mentioned the matter.'

'Could you get in to see the notes, listen to the tapes?' he asked.

'In the middle of the night? There would be questions asked.'

'Make an excuse, darling. Any excuse. You want to start and finish your work early, so as to get away.'

'I will try,' she said eventually. 'I will try, for you, Adam, not for those men in London.'

'I know those men in London,' said Adam Munro. 'They will bring you and Sasha out if you help them now. This will be the last risk, truly the last.'

She seemed not to have heard him, and to have overcome, for a while, her fear of the KGB, exposure as a spy, the awful consequences of capture unless she could escape in time. When she spoke, her voice was quite level.

'You know Dyetsky Mir? The soft toys counter. At ten o'clock this morning.'

He stood on the black tarmac and watched her tail lights drive away. It was done. They had asked him to do it, demanded that he do it, and he had done it. He had diplomatic protection to keep him out of Lubyanka. The worst that could happen would be his ambassador summoned to the Foreign Ministry on Monday morning to receive an icy protest and demand for his removal from Dmitri Rykov. But Valentina was walking right into the secret archives, without even the disguise of normal, accustomed, justified behaviour to protect her. He looked at his watch. Seven hours, seven hours to go, seven hours of knotted stomach muscles and ragged nerve ends. He walked back to his car.

Ludwig Jahn stood in the open gateway of Tegel Jail and watched the tail lights of the armoured van bearing Mishkin and Lazareff disappear down the street.

Unlike Munro, for him there would be no more waiting, no tension stretching through the dawn and into the morning. For him the waiting was over.

He walked carefully to his office on the first floor and

closed the door. For a few moments he stood by the open window, then drew back one hand and hurled the first of the cyanide pistols far into the night. He was fat, overweight, unfit. A heart attack would be accepted as possible, provided no evidence was found.

Leaning far out of the window he thought of his nieces over the Wall in the East, their laughing faces when Uncle Ludo had brought the presents four months ago at Christmas. He closed his eyes, held the other tube beneath his nostrils and pressed the trigger-button.

The pain slammed across his chest like a giant hammer. The loosened fingers dropped the tube, which fell with a tinkle to the street below. Jahn slumped, hit the window sill and caved backwards into his office, already dead. When they found him, they would assume he had opened the window for air when the first pain came. Kukushkin would not have his triumph. The chimes of midnight were drowned by the roar of a lorry which crushed the tube in the gutter to fragments.

The hijacking of the *Freya* had claimed its first victim.

15

Midnight to 0800

The resumed West German Cabinet meeting assembled in the chancellery at 1 a.m., and the mood when the ministers heard from Dietrich Busch the plea from Washington varied between exasperation and truculence.

'Well, why the hell won't he give a reason?' asked the defence minister. 'Doesn't he trust us?'

'He claims he has a reason of paramount importance, but cannot divulge it even over the hot line,' replied Chancellor Busch. 'That gives us the opportunity of either believing him, or calling him a liar. At this stage I cannot do the latter.'

'Has he any idea what the terrorists will do when they learn Mishkin and Lazareff are not to be released at dawn?' queried another.

'Yes, I think he has. At least, the text of all the exchanges between the *Freya* and Maas Control are in his hands. As we all know, they have threatened either to kill another seaman, or vent twenty thousand tons of crude, or both.'

'Well, then, let him carry the responsibility,' urged the interior minister. 'Why should we take the blame if that happens?'

'I haven't the slightest intention that we should,' replied Busch, 'but that doesn't answer the question. Do we grant President Matthews' request or not?'

There was silence for a while. The foreign minister broke it. 'How long is he asking for?'

'As long as possible,' said the Chancellor. 'He seems to

have some plan afoot to break the deadlock, to find a third alternative. But what the plan is, or what the alternative could be, he alone knows; he and a few people he evidently trusts with the secret,' he added with some bitterness. 'But that doesn't include us for the moment.'

'Well, personally I think it is stretching the friendship between us a bit far,' said the foreign minister, 'but I think we ought to grant him an extension, while making plain, at least unofficially, that it is at his request, not ours.'

'Perhaps he has an idea to storm the *Freya*,' suggested Defence.

'Our own people say that would be extremely risky,' replied the interior minister. 'It would require an underwater approach for at least the last two miles; a sheer climb up smooth steel from the sea to the deck, a penetration of the superstructure without being observed from the funnel, and the selection of the right cabin with the leader of the terrorists in it. If, as we suspect, the man holds a remote-control detonating mechanism in his hand, he'd have to be shot and killed before he could press the button.'

'In any case, it is too late to do it before dawn,' said the defence minister. 'It would have to be in darkness, and that means ten p.m. at the earliest, twenty-one hours from now.'

At a quarter to three the German Cabinet finally agreed to grant President Matthews his request: an indefinite delay on the release of Mishkin and Lazareff while reserving the right to keep the consequences under constant review and reverse that decision if it became regarded in Western Europe as impossible to continue to hold the pair.

At the same time the government spokesman was quietly asked to leak the news to two of his most reliable media contacts that only massive pressure from Washington had caused the about-face in Bonn.

It was 11 p.m. in Washington, 4 a.m. in Europe, when the news from Bonn reached President Matthews. He sent back his heartfelt thanks to Chancellor Busch and asked David

Lawrence: 'Any reply from Jerusalem yet?'

'None,' said Lawrence. 'We only know that our ambassador there has been granted a personal interview with Benyamin Golen.'

When the Israeli premier was disturbed for the second time during the Sabbath night, his tetchy capacity for patience was wearing distinctly thin. He received the US ambassador in his dressing gown and the reception was frosty. It was 3 a.m. in Europe, but 5 a.m. in Jerusalem and the first thin light of Saturday morning was on the hills of Judea.

He listened without reaction to the ambassador's personal plea from President Matthews. His private fear was for the identity of the terrorists aboard the *Freya*. No terrorist action aimed at delivering Jews from a prison cell had ever been mounted since the days of his own youth, fighting right here on the soil where he stood. Then, it had been to free condemned Jewish partisans from a British jail at Acre, and he had been a part of that fight. Thirty-five years had elapsed and the perspectives had changed. Now it was Israel who roundly condemned terrorism, the taking of hostages, the blackmail of regimes. And yet. . . .

And yet, hundreds of thousands of his own people would secretly sympathize with two youths who had sought to escape the terror of the KGB the only way left open to them. The same voters would not openly hail the youths as heroes, but neither would they condemn them as murderers. As to the masked men on the *Freya*, there was a chance that they too were Jewish, possibly (heaven forbid) Israelis. He had hoped the previous evening that the affair would be over by sundown of the Sabbath, the prisoners of Berlin inside Israel, the terrorists of the *Freya* captured or dead. There would be a fuss, but it would die down.

Now he was learning that there would be no release. The news hardly inclined him to the American request, which was in any case impossible. When he had heard the ambassador out, he shook his head.

'Please convey to my good friend William Matthews my heartfelt wish that this appalling affair can be concluded without further loss of life,' he replied. 'But on the matter of Mishkin and Lazareff my position is this: if, on behalf of the government and the people of Israel, and at the urgent request of West Germany, I give a solemn, public pledge not to imprison them here or return them to Berlin, then I shall have to abide by that pledge. I'm sorry, but I cannot do as you ask and return them to jail in Germany as soon as the *Freya* has been released.'

He did not need to explain what the American ambassador already knew; that, apart from any question of national honour, even the explanation that promises extracted under duress were not binding would not work in this case. The outrage from the National Religious Party, the Gush Emunim extremists, the Jewish Defense League and the 100,000 Israeli voters who had come from the USSR in the past decade; all these alone would prevent any Israeli premier from reneging on an international pledge to set Mishkin and Lazareff free.

'Well, it was worth a try,' said President Matthews when the cable reached Washington an hour later.

'It now ranks as one possible third option that no longer exists,' remarked David Lawrence, 'even if Maxim Rudin would have accepted it, which I doubt.'

It was one hour to midnight; lights were burning in five government departments, scattered across the capital, as they burned in the Oval Office and a score of other rooms throughout the White House where men and women sat at telephones and teleprinters waiting the news from Europe. The four men in the Oval Office settled to wait the reaction from the *Freya*.

Doctors say three in the morning is the lowest ebb of the human spirit, the hour of weariness, slowest reactions and gloomiest depression. It also marked one complete cycle of the sun and moon for the two men who faced each other in the captain's cabin of the *Freya*. Neither had slept that night nor the previous one; each had been forty-four hours without rest; each was drawn and red-eyed.

Thor Larsen, at the epicentre of a whirling storm of international activity, of cabinets and councils, embassies and meetings, plottings and consultations that kept the lights burning through three continents from Jerusalem to Washington, was playing his own game. He was pitting his own capacity to stay awake against the will of the fanatic who faced him, knowing that at stake if he failed was his crew and his ship.

Larsen knew that the man who called himself Svoboda, younger and consumed by his own inner fire, nerves tightened by a combination of black coffee and the tension of his gamble against the world, could have ordered the Norwegian captain to be tied up while he himself sought rest. So the bearded mariner sat facing the barrel of a gun and played on his captor's pride, hoping that the man would take his challenge, refuse to back down and concede defeat in the game of beating sleep.

It was Larsen who proposed the endless cups of strong black coffee, a drink he only took with milk and sugar two or three times a day. It was he who talked, through the day and the night, provoking the Ukrainian with suggestions of eventual failure, then backing off when the man became too irritable for safety. Long years of experience, nights of yawning, gritty-mouthed training as a sea captain, had taught the bearded giant to stay awake and alert through the night watches, when the cadres drowsed and the deckhands dozed.

So he played his own solitary game, without guns or ammunition, without teleprinters or night-sight cameras, without support and without company. All the superb technology the Japanese had built into his new command was as much use as rusty nails to him now. If he pushed the man across the table too far, he might lose his temper and shoot to kill. If he was frustrated too often he could order the execution of another crewman. If he felt himself becoming too drowsy, he might have himself relieved by another, fitter terrorist while he himself took sleep and undid all that Larsen was trying to do to him.

That Mishkin and Lazareff would be released at dawn, Larsen still had reason to believe. After their safe arrival in Tel Aviv, the terrorists would prepare to quit the *Freya*. Or would they? Could they? Would the surrounding warships let them go so easily? Even away from the *Freya*, attacked by the NATO navies, Svoboda could press his button and blow the *Freya* apart.

But that was not all of it. This man in black had killed one of the crew. Thor Larsen wanted him for that, and he wanted him dead. So he talked the night away to the man opposite him, denying them both sleep.

Whitehall was not sleeping either. The crisis management committee had been in session since 3 a.m., and within an hour the progress reports were complete.

Across southern England the bulk tanker lorries, commandeered from Shell, British Petroleum and a dozen other sources, were filling up with emulsifier concentrate at the Hampshire depot. Bleary-eyed drivers rumbled through the night, empty towards Hampshire or loaded towards Lowestoft, moving hundreds of tons of the concentrate to the Suffolk port. By 4 a.m. the stocks were empty; all 1000 tons of the national supply was headed east to the coast.

So also were inflatable booms to try to hold the vented oil away from the coast until the chemicals could do their work. The factory that made the emulsifier had been geared for maximum output until further notice.

At 3.30 a.m. the news had come from Washington that the Bonn Cabinet had agreed to hold Mishkin and Lazareff for a while longer.

'Does Matthews know what he's doing?' someone asked.

Sir Julian Flannery's face was impassive. 'We must assume that he does,' he said smoothly. 'We must also assume that a venting by the *Freya* will probably now take place. The efforts of the night have not been in vain. At least we are now almost ready.'

'We must also assume,' said the civil servant from the Foreign Ministry, 'that when the announcement becomes public, France, Belgium and Holland are going to ask for assistance in fighting any oil-slick that may result.'

'Then we shall be ready to do what we can,' said Sir Julian. 'Now, what about the spraying aircraft and the fire-fighting tugs?'

The report in the Unicorne room mirrored what was happening at sea. From the Humber estuary tugs were churning south towards Lowestoft harbour, while from the Thames and even as far round as the navy base at Lee other tugs capable of spraying liquid on to the surface of the sea were moving to rendezvous point on the Suffolk coast.

They were not the only things moving round the south coast that night. Off the towering cliffs of Beachy Head the *Cutlass*, *Scimitar* and *Sabre*, carrying the assorted, complex and lethal hardware of the world's toughest team of assault frogmen, were pointing their noses north of east to bring them past Sussex and Kent towards where the cruiser *Argyll* lay at anchor in the North Sea.

The boom of their engines echoed off the chalk battlements of the southern coast and light sleepers in Eastbourne heard the rumble out to sea.

Twelve marines of the Special Boat Service clung to the rails of the bucking craft, watching over their precious kayaks and the crates of diving gear, weapons and unusual explosives that made up the props of their trade. It was all being carried as deck cargo.

'I hope,' shouted the young lieutenant commander who skippered the *Cutlass* to the marine beside him, the second-in-command of the team, 'that those whizz-bangs you're carrying back there don't go off.'

'They won't,' said the marine captain with confidence. 'Not until we use them.'

In a room adjoining the main conference centre beneath the Cabinet Office their commanding officer was poring over photographs of the *Freya*, taken by night and by day. He was comparing the configuration shown by the Nimrod's pictures with the scale-plan provided by Lloyd's and the model of the British *Princess* supertanker loaned by BP.

'Gentlemen,' said Colonel Holmes to the assembled men next door, 'I think it's time we considered one of the less palatable choices we may have to face.'

'Ah, yes,' said Sir Julian regretfully, 'the hard option.'

'If,' pursued Holmes, 'President Matthews continues to object to the release of Mishkin and Lazareff and West Germany continues to accede to that demand, the moment may well come when the terrorists realize the game is up; that their blackmail is not going to work. At that moment they may well refuse to have their bluff called, and blow the *Freya* to pieces. Personally, it seems to me this will not happen before nightfall, which gives us about sixteen hours.'

'Why nightfall, colonel?' asked Sir Julian.

'Because, sir, unless they are all suicide candidates, which they may be, one must assume that they will seek their own escape in the confusion. Now, if they wish to try to live, they may well leave the ship and operate their remote-control detonator from a certain distance from the ship's side.'

'And your proposal, colonel?'

'Twofold, sir. Firstly, their launch. It is still moored beside the courtesy ladder. As soon as darkness falls, a diver could approach that launch and attach a delayed-action explosive device to it. If the *Freya* should blow up, nothing within a half-mile radius would be safe. Therefore I propose a charge detonated by a mechanism operated by water pressure; as the launch moves away from the ship's side, the forward thrust of the launch will cause water to enter a funnel beneath the keel. This water will operate a trigger, and sixty seconds later the launch will blow up, before the terrorists have reached a point half a mile from the *Freya*, and therefore before they can operate their own detonator.'

There was a murmur of relief around the table.

'Would the exploding of their launch not detonate the charges on the *Freya*?' asked someone.

'No. If they have a remote-control detonator, it must be electronically operated. The charge would blow the launch carrying the terrorists to smithereens. No one would survive.'

'But if the detonator sank, would not the water pressure depress the button?' asked one of the scientists.

'No. Once under the water the remote-control detonator would be safe. It could not beam its radio message to the larger charges in the ship's tanks.'

'Excellent,' said Sir Julian. 'Can this plan not operate before darkness falls?'

'No, it cannot,' answered Holmes. 'A frogman diver leaves a trail of bubbles. In stormy weather this might not be noticed, but on a flat sea it would be too obvious. One of the lookouts could spot the bubbles rising. It would provoke what we are trying to avoid.'

'After dark it is, then,' said Sir Julian.

'Except for one thing, which is why I oppose the idea of sabotaging their escape launch as the only ploy. If, as may well happen, the leader of the terrorists is prepared to die with the *Freya*, he may not leave the ship with the rest of his team. So I believe we may have to storm the ship during a night attack and get to him before he can use his device.'

The Cabinet secretary sighed.

'I see. Doubtless you have a plan for that as well?'

'Personally, I do not. But I would like you to meet Major Simon Fallon, commanding the Special Boat Service.'

It was all the stuff of Sir Julian Flannery's nightmares. The marine major was barely five feet eight inches tall, but he seemed about the same across the shoulders and was evidently of that breed of men who talk about reducing other humans to their component parts with the same ease that Lady Flannery talked of dicing vegetables for one of her famous Provençal salads.

In at least three encounters the peace-loving Cabinet secretary had had occasion to meet officers from the SAS, but this was the first time he had seen the commander of the other, smaller specialist unit, the SBS. They were, he observed to himself, of the same breed.

The SBS had originally been formed for conventional war, to act as specialists in attacks on coastal installations arriving from the sea. That was why they were drawn from the marine commandos. As basic requirement they were physically fit to a revolting degree, experts in swimming, canoeing, diving, climbing, marching and fighting.

From there they went on to become proficient in parachuting, explosives, demolition and the seemingly limitless techniques of cutting throats or breaking necks with knife, wire-loop or simply bare hands. In this, and their capacity for living in self-sufficiency on or rather off the countryside for extended periods and leaving no trace of their presence, they simply shared the skills of their cousins in the SAS.

It was in their underwater skills that the SBS men were different. In frogman gear they could swim prodigious distances, lay explosive charges, or drop their swimming gear while treading water without a ripple, and emerge from the sea with their arsenal of special weapons wrapped about them.

Some of their weaponry was fairly routine: knives and cheese-wire. But since the start of that rash of outbreaks of terrorism in the late sixties, they had acquired fresh toys which delighted them. Each was an expert marksman with his high-precision, hand-tooled Finlanda rifle, a Norwegian-made piece that had been evaluated as perhaps the best rifle in the world. It could be and usually was fitted with image-intensifier, a sniper-scope as long as a bazooka and a completely effective silencer and flash-guard.

For taking doors away in half a second, they tended like the SAS towards short-barrelled pump-action shotguns firing solid charges. These they never aimed at the lock, for there could be other bolts behind the door; they fired two simultaneously to take off both hinges, kicking the door down and opening fire with the silenced Ingram machine-pistols.

Also in the arsenal that had helped the SAS assist the Germans at Mogadishu were their flash-bang-crash grenades, a sophisticated development of the 'stun' grenades. These did more than just stun, they paralysed. With a half-second delay after pulling the pin, these grenades, thrown into a confined space containing both terrorists and hostages, had three effects. The flash blinded anyone looking in that direction for at least thirty seconds, the bang blew the eardrums out, causing instant pain and a certain loss of concentration, and the crash was a tonal sound that entered the middle ear and caused a ten-second paralysis of all muscles.

During tests one of their own men had tried to pull the trigger of a gun pressed into a companion's side while the grenade went off. It was impossible. Both terrorists and hostages lost their eardrums, but they can grow again. Dead hostages cannot.

While the paralytic effect lasts, the rescuers spray bullets four inches over head height while their colleagues dive for the hostages, dragging them to the floor. At this point the firers drop their aim by six inches.

The exact position of hostage and terrorist in a closed room can be determined by the application of an electronic stethoscope to the outside of the door. Speech inside the room is not necessary; breathing can be heard and located accurately. The rescuers communicate in an elaborate sign-language that permits of no misunderstanding.

Major Fallon placed the model of the *Princess* on the conference table, aware he had the attention of everyone present.

'I propose,' he began, 'to ask the cruiser *Argyll* to turn herself broadside on to the *Freya*, and then before dawn park the assault boats containing my men and equipment close up in the lee of the *Argyll* where the lookout, here on top of the *Freya*'s funnel, cannot see them, even with binoculars. That will enable us to make our preparations through the afternoon unobserved. In case of aeroplanes hired by the press, I would like the sky cleared, and any detergent-spraying tugs within visual range of what we are doing to keep silent.'

There was no dissent to that. Sir Julian made two notes.

'I would approach the *Freya* with four two-man kayaks, halting at a range of three miles, in darkness, before the rising of the moon. Her radars will not spot kayaks. They are too small, too low in the water: they are of wood and canvas construction, which does not effectively register on radar. The paddlers will be in rubber, leather, wool undervests, etcetera, and all buckles will be in plastic. Nothing should register on the *Freya*'s radar.

'The men in the rear seats will be frogmen; their oxygen bottles have to be of metal, but at three miles will not register larger than a floating oil drum, not enough to cause alarm on the *Freya*'s bridge. At a range of three miles the divers take a compass bearing on the *Freya*'s stern, which they can see because it is illuminated, and drop overboard. They have luminescent wrist-compasses and swim by these.'

'Why not go for the bow?' asked the air force group captain. 'It's darker there.'

'Partly because it would mean eliminating the man on lookout high up on the fo'c's'le and he may be in walkie-talkie contact with the bridge,' said Fallon. 'Partly because that's a hell of a long walk down that deck, and they have a spotlight operable from the bridge. Partly because the superstructure, approached from the front, is a steel wall five storeys high. We would climb it, but it has windows, to cabins some of which may be occupied.

'The four divers, one of whom will be me, rendezvous at the stern of the *Freya*. There should be a tiny overhang of a few feet. Now, there's a man on top of the funnel, a hundred feet up. But people a hundred feet up tend to look outwards rather than straight down. To help him in this, I want the *Argyll* to start flashing her searchlight to another nearby vessel, creating a spectacle for the man to wach. We will come up the stern from the water, having shed flippers, masks, oxygen bottles and weighted belts. We will be bare-headed, barefoot, in rubber wet-suits only. All weaponry carried in wide webbing belts round the waist.'

'How do you get up the side of the *Freya* carrying forty pounds of metal after a three-mile swim?' asked one of the ministry men.

Fallon smiled. 'It's only thirty feet at most to the taffrail,' he said. 'While practising on the North Sea oil rigs we've climbed a hundred and sixty feet of vertical steel in four minutes.'

He saw no point in explaining the details of the fitness necessary for such a feat, nor the equipment that made it possible. The boffins had long ago developed for the SBS some remarkable climbing gear. Included among it were the magnetic climbing clamps. These were like dinner plates, fringed with rubber so that they could be applied to metal without making a sound. The plate itself was rimmed with steel beneath the rubber, and this steel ring could be magnetized to enormous strength. The magnetic force could be turned on or off by a thumb switch by the hand of the man holding the grip on the back of the plate. The electrical charge came from a small but reliable nickel-cadmium battery inside the climbing plate.

The divers were trained to come out of the sea, reach upwards and affix the first plate, then turn on the current. The magnet jammed the plate to the steel structure. Hanging on this, they reached higher and hung the second plate. Only when it was secure did they unlock the first disc, reach higher still and re-affix it. Hand over hand, hanging on by fist-grip, wrist and forearm, they climbed out of the sea and upwards, body, legs, feet and equipment swinging free, pulling against the hands and wrists.

So strong were the magnets, so strong also the arms and shoulders, that the commandos could climb an overhang of forty-five degrees if they had to.

'The first man goes up with the special clamps,' said Fallon, 'trailing a rope behind him. If it is quiet on the poop deck, he fixes the rope and the other three can be on deck inside ten seconds. Now, here, in the lee of the funnel assembly, this turbine housing should cast a shadow in the light thrown by the lamp above the door to the superstructure at "A" deck level. We group in this shadow. We'll have black wet-suits, black hands, feet and faces.

'The first major hazard is getting across this patch of illuminated after deck from the shadow of the turbine housing to the main superstructure with all its living quarters.'

'So how do you do it?' asked the vice-admiral, fascinated by this return from technology to the days of Nelson.

'We don't, sir,' said Fallon. 'We will be on the side of the funnel assembly away from where the *Argyll* is stationed. Hopefully the lookout atop the funnel will be looking at the *Argyll*, away from us. We move across from the shadow of the turbine housing, round the corner of the superstructure to this point here, outside the window of the dirty linen store. We cut the plate-glass window in silence with a miniature blow-torch working off a small gas bottle, and go in through the window. The chances of the door of such a store being locked are pretty slim. No one pinches dirty linen, so no one locks such doors. By this time we will be inside the superstructure, emerging to a passage a few yards from the main stairway leading up to "B", "C" and "D" deck, and the bridge.'

'Where do you find the terrorist leader,' asked Sir Julian Flannery, 'the man with the detonator?'

'On the way up the stairs we listen at every door for sounds of voices,' said Fallon. 'If there are any, we open the door and eliminate everyone in the room with silenced automatics. Two men entering the cabin, two men outside on guard. All the way up the structure. Anyone met on the stairs, the same thing. That should bring us to "D" deck unobserved. Here we have to take a calculated gamble. One choice is the captain's cabin; one man will take that choice. Open the door, step inside and shoot without any question. Another man will take the chief engineer's cabin on the same floor, other side of the ship. Same procedure. The last two men take the bridge itself; one with grenades, the second with the Ingrams. It's too big an area, that bridge, to pick targets. We'll just have to sweep it with the Ingram and take everybody in the place after the grenade has paralysed them.'

'What if one of them is Captain Larsen?' asked a ministry man.

Fallon studied the table. 'I'm sorry, there's no way of identifying targets,' he said.

'Suppose neither of the two cabins or the bridge contain the leader? Suppose the man with the remote control detonator is somewhere else? Out on deck taking the air? In the lavatory? Asleep in another cabin?'

Major Fallon shrugged. 'Bang,' he said, 'big bang.'

'There are twenty-nine crewmen locked down below,' protested a scientist. 'Can't you get them out? Or at least up on deck where they could have a chance to swim for it?'

'No, sir. I've tried every way of getting down to the paint locker, if they are indeed in the paint locker. To attempt to get down through the deck housing would give the game away; the bolts could well squeak, the opening of the steel door would flood the poop deck with light. To go down through the main superstructure to the engine room and try to get them that way would split my force. Moreover the engine room is vast; three levels of it, vaulted like a cathedral. One single man down there, in communication with his leader before we could silence him, and everything would be lost. I believe getting the man with the detonator is our best chance.'

'If she does blow up, with you and your men topsides I suppose you can dive over the side and swim for the *Argyll*?' suggested another of the ministry civil servants.

Major Fallon looked at the man with anger in his suntanned face.

'Sir, if she blows up, any swimmer within two hundred yards of her will be sucked down into the currents of water pouring into her holes.'

'I'm sorry, Major Fallon,' interposed the Cabinet secretary hurriedly. 'I am sure my colleague was simply concerned for your own safety. Now the question is this: the percentage chance of your hitting the holder of the detonator is a highly problematical figure. Failure to stop the man setting off his charges would provoke the very disaster we are trying to avoid. . . .'

'With the greatest respect, Sir Julian,' cut in Colonel Holmes, 'if the terrorists threaten during the course of the day to blow up the *Freya* at a certain hour tonight, and Chancellor Busch will not weaken in the matter of releasing Mishkin and Lazareff, surely we will have to try Major Fallon's way. We'll be on a hiding to nothing by then anyway. We'll have no alternative.'

The meeting murmured assent. Sir Julian conceded.

'Very well. Defence ministry will please make to *Argyll*; she should turn herself broadside to the *Freya* and provide a lee shelter for Major Fallon's assault boats when they arrive. Environment will instruct air traffic controllers to spot and turn back all aircraft trying to approach the *Argyll* at any altitude; various responsible departments will instruct the tugs and other vessels near the *Argyll* not to betray Major Fallon's preparations to anyone. What about you personally, Major Fallon?'

The marine commando glanced at his watch. It was five-fifteen.

'The navy is lending me a helicopter from the Battersea Heliport to the after deck of the *Argyll*,' he said. 'I'll be there when my men and equipment arrive by sea, if I leave now. . . .'

'Then be on your way, and good luck to you, young man.'

The men at the meeting stood up as a somewhat embarrassed major gathered his model ship, his plans and photographs and left with Colonel Holmes for the helicopter pad beside the Thames Embankment.

A weary Sir Julian Flannery left the smoke-charged room to ascend to the chill of the pre-dawn of another spring day and report to his Prime Minister.

At 6 a.m. a simple statement from Bonn was issued to the effect that after due consideration of all the factors involved, the Federal German government had come to the conclusion that it would after all be wrong to accede to blackmail and that therefore the policy of releasing Mishkin and Lazareff at 8 a.m. had been reconsidered.

Instead, the statement continued, the Federal government would do all in its power to enter into negotiations with the captors of the *Freya* with a view to seeking the release of the ship and its crew by alternative proposals.

The European allies of West Germany were informed of this statement just one hour before it was issued. Each and every premier privately asked the same question:

'What the hell is Bonn up to?'

The exception was London, who knew already. But unofficially, each government was informed that the reversal of position stemmed from urgent American pressure on Bonn during the night, and they were further informed that Bonn had only agreed to delay the release, pending further and, it was hoped, more optimistic developments.

With the breaking of the news, the Bonn government spokesman had two brief and very private working breakfasts with influential German journalists, during which each pressman was given to understand in oblique terms that the change of policy stemmed only from brutal pressure from Washington.

The first radio newscasts of the day carried the fresh statement out of Bonn even as the listeners were picking up their newspapers, which confidently announced the release at breakfast time of the two hijackers. The newspapers' editors were not amused and bombarded the government's news office for an explanation. None was forthcoming that satisfied anyone. The Sunday papers, due for preparation that Saturday, geared themselves for an explosive issue the following morning.

On the *Freya*, the news from Bonn came over the BBC world service to which Drake had tuned his portable radio, at 6.30. Like many another interested party in Europe that morning, the Ukrainian listened to the news in silence, then burst out:

'What the hell do they think they're up to?'

'Something has gone wrong,' said Thor Larsen flatly. 'They've changed their minds. It's not going to work.'

For answer Drake leaned far across the table and pointed his handgun straight at the Norwegian's face.

'Don't you gloat,' he shouted. 'It's not just my friends in Berlin they're playing silly games with. It's not just me. It's your precious ship and crew they're playing with. And don't you forget it.'

He went into deep thought for several minutes, then used the captain's intercom to summon one of his men from the bridge. The man, when he came to the cabin, was still masked, and spoke to his chief in Ukrainian, but the tone sounded worried. Drake left him to guard Captain Larsen and was away for fifteen minutes. When he returned he brusquely beckoned the *Freya*'s skipper to accompany him to the bridge.

The call came in to Maas Control just a minute before seven. Channel twenty was still reserved for the *Freya* alone, and the duty operator was expecting something, for he too had heard the news from Bonn. When the *Freya* called up, he had the tape recorders spinning.

Larsen's voice sounded tired, but he read the statement from his captors in an unemotional tone. ' "Following the stupid decision of the government in Bonn to reverse its agreement to release Lev Mishkin and David Lazareff at oh eight hundred hours this morning, those who presently hold the *Freya* announce the following: in the event that Mishkin and Lazareff are not released and airborne on their way to Tel Aviv by noon today, the *Freya* will, on the stroke of noon, vent twenty thousand tons of crude oil into the North Sea. Any attempt to prevent this, or interfere with the process, and any attempt by ships or aircraft to enter the area of clear water round the *Freya*, will result in the immediate destruction of the ship, her crew and cargo." '

The transmission ceased and the channel was cut off. No questions were asked. Almost a hundred listening posts heard the message, and it was contained in news flashes on the breakfast radio shows across Europe within fifteen minutes.

·

President Matthews' Oval Office was beginning to adopt the aspect of a council of war by the small hours of the morning.

All four men in it had taken their jackets off and loosened ties. Aides came and went with messages from the communications room for one or other of the presidential advisers. The corresponding communication rooms at Langley and State Department had been patched through to the White House. It was 7.15 European time but 2.15 in the morning when the news of Drake's ultimatum was brought into the office and handed to Robert Benson. He passed it without a word to President Matthews.

'I suppose we should have expected it,' said the President wearily, 'but it makes it no easier to learn.'

'Do you think he'll really do it, whoever he is?' asked Secretary David Lawrence.

'He's done everything else he promised so far, damn him,' replied Stanislaw Poklewski.

'I assume Mishkin and Lazareff are under extra heavy guard in Tegel,' said Lawrence.

'They're not in Tegel any more,' replied Benson. 'They were moved just before midnight, Berlin time, to Moabit. It's more modern and more secure.'

'How do you know, Bob?' asked Poklewski.

'I've had Tegel and Moabit under surveillance since the *Freya*'s noon broadcast,' said Benson.

Lawrence, the old-style diplomat, looked exasperated.

'Is it the new policy to spy even on our allies?' he snapped.

'Not quite,' replied Benson. 'We've always done it.'

'Why the change of jail, Bob?' asked Matthews. 'Does Dietrich Busch think the Russians would try and get at Mishkin and Lazareff?'

'No, Mr President, he thinks I will,' said Benson.

'There seems to me a possibility here that maybe we hadn't thought of,' interposed Poklewski. 'If the terrorists on the *Freya* go ahead and vent twenty thousand tons of crude, and threaten to vent a further fifty thousand tons later in the day, the pressures on Busch could become overwhelming. . . .'

'No doubt they will,' observed Lawrence.

'What I mean is, Busch might simply decide to go it alone and release the hijackers unilaterally. Remember, he doesn't know that the price of such an action would be the destruction of the Treaty of Dublin.'

There was silence for several seconds.

'There's nothing I can do to stop him,' said President Matthews quietly.

'There is, actually,' said Benson. He had the instant attention of the other three. When he described what it was, the faces of Matthews, Lawrence and Poklewski showed disgust.

'I couldn't give that order,' said the President.

'It's a pretty terrible thing to do,' agreed Benson, 'but it's the only way to pre-empt Chancellor Busch. And we will know if he tries to make secret plans to release the pair prematurely. Never mind how; we *will* know. Let's face it; the alternative would be the destruction of the treaty, and the consequences in terms of a resumed arms race that this must bring. If the treaty is destroyed, presumably we will not go ahead with the grain shipments to Russia. In that event Rudin may fall. . . .'

'Which makes his reaction over this business so crazy,' Lawrence pointed out.

'Maybe so, but that *is* his reaction, and until we know why we can't judge how crazy he is,' Benson resumed. 'Until we do know, Chancellor Busch's private knowledge of the proposal I have just made should hold him in check a while longer.'

'You mean we could just use it as something to hold over Busch's head?' asked Matthews hopefully. 'We might never actually have to do it?'

At that moment a personal message arrived for the President from Prime Minister Carpenter in London.

'That's some woman,' he said when he had read it. 'The British reckon they can cope with the first oil slick of twenty thousand tons, but no more. They're preparing a plan to storm the *Freya* with specialist frogmen after sundown and silence the man with the detonator. They give themselves a better than even chance.'

'So we only have to hold the German Chancellor in line for another twelve hours,' said Benson. 'Mr President, I urge you to order what I have just proposed. The chances are it will never have to be activated.'

'But if it must be, Bob? If it must be?'

'Then it must be.'

William Matthews placed the palms of his hands over his face and rubbed tired eyes with his fingertips.

'Dear God, no man should be asked to give orders like that,' he said. 'But if I must. . . . Bob, give the order.'

The sun was just clear of the horizon, away to the east over the Dutch coast. On the after deck of the cruiser *Argyll*, now turned broadside to where the *Freya* lay, Major Fallon stood and looked down at the three fast assault craft tethered to her lee side. From the lookout on the *Freya's* funnel top all three would be out of vision. So too the activity on their decks, where Fallon's team of marine commandos were preparing their kayaks and unpacking their unusual pieces of equipment. It was a bright, clear sunrise, giving promise of another warm and sunny day. The sea was a flat calm. Fallon was joined by the *Argyll*'s skipper, Captain Richard Preston.

They stood side by side looking down at the three sleek sea greyhounds that had brought the men and equipment from Poole in eight hours. The boats rocked in the swell of a warship passing several cables to the west of them. Fallon looked up. 'Who's that?' he asked, nodding towards the grey warship flying the stars and stripes that was moving to the south.

'The American navy has sent an observer,' said Captain Preston. 'The USS *Moran*. She'll take up station between us and the *Montcalm*.' He glanced at his watch.

'Seven-thirty. Breakfast is being served in the wardroom, if you'd care to join us.'

It was seven-fifty when there was a knock at the door of the cabin of Captain Mike Manning, commanding the *Moran*.

She was at anchor after her race through the night and Manning, who had taken the bridge throughout the night, was running a shaver over his stubble. When the telegraphist entered, Manning took the proffered message and gave it a glance, still shaving. He stopped and turned to the rating.

'It's still in code,' he said.

'Yes, sir. It's tagged for your eyes only, sir.'

Manning dismissed the man, went to his wall-safe and took out his personal decoder. It was unusual, but not unheard of. He began to run a pencil down columns of figures, seeking the groups on the message in front of him and their corresponding letter-combinations. When he had finished decoding, he just sat at his table and stared at the message for a fault. He rechecked the beginning of the message, hoping it was a practical joke. But there was no joke. It was for him, via STANFORLANT through Navy Department, Washington. And it was a presidential order, personal to him from the commander-in-chief, US armed forces, White House, Washington.

'He can't ask me to do that,' he breathed. 'No man can ask a sailor to do that.'

But the message did, and it was unequivocal.

In the event the West German government seeks to release the hijackers of Berlin unilaterally, the USS *Moran* is to sink the supertanker *Freya* by shellfire, using all possible measures to ignite cargo and minimize environmental damage. This action will be taken on receipt by USS *Moran* of the signal 'THUNDERBOLT' repeat 'THUNDERBOLT'. Destroy message.

Mike Manning was forty-three years old, married with four children, all living with their mother outside Norfolk, Virginia. He had been twenty-one years a serving officer in the US Navy and had never before thought to query a service order.

He walked to the porthole and looked across the five miles of ocean to the low outline between him and the climbing sun. He thought of his magnesium-based starshells slamming into her unprotected skin, penetrating to the volatile crude oil beneath. He thought of twenty-nine men, crouched deep beneath the water-line, eighty feet beneath the waves, in a steel coffin, waiting for rescue, thinking of their own families in the forests of Scandinavia. He crumpled the paper in his hand.

'Mr President,' he whispered, 'I don't know if I can do that.'

16

0800 to 1500

Dyetski Mir means 'Children's World' and is Moscow's premier toyshop, four storeys of dolls and playthings, puppets and games. Compared to a Western equivalent the layout is drab and the stock shabby, but it is the best the Soviet capital has, apart from the hard-currency Beriozka shops where mainly foreigners go.

By an unintended irony it is across Dzerzhinsky Square from the KGB headquarters, which is definitely not a children's world. Adam Munro was at the ground-floor soft toys counter just before 10 a.m., Moscow time, two hours later than North Sea time. He began to examine a nylon bear as if debating whether to buy it for his offspring.

Two minutes after ten someone moved to the counter beside him. Out of the corner of his eye he saw that she was pale, her normally full lips drawn, tight, the colour of cigarette ash.

She nodded. Her voice was pitched as his own, low, conversational, uninvolved.

'I managed to see the transcript, Adam. It's serious.'

She picked up a hand-puppet shaped like a small monkey in artificial fur, and told him quietly what she had discovered.

'That's impossible,' he muttered. 'He's still convalescing from a heart attack.'

'No. He was shot dead last October 31st in the middle of the night in a street in Kiev.'

Two salesgirls leaning against the wall twenty feet away

eyed them without curiosity and returned to their gossip. One of the few advantages of shopping in Moscow is that one is guaranteed complete privacy by the sales staff.

'And those two in Berlin were the ones?' asked Munro.

'It seems so,' she said dully. 'The fear is that if they escape to Israel they will hold a press conference and inflict an intolerable humiliation on the Soviet Union.'

'Causing Maxim Rudin to fall,' breathed Munro. 'No wonder he will not countenance their release. He cannot. He too has no alternative. And you, are you safe, darling?'

'I don't know. I don't think so. There were suspicions. Unspoken, but they were there. Soon the man on the telephone switchboard will report about your call; the gateman will tell his superiors about my drive in the small hours. It will all come together.'

'Listen, Valentina, I will get you out of here. Quickly, in the next few days.'

For the first time, she turned and faced him. He saw that her eyes were brimming.

'It's over, Adam. I've done what you asked of me, and now it's too late.' She reached up and kissed him briefly, before the astonished gaze of the salesgirls. 'Good-bye, Adam, my love. I'm sorry.'

She turned, paused for a moment to collect herself, and walked away, through the glass doors to the street, back through the gap in the Wall into the East. From where he stood with a plastic-faced milkmaid doll in his hand, he saw her reach the pavement and turn out of sight. A man in a grey trenchcoat, who had been wiping the windscreen of a car, straightened, nodded to the colleague behind the windscreen, and strolled after her.

Adam Munro felt the grief and the anger rising in his throat like a ball of sticky acid. The sounds of the shop muted as a roaring invaded his ears. His hand closed round the head of the doll, crushing, cracking, splintering the smiling pink face beneath the lace cap.

A salesgirl appeared rapidly at his side. 'You've broken it,' she said. 'That will be four roubles.'

Compared with the whirlwind of public and media concern that had concentrated on the West German Chancellor the previous afternoon, the recriminations that poured upon Bonn that Saturday morning were more like a hurricane.

The Foreign Ministry received a continual stream of requests couched in the most urgent terms from the embassies of Finland, Norway, Sweden, Denmark, France, Holland and Belgium, each asking that their ambassadors be received. Each wish was granted, and each ambassador asked in the courteous phraseology of diplomacy the same question: What the hell is going on?

Newspapers, television and radio operations called in all their staffers from weekend leave and tried to give the affair saturation coverage, which was not easy. There were no pictures of the *Freya* since the hijack, save those taken by the French freelancer, who was under arrest, and his pictures confiscated. In fact the same pictures were in Paris under study, but the shots from the successive Nimrods were just as good, and the French government was receiving them anyway.

For lack of hard news, the papers hunted anything they could go for. Two enterprising Englishmen bribed Hilton Hotel staff in Rotterdam to lend them their uniforms, and tried to reach the penthouse suite where Harry Wennerstrom and Lisa Larsen were under siege.

Others sought out former prime ministers, cabinet office holders and tanker captains for their views. Extraordinary sums were waved in the faces of the wives of the crewmen, almost all of whom had been traced, to be photographed praying for their husbands' deliverance.

One former mercenary commander offered to storm the *Freya* alone for a $1,000,000 fee; four archbishops and seventeen parliamentarians of varying persuasions and ambitions offered themselves as hostages in exchange for Captain Larsen and his crew.

'Separately, or in job lots?' snapped Dietrich Busch when he was informed. 'I wish William Matthews was on board instead of thirty good sailors. I'd hold out till Christmas.'

By mid-morning the leaks to the two German stars of press and radio were beginning to have their effect. Their respective comments in German radio and television were picked up by the news agencies and Germany-based correspondents and given wider coverage. The view began to percolate that Dietrich Busch had in fact been acting in the hours before dawn under massive American pressure.

Bonn declined to confirm this, but refused to deny it either. The sheer evasiveness of the government spokesman there told the press its own story.

As dawn broke over Washington, five hours behind Europe, the emphasis switched to the White House. By 6 a.m. in Washington the White House press corps was clamouring for an interview with the President himself. They had to be satisfied, but were not, with a harassed and evasive official spokesman. The spokesman was evasive only because he did not know what to say; his repeated appeals to the Oval Office brought only further instructions that he tell the newshounds the matter was a European affair and the Europeans must do as they thought best. Which threw the affair back into the lap of an increasingly outraged German Chancellor.

'How much longer the hell can this go on?' shouted a thoroughly shaken William Matthews to his advisers as he pushed away a plate of scrambled egg just after 6 a.m. Washington time.

The same question was being asked, but not answered, in a score of offices across America and Europe that unquiet Saturday forenoon.

From his office in Texas the owner of the one million tons of Mubarraq crude, lying dormant but dangerous beneath the *Freya*'s deck, was on the line to Washington.

'I don't care what the hell time of the morning it is,' he shouted to the party campaign manager's secretary. 'You get him on the line and tell him this is Clint Blake, ya hear?'

When the campaign manager of the political party to which the President belonged finally came on the line, he was not a happy man. When he put the machine back in its cradle he was downright morose. A $1,000,000 campaign contribution is no small potatoes in any country, and Clint Blake's threat to withdraw it from his own party and donate it to the opposition was no joke.

It seemed to matter little to him that the cargo was fully insured against loss by Lloyds. He was one very angry Texan that morning.

Harry Wennerstrom was on the line most of the morning from Rotterdam to Stockholm, calling every one of his friends and contacts in shipping, banking and government to bring pressure on the Swedish premier. The pressure was effective and it was passed on to Bonn.

In London the chairman of Lloyd's, Sir Murray Kelso, found the permanent under-secretary to the Department of the Environment still at his desk in Whitehall. Saturday is normally not a day when the senior members of Britain's Civil Service are to be found at the desks, but this was no normal Saturday. Sir Rupert Mossbank had driven hastily back from his country home before dawn when the news came from Downing Street that Mishkin and Lazareff were not to be released. He showed his visitor to a chair.

'Damnable business,' said Sir Murray.

'Perfectly appalling,' agreed Sir Rupert.

He proffered the Butter Osbornes and the two knights sipped their tea.

'The thing is,' said Sir Murray at length, 'the sums involved are really quite vast. Close to a thousand million dollars. Even if the victim countries from the oil spillage if the *Freya* blows up were to sue West Germany rather than us, we'd still have to carry the loss of the ship, cargo and crew. That's about four hundred million dollars.'

'You'd be able to cover it, of course,' said Sir Rupert anxiously. Lloyd's was more than just a company, it was an institution and as Sir Rupert's department covered merchant shipping he was concerned.

'Oh yes, we would cover it. Have to,' said Sir Murray.

'Thing is, it's such a sum it would have to be reflected in the country's invisible earnings for the year. Probably tip the balance, actually. And what with the new application for another IMF Loan. . . .'

'It's a German question, you know,' said Mossbank. 'Not really up to us.'

'Nevertheless, one might press the Germans a bit over this one. Hijackers are bastards, of course, but in this case, why not just let those two blighters in Berlin go. Good riddance to them.'

'Leave it to me,' said Mossbank. 'I'll see what I can do.'

Privately he knew he could do nothing. The confidential file locked in his safe told him Major Fallon was going in by kayak in eleven hours, and until then the Prime Minister's orders were that the line had to hold.

Chancellor Dietrich Busch received the news of the intended underwater attack during the mid-morning in a face-to-face interview with the British ambassador. He was slightly mollified.

'So that's what it's all about,' he said when he had examined the plan unfolded before him. 'Why could I not have been told of this before?'

'We were not sure whether it would work before,' said the ambassador smoothly. Those were his instructions. 'We were working on it through the afternoon of yesterday and last night. By dawn we were certain it was perfectly feasible.'

'What chance of success do you give yourselves?' asked Dietrich Busch.

The ambassador cleared his throat. 'We estimate the chances at three to one in our favour,' he said. 'The sun sets at seven-thirty. Darkness is complete by nine. The men are going in at ten tonight.'

The Chancellor looked at his watch. Twelve hours to go. If the British tried and succeeded, much of the credit would go to their frogmen-killers, but much also to him for keeping his nerve. If they failed, theirs would be the responsibility.

'So it all depends now on this Major Fallon. Very well, ambassador, I will continue to play my part until ten tonight.'

Apart from her batteries of guided missiles, the USS *Moran* was armed with two five-inch Mark 45 naval guns, one forward, one aft. They were of the most modern type available, radar-aimed and computer-controlled. Each could fire a complete magazine of twenty shells in rapid succession without reloading, and the sequence of various types of shell could be pre-set on the computer.

The old days when naval guns' ammunition had to be manually hauled out of the deep magazine, hoisted up to the gun turret by steam power, and rammed into the breech by sweating gunners were long gone. In the *Moran* the shells would be selected by type and performance from the stock on the magazine by the computer, the shells brought to the firing turret automatically, the five-inch guns loaded, fired, voided, reloaded and fired again without a human hand.

The aiming was by radar; the invisible eyes of the ship would seek out the target according to the programmed instructions, adjust for wind, range and the movement of either target or firing platform, and, once locked on, hold that aim until given fresh orders. The computer would work together with the eyes of radar, absorbing within fractions of a second any tiny shift of the *Moran* herself, the target, or the wind strength between them. Once locked on, the target could begin to move, the *Moran* could go anywhere she liked; the guns would simply move on silent bearings, keeping their deadly muzzles pointed to just where the shells should go. Wild seas could force the *Moran* to pitch and roll; the target could yaw and swing; it made no difference because the computer compensated. Even the pattern in which the homing shells should fall could be pre-set.

As a back-up, the gunnery officer could scan the target visually with the aid of a camera mounted high aloft, and issue fresh instructions to both radar and computer when he wished to change target.

Captain Mike Manning surveyed the *Freya* from where he stood by the rail with grim concentration. Whoever had advised the President must have done his homework well. The environmental hazard in the death of the *Freya* lay in the escape in crude oil form of her million-ton cargo. But if that cargo was ignited while still in the holds, or within a few seconds of the ship's rupture, it would burn. In fact it would more than burn – it would explode.

Normally crude oil is exceptionally difficult to burn, but if heated enough it will inevitably reach its flashpoint and take fire. The Mubarraq crude the *Freya* carried was the lightest of them all, and to plunge lumps of blazing magnesium, burning at more than 1000° C, into her hull would do the trick with margin to spare. Up to ninety per cent of her cargo would never reach the ocean in crude oil form; it would flame, making a fireball over 10,000 feet high.

What would be left of the cargo would be scum, drifting on the sea's surface, and a black pall of smoke as big as the cloud that once hung over Hiroshima. Of the ship herself, there would be nothing left, but the environmental problem would have been reduced to manageable proportions. Mike Manning summoned his gunnery officer, Lieutenant Commander Chuck Olsen, to join him by the rail.

'I want you to load and lay the forward gun,' he said flatly. Olsen began to note the commands.

'Ordnance: three semi-armour-piercing, five magnesium starshell, two high-explosive. Total, ten. Then repeat that sequence. Total, twenty.'

'Yes, sir. Three SAP, five Star, two HE. Fall pattern?'

'First shell on target, next shell two hundred metres further; third shell two hundred metres further still. Backtrack in forty-metre drops with the five starshells. Then forward again with the high-explosive, one hundred metres each.'

Lieutenant Commander Olsen noted the fall pattern his captain required. Manning stared over the rail. Five miles away the bows of the *Freya* were pointing straight at the *Moran*. The fall pattern he had dictated would cause the shells to drop in a line from the peak of the *Freya* to the base of her superstructure, then back to the bow, then back again with the explosive towards the superstructure. The semi-armour piercing would cut open her tanks through the deck-metal as a scalpel opens skin; the starshells would drop in a line of five down the cuts; the explosive would push the blazing crude oil outwards into all the port and starboard holds.

'Got it, captain. Fall point for first shell?'

'Ten metres over the bow of the *Freya*.'

Olsen's pen halted above the paper of his clipboard. He stared at what he had written, then raised his eyes to the *Freya* five miles away.

'Captain,' he said slowly, 'if you do that, she won't just sink; she won't just burn; she won't just explode. She'll vapourize.'

'Those are my orders, Mr Olsen,' said Manning stonily.

The young Swedish-American by his side was pale. 'For Christ's sake, there are thirty Scandinavian seamen on that ship.'

'Mr Olsen, I am aware of the facts. You will either carry out my orders and lay that gun, or announce to me that you refuse.'

The gunnery officer stiffened to attention.

'I'll load and lay your gun for you, Captain Manning,' he said, 'but I will not fire it. If the fire button has to be pressed, you must press it yourself.'

He snapped up a perfect salute and marched away to the fire-control station below decks.

You won't have to, thought Manning, by the rail. If the President himself orders me, I will fire it. Then I will resign my commission.

An hour later the Westland Wessex from the *Argyll* came overhead and winched a Royal Navy officer to the deck of the *Moran*. He asked to speak to Captain Manning in private and was shown to the American's cabin.

'Compliments of Captain Preston, sir,' said the ensign, and handed Manning a letter from Preston. When he had finished reading it, Manning sat back like a man reprieved from the gallows. It told him that the British were sending in a team of armed frogmen at ten that night, and all governments had agreed to undertake no independent action in the meantime.

While the two officers were talking aboard the USS *Moran*, the airliner bearing Adam Munro back to the West was clearing the Soviet-Polish border.

From the toyshop on Dzerzhinsky Square, Munro had gone to a public call box and telephoned the head of chancery at his embassy. He had told the amazed diplomat in coded language that he had discovered what his masters wanted to know, but would not be returning to the embassy. Instead he was heading straight for the airport to catch the noon plane.

By the time the diplomat had informed the Foreign Office of this, and the FO had told the SIS, the message back to the effect that Munro should cable his news was too late. Munro was boarding.

'What the devil's he doing?' asked Sir Nigel Irvine of Barry Ferndale in the SIS head office in London when he learned his storm petrel was flying home.

'No idea,' replied the controller of Soviet Section. 'Perhaps the Nightingale's been blown and he needs to get back urgently before the diplomatic incident blows up. Shall I meet him?'

'When does it land?'

'One forty-five, London time,' said Ferndale. 'I think I ought to meet him. It seems he has the answer to President Matthews' question. Frankly, I'm curious to find out what the devil it can be.'

'So am I,' said Sir Nigel. 'Take a car with scrambler phone and stay in touch with me personally.'

At a quarter to twelve Drake sent one of his men to bring the *Freya*'s pumpman back to the cargo control room on 'A' deck. Leaving Thor Larsen under the guard of another terrorist, Drake descended to cargo control, took the fuses from his pocket and replaced them. Power was restored to the cargo pumps.

'When you discharge cargo, what do you do?' he asked the crewman. 'I've still got a submachine gun pointing at your captain, and I'll order it to be used if you play any tricks.'

'The ship's pipeline system terminates at a single point, a cluster of pipes which we call the manifold,' said the pumpman. 'Hoses from the shore installation are coupled up to the manifold. After that, the main gate valves are opened at the manifold, and the ship begins to pump.'

'What's your rate of discharge?'

'Twenty thousand tons per hour,' said the man. 'During discharge the ship's balance is maintained by venting several tanks at different points on the ship simultaneously.'

Drake had noted that there was a slight, one-knot tide flowing past the *Freya*, northeast towards the Dutch Friesian islands. He pointed to a tank amidships on the *Freya*'s port side.

'Open the master valve on that one,' he said. The man paused for a second, then obeyed.

'Right,' said Drake, 'when I give the word, switch on the cargo pumps and vent the entire tank.'

'Into the sea?' asked the pump man incredulously.

'Into the sea,' said Drake grimly. 'Chancellor Busch is about to learn what international pressure really means.'

As the minutes ticked away to midday of Saturday, 2nd April, Europe held its breath. So far as anyone knew, the terrorist had already executed one seaman for a breach of the airspace above them, and had threatened to do it again, or vent crude oil, on the stroke of noon.

The Nimrod that had replaced Squadron Leader Latham the previous midnight had run short of fuel by 11 a.m., so Latham was back on duty, cameras whirring as the minutes to noon ticked away.

Many miles above him a Condor spy satellite was on station, bouncing its continuous stream of picture images across the globe to where a haggard American President sat in the

Oval Office watching a television screen. On the TV the *Freya* inched gently into frame from the bottom rim like a pointing finger.

In London men of rank and influence grouped round a screen in the Cabinet Office briefing room on which was presented what the Nimrod was seeing. The Nimrod was on continuous camera-roll from five minutes before twelve, her pictures passing to the Datalink on the *Argyll* beneath her, and from there to Whitehall.

Along the rails of the *Montcalm, Breda, Brunner, Argyll* and *Moran*, sailors of five nations passed binoculars from hand to hand. Their officers stood as high aloft as they could get, with telescopes to eye.

On the BBC World Service the bell of Big Ben struck noon. In the Cabinet Office two hundred yards from Big Ben and two floors beneath the street, someone shouted, 'Christ, she's venting.' Three thousand miles away four shirtsleeved Americans in the Oval Office watched the same spectacle.

From the side of the *Freya*, amidships to port, a column of sticky, ochre-red crude oil erupted.

It was as thick as a man's torso. Impelled by the power of the *Freya*'s mighty pumps, the oil leapt the port rail, dropped twenty-five feet and thundered into the sea. Within seconds the blue-green water was discoloured, putrefied. As the oil bubbled back to the surface, a stain began to spread, moving out and away from the ship's hull on the tide.

For sixty minutes the venting went on, until the single tank was dry. The great stain formed the shape of an egg, broad nearest the Dutch coast and tapering near to the ship. Finally the mass of oil parted company with the *Freya* and began to drift. The sea being calm, the oil slick stayed in one piece, but it began to expand as the light crude ran across the surface of the water. At 2 p.m., an hour after the venting ended, the slick was ten miles long and seven miles wide at its broadest.

In Washington the Condor passed on and the slick moved off screen. Stanislaw Poklewski switched off the set.

'That's just one fiftieth of what she carries,' he said. 'Those Europeans will go bloody mad.'

Robert Benson took a telephone call and turned to President Matthews.

'London just checked in with Langley,' he said. 'Their man from Moscow has cabled that he has the answer to our question. He claims he knows why Maxim Rudin is threatening to tear up the Treaty of Dublin if Mishkin and Lazareff go free. He's flying personally with the news from Moscow to London, and he should land in one hour.'

Matthews shrugged.

'With this man Major Fallon going in with his divers in nine hours, maybe it doesn't matter any more,' he said, 'but I'd sure be interested to know.'

'He'll report to Sir Nigel Irvine, who will tell Mrs Carpenter. Maybe you could ask her to use the hot line the moment she knows,' suggested Benson.

'I'll do that,' said the President.

It was just after 8 a.m. in Washington but past 1 p.m. in Europe when Andrew Drake, who had been pensive and withdrawn while the oil was being vented, decided to make contact again.

By twenty-past one Captain Thor Larsen was speaking again to Maas Control, from whom he asked at once to be patched through to the Dutch premier, Mr Jan Grayling. The patch-through to The Hague took no time; the possibility had been foreseen that sooner or later the premier might get a chance to talk to the leader of the terrorists personally and appeal for negotiations on behalf of Holland and Germany.

'I am listening to you, Captain Larsen,' said the Dutchman to the Norwegian in English. 'This is Jan Grayling speaking.'

' "Prime Minister, you have seen the venting of twenty thousand tons of crude oil from my ship?" ' asked Larsen, the gun barrel an inch from his ear.

'With great regret, yes,' said Grayling.

' "The leader of the partisans proposes a conference." '

The captain's voice boomed through the premier's office in The Hague. Grayling looked up sharply at the two senior civil servants who had joined him. The tape recorder rolled impassively.

'I see,' said Grayling, who did not see at all but was stalling for time. 'What kind of conference?'

' "A face-to-face conference with the representatives of the coastal nations and other interested parties," ' said Larsen, reading from the paper in front of him.

Jan Grayling clapped his hand over the mouthpiece.

'The bastard wants to talk,' he said excitedly, and then, down the telephone he said, 'On behalf of the Dutch government, I accept to be host to such a conference. Please inform the partisan leader of this.'

On the bridge of the *Freya* Drake shook his head and placed his hand over the mouthpiece. He had a hurried discussion with Larsen.

'Not on land,' said Larsen down the phone. 'Here at sea. What is the name of that British cruiser?'

'She's called the *Argyll*,' said Grayling.

' "She has a helicopter," ' said Larsen at Drake's instruction. ' "The conference will be aboard the *Argyll*. At three p.m. Those present should include yourself, the German ambassador, and the captains of the five NATO warships. No one else." '

'That is understood,' said Grayling. 'Will the leader of the partisans attend in person? I would need to consult the British about a guarantee of safe-conduct.'

There was silence as another conference took place on the bridge of the *Freya*. Captain Larsen's voice came back.

'No, the leader will not attend. He will send a representative. "At five minutes before three the helicopter from the *Argyll* will be permitted to hover over the helipad of the *Freya*. There will be no soldiers or marines on board. Only the pilot and the winchman, both unarmed. The scene will be observed from the bridge. There will be no cameras. The helicopter will not descend lower than twenty feet. The winchman will lower a harness and the emissary will be lifted off the main deck and across to the *Argyll*. Is that understood?" '

'Perfectly,' said Grayling. 'May I ask who the representative will be?'

'One moment,' said Larsen and the line went dead.

On the *Freya*, Larsen turned to Drake and asked: 'Well, Mr Svoboda, if not yourself, who are you sending?'

Drake smiled briefly.

'You,' he said. 'You will represent me. You are the best person I can think of to convince them I am not joking either about the ship or the crew or the cargo. And that my patience is running short.'

The phone in Premier Grayling's hand crackled to life.

'I am informed it will be me,' said Larsen, and the line was cut.

Jan Grayling glanced at his watch.

'One forty-five,' he said. 'Seventy-five minutes to go. Get Konrad Voss over here; prepare a helicopter to take off from the nearest point to this office. I want a direct line to Mrs Carpenter in London.'

He had hardly finished speaking before his private secretary told him Harry Wennerstrom was on the line. The old millionaire in the penthouse above the Hilton in Rotterdam had acquired his own radio receiver during the night and had mounted a permanent watch on channel twenty.

'You'll be going out to the *Argyll* by helicopter,' he told the Dutch premier without preamble. 'I'd be grateful if you would take Mrs Lisa Larsen with you.'

'Well, I don't know. . . .' began Grayling.

'For pity's sake, man,' boomed the Swede, 'the terrorists will never know. And if this business isn't handled right, it may be the last time she ever sees him.'

'Get her here in forty minutes,' said Grayling. 'We take off at half-past two.'

The conversation on channel twenty had been heard by every intelligence network and most of the media. Lines were already buzzing between Rotterdam and nine European capitals. The National Security Agency in Washington had a transcript clattering off the White House teleprinter for President Matthews. An aide was darting across the lawn from the Cabinet Office to Mrs Carpenter's study in 10 Downing Street. The Israeli ambassador in Bonn was urgently asking Chancellor Busch to ascertain for Prime Minister Golen from Captain Larsen whether the terrorists were Jews or not, and the German government chief promised to do this.

The afternoon newspapers, radio and TV shows across Europe had their headlines for the 5 p.m. edition and frantic calls were made to four navy ministries for a report on the conference if and when it took place.

As Jan Grayling put down the telephone on Thor Larsen, the jet airliner carrying Adam Munro from Moscow touched the tarmac of runway One at London's Heathrow Airport.

Barry Ferndale's Foreign Office pass had brought him to the foot of the aircraft steps and he ushered his bleak-faced colleague from Moscow into the back seat. The car was better than most that the firm used; it had a screen between driver and passengers, and a telephone linked to head office.

As they swept down the tunnel from the airport to the M4 motorway, Ferndale broke the silence.

'Rough trip, old boy.' He was not referring to the aeroplane journey.

'Disastrous,' snapped Munro. 'I think the Nightingale is blown. Certainly followed by the opposition. May have been picked up by now.'

Ferndale clucked sympathy.

'Bloody bad luck,' he said. 'Always terrible to lose an agent. Damned upsetting. Lost a couple myself, you know. One died damned unpleasantly. But that's the trade we're in, Adam. That's part of what Kipling used to call the Great Game.'

'Except this is no game,' said Munro, 'and what the KGB will do to the Nightingale is no joke.'

'Absolutely not. Sorry. Shouldn't have said that.' Ferndale paused expectantly as their car joined the M4 traffic stream.

'But you did get the answer to our questions? Why is Rudin so pathologically opposed to the release of Mishkin and Lazareff?'

'The answer to Mrs Carpenter's question,' said Munro grimly. 'Yes, I got it.'

'And it is?'

'She asked it,' said Munro, 'she'll get the answer. I hope she'll like it. It cost a life to get it.'

'That might not be wise, Adam, old son,' said Ferndale. 'You can't just walk in on the PM, you know. Even the Master has to make an appointment.'

'Then ask him to make one,' said Munro gesturing to the telephone.

'I'm afraid I'll have to,' said Ferndale quietly. It was a pity to see a talented man blow his career to bits, but Munro had evidently reached the end of his tether. Ferndale was not going to stand in his way; the Master had told him to stay in touch. He did exactly that.

Ten minutes later Mrs Joan Carpenter listened carefully to the voice of Sir Nigel Irvine on the scrambler telephone.

'To give the answer to me personally, Sir Nigel?' she asked. 'Isn't that rather unusual?'

'Extremely so, ma'am. In fact it's unheard of. I fear it has to mean Mr Munro and the Service parting company. But short of asking the specialists to require the information out of him, I can hardly force him to tell me. You see, he's lost an agent who seems to have become a personal friend over the past nine months, and he's just about at the end of his tether.'

Joan Carpenter thought for several moments.

'I am deeply sorry to have been the cause of so much distress,' she said. 'I would like to apologize to your Mr Munro for what I had to ask him to do. Please ask his driver to bring him to Number Ten. And join me yourself immediately.'

The line went dead. Sir Nigel Irvine stared at the receiver for a while. That woman never ceases to surprise me, he thought. All right, Adam, you want your moment of glory, son, you'll have it. But it'll be your last. After that it's pastures new for you. Can't have prima donnas in the Service.

As he descended to his car Sir Nigel reflected that however interesting the explanation might be, it was academic, or soon would be. In seven hours Major Simon Fallon would steal aboard the *Freya* with three companions and wipe out the terrorists. After that Mishkin and Lazareff would stay where they were for fifteen years.

At two o'clock, back in the day cabin, Drake leaned forward towards Thor Larsen and told him: 'You're probably wondering why I set up this conference on the *Argyll*. I know that while you are there you will tell them who we are and how many we are. What we are armed with and where the charges are placed. Now listen carefully, because this is what you must also tell them, if you want to save your crew and ship from instant destruction.'

He talked for over thirty minutes. Thor Larsen listened impassively, drinking in the words and their implications. When he had finished the Norwegian captain said: 'I'll tell them. Not because I aim to save your skin, Mr Svoboda, but because you are not going to kill my crew and my ship.'

There was a trill from the intercom in the soundproof cabin. Drake answered it and looked out through the windows to the distant fo'c's'le. Approaching from the seaward side, very slowly and carefully, was the Wessex helicopter from the *Argyll*, the Royal Navy markings clear along her tail.

Five minutes later, under the eyes of cameras that beamed their images across the world, watched by men and women in subterranean offices hundreds and even thousands of miles away, Captain Thor Larsen, master of the biggest ship ever built, stepped out of her superstructure into the open air. He had insisted on donning his black trousers and had buttoned his merchant navy jacket with the four gold rings of a sea captain over his white sweater. On his head was the braided cap with the Viking-helmet emblem of the Nordia Line. He was in the uniform he would have worn the previous evening to meet the world's press for the first time. Squaring his wide shoulders, he began the long, lonely walk down the vast expanse of his ship to where the harness and cable dangled from the helicopter a third of a mile in front of him.

17

1500 to 2100

Sir Nigel Irvine's personal limousine, bearing Barry Ferndale and Adam Munro, arrived at 10 Downing Street a few seconds before three o'clock. When the pair were shown into the anteroom leading to the Prime Minister's study, Sir Nigel himself was already there. He greeted Munro coolly.

'I do hope this insistence on delivering your report to the PM personally will have been worth all the effort, Munro,' he said.

'I think it will, Sir Nigel,' replied Munro.

The director-general of the SIS regarded his staffer quizzically. The man was evidently exhausted and had had a rough deal over the Nightingale affair. Still, that was no excuse for breaking discipline. The door to the private study opened and Sir Julian Flannery appeared.

'Do come in, gentlemen,' he said.

Adam Munro had never met the Prime Minister personally. Despite not having slept for two days, she appeared fresh and collected. She greeted Sir Nigel first then shook hands with the two men she had not met before, Barry Ferndale and Adam Munro.

'Mr Munro,' she said, 'let me state at the outset my deep personal regret that I had to cause you both personal hazard and possible exposure to your agent in Moscow. I had no wish to do so, but the answer to President Matthews' question was of a truly international importance, and I do not use that phrase lightly.'

'Thank you for saying so, ma'am,' replied Munro.

She went on to explain that even as they talked the Captain of the *Freya*, Thor Larsen, was landing on the after deck of the cruiser *Argyll* for a conference; and that, scheduled for ten that evening, a team of SBS frogmen was going to attack the *Freya* in an attempt to wipe out the terrorists and their detonator.

Munro's face was set like granite when he heard.

'If, ma'am,' he said clearly, 'these commandos are successful, then the hijack will be over, the two prisoners in Berlin will stay where they are, and the probable exposure of my agent will have been in vain.'

She had the grace to look thoroughly uncomfortable.

'I can only repeat my apology, Mr Munro. The plan to storm the *Freya* was only devised in the small hours of this morning, eight hours after Maxim Rudin delivered his ultimatum to President Matthews. By then you were already consulting the Nightingale. It was impossible to call that agent back.'

Sir Julian entered the room and told the premier: 'They're coming on patch-through now, ma'am.'

The Prime Minister asked her three guests to be seated. In the corner of her office a box speaker had been stood, and wires led from it to a neighbouring anteroom.

'Gentlemen, the conference on the *Argyll* is beginning. Let us listen to it, and then we will learn from Mr Munro the reason for Maxim Rudin's extraordinary ultimatum.'

As Thor Larsen stepped from the harness at the end of his dizzying five-mile ride through the sky beneath the Wessex on to the after deck of the British cruiser, the roar of the engines above his head was penetrated by the shrill welcome of the bo'sun's pipes.

The *Argyll*'s captain stepped forward, saluted and held out his hand.

'Richard Preston,' said the navy captain. Larsen returned the salute and shook hands.

'Welcome aboard, captain,' said Preston.

'Thank you,' said Larsen.

'Would you care to step down to the ward-room?'

The two captains descended from the fresh air into the largest cabin in the cruiser, the officers' ward-room. There Captain Preston made the formal introductions.

'The Right Honourable Jan Grayling, Prime Minister of the Netherlands. You have spoken on the telephone already, I believe ... His Excellency Konrad Voss, ambassador of the German Federal Republic ... Captains Desmoulins of the French navy, de Jong of the Dutch navy, Hasselmann of the German navy, and Captain Manning of the US Navy.'

Mike Manning put out his hand and stared into the eyes of the bearded Norwegian.

'Good to meet you, captain.' The words stuck in his throat. Thor Larsen looked into his eyes a fraction longer than he had for the other naval commanders, and passed on.

'Finally,' said Captain Preston, 'may I present Major Simon Fallon of the Royal Marine commandos.'

Larsen looked down at the short, burly marine and felt the man's hard fist in his own. So, he thought, Svoboda was right after all.

At Captain Preston's invitation they all seated themselves at the expansive dining table.

'Captain Larsen, I should make plain that our conversation has to be recorded, and will be transmitted in uninterceptable form directly from this cabin to Whitehall where the British Prime Minister will be listening.'

Larsen nodded. His gaze kept wandering to the American; everyone else was looking at him with interest; the US Navy man was studying the mahogany table.

'Before we begin, may I offer you anything?' asked Preston. 'A drink perhaps? Food? Tea or coffee?'

'Just a coffee, thank you. Black, no sugar.'

Captain Preston nodded to a steward by the door who disappeared.

'It has been agreed that to begin with I shall ask the questions that interest and concern all our governments,' continued Captain Preston. 'Mr Grayling and Mr Voss have graciously conceded this. Of course anyone may pose a question that I may have overlooked. Firstly, may we ask you, Captain Larsen, what happened in the small hours of yesterday morning.'

Was it only yesterday, Larsen thought. Yes, three a.m. on Friday morning; and it was now five past three on Saturday afternoon. Just thirty-six hours. It seemed like a week.

Briefly and clearly he described the takeover of the *Freya* during the night watch, how the attackers came so effortlessly aboard and herded the crew down to the paint locker.

'So there are seven of them?' asked the Marine major. 'You are quite certain there are no more?'

'Quite certain,' said Larsen. 'Just seven.'

'And do you know who they are?' asked Preston. 'Jews? Arabs? Red Brigades?'

Larsen stared at the ring of faces in surprise. He had forgotten that outside the *Freya* no one knew who the hijackers were.

'No,' he said. 'They're Ukrainians. Ukrainian nationalists. The leader calls himself simply Svoboda. He said it means "freedom" in Ukrainian. They always talk to each other in what seems to be Ukrainian. Certainly it's Slavic.'

'Then what the hell are they seeking the liberation of two Russian Jews from Berlin for?' asked Jan Grayling in exasperation.

'I don't know,' said Larsen. 'The leader claims they are friends of his.'

'One moment,' said Ambassador Voss. 'We have all been mesmerized by the fact that Mishkin and Lazareff are Jews and wish to go to Israel. But of course they both come from the Ukraine, the city of Lvov. It did not occur to my government that they could be Ukrainian partisan fighters as well.'

'Why do they think the liberation of Mishkin and Lazareff will help their Ukrainian nationalist cause?' asked Preston.

'I don't know,' said Larsen. 'Svoboda won't say. I asked him; he nearly told me, but then shut up. He would only say that the liberation of those two men would cause such a blow to the Kremlin, it could start a widespread popular uprising.'

There was blank incomprehension on the faces of the men around him. The final questions about the layout of the ship, where Svoboda and Larsen stayed, the deployment of the terrorists, took a further ten minutes. Finally, Captain Preston looked round at the other captains and representatives of Holland and Germany. The men nodded. Preston leaned forward.

'Now, Captain Larsen, I think it is time to tell you. Tonight Major Fallon here and a group of his colleagues are going to approach the *Freya* underwater, scale her sides and wipe out Svoboda and his men.'

He sat back to watch the effect.

'No,' said Thor Larsen slowly, 'they are not.'

'I beg your pardon?'

'There will be no underwater attack unless you wish to have the *Freya* blown up and sunk. That is what Svoboda sent me here to tell you.'

Item by item, Captain Larsen spelled out Svoboda's message to the West. Before sundown every single floodlight on the *Freya* would be switched on. The man in the fo'c's'le would be withdrawn; the entire foredeck from the bow to the base of the superstructure would be bathed in light.

Inside the accommodation, every door leading outside would be locked and bolted on the inside. Every interior door would also be locked, to prevent access via a window.

Svoboda himself, with his detonator, would remain inside the superstructure, but would select one of the more than fifty cabins to occupy. Every light in every cabin would be switched on, and every curtain drawn.

One terrorist would remain on the bridge, in walkie-talkie contact with the man atop the funnel. The other four men would ceaselessly patrol the taffrail round the entire stern area of the *Freya* with powerful torches, scanning the surface of the sea. At the first trace of a stream of bubbles, or someone climbing the vessel's side, the terrorist would fire a shot. The man on top of the funnel would alert the bridge-watch, who would shout a warning down the telephone to the cabin where Svoboda hid. This telephone line would be kept open all night. On hearing the word of alarm, Svoboda would press his red button.

When he had finished, there was silence round the table.

'Bastard,' said Captain Preston with feeling. The group's eyes swivelled to Major Fallon, who stared unblinkingly at Larsen.

'Well, major?' asked Grayling.

'We could come aboard at the bow instead,' said Fallon.

Larsen shook his head. 'The bridge-watch would see you in the floodlights,' he said. 'You wouldn't get halfway down the foredeck.'

'We'll have to booby-trap their escape launch anyway,' said Fallon.

'Svoboda thought of that, too,' said Larsen. 'They are going to pull it round to the stern where it is in the glare of the deck lights.'

Fallon shrugged.

'That just leaves a frontal assault,' he said. 'Come out of the water firing, use more men, come aboard against the opposition, beat in the door and move through the cabins one by one.'

'Not a chance,' said Larsen firmly. 'You won't be over the rail before Svoboda has heard you and blown us all to Kingdom come.'

'I'm afraid I have to agree with Captain Larsen,' said Jan Grayling. 'I don't believe the Dutch government would agree to a suicide mission.'

'Nor the West German government,' said Voss.

Fallon tried one last move.

'You are alone with him personally for much of the time, Captain Larsen. Would you kill him?'

'Willingly,' said Larsen, 'but if you are thinking of giving me a weapon, don't bother. On my return I am to be skin-searched, well out of Svoboda's reach. Any weapon found, and another of my seamen is executed. I'm not taking anything back on board. Not weapons, not poison.'

'I'm afraid it's over, Major Fallon,' said Captain Preston

gently. 'The hard option won't work.'

He rose from the table.

'Well, gentlemen, barring further questions to Captain Larsen, I believe there is little more we can do. It now has to be passed back to the concerned governments. Captain Larsen, thank you for your time and your patience. In my personal cabin there is someone who would like to speak with you.'

Thor Larsen was shown from the silent ward-room by a steward. Mike Manning watched him go with anguish. The destruction of the plan of attack by Major Fallon's party now brought back to terrible possibility the order he had been given that morning from Washington.

The steward showed the Norwegian captain through the door of Preston's personal living quarters. Lisa Larsen rose from the edge of the bed where she had been sitting, staring out of the porthole at the dim outline of the *Freya*.

'Thor,' she said. Larsen kicked back and slammed the door shut. He opened his arms and caught the running woman in a hug.

'Hallo, little snow-mouse.'

In the Prime Minister's private office in Downing Street, the transmission from the *Argyll* was switched off.

'Blast,' said Sir Nigel, expressing the views of them all.

The Prime Minister turned to Munro. 'Now, Mr Munro, it seems that your news is not so academic after all. If the explanation can in any way assist us to solve this impasse, your risks will not have been run in vain. So, in a sentence, why is Maxim Rudin behaving in this way?'

'Because, ma'am, as we all know his supremacy in the Politburo hangs by a thread and has done so for months. . . .'

'But on the question of arms concessions to the Americans, surely,' said Mrs Carpenter. 'That is the issue on which Vishnayev wishes to bring him down.'

'Ma'am, Yefrem Vishnayev has made his play for supreme power in the Soviet Union and cannot go back now. He will bring Rudin down any way he can, for if he does not, then following the signature of the Treaty of Dublin in eight days' time Rudin will destroy him. These two men in Berlin can deliver to Vishnayev the instrument he needs to swing one or two members of the Politburo to change their votes and join his faction of hawks.'

How?' asked Sir Nigel.

'By speaking. By opening their mouths. By reaching Israel alive and giving an international press conference. By inflicting on the Soviet Union a massive public and international humiliation.'

'Not for killing an airline captain no one had ever heard of?' asked the PM.

'No. Not for that. The killing of Captain Rudenko in that cockpit was genuinely an accident. The escape to the West was indispensable if they were to give their real achievement the worldwide publicity it needed. You see, ma'am, on the night of 31st of October last, in a street in Kiev, Mishkin and Lazareff assassinated Yuri Ivanenko, the head of the KGB.'

Sir Nigel Irvine and Barry Ferndale sat bolt upright as if stung.

'So that's what happened to him,' breathed Ferndale, the Soviet expert. 'I thought he must be in disgrace.'

'Not disgrace, a grave,' said Munro. 'The Politburo knows it, of course, and at least one, maybe two, of Rudin's faction have threatened they will change sides if the assassins escape scot free and humiliate the Soviet Union.'

'Does that make sense, in Russian psychology, Mr Ferndale?' the Prime Minister asked.

Ferndale's handkerchief whirled in circles across the lenses of his glasses and he polished furiously.

'Perfect sense, ma'am,' he said excitedly. 'Internally and externally. In times of crisis, such as food shortages, it is imperative that the KGB inspire awe in the people, especially the non-Russian nationalities, to hold them in check. If that awe were to vanish, if the terrible KGB were to become a laughing-stock, the repercussions could be appalling – seen from the Kremlin of course.

'Externally, and especially in the Third World, the impression that the power of the Kremlin is an impenetrable fortress is of paramount importance to Moscow in maintaining its hold, and its steady advance.

'Yes, those two men are a time-bomb for Maxim Rudin. The fuse is lit by the *Freya* affair, and the time is running out.'

'Then why cannot Chancellor Busch be told of Rudin's ultimatum?' asked Munro. 'He'd realize that the Treaty of Dublin, which affects his country massively, is more important than the *Freya*.'

'Because,' cut in Sir Nigel, 'even the news that Rudin has made the ultimatum is secret. If even that got out, the world would realize the affair must concern more than just a dead airline captain.'

'Well, gentlemen, this is all very interesting,' said Mrs Carpenter, 'fascinating indeed. But it does not help solve the problem. President Matthews faces two alternatives: permit Chancellor Busch to release Mishkin and Lazareff, and lose the treaty; or, require these two men to remain in jail, and lose the *Freya* while gaining the loathing of nearly a dozen European governments and condemnation of the world.

'So far, he has tried a third option: that of asking Prime Minister Golen to return the two men to jail in Germany after the release of the *Freya*. The idea was to seek to satisfy Maxim Rudin. It might have, it might not. In fact Benyamin Golen refused. So that was that.

'Then we tried another way: storm the *Freya* and liberate her. Now that has become impossible. I fear there are no more options, short of doing what we suspect the Americans have in mind.'

'And what is that?' asked Munro.

'Blowing her apart by shellfire,' said Sir Nigel Irvine. 'We have no proof of it, but the guns of the *Moran* are trained right on the *Freya*.'

'Actually, there *is* a third option. It might satisfy Maxim Rudin, and it should work.'

'Then please explain it,' commanded the Prime Minister.

Munro did so. It took barely five minutes. There was silence.

'I find it utterly repulsive,' said Mrs Carpenter at last.

'Ma'am, with all respect, so did I betraying my agent to the KGB,' Munro replied stonily. Ferndale shot him a warning look.

'Do we have such devilish equipment available?' Mrs Carpenter asked Sir Nigel.

He studied his fingertips. 'I believe the specialist department may be able to lay its hands on that sort of thing,' he said quietly.

Joan Carpenter inhaled deeply.

'It is not, thank God, a decision I would need to make. It is a decision for President Matthews. I suppose it has to be put to him. But it should be explained person to person. Tell me, Mr Munro, would you be prepared to carry out this plan?'

Munro thought of Valentina walking out into the street, to the waiting men in grey trenchcoats.

'Yes,' he said, 'without a qualm.'

'Time is short,' she said briskly, 'if you are to reach Washington tonight. Sir Nigel, have you any ideas?'

'There is the five o'clock Concorde, the new service to Boston,' he said. 'It could be diverted to Washington if the President wanted it.'

Mrs Carpenter glanced at her watch. It read 4 p.m.

'On your way, Mr Munro,' she said. 'I will inform President Matthews of the news you have brought from Moscow, and ask him to receive you. You may explain to him personally your somewhat macabre proposal. If he will see you at such short notice.'

Lisa Larsen was still holding her husband five minutes after he entered the cabin. He asked her about home, and the children. She had spoken to them two hours earlier; there was no school on Saturday, so they were at home with the Dahl family. They were fine, she said. They had just come back from feeding the rabbits at Bogneset. The small talk died away.

'Thor, what is going to happen?'

'I don't know. I don't understand why the Germans will not release those two men. I don't understand why the Americans will not allow it. I sit with prime ministers and ambassadors, and they can't tell me either.'

'If they don't release the men, will that terrorist . . . do it?' she asked.

'He may,' said Larsen thoughtfully. 'I believe he will try. And if he does, I shall try to stop him. I have to.'

'Those fine captains out there, why won't they help you?'

'They can't, snow-mouse. No one can help me. I have to do it myself, or no one else will.'

'I don't trust that American captain,' she whispered. 'I saw him when I came on board with Mr Grayling. He would not look me in the face.'

'No, he cannot. Nor me. You see, he has orders to blow the *Freya* out of the water.'

She pulled away from him and looked up, eyes wide.

'He couldn't,' she said. 'No man would do that to other men.'

'He will, if he has to. I don't know for certain, but I suspect so. The guns of his ship are trained on us. If the Americans thought they had to do it, they would do it. Burning up the cargo would lessen the ecological damage, destroy the blackmail weapon.'

She shivered and clung to him. She began to cry.

'I hate him,' she said.

Thor Larsen stroked her hair, his great hand almost covering her small head. 'Don't hate him,' he rumbled. 'He has his orders. They all have their orders. They will all do what the men far away in the chancelleries of Europe and America tell them to do.'

'I don't care. I hate them all.'

He laughed and he stroked her, gently reassuring.

'Do something for me, snow-mouse.'

'Anything.'

'Go back home. Go back to Alesund. Get out of this place. Look after Kurt and Kristina. Keep the house ready for me. When this is over, I am going to come home. You can believe that.'

'Come back with me. Now.'

'You know I have to go. The time is up.'

'Don't go back to the ship,' she begged him. 'They'll kill you there.'

She was sniffing furiously, trying not to cry, trying not to hurt him.

'It's my ship,' he said gently. 'It's my crew. You know I have to go.'

He left her in Captain Preston's armchair.

As he did so the car bearing Adam Munro swung out of Downing Street, past the crowd of sightseers who hoped to catch a glimpse of the high and the mighty at this moment of crisis, and turned through Parliament Square for the Cromwell Road and the motorway to Heathrow.

Five minutes later Thor Larsen was buckled by two Royal Navy seamen, their hair awash from the rotors of the Wessex above them, into the harness.

Captain Preston, with six of his officers and the four NATO captains stood in a line a few yards away. The Wessex began to lift.

'Gentlemen,' said Captain Preston. Five hands rose to five braided caps in simultaneous salute.

Mike Manning watched the bearded sailor in the harness being borne away from him. From a hundred feet up, the Norwegian seemed to be looking down, straight at him.

He knows, thought Manning with horror. Oh, Jesus and Mary, he knows.

Thor Larsen walked into the day cabin of his own suite on the *Freya* with a submachine carbine at his back. Svoboda was in his usual chair. Larsen was directed into the one at the far end of the table.

'Did they believe you?' asked the Ukrainian.

'Yes,' said Larsen. 'They believed me. And you were right. They were preparing an attack by frogmen after dark. It's been called off.'

Drake snorted.

'Just as well,' he said. 'If they had tried it, I'd have pressed this button without hesitation, suicide or no suicide. They'd have left me no alternative.'

At ten minutes before noon, President William Matthews laid down the telephone that had joined him for fifteen minutes to the British premier in London, and looked at his three advisers. They had each heard the conversation on the amplivox.

'So that's it,' he said. 'The British are not going ahead with their night attack. Another of our options gone. That just about leaves us with the plan of blowing the *Freya* to pieces ourselves. Is the warship on station?'

'In position, guns laid and loaded,' confirmed Stanislaw Poklewski.

'Unless this man Munro has some idea that would work,' suggested Robert Benson. 'Will you agree to see him, Mr President?'

'Bob, I'll see the Devil himself if he can propose some way of getting me off this hook,' said Matthews.

'One thing at least we may now be certain of,' said David Lawrence. 'Maxim Rudin was not over-reacting. He could do nothing other than he has done, after all. In his fight with Yefrem Vishnayev, he too has no aces left. How the hell did those two in Moabit Jail ever get to shoot Yuri Ivanenko?'

'We have to assume the one who leads that group on the *Freya* helped them,' said Benson. 'I'd dearly love to get my hands on that Svoboda.'

'No doubt you'd kill him,' said Lawrence with distaste.

'Wrong,' said Benson. 'I'd enlist him. He's tough, ingenious and ruthless. He's taken ten European governments and made them dance like puppets.'

It was noon in Washington, 5 p.m. in London as the late-afternoon Concorde hoisted its stiltlike legs over the concrete of Heathrow, lifted its drooping spear of a nose towards the western sky and climbed through the sound barrier towards the sunset.

The normal rules about not creating the sonic boom until well out over the sea had been overruled by orders from Downing Street. The pencil-slim dart pushed its four screaming Olympus engines to full power just after take-off and 150,000 pounds of thrust flung the airliner towards the stratosphere.

The captain had estimated three hours to Washington, two hours ahead of the sun. Halfway across the Atlantic he told his Boston-bound passengers with deep regret that the Concorde would make a stopover of a few moments at Dulles International Airport, Washington, before heading back to Boston, due to the cover-all 'operational reasons'.

It was 7 p.m. in Western Europe but 9 in Moscow when Yefrem Vishnayev finally got the personal and highly unusual Saturday evening meeting with Maxim Rudin for which he had been clamouring all day.

The old dictator of Soviet Russia agreed to meet his party theoretician in the Politburo meeting room on the third floor of the arsenal building.

When he arrived, Vishnayev was backed by Marshal Nikolai Kerensky, but he found Rudin supported by his allies Dmitri Rykov and Vassili Petrov.

'I note that few appear to be enjoying this brilliant spring weekend in the countryside,' he said acidly.

Rudin shrugged, 'I was in the midst of enjoying a private dinner with two friends,' he said. 'What brings you, Comrades Vishnayev and Kerensky, to the Kremlin at this hour?'

The room was bare of secretaries and guards; it contained just the five power bosses of the union in angry confrontation beneath the globe lights in the high ceiling.

'Treason,' snapped Vishnayev. 'Treason, Comrade Secretary-General.'

The silence was ominous, menacing.

'Whose treason?' asked Rudin. Vishnayev leaned across the table and spoke two feet from Rudin's face.

'The treason of two filthy Jews from Lvov,' hissed Vishnayev. 'The treason of two men now in a jail in Berlin. Two men whose freedom is being sought by a gang of murderers on a tanker in the North Sea. The treason of Mishkin and Lazareff.'

'It is true,' said Rudin carefully, 'that the murder last December by these two of Captain Rudenko of Aeroflot constitutes –'

'Is it not also true,' asked Vishnayev menacingly, 'that these two murderers killed Yuri Ivanenko?'

Maxim Rudin would dearly have liked to shoot a sideways glance at Vassili Petrov by his side. Something had gone wrong. There had been a leak.

Petrov's lips set in a hard, straight line. He too, now controlling the KGB through General Abrassov, knew that the circle of men aware of the real truth was small, very small. The man who had spoken, he was sure, was Colonel Kukushkin, who had first failed to protect his master, and then failed to liquidate his master's killers. He was trying to buy his career, perhaps even his life, by changing camps and confiding in Vishnayev.

'It is certainly suspected,' said Rudin carefully. 'Not a proven fact.'

'I understand it *is* a proven fact,' snapped Vishnayev. 'These two men have been positively identified as the killers of our dear comrade Yuri Ivanenko.'

Rudin reflected how intensely Vishnayev had loathed Ivanenko and wished him dead and gone.

'The point is academic,' said Rudin. 'Even for the killing of Captain Rudenko, the two murderers are destined to be liquidated inside their Berlin jail.'

'Perhaps not,' said Vishnayev with well-simulated outrage. 'It appears they may be released by West Germany and sent to Israel. The West is weak, it cannot hold out for long against the terrorists on the *Freya*. If those two reach Israel alive, they will talk. I think, my friends, oh, yes, I truly think we all know what they will say.'

'What are you asking for?' said Rudin.

Vishnayev rose. Taking his example, Kerensky rose too. 'I am demanding,' said Vishnayev, 'an extraordinary plenary meeting of the full Politburo here in this room tomorrow night at this hour, nine o'clock. On a matter of exceptional national urgency. That is my right, Comrade Secretary-General?'

Rudin's shock of grey hair nodded slowly. He looked up at Vishnayev from under his eyebrows.

'Yes,' he growled, 'that is your right.'

'Then until this hour tomorrow,' snapped the theoretician, and stalked from the chamber.

Rudin turned to Petrov.

'Colonel Kukushkin?' he asked.

'It looks like it. Either way, Vishnayev knows.'

'Any possibility of eliminating Mishkin and Lazareff inside Moabit?'

Petrov shook his head.

'Not by tomorrow. No chance of mounting a fresh operation under a new man in that time. Is there any way of pressuring the West not to release them at all?'

'No,' said Rudin shortly, 'I have brought every pressure on Matthews that I know how. There is nothing more I can bring to bear on him. It is up to him now, him and that damned German Chancellor in Bonn.'

'Tomorrow,' said Rykov soberly, 'Vishnayev and his people will produce Kukushkin and demand that we hear him out. And if by then Mishkin and Lazareff are in Israel. . . .'

At 8 p.m., European time, Andrew Drake, speaking through Captain Thor Larsen from the *Freya*, issued his final ultimatum.

At 0900 the following morning, in thirteen hours, the *Freya* would vent 100,000 tons of crude oil into the North Sea, unless Mishkin and Lazareff were airborne and on their way to Tel Aviv. At 2000 unless they were in Israel and identified as genuine, the *Freya* would blow herself apart.

'That's bloody well the last straw,' shouted Dietrich Busch when he heard the ultimatum ten minutes after it was broadcast from the *Freya*. 'Who does William Matthews think he is? No one, but no one, is going to force the Chancellor of Germany to carry on with this charade. It is over.'

At twenty past eight the Federal German government announced that it was unilaterally releasing Mishkin and Lazareff the following morning at 8 a.m.

At 8.30 p.m. a personal coded message arrived on the USS *Moran* for Captain Mike Manning. When decoded it read simply: 'Prepare for fire order 0700 tomorrow.'

He screwed it into a ball in his fist and looked out through the porthole towards the *Freya*. She was lit like a Christmas tree, flood and arc lights bathing her towering superstructure in a glare of white light. She sat on the ocean five miles away, doomed, helpless; waiting for one of her two executioners to finish her off.

While Thor Larsen was speaking on the *Freya*'s radio-telephone to Maas Control, the Concorde bearing Adam Munro swept over the perimeter fence at Dulles Airport, flaps and undercarriage hanging, nose high, a delta-shaped bird of prey seeking to grip the runway.

The bewildered passengers, like goldfish peering through the tiny windows, noted only that she did not taxi towards the terminal building, but simply hove-to, engines running, in a parking bay beside the taxi track. A gangway was waiting, along with a black limousine.

A single passenger, carrying no mackintosh and no hand luggage, rose from near the front, stepped out of the open door and ran down the steps. Seconds later the gangway was withdrawn, the door closed and the apologetic captain announced that they would take off at once for Boston.

Adam Munro stepped into the limousine beside the two burly escorts and was immediately relieved of his passport.

The two presidential Secret Service agents studied it intently as the car swept across the expanse of tarmac to where a small helicopter stood in the lee of a hangar, rotors whirling.

The agents were formal, polite. They had their orders. Before he boarded the helicopter Munro was exhaustively frisked for hidden weapons. When they were satisfied, they escorted him aboard and the whirlybird lifted off, heading for Washington across the Potomac, and the spreading lawns of the White House. It was half an hour after touchdown at Dulles, three-thirty on a warm Washington spring afternoon, when they landed barely a hundred yards from the Oval Office windows.

The two agents escorted Munro across the lawns to where a narrow street ran between the big, grey Executive Office building, a Victorian monstrosity of porticos and columns intersected by a bewildering variety of different types of window, and the much smaller, white West Wing, a squat box partly sunken below ground level.

It was to a small door at the basement level that the two agents led Munro. Inside, they identified themselves and their visitor to a uniformed policeman sitting at a tiny desk. Munro was surprised; this was all a far cry from the sweeping façade of the front entrance to the residence on Pennsylvania Avenue, so well-known to tourists and beloved of Americans.

The policeman checked with someone by house-phone, and a female secretary came out of a lift several minutes later. She led the three past the policeman and down a corridor, at the end of which they mounted a narrow staircase. One floor up, they were at ground level, stepping through a door into a thickly carpeted hallway, where a male aide in charcoal grey suit glanced with raised eyebrows at the unshaven, dishevelled Englishman.

'You're to come straight through, Mr Munro,' he said, and led the way. The two Secret Service agents stayed with the girl.

Munro was led down the corridor, past a small bust of Abraham Lincoln. Two staffers coming the other way passed in silence. The man leading him veered to the left and confronted another uniformed policeman sitting at a desk outside a white, panelled door, set flush with the wall. The policeman examined Munro's passport again, looked at his appearance with evident disapproval, reached under his desk and pressed a button. A buzzer sounded and the aide pushed at the door. When it opened, he stepped back and ushered Munro past him. Munro took two paces forward and found himself in the Oval Office. The door clicked shut behind him.

The four men in the room were evidently waiting for him, all four staring towards the curved door now set back in the wall where he stood. He recognized President William Matthews, but this was a President as no voter had ever seen him; tired, haggard, ten years older than the smiling, confident, mature but energetic, image on the posters.

Robert Benson rose and approached him.

'I'm Bob Benson,' he said. He drew Munro towards the desk. William Matthews leaned across and shook hands. Munro was introduced to David Lawrence and Stanislaw Poklewski, both of whom he knew from their newspaper pictures.

'So,' said President Matthews, looking with curiosity at the English agent across his desk, 'you're the man who runs the Nightingale.'

'Ran the Nightingale, Mr President,' said Munro. 'As of twelve hours ago, I believe that asset is blown to the KGB.'

'I'm sorry,' said Matthews. 'You know what a hell of an ultimatum Maxim Rudin put to me over this tanker affair? I had to know why he was doing it.'

'Now we know,' said Poklewski, 'but it doesn't seem to change much, except to prove that Rudin is backed right into a corner, as we are here. The explanation is fantastic, the murder of Yuri Ivanenko by two amateur assassins in a street in Kiev. But we are still on that hook. . . .'

'We don't have to explain to Mr Munro the importance of the Treaty of Dublin, or the likelihood of war if Yefrem Vishnayev comes to power,' said David Lawrence. 'You've read all those reports of the Politburo discussions that the Nightingale delivered to you, Mr Munro?'

'Yes, Mr Secretary,' said Munro. 'I read them in the original Russian just after they were handed over. I know what is at stake, on both sides.'

'Then how the hell do we get out of it?' asked President Matthews. 'Your Prime Minister asked me to receive you because you had some proposal she was not prepared to discuss over the telephone. That's why you're here, right?'

'Yes, Mr President.'

At that point the phone rang. Benson listened for several seconds, then put it down.

'We're moving towards the crunch,' he said. 'That man Svoboda on the *Freya* has just announced he is venting a hundred thousand tons of oil tomorrow morning at nine European time, that's four a.m. our time. Just over twelve hours from now.'

'So what's your suggestion, Mr Munro?' asked President Matthews.

'Mr President, there are two basic choices here. Either Mishkin and Lazareff are released to fly to Israel, in which case they talk when they arrive there and destroy Maxim Rudin and the Treaty of Dublin; or they stay where they are, in which case the *Freya* will either destroy herself or will have to be destroyed with all her crew on board her.'

He did not mention the British suspicion concerning the real role of the *Moran*, but Poklewski shot the impassive Benson a sharp glance.

'We know that, Mr Munro,' said the President.

'But the real fear of Maxim Rudin does not really concern the geographical location of Mishkin and Lazareff. His real concern is whether they have the opportunity to address the world on what they did in that street in Kiev five months ago.'

William Matthews sighed.

'We thought of that,' he said. 'We have asked Prime Minister Golen to accept Mishkin and Lazareff, hold them incommunicado until the *Freya* was released, then return them to Moabit Jail, even hold them out of sight and sound inside an Israeli jail for another ten years. He refused. He said if he made the public pledge the terrorists demanded, he would not go back on it. And he won't. Sorry, it's been a wasted journey, Mr Munro.'

'That was not what I had in mind,' said Munro. 'During the flight I wrote the suggestion in memorandum form on airline notepaper.'

He withdrew a sheaf of papers from his inner pocket and laid it on the President's desk.

The United States President read the memorandum with an expression of increasing horror.

'This is appalling,' he said when he had finished. 'I have no choice here. Or rather, whichever option I choose, men are going to die.'

Adam Munro looked across at him with no sympathy. In his time he had learned that, in principle, politicians have little enough objection to loss of life, provided that they personally cannot be seen publicly to have had anything to do with it.

'It has happened before, Mr President,' he said firmly, 'and no doubt it will happen again. In the firm we call it "the Devil's Alternative".'

Wordlessly President Matthews passed the memorandum to Robert Benson who read it quickly.

'Ingenious,' he said. 'It might work. Can it be done in time?'

'We have the equipment,' said Munro. 'The time is short, but not too short. I would have to be back in Berlin by seven a.m. Berlin time, ten hours from now.'

'But even if we agree, will Maxim Rudin go along with it?' asked the President. 'Without his concurrence the Treaty of Dublin would be forfeit.'

'The only way is to ask him,' said Poklewski, who had finished the memorandum and passed it to David Lawrence.

The Bostonian secretary of state put the papers down as if they would soil his fingers. 'I find the idea cold-blooded and repulsive,' he said. 'No United States government could put its imprimatur to such a scheme.'

'Is it worse than sitting back as thirty innocent seamen in the *Freya* are burned alive?' asked Munro.

The phone rang again. When Benson replaced it he turned to the President.

'I feel we may have no alternative but to seek Maxim Rudin's agreement,' he said. 'Chancellor Busch has just announced Mishkin and Lazareff are being freed at oh eight hundred hours, European time. And this time he will not back down.'

'Then we have to try it,' said Matthews. 'But I am not taking sole responsibility. Maxim Rudin must agree to permit the plan to go ahead. He must be forewarned. I shall call him personally.'

'Mr President,' said Munro, 'Maxim Rudin did not use the hot line to deliver his ultimatum to you. He is not sure of the loyalties of some of his inner staff inside the Kremlin. In these faction fights, even some of the small fry change sides and support the opposition with classified information. I believe this proposal should be for his ears alone, or he will feel bound to refuse it.'

'Surely there is not the time for you to fly to Moscow through the night and be back in Berlin by dawn?' objected Poklewski.

'There is one way,' said Benson. 'There is a Blackbird based at Andrews which would cover the distance in the time.'

President Matthews made up his mind.

'Bob, take Mr Munro personally to Andrews base. Alert the crew of the Blackbird there to prepare for take-off in one hour. I will personally call Maxim Rudin and ask him to permit the airplane to enter Soviet airspace and to receive Adam Munro as my personal envoy. Anything else, Mr Munro?'

Munro took a single sheet from his pocket.

'I would like the company to get this message urgently to Sir Nigel Irvine so that he can take care of the London and Berlin ends,' he said.

'It will be done,' said the President. 'Be on your way, Mr Munro. And good luck to you.'

18

2100 to 0600

When the helicopter rose from the White House lawn, the Secret Service agents were left behind. An amazed pilot found himself bearing the mysterious Englishman in rumpled clothes, and the director of the CIA. To their right, as they rose above Washington, the Potomac River glittered in the late afternoon sun. The pilot headed due southeast for Andrews air force base.

Inside the Oval Office Stanislaw Poklewski, invoking the personal authority of President Matthews in every sentence, was speaking to the base commander there. That officer's protestations died slowly away. Finally, the National Security Adviser handed the phone to William Matthews.

'Yes, general, this is William Matthews and those are my orders. You will inform Colonel O'Sullivan that he is to prepare a flight plan immediately for a polar route direct from Washington to Moscow. Clearance to enter Soviet airspace unharmed will be radioed to him before he quits Greenland.'

The President went back to his other telephone, the red machine on which he was trying to speak directly to Maxim Rudin in Moscow.

At Andrews base, the commander himself met the helicopter as it touched down. Without the presence of Robert Benson, whom the air force general knew by sight, it was unlikely he would have accepted the unknown Englishman as a passenger on the world's fastest reconnaissance jet, let alone his orders to allow that jet to take off for Moscow. Ten years after it entered service, it was still on the secret list, so sophisticated were its components and systems.

'Very well, Mr Director,' he said finally, 'but I have to tell you in Colonel O'Sullivan we have one very angry Arizonan.'

He was right. While Adam Munro was taken to the pilot clothing store to be issued with a G-suit, boots, and goldfish-bowl oxygen helmet, Robert Benson found Colonel George T. O'Sullivan in the navigation room, cigar clamped in his teeth, poring over maps of the Arctic and eastern Baltic. The director of central intelligence may have outranked him, but he was evidently in no mood to be polite.

'Are you seriously ordering me to fly this bird clean across Greenland and Scandinavia, and into the heart of Rooshia?' he demanded truculently.

'No, colonel,' said Benson reasonably, 'the President of the United States is ordering you to do it.'

'Without my navigator/systems operator? With some goddam Limey sitting in his seat?'

'The goddam Limey happens to bear a personal message of President Matthews to President Rudin of the USSR which has to reach him tonight and cannot be discussed in any other way,' said Benson.

The air force colonel stared at him for a moment.

'Well,' he conceded, 'it better be goddam important.'

At twenty minutes before six, Adam Munro was led into the hangar where the aircraft stood, swarming with ground technicians preparing her to fly.

He had heard of the Lockheed SR-71, nicknamed the Blackbird due to its colour; he had seen pictures of it, but never the real thing. It was certainly impressive. On a single, thin nosewheel assembly, the bulletlike nosecone thrust upwards at a shallow angle. Far down the fuselage wafer-thin wings sprouted, delta-shaped, being both wings and tail controls all in one.

Almost at each wingtip the engines were situated, sleek pods housing the Pratt and Whitney JT-11-D turbofans, each capable with afterburner of throwing out 32,000 pounds of thrust. Two knifelike rudders rose, one from atop each engine, to give directional control. Body and engines resembled three hypodermic syringes, linked only by the wing.

Small white US stars in their white circles indicated its nationality; otherwise the SR-71 was black from nose to tail.

Ground assistants helped him into the narrow confines of the rear seat. He found himself sinking lower and lower until the side walls of the cockpit rose above his ears. When the canopy came down it would be almost flush with the fuselage to cut down drag effect. Looking out, he would only see directly upwards to the stars.

The man who should have occupied that seat would have understood the bewildering array of radar screens, electronic counter-measure systems and camera controls, for the SR-71 was essentially a spyplane, designed and equipped to cruise at altitudes far beyond the reach of most interceptor fighters and rockets, photographing what it saw beneath.

Helpful hands linked the tubes sprouting from his suit to the aircraft's systems; radio, oxygen, anti-G-force. In front of him he watched Colonel O'Sullivan lower himself into the front seat with accustomed ease and begin attaching his own life-support systems. When the radio was connected the Arizonan's voice boomed in his ears.

'You Scotch, Mr Munro?'

'Scottish, yes.' said Munro into his helmet.

'I'm Irish,' said the voice in his ears. 'You a Catholic?'

'A what?'

'A Catholic, for Christ's sake!'

Munro thought for a moment. He was not really religious at all.

'No,' he said, 'Church of Scotland.'

There was evident disgust up front.

'Jesus, twenty years in the United States Air Force and I get to chauffeur a Scotch Protestant.'

The triple-perspex canopy capable of withstanding the tremendous air pressure differences of ultra-high altitude flight was closed upon them. A hiss indicated the cabin was now fully pressurized. Drawn by a tractor somewhere ahead of the nosewheel, the SR-71 emerged from the hangar into the evening light.

From inside, the engines once started made only a low whistle. Outside, ground crew shuddered even in their earmuffs as the boom echoed through the hangars.

Colonel O'Sullivan secured immediate clearance for take-off even while he was running through his seemingly innumerable pre-take-off checks. At the start of the main runway the Blackbird paused, rocked on its wheels as the colonel lined her up, then Munro heard his voice:

'Whatever God you pray to, start now and hold tight.'

In the rear seat Munro braced himself.

Something like a runaway train hit him squarely across the broad of the back; it was the moulded seat in which he was strapped. He could see no buildings to judge his speed, just the pale blue sky above. When the jet reached 150 knots, the nose left the tarmac; half a second later the main wheels parted company, and O'Sullivan lifted the undercarriage into their bays.

Clean of encumbrances, the SR-71 tilted back until its jet efflux pipes were pointing directly down at Maryland, and it climbed. It climbed almost vertically, powering its way to the sky like a rocket, which was almost what it was. Munro was on his back, feet towards the sky, conscious only of the steady pressure of the seat on his spine as the Blackbird streaked towards a sky that was soon turning to dark blue, to violet and finally to black.

In the front seat Colonel O'Sullivan was navigating himself, which is to say, following the instructions flashed before him in digital display by the aircraft's on-board computer. It was feeding him altitude, speed, rate of climb, course and heading, external and internal temperatures, engine and jet-pipe temperatures, oxygen flow rates and approach to the speed of sound.

Somewhere below them, Philadelphia and New York went by like toy towns; over northern New York State they went through the sound barrier, still climbing and still accelerating. At 80,000 feet, five miles higher than the Concorde, Colonel

O'Sullivan cut out the afterburners and levelled his flight attitude.

Though it was still not quite sundown, the sky was a deep black, for at these altitudes there are so few air molecules from which the sun's rays can reflect that there is no light. But there are still enough such molecules to cause skin friction on a plane like the Blackbird. Before the state of Maine and the Canadian frontier passed beneath them, they had adopted a fast-cruise speed of almost three times the speed of sound. Before Munro's amazed eyes, the black skin of the SR-71, made of pure titanium, began to glow cherry red in the heat.

Within the cockpit, the aircraft's own refrigeration system kept its occupants at a comfortable body temperature.

'Can I talk?' asked Munro.

'Sure,' said the laconic voice of the pilot.

'Where are we now?'

'Over the Gulf of St Lawrence,' said O'Sullivan, 'heading for Newfoundland.'

'How many miles to Moscow?'

'From Andrews base, four thousand, eight hundred and fifty-six miles.'

'How long for the flight?'

'Three hours and fifty minutes.'

Munro calculated. They had taken off at 6 p.m. Washington time, 11 p.m. European time. That would be 1 a.m. in Moscow on Sunday, 3rd April. They would touch down at around 5 a.m. Moscow time. If Rudin agreed to his plan, and the Blackbird could bring him back to Berlin, they would gain two hours by flying the other way. There was just time to make Berlin by dawn.

They had been flying for just under one hour when Canada's last landfall at Cape Harrison drifted far beneath them and they were over the cruel North Atlantic, bound for the southern tip of Greenland, Cape Farewell.

'President Rudin, please hear me out,' said William Matthews. He was speaking earnestly into a small microphone on his desk, the so-called hot line, which in fact is not a telephone at all. From an amplifier to one side of the microphone the listeners in the Oval Office could hear the mutter of the simultaneous translator speaking into Rudin's ear in Moscow in Russian.

'Maxim Andreivitch, I believe we are both too old in this business, that we have worked too hard and too long to secure peace for our peoples, to be frustrated and cheated at this late stage by a gang of murderers on a tanker in the North Sea.'

There was silence for a few seconds, then the gruff voice of Rudin came down the line, speaking in Russian. By the President's side a young aide from State Department rattled off the translation in a low voice.

'Then William, my friend, you must destroy the tanker, take away the weapon of blackmail, for I can do no other than I have done.'

Bob Benson shot the President a warning look. There was no need to tell Rudin the West already knew the real truth about Ivanenko.

'I know this,' said Matthews into the mike. 'But I cannot destroy the tanker either. To do so would destroy me. There may be another way. I ask you with all my heart to receive this man who is even now airborne from here and heading for Moscow. He has a proposal that may be the way out for us both.'

'Who is this American?' asked Rudin.

'He is not American, he is British,' said President Matthews. 'His name is Adam Munro.'

There was silence for several moments. Finally the voice from Russia came back grudgingly.

'Give my staff the details of his flight plan – height, speed, course. I will order that his airplane be allowed through and will receive him personally when he arrives. *Spakoinyo notch*, William.'

'He wishes you a peaceful night, Mr President,' said the translator.

'He must be joking,' said William Matthews. 'Give his

people the Blackbird's flight path, and tell Blackbird to proceed on course.'

On board the *Freya* it struck midnight. Captives and captors entered their third and last day. Before another midnight struck, Mishkin and Lazareff would be in Israel, or the *Freya* and all aboard her would be dead.

Despite his threat to choose a different cabin, Drake was confident there would be no night attack from the marines and elected to stay where he was.

Thor Larsen faced him grimly across the table in the day cabin. For both men the exhaustion was almost total. Larsen, fighting back the waves of weariness that tried to force him to place his head in his arms and go to sleep, continued his solo game of seeking to keep Svoboda awake too, pin-pricking the Ukrainian to make him reply.

The surest way of provoking Svoboda, he had discovered, the surest way of making him use up his last remaining reserve of nervous energy, was to draw the conversation to the question of Russians.

'I don't believe in your popular uprising, Mr Svoboda,' he said. 'I don't believe the Russians will ever rise against their masters in the Kremlin. Bad, inefficient, brutal they may be; but they only have to raise the spectre of the foreigner, and they can rely on that limitless Russian patriotism.'

For a moment it seemed the Norwegian might have gone too far. Svoboda's hand closed over the butt of his gun, his face went white with rage.

'Damn and blast their patriotism,' he shouted, rising to his feet. 'I am sick and tired of hearing Western writers and liberals go on and on about this so-called marvellous Russian patriotism.

'What kind of patriotism is it that can only feed on the destruction of other people's love of homeland? What about *my* patriotism, Larsen? What about the Ukrainians' love for their enslaved homeland? What about Georgians, Armenians, Lithuanians, Estonians, Latvians? Are they not allowed any patriotism? Must it all be sublimated to this endless and sickening love of Russia?

'I hate their bloody patriotism. It is mere chauvinism and always has been, since Peter and Ivan. It can only exist through conquest and slavery of other surrounding nations.'

He was standing over Larsen, halfway round the table, waving his gun, panting from the exertion of shouting. He took a grip on himself and returned to his seat. Pointing the gun barrel at Thor Larsen like a forefinger he told him:

'One day, maybe not too long from now, the Russian empire will begin to crack. One day soon, the Romanians will exercise *their* patriotism, and the Poles and Czechs. Followed by the Germans and Hungarians. And the Balts and Ukrainians, the Georgians and Armenians. The Russian empire will crack and crumble, the way the Roman and British empires cracked, because at last the arrogance of their mandarins became insufferable.

'Within twenty-four hours I am personally going to put the cold chisel into the mortar and swing one gigantic hammer on to it. And if you or anyone else gets in my way, you'll die. And you'd better believe it.'

He put the gun down and spoke more softly.

'In any case, Busch has acceded to my demands and this time he will not go back on it. This time Mishkin and Lazareff *will* reach Israel.'

Thor Larsen observed the younger man clinically. It had been risky, he had nearly used his gun. But he had nearly also dropped concentration; he had nearly come within range. One more time, one single further attempt, in the sad hour just before dawn. . . .

Coded and urgent messages had passed all night between Washington and Omaha, and from there to the many radar stations that make up the eyes and ears of the Western Alliance in an electronic ring round the Soviet Union. Unseen eyes had watched the shooting star of the blip from the Blackbird moving east of Iceland towards Scandinavia on its route to Moscow. Forewarned, the watchers raised no alarm.

On the other side of the Iron Curtain, messages out of Moscow alerted the Soviet watchers to the presence of the incoming plane. Forewarned, no interceptors scrambled to intercept it. An air highway was cleared from the Gulf of Bothnia to Moscow, and the Blackbird stuck to its route.

But one fighter base had apparently not heard the warning; or hearing it had not heeded it; or had been given secret orders from somewhere deep inside the Defence Ministry, countermanding the Kremlin.

High in the Arctic, east of Kirkenes, two MIG-25s clawed their way from the snow towards the stratosphere on an interception course. These were the 25-E versions, ultra-modern, better powered and armed than the older version of the 1970s, the 25-A.

They were capable of 2.8 times the speed of sound, and with a maximum altitude of 80,000 feet. But the six 'Acrid' air-to-air missiles that each had slung beneath its wings would roar on, another 20,000 feet above that. They were climbing on full power with afterburner, leaping upwards at over 10,000 feet per minute.

The Blackbird was over Finland, heading for Lake Ladoga and Leningrad when Colonel O'Sullivan grunted into the microphone.

'We have company.'

Munro came out of his reverie. Though he understood little of the technology of the SR-71, the small radar screen in front of him told its own story. There were two small blips on it, approaching fast.

'Who are they?' he asked, and for a moment a twinge of fear moved in the pit of his stomach. Maxim Rudin had given his personal clearance. He wouldn't, surely? But would someone else?

Up front, Colonel O'Sullivan had his own duplicate radar scanner. He watched the speed of approach for several seconds.

'Mig Twenty-fives,' he said. 'At sixty thousand feet and climbing fast. Those goddam Rooshians; knew we should never have trusted them.'

'You turning back to Sweden?' asked Munro.

'Nope,' said the colonel. 'President of the US of A said to git you to Moscow, Limey, and you are going to Moscow.'

Colonel O'Sullivan threw his two afterburners into the game; Munro felt a kick as from a mule in the base of the spine as the power increased. The Mach counter began to move upwards, towards and finally through the mark representing three times the speed of sound. On the radar screen the approach of the blips slowed and halted.

The nose of the Blackbird rose slightly; in the rarefied atmosphere, seeking a tenuous lift from the weak air around her, the aircraft slid through the 80,000 feet mark and kept climbing.

Below them, Major Pyotr Kuznetsov, leading the two-plane detail, pushed his two Tumansky single-shaft jet engines to the limit of performance. His Soviet technology was good, the best available, but he was producing 5000 pounds less of thrust with his two engines than the twin American jets above him. Moreover he was carrying external weaponry, whose drag was acting as a brake on his speed.

Nevertheless the two Migs swept through 70,000 feet and approached rocket range. Major Kuznetsov armed his six missiles and snapped an order to his wing-man to follow suit.

The Blackbird was nudging 90,000 feet and Colonel O'Sullivan's radar told him his pursuers were over 75,000 feet and nearly within rocket range. In straight pursuit they could not hold him on speed and altitude, but they were on an intercept course, cutting the corner from their flight path to his.

'If I thought they were escorts,' he said to Munro, 'I'd let the bastards come close. But I just never did trust Rooshians.'

Munro was sticky with sweat beneath his thermal clothing. He had read the Nightingale file, the colonel had not.

'They're not escorts,' he said. 'They have orders to see me dead.'

'You don't say?' came the drawl in his ear. 'Goddam conspiring bastards. President of the US of A wants you alive, Limey. In Moscow.'

The Blackbird pilot threw on the whole battery of his electronic counter-measures. Rings of invisible jamming waves radiated out from the speeding black jet, filling the atmosphere for miles around with the radar equivalent of a bucket of sand in the eyes.

The small screen in front of Major Kuznetsov became a seething snowfield like a television set when the main tube blows out. The digital display showing him he was closing with his victim and when to fire his rockets was still fifteen seconds short of fire-time. Slowly, it began to unwind, telling him he had lost his target somewhere up there in the freezing stratosphere.

Thirty seconds later the two hunters keeled on to their wing-tips and dropped away down the sky to their Arctic base.

Of the five airports that surround Moscow, one of them, Vnukovno II, is never seen by foreigners. It is reserved for the Party elite and their fleet of jets maintained at peak readiness by the air force. It was here, at 5 a.m. local time, that Colonel O'Sullivan put the Blackbird on to Russian soil.

When the cooling jet reached the parking bay it was surrounded by a group of officers wrapped in thick coats and fur hats, for early April is still bitter in Moscow before dawn. The Arizonan lifted the cockpit canopy on its hydraulic struts and gazed at the surrounding crowd with horror.

'Rooshians,' he breathed. 'Messing all over my bird.' He unbuckled and stood up. 'Hey, get your mother-loving hands off this machine, ya hear?'

Adam Munro left the desolate colonel trying to prevent the Russian Air Force from finding the flush-caps leading to the re-fuelling valves, and was whisked away in a black limousine, accompanied by two bodyguards from the Kremlin staff. In the car he was allowed to peel off his G-suit and dress again in his trousers and jacket, both of which had spent the journey rolled up between his knees and looked as if they had just been machine-washed.

Forty-five minutes later the Zil, preceded by the two motor cycle outriders who had cleared the roads into Moscow, shot through the Borovitsky Gate into the Kremlin, skirted the

Grand Palace and headed for the side door to the arsenal building. At two minutes to six Adam Munro was shown into the private apartment of the leader of the USSR, to find an old man in a dressing gown, nursing a cup of warm milk. He was waved to an upright chair. The door closed behind him.

'So you are Adam Munro,' said Maxim Rudin. 'Now what is this proposal from President Matthews?'

Munro sat in the straight-backed chair and looked across the desk at Maxim Rudin. He had seen him several times at state functions, but never this close. The old man looked wearied and strained.

There was no interpreter present. Rudin spoke no English. In the hours while he had been in the air, Munro realized, Rudin had checked his name and knew perfectly well he was a diplomat from the British embassy and spoke Russian.

'The proposal, Mr Secretary-General,' Munro began in fluent Russian, 'is a possible way whereby the terrorists on the supertanker *Freya* can be persuaded to leave that ship without having secured what they came for.'

'Let me make one thing clear, Mr Munro, there is to be no more talk of the liberation of Mishkin and Lazareff.'

'Indeed not, sir. In fact I had hoped we might talk of Yuri Ivanenko.'

Rudin stared back at him, face impassive. Slowly he lifted his glass of milk and took a sip.

'You see, sir, one of those two *has* let something slip already,' said Munro. He was forced, to strengthen his argument, to let Rudin know that he too was aware what had happened to Ivanenko. But he would not indicate he had learned from someone inside the Kremlin hierarchy, just in case Valentina was still free.

'Fortunately,' he went on, 'it was to one of our people, and the matter has been taken care of.'

'Your people?' mused Rudin. 'Ah, yes, I think I know who your people are. How many others know?'

'The director-general of my organization, the British Prime Minister, President Matthews and three of his senior advisers. No one who knows has the slightest intention of revealing this for public consumption. Not the slightest.'

Rudin seemed to ruminate for a while.

'Can the same be said for Mishkin and Lazareff?' he asked.

'That is the problem,' said Munro. 'That has always been the problem since the terrorists, who are Ukrainian emigrés by the way, stepped on to the *Freya*.'

'I told William Matthews, the only way out of this is to destroy the *Freya*. It would cost a handful of lives, but save a lot of trouble.'

'It would have saved a lot of trouble if the airliner in which these two young killers escaped had been shot down,' rejoined Munro.

Rudin looked at him keenly from under beetle eyebrows.

'That was a mistake,' he said flatly.

'Like the mistake tonight in which two Mig Twenty-fives almost shot down the plane in which I was flying?'

The old Russian's head jerked up.

'I did not know,' he said. For the first time Munro believed him.

'I put it to you, sir, that destroying the *Freya* would not work. That is, it would not solve the problem. Three days ago Mishkin and Lazareff were two insignificant escapees and hijackers, serving fifteen years in jail. Now they are already celebrities. But it is assumed their freedom is being sought for its own sake. We know different.

'If the *Freya* were destroyed,' Munro went on, 'the entire world would wonder why it had been so vital to keep them in jail. So far no one realizes that it is not their imprisonment that is vital, it is their silence. With the *Freya*, her cargo and crew destroyed in order to keep them in jail, they would have no further reason to stay silent. And because of the *Freya*, the world would believe them when they spoke about what they had done. So simply keeping them in jail is no use any more.'

Rudin nodded slowly.

'You are right, young man,' he said. 'The Germans would give them their audience; they would have their press conference.'

'Precisely,' said Munro. 'This then is my suggestion.'

He outlined the same train of events that he had described to Mrs Carpenter and President Matthews over the previous twelve hours. The Russian showed neither surprise nor horror, just interest.

'Would it work?' he asked at last.

'It has to work,' said Munro. 'It is the last option. They have to be allowed to go to Israel.'

Rudin looked at the clock on the wall. It was past 6.45 a.m. Moscow time. In fourteen hours he would have to face Vishnayev and the rest of the Politburo. This time there would be no oblique approach; this time the Party theoretician would put down a formal motion of no confidence.

His grizzled head nodded. 'Do it, Mr Munro,' he said. 'Do it and make it work. For if it doesn't, there will be no more Treaty of Dublin, and no more *Freya* either.'

He pressed a bell-push and the door opened immediately. An immaculate major of the Kremlin praetorian guard stood there.

'I shall need to deliver two signals, one to the Americans, one to my own people,' said Munro. 'A representative of each embassy is waiting outside the Kremlin walls.'

Rudin issued his orders to the guard major, who nodded and escorted Munro out. As they were in the door, Maxim Rudin called:

'Mr Munro.'

Munro turned. The old man was as he had found him, hands cupped round his glass of milk.

'Should you ever need another job, Mr Munro,' he said grimly, 'come and see me. There is always a place here for men of talent.'

As the Zil limousine left the Kremlin by the Borovitsky Gate at 7 a.m. the morning sun was just tipping the spire of St Basil's Cathedral. Two long black cars waited by the kerb. Munro descended from the Zil and approached each in turn. He passed one message to the American diplomat and one to the British. Before he was airborne for Berlin, the instructions would be in London and Washington.

On the dot of eight o'clock the bullet nose of the SR-71

lifted from the tarmac of Vnukovno II Airport and turned due west for Berlin, a thousand miles away. It was flown by a thoroughly disgusted Colonel O'Sullivan, who had spent three hours watching his precious bird being refuelled by a team of Soviet Air Force mechanics.

'Where do you want to go now?' he called down the intercom. 'I can't bring this into Tempelhof, ya know. Not enough room.'

'Make a landing at the British base at Gatow,' said Munro.

'First Rooshians, now Limeys,' grumbled the Arizonan. 'Dunno why we don't put this bird on public display. Seems everyone is entitled to have a good look at her today.'

'If this mission is successful,' said Munro, 'the world may not need the Blackbirds any more.'

Colonel O'Sullivan, far from being pleased, regarded the suggestion as a disaster.

'Know what I'm going to do if that happens?' he called. 'I'm going to become a goddam cab driver. I'm sure getting enough practice.'

Far below, the city of Vilnius in Lithuania went by. Flying at twice the speed of the rising sun, they would be in Berlin at 7 a.m. local time.

It was half-past five on the *Freya*, while Adam Munro was in a car between the Kremlin and the airport, that the intercom from the bridge rang in the day cabin.

The man called Svoboda answered it, listened for a while and replied in Ukrainian. From across the table Thor Larsen watched him through half-closed eyes.

Whatever the call was, it perplexed the terrorist leader, who sat with a frown, staring at the table, until one of his men came to relieve him in the guarding of the Norwegian skipper.

Svoboda left the captain under the barrel of the submachine gun in the hands of his masked subordinate and went up to the bridge. When he returned ten minutes later he seemed angry.

'What's the matter?' asked Larsen. 'Something gone wrong again?'

'The German ambassador on the line from The Hague,' said Svoboda. 'It seems the Russians have refused to allow any West German jet, official or private, to use the air corridors out of West Berlin.'

'That's logical,' said Larsen. 'They're hardly likely to assist in the escape of the two men who murdered their airline captain.'

Svoboda dismissed his colleague who closed the door behind him and returned to the bridge. The Ukrainian resumed his seat. 'The British have offered to assist Chancellor Busch by putting a communications jet from the Royal Air Force at their disposal to fly Mishkin and Lazareff from Berlin to Tel Aviv.'

'I'd accept,' said Larsen. 'After all, the Russians aren't above diverting a German jet, even shooting it down and claiming an accident. They'd never dare fire on an RAF military jet in one of the air corridors. You're on the threshold of victory; don't throw it away for a technicality. Accept the offer.'

Svoboda regarded the Norwegian, bleary-eyed from weariness, slow from lack of sleep.

'You're right,' he conceded, 'they might shoot down a German plane. In fact, I have accepted.'

'Then it's over bar the shouting,' said Larsen, forcing a smile. 'Let's čelebrate.'

He had two cups of coffee in front of him, poured while he was waiting for Svoboda to return. He pushed one halfway down the long table; the Ukrainian reached for it. In a well-planned operation it was the first mistake he made. . . .

Thor Larsen came at him down the length of the table with all the pent-up rage of the past fifty hours unleashed in the violence of a maddened bear.

The partisan recoiled, reached for his gun, had it in his hand and was about to fire. A fist like a log of spruce caught him on the left temple, flung him out of his chair and backwards across the cabin floor.

Had he been less fit, he would have been out cold. He was very fit, and younger than the seaman. As he fell, the gun slipped from his hand and skittered across the floor. He came up empty-handed, fighting, to meet the charge of the Norwegian, and the pair of them went down again in a tangle of arms and legs, fragments of a shattered chair and two broken coffee cups.

Larsen was trying to use his weight and strength, the Ukrainian his youth and speed. The latter won. Evading the grip of the big man's hands, Svoboda wriggled free and went for the door. He almost made it; his hand was reaching for the knob when Larsen launched himself across the carpet and brought both his ankles out from under him.

The two men came up again together, a yard apart, the Norwegian between Svoboda and the door. The Ukrainian lunged with a foot, caught the bigger man in the groin with a kick that doubled him over. Larsen recovered, rose again and threw himself at the man who had threatened to destroy his ship.

Svoboda must have recalled that the cabin was virtually soundproof. He fought in silence, wrestling, biting, gouging, kicking, and the pair rolled over the carpet among the broken furniture and crockery. Somewhere beneath them was the gun that could have ended it all; in Svoboda's belt was the oscillator which, if the red button on it were pressed, would certainly end it all.

In fact it ended after two minutes; Thor Larsen pulled one hand free, grasped the head of the struggling Ukrainian and slammed it into the leg of the table. Svoboda went rigid for half a second, then slumped limp. From under his hairline a thin trickle of blood seeped down his forehead.

Panting with weariness, Thor Larsen raised himself from the floor and looked at the unconscious man. Carefully, he eased the oscillator from the Ukrainian's belt, held it in his left hand and crossed to the one window in the starboard side of his cabin which was secured closed with butterfly-headed bolts. One-handed, he began to unwind them. The first one flicked open; he started on the second. A few more seconds, a single long throw, and the oscillator would sail out of the porthole, across the intervening ten feet of steel deck and into the North Sea.

On the floor behind him the young terrorist's hand inched over the carpet to where his discarded gun lay. Larsen had the second bolt undone and was swinging the brass-framed window inwards when Svoboda lifted himself painfully on to one shoulder, reached round the table and fired.

The crash of the gun in the enclosed cabin was earsplitting. Thor Larsen reeled back against the wall by the open window and looked first at his left hand, then at Svoboda. From the floor the Ukrainian stared back, in disbelief.

The single shot had hit the Norwegian captain in the palm of his left hand, the hand that held the oscillator, driving shards of plastic and glass into the flesh. For ten seconds both men stared at each other, waiting for the series of rumbling explosions that would mark the end of the *Freya*.

They never came. The soft-nosed slug had fragmented the detonator device into small pieces, and in shattering it had not had time to reach the tonal pitch needed to trigger the detonators in the bombs below decks.

Slowly the Ukrainian climbed to his feet, holding on to the table for support. Thor Larsen looked at the steady stream of blood running from his broken hand down to the carpet. Then he looked across at the panting terrorist.

'I have won, Mr Svoboda. I have won. You cannot destroy my ship and my crew.'

'You may know that, Captain Larsen,' said the man with the gun, 'and I may know that. But they . . .' he gestured to the open porthole and the lights of the NATO warships in the pre-dawn gloom across the water, ' . . . they don't know that. The game goes on. Mishkin and Lazareff *will* reach Israel.'

19

0600 to 1600

Moabit Jail in West Berlin is in two parts. The older part pre-dates the Second World War. But during the sixties and early seventies, when the Baader-Meinhof gang spread a wave of terror over Germany, a new section was built. Into it were included ultra-modern security systems, the toughest steel and concrete, television scanners, electronically controlled doors and grills.

On the upper floor, David Lazareff and Lev Mishkin were woken in their separate cells by the governor of Moabit at 6 a.m. on the morning of Sunday, 3rd April 1983.

'You are being released,' he told them brusquely. 'You are being flown to Israel this morning. Take-off is scheduled for eight o'clock. Get ready to depart; we leave for the airfield at seven-thirty.'

Ten minutes later the military commandant of the British Sector was on the telephone to the governing mayor.

'I'm terribly sorry, Herr Burgomeister,' he told the West Berliner, 'but a take-off from the civil airport at Tegel is out of the question. For one thing the aircraft, by agreement between our governments, will be a Royal Air Force jet, and the re-fuelling and maintenance facilities for our aircraft are far better at our own airfield at Gatow. For a second reason we are trying to avoid the chaos of an invasion by the press, which we can easily prevent at Gatow. It would be hard for you to do this at Tegel Airport.'

Privately the governing mayor was somewhat relieved. If

the British took over the whole operation, any possible disasters would be their responsibility; and with the regional elections coming up, Berlin was included.

'So what do you want us to do, general?' he asked.

'London has asked me to suggest to you that these blighters be put in a closed and armoured wagon inside Moabit, and driven straight into Gatow. Your chaps can hand them over to us in privacy inside the wire, and of course we'll sign for them.'

The press was less than happy. Over four hundred reporters and cameramen had camped outside Moabit Jail since the announcement from Bonn the previous evening that release would take place at eight. They desperately wanted pictures of the pair leaving for the airport. Other teams of pressmen were staking out the civilian airport at Tegel, seeking vantage points for their telephoto lenses high on the observation terraces of the terminal building. They were all destined to be frustrated.

The advantage of the British base at Gatow is that it occupies one of the most outlying and isolated sites inside the fenced perimeter of West Berlin, situated on the western side of the broad Havel River, close up against the border with Communist East Germany which surrounds the beleaguered city on all sides.

Inside the base there had been controlled activity for hours before dawn. Between three and four o'clock an RAF version of the HS 125 executive jet, which the air force calls the Dominie, had flown in from Britain. It was fitted with long-range fuel tanks which would extend its range to give it ample reserves to fly from Berlin to Tel Aviv over Munich, Venice and Athens without ever entering Communist airspace. Its 500 m.p.h. cruising speed would enable the Dominie to complete the 2200-mile journey in just over four hours.

Since landing, the Dominie had been towed to a quiet hangar where it had been serviced and re-fuelled.

So keen were the press on observing the jail of Moabit and the airport at Tegel that no one noticed a sleek black SR-71 sweep over the East Germany–West Berlin border in the extreme corner of the city and drop on to the main runway at Gatow just three minutes after seven o'clock. This aircraft too was quickly towed to an empty hangar where a team of mechanics from the USAF at Tempelhof hurriedly closed the doors against prying eyes and began to work on it. The SR-71 had done its job. A relieved Colonel O'Sullivan found himself at last surrounded by his fellow-countrymen, next destination his beloved US of A.

His passenger left the hangar and was greeted by a youthful squadron leader waiting with a Land-Rover.

'Mr Munro?'

'Yes.' Munro produced his identification which the air force officer scanned closely.

'There are two gentlemen waiting to see you in the mess, sir.'

The two gentlemen could, if challenged, have proved that they were low-grade civil servants attached to the Ministry of Defence. What neither would have cared to concede was that they were concerned with experimental work in a very secluded laboratory whose findings, when such were made, went immediately into a Top Secret classification.

Both men were neatly dressed and carried attaché cases. One wore rimless glasses and had medical qualifications, or had had until he and the profession of Hippocrates parted company. The other was his subordinate, a former male nurse.

'You have the equipment I asked for?' said Munro without preamble.

For answer, the senior man opened his attaché case and extracted a flat box no larger than a cigar case. He opened it and showed Munro what nestled on a bed of cotton wool inside.

'Ten hours,' he said. 'No more.'

'That's tight,' said Munro. 'Very tight.'

It was seven-thirty on a bright, sunny morning.

The Nimrod from Coastal Command still turned and turned

15,000 feet above the *Freya*. Apart from observing the tanker, its duties also included that of watching the oil slick of the previous noon. The gigantic stain was still moving sluggishly on the face of the water, still out of range of the detergent-spraying tugs who were not allowed to enter the area immediately round the *Freya* herself.

After spillage the slick had drifted gently northeast of the tanker on the one-knot tide towards the northern coast of Holland. But during the night it had halted, the tide had moved to the ebb and the light breeze had shifted several points. Before dawn the slick had come back, until it had passed the *Freya* and lay just south of her, two miles away from her side in the direction of Holland and Belgium.

On the tugs and fireships, each loaded with their maximum capacity of emulsifier-concentrate, the scientists loaned from Warren Springs prayed the sea would stay calm and the wind light until they could move into operation. A sudden change in wind, a deterioration of the weather, and the giant slick could break up, driven before the storm towards the beaches either of Europe or Britain.

Meteorologists in Britain and Europe watched with apprehension the approach of a cold front coming down from the Denmark Strait, bringing cold air to dispel the unseasonal heatwave, and possibly wind and rain. Twenty-four hours of squalls would shatter the calm sea and make the slick uncontrollable. The ecologists prayed the descending cold snap would bring no more than a sea fog.

On the *Freya*, as the minutes to eight o'clock ticked away, nerves became even more strained and taut. Andrew Drake, supported by two men with submachine guns to prevent another attack from the Norwegian skipper, had allowed Captain Larsen to use his own first-aid box on his hand. Grey-faced with pain, the captain had plucked from the pulped meat of his palm such pieces of glass and plastic as he could, then bandaged the hand and placed it in a rough sling round his neck. Svoboda watched him from across the cabin, a small plaster covering the cut on his forehead.

'You're a brave man, Thor Larsen, I'll say that for you,' he said. 'But nothing has changed. I can still vent every ton of oil on this ship with her own pumps, and before it's halfway through the navy out there will open fire on her and complete the job. If the Germans renege again on their promise, that's just what I'll do at nine.'

At precisely seven-thirty the journalists outside Moabit Prison were rewarded for their vigil. The double gates on Klein Moabit Strasse opened for the first time and the nose of a blank-sided armoured van appeared. From apartment windows across the road the photographers got what pictures they could, which were not very much, and the stream of press cars started up, to follow the van wherever it would go.

Simultaneously, outside broadcast units rolled their cameras and radio reporters chattered excitedly into their microphones. Even as they spoke, their words went straight to the various capital cities from which they hailed, including that of the BBC man. His voice echoed into the day cabin of the *Freya* where Andrew Drake, who had started it all, sat listening to his radio.

'They're on their way,' he said with satisfaction. 'Not long to wait now. Time to tell them the final details of their reception in Tel Aviv.'

He left for the bridge; two men remained to cover the *Freya*'s captain, slumped in his chair at the table, struggling with an exhausted brain against the waves of pain from his bleeding and broken hand.

The armoured van, preceded by motorcycle outriders with howling sirens, swept through the twelve-foot-high steel mesh gates of the British base at Gatow and the pole-barrier descended fast as the first car bulging with pressmen tried to follow through. The car stopped with a squeal of tyres. The double gates swung to. Within minutes a crowd of protesting reporters and photographers were at the wire clamouring for admittance.

Gatow not only contains an air base; it has an army unit as well, and the commandant was an army brigadier. The men on the gate were from the military police, four giants with red-topped caps, peaks down to the bridge of the nose, immovable and immune.

'You cannot do this,' yelled an outraged photographer from *Spiegel*. 'We demand to see the prisoners take off.'

'That's all right, Fritz,' said Staff Sergeant Farrow comfortably, 'I've got my orders.'

Reporters rushed to public telephones to complain to their editors. They complained to the governing mayor, who sympathized earnestly and promised to contact the base commander at Gatow immediately. When the phone was quiet, he leaned back and lit a cigar.

Inside the base, Adam Munro walked into the hangar where the Dominie stood, accompanied by the wing commander in charge of aircraft maintenance.

'How is she?' Munro asked of the warrant officer (Technical) in charge of the fitters and riggers.

'Hundred per cent, sir,' said the veteran mechanic.

'No, she's not,' said Munro. 'I think if you look under one of the engine cowlings, you'll find an electrical malfunction that needs quite a bit of attention.'

The warrant officer looked at the stranger in amazement, then across to his superior officer.

'Do as he says, Mr Barker,' said the wing commander. 'There has to be a technical delay. The Dominie must not be ready for take-off for a while. But the German authorities must believe it's genuine. Open her up and get to work.'

Warrant Officer Barker had spent thirty years maintaining aircraft for the Royal Air Force. Wing commander's orders were not to be disobeyed, even if they did come from a scruffy civilian who ought to be ashamed of the way he was dressed, not to mention being unshaven.

Prison Governor Alois Bruckner had arrived in his own car to witness the handover of his prisoners to the British and their take-off for Israel. When he heard the aircraft was not yet ready, he was incensed and demanded to see it for himself.

He arrived in the hangar escorted by the RAF base commander, to find W/O Barker head and shoulders into the starboard engine of the Dominie.

'What is the matter?' he asked in exasperation.

Warrant Officer Barker pulled his head out.

'Electrical short circuit, sir,' he told the official. 'Spotted it during test run of the engines just now. Shouldn't be too long.'

'These men must take off at eight o'clock, in ten minutes' time,' said the German. 'At nine o'clock the terrorists on the *Freya* are going to vent a hundred thousand tons of oil.'

'Doing my best, sir. Now, if I could just get on with my job,' said the warrant officer.

The base commander steered Herr Bruckner out of the hangar. He too had no idea what the orders from London meant, but orders they were and he intended to obey them.

'Why don't we step across to the officers' mess for a nice cup of tea?' he suggested.

'I don't want a nice cup of tea,' said the frustrated Herr Bruckner. 'I want a nice take-off for Tel Aviv. But first I must telephone the governing mayor.'

'Then the officers' mess is just the place,' said the wing commander. 'By the way, since the prisoners can't really remain in that van much longer, I've ordered them to the military police station cells in Alexander Barracks. They'll be nice and comfortable there.'

It was five to eight when the BBC radio correspondent was given a personal briefing by the RAF base commander about the technical malfunction in the Dominie, and his report cut clean into the 8 a.m. news as a special flash seven minutes later. It was heard on the *Freya*.

'They'd better hurry up,' said Svoboda.

Adam Munro and the two civilians entered the military police cells just after eight o'clock. It was a small unit, only used for the occasional army prisoner, and there were four cells in a row. Mishkin was in the first, Lazareff in the fourth. The junior civilian let Munro and his colleague enter the corridor leading to the cells, then closed the corridor door and stood with his back to it.

'Last minute interrogation,' he told the outraged MP sergeant in charge. 'Intelligence people.' He tapped the side of his nose. The MP sergeant shrugged and went back to his orderly room.

Munro entered the first cell. Lev Mishkin, in civilian clothes, was sitting on the edge of the bunk bed smoking a cigarette. He had been told he was going to Israel at last, but he was still nervous and uninformed about most of what had been going on these past three days.

Munro stared at him. He had almost dreaded meeting him. But for this man and his crazy schemes to assassinate Yuri Ivanenko in pursuit of some far-off dream, his beloved Valentina would even now be packing her bags, preparing to leave for Romania, the Party conference, the holiday at Mamaia Beach and the boat that would take her to freedom. He saw again the back of the woman he loved going through the plate-glass doors to the street of Moscow, the man in the trenchcoat straighten up and begin to follow her.

'I am a doctor,' he said in Russian. 'Your friends the Ukrainians who have demanded your release have also insisted you be medically fit to travel.'

Mishkin stood up and shrugged. He was unprepared for the four rigid fingertips that jabbed him in the solar plexus, not expecting the small canister held under his nose as he gasped for air, unable to prevent himself inhaling the aerosol vapour that sprayed from the nozzle of the can as he inhaled. When the knock-out gas hit the lungs his legs buckled without a sound and Munro caught him beneath the armpits before he reached the floor. Carefully, he was laid on the bed.

'It'll act for five minutes, no more,' said the civilian from the ministry, 'then he'll wake with a fuzzy head but no ill effects. You'd better move fast.'

Munro opened the attaché case and took out the box containing the hypodermic syringe, the cotton wool and a small bottle of ether. Soaking the cotton wool in the ether he swabbed a portion of the prisoner's right forearm to sterilize the skin, and held the syringe to the light and squeezed until a fine jet of liquid rose into the air, expelling the last bubbles.

The injection took less than three seconds, and ensured Lev Mishkin would remain under its effects for almost two hours, longer than necessary but a period that could not be reduced.

The two men closed the cell door behind them and went down to where David Lazareff, who had heard nothing, was pacing up and down full of nervous energy. The aerosol spray worked with the same instantaneous effect. Two minutes later he also had had his injection.

The civilian accompanying Munro reached into his breast pocket and took out a flat tin. He held it out.

'I leave you now,' he said coldly. 'This isn't what I am paid for.'

Neither hijacker knew or would ever know what had been injected into them. In fact it was a mixture of two narcotics called pethidene and hyacine by the British, or meperidine and scopolamine by the Americans. In combination they have remarkable effects.

They cause the patient to remain awake, albeit slightly sleepy, willing and able to be obedient to instructions. They also have the effect of telescoping time, so that coming out from their effects after almost two hours, the patient has the impression of having suffered a dizzy spell for several seconds. Finally, they cause complete amnesia so that when the effects wear off the patient has not the slightest recall of anything that happened during the intervening period. Only a reference to a clock will tell him that time has passed at all.

Munro re-entered Mishkin's cell. He helped the young man into a sitting position on his bed, back to the wall.

'Hello,' he said.

'Hello,' said Mishkin and smiled. They were speaking in Russian, but Mishkin would never remember it.

Munro opened his flat tin box, extracted two halves of a long torpedo-shaped capsule called a spansule, such as are often used as cold remedies, and screwed the two ends together.

'I want you to take this pill,' he said, and held it out with a glass of water.

'Sure,' said Mishkin, and swallowed it without demur.

From his attaché case Munro took a battery-operated wall clock and adjusted a timer at the back. Then he hung it on the wall. The hands read eight o'clock but were not in motion. He left Mishkin sitting on his bed and returned to the cell of the other man. Five minutes later the job was finished. He repacked his bag and left the cell corridor.

'They're to remain in isolation until the aircraft is ready for them,' he told the MP sergeant at the orderly room desk as he passed through. 'No one is to see them at all. Base commander's orders.'

For the first time Andrew Drake was speaking in his own voice to the Dutch premier, Jan Grayling. Later English linguistics experts would place the tape-recorded voice as having originated within a twenty-mile radius of the city of Bradford, England, but by then it would be too late.

'These are the terms for the arrival of Mishkin and Lazareff in Israel,' said Drake. 'I shall expect no later than one hour after the take-off from Berlin an assurance from Premier Golen that they will be abided by. If they are not, the release of my friends will be regarded as null and void.

'One: the two are to be led from the aircraft on foot and at a slow pace past the observation terrace on top of the main terminal building at Ben Gurion Airport. Two: access to that terrace is to be open to the public. No controls of identity or screening of the public is to take place by the Israeli security force. Three: if there has been any switch of the prisoners, if any look-alike actors are playing their part, I shall know within hours. Four: three hours before the airplane lands at Ben Gurion, the Israeli radio is to publish the time of its arrival and inform everyone that any person who wishes to come and witness their arrival is welcome to do so. The broadcast is to be in Hebrew and English, French and German. That is all.'

'Mr Svoboda,' Jan Grayling cut in urgently, 'all these demands have been noted and will be passed immediately to the Israeli government. I am sure they will agree. Please do not cut contact. I have urgent information from the British in West Berlin.'

'Go ahead,' said Drake shortly.

'The RAF technicians working on the executive jet in the hangar at Gatow Airfield have reported a serious electrical fault which developed this morning in one of the engines during testing. I implore you to believe this is no trick. They are working frantically to put the fault right. But there will be a delay of an hour or two.'

'If this is a trick, it's going to cost your beaches a deposit of one hundred thousand tons of crude oil,' snapped Drake.

'It is not a trick,' said Grayling urgently. 'All aircraft occasionally suffer a technical fault. It is disastrous that this should happen to the RAF plane right now. But it has; and it will be mended, is being mended, even as we speak.'

There was silence for a while as Drake thought.

'I want take-off witnessed by four different national radio reporters, each in live contact with his head office. I want live reports by each of that take-off. They must be from Voice of America, Voice of Germany, the BBC and France's ORTF. All in English and all within five minutes of take-off.'

Jan Grayling sounded relieved.

'I will ensure the RAF personnel at Gatow permit these four reporters to witness the take-off,' he said.

'They had better,' said Drake. 'I am extending the venting of the oil by three hours. At noon we start pumping one hundred thousand tons into the sea.'

There was a click as the line went dead.

Premier Benyamin Golen was at his desk in his office in Jerusalem that Sunday morning. The Sabbath was over and it was a normal working day; it was also past ten o'clock, two hours later than in Western Europe.

The Dutch Prime Minister was barely off the telephone

before the small unit of Mossad agents who had established themselves in an apartment in Rotterdam were relaying the message from the *Freya* back to Israel. They beat the diplomatic channels by more than an hour.

It was the premier's personal adviser on security matters who brought him the transcript of the *Freya* broadcast and laid it silently on his desk. Golen read it quickly.

'What are they after?' he enquired.

'They are taking precautions against a switch of the prisoners,' said the adviser. 'It would have been an obvious ploy; to make up two young men to pass for Mishkin and Lazareff at first glance, and effect a substitution.'

'Then who is going to recognize the real Mishkin and Lazareff here in Israel?'

The security adviser shrugged.

'Someone on that observation terrace,' he said. 'They have to have a colleague here in Israel who can recognize the men on sight; more probably someone whom Mishkin and Lazareff can recognize.'

'And after recognition?'

'Some message or signal will presumably have to be passed to the media for broadcasting, to confirm to the men on the *Freya* that their friends have reached Israel safely. Without that message, they will think they have been tricked and go ahead with their deed.'

'Another of them? Here in Israel? I'm not having that,' said Benyamin Golen. 'We may have to play host to Mishkin and Lazareff, but not to any more. I want that observation terrace put under clandestine scrutiny. If any watcher on that terrace receives a signal from these two when they arrive, I want him followed. He must be allowed to pass his message, then arrest him.'

On the *Freya* the morning ticked by with agonizing slowness. Every fifteen minutes Andrew Drake, scanning the wavebands of his portable radio, picked up English-language news broadcasts from Voice of America or the BBC World Service.

Each bore the same message: there had been no take-off. The mechanics were still working on the faulty engine of the Dominie.

Shortly after nine o'clock the four radio reporters designated by Drake as the witnesses to the take-off were admitted to Gatow base and escorted by military police to the officers' mess where they were offered coffee and biscuits. Direct telephone facilities were established to their Berlin offices, from whence radio circuits were held open to their native countries. None of them met Adam Munro who had borrowed the base commander's private office and was speaking to London.

In the lee of the cruiser *Argyll* the three fast patrol boats *Cutlass, Sabre* and *Scimitar* waited at their moorings. On the *Cutlass* Major Fallon had assembled his group of twelve Special Boat Service commandos.

'We have to assume the powers-that-be are going to let the bastards go,' he told them. 'Some time in the next couple of hours they'll take off from West Berlin for Israel. They should arrive about four and a half hours later. So during this evening or tonight, if they keep their word, those terrorists are going to quit the *Freya*.

'Which way they'll head, we don't know yet, but probably towards Holland. The sea is empty of ships on that side. When they are three miles from the *Freya*, and out of possible range for a small, low-power transmitter-detonator to operate the explosives, Royal Navy experts are going to board the *Freya* and dismantle the charges. But that's not our job.

'We're going to take those bastards, and I want that man Svoboda. He's mine, got it?'

There was a series of nods and several grins. Action was what they had been trained for, and they had been cheated of it. The hunting instinct was high.

'The launch they've got is much slower than ours,' Fallon resumed. 'They'll have an eight-mile start, but I reckon we can take them three to four miles before they reach the coast. We have the Nimrod overhead, patched in to the *Argyll*. The *Argyll* will give us the directions we need. When we get close to them we'll have our searchlights. When we spot them, we take them out. London says no one is interested in prisoners. Don't ask me why; maybe they want them silenced for reasons we know nothing about. They've given us the job, and we're going to do it.'

A few miles away Captain Mike Manning was also watching the minutes tick away. He too waited on news from Berlin that the mechanics had finished their work on the engine of the Dominie. The news in the small hours of the morning, while he sat sleepless in his cabin awaiting the dreaded order to fire his shells and destroy the *Freya* and her crew, had surprised him. Out of the blue, the United States government had reversed its attitude of the previous sundown; far from objecting to the release of the men of Moabit; far from being prepared to wipe out the *Freya* to prevent that release, Washington now held no objection. But his main emotion was relief; waves of pure relief that his murderous orders had been rescinded, unless.... Unless something could still go wrong. Not until the two Ukrainian Jews had touched down at Ben Gurion Airport would he be completely satisfied that his orders to shell the *Freya* to a funeral pyre had become part of history.

At a quarter to ten, in the cells below Alexander Barracks, Gatow base, Mishkin and Lazareff came out from the effects of the narcotic they had ingested at eight o'clock. Almost simultaneously the clocks Adam Munro had hung on the walls of each cell came to life. The sweep hands began to move round the dials.

Mishkin shook his head and rubbed his eyes. He felt sleepy, slightly muzzy in the head. He put it down to the broken night, the sleepless hours, the excitement. He glanced at the clock on the wall; it read two minutes past eight. He knew that when he and David Lazareff had been led through the orderly room towards the cells, the clock there had said eight exactly. He stretched, swung himself off the bunk and began to pace the cell. Five minutes later at the other end of the corridor Lazareff did much the same.

Adam Munro strolled into the hangar where Warrant Officer Barker was still fiddling with the starboard engine of the Dominie.

'How is it going, Mr Barker?' asked Munro.

The long-service technician withdrew himself from the guts of the engine and looked down at the civilian with exasperation.

'May I ask, sir, how long I am supposed to keep up this play-acting? The engine's perfect.'

Munro glanced at his watch.

'Ten-thirty,' he said. 'In one hour exactly I'd like you to telephone the aircrew room and the officers' mess and report that she's fit and ready to fly.'

'Eleven-thirty it is, sir,' said W/O Barker.

In the cells, David Lazareff glanced again at the wall clock. He thought he had been pacing for thirty minutes, but the clock said nine. An hour had gone by, but it had seemed a very short one. Still, in isolation in a cell, time plays strange tricks on the senses. Clocks, after all, are accurate. It never occurred to him or Mishkin that their clocks were moving at double-speed to catch up on the missing hundred minutes in their lives, or that they were destined to synchronize with the clocks outside the cells at eleven-thirty precisely.

At eleven Premier Jan Grayling from The Hague was on the telephone to the governing mayor of West Berlin.

'What the devil is going on, Herr Burgomeister?'

'I don't know,' shouted the exasperated Berlin official. 'The British say they are nearly finished with their damn engine. Why the hell they can't use a British Airways airliner from the civil airport I don't understand. We would pay for the extra cost of taking one out of service to fly to Israel with two passengers only.'

'Well, I'm telling you that in one hour those madmen on the *Freya* are going to vent a hundred thousand tons of oil,' said Jan Grayling, 'and my government will hold the British responsible.'

'I entirely agree with you,' said the voice from Berlin. 'The whole affair is madness.'

At eleven-thirty Warrant Officer Barker closed the cowling of the engine and climbed down. He went to a wall phone and called the officers' mess. The base commander came on the line.

'She's ready, sir,' said the technician.

The RAF officer turned to the men grouped around him, including the governor of Moabit Jail and four radio reporters holding telephones linked to their offices.

'The fault has been put right,' he said. 'She'll be taking off in fifteen minutes.'

From the windows of the mess they watched the sleek little executive jet being towed out into the sunshine. The pilot and co-pilot climbed aboard and started both engines.

The prison governor entered the cells of the prisoners and informed them they were about to take off. His watch said 11.35. So did the wall clocks.

Still in silence, the two prisoners were marched to the MP Land-Rover and driven with the German prison official across the tarmac to the waiting jet. Followed by the air quartermaster sergeant who would be the only other occupant of the Dominie on its flight to Ben Gurion, they went up the steps without a backward glance and settled into their seats.

At 11.45 Wing Commander Jarvis opened both the throttles and the Dominie climbed away from the runway of Gatow Airfield. On instructions from the air traffic controller, it swung cleanly into the southbound air corridor from West Berlin to Munich and disappeared into the blue sky.

Within two minutes all four radio reporters were speaking to their audiences live from the officers' mess at Gatow. Their voices went out across the world to inform their listeners that forty-eight hours after the demands were originally made from the *Freya*, Mishkin and Lazareff were airborne and on their way to Israel and freedom.

In the homes of thirty officers and seamen from the *Freya* the broadcasts were heard; in thirty houses across the four countries of Scandinavia mothers and wives broke down and children asked why mummy was crying.

In the small armada of tugs and detergent-spraying vessels lying in a screen west of the *Argyll* the news came through and there were sighs of relief. Neither the scientists nor the seamen had the slightest doubt they could never have coped with 100,000 tons of crude oil spilling into the sea.

In Texas oil tycoon Clint Blake caught the news from NBC over his Sunday morning breakfast in the sun and shouted, 'About goddam time, too.'

Harry Wennerstrom heard the BBC broadcast in his penthouse suite high over Rotterdam and grinned with satisfaction.

In every newspaper office from Ireland to the Iron Curtain the Monday morning editions of the dailies were in preparation. Teams of writers were putting together the whole story from the first invasion of the *Freya* in the small hours of Friday until the present moment. Space was left for the arrival of Mishkin and Lazareff in Israel, and the freeing of the *Freya* herself. There would be time before the first editions went to press at 10 p.m. to include most of the end of the story.

At twenty minutes past twelve, European time, the State of Israel agreed to abide by the demands made from the *Freya* for the public and identifiable reception of Mishkin and Lazareff at Ben Gurion Airport in four hours' time.

In his sixth-floor hotel room at the Avia Hotel, three miles from Ben Gurion Airport, Miroslav Kaminsky heard the news on the piped-in radio. He leaned back with a sigh of relief. Having arrived in Israel on the late afternoon of the previous Friday, he had expected to see his old fellow partisans arrive on the Saturday. Instead, he had listened by radio to the change of heart by the German government in the small hours, the delay through Saturday and the venting of the oil at noon. He had bitten his fingernails down, helpless to assist, unable to rest, until the final decision to release them after all. Now for him too the hours were ticking away until touch-down of the Dominie at four-fifteen European time, six-fifteen in Tel Aviv.

On the *Freya*, Andrew Drake heard the news of the take-off with a satisfaction that cut through his weariness. The agreement of the State of Israel to his demands thirty-five minutes later was in the way of a formality.

'They're on their way,' he told Larsen. 'Four hours to Tel Aviv and safety. Another four hours after that, even less if the fog closes down, and we'll be gone. The navy will come on board and release you. You'll have proper medical help for that hand, and you'll have your crew and your ship back. . . . You should be happy.'

The Norwegian skipper was leaning back in his chair, deep black smudges under his eyes, refusing to give the younger man the satisfaction of seeing him fall asleep. For him it was still not over; not until the poisonous explosive charges had been removed from his holds, not until the last terrorist had left his ship. He knew he was close to collapse. The searing pain from his hand had settled down to a dull, booming throb that thumped up the arm to the shoulder, and the waves of exhaustion swept over him until he was dizzy. But still he would not close his eyes.

He raised his eyes to the Ukrainian with contempt. 'And Tom Keller?' he asked.

'Who?'

'My third officer, the man you shot out on the deck on Friday morning.'

Drake laughed. 'Tom Keller is down below with the others,' he said. 'The shooting was a charade. One of my own men in Keller's clothes. The bullets were blank.'

The Norwegian grunted. Drake looked across at him with interest.

'I can afford to be generous,' he said, 'because I have won. I brought against the whole of Western Europe a threat they could not face, and an exchange they could not wriggle out of. In short I left them no alternative. But you nearly beat me; you came within an inch of it.

'From six o'clock this morning when you destroyed the detonator, those commandos could have stormed this ship any time they pleased. Fortunately, they don't know that. But they might have done if you'd signalled to them. You're a brave man, Thor Larsen. Is there anything you want?'

'Just get off my ship,' said Larsen.

'Soon now, very soon, captain.'

High over Venice Wing Commander Jarvis moved the controls slightly and the speeding silver dart turned a few points east of south for the long run down the Adriatic.

'How are the clients?' he asked the quarter-master sergeant.

'Sitting quietly, watching the scenery,' said the QMS over his shoulder.

'Keep 'em like that,' said the pilot. 'The last time they took a plane trip, they ended up shooting the captain.'

The QMS laughed.

'I'll watch 'em,' he promised.

The co-pilot tapped the route chart on his knee.

'Three hours to touch-down,' he said.

The broadcasts from Gatow had also been heard elsewhere in the world. In Moscow the news was translated into Russian and brought to the table in a private apartment at the privileged end of Kutuzovsky Prospekt where two men sat at lunch shortly after 2 p.m. local time.

Marshal Nikolai Kerensky read the typed message and slammed a meaty fist on to the table.

'They've let them go,' he shouted. 'They've given in. The Germans and the British have caved in. The two Jew-boys are on their way to Tel Aviv.'

Silently Yefrem Vishnayev took the message from his companion's hand and read it. He permitted himself a wintry smile.

'Then tonight, when we produce Colonel Kukushkin and his evidence before the Politburo, Maxim Rudin will be finished,' he said. 'The censure motion will pass, there is no doubt of it. By midnight, Nikolai, the Soviet Union will be ours. And in a year, all of Europe.'

The marshal of the Red Army poured two generous slugs of Stolichnaya vodka. Pushing one towards the Party theoretician, he raised his own.

'To the triumph of the Red Army.'

Vishnayev raised his glass, a spirit he seldom touched. But there were exceptions.

'To a truly Communist world.'

20

1600 to 2000

Off the coast south of Haifa the little Dominie turned its nose for the last time and began dropping on a straight course for the main runway at Ben Gurion Airport inland from Tel Aviv.

It touched down after exactly four hours and thirty minutes of flight, at four-fifteen European time. It was six-fifteen in Israel.

At Ben Gurion the upper terrace of the passenger building was crowded with curious sightseers, surprised in a security-obsessed country to be allowed free access to such a spectacle.

Despite the earlier demands of the terrorists on the *Freya* that there be no police presence, the Israeli Special Branch were there. Some were in the uniform of El Al staff, others selling soft drinks, or sweeping the forecourt, or at the wheels of taxis. Detective Inspector Avram Hirsch was in a newspaper van, doing nothing in particular with bundles of evening newspapers that might or might not be destined for delivery to the kiosk in the main concourse.

After touch-down the Royal Air Force plane was led by a ground-control jeep to the apron of tarmac in front of the passenger terminal. Here a small knot of officials waited to take charge of the two passengers from Berlin.

Not far away an El Al jet was also parked, and from its curtained portholes two men with binoculars peered through the cracks in the fabric at the row of faces atop the passenger building. Each had a walkie-talkie set to hand.

Somewhere in the crowd of several hundred on the observation terrace Miroslav Kaminsky stood, indistinguishable from the other innocent sightseers.

One of the Israeli officials mounted the few steps to the Dominie and went inside. After two minutes he emerged, followed by David Lazareff and Lev Mishkin. Two young hotheads from the Jewish Defense League on the terrace unfurled a placard they had secreted in their coats and held it up. It read simply 'Welcome' and was written in Hebrew. They also began to clap, until several of their neighbours told them to shut up.

Mishkin and Lazareff looked up at the crowd on the terrace above them as they were led along the front of the terminal building, preceded by a knot of officials and with two uniformed policemen behind them. Several of the sightseers waved; most watched in silence.

From inside the parked airliner the Special Branch men peered out, straining to catch any sign of recognition from the refugees towards one of those at the railing.

Lev Mishkin saw Kaminsky first and muttered something quickly in Ukrainian out of the side of his mouth. It was picked up at once by a directional microphone aimed at the pair of them from a catering van a hundred yards away. The man squinting down the riflelike microphone did not hear the phrase; the man next to him in the cramped van, with the earphones over his head, did. He had been picked for his knowledge of Ukrainian. He muttered into a walkie-talkie, 'Mishkin just made a remark to Lazareff. He said, quote there he is, near the end with the blue tie, unquote.'

Inside the parked airliner the two watchers swung their binoculars towards the end of the terrace. Between them and the terminal building the knot of officials continued their solemn parade past the sightseers.

Mishkin, having spotted his fellow-Ukrainian, diverted his eyes. Lazareff ran his eyes along the line of faces above him, spotted Miroslav Kaminsky and winked. That was all Kaminsky needed; there had been no switch of prisoners.

One of the men behind the curtains in the airliner said,

'Got him' and began to talk into his hand-held radio.

'Medium height, early thirties, brown hair, brown eyes, dressed in grey trousers, tweed sports jacket and blue tie. Standing seven or eight from the far end of the observation terrace, towards the control tower.'

Mishkin and Lazareff disappeared into the building. The crowd on the roof, the spectacle over, began to disperse. They poured down the stairwell to the interior of the main concourse. At the bottom of the stairs a grey-haired man was sweeping cigarette butts into a trash can. As the column swept past him, he spotted a man in tweed jacket and blue tie. He was still sweeping as the man strode across the concourse floor.

The sweeper reached into his barrow, took out a small black box and muttered, 'Suspect moving on foot towards exit gate five.'

Outside the building Avram Hirsch hefted a bundle of evening newspapers from the back of the van and swung them on to a trolley held by one of his colleagues. The man in the blue tie walked within a few feet of him, looking neither to right nor left, made for a parked hire-car and climbed in.

Detective Inspector Hirsch slammed the rear doors of his van, walked to the passenger door and swung himself into the seat.

'The Volkswagen Golf over there in the car park,' he said to the van driver, Detective Constable Bentsur. When the rented car left the park en route for the main exit from the airport complex, the newspaper van was two hundred yards behind it.

Ten minutes later Avram Hirsch alerted the other police cars coming up behind him. 'Suspect entering Avia Hotel car park.'

Miroslav Kaminsky had his room key in his pocket. He passed quickly through the foyer and took the lift to his sixth-floor room. Sitting on the edge of the bed he lifted the telephone and asked for an outside line. When he got it he began to dial.

'He's just asked for an outside line,' the switchboard

operator told Inspector Hirsch, who was by her side.

'Can you trace the number he's dialling?'

'No, it's automatic for local calls.'

'Blast,' said Hirsch. 'Come on.' He and DC Bentsur ran for the lift.

The telephone in the Jerusalem office of the BBC answered at the third ring.

'Do you speak English?' asked Kaminsky.

'Yes, of course,' said the Israeli secretary at the other end.

'Then listen,' said Kaminsky. 'I'll only say this once. If the supertanker *Freya* is to be released unharmed, the first item in the six o'clock news on the BBC World Service, European time, must include the phrase "no alternative". If that phrase is not included in the first news item of the broadcast, the ship will be destroyed. Have you got that?'

There were several seconds of silence as the young secretary to the Jerusalem correspondent scribbled rapidly on a pad.

'Yes, I think so. Who is that?' she asked.

Outside the bedroom door in the Avia, Avram Hirsch was joined by two other men. One had a short-barrelled shotgun. Both were dressed in airport staff uniform. Hirsch was still in the uniform of the newspaper delivery company, green trousers, green shirt and green peaked cap. He listened at the door till he heard the tinkle of the telephone being replaced. Then he stood back, drew his service revolver and nodded to the man with the shotgun.

The gunner aimed once, carefully, at the door lock and blew the whole assembly out of the woodwork. Avram Hirsch went past him at a run, moved three paces into the room, dropped to a crouch, gun held forward in both hands, pointed straight at the target, and called on the room's occupant to freeze.

Hirsch was a sabra, born in Israel thirty-four years earlier, the son of two immigrants who had survived the death-camps of the Third Reich. Around the house in his childhood the language spoken was always Yiddish or Russian, for both his parents were Russian Jews.

He supposed the man in front of him was Russian; he had no reason to think otherwise. So he called to him in Russian. '*Stoi*. . . .' His voice echoed through the small bedroom.

Miroslav Kaminsky was standing by the bed, the telephone directory in his hand. When the door crashed open he dropped the book, which closed, preventing any searcher from seeing which page it had been open at, or what number he might have called.

When the cry came, he did not see a hotel bedroom outside Tel Aviv; he saw a small farmhouse in the foothills of the Carpathians, heard again the shouts of the men in the green uniforms closing in on the hideaway of his group. He looked at Avram Hirsch, took in the green peaked cap and uniform, and began to move towards the open window.

He could hear them again coming at him through the bushes shouting their endless cry: '*Stoi* . . . *Stoi* . . . *Stoi*. . . .' There was nothing to do but run, run like a fox with the hounds behind him, out through the back door of the farmhouse and into the undergrowth.

He was running backwards, through the open glass door to the tiny balcony when the balcony rail caught him in the small of the back and flipped him over. When he hit the car park fifty feet below it broke his back, pelvis and skull. From over the balcony rail, Avram Hirsch looked down at the broken body and turned to Constable Bentsur.

'What the hell did he do that for?'

The service aircraft that had brought the two specialists to Gatow from Britain the previous evening returned westwards soon after the take-off of the Dominie from Berlin for Tel Aviv. Adam Munro hitched a lift on it, but used his clearance from the Cabinet Office to require that it drop him off at Amsterdam before going on to England.

He had also ensured that the Wessex helicopter from the *Argyll* would be at Schiphol to meet him. It was half-past four when the Wessex settled back on to the after deck of the missile cruiser. The officer who welcomed him aboard glanced with evident disapproval at his appearance, but took him to meet Captain Preston.

All the navy officer knew was that his visitor was from the Foreign Office and had been in Berlin supervising the departure of the hijackers to Israel.

'Care for a wash and brush-up?' he asked.

'Love one,' said Munro. 'Any news of the Dominie?'

'Landed fifteen minutes ago at Ben Gurion,' said Captain Preston. 'I could have my steward press your suit, and I'm sure we could find you a shirt that fits.'

'I'd prefer a nice thick sweater,' said Munro. 'It's turned damn cold out there.'

'Yes, that may prove a bit of a problem,' said Captain Preston. 'There's a belt of cold air moving down from Norway. We could get a spot of sea-mist this evening.'

The sea-mist when it came, just after five o'clock, was a rolling bank of fog that drifted out of the north as the cold air followed the heatwave and came in contact with the warm land and sea.

When Adam Munro, washed, shaved and dressed in borrowed thick white sweater and black serge trousers, joined Captain Preston on the bridge just after five, the fog was thickening.

'Damn and blast,' said Preston. 'These terrorists seem to be having everything their own way.'

By half-past five the fog had blotted out the *Freya* from vision and swirled around the stationary warships, none of whom could see each other, except on radar. The circling Nimrod above could see them all, and the *Freya*, on its radar, and was still flying in clear air at 15,000 feet. But the sea itself had vanished in a blanket of grey cotton wool. Just after five the tide turned again and began to move back to the north-east, bearing the drifting oil slick with it, somewhere between the *Freya* and the Dutch shore.

The BBC correspondent in Jerusalem was a staffer of long experience in the Israeli capital and had many and good contacts. As soon as he learned of the telephone call his secretary had taken, he called a friend in one of the security services.

'That's the message,' he said, 'and I'm going to send it to London right now. But I haven't a clue who telephoned it.'

There was a chuckle at the other end.

'Send the message,' said the security man. 'As to the man on the telephone, we know. And thanks.'

It was just after four-thirty when the news flash was broadcast on the *Freya* that Mishkin and Lazareff had landed at Ben Gurion.

Andrew Drake threw himself back in his chair with a shout.

'We've done it,' he yelled at Thor Larsen. 'They're in Israel.'

Larsen nodded slowly. He was trying to close his mind to the steady agony from his wounded hand.

'Congratulations,' he said sardonically. 'Now perhaps you can leave my ship and go to hell.'

The telephone from the bridge rang. There was a rapid exchange in Ukrainian, and Larsen heard a whoop of joy from the other end.

'Sooner than you think,' said Drake. 'The lookout on the funnel reports a thick bank of fog moving towards the whole area from the north. With luck we won't even have to wait until dark. The fog will be even better for our purpose. But when we do leave, I'm afraid I'll have to handcuff you to the table leg. The navy will rescue you in a couple of hours.'

At five o'clock the main newscast brought a despatch from Tel Aviv to the effect that the demands of the hijackers of the *Freya* in the matter of the reception at Ben Gurion Airport of Mishkin and Lazareff had been abided by. Meanwhile, the Israeli government would keep the two from Berlin in custody until the *Freya* was released safe and unharmed. In the event that she was not, the Israeli government would regard its pledges to the terrorists as null and void, and return Mishkin and Lazareff to jail.

In the day cabin on the *Freya*, Drake laughed.

'They won't need to,' he told Larsen. 'I don't care what happens to me now. In twenty-four hours those two men are going to hold an international press conference. And when they do, Captain Larsen, when they do, they are going to blow the biggest hole ever made in the walls of the Kremlin.'

Larsen looked out of the windows at the thickening fog.

'The commandos might use this fog to storm the *Freya*,' he said. 'Your lights would be no use. In a few minutes you won't be able to see any bubbles from frogmen underwater.'

'It doesn't matter any more,' said Drake. 'Nothing matters any more. Only that Mishkin and Lazareff get their chance to speak. That was what it was all about. That is what makes it all worthwhile.'

The two Jewish-Ukrainians had been taken from Ben Gurion Airport in a police van to the central police station in Tel Aviv and locked in separate cells. Prime Minister Golen was prepared to abide by his part of the bargain – the exchange of the two men for the safety of the *Freya*, her crew and cargo. But he was not prepared to have the unknown Svoboda play him a trick.

For Mishkin and Lazareff it was the third cell in a day, but both knew it would be the last. As they parted in the corridor, Mishkin winked at his friend and called in Ukrainian, 'Not next year in Jerusalem – tomorrow.'

From an office upstairs the chief superintendent in charge of the station made a routine call to the police doctor to give the pair a medical examination, and the doctor promised to come at once. It was half-past seven Tel Aviv time.

The last thirty minutes before six o'clock dragged by like snails on the *Freya*. In the day cabin Drake had tuned his radio to the BBC World Service and listened impatiently for the six o'clock newscast.

Azamat Krim, assisted by three of his colleagues, shinned down a rope from the taffrail of the tanker to the sturdy fishing launch that had bobbed beside the hull for the past two and half days. When the four of them were standing in the launch's open waist, they began preparations for the departure of the group from the *Freya*.

At six o'clock the chimes of Big Ben rang out from London and the evening news broadcast began.

'This is the BBC World Service. The time is six o'clock in London, and here is the news, read to you by Peter Chalmers.'

A new voice came on. It was heard in the wardroom of the *Argyll* where Captain Preston and most of his officers grouped around the set. Captain Mike Manning tuned in on the USS *Moran*; the same newscast was heard in Downing Street, The Hague, Washington, Paris, Brussels, Bonn and Jerusalem. On the *Freya*, Andrew Drake sat motionless, watching the radio unblinkingly.

'In Jerusalem today, Prime Minister Benyamin Golen said that following the arrival earlier from West Berlin of the two prisoners David Lazareff and Lev Mishkin, he would have no alternative but to abide by his pledge to free the two men, provided the supertanker *Freya* was freed with her crew unharmed. . . .'

' "No alternative",' shouted Drake. 'That's the phrase. Miroslav has done it.'

'Done what?' asked Larsen.

'Recognized them. It's them all right. No switching has taken place.'

He slumped back in his chair and exhaled a deep sigh.

'It's over, Captain Larsen. We're leaving, you'll be glad to hear.'

The captain's personal locker contained one set of handcuffs, with keys, in case of the necessity physically to restrain someone on board. Cases of madness have been known on ships. Drake slipped one of the cuffs round Larsen's right wrist and snapped it shut. The other went round the table leg. The table was bolted to the floor. Drake paused in the doorway, and laid the keys to the handcuffs on top of a shelf.

'Good-bye, Captain Larsen. You may not believe this, but

I'm sorry about the oil slick. It need never have happened if the fools out there had not tried to trick me. I'm sorry about your hand, but that too need not have happened. We'll not see each other again, so good-bye.'

He closed and locked the cabin door behind him and ran down the three flights of stairs to 'A' deck and outside to where his men were grouped on the after deck. He took his transistor radio with him.

'All ready?' he asked Azamat Krim.

'As ready as we'll ever be,' said the Crimean Tatar.

'Everything OK?' he asked the American-Ukrainian who was an expert in small boats.

The man nodded. 'All systems go,' he replied.

Drake looked at his watch. It was twenty past six.

'Right. Six forty-five Azamat hits the ship's siren, and the launch and the first group leave simultaneously. Azamat and I leave ten minutes later. You've all got papers and clothes. After you hit the Dutch coast, everyone scatters. It's every man for himself.'

He looked over the side. By the fishing launch two inflatable Zodiac speedboats bobbed in the foggy water. Each had been dragged out from the fishing launch and inflated in the previous hour. One was the fourteen-foot model, big enough for five men. The smaller ten-foot model would take two comfortably. With the forty-horsepower outboards behind them, they would make thirty-five knots over a calm sea.

'They won't be long now,' said Major Simon Fallon, standing on the forward rail of the *Cutlass*.

The three fast patrol boats, long since invisible from the *Freya*, had been pulled clear of the western side of the *Argyll* and now lay tethered beneath her stern, noses pointed to where the *Freya* lay, five miles away through the fog.

The marines of the SBS were scattered, four to each boat, all armed with submachine carbines, grenades and knives. One boat, the *Sabre*, also carried on board four Royal Navy explosives experts, and this boat would make straight for the

Freya to board and liberate her as soon as the circling Nimrod had spotted the terrorist launch leaving the side of the supertanker and achieving a distance of three miles from her. The *Cutlass* and *Scimitar* would pursue the terrorists and hunt them down before they could lose themselves in the maze of creeks and islands that make up the Dutch coast south of the Maas.

Major Fallon would head the pursuit group in the *Cutlass*. Standing beside him, to his considerable disgust, was the man from the Foreign Office, Mr Munro.

'Just stay well out of the way when we close with them,' Fallon said. 'We know they have submachine carbines and handguns, maybe more. Personally, I don't see why you insist on coming at all.'

'Let's just say I have a personal interest in these bastards,' said Munro, 'especially Mr Svoboda.'

'So have I,' growled Fallon. 'And Svoboda's mine.'

Aboard the USS *Moran*, Mike Manning had heard the news of the safe arrival of Mishkin and Lazareff in Israel with as much relief as Drake on the *Freya*. For him, as for Thor Larsen, it was the end of a nightmare. There would be no shelling of the *Freya* now. His only regret was that the fast patrol boats of the Royal Navy would have the pleasure of hunting down the terrorists when they made their break. For Manning the agony he had been through for a day and a half parlayed itself into anger.

'I'd like to get my hands on that Svoboda,' he told Commander Olsen. 'I'd happily wring his bloody neck.'

As on the *Argyll*, the *Brunner*, the *Breda* and the *Montcalm*, the ship's radar scanners swept the ocean for signs of the launch moving away from the *Freya*'s side. Six-fifteen came and went and there was no sign.

In its turret the forward gun of the *Moran*, still loaded, moved away from the *Freya* and pointed at the empty sea three miles to the south of her.

At ten past eight, Tel Aviv time, Lev Mishkin was standing in his cell beneath the streets of Tel Aviv when he felt a pain in his chest. Something like a rock seemed to be growing fast inside him. He opened his mouth to scream, but the air was cut off. He pitched forward, face down, and died on the floor of the cell.

There was an Israeli policeman on permanent guard outside the door of the cell, and he had orders to peer inside at least every two or three minutes. Less than sixty seconds after Mishkin died, his eye was pressed to the judas-hole. What he saw caused him to let out a yell of alarm, and he frantically rattled the key in the lock to open the door. Further up the corridor, a colleague in front of Lazareff's door heard the yell and ran to his assistance. Together they burst into Mishkin's cell and bent over the prostrate figure.

'He's dead,' breathed one of the men. The other rushed into the corridor and hit the alarm button. Then they ran to Lazareff's cell and hurried inside.

The second prisoner was doubled up on the bed, arms wrapped round himself as the paroxysms struck him.

'What's the matter?' shouted one of the guards, but he spoke in Hebrew, which Lazareff did not understand. The dying man forced out four words in Russian. Both guards heard him clearly and later repeated the phrase to senior officers, who were able to translate it.

'Head ... of ... KGB ... dead.'

That was all he said. His mouth stopped moving; he lay on his side on the cot, sightless eyes staring at the blue uniforms in front of him.

The ringing bell brought the chief superintendent, a dozen other officers of the station staff and the doctor who had been taking a coffee in the police chief's office.

The doctor examined each rapidly, searching mouths, throats and eyes, feeling pulses and chests. When he had done, he stalked from the second cell. The superintendent followed him into the corridor; he was a badly worried man.

'What the hell's happened?' he asked the doctor.

'I can do a full autopsy later,' said the doctor, 'or maybe it will be taken out of my hands. But as to what has happened, they've been poisoned, that's what happened.'

'But they haven't eaten anything,' protested the policeman. 'They haven't drunk anything. They were just going to have supper. Perhaps at the airport ... on the plane ... ?'

'No,' said the doctor, 'a slow-acting poison would not work with such speed, and simultaneously. Body systems vary too much. Each either administered to himself, or was administered, a massive dose of instantaneous poison, which I suspect to be potassium cyanide, within the five to ten seconds before they died.'

'That's not possible,' shouted the police chief. 'My men were outside the cells all the time. Both prisoners were frisked and searched before they entered the cells. Mouths, anuses, the lot. There were no hidden poison capsules. Besides, why would they commit suicide? They've just arrived in freedom.'

'I don't know,' said the doctor, 'but they both died within seconds of that poison hitting them.'

'I'm phoning the Prime Minister's office at once,' said the chief superintendent grimly, and strode off to his office.

The Prime Minister's personal security adviser, like almost everyone else in Israel, was an ex-soldier. But the man whom those within a five-mile radius of the Knesset called simply 'Barak' had never been an ordinary soldier. He had started as a paratrooper under the para commander Rafael Eytan, the legendary Raful. Later he had transferred, to become a major in General Arik Sharon's elite 101 Unit, until he stopped a bullet in the kneecap during a dawn raid on a Palestinian apartment block in Beirut.

Since then he had specialized in the more technical side of security operations, using his knowledge of what he would have done to kill the Israeli premier and then reversing it, to protect his master. It was he who took the call from Tel Aviv and entered the office where Benyamin Golen was working late to break the news to him.

'Inside the cell itself?' echoed a stunned premier. 'Then they must have taken the poison themselves.'

'I don't think so,' said Barak, 'they had every reason to want to live.'

'Then they were killed by others?'

'It looks like it, Prime Minister.'

'Then who would want them dead?'

'The KGB, of course. One of them muttered something about the KGB, in Russian. It seems he was saying the head of the KGB wanted them dead.'

'But they haven't been in the hands of the KGB. Twelve hours ago they were in Moabit Jail. Then for eight hours in the hands of the British. Then two hours with us. In our hands they ingested nothing; no food, no drink, nothing. So how did they take in an instant-acting poison?'

Barak scratched his chin, a dawning gleam in his eye.

'There is a way, Prime Minister. A delayed-action capsule.'

He took a sheet of paper and drew a diagram.

'It is possible to design and make a capsule like this. It has two halves; one is threaded so that it screws into the other half just before it is swallowed.'

The Prime Minister looked at the diagram with growing anger.

'Go on,' he commanded.

'One half of the capsule is of a ceramic substance, immune both to the acidic effects of the gastric juices of the human stomach, and to the effects of the much stronger acid inside it. And strong enough not to be broken by the muscles of the throat when it is swallowed.

'The other half is of a plastic compound, tough enough to withstand the digestive juices, but not enough to resist the acid. In the second portion lies the cyanide. Between the two is a copper membrane. The two halves are screwed together; the acid begins to burn away at the copper wafer. The capsule is swallowed. Several hours later, depending on the thickness of the copper, the acid burns through. It is the same principle as certain types of acid-operated detonators.

'When the acid penetrates the copper membrane, it quickly

cuts through the plastic of the second chamber, and the cyanide floods out into the body system. I believe it can be extended up to ten hours, by which time the indigestible capsule has reached the lower bowel. Once the poison is out, the blood absorbs it quickly and carries it to the heart.'

Barak had seen his premier annoyed before, even angry. But he had never seen him white and trembling with rage.

'They send me two men with poison pellets deep inside them,' he whispered, 'two walking time bombs, triggered to die when they are in our hands? Israel will not be blamed for this outrage. Publish the news of the deaths immediately, do you understand, at once. And say a pathology examination is under way at this very moment. That is an order.'

'If the terrorists have not yet left the *Freya*,' suggested Barak, 'that news could reverse their plans to leave.'

'The men responsible for poisoning Mishkin and Lazareff should have thought of that,' snapped Premier Golen. 'But any delay in the announcement, and Israel will be blamed for murdering them. And that I will not tolerate.'

The fog rolled on. It thickened, it deepened. It covered the sea from the coast of East Anglia across to the Walcherens. It embalmed the flotilla of dispersant tugs sheltering west of the warships, and the navy vessels themselves. It whirled around the *Cutlass, Sabre* and *Scimitar* as they lay under the stern of the *Argyll*, engines throbbing softly, straining to be up and away to track down their prey. It shrouded the biggest tanker in the world at her mooring between the warships and the Dutch shore.

At six forty-five all the terrorists but two climbed down into the larger of the inflatable speedboats. One of them, the American-Ukrainian, jumped into the old fishing launch that had brought them to the middle of the North Sea, and glanced upwards.

From the rail above him, Andrew Drake nodded. The man pushed the starter button and the sturdy engine coughed into life. The prow of the launch was pointed due west, her wheel lashed with cord to hold her steady on course. The terrorist steadily increased the power of the engine, holding her in neutral gear.

Across the water keen ears, human and electronic, had caught the sound of the motor; urgent commands and questions flashed from the warships to each other, and from the *Argyll* to the circling Nimrod overhead. The spotter plane looked to its radar, but detected no movement on the sea below.

Drake spoke quickly into his hand-held radio, and far up on the bridge Azamat Krim hit the *Freya*'s siren button.

The air filled with the booming roar of sound as the siren blew away the silence of the surrounding fog and the lapping water.

On his bridge on the *Argyll* Captain Preston snorted with impatience.

'They're trying to drown the sound of the launch engine,' he observed. 'No matter, we'll have it on radar as soon as it leaves the *Freya*'s side.'

Seconds later the terrorist in the launch slammed the gear into forward and the fishing boat, its engine revving high, pulled violently away from the *Freya*'s stern. The terrorist leapt for the swinging rope above him, lifted his feet and let the empty boat churn out from under him. In two seconds it was lost in the fog, ploughing its way strongly towards the warships to the west.

The terrorist swung on the end of his rope, then lowered himself into the speedboat where his four companions waited. One of them jerked at the engine's lanyard; the outboard coughed and roared. Without a wave, the five men in it gripped the handholds and the helmsman pushed on the power. The inflatable dug its motor into the water, cleared the stern of the *Freya*, lifted its blunt nose high and tore away across the calm water towards Holland.

The radar operator in the Nimrod high above spotted the steel hull of the fishing launch instantly; the rubber-compound speedboat gave no reflector signal.

'The launch is moving,' he told the *Argyll* below him. 'Hell, they're coming straight at you.'

Captain Preston glanced at the radar display on his own bridge.

'Got 'em,' he said, and watched the blip separating itself from the great white blob that represented the *Freya* herself.

'He's right, she's boring straight at us. What the hell are they trying to do?'

On full power and empty, the fishing launch was making fifteen knots. In twenty minutes it would be among the navy ships, then through them and in the flotilla of tugs behind them.

'They must think they can get through the screen of warships unharmed, and then lose themselves among the tugs in the fog,' suggested the first officer beside Captain Preston. 'Shall we send the *Cutlass* to intercept?'

'I'm not risking good men, however much Major Fallon may want his personal fight,' said Preston. 'Those bastards have already shot one seaman on the *Freya*, and orders from Admiralty are quite specific. Use the guns.'

The procedure that was put into effect on the *Argyll* was smooth and practised. The other four NATO warships were politely asked not to open fire, but to leave the job to the *Argyll*. Her fore and aft five-inch guns swung smoothly on to target and opened fire.

Even at three miles, the target was small. Somehow it survived the first salvo, though the sea around it erupted in spouts of rising water when the shells dropped. There was no spectacle for the watchers on the *Argyll*, nor for those crouched on the three patrol boats beside her. Whatever was happening out there in the fog was invisible; only the radar could see every drop of every shell, and the target boat rearing and plunging in the maddened water. But the radar could not tell its masters that no figure stood at the helm, no men crouched terrified in her stern.

Andrew Drake and Azamat Krim sat quietly in their two-man speedboat close by the *Freya* and waited. Drake held on to the rope that hung from her rail high above. Through the fog they both heard the first muffled boom of the *Argyll*'s guns. Drake nodded at Krim, who started the outboard engine. Drake released the rope and the inflatable sped away, light as a feather, skimming the sea as the speed built up, its engine noise drowned by the roar of the *Freya*'s siren.

Krim looked at his left wrist where a waterproof compass was strapped, and altered course a few points to south. He had calculated forty-five minutes at top speed from the *Freya* to the maze of islands that make up North and South Beveland.

At five minutes to seven the fishing launch stopped the *Argyll*'s sixth shell, a direct hit. The explosive tore the launch apart, lifting it half out of the water and rolling both stern and aft sections over. The fuel tank blew up and the steel-hulled boat sank like a stone.

'Direct hit,' reported the gunnery officer from deep inside the *Argyll* where he and his gunners watched the uneven duel on radar. 'She's gone.'

The blip faded from the screen, the illuminated sweep arm went round and round, but only showed the *Freya* at five miles. On the bridge four officers watched the same display, and there were a few moments of silence. It was the first time for any of them that their ship had actually killed anybody.

'Let the *Sabre* go,' said Captain Preston quietly. 'They can board and liberate the *Freya* now.'

The radar operator in the darkened hull of the Nimrod peered closely at his screen. He could see all the warships, all the tugs, and the *Freya* to the east of them. But somewhere beyond the *Freya*, shielded by the tanker's bulk from the navy vessels, a tiny speck seemed to be moving away to the south-east. It was so small it could almost have been missed; it was no bigger than the blip that would have been made by a medium-sized tin can; in fact it was the metallic cover to the outboard engine of a speeding inflatable. Tin cans do not move across the face of the ocean at thirty knots.

'Nimrod to *Argyll*, Nimrod to *Argyll*. . . .'

The officers on the bridge of the guided missile cruiser listened to the news from the circling aircraft with shock. One of them ran to the wing of the bridge and shouted the information down to the sailors from Portland who waited on their patrol launches.

Two seconds later the *Cutlass* and the *Scimitar* were away, the booming roar of their twin diesel marine engines filling the fog around them. Long white plumes of spray rose from their prows, the noses rose higher and higher, the sterns deeper in the wake as the bronze screws whipped through the foaming water.

'Damn and blast them,' shouted Major Fallon to the navy commander who stood with him in the tiny wheelhouse of the *Cutlass*. 'How fast can we go?'

'On water like this, over forty knots,' the commander shouted back.

Not enough, thought Adam Munro, both hands locked to a stanchion as the vessel shuddered and bucked like a runaway horse through the fog. The *Freya* was still five miles away, the terrorists' speedboat another five beyond that. Even if they overhauled at ten knots, it would take an hour to come level with the inflatable carrying Svoboda to safety in the creeks of Holland where he could lose himself. But he would be there in forty minutes, maybe less.

Cutlass and *Scimitar* were driving blind, tearing the fog to shreds, only to watch it form behind them. In any crowded sea it would be lunacy to use such speed in conditions of zero visibility. But the sea was empty. In the wheelhouse of each launch, their commanders listened to a constant stream of information from the Nimrod via the *Argyll*; their own position and that of the other fast-patrol launch; position in the fog ahead of them of the *Freya* herself; position of the *Sabre*, well away to their left, heading towards the *Freya* at a slower speed; and the course and speed of the moving dot that represented Svoboda's escape.

Well east of the *Freya*, the inflatable in which Andrew Drake and Azamat Krim were making for safety seemed to be in luck. Beneath the fog the sea had become even calmer, and the sheet-like water enabled them to increase speed even more. Most of their craft was out of the water, only the shaft of the howling engine being deep beneath the surface. A few feet away in the fog, passing by in a blur, Drake saw the last remaining traces of the wake made by their companions ten minutes ahead of them. It was odd, he thought, for the traces to remain on the sea's surface for so long.

On the bridge of the USS *Moran*, lying south of the *Freya*, Captain Mike Manning also studied his radar scanner. He could see the *Argyll* away to the northwest of him, and the *Freya* a mite east of north.

Between them, the *Cutlass* and the *Scimitar* were visible, closing the gap fast. Away to the east he could spot the tiny blip of the racing speedboat, so small it was almost lost among the milky complexion of the screen. But it was there. Manning looked at the gap between the refugee and the hunters charging after it.

'They'll never make it,' he said, and gave an order to his executive officer. The five-inch forward gun of the *Moran* began to traverse slowly to the right, seeking a target somewhere through the fog.

A seaman appeared at the elbow of Captain Preston, still absorbed in the pursuit through the fog as shown by his own scanner. His guns, he knew, were useless; the *Freya* lay almost between him and the target, so any shooting would be too risky. Besides, the bulk of the *Freya* masked the target from his own radar scanner, which could therefore not pass the correct aiming information to the guns.

'Excuse me, sir,' said the seaman.

'What is it?'

'Just come over the news, sir. Those two men who were flown to Israel today, sir. They're dead. Died in their cells.'

'Dead?' queried Captain Preston incredulously. 'Then the whole bloody thing was for nothing. Wonder who the hell could have done that? Better tell that Foreign Office chappie when he gets back. He'll be interested.'

The sea was still flat calm for Andrew Drake. There was a slick, oily flatness to it that was unnatural in the North Sea. He and Krim were almost halfway to the Dutch coast when their engine coughed for the first time. It coughed again several seconds later, then repeatedly. The speed slowed, the power reduced.

Azamat Krim gunned the engine urgently. It fired, coughed again, and resumed running but with a throaty sound.

'It's overheating,' he shouted to Drake.

'It can't be,' yelled Drake. 'It should run at full power for at least an hour.'

Krim leaned out of the speedboat and dipped his hand in the water. He examined the palm and showed it to Drake. Streaks of sticky brown crude oil ran down to his wrist.

'It's blocking the cooling ducts,' said Krim.

'They seem to be slowing down,' the operator in the Nimrod informed the *Argyll*, who passed the information to the *Cutlass*.

'Come on,' shouted Major Fallon, 'we can still get the bastards.'

The distance began to close rapidly. The inflatable was down to ten knots. What Fallon did not know, or the young commander who stood at the wheel of the racing *Cutlass*, was that they were speeding towards the edge of a great lake of oil lying on the surface of the ocean. Or that their prey was chugging right through the centre of it.

Ten seconds later Azamat Krim's engine cut out. The silence was eerie. Far away they could hear the boom of the engines of *Cutlass* and *Scimitar* coming towards them through the fog.

Krim scooped a double handful from the surface of the sea and held it out to Drake.

'It's our oil, Andrew, it's the oil we vented. We're right in the middle of it.'

'They've stopped,' said the commander on the *Cutlass* to Fallon beside him. 'The *Argyll* says they've stopped. God knows why.'

'We'll get 'em,' shouted Fallon gleefully, and unslung his Ingram submachine gun.

On the USS *Moran* Gunnery Officer Chuck Olsen reported to Manning, 'We have range and direction.'

'Open fire,' said Manning calmly.

Seven miles to the south of the *Cutlass* the forward gun of the *Moran* began to crash out its shells in steady, rhythmic sequence. The commander of the *Cutlass* could not hear the shells, but the *Argyll* could, and told him to slow down. He was heading straight into the area where the tiny speck on the radar screens had come to rest, and the *Moran* had opened fire on the same area. The commander eased back on his twin throttles, the bucking launch slowed, then settled, chugging gently forward.

'What the hell are you doing?' shouted Major Fallon. 'They can't be more than a mile or so ahead.'

The answer came from the sky. Somewhere above them, a mile forward from the prow, there was a sound like a rushing train as the first shells from the *Moran* homed in on their target.

The three semi-armour-piercing shells went straight into the water, raising spouts of foam but missing the bobbing inflatable by a hundred yards.

The starshells had proximity fuses. They exploded in blinding sheets of white light a few feet above the ocean surface, showering gentle, soft gobbets of burning magnesium over a wide area.

The men on the *Cutlass* were silent, seeing the fog ahead of them illuminated. Four cables to starboard the *Scimitar* was also hove-to, on the very edge of the oil slick.

The magnesium dropped on to the crude oil, raising its temperature to and beyond its flashpoint. The light fragments of blazing metal, not heavy enough to penetrate the scum, sat and burned in the oil.

Before the eyes of the watching sailors and marines the sea caught fire; a gigantic plain, miles long and miles wide, began to glow, ruddy red at first, then brighter and hotter.

It only lasted for fifteen seconds. In that time the sea blazed. Over half of a spillage of 20,000 tons of oil caught fire and burned. For several seconds it reached 5000°C. The sheer heat of it burned off the fog for miles around in a tenth of a minute, the white flames reaching four to five feet high off the surface of the water.

In utter silence the sailors and marines gazed at the blistering inferno starting only a hundred yards ahead of them; some had to shield their faces or be scorched by the heat.

From the midst of the fire a single candle spurted, as if a petrol tank had exploded. The burning oil made no sound as it shimmered and glowed for its brief life.

From the heart of the flames, carrying across the water, a single human scream reached the ears of the sailors.

'*Shche ne vmerla Ukraina. . . .*'

Then it was gone. The flames died down, fluttered and waned. The fog closed in.

'What the hell did that mean?' whispered the commander of the *Cutlass*. Major Fallon shrugged.

'Don't ask me. Some foreign lingo.'

From beside them Adam Munro gazed at the last flickering glow of the dying flames.

'Roughly translated,' he said, 'it means "Ukraine will live again".'

Epilogue

It was 8 p.m. in Western Europe but 10 in Moscow, and the Politburo meeting had been in session for an hour.

Yefrem Vishnayev and his supporters were becoming impatient. The Party theoretician knew he was strong enough; there was no point in further delay. He rose portentously to his feet.

'Comrades, general discussion is all very well, but it brings us nowhere. I have asked for this special meeting of the Praesidium of the Supreme Soviet for a purpose, and that is to see whether the Praesidium continues to have confidence in the leadership of our esteemed Secretary-General, Comrade Maxim Rudin.

'We have all heard the arguments for and against the so-called Treaty of Dublin, concerning the grain shipments the United States had promised to make to us, and the price – in my view the inordinately high price – we have been required to pay for them.

'And finally we have heard of the escape to Israel of the murderers Mishkin and Lazareff, men who it has been proved to you beyond a doubt were responsible for assassinating our dear comrade Yuri Ivanenko. My motion is as follows: that the Praesidium of the Supreme Soviet can no longer have confidence in the continued direction of the affairs of our great nation by Comrade, Rudin. Mr Secretary-General, I demand a vote on the motion.'

He sat down. There was silence. Even for those participating, far more for the smaller fry present, the fall of a giant from Kremlin power is a terrifying moment.

'Those in favour of the motion. . . .' said Maxim Rudin.

Yefrem Vishnayev raised his hand. Marshal Nikolai Kerensky followed suit. Vitautas the Lithuanian did likewise. There was a pause of several seconds. Mukhamed the Tadjik raised his hand. The telephone rang. Rudin answered it, listened and replaced the receiver.

'I should not, of course,' he said impassively, 'interrupt a vote, but the news just received is of some passing interest.

'Two hours ago Mishkin and Lazareff both died, instantaneously, in cells beneath the central police station of Tel Aviv. A colleague fell to his death from a hotel balcony window outside that city. One hour ago the terrorists, who had hijacked the *Freya* in the North Sea to liberate these men, died in a sea of blazing petrol. None of them ever opened their mouths. And now none of them ever will.

'We were, I believe, in the midst of voting for Comrade Vishnayev's resolution. . . .'

Eyes studiously averted themselves; gazes were upon the tablecloth.

'Those against the motion?' murmured Rudin.

Vassili Petrov and Dmitri Rykov raised their hands. They were followed by Chavadze the Georgian, Shushkin and Stepanov.

Petryanov, who had once voted for the Vishnayev faction, glanced at the raised hands, caught the drift of the wind and raised his own.

'May I,' said Komarov of Agriculture, 'express my personal pleasure at being able to vote with the most complete confidence in favour of our Secretary-General.' He raised his hand.

Rudin smiled at him. Slug, thought Rudin, I am personally going to stamp you into the garden path.

'Then with my own vote the issue is denied by eight votes to four,' said Rudin. 'I don't think there is any other business?'

There was none.

Twelve hours later, Captain Thor Larsen stood once again on the bridge of the *Freya* and scanned the sea around him.

It had been an eventful night. The British marines had found and freed him twelve hours before, on the verge of collapse. Navy demolitions experts had carefully lowered themselves into the holds of the supertanker and plucked the detonators from the dynamite, bringing the charges gently up from the bowels of the ship to the deck, whence they were removed.

Strong hands had turned the steel cleats to the door behind which his crew had been imprisoned for sixty-four hours and the liberated seamen had whooped and danced for joy. All night they had been putting through personal calls to their parents and wives.

Gentle hands of a navy doctor had laid Thor Larsen on his own bunk and tended the wounds as best the conditions would allow.

'You'll need surgery, of course,' the doctor told the Norwegian. 'And it'll be set up for the moment you arrive by helicopter in Rotterdam, OK?'

'Wrong,' said Larsen on the brink of unconsciousness. 'I will go to Rotterdam, but I will go in the *Freya*.'

The doctor had cleaned and swabbed the broken hand, sterilizing against infection and injecting morphine to dull the pain. Before he was finished, Thor Larsen slept.

Skilled hands had piloted the stream of helicopters that rose and landed on the *Freya*'s helipad amidships through the night, bringing Harry Wennerstrom to inspect his ship, and the berthing crew to help her dock. The pumpman had found his spare fuses and repaired his cargo control pumps. Crude oil had been pumped from one of the full holds to the vented one to restore the balance; the valves had all been closed.

While the captain slept, the first and second officers had examined every inch of the *Freya* from stem to stern. The chief engineer had gone over his beloved engines foot by foot, testing every system to make sure nothing had been damaged.

During the dark hours the tugs and fireships had started to spray their emulsifier-concentrate on to the area of sea where the scum of the vented oil still clung to the water. Most had burned off in the single, brief holocaust caused by the magnesium shells of Captain Manning.

Just before dawn Thor Larsen had woken. The chief steward had helped him gently into his clothes, the full uniform of a senior captain of the Nordia Line that he insisted on wearing. He had slipped his bandaged hand carefully down the sleeve with the four gold rings, then hung the hand back in the sling round his neck.

At 8 a.m. he stood beside his first and second officer on the bridge. The two pilots from Maas Control were also there, the senior pilot with his independent 'brown box' navigational aid system.

To Thor Larsen's surprise the sea to the north, south and west of him was crowded. There were trawlers from the Humber and the Scheldt, fishermen up from Lorient and St Malo, Ostend and the coast of Kent. Merchant vessels flying a dozen flags mingled with the warships of five NATO navies, all hove-to within a radius of three miles and outwards from that.

At two minutes past eight the gigantic propellers of the *Freya* began to turn, the massive anchor cable rumbled up from the ocean floor. From beneath her stern a maelstrom of white water appeared.

In the sky above, four aircraft circled, bearing television cameras that showed a watching world the sea goddess coming under way.

As the wake broadened behind her, and the Viking helmet emblem of her company fluttered out from her yardarm the North Sea exploded in a burst of sound.

Little sirens like tin whistles, booming roars and shrill whoops echoed across the water as over a hundred sea captains commanding vessels from the tiny to the grand, from the harmless to the deadly, gave the *Freya* the traditional sailor's greeting.

Thor Larsen looked at the crowded sea about him and the empty lane leading to Euro Buoy Number One. He turned to the waiting Dutch pilot.

'Mr Pilot, pray set course for Rotterdam.'

On Sunday, 10th April, in Saint Patrick's Hall, Dublin Castle, two men approached the great oak refectory table that had been brought in for the purpose, and took their seats.

In the Minstrel Gallery the television cameras peered through the arcs of white light that bathed the table and beamed their images across the world.

Dmitri Rykov carefully scrawled his name for the Soviet Union on both copies of the Treaty of Dublin and passed the copies, bound in red Morocco leather, to David Lawrence, who signed for the United States.

Within hours the first grain ships, waiting off Murmansk and Leningrad, Sebastopol and Odessa, moved forward to their berths.

A week later the first combat units along the Iron Curtain began to load their gear to pull back from the barbed wire line.

On Thursday the 14th the routine meeting of the Politburo in the arsenal building of the Kremlin was far from routine.

The last man to enter the room, having been delayed outside by a major of the Kremlin Guard, was Yefrem Vishnayev. When he came through the doorway, he observed that the faces of the other eleven members were all turned towards him. Maxim Rudin brooded at the centre place at the top of the T-shaped table. Down each side of the stem were five chairs, and each was occupied. There was only one chair left vacant. It was the one at the far end of the stem of the table, facing up the length of it.

Impassively, Yefrem Vishnayev walked slowly forward to take that seat, known simply as the penal chair. It was to be his last Politburo meeting.

On 18th April a small freighter was rolling in the Black Sea swell, ten miles off the shore of Romania. Just before 2 a.m. a fast speedboat left the freighter and raced towards the shore. At three miles it halted and a marine on board took a powerful torch, pointed it towards the invisible sands and flashed a signal; three long dashes and three short ones. There was no answering light from the beach. The man repeated his signal four times. Still there was no answer.

The speedboat turned back and returned to the freighter. An hour later it was stowed below decks and a message was transmitted to London.

From London another message went in code to the British embassy in Moscow. 'Regret. Nightingale has not made the rendezvous. Suggest you return to London.'

On 25th April there was a plenary meeting of the full Central Committee of the Communist Party of the Soviet Union in the Palace of Congresses inside the Kremlin. The delegates had come from all over the union, some of them many thousands of miles.

Standing on the podium beneath the outsized head of Lenin, Maxim Rudin made them his farewell speech.

He began by outlining to them all the crisis that had faced their country twelve months earlier; he painted a picture of famine and hunger to make their hair stand on end. He went on to describe the brilliant feat of diplomacy by which the Politburo had instructed Dmitri Rykov to meet the Americans in Dublin and gain from them grain shipments of unprecedented size, along with imports of technology and computers, all at minimal cost. No mention was made of concessions on arms levels. He received a standing ovation for ten minutes.

Turning his attention to the matter of world peace, he reminded one and all of the constant danger to peace that was posed by the territorial and imperial ambitions of the capitalist West, occasionally aided by enemies of peace right here within the Soviet Union.

This was too much; consternation was unconfined. But, he

went on with an admonishing finger, these secret co-plotters with the imperialists had been uncovered and rooted out, thanks to the eternal vigilance of the tireless Yuri Ivanenko, who had died a week earlier in a sanatorium after a long and gallant struggle against heart ailment.

There were cries of horror and condolence for the departed comrade, who had saved them all, when the news of his death broke. Rudin raised a regretful hand for silence.

But, he told them, Ivanenko had been ably assisted before his heart attack last October, and replaced since his infirmity began, by his ever loyal comrade in arms, Vassili Petrov, who had completed the task of safe-guarding the Soviet Union as the world's first champion of peace. There was an ovation for Vassili Petrov.

Because the conspiracies of the anti-peace faction, both inside and outside the Soviet Union, had been exposed and destroyed, Rudin went on, it had been possible for the USSR, in its unending search for détente and peace, to curb its arms-building programmes for the first time in years. More of the national effort could thenceforward be directed towards the production of consumer goods and social improvement, thanks solely to the vigilance of the Politburo in spotting the anti-peace faction for what they were.

This time the applause extended for another ten minutes.

Maxim Rudin waited till the clapping was almost over before he raised his hands, and dropped his speaking tone.

As for him, he said, he had done what he could, but the time had come for him to depart.

The stunned silence was tangible.

He had toiled long, too long perhaps, bearing on his shoulders the harshest burdens, and it had sapped his strength and his health.

On the podium, his shoulders slumped with the weariness of it all. There were cries of 'No ... no....'

He was an old man, Rudin said. What did he want? Nothing more than any old man wanted. To sit by the fire's corner on a winter night and play with his grandchildren....

In the diplomatic gallery the British head of chancery whispered to the ambassador: 'I say, that's going a bit strong. He's had more people shot than I've had hot dinners.'

The ambassador raised a single eyebrow and muttered back: 'Think yourself lucky. If this was America he'd produce his bloody grandchildren on the stage.'

And so, concluded Rudin, the time had come for him to admit openly to his friends and comrades that the doctors had informed him he had only a few more months to live. With his audience's permission he would lay down the burden of office and spend what little time remained to him in the countryside he loved so much, with the family who were the sun and the moon to him.

Several of the women delegates were crying openly by now.

One last question remained, said Rudin. He wished to retire in five days, on the last day of the month. The following morning was May Day, and a new man would stand atop Lenin's Mausoleum to take the salute of the great parade. Who would that man be?

It should be a man of youth and vigour, of wisdom and unbounded patriotism; a man who had proved himself in the highest councils of the land, but was not yet bowed with age. Such a man, Rudin proclaimed, the peoples of the fifteen socialist republics were lucky to have, in the person of Vassili Petrov. . . .

The election of Petrov to succeed Rudin was carried by acclamation. Supporters of alternative candidates would have been shouted down had they tried to speak. They did not even bother.

Following the climax of the hijack in the North Sea, Sir Nigel Irvine had wished Adam Munro to remain in London, or at least not to return to Moscow. Munro had appealed personally to the Prime Minister to be allowed one last chance to ensure that his agent, the Nightingale, was safe at least. In view of his role in ending the crisis, his wish had been granted.

Since his meeting in the small hours of 3rd April with

Maxim Rudin, it was evident that his cover was completely blown and that as an agent in Moscow he could not function.

The ambassador and head of chancery regarded his return with considerable misgivings, and it was no surprise when his name was carefully excluded from any diplomatic invitations, nor that he could not be received by any representative of the Soviet Ministry of Foreign Trade. He hung about like a forlorn and unwanted party guest, hoping against hope that Valentina would contact him to indicate she was safe.

Once he tried her private telephone number. There was no answer. She could have been out, but he dared not risk it again. Following the fall of the Vishnayev faction, he was told he had until the end of the month. Then he would be recalled to London, and his resignation from the Service would be gratefully accepted.

Maxim Rudin's farewell speech caused a furore in the diplomatic missions, as each informed its home government of the news of Rudin's departure and prepared position-papers on his successor, Vassili Petrov. Munro was excluded from this whirl of activity.

It was therefore all the more surprising when, following the announcement of a reception in St George's Hall in the Kremlin Great Palace on the evening of 30th April, invitations arrived at the British embassy for the ambassador, the head of chancery, and Adam Munro. It was even hinted during a phone call from the Soviet Foreign Ministry to the embassy that Munro was confidently expected to attend.

The state reception to bid farewell to Maxim Rudin was a glittering affair. Over a hundred of the elite of the Soviet Union mingled with four times that number of foreign diplomats from the Socialist world, the West and the Third World. Fraternal delegations from Communist parties outside the Soviet bloc were also there, ill-at-ease among the full evening dress, military uniforms, stars, orders and medals. It could have been a tsar who was abdicating rather than a leader of a classless workers' paradise.

The foreigners mingled with their Russian hosts beneath the 3000 lights of the six spreading chandeliers, exchanging gossip and congratulations in the niches where the great tsarist war heroes were commemorated with the other Knights of St George. Maxim Rudin moved among them like an old lion, accepting the plaudits of well-wishers from 150 countries as no more than his due.

Munro spotted him from afar, but he was not included in the list of those presented personally, nor was it wise for him to approach the outgoing Secretary-General. Before midnight, pleading a natural tiredness, Rudin excused himself and left the guests to the care of Petrov and the others from the Politburo.

Twenty minutes later Adam Munro felt a touch at his arm. Standing behind him was an immaculate major in the uniform of the Kremlin's own praetorian guard. Impassive as ever, the major spoke to him in Russian.

'Mr Munro, please come with me.'

His tone permitted no expostulation. Munro was not surprised; evidently his inclusion in the guest list had been a mistake, it had been spotted and he was being asked to leave.

But the major headed away from the main doors, passed through into the high, octagonal Hall of St Vladimir, up a wooden staircase guarded by a bronze grill and out into the warm starlight of Upper Saviour Square.

The man walked with completely confident tread, at ease among passages and doorways well known to him although unseen by most.

Still following, Munro went across the square and into the Terem Palace. Silent guards were at every door; each opened as the major approached and closed as they passed through. They walked straight across the Front Hall Chamber and to the end of the Cross Chamber. Here, at a door at the far end, the major paused and knocked. There was a gruff command from inside. The major opened the door, stood aside and indicated that Munro should enter.

The third chamber in the Terem Palace, the so-called Palace of Chambers, is the Throne Room, the holy of holies of the old tsars, most inaccessible of all the rooms. In red, gilt and mosaic tiles, with parquet floor and deep burgundy carpet, it is lush; smaller and warmer than most of the other rooms. It was the place where the tsars worked or received emissaries in complete privacy. Standing staring out through the Petition Window was Maxim Rudin. He turned as Munro entered.

'So Mr Munro, you will be leaving us, I hear.'

It had been twenty-seven days since Munro had seen him before, in dressing gown, nursing a glass of milk, in his personal apartments in the arsenal. Now he was in a beautifully cut charcoal-grey suit, almost certainly made in Savile Row, London, bearing the two Orders of Lenin and Hero of the Soviet Union on the left lapel. The Throne Room suited him better this way.

'Yes, Mr President,' said Munro.

Maxim Rudin glanced at his watch.

'In ten minutes, Mr ex-President,' he remarked. 'Midnight I officially retire. You also, I presume, will be retiring?'

The old fox knows perfectly well that my cover was blown the night I met him, thought Munro, and that I also have to retire.

'Yes, Mr President, I shall be returning to London tomorrow, to retire.'

Rudin did not approach him or hold out his hand. He stood across the room, just where the tsars had once stood, in the room representing the pinnacle of the Russian Empire, and nodded.

'Then I shall wish you farewell, Mr Munro.'

He pressed a small onyx bell on a table, and behind Munro the door opened.

'Good-bye, sir,' said Munro. He had half turned to go when Rudin spoke again.

'Tell me, Mr Munro, what do you think of our Red Square?'

Munro stopped, puzzled. It was a strange question for a man saying farewell. Munro thought, and answered carefully.

'It is very impressive.'

'Impressive, yes,' said Rudin, as if weighing the word. 'Not perhaps as elegant as your Berkeley Square, but sometimes, even here, you can hear a nightingale sing.'

Munro stood motionless as the painted saints on the ceiling above him. His stomach turned over in a wave of nausea. They had got her, and, unable to resist, she had told them all, even the code-name and the reference to the old song about the nightingale in Berkeley Square.

'Will you shoot her?' he asked dully.

Rudin seemed genuinely surprised.

'Shoot her? Why should we shoot her?'

So, it would be the labour camps, the living death, for the woman he loved and had been so near to marrying in his native Scotland.

'Then what will you do to her?'

The old Russian raised his eyebrows in mock surprise.

'Do? Nothing. She is a loyal woman, a patriot. She is also very fond of you, young man. Not in love, you understand, but genuinely fond. . . .'

'I don't understand,' said Munro. 'How do you know?'

'She asked me to tell you,' said Rudin. 'She will not be a housewife in Edinburgh. She will not be Mrs Munro. She cannot see you again – ever. But she does not want you to worry for her, to fear for her. She is well, privileged, honoured, among her own people. She asked me to tell you not to worry.'

The dawning comprehension was almost as dizzying as the fear. Munro stared at Rudin as the disbelief receded.

'She was yours,' he said flatly, 'she was yours all along. From the first contact in the woods, just after Vishnayev made his bid for war in Europe. She was working for you. . . .'

The grizzled old Kremlin fox shrugged.

'Mr Munro,' growled the old Russian, 'how else could I get my messages to President Matthews with the absolute certainty that they would be believed?'

The impassive major with the cold eyes drew at his elbow; he was outside the Throne Room and the door closed behind him. Five minutes later he was shown out, on foot, through a small door in the Saviour Gate on to Red Square. The parade marshals were rehearsing their roles for May Day. The clock above his head struck midnight.

He turned left towards the National Hotel to find a taxi. A hundred yards later, as he passed Lenin's Mausoleum, to the surprise and outrage of a militiaman, he began to laugh.

THE FOURTH PROTOCOL

For Shane Richard, age five,
without whose loving attentions
this book would have been written
in half the time.

Part One

1

The man in grey decided to take the Glen suite of diamonds at midnight. Provided they were still in the apartment safe and the occupants away. This he needed to know. So he watched and he waited. At half past seven he was rewarded.

The big, wide limousine swooped up from the subterranean car park with the powerful grace implied by its name. It paused for an instant in the mouth of the cavern as its driver checked the street for traffic, then turned into the road and headed towards Hyde Park Corner.

Sitting across from the luxury apartment block, dressed in a hired chauffeur's uniform at the wheel of the rented Volvo estate, Jim Rawlings breathed a sigh of relief. Gazing unobserved across the Belgravia street he had seen what he had hoped for: the husband had been at the wheel with his wife beside him. He already had the engine running and the heater on to keep out the cold. Moving the automatic shift into drive, he eased out of the line of parked cars and went after the Daimler-Jaguar.

It was a crisp and bright morning, with a pale wash of light over Green Park in the east and the street lights still on. Rawlings had been at the stakeout since five o'clock and although a few people had passed down the street no-one had taken any notice of him. A chauffeur in a big car in Belgravia, richest of London's West End districts, attracts no attention, least of all with four suitcases and a hamper in the back, on the morning of 31 December. Many of the rich would be preparing to leave the capital to celebrate the festivities at their country homes.

He was fifty yards behind the Jaguar at Hyde Park Corner, allowing a truck to move between them. Up Park Lane Rawlings had one momentary misgiving: there was a branch of Coutts Bank there and he feared the couple in the Jaguar might pause to drop the diamonds into the night safe.

At Marble Arch he breathed a second sigh of relief. The limousine ahead of him made no turn around the arch to take the southbound carriageway back down Park Lane towards the bank. It sped straight up Great Cumberland Place, joined Gloucester Place and kept on north. So, the occupants of the luxury apartment on the eighth floor of Fontenoy House were not leaving the items with Coutts; either they had them in the car and were taking them to the country, or they were leaving them for the New Year period in the apartment. Rawlings was confident it would be the latter.

He tailed the Jaguar to Hendon, watched it speeding into the last mile before the M1 motorway and then turned back towards central London. Evidently, as he had hoped, they were going to join the wife's brother, the Duke of Sheffield, at his estates in North Yorkshire, a full six-hour drive away. That would give him a minimum of twenty-four hours, more than he needed. He had no doubts he could 'take' the apartment at Fontenoy House; he was, after all, one of the best cracksmen in London.

By mid-morning he had returned the Volvo to the rental company, the uniform to the costumiers, and the empty suitcases to the cupboard. He was back in his top-floor flat, a comfortable and expensively furnished pad atop a converted tea warehouse in his native Wandsworth. However he prospered, he was a south Londoner, born and bred, and though Wandsworth might not be as chic as Belgravia or Mayfair, it was his 'manor'. Like all of his kind, he hated to leave the security of his own manor. Within it he felt reasonably safe, even though to the local underworld and the police he was known as a 'face', underworld slang for a criminal or villain.

Like all successful villains, he kept a low profile around the manor, driving an unobtrusive car, his sole indulgence being the elegance of his apartment. He cultivated a deliberate vagueness among the lower orders of the underworld as to exactly what he did, and although the police accurately suspected his speciality, his 'form book' was clean, apart from a short stretch of porridge as a teenager. His evident success and the vagueness about how he achieved it evoked reverence among the young aspirants in the game, who were happy to perform small errands for him. Even the heavy mobs who took out wage offices in broad daylight with shotguns and pickaxe handles left him alone.

As was necessary, he had to have a 'front' occupation to account for the money. All the successful 'faces' had some form of legitimate business. The favoured ones have always been minicab driving or owning greengrocer shops, or a scrap metal and general dealership. All these fronts permit a lot of hidden profits, cash dealing, spare time, a range of hiding places and the facility to employ a couple of 'heavies' or 'slags'. These are hard men of little brain but considerable strength who also need an apparently legitimate employment to supplement their habitual profession as muscle hire.

Rawlings in fact had a scrap-metal dealership and car-wrecking yard. It gave him access to a well-equipped machine workshop, metal of all kinds, electrical wiring, battery acid and the two big thugs he employed both in the yard and as backup should he ever run into any aggro from villains who might decide to make trouble for him.

Showered and shaved, Rawlings stirred demerara crystals into his second espresso of the morning and studied again the sketch drawings Billy Rice had left him.

Billy was his apprentice, a smart twenty-three-year-old who would one day become good, even very good. He was still starting out on the fringe of the underworld and eager to do favours for a man of prestige, apart from the invaluable instructions he would get in the process. Twenty-four hours earlier Billy had knocked at the door of the eighth-floor apartment of Fontenoy House, dressed in the livery of an expensive flower shop and carrying a large bouquet of flowers. The props had got him effortlessly past the commissionaire in the lobby, where he had also noted the exact layout of the entrance hall, the porter's lodge and the way to the stairs.

It was her ladyship who had answered the door personally, her face lighting up with surprise and pleasure at the sight of the flowers. They purported to come from the committee of the Distressed Veterans Benevolent Fund, of which Lady Fiona was one of the patronesses and whose gala ball she was due to attend that very night, 30 December 1986. Rawlings figured that even if, at the ball itself, she mentioned the bouquet to any one of the committee members, he would simply assume it had been sent by another member on behalf of them all.

At the door she had examined the attached card, exclaimed, 'Oh, how perfectly lovely,' in the bright cut-crystal accents of her class, and taken the bouquet. Then Billy had held out his receipt pad and ballpoint pen. Unable to manage all three items together, Lady Fiona had withdrawn flustered into the sitting-room to put down the bouquet, leaving Billy unattended for several seconds in the small hallway.

With his boyish looks, fluffy blond hair, blue eyes and shy smile, Billy was a gift. He reckoned he could work his way past any middle-aged housewife in the metropolis. But his baby blue eyes missed very little.

Before even pressing the doorbell, he had spent a full minute scanning the outside of the door, its frame and surrounding wall area in the passage. He was looking for a small buzzer no larger than a walnut, or a black button or switch with which to turn the buzzer off. Only when satisfied there was none did he ring the bell.

Left alone in the doorway, he did the same again, searching the inner side of the frame and the walls for buzzer or switch. Again there was none. By the time the lady of the house returned to the hall to sign the receipt, Billy knew the door was secured by a shunt lock, which he had gratefully identified as a Chubb rather than a Bramah, which is reputedly unpickable.

Lady Fiona took the pad and pen and tried to sign for the flowers. No chance. The ballpoint pen had long had its cartridge removed and any remaining ink expended on a blank piece of paper. Billy apologized profusely. With a bright smile, Lady Fiona told him it was of no account, she was sure she had one in her bag, and returned beyond the sitting-room door. Billy had already noted what he sought. The door was indeed linked to an alarm system.

Protruding from the edge of the open door, high up on the hinge side, was a small plunger contact. Opposite it, set in the door jamb, was a tiny socket. Inside that socket, he knew, would be a Pye microswitch. With the door in the closed position the plunger would enter the socket and make a contact.

With the burglar alarm set and activated, the microswitch would trigger the alarm if the contact were broken, that is, if the door were opened. It took Billy less than three seconds to bring out his tube of superglue, squirt a hefty dollop into the orifice containing the microswitch and tamp the whole thing down with a small ball of plasticine and glue compound. In four seconds more it was rock hard, the microswitch blanked off from the entering plunger in the edge of the door.

When Lady Fiona returned with the signed receipt she found the nice young man leaning against the door jamb, from which he straightened up with an apologetic smile, smearing any surplus from the ball of his thumb as he did so. Later, Billy had given Jim Rawlings a complete description of the layout of the entrance, porter's lodge, location of the stairs and elevators, the passage to the apartment door, the small hallway behind the door and what part of the sitting-room he had been able to see.

As he sipped his coffee Rawlings was confident that four hours earlier the apartment owner had carried his suitcases into the corridor and returned to his own hallway to set his alarm. As usual it had made no sound. Closing the front door after him, he would have turned the key fully in the mortise lock, satisfied his alarm was now set and activated. Normally, the plunger would have been in contact with the Pye microswitch. The turning of the key would have established the complete link, activating the whole system. But with the plunger blanked off from the microswitch, the door system at least would be inert. Rawlings was certain he could take that door lock inside thirty minutes. In the apartment itself there would be other traps. He would cope with those when he met them.

Finishing his coffee, he reached for his file of newspaper cuttings. Like all jewel thieves, Rawlings followed the society gossip columns closely. This particular file was entirely about the social appearances of Lady Fiona and the suite of perfect diamonds she had worn to the gala ball the previous evening, so far as Jim Rawlings was concerned, for the last time.

A thousand miles to the east the old man standing at the window of the sitting-room in the third-floor front apartment at Prospekt Mira 111 was also thinking of midnight. It would herald 1 January 1987, his seventy-fifth birthday.

The hour was well past midday but he was still in a robe; there was little enough cause these days to rise early or spruce up to go to the office. There was no office to go to. His Russian wife Erita, thirty years his junior, had taken their two boys skating along the flooded and frozen lanes of Gorki Park, so he was alone.

He caught a glance of himself in a wall mirror and the prospect brought him no more joy than to contemplate his life, or what was left of it. The face, always lined, was now deeply furrowed. The hair, once thick and dark, was now snow white, skimpy and lifeless. The skin, after a lifetime of titanic drinking and chain-smoking, was blotched and mottled. The eyes gazed back miserably. He returned to the window and looked down at the snow-choked street. A few muffled, huddled babushkas were sweeping away the snow, which would fall again tonight.

It had been so long, he mused, twenty-four years almost to the day, since he had quit his non-job and pointless exile in Beirut to come here. There had been no point in staying, Nick Elliot and the rest at the Firm had got it all together by then; he had finally admitted it to them himself. So he had come, leaving wife and children to join him later if they wished.

At first he thought it was like coming home, to a spiritual and moral home. He had thrown himself into the new life, he had truly believed in the philosophy and its eventual triumph. Why not? He had spent twenty-seven years serving it. He had been happy and fulfilled those first, early years of the mid-sixties. There had been the extensive debriefing, of course, but he had been revered within the Committee of State Security. He was, after all, one of the Five Stars, the greatest of them all, with Burgess, Maclean, Blunt and Blake, the ones who had burrowed into the inner core of the British establishment and betrayed it all.

Burgess, drinking and buggering his way to an early grave, had been in it before he had arrived. Maclean had lost his illusions first, but then he had been in Moscow since 1951. By 1963 he was sour and embittered, taking it out on Melinda, who had finally quit to come here, to this apartment. Maclean had gone on, somehow, utterly disillusioned and resentful, until the cancer got him, by which time he hated his hosts and they hated him. Blunt had been blown and disgraced back in England. That left him and Blake, the old man thought. In a way he envied Blake, completely assimilated, utterly content, who had invited him and Erita round for New Year's Eve. Of course, Blake had had a cosmopolitan background, Dutch father, Jewish mother.

For him personally there could be no assimilation; he had known that after the first five years. By then he had learned fluent Russian, written and spoken, but he still retained a remarkable English accent. Apart from that, he had come to hate the society. It was a completely, irreversible and unalterably alien society.

That was not the worst of it: within seven years of arriving he had lost his last politicial illusions. It was all a lie, and he had been smart enough to see through it. He had spent his youth and manhood serving a lie, lying for the lie, betraying for the lie, abandoning that 'green and pleasant land', and all for a lie.

For years, provided as of right with every British magazine and newspaper, he had followed the cricket scores while advising on the inspiration of strikes, looked at the old familiar places in the magazines while preparing disinformation aimed at bringing it all to ruin, perched unobserved on a barstool in the National to listen to the Brits laughing and joking in his language, while counselling the top men of the KGB, including even the Chairman himself, on how best to subvert that little island. And all the time, deep inside, these past fifteen years, there had been a great void of despair that not even the drink and the many women had been able to blank out. It was too late; he could never go back, he told himself. And yet, and yet . . .

The doorbell rang. It puzzled him. Prospekt Mira 111 is a totally KGB-owned block in a quiet back street of central Moscow, with mainly senior KGB tenants and a few Foreign Ministry people. A visitor would have to check in with the concierge. It could not be Erita – she had her own key.

When he opened the door a man stood there alone. He was youthful and looked fit, sheathed in a well-cut greatcoat and with a warm fur *shapka*, without insignia, on his head. His face was coldly impassive, but not from the freezing wind outside, for his shoes indicated he had stepped from a warm car into a warm apartment block, not trudged through icy snow. Blank blue eyes stared at the old man with neither friendship nor hostility.

'Comrade Colonel Philby?' he asked.

Philby was surprised. Close personal friends, the Blakes

and half a dozen others, called him Kim. For the rest, he had lived under a pseudonym for many, many years. Only to a few at the very top was he Philby, a full KGB colonel on the retired list.

'Yes'.

'I am Major Pavlov, of the Ninth Directorate, attached to the personal staff of the General Secretary of the CPSU.'

Philby knew the Ninth Directorate of the KGB. It provided the bodyguards for all the top Party personnel and the buildings in which they worked and lived. In uniform, nowadays confined to inside the Party buildings and for ceremonial occasions, they would wear the distinctive electric-blue cap bands, shoulder boards and lapel tabs, and be also known as the Kremlin Guards. Attached as personal bodyguards, they would wear beautifully cut civilian clothes; they would also be utterly fit, highly trained, icily loyal, and armed.

'Indeed,' said Philby.

'This is for you, Comrade Colonel.'

The major held out a long envelope of high-quality paper. Philby took it.

'This also,' said Major Pavlov and held out a small square of pasteboard with a phone number on it.

'Thank you,' said Philby. Without a further word the major inclined his head briefly, turned on his heel and went back down the corridor. Seconds later, from his window, Philby watched the sleek black Chaika limousine with its distinctive Central Committee number plates, beginning with the letters MOC, slide away from the front entrance.

Jim Rawlings peered down at the society magazine photograph through a magnifying glass. The picture showed the woman he had seen driving north out of London that morning with her husband, albeit taken a year earlier. She was standing in a presentation line while the woman next to her greeted Princess Alexandra. And she was wearing the stones. Rawlings, who studied for months before he made a hit, knew their provenance better than his own birth date.

In 1905 the young Earl of Margate had returned from South Africa bearing with him four magnificent but uncut stones. On his marriage in 1912 he had had Cartier of London cut and set the stones as a present to his young wife. Cartier had them cut by Aascher's of Amsterdam, still then regarded as the finest cutters in the world following their triumph in the cutting of the massive Cullinan stone. The four original gems emerged as two matching pairs of pear-shaped fifty-eight-facet stones, one pair weighing in at ten carats each, the other pair at twenty carats each.

Back in London Cartier had set these stones in white gold, surrounded by a total of forty much smaller stones, to create a suite composed of a tiara with as its centrepiece one of the larger of the pear-shaped gems, a pendant with the other as its centrepiece, and two matching pendant earrings with the two smaller stones. Before they were ready the Earl's father, the seventh Duke of Sheffield, died and the Earl succeeded to the title. The diamonds became known as the Glen Diamonds, after the family name of the House of Sheffield.

The eighth Duke had passed them on his death in 1936 to his son and he in turn had had two children, a daughter born in 1944 and a son born in 1949. It was this daughter, now aged forty-two, whose image was beneath Jim Rawlings's magnifying glass.

'You won't be wearing them again, darling,' said Rawlings to himself. Then he began checking once again his equipment for the evening.

Harold Philby slit the envelope with a kitchen knife, extracted the letter and spread it on the sitting-room table. He was impressed; it was from the General Secretary of the CPSU personally, handwritten in the Soviet leader's neat, clerkish script and, of course, in Russian.

The paper was of fine quality like the matching

envelope, and unheaded. He must have written it from his personal apartment in number 26 Kutuzovsky Prospekt, the huge block which since the time of Stalin had contained in its sumptuous quarters the Moscow homes of the very top level of the Party hierarchs.

In the top right-hand corner were the words: 'A.m. Wednesday, 31 December 1986'. The text came below. It read:

Dear Philby,

My attention has been drawn to a remark made by you at a recent dinner party in Moscow. To wit, that 'the political stability of Great Britain is constantly overestimated here in Moscow and never more so than at the present time'.

I would be happy to receive from you an expansion and clarification of this remark. Put this explanation in written form and direct it to me personally, without retaining any copies or using secretaries.

When it is ready call the number Major Pavlov has given you, ask to speak to him personally, and he will come to your residence to collect it.

My felicitations upon your birthday tomorrow.

Sincerely . . .

The letter ended with the signature.

Philby let out his breath slowly. So, Kryuchkov's dinner on the 26th for senior officers of the KGB had been bugged after all. He had half suspected it. As First Deputy Chairman of the KGB and head of its First Chief Directorate, Vladimir Alexandrovitch Kryuchkov was the General Secretary's creature, body and soul. Although styled a Colonel-General, Kryuchkov was no military man nor even a professional intelligence officer; he was a Party apparatchik to his bootstraps, one of those brought in by the present Soviet leader when he had been Chairman of the KGB.

Philby read the letter again, then pushed it away from him. The old man's style hadn't changed, he thought. Brief to the point of starkness, clear and concise, devoid of elaborate courtesies, inviting no contradiction. Even the reference to Philby's birthday was brief enough simply to show he had called for the file and little more.

Still, Philby was impressed. A personal letter from this most glacial and remote of men was unusual and would have had many men trembling at the honour. Years ago it had been different. When the present Soviet leader had arrived at the KGB as Chairman, Philby had already been there for years and was considered something of a star. He lectured on the Western intelligence agencies in general and on the British SIS in particular.

Like all incoming Party men set to command professionals of another discipline the new Chairman had looked to put his own placemen in key posts. Philby, even though respected and admired as one of the Five Stars, realized that a patron in very high places would be useful in this most conspiratorial of societies. The Chairman, a highly intelligent and cultured man, had shown a curiosity, short of fascination but above mere interest, in Britain.

Many times, over those years, he had asked Philby for an interpretation or analysis of events in Britain, its personalities and likely reactions, and Philby had been happy to oblige. It was as if the KGB Chairman wanted to check what reached his desk from the in-house 'Britain' experts and from those at his old office, the International Department of the Central Committee under Boris Ponomarev, against another critique. Several times he had heeded Philby's quiet advice on matters pertaining to Britain.

It had been some time since Philby had seen the new czar of all the Russias face to face. That was when he had attended a reception to mark the Chairman's departure from the KGB back to the Central Committee, apparently as a Secretary, in fact to prepare for his predecessor's coming death and to mastermind his own advancement. And now he was seeking Philby's interpretation again.

His reverie was interrupted by the return of Erita and the boys, flushed from skating and noisy as ever. Back in 1975, long after Melinda Maclean's departure, when the higher-ups at the KGB had decided his desultory whoring and drinking had lost their charms (for the apparat, at least), Erita had been ordered to move in with him. She was a KGB girl then, unusually also Jewish, aged thirty-four, dark and solid. They had married the same year.

After the marriage his notable personal charm had taken its toll. She had genuinely fallen in love with him and had roundly refused to report on him any more to the KGB. The case officer had shrugged, reported back and been told to drop the matter. The boys had come two and three years later.

'Anything important, Kim?' she asked, as he stood and pushed the letter into his pocket. He shook his head. She went on pulling the thick, quilted jackets off the boys.

'Nothing, my love,' he said.

But she could see he was absorbed by something. She knew better than to insist, but she came over and kissed him on the cheek. 'Please don't drink too much at the Blakes' tonight.'

'I'll try,' he said with a smile.

In fact he was going to permit himself one last bender. A lifelong toper who, when he started drinking at a party, would usually go on until he collapsed, he had ignored a hundred doctors' warnings to quit. They had forced him to stop the cigarettes, and that had been bad enough. But not the booze; he could still quit it when he wanted and he knew that he would have to stop for a while after this evening's party.

He recalled the remark he had made at Kryuchkov's dinner table and the thoughts that had prompted it. He knew what was going on, and what was intended, deep inside the heart of Britain's Labour Party. Others had received the mass of raw intelligence that he had studied over the years, and which was still passed to him as a sort of favour. But only he had been able to put all the pieces together, assembling them within the framework of British mass psychology, to come up with the real picture. If he was going to do justice to the idea forming in his mind, he was going to have to describe that picture in words; prepare for the Soviet leader one of the best pieces he had ever penned. At the weekend he could send Erita and the boys to the dacha. He would start, alone in the apartment, at the weekend. Before then, one last bender.

Jim Rawlings spent the hour between nine and ten that night sitting in another, smaller rented car outside Fontenoy House. He was dressed in a beautifully cut dinner jacket and attracted no attention. What he was studying was the pattern of lights high up in the apartment block. The flat he had targeted was, of course, in darkness, but he was happy to see that lights were on in the apartments above and below it. In each, to judge from the appearances of guests at the windows, New Year parties were getting under way.

At ten, with his car parked discreetly in a side street two blocks away, he sauntered into the front entrance of Fontenoy House. There had been so many people going in and out that the doors were closed but not locked. Inside the lobby, on the left-hand side, was the porter's lodge, just as Billy Rice had said. Inside it the night porter was watching his Japanese portable. He rose and came to his doorway, as if to speak.

Rawlings was carrying a bottle of champagne decorated with a huge ribbon bow. He waved a hand in tipsy greeting. 'Evening,' he called, and added, 'Oh, and Happy New Year.'

If the old porter was thinking of asking for identification or destination, he thought better of it. There were at least six parties going on in the block. Half of them seemed to be open house, so how was *he* to check guest lists?

'Oh, er, thank you, sir. Happy New Year, sir,' he

called, but the dinner-jacketed back had gone down the corridor. He returned to his movie.

Rawlings used the stairs to the first floor, then the lift to the eighth. At five past ten he was outside the door of the apartment he sought. As Billy had reported, there was no buzzer and the lock was a Chubb mortise. There was a secondary, self-closing Yale lock twenty inches above the Chubb for everyday use.

The Chubb mortise has a total of 17,000 computations and permutations. It is a five-lever lock but for a good keyman not an insuperable problem, since only the first two and a half levers need to be ascertained; the other two and a half are the same, but in reverse, so that the owner's key will operate equally well when introduced from the other side of the door.

After leaving school at sixteen, Rawlings had spent ten years working with and under his Uncle Albert in the latter's hardware shop. It was a good front for the old man, himself a notable cracksman in his day. It gave the eager young Rawlings access to every known lock on the market and most of the smaller safes. After ten years of endless practice and with Uncle Albert's expert coaching, Rawlings could take just about any lock in manufacture.

From his trouser pocket he produced a ring of twelve skeleton keys, all made up in his own workshop. He selected and tested three, one after the other, and settled for the sixth on the ring. Inserting it into the Chubb, he began to detect the pressure points inside the lock. Then, using a flat pack of slim steel files from his top pocket he started to work on the softer metal of the skeleton. Within ten minutes he had the first two and a half levers, the configuration or 'profile' that he needed. In another fifteen minutes he had reproduced the same two and a half lever pattern in reverse. Inserting the finished skeleton into the Chubb lock, he turned it slowly and carefully.

It went fully back. He waited for sixty seconds, just in case Billy's tamp of plasticine and super-glue compound had not held inside the door jamb. No bells. He let out a sigh and went to work on the Yale with a fine steel spike. That took sixty seconds and the door swung quietly open. It was dark inside, but the light from the corridor gave him the outlines of the empty hallway. It was about eight feet square and carpeted.

He suspected there would be a pressure pad somewhere, but not too close to the door, lest the owner should trigger it himself. Stepping into the hall, close to the wall, he eased the door closed behind him and put on the hall light. To his left was a door, partly open, through which he could see a lavatory. To his right, another door, almost certainly the cloaks cupboard containing the alarm control system, which he would leave alone. Taking a pair of pliers from his breast pocket, he stooped and lifted the carpet from its smooth-edge beading. As the square of carpet rose he spotted the pressure pad in the dead centre of the hall. Just the one. Letting the carpet gently back in place, he stepped around it and opened the large door ahead of him. As Billy had said, it was the door to the sitting-room.

He stood for several minutes on the threshold of the sitting-room before identifying the light switch and putting on the lights. It was a risk, but he was eight floors above the street, the owners were in Yorkshire and he did not have the time to work in a booby-trapped room by pencil torch.

The room was oblong, about twenty-five feet by eighteen, carpeted and richly furnished. Ahead of him were the double-glazed picture windows facing south and over the street. To his right was a wall containing a stone fireplace and gas-log fire with, in one corner, a door presumably leading to the master bedroom suite. To his left, the opposite wall contained two doors, one open to the passage leading to the guest bedrooms, the other closed, perhaps to the dining-room and kitchen.

He spent another ten minutes standing motionless scanning the walls and ceiling. His reason was simple: there could well be a static movement alarm that Billy Rice had not seen, but which would detect any body heat or movement entering the room. If bells went off, he could be out of there in three seconds. There were no bells; the system was based on a wired-up door, probably windows which he did not intend to touch anyway, and a system of pressure pads.

The safe, he was sure, would be in this room or the master bedroom, and it would be on an outside wall, since interior walls would not be thick enough. He spotted it just before eleven o'clock. Right in front of him, in an eight-foot piece of wall between the two wide windows, was a gilt-framed mirror, not hanging slightly away from the wall like the pictures, casting a narrow shadow at the edge, but too flat to the wall, as if hinged.

Using his pliers to lift the edge of the carpet, he worked his way round the walls, unveiling the thread-like wires leading from the skirting board to the pads, somewhere out towards the centre of the room.

When he reached the mirror he saw there was one pressure pad directly beneath it. He thought of moving it, but instead lifted a large, low coffee table from nearby and placed it over the pad, its legs clear of the edges. He now knew that if he stayed close to the walls, or stood on pieces of furniture (no furniture can stand on a pressure pad) he would be safe.

The mirror was kept close to the wall by magnetic catch, also wired up. That was no problem. He slipped a flat wafer of magnetized steel between the two magnets of the catch, one in the mirror frame and the other in the wall. Keeping his substitute flat to the wall-based magnet, he eased the mirror away from the wall. The wall magnet made no protest; it was still in contact with another magnet, so it did not report that any contact had been broken.

Rawlings smiled. The wall safe was a nice little Hamber Model D. He knew the door was made of half-inch-thick, high-tensile, hardened steel: the hinge was a vertical rod of hardened steel, going into the frame upwards and downwards from the door itself. The securing mechanism consisted of three hardened-steel bolts emerging from the door and entering the frame to a depth of 1½ inches. Behind the steel face of the door was a 2-inch-deep tinplate box containing the three locking bolts, the vertical control bolt that governed their movements and the three-wheel combination lock whose face was now staring at him.

Rawlings did not intend to tamper with any of this. There was an easier way – to cut the door from top to bottom just on the hinge side of the combination dial. That would leave 60 per cent of the door, containing the combination lock and three locking bolts, jammed into the safe's door frame. The other 40 per cent of the door would swing open, giving him enough space to get his hand inside and the contents out.

He worked his way back to the hall, where he had left his bottle of champagne, and returned with it. Squatting on the coffee table, he unscrewed the bottom of the false bottle and emptied out his supplies. Apart from an electric detonator, ensconced in cotton wool in a small box, a collection of small magnets and a reel of ordinary household 5-amp flex, he had brought a length of CLC.

Rawlings knew the best way to cut half-inch steel plate was to use the Monroe theory, named after the inventor of the 'shaped charge' principle. What he was holding was called in the trade Charge-Linear-Cutting, or CLC; a V-shaped length of metal, stiff but just pliable, encased in plastic explosive. It was manufactured by three companies in Britain, one government-owned and the other two in the private sector. CLC was definitely not available except under stringent licence, but as a professional cracksman Rawlings had a contact, a bent employee in one of the private-sector companies.

Quick and expertly, Rawlings prepared the length he needed and applied it to the outside of the Hamber's door, from top to bottom, just one side of the combination dial. Into one end of the CLC he inserted the detonator, from which protruded two twisted copper wires. These he untwisted and separated widely, to prevent a short-circuit later. To each wire he attached one of the strands from his domestic flex, which itself terminated in a three-pin domestic plug.

Unravelling this carefully, he worked his way backwards round the room and into the corridor leading to the guest bedrooms. The lee of the passage would give him protection from the blast. Making his way gingerly to the kitchen, he filled with water a large polythene bag from his pocket. This he fixed to the wall with thumb tacks to hang over the explosive on the safe's door. Feather cushions, Uncle Albert had told him, are for the birds and TV. There is no shock absorber like water.

It was twenty to midnight. Above him the party was getting noisier and noisier. Even in this luxury block with its accent on privacy he could clearly hear the shouting and dancing. His last act before retiring to the corridor was to turn on the television set. Inside the corridor he located a wall plug, made sure the switch was off and plugged in his flex. Then he waited.

By one minute to midnight the noise above was horrendous. Then suddenly it quietened as somebody roared for silence. In the quiet Rawlings could hear the television he had switched on in the sitting-room. The traditional Scottish programme, with its ballads and Highland dancing changed to a static image of the clock mistakenly called Big Ben atop London's Houses of Parliament. Behind the clock's facade was the giant bell, the real Big Ben. The TV commentator chattered away the seconds to midnight as people across the kingdom charged their glasses. Then the quarters began to sound.

After the quarters there was a pause. Then Big Ben spoke: BONG, the thunderous boom of the first stroke of midnight. It echoed in twenty million homes across the land; it crashed through the apartment on the ninth floor of Fontenoy House and was itself eclipsed by the roar of cheering and 'Auld Lang Syne'. As the first boom rang out on the eighth floor, Jim Rawlings flicked the electric switch to 'on'.

The flat crack went unnoticed, save by himself. He waited sixty seconds, then unplugged his lead and began to work his way back to the safe, tidying up his gear as he went. The plumes of smoke were clearing. Of the plastic cushion and its gallon of water there was nothing left but a few damp patches. The door of the safe looked as if it had been cleft from top to bottom by a blunt axe wielded by a giant. Rawlings blew away a few plumes of smoke and with gloved hand pulled the smaller part of the door back on its hinges. The tinplate box had been torn apart by the blast, but all the bolts in the other section of the door were in their sockets. The part he had opened was large enough for him to peer inside. A cash box and a velvet bag; he eased out the bag, undid the drawstring and emptied the contents on to the coffee table.

They glittered and flared in the light, as if they contained their own fire. The Glen Diamonds. Rawlings put the remainder of his equipment back in the false champagne bottle, the flex, the empty detonator box, the thumb tacks and remainder of the CLC, before he realized he had an unforeseen problem. The pendant and earrings would slip into his trouser pockets, but the tiara was wider and higher than he had thought. He glanced round for a receptacle that would attract no attention. It was lying on top of the bureau a few feet away.

He emptied the contents of the attaché case into the bowl of an armchair – a collection of wallets, credit cards, pens, address books and a couple of folders.

It was exactly right. The case took all the Glen suite and the champagne bottle, which might have seemed odd if seen *leaving* a party. With a last glance around the sitting-room, Rawlings switched off the light, stepped back into the hall and closed the door. Once in the corridor he relocked the main door with the Chubb lock and sixty seconds later strolled past the porter's lodge and out into the night. The man did not even look up.

It was nearly midnight that first day of January when

Harold Philby sat down at the sitting-room table in his Moscow flat. He had had his bender the previous evening at the Blakes' party, but had not even enjoyed it. His thoughts were too locked into what he would have to write. During the morning he had recovered from the inevitable hangover and now, with Erita and the boys in bed asleep, he had the peace and quiet to try to think things out.

There was a 'coo' from across the room; Philby rose and went over to the large cage in the corner and gazed through the bars at a pigeon with one leg in splints. He had always adored pets, from his vixen in Beirut through a range of canaries and parakeets in this very apartment. The pigeon waddled across the floor of its cage, the splinted leg impeding its passage.

'All right, old fellow,' said Philby through the bars, 'we'll have them off soon and you can fly again.'

He returned to the table. It had got to be good, he told himself for the hundredth time. The General Secretary was a bad man to cross and a hard one to deceive. Some of those senior Air Force men who had made such a dog's breakfast of the tracking and downing of the Korean jet-liner back in 1983 had, on his personal recommendation, ended up in cold graves beneath the permafrost of the Kamchatka. Wracked by health problems, confined to a wheelchair part of the time he might be, but he was still the undisputed master of the USSR, his word was law, his brain was still razor sharp and his pale eyes missed nothing.

Taking paper and pencil, Philby began to rough out the first draft of his reply.

Four hours later, but at the same period just before midnight in London, the owner of the apartment at Fontenoy House returned alone to the capital. A tall, greying and distinguished man in his mid-fifties, he drove straight into the basement car park using his own plastic admission card and took his own suitcase in the elevator to the eighth floor. He was in a foul mood.

He had driven for six hours, having left his brother-in-law's stately home three days prematurely following a blazing row with his wife. She, angular and horsy, adored the countryside as much as he loathed it. Content to stride the bleak Yorkshire moors in mid-winter, she had left him miserably cooped up indoors with her brother, the tenth Duke. Which was in a way worse, for the apartment owner, who prided himself on his appreciation of the manly virtues was convinced the wretched fellow was gay.

The New Year's Eve dinner had been appalling for him, surrounded as he was by his wife's cronies who talked hunting, shooting and fishing the entire time, the whole being punctured by the high, wittering laugh of the Duke and his too handsome pals. That morning he had made some remark to his wife and she had gone off the deep end. The result was, it had been agreed he could drive south alone after tea; she would remain as long as she wished, which might be a month.

He entered the hall of his apartment and paused; the alarm system should be emitting a loud, repeated 'peep' which should last for thirty seconds before the full alarm sounded, during which time he could reach the master box and turn it off. Damn thing, he thought, probably out of order. He went into the cloaks cupboard and turned the whole system off with his personal key. Then he entered the sitting-room and threw on the light.

He stood, with his bag behind him in the hall, and stared at the scene in open-mouthed horror. The damp patches had evaporated in the warmth, and the television was not on. What caught his eye at once was the scorched wall and cloven safe door right ahead of him. He crossed the room in several strides and peered into the safe. There was no doubt; the diamonds were gone. He looked around again, saw his possessions scattered in the armchair by the fire and the carpet lifted from its smooth-edge all round the walls. He sank into the other fireside armchair, as white as a sheet.

'Oh, my God,' he breathed. He seemed stunned by the

nature of the disaster and remained in the chair for ten minutes, breathing heavily and staring at the disarray.

Finally he rose and went to the telephone. With a trembling forefinger he dialled a number. At the other end it rang and rang, but there was no reply.

The following morning, just before eleven, John Preston walked down Curzon Street towards the headquarters of the department he worked for, round the corner from the Mirabelle Restaurant, in which few of the department's employees could afford to dine.

Most of the civil service that Friday morning were being allowed to bridge over from Thursday, the New Year's Day which was a public holiday anyway, into the weekend. But Brian Harcourt-Smith had asked him to come in especially, so he had come. He suspected he knew what the Deputy Director-General of MI5 wanted to talk about.

For three years, over half the time he had spent with MI5 since joining them as a late entrant in the summer of 1981, John Preston had been in 'F' Branch of the service, dealing with surveillance of extremist political organizations, Left and Right; with research into these bodies and the running of agents within them. For two of those years he had been in F.1, heading up (D) Section, concerned with the penetration of extreme Left-wing elements into Britain's Labour Party. The result of his investigations, his report, had been submitted two weeks earlier, just before Christmas. He was surprised it had been read and digested so quickly.

He presented himself at the front desk, proffered his card, was vetted, checked out with the DDG's office as an expected visitor, and allowed to proceed to the top of the building.

He was sorry he would not be seeing the Director-General personally. He liked Sir Bernard Hemmings, but it was an open secret inside 'Five' that the old man was ill and spending less and less time in the office. In his absences the day-to-day running of the department was passing more and more into the hands of his ambitious deputy, a fact which did not please some of the older veterans of the service.

Sir Bernard was a 'Five' man from way back, and had done his fieldwork. He could establish empathy with the men who went out on the streets, staked out suspects, tailed hostile couriers and penetrated subversive organizations. Harcourt-Smith was of the university intake, with a first-class degree, and had been mainly a head-office man, moving smoothly between the departments and steadily up the promotion ladder.

He received Preston warmly in his office immaculately dressed as ever. Preston was wary of the warmth. Others had been received just as warmly, so went the stories, and had been out of service a week later. Harcourt-Smith seated Preston in front of his desk and himself behind it. Preston's report lay on the blotter.

'Now, John, this report of yours. You'll understand, of course, that I take it, along with all your work, extremely seriously.'

'Thank you,' said Preston.

'So much so,' Harcourt-Smith went on, 'that I've spent a good part of the festivities break right here in this office to reread it and consider it.'

Preston thought it wiser to remain silent.

'It is, how shall I put it, pretty radical . . . no holds barred, eh? The question is, and this is the question I have to ask myself before this department proposes any kind of policy based upon it, is it all absolutely true? Can it be verified? This is what *I* should be asked.'

'Look Brian, I've spent two years on that investigation. My people went deep, very deep. The facts, where I've stated them as facts, are true.'

'Ah, John. I'd never dispute any facts presented by you. But the conclusions drawn from them . . .'

'Are based on logic, I think,' said Preston.

'A great discipline, I used to study it,' resumed

Harcourt-Smith. 'But not always supported by hard evidence, wouldn't you agree? Let's take this thing here . . .' He found the place in the report and his finger ran along one line. 'The MBR. Pretty extreme, wouldn't you say?'

'Oh yes, Brian, it's extreme. These are pretty extreme people.'

'No doubt about it. But wouldn't it have been helpful to have a copy of the MBR attached to your report?'

'So far as I could discover, it hasn't been written down. It's a series of intentions, albeit very firm intentions, in the minds of certain people.'

Harcourt-Smith sucked regretfully at a tooth. 'Intentions,' he said as though the word intrigued him, 'yes, intentions. But you see, John, there are a lot of intentions in the minds of a lot of people vis-à-vis this country, not all of them friendly. But we can't propose policy, measures or counter-measures on the basis of these intentions . . .'

Preston was about to speak, but Harcourt-Smith swept on, rising to indicate the interview was over. 'Look, John, leave this with me a while longer. I'll have to think on it and perhaps take a few soundings before I decide where I can best place it. By the by, how do you like F.1(D)?'

'I like it fine,' said Preston, rising also.

'I may have something for you that you'll like even more,' said Harcourt-Smith.

When Preston had gone Harcourt-Smith stared for several minutes at the door through which he had passed. He seemed lost in thought.

Simply to shred the file, which he privately regarded as embarrassing and possibly one day dangerous, was not possible. It had been formally presented by a section head. It had a file number. He thought long and hard. Then he took his red-ink pen and wrote carefully on the cover of the Preston Report. He pressed his buzzer for his secretary.

'Mabel,' he said when she entered, 'take this down to Registry yourself please. Right now.'

The girl glanced at the cover of the file. Across it were written the letters NFA and Brian Harcourt-Smith's initials. In the service NFA stands for 'No Further Action'. The report was to be buried.

2

It was not until 4 January, the following Sunday, that the apartment owner at Fontenoy House was able to get an answer from the number he had been ringing every hour for three days. It was a brief conversation when it took place, but it resulted in his meeting with another man just before the hour of luncheon in a recessed alcove of one of the public rooms in a very discreet West End hotel.

The newcomer was about sixty, with iron-grey hair, soberly dressed and with the air of a kind of civil servant, which in a way he was. He was the second to arrive and seated himself with an immediate apology.

'I'm terribly sorry I wasn't available these past three days,' he said. 'Being a single man, I was invited by some kind friends to spend the New Year period with them out of town. Now, what seems to be the problem?'

The apartment owner told him in short, clear sentences. He had had time to think exactly how he would convey the enormity of what had happened and he chose his phrases well. The other man considered the narrative with deepening gravity.

'You're quite right, of course,' he said at length. 'It could be very serious. When you returned on Thursday night, did you call the police? Or at any time since?'

'No, I thought it better to talk to you first.'

'Ah, a pity in a way. It's too late now anyway. Their forensic people would establish the blowing of the safe was three or four days old. Hard to explain that. Unless . . .'

'Yes?' asked the apartment owner eagerly.

'Unless you could maintain that the mirror was back in its place and everything in such apple-pie order that you could live there for three days and not know you had been burgled?'

'Hardly,' said the apartment owner. 'The carpet had been taken up all round the edges. The bastard must have walked around the walls to avoid the pressure pads.'

'Yes,' mused the other. 'They'd hardly credit a burglar so neat he even replaces the carpet as well as the mirror. So that won't work. Nor, I fear, could one pretend you had spent the intervening three days somewhere else.'

'But where? I would have been seen. But I haven't. Club? Hotel? I would have had to check in.'

'Precisely,' said the confidant. 'No, it won't work. For better or worse the die is cast. It's too late to call in the police now.'

'Then what the hell do I do?' asked the apartment owner. 'They have simply *got* to be recovered.'

'How long will your wife remain away from London?' asked the other.

'Who knows? She enjoys it up in Yorkshire. Some weeks, I hope.'

'Then we shall have to effect a replacement of the damaged safe with a new and identical model. Also a replica set of the Glen Diamonds. It will take time to arrange.'

'But how about what has been stolen?' asked the apartment owner desperately. 'They can't just be left somewhere out there on the loose. I've got to have them back.'

'True,' nodded the other. 'Look, as you may imagine, my people have some contacts in the world of diamonds. I'll cause enquiries to be made. The gems will almost certainly be passed to one of the main centres for reshaping. They could not be marketed as they are. Too identifiable. I'll see if the burglar can be traced and the things recovered.'

The man rose and prepared to leave. His friend remained seated, evidently deeply worried. The sober-suited man was equally dismayed but he hid it better.

'Do nothing and say nothing untoward,' he advised. 'Keep your wife in the country as long as possible. Behave perfectly normally. Rest assured, I shall be in touch.'

The following morning John Preston was one of those who joined the great throng of people surging back into central London after the too-long five day break. As he lived in South Kensington it suited him to come to work on the Underground. He disembarked at Goodge Street and made his way the remaining five hundred yards on foot, an unnoticeable man of medium height and build, aged forty-six, in a grey raincoat and hatless despite the chill.

Near the top of Gordon Street he turned into the entrance of an equally unnoticeable building that could have been an office block like any other, solid but not modern, and purporting to house an insurance enterprise. Only inside the hallway were the differences from other office blocks in the neighbourhood discernible.

For one thing there were three men in the lobby, one on the door, one behind the reception desk and one by the lift doors; all were of a size and muscularity not normally associated with the underwriting of insurance policies. Any stray citizen seeking to do business with this particular company, and declining to be directed elsewhere, would have learned the hard way that only those presenting an identification that could pass the scrutiny of the small computer terminal beneath the reception desk were permitted beyond the lobby.

The British Security Service, better known as MI5, does not live in one single building. Discreetly but inconveniently, it is split up into four office blocks. The headquarters are in Charles Street, and no longer at the old HQ, Leconfield House, so habitually mentioned in the newspapers.

The next biggest block is in Gordon Street, known simply as 'Gordon' and nothing else, just as the head office is known as 'Charles'. The other two premises are in Cork Street (known as 'Cork') and a humble annexe in Marlborough Street, again known simply by the street name.

The department is divided into six branches scattered throughout the buildings. Again, discreetly but confusingly, some of the branches have sections in different buildings. In order to avoid an inordinate use of shoe leather, all are linked by extremely secure telelphone lines, with a flawless system for identification of the credentials of the caller.

'A' Branch handles in its various sections Policy, Technical Support, Property Establishment, Registry, Data Processing, the office of the Legal Adviser and the Watcher Service. The last named is the home of that idiosyncratic group of men and (some) women, of all ages and types, street wise and ingenious, who can mount the finest personal surveillance teams in the world. Even 'hostiles' have had to concede that on their own ground MI5's watchers are just about unbeatable.

Unlike the Secret Intelligence Service (MI6) which handles foreign intelligence and has absorbed a number of Americanisms into its in-house jargon, the Security Service (MI5), covering internal counter-intelligence, bases most of its jargon on former police phrases. It avoids terms like 'surveillance operative' and still calls its tracker teams simply 'the watchers'.

'B' Branch handles Recruitment, Personnel, Vetting, Promotions, Pensions and Finance (meaning salaries and operational expenses).

'C' Branch concerns itself with the security of the Civil Service (its staffers and its buildings), the security of Contractors (mainly those civilian firms handling defence and communications work), Military Security (in close liaison with the Armed Forces' own internal security staffs) and Sabotage (in reality or prospect).

There used to be a 'D' Branch, but with the arcane logic known only to its practitioners in the intelligence world, it was long ago renamed 'K' Branch. It is one of the biggest, and its biggest section is just called Soviet, being subdivided into Operations, Field Investigations and Order of Battle. Next in 'K' comes Soviet Satellites, also divided into the same three subsections, then Research and finally Agents.

As may be imagined, 'K' devotes its not inconsiderable labours to keeping track of the huge number of Soviet and satellite agents who operate, or try to, out of the various embassies, consulates, legations, trade missions, banks, news agencies and commercial enterprises that a lenient British government has allowed to be scattered all over the capital and (in the case of consulates) the provinces.

Also inside 'K' Branch is a modest office inhabited by the officer whose job is to liaise between MI5 and its sister service MI6. This officer is in fact a 'Six' man, on secondment to Charles Street in order to carry out his liaison duties. The section is known simply as K.7.

'E' Branch (the alphabetical sequence resumes with E) covers international communism and its adherents who may wish to visit Britain for nefarious reasons, or the home-grown variety who may wish to go abroad for the same purposes. Also inside 'E', Far East maintains liaison officers in Hong Kong, New Delhi, Canberra and Wellington, while All Regions does the same in Washington, Ottawa, the West Indies and other friendly capitals.

Finally 'F' Branch, to which John Preston belonged, at least until that morning, covering Political Parties (extreme Left-wing), Political Parties (extreme Right-wing), Research and Agents.

'F' Branch lives at Gordon, on the fourth floor, and it was to his office there that John Preston made his way that January morning. He might not have thought his report of three weeks earlier would establish him as Brian Harcourt-Smith's flavour of the month, but he still believed his report would go to the desk of the Director-General himself, Sir Bernard Hemmings.

Hemmings, he was confident, would feel able to impart its information and admittedly part-conjectural findings to the Chairman of the Joint Intelligence Committee or the Permanent Under Secretary at the Home Office, the political ministry commanding MI5. A good PUS would probably feel his Minister should glance at it, and the Home Secretary could have drawn the attention of the Prime Minister to it.

The memorandum on his desk when he arrived indicated this was not going to happen. After reading the sheet he sat back lost in thought. He was prepared to stand by that report, and if it had gone higher there would have been questions to answer. He could have answered them, would have answered them, for he was convinced he was right. He could have answered them, that is, as Head of F.1(D), but not after being transferred to another department.

After a transfer, it would be the new Head of F.1(D) who would be the one to raise the issue of the Preston Report, and he was satisfied the man appointed to succeed him, almost certain to be one of Harcourt-Smith's most loyal protégés, would do no such thing.

He made one call to Registry. Yes, it had been filed. He noted the registry file number, just for future reference, if any.

'What do you mean, NFA?' he asked incredulously. 'All right, sorry, yes, I know it's not down to you, Charlie. I was just asking; a bit surprised, that's all.'

He replaced the receiver and sat back thinking deeply. Thoughts a man should not think about his superior officer, even if there was no personal empathy between them. But the thoughts would not go away. It was possible, he conceded, that if his report had gone higher its general burden might eventually have been imparted to Neil Kinnock, leader of the Labour Party Opposition in Parliament, who might not have been best pleased.

It was also possible that at the next election, due within seventeen months at the outside, Labour could win and that Brian Harcourt-Smith was entertaining the hope that one of the new government's first acts would be to confirm him as Director-General of MI5. Not offending powerful politicians in office, or who might come to office, was nothing new. For a man of weak and tremulous disposition or of vaulting ambition, refusal to impart the bad news could be a powerful motive for inertia.

Everyone in the service recalled the affair of a former Director-General, Sir Roger Hollis. Even to this day the mystery had never been completely solved, though partisans on both sides had their convinced opinions.

Back in 1962 and 1963 Roger Hollis had known almost from the outset of the business the full details of the Christine Keeler affair, as it came to be known. He had had on his desk, weeks if not months before the scandal blew open, reports of the Cliveden parties, of Stephen Ward who provided the girls and who was in any case reporting back, of Soviet attaché Ivanov sharing the favours of the same girl as Britain's own War Minister. Yet he had sat back as the evidence mounted and never sought, as was his duty, a personal meeting with his own Prime Minister, Harold Macmillan.

Without that warning, Macmillan had walked into the scandal leading with his jaw. The affair had festered and suppurated through the summer of 1963, hurting Britain at home and abroad, for all the world as if it had been scripted in Moscow.

Years later the argument still raged: had Roger Hollis been a supine incompetent, or had he been much, much worse . . . ?

'Bollocks,' said Preston to himself and banished his thoughts. He reread the memorandum again.

It was from the head of B.4 (Promotions) personally and advised him that he was as of that day transferred and promoted to Head of C.1 (A). The tone was in the cosy friendliness that is supposed to soften the blow.

'I am advised by the DDG that it would be so helpful if the New Year could begin with all fresh postings occupied . . . most grateful if you could tidy up any outstanding things and hand over to young Maxwell without too much delay, even within a couple of days if possible . . . my warmest best wishes for your satisfaction with the new post . . .'

'Blah, blah, blah,' thought Preston. C.1 he knew as Civil Service Personnel and Buildings, and 'A' Section meant within the capital. He was to be in charge of security in all Her Majesty's ministries in London.

'It's a bloody policeman's job,' he snorted, and began to call up his team to say goodbye.

A mile away across London Jim Rawlings opened the door of a small but exclusive jewellery shop in a side road not two hundred yards from the surging traffic of Bond Street. The shop was dark but its discreet lights fell on showcases containing Georgian silver and in the illuminated counter display cabinets could be seen jewellery of a bygone era. Evidently the emporium specialized in antique pieces rather than their modern counterparts.

He was wearing a neat dark suit, silk shirt and muted tie, and carried a dully gleaming attaché case. The girl behind the counter looked up and took him in with a glance of appreciation. At thirty-six he looked lean and fit with an aura that was part gentleman, part tough, always a useful combination. She pushed out her chest and flashed a bright smile. 'Can I help you?'

'I'd like to see Mr Zablonsky. Personal.' His Cockney accent indicated he was unlikely to be a customer.

Her face fell. 'You a rep?' she asked.

'Just say Mr James would like to speak to him,' said Rawlings.

But at that moment the mirrored door at the rear of the shop opened and Louis Zablonsky came out. He was a short, wizened man of fifty-six, but looked older.

'Mr James,' he beamed, 'how nice to see you. Please come into my office. How have you been keeping?' He ushered Rawlings through the counter and into his inner sanctum. 'That's all right, Sandra, my dear.'

Inside his small and cluttered office he closed and locked the mirrored door, through which a view of the outer shop could be seen. He gestured Rawlings to the chair in front of his antique desk and took the swivel chair behind it. A single spotlight beamed down on the blotter. He eyed Rawlings keenly. 'Well now, Jim, what have you been up to?'

'Got something for you, Louis, something you'll like. So don't tell me it's rubbish.' Rawlings flicked open his attaché case. Zablonsky spread his hands. 'Jim, would I . . . ?' His words were cut off as he saw what Rawlings was placing on the blotter. When they were all there he stared at them in disbelief.

'The Glen suite,' he breathed, 'you've gone and nicked the Glen Diamonds. It's not even been in the papers yet.'

'So maybe they're still away from London,' said Rawlings. 'There was no alarm raised. I'm good, you know that.'

'The best, Jim, the best. But the Glen suite. Why didn't you tell me?'

Rawlings knew it would have been easier for all if a route for the Glen suite had been set up before the robbery. But he worked in his own way, which was extremely carefully. He trusted no-one, least of all a fence, even a blue-chip top-of-the-market fence like Louis Zablonsky. A fence, hit by a police raid and facing a long stretch of porridge, would be quite able to trade information on a coming heist against a let-off for himself. The Serious Crime Squad down at Scotland Yard knew about Zablonsky, even if he had never seen the inside of one of HM Prisons. That was why Rawlings never pre-announced one of his jobs and always arrived unheralded. So he did not answer.

Zablonsky in any case was lost in contemplation of the jewels that sparkled on his blotter. He too knew their provenance without being told.

Inheriting the suite in 1936, the ninth Duke of Sheffield had had two offspring, a boy and a girl, Lady Fiona Glen. When he in turn died in 1980, he bequeathed them not to his son, the heir to the title, but to his daughter.

The saddened Duke had been forced to realize by 1974, when his son was twenty-five, that the exotic young man was what gossip columnists are pleased to call one of nature's bachelors. There would be no more pretty young countesses of Margate or duchesses of Sheffield to wear the famed Glen Diamonds. So they had gone to the daughter.

Zablonsky knew that, after the Duke's death, Lady Fiona had taken to wearing them occasionally, with the insurers' grudging permission, usually for charity galas at which she was a not infrequent presence. The rest of the time they lay where they had spent so many years, in darkness in the vaults of Coutts on Park Lane. He smiled.

'The charity gala at Grosvenor House just before the New Year?' he asked. Rawlings shrugged. 'Oh, you're a naughty boy, Jim. But such a talented one.'

Although he spoke fluent Polish, Yiddish and Hebrew, Louis Zablonsky after forty years in Britain had never quite mastered English, which he spoke with a discernible Polish accent. He also, because he had learned them from books written years earlier, mistakenly used phrases that nowadays could be regarded as 'camp'. Rawlings knew there was nothing gay about Louis Zablonsky. In fact Rawlings knew, because Beryl Zablonsky had told him, that the old man had been neutered in one of the concentration camps as a boy.

Zablonsky was still admiring the diamonds as a true connoisseur will admire any masterpiece. He recalled vaguely having read somewhere that in the mid-sixties Lady Fiona Glen had married a rising young civil servant who by the mid-eighties had become a senior mandarin in one of the ministries and that the couple lived somewhere in the West End at a most elegant and luxurious standard maintained largely by the wife's private fortune.

'So what do you think, Louis?'

'I'm impressed, my dear Jim. Very impressed. But also perplexed. These are not just ordinary stones. These are identifiable anywhere in the diamond world. What am I to do with them?'

'So you tell me,' said Rawlings.

Louis Zablonsky spread his hands wide. 'I will not lie to you, Jim. I will tell you straight. The Glen Diamonds probably have an insured value of £750,000, which is roughly what they would fetch if sold legitimately on the open market by Cartier. But they can't be sold like that, obviously.

'That leaves two options. One is to find a very rich buyer who would want to buy the famous Glen Diamonds knowing he could never display them or admit ownership – a rich miser content to gloat over them in privacy. There are such people – but very few. From such a person one could get perhaps half the price I have named.'

'When could you find a buyer like that?'

Zablonsky shrugged. 'This year, next year, sometime, never. You can't just advertise in the personal columns.'

'Too long,' said Rawlings. 'The other way?'

'Prise them out of their settings – that act alone would reduce the value to £600,000; repolish them and sell them separately as four unmatched, individual gems. One might get £300,000, but the repolisher would want his cut. If I carried those costs personally, I think I could let you have £100,000 – but at the end of the day. After the sales had been completed.'

'So what can you let me have up front? I can't live on fresh air, Louis.'

'Who can?' said the old fence. 'Look, for the white gold setting I can get maybe £2,000 on the scrap market. For the forty small stones, put through the legitimate market, say £12,000. That's £14,000 which I can recover quickly. I can let you have half up front, in cash, now. What do you say?'

They talked for another thirty minutes and clinched their deal. From his safe Louis Zablonsky took £7,000 in cash. Rawlings opened the attaché case and laid the wads of used notes inside.

'Nice,' said Zablonsky. 'You treat yourself?'

Rawlings shook his head. 'Came with the heist,' he said.

Zablonsky tut-tutted and wagged a finger under

Rawlings's nose. 'Get rid of it, Jim. Never keep anything from a job. Not worth the risk.'

Rawlings considered, nodded, made his farewells and left.

John Preston had spent the entire day seeking out the various members of his investigative team to make his farewells. They were gratifyingly sorry to see him go. Then there was the paperwork. Bobby Maxwell had come in to say hello.

Preston knew him vaguely. He was an agreeable enough young man, eager to make a career in 'Five' and seeing his best chances of promotion as lying in a policy of hitching his waggon to the rising star of Brian Harcourt-Smith. Preston could not hold that against him.

He himself was a late entrant, having been inducted into the service direct from the Army Intelligence Corps in 1981 at the age of forty-one. He knew he would never get to the top. Head of section was about the limit for late entrants.

Just occasionally the post of the outgoing Director-General went to someone from quite outside the service if there was no obviously suitable candidate from within, always to the dismay of the people who worked in 'Five'. But the DDG, all the directors of the six branches and most of the departments within the branches were by tradition lifelong staffers.

He had agreed with Maxwell that he would spend Monday finishing off his paperwork, and the whole of the next day briefing his successor on every current file and investigation. They had parted on that note with mutual good wishes until the morning.

He glanced at his watch. It would be a late night. From his personal office safe he would have to get out every current file, check those that could safely go back to Registry and spend half the night going through the current bumph page by page ready to brief Maxwell in the morning.

First he needed a decent drink. He took the lift down to the sub-basement where Gordon had a well-stocked and cosy bar.

Louis Zablonsky worked through the whole of Tuesday locked in his back room. Only twice did he have to emerge to see a customer personally. It was a slack day for which, unusually, he was thankful.

He worked with jacket off and shirt sleeves rolled up over his almost hairless forearms, carefully easing the Glen Diamonds from their white gold settings. The four principal stones, the two ten-carat gems from the earrings and the matched pair from the tiara and the pendant, came easily and took little time.

When they were out of their beds he could examine them more closely. They were truly beautiful, flaming and sparkling in the light. They were already known to be blue-whites, once also called Top River, but now reclassified under the standardized GIA gradings as 'D-flawless'. These four, when he had finished admiring them, he dropped into a small velvet bag. That done, he began the time-consuming task of easing the forty smaller stones out of the gold. As he worked, the light occasionally caught a faded mark in the form of a five-figure number on the underside of his left forearm. To anyone who knew the significance of such marks, the number meant only one thing. It was the brand of Auschwitz.

Zablonsky had been born in 1930, the third son of a Polish–Jewish jeweller of Warsaw. He was nine when the Germans invaded and by 1940 the ghetto of Warsaw had been enclosed; incarcerated inside it were close to 400,000 Jews and rations were fixed at well below starvation level.

On 19 April 1943 the 90,000 surviving ghetto inhabitants, led by the few able-bodied men left among them, rose in revolt. Louis Zablonsky was just turned thirteen, but so thin and emaciated he could well have appeared five years younger.

When the ghetto finally fell to the Waffen-SS troops of

General Juergen Stroop on 16 May, he was one of the few who lived through the mass shootings. The bulk of the inhabitants, some 60,000, were already dead, from bullet, shot, shell, crushed beneath falling buildings or executed. The remaining 30,000 were almost exclusively aged, with women and small children. Into these Zablonsky was herded. Most went off to Treblinka and died.

But in one of those freaks of circumstance that occasionally decide between life and death, the engine of the train hauling Zablonsky's cattle truck broke down. The truck was attached to another engine and ended up at Auschwitz.

Though destined for death, he was spared when he gave his profession as jeweller and was put to work sorting and classifying the trinkets still being found upon the persons of Jews in each fresh intake. Then one day he was summoned to the camp hospital and into the hands of that smiling blond man whom they called 'the Angel' and who was still carrying out his manic experiments on the genitalia of pubescent Jewish youths. It was on Josef Mengele's operation table that, without anaesthetic, Louis Zablonsky was castrated.

He tugged the last of the forty smaller stones from the gold settings and checked to see he had missed none. He counted the stones and began to weigh them. Forty in all; averaging half a carat but mostly smaller. Engagement-ring stuff, but about £12,000 in all. He could pass them through Hatton Garden and no-one the wiser. Cash deals; he knew his dealers. Then he began to crush the white gold settings into a shapeless mass.

In late 1944 the survivors of Auschwitz were force-marched westwards and Zablonsky ended up in Bergen-Belsen where, more dead than alive, he was finally freed by the British Army.

After intensive hospitalization Zablonsky was brought to Britain, sponsored by a north London rabbi, and after further rehabilitation became a jeweller's apprentice. In the early 1960s he left his employer and opened his own jewellery shop, first in the East End and ten years later the present, more prosperous establishment in the West End.

It was in the East End, down among the dockland, that he had first started to handle gems imported by seamen – emeralds from Ceylon, diamonds from Africa, rubies from India and opals from Australia. By the mid-1980s he was a wealthy man from both his enterprises, the legitimate and the illicit, one of the top fences in London, a specialist in diamonds, with a large detached house in Golders Green, and a pillar of his community there.

When the white gold settings were a mangled blob of metal he dropped the lump into his lemel bag along with other scrap. He saw Sandra off the premises, closed the shop, tidied up his office and left, taking the four primary stones with him. On the way home he made a phone call from a public box to a number outside Antwerp in Belgium, a number situated in a small village called Nijlen. When he got home he rang British Airways and booked a flight for the morrow to Brussels.

Along the shore of the River Thames, on its southern bank, where once had stood the rotting wharves of a dying dockland, a huge redevelopment programme had been continuing through the early and mid-1980s. The programme left great swathes of demolished rubble between the new buildings, moonscapes where the rank grass tangled with the fallen bricks and dust. One day it was intended all would be covered by the new apartment blocks, shopping malls and multi-storey car parks, but when that would be was anybody's guess.

In warm weather the winos camped out among these wastelands and any south London 'face' wishing to lose a piece of evidence had but to take the article to the centre of these abandoned places and burn it to extinction.

Late on the evening of that Tuesday, 6 January, Jim Rawlings was walking across an area of several acres, stumbling in the dark as he tripped over unseen chunks of masonry. Had anyone been observing him, which they were not, they would have seen he carried in one hand a two-gallon can of petrol and in the other a beautiful hand-crafted calfskin attaché case.

Louis Zablonsky went through Heathrow Airport on the Wednesday morning with no trouble. With heavy great-coat and soft tweed hat, handgrip and big briar pipe jutting from his jaw, he joined the daily flow of business-men from London to Brussels.

On the plane one of the stewardesses leaned over him and whispered, 'I'm afraid we can't allow you to light the pipe inside the cabin, sir.'

Zablonsky apologized profusely and stuffed the briar in his pocket. He did not mind. He did not smoke, and even if he had lit it, it would not have drawn very well. Not with four pear-shaped fifty-eight-facet diamonds crammed into the base below the tamped tobacco.

At Brussels National he rented a car and headed north up the motorway out of Zaventem towards Mechelen, where he pulled right and northeast to Lier and Nijlen.

The bulk of the diamond industry in Belgium is centred upon Antwerp and is specifically located in and around the Pelikaanstraat, where the big enterprises have their showrooms and workshops. But like most industries, the diamond business depends for a part of its functioning upon a mass of small suppliers and outworkers, one-man operations working out of their ateliers, to whom can be subcontracted some of the manufacture of settings, cleaning and repolishing.

Some of these outworkers also live in Antwerp, with the Jews, many of East European origin, predominant among them. But east of Antwerp lies an area known as Kempen, a cluster of neat villages in which are also located scores of these small workshops who undertake outwork for the Antwerp industry. In the centre of Kempen lies Nijlen astride the main road and rail lines from Lier to Herentals.

Halfway down the Molenstraat lived one Raoul Levy, a Polish Jew who had settled in Belgium after the war and who also happened to be a second cousin of Louis Zablonsky of London. Levy was a diamond-polisher, a widower who lived alone in one of the small, neat, red-brick bungalows that line the western side of the Molenstraat. At the back of the house was his workshop. It was to here that Zablonsky drove and met his relative a little after lunchtime.

They argued for an hour and struck their deal. Levy would repolish the stones, losing as little of their weight as possible, but enough to disguise their identity. They settled at a fee of £50,000, half up front and half upon sale of the fourth stone. Zablonsky left and returned to London.

The trouble with Raoul Levy was not that he lacked skill; it was that he was lonely. So each week he looked forward to his one expedition. He loved to take the train into Antwerp, go to his favourite café where all his cronies met in the evenings, and talk shop. Three days later he went there and talked shop once too often.

While Louis Zablonsky was in Belgium, John Preston was installing himself in his new office on the second floor. He was glad he did not have to leave Gordon for another building.

His predecessor had retired at the end of the year, and the deputy head of C.1(A) had been in charge for a few days, no doubt hoping he would be confirmed in the top man's post. He took his disappointment well and briefed Preston copiously on what the job entailed, which seemed to Preston to be mainly grinding routine.

Left alone that afternoon, Preston cast his eye down the list of ministry buildings that came under his Section A. It was longer than might be imagined, but most were not security-sensitive, save for leakages that might be politically embarrassing. Document leaks concerning, for example, intended social security cuts were always a hazard since the civil-service unions had recruited so many staffers with extreme-Left political views, but they could usually be left to the Ministry's in-house security people.

The big ones for him were the Foreign Office, Cabinet Office and Defence, all of which received cosmic-rated papers. But each had pretty tight security handled by its own internal security team. Preston sighed. He started to make a series of phone calls, setting up getting-to-know-you meetings with the security chiefs in each of the main ministries.

Between calls he glanced at the pile of personal stuff he had brought down from his old office two floors above. Waiting for a callback from some official otherwise engaged, he rose, unlocked his new personal safe, and put the files one by one inside. The last of them was his report of the previous month, his own personal copy. Other than the one he knew to be NFA-ed in the Registry, it was the only copy in existence. He shrugged and put it at the back of the safe. It would probably never be examined again, but he did not see why he should not keep it, for old time's sake. After all, it had taken a hell of a lot of sweat to put it together.

3

Moscow
Wednesday, 7 January 1987

From: H.A.R. Philby
To: General Secretary of the CPSU

Permit me to begin, Comrade General Secretary, with a brief outline of the history of the British Labour Party and its steady penetration and successful eventual domination by the Hard Left over the past twenty-five years. Only, I believe, on the basis of such a narration can the events of the past few years and those intended for the next few months be seen in their perspective.

Since Hugh Gaitskell was impregnated with the untraceable viral toxin that finally killed him, the development of Britain's Labour Party could hardly have followed a more hopeful course of development had its historical scenario been written here in Moscow.

One must be quite aware, of course, that there always has been a dedicated, ardently pro-Soviet Marxist-Leninist wing deep within the Labour Party. But for most of the history of that Party it was a tiny minority and impotent to influence the course of events, the formulation of policies or, most importantly, the selection of candidates and the leadership of the Party itself.

So long as the Party was under the commanding influence of the decisive Clement Attlee or the passionate Hugh Gaitskell that situation was bound to continue.

Both men staunchly maintained the Proscribed List, under whose terms a whole range of bodies of Marxist-Leninist, Trotskyite or revolutionary persuasions were anathema to the Labour Party and whose members were prohibited from joining the Labour Party, let alone standing for office within it.

After Hugh Gaitskell, the man who at Scarborough in 1960 brought the Party Conference to its feet with his avowal to 'fight, fight and fight again' for the (traditional) soul of the Party, died in January 1963, the leadership of the Party passed into the hands of Harold Wilson, who held it for thirteen years. He was a man dominated by two characteristics that had much to do with what happened to the Party in those thirteen years.

Unlike Attlee, he possessed a personal vanity of almost cosmic proportions, and unlike Gaitskell he would go to almost any lengths to avoid a fight. Sensing this, our friends within the Party began to undertake the long-awaited and immensely careful campaign to move deeper and in greater numbers into the Party fabric.

For some years this was hard, back-breaking work.

Then in 1972 our pro-Soviet friends on the National Executive Committee (hereafter called the NEC) tested the temperature of the water by helping to pass a resolution removing the Labour Research Department from the Proscribed List. The Labour Research Department, despite its deliberately misleading name, had nothing to do with the Labour Party, being a Communist-controlled body. Happily, there was no backlash from the Centrists to this move. The following year, 1973, the Hard Left on the NEC managed to abolish the Proscribed List completely.

The effect was beyond the dreams of the Marxist-Leninist group within the Party. Few of them even then were spring chickens; most dated back to their original conversions to pro-Soviet Marxist-Leninism in the thirties. They needed to increase their numbers within the Party; they knew many of their, and our, fellow-travellers were excluded from Party membership and that there was a whole new generation of Hard Left political activists looking for a political home. With the floodgates open, it was these, in all age groups, who now swarmed into the Party ranks.

With the passing of the years most of the old stagers, who kept the flame alight inside the party throughout the seemingly hopeless years of Attlee and Gaitskell, have had to move into retirement. But they served their purpose; they opened the gates from the inside. And now it is the new generation, youthful fifteen years ago but now mature, who form the Hard Left; and who have not simply a handsome share of the Party, but have in effect taken it over at almost every level.

Since 1973 the absolutely vital NEC has seldom been out of the hands of a Hard Left majority and it has been through the skilful use of this tool that the constitution of the Party and its composition at the higher levels have been changed out of all recognition.

A brief word of digression, Comrade General Secretary, to explain precisely whom I mean by 'our friends' within the British Labour Party and trade-union movement. They fall into two categories, the deliberate and the unwitting. With the first category I am referring to people not of the so-called Soft Left, nor of the Trotskyite aberration, both of whom abhor Moscow, albeit for different reasons. I refer to those of the Ultra-Hard Left. These are dedicated, dyed-in-the-wool Marxist-Leninists, who would not appreciate being called Communists since this implies membership of the quite useless British Communist Party. They are nevertheless staunch friends of Moscow and in nine cases out of ten will act in accordance with Moscow's wishes, even though those wishes may remain unexpressed and even though the person concerned would stoutly claim he was acting for 'conscientious' or 'British' reasons.

The second group of friends inside, and now dominating, the British Labour Party, the Hard Left, are as such: a person with a deep political and emotional commitment to a form of socialism so far Left as to qualify as Marxist-Leninism; who will, in any given set of circumstances or in any contingency, fortuitously react quite spontaneously in a manner completely parallel to, or convergent with, the desires of Soviet foreign policy vis-à-vis Britain and/or the Western Alliance; a person who needs no briefing or instructions whatsoever, and who would probably be offended if such were proposed; a person who, wittingly or unwittingly, whether impelled by conviction, a warped patriotism, a desire to destroy, gain self-advancement, fear of intimidatory pressure, self-importance or desire to move with the herd, will conduct himself in a manner that suits our Soviet interests perfectly. They all constitute agents of influence to our benefit.

They all, of course, claim to be seekers after democracy. Happily, the overwhelming majority of Britishers today still understand by the word 'democracy' a pluralist (multi-party) state, whose governing body shall be chosen by universal adult suffrage based upon the secret ballot at periodic intervals. Obviously our Hard Left friends over there, being people who eat, drink, breathe, sleep, dream and work at Left-wing policies every waking hour of every day, mean a 'democracy of the committed' with its controlling roles performed by themselves and like thinkers. The British press fortunately take few steps to correct this misapprehension.

I must now mention, Comrade General Secretary, and dispose of, the issue which for many years divided the thrust of the Hard Left in the British labour movement. This was the dichotomy of the two perceived 'roads to socialism' that ran in parallel through Hard Left thinking in Britain for decades and was only resolved in the climactic year of 1976, almost a decade ago to the day as I write.

The twin, and competing, ways for the Hard Left to progress inside Britain were for many years the 'parliamentary road to Socialism' and the 'industrial road to Socialism'. The first saw the better chances as lying in a stealthy takeover of the British Labour Party, which was then to be used as the instrument to gain power and produce the truly revolutionary society. The latter saw the better chance as lying in the mass mobilization of the working class behind the trade-union movement, the eventual bringing of that working class on to the streets and the production of the revolutionary society that way.

One should never forget that the true bedrock of Marxist-Leninism in Britain has always lain inside the trade-union movement. For one thing, the union bedrock was always much more numerous than inside the Parliamentary Labour Party, which was why for years it was the trade-union side that made all the running, culminating in the absolute peak of its power in 1976.

By the time he returned to power in 1974 after the collapse of the Heath Government, Wilson knew he could not take on the unions. If he confronted them he split the Party and lost office. By then also Britain was sinking fast, industrially, commercially and financially, in face of union-engineered strikes, rising wage claims, falling productivity, spiralling unit costs and sky-high personal taxation.

By April 1976 Harold Wilson had lost control – of the unions and the economy. The cataclysm was coming; the economists knew it. He resigned, announcing health reasons, and handed over to James Callaghan.

By the late summer Britain was heading straight towards bankruptcy and needed a large and fast loan from the International Monetary Fund. But the IMF was adamant: there had to be conditions. At that October's Labour Party Conference the British Chancellor of the Exchequer literally had to plead with the union barons for wage restraint and the acceptance of public-sector spending cuts.

Philby rose and walked to the window. He recalled that traumatic autumn well, and sighed regretfully. He had been a secret listener and closet adviser when the British trade unionists had made their contacts and been instructed by Moscow what had to be done. It was a pity; not since the Civil War of the seventeenth century, he knew, had Britain come closer to being in the grip of a revolutionary regime; not since then had it been so close to complete extra-parliamentary rule. He returned to his typewriter.

You will recall with no less regret than I that Moscow's advice had to be that the unions heed the Callaghan Government's call for moderation. Within a fortnight the union belligerency had collapsed, to give way to the government-union agreed Social Contract.

To this day the British themselves do not understand why. So just permit me to reiterate what must be known to you, since it has a bearing on what must follow.

The Chancellor's plea had *to be heeded and the chance of bringing millions of workers on to the streets to confront their own army and police had to be abandoned. There was and remains one reason and one reason only for this. As Professor Krilov so persuasively argued then, all history teaches that soundly based democracies can only be toppled by mass action in the streets when the police and armed forces have been sufficiently penetrated by the revolutionaries that large numbers of them can be expected to refuse to obey the orders of their officers and side instead with the demonstrators.*

And this was what was wrong with Britain. Despite repeated attempts over the years to secure the right to 'organize' on a union basis (i.e. infiltrate union activists), this has never been achieved in Britain. It was calculated then, and I still think correctly, that the British soldiers and policemen would stay loyal to the Queen, Throne, Crown (call it what one will) and obey the orders of their officers.

Had that happened, the attempt to change the course of British history from the streets instead of from the Houses of Parliament must have failed. And, in failing, must have set back the cause of our true friends by decades, if not half a century.

Since then, further efforts have been made to remedy this lacuna in Britain's revolutionary possibilities, and to establish trade-union activism within the police and the armed forces. But to no avail. James Callaghan, a former consultant to the Police Federation, would have none of it. With the arrival of Margaret Thatcher in May 1979 the whole issue went out the window.

Our friends have done what they can. Since taking control of numerous large metropolitan authorities, through the press and the media, at every level high and low, they have either themselves, or using the wild young people of the Trotskyite splinter factions as shock troops, carried out an unrelenting campaign to denigrate, vilify and undermine the British police. The aim, of course, is to vitiate or destroy the confidence of the British public in their police, which unfortunately remains the most affable and disciplined in the world.

The results have been patchy; there have been occasional successes in exploiting local grievances, genuine abuses in the areas of corruption or police brutality, and the occasional well-organized riot. But overall the British working class remains infuriatingly wedded to the law-and-order issue, and the middle class still seems foursquare behind the police.

I have narrated all this only to substantiate one argument; that the 'industrial road' to socialism, the mass mobilization of millions on the streets to topple elective government, is as dead as the dodo. The path now lies through the 'parliamentary road', quieter, more covert, but probably all in all more effective.

It is this pursuit over the succeeding years of the parliamentary road to true revolutionary socialism that has now come to the threshold of success. It has come this far due to the largely successful campaign of the Hard Left to take over the Labour Party from inside; to several key changes in the Party constitution; and to the success of the self-denying programme our true friends have forced themselves to adopt since the electoral disaster of 1983.

With the diversion of the industrial road once disposed of in the autumn of 1976, our Marxist-Leninist friends in the Labour Party were able to devote themselves single-mindedly to the struggle to capture the Party covertly, a programme made so feasible by the abolition of the Proscribed List three years earlier.

The Labour Party has always stood like a tripod on three legs: the trade unions, the constituency Labour parties (one each in the constituencies that make up the British electoral pattern), and the Parliamentary Labour Party, the group of Labour MPs who were elected at the previous general election. The Party leader is always drawn from among these.

The trade unions are the most powerful of the three and exercise this power in two ways. One, they are the Party's paymasters, funding the coffers from political levies deducted from millions of workers' pay packets. Two, they dispose at Party Conference of huge 'block votes', cast by the union National Executive on behalf of millions of uncanvassed members. These block votes can ensure the passage of any resolution and elect up to a third of the Party's all-important National Executive Commitee.

These vote-casting union executive committees are absolutely vital; they comprise the full-time union activists and officials who decide union policy. They stand at the peak of the pyramid of which the middle ranks are the area officials and the lower ranks the branch officials. Thus the effective takeover by Hard Left activists of great swathes of trade-union officialdom was clearly essential, and has in fact been achieved.

The great ally of our friends in this task has always been the apathy of the largely moderate rank-and-file union members, who cannot be bothered to attend union branch meetings. Thus the activists, who attend everything, have been able to take over thousands of branches, hundreds of areas and the cream of the National Executive Committees. At present the biggest ten of the eighty unions affiliated to the

Labour Party control over half the union movement's votes; nine of those ten have Hard Left control at the top, as against two in the early seventies. All this has been achieved over the heads of millions of British workers by no more than ten thousand dedicated men.

The importance of this Hard Left-dominated union vote will become plain when I describe the Electoral College that chooses the new Party leader; the unions hold 40 per cent of the votes in this so-called College.

Next, the constituency Labour parties, or CLPs. At the core of these lie the general management committees, which, apart from running the day-to-day business of the Party within the constituency, have one other vital function: they choose the Labour candidate for Parliament. Over the decade 1973 to 1983, hard-line activist young people of the extreme Left began to move into the constituencies, and by assiduous attendance at dull and sparsely filled CLP meetings ousted the old-time officials to gain control of one general management committee after another.

As each successive constituency fell to the new Hard Left activist control, the position of the largely Centrist MPs representing those constituencies became tougher and tougher. Still, they could not be easily ousted. For the true triumph of the Hard Left it was necessary to weaken, indeed emasculate, the independence of conscience of a Member of Parliament; to transform him from the trustee of all his constituents' interests into a mere legate of his general management committee.

This was brilliantly achieved by the Hard Left at Brighton in 1979 and with the passage of the new rule requiring the annual reselection (or deselection) of MPs by their management committees. The rule caused a massive switch of power. A whole group of Centrists quit to form the Social Democratic Party; others were deselected and left politics; some of the ablest Centrists were harassed into resignation. Still, the Parliamentary Labour Party, though emasculated and humiliated, was left with one vital function: the MPs and they alone could elect the Labour Party leader. It was crucial, to complete the three-prong capture, to take that power away from them. This was achieved, again at the urging of the Hard Left, in 1981 with the creation of the Electoral College in which 30 per cent of the votes are held by the Parliamentary Party, 30 per cent by the constituency parties and 40 per cent by the trade unions. The College will elect each new leader as and when needed, and reconfirm him annually. This last function is crucial to the plans now afoot, and which I will describe.

The struggle for control that I have described brings the story to the general election of 1983. The takeover was almost complete but our friends had made two errors, aberrations from the Leninist doctrine of caution and dissimulation. They had come out too openly, too visibly, to win those titanic struggles and the premature call for the general election caught them on the hop. The Hard Left needed one extra year to consolidate, mollify, unify. They did not get it. The Party, saddled too early with the most extreme Hard Left manifesto in history, was in complete disarray. Worse, the British public had seen the real face of the Hard Left.

As you will recall, the 1983 election was apparently a disaster for the by now Hard Left-dominated Labour Party. Yet I suggest the outcome was in fact a blessing in disguise. For it led to the gritty and self-denying realism to which our true friends in the Party have agreed to submit themselves over the past forty months.

Briefly, out of 650 constituencies in Britain in 1983, the Labour Party won only 209. But it was not quite as bad as it looked. For one thing, of those 209 sitting Labour MPs, a hundred were now firmly on the Left, forty of them of the Hard Left. It may be small, but today's Parliamentary Labour Party is the furthest Left that has ever sat in the House of Commons.

Secondly, the defeat at the polls gave a jolt to those fools who thought the struggle for total control was already over. They soon realized that after the bitter but necessary struggles by our friends to win control of the Party between 1979 and 1983, the time had come to re-establish unity and to repair the damaged power base in the country, with an eye to the next election. This programme began under Hard Left orchestration at the October 1983 Party Conference, and has been unswerving ever since.

Thirdly, they all saw the necessity to return to that clandestinity demanded by Lenin of true believers operating inside a bourgeois society. Thus the leitmotif of the whole span of the Hard Left's conduct these past forty months has been a return to that clandestinity that worked so well through the early and mid-seventies. This has been coupled with a reversion to an apparent and surprising degree of moderation. It has taken a vast effort in self-discipline to achieve this, but again the comrades have not been found wanting in this regard.

The Hard Left has effectively since October 1983 taken on the clothes of courtesy, tolerance and moderation; stress is eternally laid upon the primordial importance of Party unity and a number of hitherto impossible concessions have been made in Hard Left dogma to achieve this. Both the Centrist wing, delighted and amicable, and the media appear to have been completely taken in by the new acceptable face of our Marxist-Leninist friends.

More covertly, the takeover of the Party has been finalized. All the lever committees are now either in the hands of the Hard Left, or could be taken over within a single emergency meeting. But, and it is an important 'but', they have usually been content to leave the chairmanship of these lever committees in the hands of a Soft Left person and even occasionally, when the voting supremacy is sufficiently overwhelming, in the hands of a Centrist.

The Centrist wing, with the exception of about a dozen sceptics, has been effectively disarmed by the new-found unity and the absence of harassment of themselves. Nevertheless, the iron fist is still very much in the velvet glove.

At constituency level the takeover of local CLPs by Hard Left elements has continued quietly and with very little public or media attention. The same thing has happened throughout the trade-union movement, as I have already mentioned. Eight out of the Big Ten and half of the remaining seventy unions belong now to the Hard Left, and here again the profile has deliberately been kept much lower than prior to 1983.

In summation, the entire Labour Party of Britain now belongs to the Hard Left, either directly, through Soft Left surrogates, through intimidated Centrists or at the holding of a fast emergency meeting of the appropriate committee; and yet neither the rank and file of the Party membership, nor of the unions, nor the media, nor the broad masses of the old Labour voters seem aware of it.

For the rest, the Hard Left has for forty months approached the next British general election like a military campaign. To win a simple majority in the British Parliament it would need 325 seats, say 330. It possesses 210 which are regarded as 'in the bag'. The other 120, lost in 1979 or 1983 or both, are regarded as winnable and have been designated target areas.

It is a fact of political life in Britain that the people, after two full terms of one kind of government, often seem to think it is time for a change, even if the incumbent government is not really unpopular. But the British will only change if they trust what they are changing towards. It has been the aim of the Labour Party these past forty months to win that trust back, albeit by subterfuge on the part of our friends within it.

To judge by recent public opinion polls, the campaign has been substantially successful, for the percentage gap between the ruling Conservatives and the Labour Party has closed to a few points. Bearing in mind also that under the British system eighty marginal seats actually control the outcome of an election, and that the marginals are swung one way or the other by the 15 per cent floating vote, the Labour Party has a chance of being returned at the next British general election as the government.

In a succeeding and concluding memorandum, Comrade Secretary General, I intend to show how, were that to happen, our friends of the Hard Left plan to topple Labour Party leader Neil Kinnock from the leadership in the hour of his victory, and impose upon Britain her first Marxist-Leninist Premier, along with a truly revolutionary socialist legislative programme.

Yours sincerely,

Harold Adrian Russell Philby

4

The men, when they came to visit Raoul Levy, were four in number: big, heavy men who arrived in two cars. The first car cruised to a halt outside Levy's bungalow in the Molenstraat while the second halted a hundred yards up the street.

The first car disgorged two of the men, who walked briskly but quietly up the short drive to the front door. The two drivers waited, lights doused, engines running. It was a bitter night, just after 7 p.m., pitch dark, and no-one walked Molenstraat that evening of 15 January.

The men who knocked on the front door were brisk and businesslike, as men with little time to waste, a job to do, and the opinion that the sooner it was over the better. They did not introduce themselves when Levy answered the door. They just stepped inside and pulled the door closed behind them. Levy's protest was hardly out of his mouth when it was cut off by four rigid fingers jabbing into his solar plexus.

The big men pulled his overcoat around his shoulders, clapped his hat on his head, left the front door on the latch and walked him expertly down the drive to the car, whose rear door opened as they approached. When they drove off with Levy sandwiched between them in the rear seat, they had taken twenty seconds.

They took him to the Kesselse Heide, a big public park just northwest of Nijlen, whose fifty acres of heather, grass, oaks and mixed conifers were completely deserted. Well off the road in the heart of the heath, the two cars stopped. The driver from the second vehicle, who was to be the interrogator, slipped into the front passenger seat.

He turned towards the rear of the car and nodded to his two colleagues. The one on Levy's right swept two arms around the small diamond polisher to hold him still, and the gloved hand of one arm went across Levy's mouth. The other man produced a pair of heavy pliers, took Levy's left hand and deftly crushed three knuckles, one after the other.

What frightened Levy more even than the shattering pain was that they did not ask him any questions. They seemed uninterested. When the fourth finger knuckle pulped in the pliers Levy was screaming to be asked questions.

The interrogator in the front nodded casually and said, 'Want to talk?'

Behind the glove Levy nodded furiously. The glove was removed. Levy let out a long, bubbling scream. When he had finished the interrogator said: 'The diamonds. From London. Where are they?'

He spoke Flemish but with a marked foreign accent. Levy told him without delay. There was no money that could compensate for losing his hands and his livelihood. The interrogator considered the information soberly.

'Keys,' he said.

They were in Levy's trouser pocket. The interrogator took them and left the car. Seconds later the second saloon crunched away across the crackling grass towards the road. It was gone fifty minutes.

During that time Levy whimpered and held his ruined hand. The men on either side of him seemed uninterested in him. The driver sat and stared ahead, gloved hands on the wheel. When the interrogator rejoined them he made no mention of the four gems that by now were in his pocket. He just said: 'One last question. The man who brought them.'

Levy shook his head. The interrogator sighed at the waste of time and nodded to the man on Levy's right. The heavy men reversed roles. The one on the right took the pliers and Levy's right hand. After the crushing of two knuckles on that hand, Levy told them. The interrogator had a couple of short supplementary questions and then he seemed satisfied. He left the car and went back to his own. In convoy the two saloons bumped back towards the road. They drove back to Nijlen.

As they went past his house, Levy saw that it was dark and closed. He hoped they would drop him off there, but they did not. They drove through the centre of the town and out to the east. The lights of the cafés, warm and snug against the freezing winter air, went past the car windows, but no-one came running out. Levy could even see the blue neon word 'Politie' above the police station across from the church, but no-one came out.

Two miles to the east of Nijlen the Looy Straat crosses the rail lines at a point where the Lier to Herentals tracks run straight as an arrow and the big diesel-electric locos go through at over 70 m.p.h. Either side of the level crossing are farm buildings. Both cars stopped short of the level crossing and doused lights and engines.

Without a word the driver opened the glove compartment, produced a bottle and handed it back to his two colleagues. One held Levy's nose closed and the other poured the white grain spirit of a local brand down the gagging throat. When threequarters of it was gone, they stopped and left him alone. Raoul Levy began to drift away in an alcoholic daze. Even the pain eased a bit. The three men in the car, and the one ahead of them, just waited.

At 11.15 the interrogator came from the first car and muttered something through the window. Levy was unconscious by then but moving fitfully. The ones beside him hauled him out of the car and half carried him towards the tracks. At 11.20 one of them hit him hard on the head with an iron bar and he died. They laid him on the tracks with his shattered hands on one of the rails and his broken head near it.

Hans Grobbelaar took the last express of the night out of Lier at 23.09 exactly, as always. It was a routine run and he would be home in his warm bed in Herentals by one o'clock. It was a nonstop freight loco and he went through

Nijlen on time at 23.19. After the crossings there he piled on the power and went down the straight towards the Looy Straat crossing at close to 70 m.p.h., the spotlight of the 6268 lighting up the track for a hundreds yards ahead.

Just short of Looy Straat he saw the huddled figure lying on the track and slammed on his brakes. Sheets of sparks flew out from his wheels. The freight train began to slow, but nowhere near enough. Mouth open, he watched through the windscreen as the headlight flew towards the crumpled figure. Two men in the yard had had it happen to them before; suicides or drunks, no-one ever knew. Not afterwards. With this kind of rig you don't even feel the thud, they had said. He didn't. The screaming loco flashed over the spot and was still doing 30 m.p.h.

When he finally stopped he could not even look. He ran to one of the farms and raised the alarm. When the police came with lanterns the mess under his wheels looked like strawberry jam. Hans Grobbelaar did not reach home until dawn.

That same morning, but four hours later, John Preston entered the lobby of the Ministry of Defence in Whitehall, approached the desk and used his universal pass to identify himself. After the inevitable check call to the man he had come to see, he was led up in the lift and down several corridors to the office of the Ministry's head of Internal Security, a room high at the back of the building overlooking the Thames.

Brigadier Bertie Capstick had changed little since Preston had last seen him, years ago in Ulster. Big, florid and genial, with apple cheeks that made him look more like a farmer than a soldier, he came forward with a roar of: 'Johnny, my boy, as I live and breathe. Come in, come in.'

Although only ten years older than Preston, Bertie Capstick had a habit of calling almost anyone his junior 'my boy', which gave him an avuncular air, matched by his appearance. But he had been a tough soldier once, moving deep into terrorist territory during the Malay campaign and later commanding a group of infiltration experts in the jungles of Borneo during what was now called the Indonesian emergency.

Capstick sat him down and produced a bottle of single malt from a filing cabinet. 'Fancy a snort?'

'Bit early,' protested Preston. It was just past eleven o'clock.

'Nonsense. For old times' sake. Anyway, the coffee they bring you here is abysmal.' Capstick sat himself down and pushed the glass towards Preston across his desk. 'So, what have they done with you, my boy?'

Preston grimaced. 'I told you on the phone what they've given me,' he said. 'Bloody policeman's job. No disrespect to you, Bertie.'

'Well, same with me, Johnny. Out to grass. Of course, I'm an RO [retired officer] now, so I'm not too bad. Took my pension at fifty-five and managed to get this slot. Not too bad. Potter up on the train every day, check up on all the security routines, make sure no-one's being a bad lad, and go home to the little woman. Could be worse. Anyway, here's to the old days.'

'Cheers,' said Preston. They both drank.

The old days had not been quite as genial as that, thought Preston. When last he had seen Bertie Capstick, then a full colonel, almost six years ago, the deceptively extroverted officer had been Deputy Director of Military Intelligence in Northern Ireland, working out of that complex of buildings at Lisburn whose data banks can tell the inquirer which IRA man had scratched his backside recently.

Preston had been one of his boys, working in civilian clothes and under cover, moving through hard-line Provo ghettoes to talk with informers or pick up packets from dead drops. It was Bertie Capstick who had loyally stuck by him in the face of the wittering civil servants from Holyrood House when Preston was 'burned' and nearly killed while on a mission for Capstick.

It was 28 May 1981 and the papers carried a few sparse details the following day. Preston had been in an unmarked car and had entered the Bogside district in Londonderry on his way to a meet with an informer. Whether there had been a leak higher up, whether the car he was driving had been used once too often, or whether his face had been 'made' by the Provo intelligence people, was never later established. Whatever, there was a foul-up. Just as he entered the Republican stronghold, a car containing four armed Provos had pulled out from a side street and followed him.

He had spotted them quickly in his mirror and called off the rendezvous at once. But the Provisionals wanted more than that. Deep inside the ghetto they swerved across his front and came tumbling out of their own car, two with Armalites and one with a pistol.

With nowhere to go but heaven or hell, Preston took the initiative. Against the odds and to the consternation of his attackers, he came out of his own door in a fast roll, just as the Armalites riddled his vehicle. He had his Browning thirteen-shot 9-millimetre in his hand, set to automatic. From the cobblestones he let them have it. They had expected him to die decently; they were too close together.

On rapid fire, he had dropped two dead in their tracks and blown a chunk out of the neck of the third. The Provo driver had let in his clutch and disappeared in a plume of burning tyres. Preston had made his way to a safe house staffed by four SAS troopers who kept him until Capstick arrived to bring him home.

Of course, there had been the devil to pay – inquiries, interrogations, worried questions from on high. There was no question of his going on. He had been well and truly burned, to use the term-of-art, that is, identified. His usefulness was over. The surviving Provo would know his face again anywhere. They would not even let him go back to his old regiment, the Paras, at Aldershot. Who knew how many Provos hung around Aldershot?

They had offered him Hong Kong or the exit door.

Then Bertie Capstick had had a talk with a friend. There was a third choice. Leave the army as a forty-one-year-old major and become a late entrant into MI5. He had gone for that one.

'Anything particular?' asked Capstick.

Preston shook his head. 'Just a round of getting-to-know-you calls,' he said.

'Don't worry, Johnny. Now I know you're in the seat, I will call if anything crops up here that looks bigger than swiping the Christmas fund. How's Julia, by the way?'

'I'm afraid she's left me. Three years ago.'

'Oh, I'm sorry to hear that.' Bertie Capstick's face puckered in genuine concern. 'Another fella?'

'No. Not then. There's someone now, I think. Just the job . . . you know.'

Capstick nodded grimly. 'My Betty's always been very good like that,' he ruminated. 'Been away from home half my life. She always stuck by. Kept the fire burning. Still, no life for a woman. Seen it happen before. Many times. Still, bad luck. See the boy?'

'Now and again,' admitted Preston.

Capstick could not have struck a more raw nerve. In his small and lonely South Kensington flat Preston kept two photographs. One showed him and Julia on their wedding day, he at twenty-six, trim in his Parachute Regiment uniform, she at twenty, beautiful in white. The other was of his son, Tommy, who meant more to him than life itself.

They had lived a normal army life in a succession of married quarters and Tommy had been born eight years later. The arrival had fulfilled John Preston, but not his wife. Soon after, Julia had begun to get bored by the chores of motherhood, compounded by the loneliness of his absences, and had begun to complain of the lack of money. She chivvied him to leave the Army and earn more in civilian life, refusing to understand that he loved his job and that the boredom of a desk in commerce or industry would have driven him to distraction.

He transferred to the Intelligence Corps, but that made

it worse. They sent him to Ulster where wives could not follow. Then he went underground and all contact was broken. After the Bogside incident she really made her feelings plain. They gave it one more try, living in the suburbs while he worked at Five, returning almost every evening to Sydenham. That had solved the separation question, but the marriage had gone sour. Julia wanted more than his salary, starting out as a late entrant in Five, could provide.

She had taken a job as a receptionist at a fashion house in the West End when Tommy, aged eight, had gone at her insistence to a local fee-paying school near their small home. That had strained the finances even more. A year later she had left completely, taking Tommy with her. Now, he knew, she was living with her boss, old enough to be her father but able to keep her in style and Tommy at a boarding preparatory school at Tonbridge. Now he hardly ever saw the twelve-year-old lad.

He had offered her a divorce, but she did not want one. With three years' separation he could have got the divorce anyway, but she had threatened that as he could not provide for the boy and pay maintenance as well, she would settle for Tommy. He was cornered and he knew it. She allowed him to have Tommy for one week in each holiday and one exeat Sunday each term.

'Well, I must be going, Bertie. You know where I am if anything big blows up.'

'Of course, of course.' Bertie Capstick lumbered to the door to see him out. 'Take care of yourself, Johnny. There aren't many of us good guys left any more.'

They parted on a jocular note and Preston went back to Gordon Street.

Louis Zablonsky knew the men who arrived in a van and knocked on his front door late that Saturday night. He was alone in the house as usual on Saturdays; Beryl was out and would not return until the small hours. He supposed they knew that.

He had been watching the late film on television when the knock came, and thought nothing of it. He answered the door and they bulled straight into the hallway, closing the door behind them. There were three of them. Unlike the four who had visited Raoul Levy two days earlier (an incident of which he knew nothing as he did not read the Belgian papers), these were muscle hire from London's East End, 'slags' in underworld parlance.

Two were brutes, simple steak-faced thugs who would do anything they were told and obey the orders of the third; he was slight, pocked, mean, with dirty blond hair. Zablonsky did not know them personally; he just 'knew' them – he had seen them in the camps, in uniform. The knowledge sapped his will to resist. He understood there was no point. Men like this always did what they wanted to people like him. There was no point in resisting or appealing.

They pushed him back into the sitting-room and threw him into his own armchair. One of the big men stood behind the chair, leaned forward and pinned Zablonsky into it. The other stood by, caressing one fist with the palm of the other. Blond-hair drew up a stool in front of the chair, squatted on it and stared at the jeweller's face.

'Hit 'im,' he said.

The slag to Zablonsky's right swung a heavy fist straight into his mouth. The man was wearing brass knuckles. The front of the jeweller's mouth dissolved in a welter of teeth, lips, blood and gum.

Blondie smiled. 'Not there,' he chided gently. 'He's supposed to talk, ain't he? Lower down.'

The thug slammed two more haymakers into Zablonsky's chest. Several ribs cracked. From Zablonsky's mouth came a high-pitched keening. Blondie smiled again. He liked it when they made a noise.

Zablonsky struggled feebly but he might as well not have bothered. The muscled arms from behind the chair held him fast, as the other arms had held him down on that stone table so long ago in southern Poland while the blond man smiled down at him.

'You bin bad, Louis,' crooned Blondie. 'You upset a friend of mine. 'E reckons you've got something of his and 'e wants it back.'

He told the jeweller what it was. Zablonsky choked back some of the blood that filled his mouth. 'Not here,' he croaked.

Blondie considered. 'Search the place,' he told his companions. 'He won't give no trouble. Take it apart.'

The two slags searched the house, leaving Blondie with the jeweller in the sitting-room. They were thorough and it took an hour. When they had finished, every closet, cupboard, drawer, nook and cranny had been turned out. Blondie contented himself with poking the old man in his broken ribs. Just after midnight the slags returned from the attic.

'Nuffink,' said one.

'So who's got it, Louis?' asked Blondie.

He tried not to tell them, so they hit him again and again until he did. When the one behind the chair released him he fell forward on to the carpet and rolled on to one side. He was going blue round the lips, his eyes starting and his breath coming in short, laboured gasps. The three men looked down at him.

'He's 'aving a heart attack,' said one curiously. 'He's croaking.'

'Hit 'im too 'ard then, di'n't ya?' said Blondie sarcastically. 'Come on, let's go. We've got the name.'

'You reckon 'e was telling us straight?' asked one of the slags.

'Yeah, 'e was telling us straight an hour ago,' said Blondie.

The three left the house, clambered into their van and drove off. On the road south from Golders Green one of the slags asked Blondie: 'So what we going to do now, then?'

'Shut up, I'm thinking,' said Blondie.

The little sadist liked to think of himself as a commander of criminals. In fact he was of limited intelligence and was in a quandary. On the one hand, the contract had been to visit just one man and recover some stolen property. On the other, they had not recovered it. Near Regent's Park he saw a telephone booth.

'Pull over,' he said, 'I got to make a phone call.'

The man who had hired him had given him a telephone number, another phone booth, and three specific hours at which to call. The first of them was only a few minutes ahead.

Beryl Zablonsky returned from her Saturday-evening treat just before two in the morning. She parked her Metro across the street and let herself in, surprised to see the lights still on.

Louis Zablonsky's wife was a nice Jewish girl of working-class origins who had early learned that to expect everything in life is stupid and selfish. Ten years earlier, when she was twenty-five, Zablonsky had plucked her from the second-row chorus line of a no-hope musical and asked her to marry him. He had told her about his inability but she had accepted him notwithstanding.

Strangely, it had been a good marriage. He had been immeasurably kind and treated her like a too indulgent father. She doted on him, almost as a daughter. He had given her everything he could – a fine house, clothes, trinkets, pocket money, security – and she was grateful.

There was one thing, of course, he could not give her, but he was understanding and tolerant. All he asked was that he never know who, or be asked to meet one. At thirty-five Beryl was a trifle overripe, a little obvious, earthy and attractive in that kind of way that appeals to younger men, a sentiment she heartily reciprocated. She maintained a small studio flat in the West End for her trysts and unashamedly enjoyed her Saturday-night treats.

Two minutes after entering the house Beryl Zablonsky was crying and giving her address down the telephone to the ambulance service. They were there six minutes later, put the dying man on a stretcher and tried to hold him in this life all the way to the Royal Free. Beryl went with him in the ambulance.

On the way he had one brief period of lucidity and beckoned her close to his bleeding mouth. Craning an ear, she caught his few words and her brow wrinkled in puzzlement. It was all he ever said. By the time they got to Hampstead Louis Zablonsky was another of the night's 'dead on arrival' cases.

Beryl Zablonsky still retained a soft spot for Jim Rawlings. She had had a brief affair with him seven years earlier before his marriage. She knew his marriage had now broken up and that he was living alone again in the top-floor apartment in Wandsworth, whose telephone number she had called often enough to have memorized it.

When she came on the line she was still crying and at first Rawlings had some trouble, dazed with sleep as he was, in making out who was calling. She was ringing from a public booth in the casualty admissions department and the pips kept going as she put in fresh coins. When he understood who it was, Rawlings listened to the message with increasing puzzlement.

'That's all he said . . . just that? All right, love. Look, I'm sorry, really very sorry. I'll come up when the fuzz have cleared out. See if there's anything I can do. Oh, and Beryl . . . thanks.'

Rawlings replaced the receiver, thought for a moment and placed two calls, one after the other. Ronnie, from the scrapyard, reached him first and Syd was there ten minutes later. Both, as instructed, were tooled up. They were just in time. The visiting party tramped up the eight flights of stairs fifteen minutes later.

Blondie had not wanted to take the second contract, but the extra money the voice on the phone had guaranteed was too much to turn down. He and his mates were East Enders and hated to go south of the river. The animosity between the gangs of the East End and the south London mobs is legendary in the capital's underworld and for a southerner to 'up East' uninvited, or the reverse, can be a ticket to a lot of trouble. Still, Blondie reckoned that at 3.30 in the morning things should be quiet enough and he could be back in his own manor with the job done before he was spotted.

When Jim Rawlings opened his door a heavy hand shoved him straight back down the corridor leading to his sitting-room. The two slags came in first, with Blondie bringing up the rear. Rawlings backed fast down the corridor to let them all in. When Blondie slammed the door behind him Ronnie came out of the kitchen and levelled the first slag with a pickaxe handle. Syd came out of the coats cupboard in a rush and used a nailbar on the cranium of the second man. Both went down like oxen.

Blondie was scrabbling at the door catch, trying to get back out to the safety of the landing when Rawlings, stepping over the bodies, caught him by the scruff and slammed him face first into a glass-fronted portrait of the Madonna, the nearest the little man had ever come to organized religion. The glass broke and Blondie collected several small shards in his cheeks.

Ronnie and Syd tied up the two heavies while Rawlings hauled Blondie into the sitting-room. Minutes later, held at the feet by Ronnie and round the waist by Syd, Blondie was protruding several feet out of the picture window, eight floors above the ground.

'See that car park down there?' Rawlings asked him.

Even in the blackness of a winter night, the man could just make out the glint of street lights on cars a long way down. He nodded.

Well, in twenty minutes that car park's going to be full of fuzz. Standing round a plastic sheet. And guess who's going to be under it, all squashed and nasty . . . ?'

Blondie, aware his life expectancy was now measurable in seconds, called from his extremity: 'All right, I'll cough.'

They brought him in and sat him down.

He tried to be ingratiating. 'Look, we know the score, squire. I was just hired to do a job, right? Recover something what got nicked . . .'

'That old man in Golders Green,' said Rawlings.

'Yeah, well, 'e said you'd got it, so I come 'ere.'

'He was a mate of mine. He's dead.'

'Well, I'm sorry, squire. I didn't know 'e 'ad an 'eart condition. The boys only tapped 'im a couple of times.'

'You crap-eater. His mouth was all over the parish and all his ribs cracked. So what did you come for?'

Blondie told him.

'The what . . . ?' asked Rawlings incredulously.

Blondie told him again. 'Don't ask me, squire. I was just paid to get it back. Or find out what happened to it.'

'Well,' said Rawlings, 'I'm very close to having you and your mates in the Thames before sun-up wearing a nice new line in concrete underpants. Only I don't need the aggro. So I'm letting you go. You tell punter it was empty. Completely empty. And I burned it . . . to a cinder. There's nothing left of it. You don't really think I'd keep something taken from a job? I'm not a complete fool. Now get out.'

At the doorway Rawlings called Ronnie back. 'See them back across the river. And give the little rat a present from me, for the old man. OK?'

Ronnie nodded. Minutes later down in the car park the more damaged of the East Enders went into the back of his own van, still trussed up. The half-conscious one was put behind the steering wheel with hands untied and told to drive. Blondie was thrown in the front passenger seat, his broken arms in his lap. Ronnie and Syd followed them to Waterloo Bridge, then turned back and went home.

Jim Rawlings was perplexed. He made himself a cup of espresso and thought things over.

He had indeed intended to burn the attaché case among the rubble. But it was so beautifully hand-tooled, the dull burnished leather glowed in the light of the flames like metal. He had examined it for any sign of an identification mark. There was none. Against his better judgement and the warning of Zablonsky, he had decided to risk keeping it.

He went to a high cupboard and brought it down. This time he went over it as a professional cracksman. It took him ten minutes to find the stud on the hinge side of the case that slid sideways when pushed hard with the ball of the thumb. From inside the case he heard a sound. When he reopened the case the base had risen half an inch at one side. With a paperknife he eased up the base and glanced inside the flat compartment between the case's real base and the false one. With tweezers he extracted the ten sheets of paper that lay within.

Rawlings was no expert on government documents, but he could understand the rubric of the Ministry of Defence and the words 'TOP SECRET' are understandable in any man's language. He sat back and whistled softly.

Rawlings was a burglar and a thief, but like much of the London underworld he would not have anyone 'rubbish' his country. It is a fact that convicted traitors in prison, along with child molesters, have to be kept in seclusion because professional 'faces' if left alone with such a man are likely to rearrange his component parts.

Rawlings knew whose apartment he had burgled, but the robbery had not been reported yet and he suspected, for reasons he could only now fathom, that it might never be. So he did not need to draw attention to it. On the other hand, with Zablonsky dead, the diamonds were probably gone for ever, and his cut of their value with it. He began to hate the man who owned that apartment.

He had already handled the papers without gloves, and he knew his own prints were on file. He dared not identify himself so he had to wipe the papers clean with a cloth, erasing the traitor's fingerprints as well.

That Sunday afternoon he mailed a plain brown envelope, well sealed and with an excess of stamps, from a post box in the Elephant and Castle. There was no collection until Monday morning and the package did not arrive until the Tuesday.

That day, 20 January, Brigadier Bertie Capstick came on the phone to John Preston at Gordon. The bluff geniality of his voice was gone.

'Johnny, remember what we were talking about the other day? If anything cropped up . . . Well, it has. And it's not the Christmas fund. It's big, Johnny. Someone has mailed me something in the post. No, not a bomb, though it might turn out worse. It looks as if we have a leak here, Johnny. And he has to be very, very high. That means it comes under your department. I think you'd better come down and take a look.'

That morning also, in the owner's absence, but by appointment and letting themselves in with provided keys, two workmen arrived at an eighth-floor apartment at Fontenoy House. During the day they chipped the damaged Hamber safe out of the wall and replaced it with an identical model. By nightfall they had redecorated the wall as it had been before. Then they left.

5

It was not until Monday, 19 January, that Harold Philby, with the boys back at school and Erita out shopping, felt able to write out the final draft of his second memorandum to the General Secretary of CPSU. He had had no word to acknowledge the receipt of the first monograph, nor any indication of how it had been viewed. It would depend on his climatic revelations in the second paper to bring the Soviet leader to the view the writer sought.

From: H.A.R. Philby
To: General Secretary of the CPSU

To conclude my two-part response to your request of New Year's Eve: On 7 May 1981 millions of Londoners went to the polls to elect a new Greater London Council. The incumbent ruling group on the GLC was then the Conservatives under the leadership of Sir Horace Cutler. The Labour group was seeking election under the leadership of Mr Andrew McIntosh, a hugely popular Centrist Labour politician of traditional Labour values. The polls closed and after the vote count it was revealed that Labour had won. McIntosh was the new leader of the GLC.

Within sixteen hours – not days or weeks or months, but sixteen hours – Andrew McIntosh was deposed from the Labour leadership in a closed-doors meeting of the Labour group's inner caucus, and replaced by a Far Left activist called Ken Livingstone of whom not more than 5 per cent of Londoners had ever even heard. It was a truly brilliant coup, of which Lenin himself would have been proud. It had taken not hours but weeks and months to cobble together the alliance of Hard Left delegates from the boroughs who formed the wafer-thin majority that toppled McIntosh, and most of the credit must go to Livingstone himself.

Although a nondescript, instantly forgettable little fellow with a nasal voice, Livingstone has shown himself to be a consummate politician in the Far Left mould. A full-time operator since his teens, content to live (at least until his appearance as leader of the GLC) in a tiny bedsitter flatlet, devoid, it would seem, of any social, leisure or family life, he lives, eats and breathes politics twenty-four hours in every day. There is no meeting so apparently unimportant that he will not attend and give his blessing and an address, so long only as there is a chance of making one fresh favour, or influencing one fresh delegate vote which may later come in useful.

As a result, using his base in County Hall as a springboard, he has managed in five years to build up a personal Far Left political machine that now spans the whole country, its tendrils far beyond the confines of London. Now a Member of Parliament, as he has been since last year, he has effectively superseded Anthony Wedgwood Benn. A brilliant committee-management man, he has become a leading mover in the Hard Left capture of the British Labour Party.

I retail all this because the Livingstone coup d'état is the model upon which is to be based the final takeover of the Labour Party leadership, not before *its electoral triumph but a few days after it. Nor are the words 'coup d'état' an exaggeration. Greater London has over eleven million people, 20 per cent of Britain's population; it is as big as Liechtenstein or Luxembourg (i.e. a mini-state) and has a budget bigger than that of eighty of the 150 nations represented at the United Nations.*

Now to specifics. Within the heart of the Hard Left of the British Labour Party and trade-union movement there is a group of twenty who, together, may be said to represent the Ultra wing.

They cannot be called a committee, because although in touch with each other, they seldom if ever meet in one place. Each has spent a lifetime working his way slowly upwards in the inner apparatus; each has at his fingertips a manipulative influence far, far beyond his apparent office or position. Each is a totally committed 'true believer' Marxist-Leninist.

There are twenty in all, nineteen men and one woman. Nine are trade unionists, six (including the woman) sitting Labour MPs, plus two academics, a peer, a lawyer and a publisher. These are the ones who will trigger and stage-manage the takeover.

Before proceeding to reveal what is intended, I must make one last digression to explain how the Labour Party leader is elected, and thus could be toppled under the new rules recently introduced. From the inception of the Electoral College in 1980 until last year the position was that, following an election, nominations for the post to Party leader closed thirty days after the MPs' oath-taking. There would then ensue three months during which the rival candidates could press their claims before the Electoral College met. In the event of a Labour victory it would be impossible for this procedure to work in favour of any candidate seeking to topple the newly elected and triumphant leader.

But in 1968 a tiny 'reform' was proposed and passed by a whisker. Under these new rules the newly triumphant Labour Prime Minister is supposed to be confirmed in leadership quickly and efficiently by these means: whenever in the year an election is held, and in the event of a Labour victory, any nominations for the Party Leadership would have to be in within three days of the national election result being declared. Then an extraordinary meeting of the Electoral College would take place within seven days of the declaration of the election result.

After the Electoral College meeting and the 'choice' of the Labour Party Leader, no further contest would be permitted for two years, the intervening year being waived. To those who had wavered in supporting the reform, it was pointed out that the procedure was simply a formality; the triumphant Party Leader, awaiting his call to Buckingham Palace to be charged by the Queen with forming a new government, would simply be massively endorsed by an unopposed re-election. It was out of the question, waverers were assured, for anyone to be so rash as to stand against such a winner.

In fact the reverse is intended. In the immediate wake of a Labour victory at the polls, before the triumphant Leader had been called to the palace, an alternative candidate would be nominated to the extraordinary meeting of the Electoral College. He would be the pre-selected Hard Left nominee to become Britain's first devout Marxist-Leninist Premier.

The outrage would be Party-wide and countrywide. But only one side would be fully prepared to cope. The triumphant Party Leader would have to contest the election with the Centrist and moderate elements in stunned disarray. The Hard Left would pull out every stop to secure the new candidate's election to the post, and they would win.

First, the unions. Some unions, before casting their vote in the Electoral College, are obliged to consult their rank-and-file members by postal ballot. Others through branch meetings; others through a national delegate conference. But inside four days this would be impossible. The National Executive Committees would have to cast the vote on behalf of all their members unconsulted and, as pointed out before, the Executives are preponderantly Hard Left.

Second, the constituencies. Here it is calculated that half would vote for the new candidate; this campaign at the grassroots would be assisted by the release of a forged letter, apparently from the Party Leader to the national agent, indicating the Leader's wish soon to revert to the old method whereby the Party Leader was elected solely by the Parliamentary Party, thus disenfranchizing the constituencies in the choice.

Finally, the Parliamentary Party. With a fresh intake of new MPs, many already of the Hard Left, all aware they held their jobs in the gift of their constituency management committees, it is calculated half would vote for the new Leader, having no allegiance to the old. But the preponderance in the unions would swing it for the new Leader.

Until recently there was one major doubt in the plan. What would be the reaction of the Throne? After profound consideration the answer, with which I concur, would be: none. For two reasons. One: precedent. When in April 1976 Harold Wilson resigned the premiership the Queen had to wait two weeks until she learned the identity of her own new Prime Minister and could invite him to Buckingham Palace for the ritual kissing-of-hands ceremony. In this instance the wait would be ten days. Two: constitution. Since the Throne had raised, as guardian of the (unwritten) British constitution, no objections to the several reforms of the Labour Party constitution at the times they took place, her advisers would have to point out that to object now that the Labour Party constitution was being required to operate would appear as an example of massive bias. So much so that it could provoke a constitutional crisis within the realm.

Thus the new Party Leader and Prime Minister would then have carte blanche, backed by a cabinet wholly in his own image and begin upon the intended legislative programme forthwith. In short, the populace would have voted for an apparently Soft Left traditionalist or at least reformist government, but a full Hard Left regime would have taken office, without the irksome necessity of an intervening election.

As for the legislative programme to which I have referred, this constitutes at this stage a plan of twenty desired measures which have not yet, for obvious reasons, been put to paper. Some of the measures are already fully part of the Labour Party manifesto as they stand; others are in the manifesto but in watered-down form; others have been seriously proposed at past Labour Party Conferences, but not adopted, though in each case the votes have moved nearer for formal adoption each time the measure has been proposed over the past ten years. All the other measures have been proposed at various times over the past twenty years within the Hard Left wing of the Labour Party.

The twenty-point plan is known as the Manifesto for the British Revolution, or MBR for short. I list below all twenty proposals, with added explanatory notes where necessary to explain what is intended. You will observe that the first fifteen refer to internal British matters and are of little direct applicability to Soviet policy, save in as much as they would reduce Britain to economic extinction and social chaos. But the last five points very much affect the Soviet Union and must constitute quite immeasurable benefits for her. Here then is the intended MBR:

1. The abolition of the entire private sector in medicine. All private clinics and hospitals, with their facilities, equipment and staff, to be taken over by the state, with compensation as and when deemed appropriate.

2. The abolition of the entire private sector in education. All schools and colleges, with their buildings, grounds, equipment and facilities, to be absorbed into the state sector, again with compensation as and when deemed appropriate.

3. The nationalization of the four major issuing banks and the twenty top merchant banks, with enabling legislation to permit an extension of nationalization to other banks in the event that they should grow in size. A ban on transfers of funds and deposits from the public to the private sector in banking.

4. The nationalization of the top 500 corporations, industrial and commercial, within the present private sector. Compensation to be based on stock value three months after nationalization and payable in Treasury bonds maturing ten years later.

5. The immediate abolition of the House of Lords and its power of legislative veto. This has already been part of the Labour Party manifesto for some years, including the phrase 'and its power of legislative veto'. Happily the British people at large have failed to spot the slip in the use of this phrase. In fact the House of Lords only has the power to delay legislation by asking the House of Commons to amend or reconsider. It retains a power of actual veto in only one case. Under Section 2 of the Parliament Act of 1911, the Lords lost its power of veto save only in the case of a Commons extending its life by an act of self-perpetuation. Thus the abolition of this power is vital to our friends in Britain. Evidently the British revolution cannot be stopped or put into reverse at the whim of the electorate. Thus there could be no further general elections, a situation that could easily be guaranteed by the passage of an Emergency Powers Act of self-perpetuation.

6. The institution of a National Committee for Editorial Guidance. The committee would have its headquarters in the national capital, but a representation in every editorial office of newspapers, magazines etc., in the land. The editorial guidance committee would comprise one member of the editorial staff, one delegate of the print union and one local appointee nominated by Central Office. Decisions as to what should be printed would depend on a simple majority among the three. The editor would sit in as an observer.

7. The institution of a new National Broadcasting Council to replace the BBC Board of Governors, the BBC Charter and the Independent Broadcasting Authority. It would have powers of guidance over all programme content and all staff appointments within all the audial and visual media.

8. The institution of a National Council for the Reform of the Courts and Judiciary, apparently to ameliorate the tiresome delays in court procedure; in reality to remove unsound judges, appoint replacements, vet and approve all public appointments within the judiciary, to shorten or abolish much of the appeal procedure and to extend the provision of in-camera hearings for offences against public order or for antisocial behaviour.

9. The institution of a Council for National Guidance in Education, with powers to approve or veto all appointments of lecturers, headmasters and assistant teachers, and to revise the nation's educational programmes so as to ensure the adoption of more socially aware curricula in schools and colleges.

10. The passage of the Trade Union (Extension to Armed Forces and Police) Bill, requiring the mandatory membership of the appropriate trade union of all members of the armed forces and the police, and the introduction into the forces and police of civilian union organizers and educators. Clearly in a closed-shop situation expulsion from the union would then require resignation from the force.

11. The passage of the Police Authorities Bill. This would subject all police forces to their local police authority which would be drawn from progressive elements in local government and the trade-union movement, who would have power of appointment of all ranks from chief constable down to sergeant, and the preponderant voice in the delineation of strategy and tactics in local community policing.

12. The passage of the Public Order (Community Safeguard) Act, whose main provision would be to bring into being the workers' militia to replace the special constabulary. The militia would support the local police in the maintenance of public order, principally in the ensuring of safe and orderly pro-government demonstrations and the disruption of any antisocial elements who might wish to dissent.

13. The Currency Exchange Control (Restoration) Bill. This speaks for itself. It would inevitably be necessary to prohibit all out-flight of funds and assets from the country.

14. The passage of the Private Wealth Accountability Act, requiring the registration of all land, pictures, jewellery, artefacts, stocks, shares, deposits, vehicles, pension funds, houses, etc., prior to their taxation or nationalization in lieu.

15. The passage of the Direction of Investment Enabling Act, requiring the registration of all corporate funds, such as those held by life offices, insurance corporations, etc., to enable the direction of future investment into state-favoured projects on the advice (mandatory) of government-appointed experts.

16. The immediate withdrawal, regardless of any treaty obligations, from the European Economic Community.

17. The down-scaling without delay of all Britain's conventional armed forces to one fifth of their present size.

18. The immediate abolition and destruction of all Britain's nuclear weapons and the dismantling of the two Advanced Weapons Research Establishments at Harwell and Aldermaston.

19. The expulsion from Britain without delay of all United States forces, nuclear and conventional, along with all their personnel and materiel.

20. The immediate withdrawal from, and repudiation of, the North Atlantic Treaty Organization.

I need hardly underline, Comrade General Secretary, that these last five proposals would wreck the defences of the Western Alliance beyond any possible hope of repair in our lifetime, if indeed ever. Obviously, everything I have outlined and described within the two memoranda depend for their full implementation upon a Labour Party victory, and for this the next election, expected in the spring of 1988, may well be the last opportunity. All the above was, in fact, what I meant by my remark at General Kryuchkov's dinner that the political stability of Britain is constantly overestimated in Moscow 'and never more so than at the present time'.

Yours sincerely,
Harold Adrian Russell Philby

The General Secretary's response to the second and final memorandum was surprisingly and gratifyingly prompt. Barely more than a day after Philby had consigned the memorandum into the hands of Major Pavlov, the inscrutable and cold-eyed young officer from the Ninth Directorate was back. He bore in his hand a single manila envelope which he handed to Philby without a word before turning away.

It was another hand-written letter from the General Secretary personally, brief and to the point as usual.

In it the Soviet leader thanked his friend Philby for his efforts. He himself had been able to confirm the bulk of the two memoranda as perfectly accurate. In consequence he estimated the victory of the British Labour Party at the next general election in that country to have become a matter of top priority for the USSR. He was calling into being a small, restricted advisory committee, responsible and answerable only to himself, to counsel him upon possible future courses. He required and requested Harold Philby to act as adviser to that committee.

6

Preston sat in the office of a very worried Bertie Capstick and examined the ten photocopied sheets spread out on the desk, reading each carefully.

'How many people have handled the envelope?' he enquired.

'The postman, obviously. God knows how many people in the sorting office. Inside the building, the front office people, the messenger who brings the morning mail up to the offices, and myself. I can't see you'll get much joy out of the envelope.'

'And the papers inside?'

'Just myself, Johnny. Of course, I didn't know what they were until I had pulled them out.'

Preston thought for a while. 'Apart from the person who mailed them they might, I suppose, contain the prints of the person who removed them. I'll have to ask Scotland Yard to check them out for prints. Don't have much hope personally. Now for the contents. It looks like very high-level stuff.'

'The tops,' said Capstick gloomily. 'Nothing short of top secret, the lot. Some of it very sensitive, concerning our NATO allies; contingency plans for NATO to counter a variety of Soviet threats – that sort of stuff.'

'All right,' said Preston, 'let's just run through the possibilities. Bear with me. Supposing this was sent back by a public-spirited citizen who for one reason or another did not want to be identified. It happens; people don't want to get involved. Where could such a person have got them? A briefcase left in a cloakroom, a taxi or a club?'

Capstick shook his head. 'Not legally, Johnny. This stuff should never under any circumstances have left the building, except possibly in the sealed bag to go across for the Foreign Office and Cabinet Office. There have been no reports of a Registry bag being tampered with. Besides, they are not marked for a destination outside this building, as they would be if they had left legitimately. The people who would even begin to have access to this sort of stuff know the rules. No-one, but no-one, may take this sort of stuff home to study. Answer your question?'

'More than somewhat,' said Preston. 'It came back from outside the Ministry. So it had to be taken outside. Illegally. Gross negligence or a deliberate attempt to leak?'

'Look at the dates of origin,' said Capstick. 'These ten sheets cover a full month. There's no chance they all arrived on a single desk in a single day. They had to be collected over a period.'

Preston, using his handkerchief, eased the ten documents back into their envelope of arrival. 'I'll have to take them to Charles Street, Bertie. May I use your phone?'

He called Charles Street and asked to be put straight through to the office of Sir Bernard Hemmings. The Director-General was in and after a delay and some insistence from Preston took the call personally. Preston simply asked for a personal appointment within minutes and got it. He put down the phone and turned to Brigadier Capstick.

'Bertie, for the moment don't do anything or say anything. To anyone. Just play out the day as if it was another routine day,' said Preston. 'I'll be in touch.'

It was out of the question to leave the Ministry with these documents but without an escort. Brigadier Capstick loaned him one of the front-hall commissionaires, a burly former guardsman.

Preston left the Ministry with the documents in his own briefcase and took a taxi to Clarges Apartments, watching the vehicle disappear down the street before walking the last two hundred yards down Clarges Street to Charles Street and his head office, where he could dismiss his escort. Sir Bernard saw him ten minutes later.

The old Spycatcher looked grey, as if he was in pain,

which he frequently was. The disease that was growing deep inside him showed nothing to the observer, but the medical tests left no doubt. A year, they had said, and not operable. He was due to retire on 1 September, which with terminal leave meant he could depart in mid-July, six weeks before his sixtieth birthday.

He would probably have gone already but for the personal responsibilities that bore upon him. He had a second wife who had brought to the marriage a step-daughter on whom the childless man doted. The girl was still at school. Early retirement would severely curtail his pension, leaving his widow and the girl in straitened circumstances. Wisely or not, he sought to carry on until the statutory retirement date and be able to leave behind his full pension. After a lifetime in the job, he had virtually no other asset to leave them.

Preston explained briefly and concisely what had happened at the Ministry of Defence that morning, and the view of Capstick regarding the feasibility of the documents' departure from the Ministry being anything other than a deliberate act.

'Oh my God, not another,' murmured Sir Bernard. Years later the memory of Vassall and Prime still rankled, as did the acid reaction of the Americans when they had been apprised. 'Well, John, where do you want to start?'

'I've told Bertie Capstick to stay silent for the moment,' said Preston. 'If we have a genuine traitor inside the Ministry, there's a second mystery. Who sent the stuff back to us? Passerby, sneak thief, wife with remorse feelings? We don't know. But if we could find that person, we might find where they got the stuff. That would short-circuit a lot of enquiry. I don't hold out much hope for the envelope – standard brown paper, sold in thousands of outlets, normal stamps, address in block capitals, felt-tip pen and already handled by a score of anonymous people. But the papers inside might have retained prints. I'd like Scotland Yard to test them all – under supervision, of course. After that, we may know where we go next.'

'Good thinking. You handle that side of it,' said Sir Bernard. 'I'll have to tell Tony Plumb and probably Perry Jones. I'll try and set up a meeting over lunch with them both. It depends on what Perry Jones thinks, of course, but we have to set up the JIC on this one. You get on with your side, John, and stay in touch with me. If the Yard comes up with anything I shall want to know.'

Down at Scotland Yard they were very helpful, putting one of their best lab men at Preston's disposal. Preston stood by the civilian technician as he carefully dusted every sheet. The man could not help reading the 'TOP SECRET' heading on each sheet.

'Someone been naughty down in Whitehall?' the technician asked archly.

Preston shook his head. 'Stupid and lazy,' he lied. 'That stuff should have been in the shredder, not a wastepaper basket. It'll be a hell of a rap on the knuckles for the clerk responsible, if we can identify the knuckles.'

The technician lost interest. When, he had finished he shook his head. 'Nothing,' he said, 'clean as a whistle. But I'll tell you one thing. They've been wiped. There's one clear set of prints, of course, probably your own.'

Preston nodded. There was no need to reveal that the single set of prints belonged to Brigadier Capstick.

'That's the point,' said the technician. 'This paper will take prints beautifully and keep them for weeks, maybe months. There ought to be at least one other set, probably more. The clerk who touched them before you, for example. But nothing. Before they went in the wastepaper basket, they were wiped with a cloth. I can see the fibres. But no prints. Sorry.'

Preston had not even offered him the envelope. Whoever had wiped them was not going to leave his own prints on the envelope. Moreover, the envelope would give the lie to his cover story about the negligent clerk. He took the ten secret documents and left. Capstick was right, he thought. It's a leak, and a bad one. It was three in the afternoon; he went back to Charles Street and waited for Sir Bernard.

Sir Bernard, with some urging, got his lunch with Sir Anthony Plumb, chairman of the Joint Intelligence Committee, the JIC, and Sir Peregrine Jones, Permanent Under-Secretary at the Defence Ministry. They met in a private room in a St James's club. Both the other senior civil servants were perturbed by the urgency of the request from the DG of 'Five' and ordered their lunch rather pensively. When the waiter had left, Sir Bernard told them what had happened. It ruined both men's appetites.

'I wish Capstick had spoken to me,' said Sir Perry Jones with some annoyance. 'Damned unsettling to be told like this.'

'I think,' said Sir Bernard, 'my man Preston asked him to stay silent a while longer because if we have a leak high in the Ministry, he mustn't be tipped off we got the documents back.'

Sir Peregrine grunted, slightly mollified.

'What do you think, Perry?' asked Sir Anthony Plumb. 'Any innocent, or simply negligent, way that stuff could have left the Ministry in photocopy form?'

The top civil servant in Defence shook his head. 'The leak needn't be all that high,' he said. 'All the top men have personal staffs. Copies have to be made – sometimes three or four men have to see an original document. But copies are listed as they are made, and later shredded. Three copies taken, three copies shredded after use. Trouble is, a senior man can't shred all his own stuff. He'll give it to one of his staff for shredding. They're vetted, of course, but no system is completely perfect.

'The thing is, those copies, spanning a whole month between them, being taken outside the Ministry, that can't be accidental, or even negligent. That has to be deliberate. Dammit . . .' He put down his knife and fork on an almost untouched meal. 'I'm sorry, Tony, but I think we've got a bad one.'

Sir Tony Plumb looked grave. 'I think I'm going to have to call into being a restricted subcommittee of the JIC,' he said. 'At this stage, very restricted. Just Home Office, Foreign Office, Defence, the Cabinet Secretary, heads of Five and Six and someone from GCHQ. I can't get it smaller.'

It was agreed he would set up the subcommittee for a meeting the next morning and Hemmings would inform them of any luck by Preston at Scotland Yard. On that note they parted.

The full JIC is a rather large committee. Apart from half a dozen ministries and several agencies, the three armed forces and the two intelligence services, it would also include the London-based representatives of Canada, Australia, New Zealand and, of course, America's CIA.

Plenary meetings tend to be rare and rather formal. Restricted subcommittees are more the rule, because those present, concerned with a specific issue, tend to know each other personally and can get through more work in less time.

The subcommittee Sir Anthony Plumb had, as chairman of the JIC and the Prime Minister's personal Coordinator of Intelligence, convened on the morning of 21 January was code-named Paragon. It met at 10 a.m. in the Cabinet Office briefing room, known as COBRA, two floors below ground level in the Cabinet Office on Whitehall, a conference room that is air-conditioned, soundproof and 'swept' daily for listening devices.

Technically their host was the Cabinet Secretary, Sir Martin Flannery, but he deferred to Sir Anthony who took the chair. Sir Perry Jones was there from Defence, Sir Patrick (Paddy) Strickland from the Foreign Office and Sir Hubert Villiers from the Home Office, which politically commands MI5.

GCHQ, the Government Communications Headquarters, the country's listening service down in Gloucestershire, so important in a highly technical age that it is almost an intelligence service in its own right, had sent its Deputy Director-General, the DG being away on vacation.

Sir Bernard Hemmings came from Charles Street, bringing with him Brian Harcourt-Smith.

'I thought it would be better if Brian were fully in the picture,' Hemmings had explained to Sir Anthony. Everyone understood he meant 'in case I cannot attend on a future occasion'.

The last man present, sitting impassively at the end of the long table opposite to Sir Anthony Plumb, was Sir Nigel Irvine, the Chief of the Secret Intelligence Service, or MI6.

Oddly, although MI5 has a Director-General, MI6 does not. It has a Chief, known throughout the intelligence world and Whitehall simply as 'C' whatever his name may be. Nor, even more oddly, does 'C' stand for Chief. The first head of MI6 was called Mansfield Cumming and the 'C' is the initial of the second half of that name. Ian Fleming, ever tongue in cheek, took the other initial 'M' for the Chief in his James Bond novels.

All in all, there were nine men round the table, seven of them knights of the realm, who between them represented more power and influence than any other seven men in the kingdom. They all knew each other well and were on first-name terms. Each could call the two Deputy Directors-General by their first name, but the DDGs would refer to the senior men as 'sir'. It was understood.

Sir Anthony Plumb opened the meeting with a brief description of the previous day's discovery, which evoked mutters of consternation, and passed the narrative to Sir Bernard Hemmings. The head of 'Five' filled in more details, including the deadend from Scotland Yard. Sir Perry Jones concluded with his insistence that there could have been no accidental or merely negligent departure of those photocopies from inside the Ministry. It would have to be deliberate and clandestine.

When he had finished there was silence round the table. Two single words hung like a spectre above them all.

Damage assessment. How long had it been going on? How many documents had gone missing? To what destination? (Though that seemed fairly obvious.) What kinds of documents had gone? How much damage had been done to Britain and the NATO alliance? And how the devil do we tell our allies?

'Who have you got handling it?' asked Sir Martin Flannery of Hemmings.

'His name's John Preston,' said Hemmings. 'He's C.1(A). The Ministry's man, Brigadier Capstick, called him when the package arrived in the mail.'

'We could, er, allocate someone more . . . experienced,' suggested Brian Harcourt-Smith.

Sir Bernard Hemmings frowned. 'John Preston is a late entrant,' he explained. 'Been with us six years. I've every confidence in him.'

'There is another reason. We have to assume there is a deliberate leak.'

Sir Perry Jones nodded glumly.

'We can also assume,' continued Hemmings, 'that the person responsible – I'll call him or her Chummy – is aware of the loss of those documents from their possession. We can hope Chummy does *not* know they have been anonymously returned to the Ministry. Still, Chummy is likely to be worried, and lying low. If I put in a whole team of ferrets, Chummy will know it's over. The last thing we need is a moonlight flit and a starring role at an international press conference in Moscow. I suggest for the moment we try to keep it low profile and see if we can get an early lead.

'As a newly appointed C.1(A), Preston can reasonably make a tour of the ministries and check, in an apparently routine fashion, on procedures. It's as good a cover as we'll get. With a bit of luck, Chummy will think nothing of it.'

From his end of the table Sir Nigel Irvine nodded. 'Makes sense,' he said.

'Any chance of a lead through one of your sources, Nigel?' asked Anthony Plumb.

'I'll put out some feelers,' he said noncommittally. Andreyev, he was thinking, he would have to set up a meet with Andreyev. 'What about our gallant allies?'

'Informing them, or some of them, will probably come to you,' Plumb reminded Irvine, 'so what do you think?'

Sir Nigel had been in his office for seven years and was in his last year. Subtle, experienced and impassive, he was held in high regard by the allied intelligence services of Europe and North America. Still, being the bearer of *these* tidings was going to be no joke. Not a good note on which to leave the game.

He was thinking of Alan Fox, the CIA's acerbic and occasionally sarcastic senior liaison man in London. Alan was going to make a five-course dinner out of this. He shrugged and smiled.

'I agree with Bernard. Chummy must be a worried man. I think we can assume he will not rush to purloin another bunch of top-secret material in the next few days. It would be nice to be able to go to our allies with some sort of progress, some kind of damage assessment. I'd like to wait and see what this man Preston can do. At least for a few days.'

'Damage assessment is of the essence,' nodded Sir Anthony. 'And that seems almost impossible until we can find Chummy and persuade him to answer a few questions. So for the moment we seem to depend on Preston's progress.'

'Sounds like the title of a book,' muttered one of the group as they broke up, the permanent under-secretaries heading to brief their ministers in closest confidence and Sir Martin Flannery knowing he was going to have an uncomfortable few moments with the redoubtable Mrs Margaret Thatcher.

The following day, in Moscow, another committee had its inaugural meeting.

Major Pavlov had called him just after lunch to say that he would collect the Comrade Colonel at six; the Comrade

General Secretary of the CPSU wished to see him. Philby supposed (rightly) that the five-hour warning was so that he could be sober and properly dressed.

The roads at that hour, in driving snow, had been clogged with crawling traffic, but the Chaika with the MOC number plates had sped down the centre lane reserved for the *vlasti*, the élite, the fat cats in what had become of Marx's dreamed-of classless society; a society rigidly structured, layered and class-ridden as only a vast bureaucratic hierarchy can be.

When they passed the Ukraina Hotel Philby had thought they might be going all the way to the dacha at Usova, but after half a mile they swung towards the barred entrance of the huge eighty-storey block at 26 Kutuzovsky Prospekt. Philby was amazed; to enter the private living quarters of the Politburo was a rare honour.

There were plain-clothes Ninth Directorate men up and down the pavement, but at the steel entrance gate they were in uniform: thick grey coats, fur *shapkas* with the earflaps down, and the blue insignia of the Kremlin Guards. Major Pavlov identified himself and the steel gates swung open. The Chaika crept into the courtyard of the hollow square and parked.

Without a word the major led him into the building, through two more identity checks, a hidden metal detector and X-ray scanner, and into the lift. At the third floor they stepped out; this entire floor belonged to the General Secretary. Major Pavlov knocked on a door; it opened to reveal a major-domo in white, who gestured Philby inside. The silent major stepped back and the door closed behind Philby. Stewards took his coat and hat and he was ushered into a large sitting-room, very warm since old men feel the cold, but surprisingly simply furnished.

Unlike Leonid Brezhnev, who had loved the ornate, the rococo and the luxurious, the General Secretary was known to be an ascetic man in his private tastes. The furniture was Swedish or Finnish whitewood, spare, clean-cut and functional. Apart from two no doubt priceless Bokhara rugs, there was nothing antique. There was a low coffee table and four chairs grouped around it, the group being open at one end to permit a fifth absent chair. Still standing – no-one was about to sit without permission – were three men. Philby knew them all, and they nodded greetings.

One was Professor Vladimir Ilich Krilov. He was a professor of modern history lecturing at Moscow University. His real importance was as a walking encyclopedia on the subject of the Socialist and Communist Parties of Western Europe, specializing in Britain. More importantly, he was a member of the Supreme Soviet, the USSR's rubber-stamp, one-party Parliament, a member of the Academy of Sciences and a frequent consultant for the International Department of the Central Committee, of which the General Secretary had once been the head.

The man in civilian clothes but with a soldierly bearing was General Pyotr Sergeivitch Marchenko, whom Philby knew only vaguely, but was aware to be a senior officer in the GRU, the Soviet armed forces' own military intelligence arm. Marchenko was an expert in the techniques of internal security and its counterpart, destabilization, and his particular study had always been the democracies of Western Europe whose police and internal security forces he had studied half his life.

The third was Dr Josef Viktorovitch Rogov, also an academician, a physicist by discipline. But his fame lay in another title – Chess Grand Master. He was known to be one of the General Secretary's few personal friends, a man on whom the Soviet leader had called several times in the past when he felt he needed to use that remarkable brain in the planning stages of certain operations.

The four men had been there two minutes when the double doors at the end of the room opened and the undisputed master of Soviet Russia, her dominions, satellites and colonies, entered.

He was in a wheelchair, pushed by a tall steward in a

white jacket. The chair was propelled to the vacant space left for it.

'Please be seated,' said the General Secretary.

Philby was surprised by the changes in the man. At seventy-five the face and the backs of the hands were blotched and mottled in the manner of very old men. The open-heart surgery of 1985 seemed to have worked and the pacemaker appeared to be doing its job. And yet he looked frail.

The white hair, thick and lustrous in the May Day portraits, making him look like every family's favourite doctor, had almost vanished. There were brown smudges round both eyes. A mile up the Kutuzovsky Prospekt near the old village of Kuntsevo, set in a huge territory inside a 2-metre timber palisade fence in the heart of a birch forest, stood the hyper-exclusive Central Committee Hospital. It was a modernization and extension of the old Kuntsevo Clinic.

In the grounds of the hospital stood Stalin's old dacha, the surprisingly modest bungalow where the tyrant had spent so much of his time and finally died. The whole of this dacha had been converted into the country's most modern intensive-care medical unit, for the benefit of one man, who now sat in his wheelchair studying them one by one.

Six top specialists were on permanent call at the dacha at Kuntsevo, and to them each week went the General Secretary for treatment. It was evident they were keeping him alive – just.

But the brain was still there, behind the chilly eyes that looked through the gold-rimmed glasses. He blinked rarely, and when he did, slowly, like a bird of prey.

He wasted no time with preamble. Philby knew he never did. Nodding to the other three he said: 'You Comrades have read the two memoranda of our friend, Comrade Colonel Philby.'

It was not a question, but the other three nodded their assent.

'Then you will experience no surprise to learn that I regard the victory of Britain's Labour Party, and thence of the ultra-Left wing of that Party, as a priority of Soviet interest. I wish you four to form a very discreet committee to advise me on any method that might occur to you that would enable us to assist, completely covertly of course, in that victory.

'You will discuss this with no-one. Documents, if any, will be prepared personally. Notes will be burned. Meetings will be held in personal residences. You will not associate in public. You will consult with no-one else. And you will report to me personally by telephoning here and speaking to Major Pavlov. I will then arrange a meeting at which you can report your proposals.'

It was clear to Philby the Soviet leader was taking the confidentiality extremely seriously. He could have held this meeting at his suite of offices in the Central Committee building, the big grey block on Novaya Ploshed where all Soviet leaders have worked since Stalin. But other Politburo members could have seen them arriving or leaving, or heard about it. The General Secretary was evidently establishing a committee that was so totally private to himself that no-one was to be allowed to know of it.

There was another odd thing. Apart from himself, and he was in retirement, there was no-one from the KGB present, yet the First Chief Directorate had massive files on Britain, and experts to match. For reasons of his own, the wily leader had chosen to keep the matter outside the service of which he had once been Chairman.

'Are there any points of query?'

Philby raised a tentative hand. The General Secretary nodded.

'Comrade General Secretary, I used to drive myself around in my own Volga. Since my stroke last year the doctors have prohibited this. Now my wife drives me. But in this instance, for the sake of confidentiality . . .'

'I will assign a KGB driver to you, for the duration,'

said the General Secretary softly. They all knew the other three men already had drivers, as of right.

There were no other points. At a nod the steward propelled the wheelchair and its occupant back through the doors. The four advisers rose and prepared to leave.

Two days later, in the country dacha of one of the two academics, the Albion Committee went into intensive session.

Book title or not, Preston *was* making some progress. Even while the inaugural session of Paragon was going on, he was ensconced in the Registry, deep under the Ministry of Defence.

'Bertie,' he had told Brigadier Capstick, 'so far as the staff here are concerned, I'm just a new broom making a bloody nuisance of himself. Put it about that I'm simply trying to make a mark with my own superiors. Routine checking of procedures, nothing to worry about, a pain in the arse.'

Capstick had done his bit, trumpeting that the new head of C.1(A) was going through all the ministries showing what an eager beaver he was. The Registry clerks rolled their eyes to heaven and cooperated with thinly veiled exasperation. But it gave Preston access to the files, the withdrawals and the returns, to whom and most importantly over what dates.

He had one early break. All the documents but one would have been available at the Foreign Office or the Cabinet Office, since they all touched upon Britain's NATO allies and the areas of joint NATO response to a variety of possible Soviet initiatives. But one document had not gone outside the Ministry. The Permanent Under-Secretary, Sir Peregrine Jones, had recently returned from talks in Washington with the Pentagon; the subject had been joint patrolling by British and American nuclear submarines in the Mediterranean and in the Central and South Atlantic and Indian oceans. He had prepared a draft paper on his talks and circulated it to a score of senior mandarins inside the Ministry. The fact that it was among the stolen papers, in photocopy form, meant at least that the leak was inside the one Ministry.

Preston began an analysis of the distribution of top-secret documents going back for months. It became clear the documents in the returned package covered a period, first to last, of four weeks. It was also plain that every mandarin who had had all those documents across his desk had also had more than these. So the thief was being selective.

There were twenty-four men who could have had access to *all* the ten documents, Preston established at the end of his second day. Then he began checking absences from office, trips abroad, incidences of flu, eliminating those who could not have had access within the period of theft.

He was hampered by two things: he had to pretend to examine a host of other withdrawals in order not to draw attention to those particular ten documents. Even Registry clerks gossip, and the leak could have been a low-level staffer, at secretary or typist level, capable of exchanging coffee-break gossip with a clerk. Secondly, he could not penetrate to the floors above to check on the number of photocopies made of originals. He knew it was common for one man to have a top-secret document officially out to him by name, but for that man to wish to take the advice of a colleague. So a photocopy would be run off, numbered and given to the colleague. On its return it would be shredded, or in this case not. The master document would then go back to Registry. But several pairs of eyes could have seen the photocopies.

To solve the second problem he returned to the Ministry with Capstick after dark and spent two nights in the upper floors, empty apart from the incurious cleaning ladies, checking the number of copies run off. More eliminations were made possible, where a document went to a senior civil servant who made no copies at all before returning it to Registry. On 27 January he reported back to Charles Street with an interim progress sheet.

* * *

It was Brian Harcourt-Smith who received him. Sir Bernard was away from the office again.

'Glad you've got something for us, John,' said Harcourt-Smith. 'I've had two calls from Anthony Plumb. It seems the Paragon people are pressing. Shoot.'

'First,' said Preston, 'the documents. They were carefully selected, as if our thief was taking the sort of stuff he had been asked for. That requires expertise. I think that counts out really low-level staffers. They would operate on the magpie syndrome, grabbing what came by. It's tentative but it cuts down the numbers. I think it's somebody of experience and with an awareness of content. Which counts out clerks and messengers. In any case, the leak isn't in the Registry. No broken bag seals, no illicit withdrawals or unauthorized copying.'

Harcourt-Smith nodded. 'So you think it's upstairs?'

'Yes, Brian, I do. Here's the second reason why. I spent two nights checking every single copy made. There are no discrepancies. So it leaves only one thing. The shredding of copies. Someone has had three copies to shred and shredded only two, smuggling the third out of the building. Now to numbers of senior men who could have done that.

'There were twenty-four who could have had access to all ten documents. I think I can count out twelve, because they only got copies, one copy each, on a give-me-your-advice basis. The rules are quite clear. A man receiving a photocopy on that basis must return it to the man who sent it to him. To retain one would be irregular and arouse suspicion. To retain ten would be unheard-of. So one comes to the twelve men who had the originals out from Registry.

'Of these, three were away for varying reasons on the days shown as the withdrawal dates on the photocopies returned by the anonymous sender. Those men made their withdrawals on other days and must be counted out. That leaves nine.

'Of those nine, four never had any copies made for advisory purposes at all, and of course unauthorized copying without logging is not possible.'

'And then there were five,' murmured Harcourt-Smith.

'Right. Now, it's only tentative, but it's the best I can do for the moment. Three of those five, during the period, had other documents on their desks that fall well within the type of the stolen papers, and which were much more interesting, but which were not stolen. By rights they ought to have been stolen. So I come down to two men. Nothing certain, just prime suspects.'

He pushed two files across the desk to Harcourt-Smith who looked at them with curiosity. 'Sir Richard Peters and Mr George Berenson,' he read. 'The first being the Assistant Under-Secretary responsible for International and Industrial Policy; and the second the Deputy Chief of Defence Procurement. Both men would have personal staffs, of course.'

'Yes.'

'But you are not listing them as suspects? May I ask why?'

'They *are* suspects,' said Preston. 'Those two men would probably rely on their staffs to make the copies and later shred them. But that widens the net to a dozen people. If one could clear the two top men, trapping the underling with the department head's cooperation would be child's play. I'd like to start with the top two.'

'What are you asking for?' said Harcourt-Smith.

'Total covert surveillance on both men for a limited period, with postal intercept and telephone tap,' said Preston.

'I'll ask the Paragon Committee,' said Harcourt-Smith. 'But these are senior men. You'd better be right.'

The second meeting of Paragon took place in the COBRA that late afternoon. Harcourt-Smith deputized for Sir Bernard Hemmings. He had a transcript of Preston's report for everyone present. The senior men read the report in silence. When all had finished, Sir Anthony Plumb asked: 'Well?'

'Seems logical,' said Sir Hubert Villiers.

'I think Mr Preston has done well in the time,' said Sir Nigel Irvine.

Harcourt-Smith smiled thinly. 'Of course, it could be neither of these two very senior men,' he said. 'A girl clerk, given the copies to shred, could just have easily taken all ten documents.'

Brian Harcourt-Smith was the product of a very minor private school and carried on his shoulder a sizeable and quite unnecessary chip. Beneath his polished veneer he had a considerable capacity for resentment. All his life he had resented the seemingly effortless ease which the men around him could bring to the business of life. He resented their endless and interwoven network of contacts and friendships, often forged long ago in schools, universities or fighting regiments, on which they could draw when they wished. It was called the 'old boy network' or the 'magic circle', and he resented most of all that he was not a member of it.

One day, he had told himself many times, when he had the Director-Generalship and his knighthood, he would sit among these men as equals, and they would listen, really listen to him.

Down the table, Sir Nigel Irvine, a receptive man, caught a look in Harcourt-Smith's eyes and was troubled. There was a capacity for anger in that man, he mused. Irvine was a contemporary of Sir Bernard Hemmings and they went back a long way. He wondered about the succession in the autumn. He wondered about the anger in Harcourt-Smith, the hidden ambition and where they might both lead, or, perhaps, already had.

'Well, we've heard what Mr Preston wants,' said Sir Anthony Plumb. 'Total surveillance. Does he get it?'

The hands went up.

Every Friday in MI5 is held what they call the 'bidding'

conference. The Director of 'K' is in the chair, head of the Joint Sections. At the bidding conference the other directors put in their request for what they think they need – finance, technical services, and surveillance of their pet suspects. The pressure is always on Director A who controls the Watchers. That week the Friday conference was pre-empted as far as the Watchers were concerned. Those attending on Friday, 30 January, found the cupboard was bare. Two days earlier Harcourt-Smith, at the requirement of Paragon, had allocated Preston the Watchers he wanted.

At six watchers to a team (four forming the 'box' and two in parked cars) and four teams in every twenty-four hours, and with two men to survey, he had taken forty-eight Watchers off other duties. There was some outrage, but nobody could do anything about it.

'There are two targets,' the briefing officers in Cork told the teams, 'this one and this one. One is married but his wife is away in the country. They live in a West End apartment and he usually walks to the Ministry every morning, about a mile and a half. The other is a bachelor and lives outside Edenbridge in Kent. He commutes by train every day. We start tomorrow.'

Technical Support took care of the telephone tap and the mail intercept, and both Sir Richard Peters and Mr George Berenson went under the microscope.

They were just too late to observe the delivery by hand of a package at Fontenoy House. It was collected from the hall porter by the addressee on his return from work. It contained a replica, using zirconium stones, of the Glen suite, and was deposited with Coutts Bank the following day.

7

Friday the 13th is supposed to be an unlucky day but for John Preston it was the opposite. It brought him his first break in the wearisome tailing of the two senior civil servants.

The surveillance had gone on for sixteen days without results. Both men were creatures of habit and neither was surveillance-conscious; that is, they did not look for a tail and therefore made the Watchers' task easy. But boring.

The Londoner left his Belgravia apartment every day at the same hour, walked to Hyde Park Corner, turned down Constitution Hill and across St James's Park. That brought him to Horse Guards Parade. He went across this, traversed Whitehall and straight into the Ministry. He sometimes lunched out, sometimes inside. He spent most evenings at home or in his club.

The commuter, who lived alone in a picturesque cottage outside Edenbridge, caught the same train to London each day, strolled from Charing Cross Station to the Ministry and disappeared inside. The Watchers 'housed' him each night and kept chilly vigil until relieved at dawn by the first day team. Neither man did anything suspicious. Mail intercept and phone taps on both men showed up only the usual bills, personal mail, banal phone calls and a modest and respectable social life. Until 13 February.

Preston, as operations controller, was in the radio-link room in the basement at Cork Street when a call came through from the 'B' team following Sir Richard Peters.

'Joe is hailing a cab. We're behind him in the cars.' In Watcher parlance, the target is always Joe, Chummy or 'our friend'.

When the 'B' team came off shift Preston had a session with its leader, Harry Burkinshaw. He was a small, rotund man, middle-aged, a veteran of his job-for-life profession, who could spend hours blended into the background of a London street and then move with remarkable speed if the target tried to slip him.

He was wearing a plaid jacket, porkpie hat, carried a raincoat and wore a camera round his neck, like an ordinary American tourist. As with all Watchers, the hat, jacket and raincoat were soft and reversible, providing six combinations. Watchers treasure their props and the various roles into which they can slip in a matter of seconds.

'So what happened, Harry?' Preston asked.

'He came out of the Ministry at the usual time. We picked him up, got him in the middle of the box. But instead of walking in the usual direction, he went as far as Trafalgar Square and hailed a cab. We were at the end of the shift. We alerted our mates on the swing shift to hold station, and set off after the cab.

'He dismissed it by Panzer's Delicatessen on Bayswater Road and ducked down Clanricarde Gardens. Halfway down he shot into a front forecourt and went down the steps to the basement. One of my lads got close enough to see there was nothing down the steps but the door of the basement flat. He had shot in there. Then my boy had to move on – Joe was coming back out again and up the steps. He went back to Bayswater Road, took another cab and headed for the West End again. After that he resumed his normal routine. We passed him to the swing shift at the bottom of Park Lane.'

'How long was he down the basement steps?'

'Thirty, forty seconds,' said Burkinshaw. 'Either he was let in damn fast, or he had his own key. No lights showing inside. Looked like he'd stopped by to pick up mail, or check for any.'

'What kind of house?'

'Dirty-looking house, dirty-looking basement. It'll all be in the log in the morning. Mind if I go now? My feet are killing me.'

Preston spent the evening wondering about the incident. Why on earth would Sir Richard Peters want to visit a seedy flat in Bayswater? For forty seconds? He couldn't see someone inside. Not enough time. Pick up mail? Or *leave* a message? He arranged for the house to be put under surveillance as well, and a car with a man and a camera in it was there within an hour.

Weekends are weekends. Preston could have roused the civilian authorities to start investigating the apartment through Saturday and Sunday, but that would have caused waves. This was an ultra-covert surveillance. He decided to wait until Monday.

The Albion Committee had agreed upon Professor Krilov as its chairman and spokesman, and it was he who alerted Major Pavlov that the committee was ready to report its considerations to the General Secretary. That was on the Saturday morning. Within hours each of the four on the committee had been told to report to the Comrade General Secretary's weekend dacha at Usovo.

The other three came in their own cars. Major Pavlov drove Philby personally, and he was able to dispense with Driver Gregoriev, the KGB pool chauffeur who had been driving him about for over two weeks.

West of Moscow, across the Uspenskoye Bridge and lying close to the banks of the Moskva River, is a complex of artificial villages round which are grouped the weekend dachas of the high and mighty in Soviet society. Even here the gradings are inflexible. At Peredelkino are the dachas of artists, academics and military men; at Zhukovka, the Central Committee and others just below the Politburo; but the last-named, the men at the supreme pinnacle, have their dachas grouped around Usovo, the most exclusive of them all.

The original Russian dacha was a country cottage, but these are veritable mansions of luxury, set in hundreds of acres of pine and birch forest, the territories patrolled round the clock by cohorts of Ninth Directorate bodyguards to ensure the utter privacy and security of the *vlasti*.

Philby knew that every member of the Politburo, on elevation to that office, has the right to four residences. There is the family apartment on Kutuzovsky Prospekt which, unless the hierarch falls in disgrace, will remain in the family for ever. Then there is the official villa in the Lenin Hills, always maintained with staff and comforts, inevitably bugged, and hardly ever used, save for the entertaining of foreign dignitaries. Thirdly comes the dacha in the forests west of Moscow, which the newly promoted big shot may design and build to his own tastes. Lastly, there is the summer retreat, often in the Crimea on the Black Sea. The General Secretary, however, had long ago had his summer retreat built at Kislovodsk, a mineral water spa in the Caucasus specializing in the treatment of abdominal ailments.

Philby had never seen the General Secretary's dacha at Usovo. As the Chaika arrived that freezing evening he observed it was long and low, of cut stone, with shingled roof, like the furniture at Kutuzovsky Prospekt owing much to Scandinavian simplicity. Inside, the temperature was very high and the General Secretary received them all in a spacious sitting-room where a roaring log fire added to the heat. After the minimal formalities the General Secretary gestured to Professor Krilov to reveal to him the Albion Committee's thinking.

'You will understand, Comrade General Secretary, that what we have sought is a means of swinging a portion of the British electorate of not less than ten per cent across the nation to two cardinal viewpoints: one is a massive loss of their popular confidence in the existing Conservative Government; the second a conviction that in the election of a Labour Government lies their best chances for contentment and security.

'In order to simplify that search, we asked ourselves if there was not perhaps one single issue which could dominate, or be brought to dominate, the entire election.

After profound consideration we have all come to the view that no economic aspect – not job losses, factory closures, increasing automation in industry, even public-service cuts – would constitute this single issue we have been seeking.

'We believe there is but one: the greatest and most emotional non-economic political issue in Britain and all Western Europe at the present time. This is the question of nuclear disarmament. This has become huge in the West, involving millions of ordinary people. It is basically a question of mass fear, and it is this we feel should become the main thrust; the issue we should covertly exploit.'

'And your specific proposals?' asked the General Secretary silkily.

'You will know, Comrade General Secretary, of our efforts so far in this field. Not millions but billions of roubles have been spent encouraging the various anti-nuclear lobbies, in proposing to the West European people that unilateral nuclear disarmanent really is synonymous with their best chance of peace. Our covert efforts and their results have been remarkable, but nothing compared to what we believe should now be sought and achieved.

'The British Labour Party is the only one of four contesting the next election that is committed to unilateral nuclear disarmament. Our view is that all the stops should now be pulled out, using funds, disinformation, propaganda, to persuade that minimum wavering ten per cent of the British electorate to switch their vote, convinced at last that the Labour vote is the Peace vote.'

The silence as they waited for the General Secretary's reaction was almost tangible. He spoke at last. 'Those efforts that we have made over eight years, and of which you spoke – have they worked?'

Professor Krilov looked as if he had been hit by an air-to-air missile. Philby caught the Soviet leader's mood and shook his head. The General Secretary noted the gesture and went on speaking: 'For eight years we have put a vast effort into destabilizing the confidence on this issue. Today, true, all the unilateralist movements are so Left-wing that by one means or another they have come under the control of our friends and work to our ends. The campaign has brought a rich harvest in agents of sympathy and influence. But . . .'

The General Secretary suddenly smacked both palms on to the arms of his wheelchair. The violent gesture in a man normally so ice cold shook his four listeners badly.

'Nothing has changed,' shouted the General Secretary. His voice then resumed its even tenor. 'Five years ago, and four years ago, all the experts in the Central Committee and the universities and the KGB analytical study groups told us that the unilateralist movements were so powerful that they could stop the deployment of Cruise and Pershing. We believe that. We were misled. At Geneva we dug our toes in, persuaded by our own propaganda that if we held on long enough the governments of Western Europe would give in to the "peace" demonstrations we were covertly supporting and refuse to deploy Pershing and Cruise. But they *did* deploy, and we had to walk out.'

Philby nodded, looking suitably modest. Back in 1983 he had stuck his neck out with a paper suggesting the 'peacenik' movement in the West, despite noisy popular demonstrations, would not swing any major election or change any government's mind. He had been proved right. Things, he suspected, were moving his way.

'It rankles, comrades, it still rankles,' said the General Secretary. 'Now you are proposing more of the same. Comrade Colonel Philby, what are the latest British public-opinion polls on this issue?'

'Not good, I'm afraid,' said Philby. 'The last suggest twenty per cent of the British now support unilateral nuclear disarmament. But even that is confusing. Among the working class, Labour's traditional voters, the figure is lower. It is a dismal fact, Comrade General Secretary, that the British working class is among the most conservative in the world. Polls also show they are among the most patriotic, in a traditionalist way. During the Falklands affair diehard trade unionists threw the rule book into the dock and worked round the clock to get the warships ready for sea.

'I'm afraid if one is going to face harsh reality, one must admit the British working man has steadily refused to see that his best interests lie with us, or at least in a weakening of Britain's defences. And there is no reason to think he will change his mind now.'

'Harsh reality, that is what I asked this committee to face,' said the General Secretary. He paused again for several more minutes. 'Go away, Comrades. Go back to your deliberations. And bring me a plan, an active measure, that will exploit that mass fear of which you spoke, as never before; something that will persuade even level-headed men and women to vote to get rid of nuclear weapons from their soil, and thus to vote Labour.'

When they had gone, the old Russian rose and with a stick walked slowly to the window. He gazed out at the crackling birch forest beneath the snow. When he had swept to power with his predecessor still unburied, he had been personally committed to the achievement of five tasks in the time left to him.

He wanted to be remembered as the man who increased food production and its efficient distribution; who doubled consumer goods in number and quality by a huge overhaul of a chronically inefficient industry; who tightened Party discipline at all levels; who extirpated the scourge of corruption that gnawed at the country's vitals; and who secured the final supremacy in men and arms over his country's serried ranks of enemies. Four years later he knew he had failed in them all.

He was an old man, and sick, and he knew time was running out. He had always prided himself on being a pragmatic man, a realistic man, within the framework of strict Marxist orthodoxy. But even pragmatic men have their dreams, and old men have their vanities. His were simple: he wanted one gigantic triumph, one great monument that was his and his alone. Just how much he wanted it, that bitter winter night, he alone knew.

On the Sunday Preston took a stroll past the house in Clanricarde Gardens, a street running due north from the Bayswater Road. Burkinshaw had been right; it was one of those once prosperous Victorian five-storey houses that had gone badly to seed, the sort now let out in bedsitters. Its small front area was weed-infested; five steps ran up to a peeling door above the street. From the front patch a set of steps led down to a tiny basement area with the top of a door just in view – the basement flat. He puzzled again as to why a senior civil servant and knight of the realm should wish to visit such a dingy place.

Somewhere in vision, he knew, would be the Watcher, probably in a parked vehicle with a long-lensed camera at the ready. He made no attempt to spot the man, but knew he himself would have been seen. (On Monday he showed up in the log as 'an undistinguished character who walked by at 11.21 and showed some interest in the house'. Thanks for nothing, he thought.)

On Monday morning he visited the local Town Hall and had a look at the list of rate-payers for that street. The address listed only one house-holder, a Mr Michael Z. Mifsud. He was grateful for the Z; there could not be many like that around. Called up on the radio, the Watcher at Clanricarde Gardens slipped across the road and checked the bell-push buttons. M. Mifsud was listed on the ground floor. Owner-occupier, thought Preston, letting out the rest of the house as furnished accommodation; tenants of unfurnished property would pay their own local rates.

In the late morning he ran Michael Z. Mifsud through the Immigration computer down at Croydon. He was from Malta, as his name implied, and had been in the country thirty years. Nothing known, but a question mark fifteen years back. Not followed up and no explanation. Scotland Yard's Criminal Records Office computer explained the question mark: the man had nearly been deported. Instead, he had served two years for living off immoral earnings. After lunch Preston went to see Armstrong in Finance at Charles Street.

'Can I be an Inland Revenue inspector tomorrow?' he asked.

Armstrong sighed. 'I'll try and fix it. Call back before closing time.'

Then he went along to the Legal Adviser. 'Would you ask Special Branch to fix me a search warrant for this address? Also I want an SB sergeant on call to front me up.'

MI5 in Britain has no powers of arrest. Only a police officer can effect an arrest, save in emergencies when a citizen's arrest is possible. When MI5 want to pick someone up, Special Branch usually oblige.

'You're not going to do a break-in?' asked the lawyer suspiciously.

'Certainly not,' said Preston. 'I want to wait until the tenant of this flat turns up, then move in and search. An arrest may be necessary, depending on the search. That's why I need the sergeant.'

'All right,' sighed the lawyer. 'I'll get on to our tame magistrate. You'll have them both tomorrow morning.'

Just before five that afternoon Preston picked up his Inland Revenue identification from Finance. Armstrong gave him another card with a telephone number. 'If there's a query, have the suspect phone that number. It's the Inland Revenue in Willesden Green. Ask for Mr Charnley. He'll vouch for you. Your name is Brent, by the way.'

'So I see,' said Preston.

Mr Michael Z. Mifsud, interviewed the next morning, was not a nice man. Unshaven, in string vest, surly and uncooperative, but he let Preston into his grubby sitting-room.

'What you tell me?' protested Mifsud. 'What income? All I make I declare.'

'Mr Mifsud, I assure you it's a routine spot check.

Happens all the time. You declare all the rents, you've got nothing to hide.'

'I got nothing to hide. So you take it up with my accountant,' said Mifsud defiantly.

'I can if you wish,' said Preston. 'But I assure you, we can ensure your accountant's fees will eventually come to an awful lot of money. Let me be frank – if the rents are in order, I just go away and do another spot check on someone else. But if, God forbid, any of these flats are let out for immoral purposes, that's different. Me, I'm concerned with income tax. But I'd be duty bound to pass my findings on to the police. You know what living off immoral earnings means?'

'What you mean?' protested Mifsud. 'Is no immoral earnings here. Is all good tenants. They pay rents, I pay taxes. Everything.'

But he had gone a shade paler and grudgingly produced the rent books. Preston pretended to be interested in them all. He noted the basement was let to a Mr Dickie at £40 per week. It took an hour to get all the details. Mifsud had never met the basement tenant. He paid by cash, regular as clockwork. But there was a typed letter originating the tenancy. It was signed by Mr Dickie. Preston took the letter with him when he left, over Mr Mifsud's protests. By lunchtime he had handed it to Scotland Yard's graphology people, along with copies of Sir Richard Peters's handwriting and signature. By close of play the Yard had rung him back. Same handwriting but diguised.

So, thought Preston, Peters himself maintains his own *pied-á-terre*. For cosy meetings with his controller? Most probably. Preston gave his orders: if Peters started heading towards the flat again, he, Preston, was to be alerted at once, wherever he was. The watch on the basement flat was to be maintained in case anyone else showed up.

Wednesday dragged by, and Thursday. Then, as he left the Ministry, Sir Richard Peters hailed a cab again and directed it towards Bayswater. The Watchers contacted

Preston in the bar at Gordon Street, whence he called Scotland Yard and hauled the designated Special Branch sergeant out of the canteen. He gave the man down the telephone the address. 'Meet me on the pavement opposite, as fast as you can, but no noise,' he said.

They all congregated in the cold darkness of the pavement opposite the suspect house. Preston had dismissed his taxi two hundred yards up the street. The Special Branch man had come in an unmarked Branch car which, with its driver, was parked with no lights around a corner. Detective Sergeant Lander turned out to be young and a bit green; it was his first bust with the MI5 people and he seemed impressed. Harry Burkinshaw materialized out of the shadows.

'How long's he been in there, Harry?'

'Fifty-five minutes,' said Burkinshaw.

'Any visitors?'

'Nope.'

Preston took out his search warrant and showed it to Lander. 'OK, let's go in,' he said.

'Is he likely to be violent, sir?' asked Lander.

'Oh, I hope not,' said Preston. 'He's a middle-aged civil servant. He might get hurt.'

They crossed the road and quietly entered the front patch. A dim light was burning behind the curtains of the basement flat. They descended the steps in silence and Preston rang the bell. There was the clack of heels inside and the door opened. Framed in the light was a woman.

When she saw the two men the smile of welcome dropped from her heavily carmined lips. She tried to shut the door but Lander pushed it open, elbowed her aside and ran past her.

She was no spring chicken, but she had done her best. Wavy black hair fell to shoulder length to frame the heavily made-up face. There had been extravagant use of mascara and shadow around the eyes, rouge on the cheeks and a smear of bright lipstick across the mouth. Before she had time to close the front of the housecoat Preston caught a glimpse of black stockings and suspenders, and a tight-waisted basque picked out in red ribbon.

He guided her by the elbow down the hall to the sitting-room and sat her down. She stared at the carpet. They sat in silence while Lander searched the flat. Lander knew fugitives sometimes hid under beds and in cupboards. He did a good job. After ten minutes he emerged from the rear area, slightly flushed.

'Not a sign of him sir. He must have done a bunk through the back and over the garden fences to the next street.'

Just then there was a ring at the front door.

'Your people, sir?' asked Lander to Preston.

Preston shook his head. 'Not with a single ring,' he replied.

Lander went to open the front door. Preston heard an oath and the sound of running footsteps. Later it transpired a man had come to the door and on seeing the detective opening it had tried to flee. Burkinshaw's people had closed in at the top of the steps and held the man until the pursuing Lander had got the cuffs on him. After that the man went quiet and was led away to the police car.

Preston sat with the woman and listened to the tumult die away. 'It's not an arrest,' he said quietly, 'but I think we should go to head office, don't you?'

The woman nodded miserably. 'Do you mind if I get changed first?'

'I think that would be a good idea, Sir Richard,' said Preston.

An hour later a burly but very gay truck driver was released from Paddington Green police station having been seriously advised on the unwisdom of answering blind-date advertisements in adult contact magazines.

John Preston escorted Sir Richard Peters to the country, stayed with him listening to what he had to say until midnight, drove back to London and spent the rest of the night writing his report. This report was in front of each member of the Paragon Committee when they met at eleven on the Friday morning. The expressions of bewilderment and distaste were general.

Good grief, thought Sir Martin Flannery, the Cabinet Secretary, to himself, first Hayman, then Trestrail, then Dunnett and now this. Can't these wretches ever keep their flies buttoned up?

The last man to finish the report looked up.

'Quite appalling,' said Sir Hubert Villiers of the Home Office.

'Don't think we'll be wanting the chap back at the Ministry,' said Sir Perry Jones of Defence.

'Where is he now?' asked Sir Anthony Plumb of MI5's Director-General, who sat next to Brian Harcourt-Smith.

'In one of our houses in the country,' said Sir Bernard Hemmings. 'He has already telephoned the Ministry, purporting to phone from his cottage at Edenbridge, to say he slipped on a patch of ice yesterday evening and cracked a bone in his ankle. He said he's in plaster and will be off for a fortnight. Doctor's orders. That should hold things for a while.'

'Aren't we overlooking one question?' murmured Sir Nigel Irvine of M16. 'Regardless of his unusual tastes, is he our man? Is he the leak?'

Brian Harcourt-Smith cleared his throat. 'Interrogation, gentlemen, is in its early stages,' he said, 'but it does seem likely that he is. Certainly he would be a prime likelihood for recruitment by blackmail.'

'Time is becoming of the very essence,' interposed Sir Patrick Strickland of the Foreign Office. 'We still have the matter of damage assessment hanging over us, and at my end the question of what and when do we tell our allies.'

'We could, er . . . intensify the interrogation,' suggested Harcourt-Smith. 'I believe that way we would have our answer within twenty-four hours.'

There was an uncomfortable silence. The thought of one of their colleagues, whatever he had done, being worked over by the 'hard' team was not a comfortable one.

Sir Martin Flannery felt his stomach turn. He had a deep personal aversion to violence.

'Surely that is not necessary at this stage?' he asked.

Sir Nigel Irvine raised his head from the report. 'Bernard, this man Preston, the investigating officer, he seems a pretty good man.'

'He is,' affirmed Sir Bernard Hemmings.

'I was wondering,' continued Irvine with deceptive diffidence, '. . . he seems to have spent some hours with Peters in the immediate aftermath of the events in Bayswater. I wonder if it might be helpful for this committee to have the opportunity of listening to him.'

'I debriefed him myself personally this morning,' interjected Harcourt-Smith rapidly. 'I am sure I can answer any questions as to what happened.'

The Chief of 'Six' was consumed with apology.

'My dear Brian, there is no doubt in my mind about that,' he said. 'It is just that . . . well . . . sometimes one can get an impression from interrogating a suspect that ill conveys itself on paper. I don't know what the committee thinks, but we are going to have to make a decision as to what happens next. I just thought it might be helpful to listen to the one man who has talked to Peters.'

There was a succession of nods around the table. Hemmings dispatched an evidently irritated Harcourt-Smith to the telephone to summon Preston. While the mandarins waited coffee was served. Preston was shown in thirty minutes later. The senior men examined him with some curiosity. He was given a chair at the centre of the table, opposite his own Director-General and DDG. Sir Anthony Plumb explained the committee's dilemma.

'Just what happened between you?' asked Sir Anthony.

Preston thought for a moment. 'In the car, on the way down to the country, he broke down,' said Preston. 'Up till then he had maintained a form of composure although under great strain. I took him down alone, driving myself. He started to cry, and to talk.'

'Yes,' prompted Sir Anthony, 'what did he say?'

'He admitted his taste for transvestite fetishism, but seemed stunned by the accusation of treason. He denied it hotly, and continued to do so until I left him with the minders.'

'Well, he would,' said Brian Harcourt-Smith. 'He could still be our man.'

'Yes, indeed he could,' agreed Preston.

'But your impression, your gut feeling?' murmured Sir Nigel Irvine.

Preston took a deep breath. 'Gentlemen, I don't think he is.'

'May we ask why?' said Sir Anthony.

'As Sir Nigel implies, it's just a gut feeling,' said Preston. 'I've seen two men whose world had shattered about them and who believed they had not much left to live for. When men in that mood spill, they tend to spill the lot. A rare man of great composure, like Philby or Blunt, can hold out. But those were ideological traitors, convinced Marxists. If Sir Richard Peters was blackmailed into treachery, I think he would either have admitted it when the house of cards came tumbling down, or at least shown no surprise at the accusation of treason. He did show complete surprise; he could have been acting, but I think he was beyond acting by then. Either that, or he ought to have an Oscar.'

It was a long speech from such a junior man in the presence of the Paragon Committee, and there was silence for a while. Harcourt-Smith was looking daggers at Preston. Sir Nigel studied Preston with interest. In view of his office, he knew about the Londonderry incident that had blown Preston's cover as an Army undercover man. He also noted Harcourt-Smith's gaze and wondered why the DDG at 'Five' seemed to dislike Preston. His own opinion was favourable.

'What do you think, Nigel?' asked Sir Anthony Plumb.

Irvine nodded. 'I too have seen the mood of utter collapse that overtakes a traitor when he is exposed. Vassall, Prime – both weak and inadequate men, and they both spilled the lot when the house came tumbling down. So, if not Peters, that seems to leave George Berenson.'

'It's been a month,' complained Sir Patrick Strickland. 'We really have got to nail the culprit one way or the other.'

'The culprit could still be a personal assistant or secretary on the staff of either of these two men,' pointed out Sir Perry Jones. 'Isn't that so, Mr Preston?'

'Quite true, sir,' said Preston.

'Then we are going to have to clear George Berenson or prove he's our man,' said Sir Patrick Strickland in some exasperation. 'Even if he's cleared, that leaves us Peters. And if *he* won't cough, we're back to square one.'

'May I make a suggestion?' asked Preston quietly.

There was some surprise. He had not been asked here to make suggestions. But Sir Anthony Plumb was a courteous man. 'Please do,' he said.

'The ten documents returned by the anonymous sender all fell within a pattern,' said Preston. The men round the table nodded. 'Seven of them,' Preston continued, 'contained material affecting Britain's and NATO's naval dispositions in the Atlantic, north and south. That seems to be an area of NATO planning of particular interest to our leak or his controllers. Would it be possible to cause to pass across Mr Berenson's desk a document of such irresistible tastiness that, if he is the guilty party, he would be sorely tempted to abstract a copy and make a move to pass it on?'

A number of heads around the table nodded thoughtfully.

'Smoke him out, you mean?' mused Sir Bernard Hemmings. 'What do you think, Nigel?'

'You know, I think I like it. It might just work. Could it be done, Perry?'

Sir Perry Jones pursed his lips. 'Actually, more realistically than you think,' he said. 'When I was in America the idea was mooted, and I haven't passed it further yet, that we might one day need to increase to refuelling and revictualling level our facilities on Ascension Island, to include facilities for our nuclear submarines. The Americans were very interested and suggested they might help with the costs if they too could have facilities. It would save our subs going back to Faslane and those endless demonstrations up there, and save the Yankees having to go back to Norfolk, Virginia.

'I suppose I could prepare a very confidential personal paper, beefing that idea up to agreed policy level and slip it across four or five desks, including Berenson's.'

'Would Berenson normally see that kind of paper?' asked Sir Paddy Strickland.

'Certainly,' said Jones. 'As Deputy Chief of Defence Procurement, his section is responsible for the nuclear side of things. He would have to get it, along with three or four others. Some copies would be run off for close colleagues' eyes only. Then returned and shredded. Original back to me, by hand.'

It was agreed. The Ascension Island Paper would land on George Berenson's desk on Tuesday.

As they left the Cabinet Office Sir Nigel Irvine invited Sir Bernard Hemmings to join him for lunch.

'Good man, that Preston,' suggested Irvine. 'Like the cut of his jib. Is he loyal to you?'

'I've every reason to think so,' said Sir Bernard, puzzled.

Ah, that might explain things, thought 'C' enigmatically.

That Sunday, the 22nd, the British Prime Minister spent at her official country residence, Chequers, in the county of Buckinghamshire. In conditions of complete secrecy she asked three of her closest advisers in the Cabinet and the chairman of the Party to drive over privately to see her.

What she had to say caused them all deep thought. That coming June she would have been in power for four years of her second term. She was determined to go for a third successive election victory. The economic indicators suggested a downturn in the autumn, accompanied by a wave of wage demands. There could be strikes. She wished to have no repeat of the 'winter of discontent' of 1978 when a wave of labour stoppages crippled the credibility of the Labour Government and led to its fall in May 1979.

Furthermore, with the Social Democrat/Liberal Alliance stuck in the public opinion polls at 20 per cent, Labour, with its newfound veneer of unity and moderation, had increased its popular rating to 37 per cent of the electorate, just six points behind the Conservatives. And the gap was closing. In short, she wanted to go for a snap June election, but without the damaging speculation that preceded and hastened her decision in 1983. A sudden, out-of-the-blue declaration and a three-week election campaign was what she wanted, not in 1988 or even the autumn of 1987, but that summer.

She bound her colleagues to silence, but the date she favoured was the penultimate Thursday in June, the 18th.

On Monday Sir Nigel Irvine had his meet with Andreyev. It was very covert, on Hampstead Heath. A screen of Irvine's own people was scattered over the heath to ensure Andreyev was himself not under surveillance by the Soviet Embassy's own KR (counter-intelligence) goons. But he was clean. Britain's own cover of the Soviet diplomat's movements had been called off.

Sir Nigel Irvine handled Andreyev as a Director's Case. These are unusual because men as high in the service (any service) as the Chief himself do not usually run an agent. It may happen because of the exceptional importance of the agent, or because original recruiting was done before the controller became his service's director and the agent refuses to be handled by anyone else. This was the problem with Andreyev.

Back in February 1972 Nigel Irvine, then plain Mr Irvine, had been Head of Station in Tokyo. In that month the Japanese counter-terrorist people had decided to take out the headquarters of the fanatical ultra-Left Red Army Faction, which was located in a villa in the snow on the slopes of Mount Otakine, at a place called Asama-so. The National Police Agency actually did the job, but under the command of the redoubtable counter-terrorist chief, Mr Sassa, who was a friend of Irvine.

Providing some of the experience gleaned by Britain's crack SAS units, Irvine was able to be of some advisory help to Mr Sassa, and some of his suggestions saved a number of Japanese lives. Aware of his country's strict neutrality, Mr Sassa could not thank Irvine in any practical way. But at a diplomtic cocktail party a month later the brilliant and subtle Japanese had caught Irvine's eye and nodded in the direction of a Russian diplomat across the room. Then he had smiled and moved away. Irvine closed on the Russian and discovered he was newly arrived in Tokyo and his name was Andreyev.

Irvine had the man tailed and discovered he was foolishly having a clandestine affair with a Japanese girl, an offence that would immediately break him with his own people. Of course the Japanese already knew this because every Soviet diplomat in Tokyo is quietly followed whenever they leave the embassy.

Irvine had set up a honey trap, acquired the appropriate photographs and tape recordings, and finally burst in on Andreyev, using the crash-bang-gotcha technique. The Russian had nearly collapsed, thinking he was being raided by his own people. As he pulled his trousers on he agreed to talk to Irvine. He was something of a catch. For one thing he was from the KGB's Illegals Directorate, a Line N man.

The First Chief Directorate of the KGB, responsible for all overseas activities, is divided into Directorates, Special Departments and Ordinary Departments. Ordinary Soviet KGB agents under diplomatic cover come from one of the 'territorial' departments – the Seventh Department happens to cover Japan. These staffers are called PR Line when on posting abroad and they do the run-of-the-mill trawling for information, making of useful contacts, reading of technical publications, etc.

But at the most secret heart of the First Chief Directorate lies the Illegals, or 'S', Directorate, which knows no territorial boundaries. The Illegals people train and run the 'illegal' agents, those not under diplomatic immunity, those who go in on the ground, under deep cover, with false papers and on secret missions. The Illegals operate outside the embassy.

Nevertheless, inside every KGB *rezidentura* in every Soviet embassy, there is usually one 'S' Directorate man known on overseas posting as Line N people. These handle special assignments only, often running spies indigenous to the country against which they are spying, or just assisting with back-up and technical support a deep-cover illegal coming in from the Soviet Bloc.

Andreyev was from the 'S' Directorate. Even more oddly, he was not a Japan expert, as all the Seventh Department colleagues in the embassy would have to be. He was an English-language expert, and the reason he was there at all was to pursue a contact with a United States Air Force master sergeant who had been talent-spotted in San Diego and transferred to the joint USAF-Japanese base at Tashikawa.

With no hope of explaining himself to his own superiors back in Moscow, Andreyev had agreed to work for Irvine. The cosy arrangement came to an end when the American sergeant, pushed beyond endurance, dispatched himself rather untidily with his service revolver in the commissary latrine and Andreyev was sent back to Moscow in a hurry. Irvine thought of burning the man there and then, but he desisted.

And then he had showed up in London. A batch of new photographs had drifted across Sir Nigel Irvine's desk six months earlier and there he was. Transferred out of the 'S' Directorate and back on to PR Line work, Andreyev was accredited as a Second Secretary in the Soviet Embassy. Sir Nigel had put the hooks in again. Andreyev had little choice but to cooperate, but he refused to be handled by anyone else, so Sir Nigel took him on as a Director's Case.

On the matter of the leak in the British Defence Ministry, he had little to offer. He knew of no such thing. If there was such a leak, then the man in the Ministry could be controlled directly from some illegal Soviet agent resident in Britain, who would contact Moscow direct, or he could be being run by one of the three Line N people inside the embassy. But such people would not discuss a case of that importance over coffee in the canteen. He personally had heard nothing, but he would keep his eyes and ears open. On that note the two men on Hampstead Heath parted.

The Ascension Island Paper was distributed on Tuesday by Sir Peregrine Jones who had spent Monday preparing it. It went to four men. Bertie Capstick had agreed to enter the Ministry each night and check on legitimate photocopies made. Preston had told his watchers he wanted to know if George Berenson scratched his neck, immediately. He told his mail-intercept people the same, and put his phone-tap team on full alert. Then they settled down to wait.

8

On the first day nothing happened. That night Brigadier Capstick with John Preston went into the Ministry of Defence while the staff were sleeping and checked the number of photocopies run off. There were seven; three by George Berenson, two each by two of the other mandarins who had had the Ascension Island Paper circulated to them and none by the fourth man.

On the evening of the second day Mr Berenson did something strange. The Watchers reported that in the middle of the evening he left his Belgravia apartment and walked to a nearby callbox. They could not tell the number he dialled, but he spoke only a few words, replaced the receiver and walked home. Why, Preston wondered, should a man do that who had a perfectly serviceable telephone in his flat, something Preston could vouch for, since he was tapping it.

On Thursday, the third day, George Berenson left the Ministry at the usual time, hailed a cab and went to St John's Wood. In the High Street of this parish, with its village-like atmosphere, was an ice-cream parlour and coffee shop. The Defence official went in, sat down and ordered a sundae, one of the specialities of the house.

John Preston sat in the basement radio room in Cork Street and listened to the Watcher team leader reporting in. It was Len Stewart, leading the 'A' team.

'I've got two people in there,' he said, 'and two more out here on the street. Plus my cars.'

'What's he doing in there?' asked Preston.

'Can't see,' said Stewart over his personal radio. 'Have to wait until the people in there with him get a chance to tell me.'

In fact Mr Berenson, ensconced in an alcove, was eating

his ice-cream sundae and filling in the last squares of the crossword in the *Daily Telegraph* which he had produced from his briefcase. He took no notice of the two jeans-clad students canoodling in the corner.

After thirty minutes the official called for his bill, took it to the cash desk, paid and left.

'He's back on the street,' called Len Stewart, 'my two have stayed inside. He's walking up the High Street. Looking for a taxi, I think. I can see my people inside now. They are paying at the desk.'

'Can you ask them what he did in there?' asked Preston. There was something odd, he thought, about the whole episode. It might be a specialist ice-cream parlour, but there were others in Mayfair and the West End, in a straight line from the Ministry to Belgravia. Why go north of Regent's Park to St John's Wood for an ice-cream?

Stewart's voice came over the air again. 'There's a taxi coming. He's hailing it. Hold on, here are my people from inside.'

There was a pause in transmission. Then: 'It seems he ate his ice-cream and completed the *Daily Telegraph* crossword. Then he paid up and left.'

'Where's the paper?' asked Preston.

'He left it when he finished . . . Hold on . . . Then the proprietor came over and cleared the table, taking the dirty bowl and paper back into the kitchen area . . . He's inside the taxi and cruising. What do we do . . . stay with him?'

Preston thought furiously. Harry Burkinshaw and the 'B' team had been taken off Sir Richard Peters and allowed a few days' rest. They had been out in rain, cold and fog for weeks. There was only one team on the job now. If he split that team and lost Berenson, who then went on to make his contact somewhere else, Harcourt-Smith would have his hide nailed to a barn door. He made his decision.

'Len, leave one car and driver to tail the taxi. I know it's not enough if he slips away on foot. But switch the rest of your people to the ice-cream parlour.'

'Will do,' said Len Stewart and went off the air.

Preston was in luck. The taxi went straight to Mr Berenson's West End club and dropped him off. He went inside. But then, thought Preston, the contact could be in there.

Len Stewart entered the ice-cream shop and sat until closing time with a coffee and *The Standard*. Nothing happened. He was asked to leave at closing time and did so. From up and down the street the four-man team saw the staff of the shop leave, the proprietor close up, the lights go out.

From Cork Street Preston was trying to get a phone tap on the ice-cream shop and a 'make' on the proprietor. He turned out to be a Signor Benotti, a legal immigrant, originally from Naples, who had led a blameless life for twenty years. By midnight Preston had a tap on the ice-cream parlour and Signor Benotti's home in Swiss Cottage. It produced nothing.

Preston spent a sleepless night in Cork Street. Stewart's relief shift had moved in at 8 p.m. and watched the ice-cream shop and Benotti's house through the night. At nine on the Friday morning Benotti walked back to his shop and at ten it opened for business. Len Stewart and the day shift took over at the same hour. At eleven Stewart called in.

'There's a small delivery van at the front door,' he told Preston. 'The vanman seems to be loading gallon tubs of ice-cream. It seems they do a customer delivery service.'

Preston stirred his twentieth cup of awful coffee. His mind was fogging with lack of sleep.

'I know,' he said, 'there's been reference to it on the telephone already. Detach a car and two people to stay with the van. Note every recipient of ice-cream deliveries.'

'It only leaves me a car and two people here, including

myself,' said Stewart, 'It's damn thin on the ground.'

'There's a bidding conference going on up at Charles. I'll try and get an extra team,' said Preston.

The ice-cream delivery van made twelve calls that morning, all in the St John's Wood/Swiss Cottage area with two as far south as Marylebone. Some of the calls were in apartment blocks where it was hard for the Watchers to appear inconspicuous, but they noted every address. Then the van drove back to the shop. It made no afternoon deliveries.

'Will you drop that list at Cork on your way home?' Preston asked Stewart.

That evening the phone-tap people reported Berenson had had four telephone calls while he was at home, including one in which the caller turned out to have a wrong number. He had made no outgoing calls. Everything was on tape. Did Preston want the tape to play over? There was nothing remotely suspicious on it. He thought he might as well.

On Saturday morning Preston played the longest shot of his life. Using a tape recorder set up by the Technical Support people, and a variety of excuses to the householders, he called up each one of the recipients of the ice-cream, asking whenever a woman answered if he might speak to her husband. Being Saturday, he got them all but one.

One voice seemed slightly familiar. What was it? A hint of accent? And where could he have heard it before? He checked the name of the householder. It meant nothing.

He ate a moody lunch in a café near Cork Street. The connection came to him over the coffee. He hurried back to Cork Street and played the tapes again. Possible; not conclusive but possible.

Scotland Yard, among the copious facilities of its forensic science department, has a section devoted to voice analysis, useful whenever a 'target' criminal, having had his phone tapped, denies it was his voice on the tape. MI5, having no forensic facilities, has to rely on Scotland Yard for this sort of thing, an arrangement usually secured via the Special Branch.

Preston called Detective Sergeant Lander, got him at home, and it was Lander who fixed a priority meeting in Scotland Yard's voice-analysis section that same Saturday afternoon. There was only one technician available; he was loath to leave his televised football game to come to work, but he did. A thin young man with pebble glasses, he played Preston's tapes half a dozen times, watching the illuminated line on the oscilloscope screen rise and fall to record the tiniest shades of tone and timbre in the voices.

'Same voice,' he said at last, 'no question about it.'

On Sunday Preston identified the owner of the accented voice by using the Diplomatic List. He also called a friend in the science department of London University, spoiled his day off by asking for a considerable favour, and finally telephoned Sir Bernard Hemmings at his Surrey home.

'I think there is something that we should report to the Paragon Committee, sir,' he said. 'Like, tomorrow morning.'

The Paragon Committee met at eleven and Sir Anthony Plumb asked Preston to make his report. There was an air of expectancy, although Sir Bernard Hemmings looked grave.

Preston detailed the events of the first two days since the distribution of the Ascension Island Paper as briefly as he could. There was a stir of interest at the news of Berenson's odd and very brief call from a public phone box on the Wednesday evening.

'Did you tape record that call?' asked Sir Peregrine Jones.

'No, sir, we couldn't get near enough,' replied Preston.

'Then what do you think it was for?'

'I believe Mr Berenson was alerting his controller to a

pending drop, probably using a code to indicate the time and place.'

'Have you any proof of that?' asked Sir Hubert Villiers of the Home Office.

'No, sir.'

Preston went on to describe the visit to the ice-cream parlour, the abandonment of the *Daily Telegraph*, and the fact it was cleared away by the proprietor personally.

'Did you manage to recover the paper?' asked Sir Paddy Strickland.

'No, sir, to have raided the ice-cream shop then might have caused the arrest of Mr Benotti, and perhaps Mr Berenson, but Benotti could have pleaded complete innocence that there was anything inside the newspaper, and Mr Berenson could have pleaded that he had made a terribly careless mistake.'

'But you believe the visit to the ice-cream shop was the drop?' asked Sir Anthony Plumb.

'I'm sure of it,' said Preston. He went on to describe the delivery of one-gallon tubs of ice-cream to a dozen customers the next morning, how he had obtained voice samples of eleven of them, and of Berenson's receipt of a 'wrong-number' call that same evening.

'The voice that dialled him that evening and established that the caller had obtained a wrong number, apologized and rang off, was the voice of one of the recipients of the ice-cream.'

There was silence round the table.

'Could it have been a coincidence?' asked Sir Hubert Villiers doubtfully. 'There are an awful lot of perfectly innocent wrong numbers dialled in this city. Get 'em myself, all the time.'

'I checked with a friend yesterday who has access to a computer,' said Preston levelly. 'The chances of a man in a city of twelve million going into a ice-cream parlour for a sundae; of that ice-cream parlour delivering to twelve customers the next morning; and of one of those customers speaking through a wrong number to the ice-cream eater by midnight are over a million to one. The telephone call on Friday evening was an acknowledgement of safe receipt.'

'Let me see if I understand,' said Sir Perry Jones. 'Berenson recovered from his three colleagues their photocopies of my fictitious paper and pretended to shred them all. In fact he retained one. He folded it inside his newspaper and left it in the ice-cream shop. The proprietor collected the paper, plastic-wrapped the classified document and delivered it next morning to the controller in a tub of ice-cream. The controller then alerted Berenson that he had got it.'

'That is what I believe happened,' said Preston.

'Chances of a million to one,' mused Sir Anthony Plumb. 'Nigel, what do you think?'

The Chief of the SIS shook his head. 'I don't believe in chances of a million to one,' he said. 'Not in our work, eh, Bernard? No, it was a drop all right, from the source to the controller via a cutout, Signor Benotti. John Preston has got it right. My congratulations. Berenson's our man.'

'So, what have you done since you made this connection, Mr Preston?' asked Sir Anthony.

'I have switched the surveillance from Mr Berenson to the controller,' said Preston. 'I've identified him. In fact this morning I joined the Watchers and followed him from his Marylebone flat, where he lives alone as a bachelor, to his office. He is a foreign diplomat. His name is Mr Jan Marais.'

'Jan? Sounds Czech,' said Sir Perry Jones.

'Not quite,' said Preston sombrely. 'Jan Marais is an accredited diplomat on the staff of the embassy of the Republic of South Africa.'

There was a stunned, disbelieving silence. Sir Paddy Strickland, in language not habitually favoured by diplomats, muttered, 'Bloody hell.' All eyes turned to Sir Nigel Irvine.

He sat at the end of the table badly shaken. If it's

true, he thought privately, I'll have his balls for cocktail olives.

He was thinking of General Henry Pienaar, head of South Africa's National Intelligence Service, successor to the late unlamented BOSS. For the South Africans to hire a few London crooks to burgle the archives of the African National Congress was one thing; to run a spy right inside the British Defence Ministry was, between services, a declaration of war.

'I think, gentlemen, with your indulgence I am going to have to ask for a few days to investigate this matter a little further,' said Sir Nigel.

Two days later, on 4 March, one of the senior Cabinet ministers in whom Mrs Thatcher had confided her desire to go for an early general election was having breakfast with his wife in their handsome town house in Holland Park, London. The wife was browsing through a sheaf of holiday brochures.

'Corfu is nice,' she said, 'or Crete.'

There was no response so she pressed her point. 'Darling, we should try and get away for a fortnight of complete rest this summer. It's been nearly two years, after all. What about June? Before the crush but when the weather is at its best.'

'Not June,' said the Minister without looking up.

'But June's beautiful,' she protested.

'Not June,' he repeated, 'anything but June.'

Her eyes widened. 'What's so important about June?'

'Never mind.'

'You cunning old fox,' she said breathlessly. 'It's Margaret, isn't it? That cosy little chat at Chequers last Sunday week. She's going to the country. Well, I'll be damned.'

'Shush,' said her husband, but after twenty-five years she knew when she had got it right.

She looked up to see Emma, their daughter, standing in the doorway. 'Are you off, darling?'

'Yeah,' said the girl, 'see you.'

Emma Lockwood was nineteen, a student at art college and subscribed with all her youthful enthusiasm to radical politics. She abominated her father's political views and sought to protest against them by her own lifestyle. To her parents' tolerant exasperation she was never missing from anti-nuclear protest. One of her areas of personal protest was to sleep with Simon Devine, a lecturer at a polytechnic college, whom she had met on a demo.

He was no great lover, but impressed her by his firebrand Trotskyism and pathological hatred of the 'bourgeoisie' which appeared to include anyone who did not agree with him. Those able to disagree more effectively than the bourgeoisie were termed Fascists. To him that evening, in his bedsitter, she vouchsafed the tip she had overheard while standing in the doorway of her parents' breakfast room.

Devine was a member of a number of revolutionary study groups and contributed articles to Hard Left publications of great passion and small circulation. Two days later he mentioned the nugget he had obtained from Emma Lockwood while he was in conference with one of the editors of a small broadsheet for whom he had prepared an article calling on all freedom-loving car workers at Cowley to destroy the production line over the issue of one of their number who had been fired for theft.

The editor advised Devine there was not enough in the rumour to make an article for the publication, but that he would discuss the information with his colleagues, and advised Devine to keep it to himself. When Devine had gone the editor did indeed discuss it with one of his colleagues, his conduit, and the conduit passed it on to the controller in the *rezidentura* inside the Soviet Embassy. On 10 March the news reached Moscow. Devine would have been appalled. As an ardent follower of Trotsky's call for instant global revolution, he hated Moscow and all it stood for.

* * *

Sir Nigel Irvine had been shaken by the revelation that the controller of a major spy within the British establishment was a South African diplomat and took up the only option left to him – a direct approach to the South African NIS to ask for an explanation.

The relationship between the British SIS and the South African NIS (and its predecessor the BOSS) would be described by a politician of either country as nonexistent. 'Arm's-length' would be more realistic. It exists, but for political reasons it is a difficult one.

Under successive British governments, because of the widespread distaste for the apartheid doctrine, the relationship has always been frowned on, more under Labour governments than Conservative. During the Labour years between 1964 and 1979 it was allowed to continue, oddly, because of the Rhodesian imbroglio. Labour Prime Minister Harold Wilson accepted that he needed all the information he could get on Ian Smith's Rhodesia to implement his sanctions, and the South Africans had most of it. By the time that affair was over the Conservatives were back in power in May 1979 and the relationship continued, this time due to concern over Namibia and Angola, where it had to be admitted the South Africans had good networks.

Nor was the relationship one-sided. It was the British who received a tip from the West Germans about the East German links of the wife of South African Navy Commodore Dieter Gerhardt – he was later arrested as a SovBloc spy. The British had also tipped off the South Africans about a couple of Soviet 'illegals' entering South Africa, using the SIS encyclopedic files on such gentlemen.

There was one unpleasant hiccough in 1967 when an agent of the BOSS, one Norman Blackburn, working as a barman at the Zambezi Club, bestowed his charms upon one of the Garden Girls. These are secretaries at 10 Downing Street, so called because they work in a room facing the garden.

The infatuated Helen (the name will suffice because she has long settled down with a family) passed several classified documents to Blackburn before the affair was discovered. It caused a stink and led to Harold Wilson's conviction ever afterwards that whatever went wrong, from corked wine to crop failure, was due to the BOSS.

After that the relationship steadied on to a more civilized course. The British maintain, therefore, a Head of Station of whom the NIS is informed, and who is normally resident in Johannesburg. No 'active measures' are conducted by the British on South African territory. The South Africans maintain several staffers at their embassy in London of whom SIS is aware, and a few outside the embassy on whom MI5 keeps a watchful eye. The task of the latter is to monitor the London-end activities of various Southern African revolutionary organizations like ANC, SWAPO and so forth. So long as the South Africans confine themselves to this, they are left alone.

It was the British Head of Station in Johannesburg who sought and got a personal interview with General Henry Pienaar and reported back to his Chief in London what the head of the NIS had to say. Sir Nigel convened a meeting of the Paragon Committee on 10 March.

'The great and good General Pienaar swears by all that he holds to be holy that he has no knowledge of Jan Marais. He claims Marais does not work for him and never has.'

'Is he telling the truth?' asked Sir Paddy Strickland.

'In this game one should never count on it,' said Sir Nigel. 'But it could be he is. For one thing, he would would have known for three days now that we have uncovered Marais. If Marais is his, he would know we would take terrible revenge. He has not moved out any of his people here, which I think he would if he knew he were guilty.'

'Then what the hell *is* Marais?' asked Sir Perry Jones.

'Pienaar claims he would like to know as much as we

would,' answered 'C'. 'In fact he has agreed to my request to receive our own investigator to carry out a joint hunt with his own people. I want to send a man down there.'

'What is the position on Berenson and Marais now?' asked Sir Anthony Plumb of Harcourt-Smith, who was representing Five.

'Both men are under discreet surveillance, but no moves have been made to close in. No break-in to either man's apartment. Just mail intercept, phone tap and the Watchers, round the clock,' replied Harcourt-Smith.

'How long do you want, Nigel?' asked Plumb.

'Ten days.'

'All right, but that's the limit. In ten days we have to move against Berenson with whatever we have got and start into damage assessment, with his willing or unwilling cooperation.'

The next day Sir Nigel Irvine called Sir Bernard Hemmings at his home outside Farnham, where the ailing man was confined. 'Bernard, that man of yours, Preston. I know it's unusual – could send one of my own people, and all that. But I like his style. Could I borrow him for the South African trip?'

Sir Bernard agreed. Preston flew to Johannesburg on the overnight flight of 12–13 March. It was not until he was airborne that the information reached the desk of Brian Harcourt-Smith. He was icily angry, but knew he had been outranked.

The Albion committee reported to the General Secretary on the evening of the 12th and was received in his apartment on Kutuzovsky Prospekt.

'And what, pray, have you got for me?' the Soviet leader asked quietly.

Professor Krilov, as chairman of the committee, gestured towards Grand Master Rogov, who opened the file in front of him and began to read.

As always in the presence of the General Secretary,

Philby was impressed, even awed, by the sheer untrammelled power of the man. During the Committee's researches the mere mention of his name as the overriding authority could have secured them anything they wanted in the USSR and no questions asked. As a student of power and its application, Philby admired the ruthless and cunning way in which the General Secretary had secured absolute power over every tendril of life in the Soviet Union.

Years earlier, when he had been given the powerful chairmanship of the KGB, it had not been as an appointee of Brezhnev, but of the unpublicized king-maker of the Politburo, the Party ideologue Mikhail Suslov. With this residual independence from Brezhnev and his personal mafia, he had ensured the KGB never became Brezhnev's unquestioning poodle. When, in May 1982, with Suslov dead and Brezhnev dying, he had quit the KGB to return to the Central Committee, he had not made the same mistake.

Behind him as Chairman of the KGB he had left General Fedorchuk, his personal placeman. From inside the Party, the General Secretary had consolidated his position with the Central Committee and then bided his time through the brief Andropov and Chernenko eras until his eventual accession. Within months of that accession he had sewn up the power sources: Party, armed forces, KGB and Interior Ministry, the MVD. With all the aces in his hands, no-one dared oppose or conspire.

'We have devised a plan, Comrade General Secretary,' said Dr Rogov, using, as they were among others, the formal term of address. 'It is a concrete plan, an active measure, a proposal to cause a destabilization among the British people that would make the Sarajevo affair and the Berlin Reichstag fire pale into insignificance. We have called it Plan Aurora.'

It took him an hour to read the full details. He glanced up occasionally to see if there was any reaction, but the General Secretary was a grand master in a much bigger game of chess and his face remained blank. At last Dr Rogov had finished. There was silence while they waited.

'It has risks,' said the General Secretary quietly. 'What guarantees are there that it would not backfire like certain . . . other operations?'

He had not mentioned the word, but they all knew what he meant. In his last year at the KGB he had been badly shaken by the dismal failure of the Wojtyla affair. It had taken three years for the rumbles and accusations to die away and it had caused the sort of global publicity the USSR definitely did not need.

In the early spring of 1981 the Bulgarian Secret Service had reported that their people among the Turkish community in West Germany had trawled a strange fish. For ethnic, cultural and historical reasons, the Bulgars, most loyal and subservient of Russia's satellites, were deeply involved in Turkey and the Turks. The man they had picked up was a dedicated terrorist killer who had been trained by the ultra-Left in Lebanon, killed for the ultra-Right Grey Wolves in Turkey, escaped from prison, and fled to West Germany. The odd thing about him was that he had expressed a personal obsession to kill the Pope. Should they throw Mehmet Ali Agca back into the ocean, or give him funds and false papers, along with a gun, and let him run?

In normal circumstances the KGB response would have been the cautious one: kill him. But circumstances were not normal. Karol Wojtyla, the world's first Polish Pope, was a major menace. Poland was in uproar; Communist rule there could soon be blown apart by the dissident Solidarity movement.

The dissident Wojtyla had already visited Poland once, with disastrous results from the Soviet point of view. He had to be stopped or discredited. The KGB replied to the Bulgars: go ahead, but we don't want to know. In May 1981, with money, false papers and a gun, Agca was escorted to Rome, pointed in the right direction and allowed his head. As a result a lot of people had lost theirs.

'With respect, I do not believe the two can be compared,' said Dr Rogov, who had principally devised Plan Aurora and was prepared to defend it. 'The Wojtyla affair was a disaster for three reasons: the target did not die; the assassin was caught alive; worst of all, there was no highly developed, in-place disinformation conspiracy to blame, for example, the Italian or American extreme Right. There should have been a tidal wave of believable evidence available for release proving to the world it was the Right who put Agca up to it.'

The General Secretary nodded like an old lizard.

'Here,' proceeded Rogov, 'the situation is different. There are fall backs and cutouts at every stage. The executant would be a top professional who would end his own life before capture. The physical artefacts are mostly harmless to look at and none can be traced back to the USSR. The executant officer cannot survive the execution of the plan. And there are subsequent subplans to place the blame firmly and convincingly on the Americans.'

The General Secretary turned to General Marchenko. 'Would it work?' he asked.

The three committee members were uncomfortable. It would have been easier to grasp the General Secretary's reaction, then agree with it. But he had given nothing away.

Marchenko took breath and nodded. 'It is feasible,' he agreed. 'I believe it would take from ten to sixteen months to put into operation.'

'Comrade Colonel?' asked the General Secretary of Philby.

Philby's stutter increased as he spoke. It always did when he was under stress. 'As to the risks, I am not best able to judge them. Nor the question of technical feasibility. As to effect – it would beyond any doubt swing over ten per cent of the British floating vote into a hasty decision to vote Labour.'

'Comrade Professor Krilov?'

'I have to oppose it, Comrade General Secretary. I regard it as extremely hazardous, in execution and in its possible consequences. It is completely contrary to the terms of the Fourth Protocol. If that is ever breached, we may all suffer.'

The General Secretary seemed lost in meditation, which no-one was about to disturb. The hooded eyes brooded behind the glittering glasses for five minutes. At length he raised his head. 'There are no notes, no tape recordings, no shreds of this plan outside this room?'

'None,' agreed the four committee men.

'Gather up the files and folders and pass them to me,' said the General Secretary. When this was done he went on, using his habitual monotone. 'It is reckless, crazy, adventurist and dangerous beyond belief,' he intoned. 'The committee is disbanded. You are to return to your professions and never mention either the Albion Committee or Plan Aurora again.'

He was still sitting there, staring at the table, when the four subdued and humbled men trooped out. They put on their coats and hats in silence, hardly meeting each other's eyes, and were led to their cars downstairs.

In the hollow courtyard they each climbed into their own car. In his personal Volga, Philby waited for Driver Gregoriev to start the engine, but the man just sat there. The other three limousines swept out of the square, under the arch and into the boulevard. There was a tap on Philby's window. He wound it down to see the face of Major Pavlov.

'Would you come with me, please, Comrade Colonel.'

Philby's heart sank. He understood now that he knew too much; he was the one foreigner in the group. The General Secretary had a reputation for tying up loose ends rather permanently. He followed Major Pavlov back into the building. Two minutes later he was shown back into the General Secretary's sitting-room. The old man was still in his wheelchair at the low coffee table. He gestured Philby to a seat. In trepidation the British traitor took it.

'What did you really think of it?' asked the General Secretary softly.

Philby swallowed hard. 'Ingenious, audacious, hazardous, but, if it worked, effective,' he said.

'It's brilliant,' murmured the General Secretary. 'And it is going ahead. But under my personal auspices. This is to be no-one else's operation, just mine. And you will be closely involved in it.'

'May I ask one thing?' Philby ventured. 'Why me? I am a foreigner, even if I have served the Soviet Union all my life and lived here for a third of it. I am still a foreigner.'

'Precisely,' replied the General Secretary, 'and you have no patronage except mine. You could not begin to conspire against me.

'You will take leave of your wife and family and dismiss your driver. You will take up residence in the guest suites at my dacha at Usovo. There you will put together the team that will undertake Plan Aurora. You will have any authority you need; it will come from my office at the Central Committee. You personally will not show yourself.' He pressed a buzzer under the table. 'You will work at all times under the eye of this man. I believe you already know him.'

The door had opened. In it stood the impassive, cold visage of Major Pavlov.

'He is highly intelligent and extremely suspicious,' said the General Secretary with approval. 'He is also totally loyal. He happens to be my nephew.'

As Philby rose to accompany the major, the General Secretary held out a slip of paper to him. It was a flimsy from the First Chief Directorate, marked for the personal attention of the General Secretary of the CPSU. Philby looked in disbelief.

'Yes,' said the General Secretary, 'it reached me yesterday. You will not have General Marchenko's ten to sixteen months. It appears Mrs Thatcher is going to make her move in June. We must make ours one week before that.'

Philby let out his breath slowly. In 1916 it had taken ten days to complete the Russian Revolution. Britain's greatest turncoat of them all was being given just ninety days to guarantee the British one.

Part Two

9

When John Preston landed at Jan Smuts Airport on the morning of the 13th, the local Head of Station, a tall, thin blond man called Dennis Grey was there to meet him. From the observation terrace two South African NIS men watched his arrival but made no move to come closer.

Customs and Immigration were a formality and within thirty minutes of touchdown the two Englishmen were speeding north to Pretoria. Preston looked at the landscape of the highveld with curiosity; it did not look much like his impression of Africa – just a modern six-lane black-top highway running across a bare plain and flanked by modern, European-style farms and factories.

'I've booked you into the Burgerspark,' said Grey. 'In central Pretoria. I was told you wanted to stay in a hotel rather than at the Residency.'

'Yes,' said Preston. 'Thank you.'

'We'll go and check in first. We have an appointment to meet the Beast at eleven.'

The not-too-affectionate title had originally been bestowed upon General Van Den Berg, a police general and head of the former Bureau of State Security, the BOSS. After the so-called Muldergate scandal of 1979 the unhappy marriage of the South African state's intelligence arm and its security police had been dissolved, to the great relief of the professional intelligence officers and the Foreign Service, some of whom had been consistently embarrassed by the BOSS's brass-knuckled tactics.

The intelligence arm had been reconstituted under the title National Intelligence Service and General Henry Pienaar had moved across from his post as head of Military Intelligence. He was not a police general but a military one, and while not a lifelong intelligence officer (IO) like

Sir Nigel Irvine, his years garnering military intelligence had taught him there were more ways to kill a cat than thumping it with blunt objects. General Van Den Berg had passed into retirement, still prepared to tell anyone who would listen to him that 'the hand of God was upon him'. Unkindly, the British had passed his nickname on to the shoulders of General Pienaar.

Preston registered into the hotel on Van Der Walt street, dumped his bags, had a quick wash and shave and joined Grey in the lobby at half past ten. From there they drove to Union Building.

The seat of most of the South African government is a huge, long, ochre-brown sandstone block, three storeys high, its 400-yard frontage studded by four colonnaded projections. It stands in central Pretoria on a hill gazing south across a valley along whose bed runs Kerk Straat, and the esplanade at the front of the block commands a panoramic view across the valley to the brown hills of the highveld to the south, topped by the squat square mass of the Voortrekker Monument.

Dennis Grey presented his identity at the reception desk and mentioned his appointment. In minutes a young official had appeared, to lead them to the office of General Pienaar. The headquarters of the NIS chief is on the top floor at the western end of the building. Grey and Preston were led down interminable corridors decorated in what appeared to be a standard South African civil-service brown and cream motif with a heavy accent on dark wood panelling. The general's office is at the end of the last corridor on the third floor, flanked by an office on the right containing two secretaries and another on the left containing two staff officers.

The official knocked on the last door, waited for the gruff command to enter, and showed the British visitors in. It was a fairly sombre, formal office, containing a large and obviously cleared desk facing the door, with a set of four leather club chairs grouped round a low table near the windows, which looked down towards Kerk Straat and across the valley to the hills. There were a number of what were apparently operational maps coyly covered in green curtains round the walls.

General Pienaar was a big, heavy man, who rose as they entered and walked forward to shake hands. Grey made the introductions and the general gestured them to the club chairs. Coffee was served, but the conversation remained at the level of small talk. Grey took the hint, made his farewells and left. General Pienaar stared at Preston for some time.

'So, Mr Preston,' he said in almost unaccented English, 'the subject of our diplomat Jan Marais. I have already told Sir Nigel and now I tell you: he does not work for me or my government, at least, not as a controller of agents in Britain. You are here to try and find out who he *does* work for?'

'That's my job, General, if I can.'

General Pienaar nodded several times. 'I have given Sir Nigel my word that you will have our complete cooperation here. And I will abide by my word.'

'Thank you, General.'

'I am going to attach to you one of my two personal staff officers. He will help you in anything you need; obtain files that you may wish to examine, interpret if necessary. You speak any Afrikaans?'

'No, General, not a word.'

'Then there will be some translating to be done. Perhaps some interpreting.'

He pressed a buzzer on the table and in seconds the door opened to admit a man of the same physical size as the general but much younger. Preston put him in his early thirties. He had ginger hair and sandy eyebrows.

'Let me introduce Captain Andries Viljoen. Andy, this is Mr John Preston from London, the one you will be working with.'

Preston rose to shake hands. He sensed a thinly veiled hostility in the young Afrikaner, perhaps a mirror of his superior's better-masked feelings.

'I have put a room at your disposal down the corridor,' said General Pienaar. 'Well, let's waste no more time, gentlemen. Please get on with it.'

When they were alone in the office set aside for them, Viljoen asked, 'What would you like to start with, Mr Preston?'

Preston sighed inwardly. The casual first-name informality back at Charles and Gordon was a lot easier to get along with.

'The personal file on Jan Marais, if you please, Captain Viljoen.'

The captain's triumph was evident as he produced it from a desk drawer. 'We have of course been going through it already,' he said. 'I took it out of Foreign Ministry Personnel Registry myself some days ago.' He placed it in front of Preston, a big fat file in a buff cover. 'Let me synthesize what we have been able to glean from it, if this will help you. Marais entered the South African Foreign Service in Cape Town in the spring of 1946. He has been in the service for forty years, a bit more, and is due to retire in December. He comes from a perfect Afrikaner background, and has never come under the slightest suspicion. That is why his behaviour in London appears such a mystery.'

Preston nodded. He did not need it spelled out any more clearly. The view here was that London had made a mistake. He opened the file. Among the top documents was a sheaf handwritten in English.

'That,' said Viljoen, 'is his hand-written autobiography, a requirement of candidates for the Foreign Service. In those days when the United Party under Jan Smuts was in power, there was a much greater use of English than today. Today such a document would be written in Afrikaans. Of course, candidates must be fluent in both languages.'

'Then I suppose we had better start with it,' said Preston. 'While I read it, could you please make a synopsis of his career while in the Service? Especially foreign postings, where, when and for how long?'

'All right,' nodded Viljoen. 'If he did go rotten, if he was turned, it probably happened somewhere abroad.'

Viljoen's stress on the word 'if' was just enough to imply his doubt, and the corrosive effect of foreigners upon good Afrikaners came out in the word 'abroad'.

Preston began to read.

I was born in August 1925 in the small farming town of Duiwelskloof in the Northern Transvaal, the only son of a farmer in the Mootseki Valley just outside the town. My father, Laurens Marais, was a pure Afrikaner, but my mother Mary was an Anglo. It was an unusual marriage in those days, but because of it I was brought up fluent in both English and Afrikaans.

My father was considerably older than my mother, who was of frail disposition and died when I was ten in one of the typhoid epidemics that in those days swept that region from time to time. My father was forty-six when I was born and my mother only twenty-five. He farmed potatoes and tobacco mainly, and also some chickens, geese, turkeys, cattle, sheep and wheat. All his life he was a strong supporter of the United Party, and I was named after Marshal Jan Smuts.

Preston broke off. 'I suppose all this would not have done his candidature any harm,' he suggested.

'No harm at all,' said Viljoen, looking over the passages. 'The United Party was still in power then. The National Party only won the country in 1948.'

Preston read on.

When I was seven I went to the local farm school in Duiwelskloof and at the age of twelve went on to the Merensky High which had been founded five years earlier. After the outbreak of war in 1939 my father, who was a keen admirer of Britain and the Empire, followed every item of news about the war in Europe on his wireless set, sitting on the stoep in the evenings after work. After my mother died we had become even closer and I too soon began to yearn to take part in the war.

Two days after my eighteenth birthday, in August 1943, I said goodbye to my father and took the train to Pietersburg and then changed for the line south to Pretoria. My father came as far as Pietersburg and my last sight of him was standing on the platform there waving me off to the war. The next day I walked into Defence headquarters in Pretoria, formally attested, signed on and was sent to Roberts Heights camp for basic training, kitting out, square-bashing and small-arms instruction. There I also volunteered to be red-tabbed.

'What does "red-tabbed" mean?' asked Preston.

Viljoen looked up from his writing. 'In those days only volunteers could be sent to fight outside the borders of South Africa,' he said. 'They could not be compelled. Those volunteering for combat overseas were given a red tab to wear.'

From Roberts Heights I was posted to the Witwatersrand Rifles/De La Rey Regiment, which had been amalgamated after the losses at Tobruk to form the Wits/De La Rey. We were sent by train to a transit camp at Hay Paddock near Pietermaritzburg and attached to reinforcements for the SA Sixth Division awaiting a transport to Italy. Finally, at Durban, we were all shipped out on the Duchess of Richmond, *up through the Suez Canal, and disembarked in late January at Taranto.*

Most of that Italian spring we were moving up towards Rome and it was with the Sixth Division, then composed of the 12th SA Motorized Brigade and the 11th SA Armoured Brigade, that we in the Wits/De La Rey went through Rome and began the move on Florence. On 13 July I was forward of Monte Benichi in the Chianti mountains with a scouting patrol from 'C' Company. In thickly wooded country I became separated from the rest of the patrol after dark and minutes later found myself surrounded by German troops of the Hermann Goering Division. I was, as they say, 'put in the bag'.

I was lucky to stay alive, but they put me in a truck with some other Allied prisoners and took us to a 'cage' or temporary camp at a place called La Tarina, north of Florence. The senior South African NCO, I recall, was Warrant Officer Snyman. It was not to be for long. As the Allies advanced through Florence we were suddenly subjected to a brutal night evacuation. It was chaos. Some prisoners tried to escape and were shot down. They were left lying in the road as the trucks rolled over them. From the trucks we were put into railcars built for cattle and went north for days, through the Alps and finally to a POW camp at Moosberg, twenty-five miles north of Munich.

Even this was not for long. After only fourteen days about half of us were marched out of Moosberg and back to the railhead, where we were entrained in cattle trucks again. With hardly any food or drink, we rolled across Germany for six days and nights, and in late August 1944 we were finally disembarked again and marched to another and much bigger camp. It was, we discovered, called Stalag 344, and was at Lamsdorf, near Breslau, in what was then German Silesia. I think Stalag 344 must have been the worst Stalag of them all. There were 11,000 Allied POWs there, on virtual starvation rations, kept alive mainly by Red Cross parcels.

As I was then a corporal I was required to join working parties, and was sent every day with many others by truck to work at a synthetic petrol factory twelve miles away. That winter in the Silesian plain was bitter. One day, just before Christmas, our truck broke down. Two POWs tried to mend it while the German guards kept them covered. Some of us were allowed to jump down near the tailboard. A young South African soldier near me stared at the pine forest only thirty yards away, looked at me and raised an eyebrow. I will never know why I did it, but the next moment we were both running through the thigh-deep snow while our comrades jostled the German guards to upset their aim. We made the forest line alive and ran on into the heart of the woods.

'Do you want to go out for lunch?' asked Viljoen. 'We have a canteen here.'

'Could we have sandwiches and coffee here, do you think?' asked Preston.

'Sure. I'll ring for them.'

Preston resumed the tale of Jan Marais.

We soon discovered that we had in effect jumped from the frying pan into the fire, except that it was not a fire but a freezing hell where the night temperatures sank to 30° below zero. We had out feet wrapped in paper inside our boots, but neither this nor our greatcoats could keep out the cold. After two days we were weak and at the point of giving ourselves up.

On the second night we were trying to sleep in a tumbled barn when we were roughly jerked awake. We thought it must be the Germans, but with Afrikaans I could understand some German words and these voices were not German. They were Polish; we had been discovered by a band of Polish partisans. They came within an inch of shooting us as German deserters, but I screamed that we were English and one of them seemed to understand.

It seemed that while most of the urban dwellers of Breslau and Lamsdorf were ethnic Germans, the peasants were of Polish stock, and as the Russian Army advanced, numbers of them had taken to the woods to harass the retreating Germans. There were two kinds of partisans: the Communist and the Catholic. We were lucky; it was a group of Catholic resistance fighters who had taken us in. They kept us through that bitter winter as the Russian guns rumbled in the east and the advance came closer. Then, in January, my comrade caught pneumonia; I tried to nurse him through it, but without antibiotics he died and we buried him in the forests.

Preston munched his sandwiches moodily and sipped his coffee. There were only a few pages left, he noted.

In March 1945 the Russian Army was suddenly upon us. In the woods we could hear their armour rumbling westwards down the roads. The Poles elected to stay in the forests, but I could take no more of it. They showed me the way to go, and one morning, with my hands above my head. I stumbled out of the forest and gave myself up to a group of Russian soldiers.

At first they thought I was a German and nearly shot me. But the Poles had told me to shout 'Angleeski', which I did repeatedly. They put up their rifles and called an officer. He spoke no English but after examining my dog tag said something to his soldiers, and they were all smiles. But if I hoped for an early repatriation, I was wrong again. They handed me over to the NKVD.

For five months, in a series of damp and icy cells, I was accorded brutal treatment, all of it in solitary confinement. I was interrogated repeatedly with third degree in an attempt to make me confess I was a spy. I refused and was sent naked back to my cell. By the late spring (the war was ending in Europe but I did not know this) my health broke completely and I was given a pallet bed to sleep on, and better food, though still uneatable by our South African standards.

Then some word must have come from the top. In August 1945, more dead than alive, I was taken many miles in a truck and finally at Potsdam in Germany handed over to the British Army. They were more kind than I can say, and after a period in a military hospital outside Bielefeld I was sent back to England. I spent a further three months at Killearn EMS Hospital, north of Glasgow, and finally in December 1945 I sailed on the Ile de France *from Southampton for Cape Town, arriving in late January this year.*

It was in Cape Town that I heard of the death of my dear father, my only relative left in the world. It caused me such distress that my health suffered a relapse and I entered the Wynberg Military Hospital here at Cape Town, where I stayed for a further two months.

I am now discharged, given a clean bill of health, and hereby apply to join the South African Foreign Service.

Preston closed the file and Viljoen looked up.

'Well,' said the South African, 'he has had a steady and blameless, if unspectacular, career since then, rising to the rank of First Secretary. He has had eight foreign postings, all the countries firmly pro-Western. That's quite a lot, but then he's a bachelor and that can make life easier in the service, except at the level of ambassador or minister, where a wife is more or less expected. You still think he went rotten somewhere along the line?'

Preston shrugged.

Viljoen leaned over and tapped the folder. 'You see what those Russian bastards did to him? That's why I think you are wrong, Mr Preston. So he likes ice cream, and he made a wrong-number phone call. A coincidence.'

'Maybe,' said Preston. 'This life story. There's something odd about it.'

Captain Viljoen shook his head. 'We've had this file in our hands ever since your Sir Nigel Irvine contacted the General. We have been over and over it. It's absolutely accurate. Every name, date, place, army camp, military unit, campaign and tiny detail. Even to the crops they used to grow before the war in the Mootseki Valley. The agriculture people confirmed that. Now they grow tomatoes and avocados up there, but in those days potatoes and tobacco. Nobody could have invented that story. No, if he went wrong at all, which I doubt, it was somewhere abroad.'

Preston looked glum. Outside the windows dusk was falling.

'All right,' said Viljoen, 'I am here to help you. Where do you want to start next?'

'I'd like to start at the beginning,' said Preston. 'This place Duiwelskloof, is it far?'

'About a four-hour drive. You want to go there?'

'Yes please. Could we start early? Say at six tomorrow morning?'

'I'll get a car from the pool and be at your hotel at six,' said Viljoen.

It's a long haul on the road north to Zimbabwe, but the motorway is modern and Viljoen had drawn a Chevair without insignia, the car usually driven by the NIS. It ate up the miles through Nylstroom and Potgietersrus to Pietersburg, which they reached in three hours. The drive gave Preston a chance to see the great limitless horizons of Africa that impress the European visitor, accustomed to smaller dimensions.

At Pietersburg they turned east and ran for 50 kilometres over flat middle veld, more endless horizons under a robin's egg blue vault of sky, until they reached the bluff called Buffalo Hill where the middle veld drops to the Mootseki Valley. As they started down the twisting gradient Preston drew in his breath in amazement.

Far below lay the valley, rich and lush, its open floor strewn with a thousand beehive-shaped African huts, the rondavels, surrounded by kraals, cattle pens and mealie gardens. Some of the rondavels were perched on the side of the Buffelberg but most were scattered across the floor of the Mootseki. Timber smoke eddied from their central smoke holes and even from the height and distance he could make out the African boys tending small groups of humped cattle and women bent over their garden patches.

This, he thought, is African Africa at last. It must have looked much the same when the *impis* of Mzilikazi, founder of the Matabele nation, marched north to escape the wrath of Chaka Zulu, to cross the Limpopo and found the kingdom of the people of the long shields. The road bucked and twisted down the bluff and into the Mootseki. Across the valley was another range of hills and in the centre a deep cleft through which the road ran. This was the gap, the Devil's Gap, the Duiwelskloof.

Ten minutes later they were into the gap and cruising

slowly past the new primary school and down Botha Avenue, the principal street of the small township.

'Where do you want to go?' asked Viljoen.

'When old Farmer Marais died, he must have left a will,' mused Preston. 'And that would have to be executed, and that means a lawyer. Can we find out if there is a lawyer in Duiwelskloof, and if he is there on a Saturday morning?'

Viljoen drew into the forecort of Kirstens Garage and pointed across the road at the Imp Inn. 'Go and have a coffee and order one for me. I'll tank up and ask around.'

He rejoined Preston in the hotel lounge five minutes later. 'There's one lawyer,' he said as he sipped his coffee, 'he's an Anglo. Name of Benson. It's right there across the street, two doors from the garage. And he'll probably be in this morning. Let's go.'

Mr Benson was in. Viljoen flashed a card in a plastic wallet at his secretary, which had an immediate effect. She talked in Afrikaans into an intercom and they were shown without delay into the office of Mr Benson, a friendly and rubicund man in a fawn suit. He greeted them both in Afrikaans. Viljoen replied in his heavily accented English.

'This is Mr Preston. He has come from London, England. He wishes to ask you some questions.'

Mr Benson bade them be seated and resumed his chair behind the desk. 'Please,' he gestured, 'anything I can do.'

'Can you tell me how old you are?' asked Preston.

Benson gazed at him in amazement. 'All the way from London to ask how old I am? As a matter of fact I'm fifty-three.'

'So in 1946 you would have been twelve?'

'Yes.'

'Can you tell me, please, who was the lawyer here in Duiwelskloof in that year?'

'Certainly. My father. Cedric Benson.'

'Is he alive?'

'Yes. He's over eighty and he handed over to me fifteen years ago. But he's pretty spry.'

'Would it be possible to talk to him?'

For answer Mr Benson reached for a telephone and dialled a number. His father must have answered, for the son explained there were visitors, one from London, who would like to talk to him. He replaced the receiver.

'He lives about six miles away, but he still drives, to the terror of all other road users. He says he'll be here directly.'

'In the interim,' asked Preston, 'could you consult your files for the year 1946 and see if you, or rather your father, executed the will of a local farmer, one Laurens Marais, who died in January of that year?'

'I'll try,' said Benson Junior. 'Of course, this Mr Marais may have been with a lawyer from Pietersburg. But local people tended to stay local in those days. The 1946 box must be around somewhere. Excuse me.'

He left the office. The secretary served coffee. Ten minutes later there were voices in the outer office. The two Bensons entered together, the son carrying a dusty cardboard box. The old man had a fuzz of white hair and looked as alert as a young kestrel. After the introductions Preston explained his problem.

Without a word the older Benson took the chair behind the desk, forcing his son to draw up another one. Old Benson placed glasses on his nose and gazed at the visitors over them. 'I remember Laurens Marais,' he said. 'And, yes, we did handle his will when he died. I did it myself.'

The son passed him a dusty and faded document tied in pink ribbon. The old man blew the dust off it, untied the ribbon and spread it out. He began to read it silently.

'Ah yes, I remember it now. He was a widower. Lived alone. Had one son, Jan. A tragic case. The boy had just come back from the Second World War. Laurens Marais was going down to Cape Town to visit him when he died. Tragic.'

'Can you tell me about the bequests?' asked Preston.

'Everything to the son,' said Benson simply. 'Farm, house, equipment, contents of house. Oh, the usual small bequests in money to the native farm workers, foreman and that sort of thing.'

'Any personal bequests, anything of a personal nature?' persisted Preston.

'Humph. One here. "To my old and good friend Joop Van Rensberg my ivory chess set in memory of the many contented evenings we spent playing together at the farm." That's all.'

'Was the son back home in South Africa when the father died?' asked Preston.

'Must have been. Old Laurens was going down to see him. A long trip in those days. No airliners then. One went by train.'

'Did you handle the sale of the farm and the other property, Mr Benson?'

'The auctioneers did the sale, right out at the farm. It went to the Van Zyls. They bought the lot. All that land belongs to Bertie Van Zyl now. But I was there as chief executor of the will.'

'Were there any personal memorabilia that did not sell?' asked Preston.

The old man furrowed his brow. 'Not much. It all went. Oh, I recall there was a photograph album. It had no commercial value. I believe I gave it to Mr Van Rensberg.'

'Who was he?'

'The schoolmaster,' cut in the son. 'He taught me, until I went to Merensky High. He ran the old farm school until they built the primary school. Then he retired, here in Duiwelskloof.'

'Is he still alive?'

'No, he died about ten years ago,' said the older Benson. 'I went to the funeral.'

'But there was a daughter,' said his son helpfully. 'Cissy. She was at Merensky with me. Must be the same age.'

'Do you know what happened to her?'

'Certainly. She married years ago. A sawmill owner out on the Tzaneen road.'

'One last question.' Preston addressed himself to the old man. 'Why did you sell up the property? Didn't the son want it?'

'Apparently not,' said the old man. 'He was in the Wynberg Military Hospital at the time. He sent me a cable. I got his address from the military authorities and they vouched for his identity. His cable asked me to realize the entire estate and cable the money to him.'

'He did not come for the funeral?'

'No time. January is our summer in South Africa. In those days there were few morgue facilities. Bodies had to be buried without delay. In fact, I don't think he ever returned at all. Understandable. With his father gone there was nothing to come back for.'

'Where is Laurens Marais buried?'

'In the graveyard up on the hill,' said Benson Senior. 'Is that all? Then I'll be off to my lunch.'

The climate east and west of the mountains at Duiwelskloof varies dramatically. West of the range the rainfall in the Mootseki is about 20 inches a year. East of the range the great clouds beat up from the Indian Ocean, drift across Mozambique and the Kruger Park and butt into the mountains, whose eastern slopes are drenched with 80 inches of rain a year. On this side the industry comes from the forests of blue gum trees. Six miles up the Tzaneen road Viljoen and Preston found the sawmill of Mr du Plessis. It was his wife, the schoolmaster's daughter, who opened the door, a plump apple-cheeked woman of about fifty, with flour on her hands and apron. She was in the throes of baking.

She listened to their problem intently, then shook her head. 'I remember as a small girl going out to the farm, and him playing chess with Farmer Marais,' she said. 'That would be about 1944 and 1945. I recall the ivory chess set, but not the album.'

'When your father died, did you not inherit his effects?' asked Preston.

'No,' said Mrs du Plessis. 'You see, my mother died in

1955, leaving Daddy a widower. I looked after him myself until I married in 1958 when I was twenty-three. After that he couldn't cope. His house was always a mess. I tried to keep going to cook and clean for him. But when the children came, it was too much.

'Then in 1960 his sister, my aunt, was widowed in her turn. She had lived at Pietersburg. It made sense for her to come and live with my father and look after him. So she did. When he died I had already asked him to leave it all to her – the house, furniture and so forth.'

'What happened to the aunt?' asked Preston.

'Oh, she still lives there. It's a modest bungalow just behind the Imp Inn back in Duiwelskloof.'

She agreed to accompany them. Her aunt, Mrs Winter, was at home, a bright, sparrow-like lady with blue-rinsed hair. When she had heard them she went to a cupboard and pulled out a flat box.

'Poor Joop used to love playing with this,' she said. It was the ivory chess set. 'Is this what you want?'

'Not quite, it's more the photograph album,' said Preston.

She looked puzzled. 'There *is* a box of old junk up in the loft,' she said. 'It went up there after he died. Just papers and things from his school-mastering days.'

Andries Viljoen went up to the attic and brought it down. At the bottom of the yellowed school reports was the Marais family album. Preston leafed through it slowly. It was all there: the frail pretty bride of 1920, the shyly smiling mother of 1930, the frowning boy astride his first pony, the father with pipe clamped in teeth, trying not to look too proud with his son by his side and a row of rabbits on the grass in front of them. At the end was a monochrome photo of a boy in cricket flannels, a handsome lad of seventeen, coming up to the wicket to bowl. The caption said 'Janni, captain of cricket, Merensky High, 1943.' It was the last entry.

'May I keep this?' said Preston.

'Certainly,' said Mrs Winter.

'Did your late brother ever talk to you about Mr Marais?'

'Sometimes,' she said. 'They were very good friends for many years.'

'Did he ever say what he died of?'

She frowned. 'Didn't they tell you at the lawyer's office? Tut. Old Cedric must be losing his wits. It was a hit-and-run accident, Joop told me. It seems old Marais had stopped to repair a puncture and he was hit by a passing truck. At the time it was thought to be some drunken kaffirs – oops—' Her hand flew to her mouth and she looked at Viljoen with embarrassment. 'I'm not supposed to say that any more. Well, anyway, they never found out who was driving the truck.'

On the way back down the hill to the main road they passed the graveyard. Preston asked Viljoen to stop. It was a pleasant quiet plot, high above the town, fringed by pine and fir, dominated in its centre by an old mwataba tree with a cleft trunk, and enclosed by a hedge of poinsettia. In one corner they found a moss-covered stone. Scraping away the moss, Preston found the motto carved in the granite: 'Laurens Marais 1879–1946. Beloved husband of Mary and father of Jan. Always with God. RIP.'

Preston strolled across to the hedge, plucked a sprig of flaming poinsettia and laid it by the stone. Viljoen looked at him oddly.

'Pretoria, I think,' said Preston.

As they were climbing the Buffelberg on the road out of the Mootseki, Preston turned to look across the valley. Dark grey storm clouds had built up behind the Devil's Gap. As he watched they closed in, blotting out the little town and its macabre secret known only to a middle-aged Englishman in a retreating car. Then he put his head back and fell asleep.

That evening Harold Philby was escorted from the guest suite to the sitting-room of the General Secretary, where the Soviet leader awaited him. Philby laid several documents in front of the old man.

The General Secretary read them and laid them down. 'There are not many people involved,' he said.

'Permit me to make two important points, Comrade General Secretary. First, because of the extreme confidentiality of Plan Aurora, I have thought it wise to keep the number of participants to an absolute minimum. On a need-to-know basis, even fewer would know what is really intended.

'Secondly, and yet conversely, because of the extreme shortness of time, there will have to be some cutting of corners. The weeks, even months, of briefing habitually required for an important active measure will have to be telescoped into days.'

The General Secretary nodded slowly. 'So explain why you need these men.'

'The key to the whole operation,' Philby continued, 'is the Executive Officer, the man who will actually go into Britain and live there for weeks as a Britisher, and who will finally carry out Aurora.

'Supplying him with what he needs will be twelve couriers or "mules". They will have to smuggle the items in, either through a Customs point or, on occasion, through an unchecked entry point. Each will know nothing of what he is carrying or why; each will have memorized a rendezvous, and another as fallback in case of a non-connect. Each will hand over the package to the Executive Officer and then return to our territory, to pass immediately into total quarantine. There will be one other man, apart from the Executive Officer, who will never return. But neither of these men should know this.

'Commanding the couriers will be the Despatching Officer with responsibility to ensure that the consignments reach the Executive Officer in Britain. He will be supported by a Procurement/Supply Officer charged with procuring the packages for delivery. This man will have four subordinates, each with one speciality.

'One will furnish the couriers' documentation and transportation; another will concern himself with obtaining the high technology; the third will provide the milled and engineered artefacts; and the fourth will assure communications. It will be vital that the Executive Officer can inform us of progress, problems and, above all, of the moment he is operationally ready; and we must be able to inform him of any change of plan, and, of course, give him the order to execute the plan.

'In the matter of communications there is one more thing to say. Because of the time element, it will not be possible to proceed through normal channels of mailed letters or personal meetings. We can communicate with the Executive Officer by coded Morse signals sent on Radio Moscow's commercial wavebands, using one-time pads. But for him to reach us urgently, he is going to need a transmitter somewhere in Britain. It's old-fashioned and risky, mainly intended for use in time of war. But it will have to be. You will see I have made mention of it.'

The General Secretary studied the documents again, identifying the executives that the plan would need. Finally he looked up. 'You will get your men,' he said. 'I will have them traced one by one, the very best we have, and transferred to special duties.

'One last thing. I do not wish anyone connected with Aurora to make contact of any form with the KGB people inside our *rezidentura* at the embassy in London. One never knows who is under surveillance, or . . .' Whatever his other fear, he left it unsaid. 'That is all.'

10

Preston and Viljoen convened in their office on the third floor of Union Building the next morning at the Englishman's request. As it was a Sunday, they had the block almost to themselves.

'Well, what next?' asked Captain Viljoen.

'I lay awake last night thinking,' said Preston, 'and there's something that doesn't fit.'

'You slept all the way back from the north,' said Viljoen grimly. 'I had to drive.'

'Ah, but you're so much fitter,' said Preston.

That pleased Viljoen, who was proud of his physique, which he exercised regularly. He unbent somewhat.

'I want to trace the other soldier,' said Preston.

'What other soldier?'

'The one Marais escaped with. He never mentions his name. Just "the other soldier" or "my comrade". Why doesn't he give him a name?'

Viljoen shrugged. 'He didn't think it necessary. He must have told the authorities at Wynberg Hospital so the next-of-kin could be informed.'

'That was verbal,' mused Preston. 'The officers who heard him would soon have scattered into civilian life. Only the written record remains, and it mentions no name. I want to trace the other soldier.'

'But he's dead,' protested Viljoen. 'He's been in a grave in a Polish forest for forty-two years.'

'Then I want to find out who he was.'

'Where the hell do we start?'

'Marais says they were kept alive in that camp mainly by Red Cross food parcels,' Preston said, as if thinking aloud. 'He also says they escaped just before Christmas. That would have upset the Germans a bit. It was usual for the whole block to be punished – loss of privileges, including food parcels. Everyone in the block would be likely to remember that Christmas for the rest of their lives. Can we find someone who was in that block?'

There is no former prisoners-of-war association in South Africa, but there is a brotherhood of war veterans, confined to those who have actually been in combat. It is called the Memorable Order of Tin Hats and its members are known as MOTHs. Each MOTH branch meeting room is called a shell hole, and the commanding officer is the Old Bill. Using a telephone each, Preston and Viljoen began to call up every shell hole in South Africa, trying to find anyone who was in Stalag 344.

It was a wearying task. Of the 11,000 Allied prisoners in that camp, the great bulk were from Britain, Canada, Australia, New Zealand or America. The South Africans were a minority.

Moreover, in the intervening years many had died. Of the MOTHs, some were out on the golf links, others away from home. They got regretful disclaimers and a host of helpful suggestions that turned out to be blind alleys. They broke for the day at sundown and started again on the Monday morning. Viljoen got his break just before noon; it came in the form of a retired meat-packer in Cape Town. Viljoen, who was speaking in Afrikaans, put his hand over the receiver. 'Guy here says he was in Stalag 344.'

Preston took over. 'Mr Anderson? Yes, my name is Preston. I am doing some research about Stalag 344 . . . Thank you, very kind . . . yes, I believe you were there. Do you remember Christmas 1944? Two young South African soldiers escaped from an outside work party . . . Ah, you do recall it. Yes, I'm sure it was pretty awful . . . Do you recall their names? Ah, not in their hut? No, of course. Well, do you remember the name of the senior South African NCO? Good, Warrant Officer Roberts. Any first name? . . . Please try to remember. What? Wally. You're sure of that? Many thanks indeed.'

Preston put the phone down. 'Warrant Officer Wally Roberts. Probably Walter Roberts. Can we go to the Military Archive?'

The South African Military Archive is found, for some reason, under the Department of Education and is situated beneath 20 Visagie Street, Pretoria. There were over a hundred Roberts listed, nineteen of them with the initial W, and seven called Walter. None fitted. They went through the rest of the W. Roberts. Nothing. Preston started with the A. Roberts files and was lucky one hour later. James Walter Roberts had been a warrant officer in the Second World War, captured at Tobruk and imprisoned in North Africa, Italy and finally eastern Germany. He had stayed on in the Army after the war and risen to the rank of colonel, retiring in 1972.

'You'd better pray he's still alive,' said Viljoen.

'If he is, he'll be drawing a pension,' said Preston. 'The Pensions people might have him.'

They did. Colonel (rtd) Wally Roberts was spending the autumn of his life at Orangeville, a small town set amid lakes and forests a hundred miles south of Johannesburg. It was dark out on Visagie Street when they emerged. They decided to drive down the next morning.

It was Mrs Roberts who opened the door of the neat bungalow and examined Captain Viljoen's identity card with flustered alarm.

'He's down by the lake feeding the birds,' she told them and pointed out the path. They found the old warrior distributing morsels of bread to a grateful flock of waterbirds. He straightened up when they approached and examined Viljoen's card. Then he nodded as if to say, 'Carry on.'

He was in his seventies, ramrod erect, in tweeds and highly polished brown shoes, a bristle of white across his upper lip. He listened gravely to Preston's question.

'Certainly I remember. I was hauled up before the German commandant who was in the devil of a rage. The whole hut lost their Red Cross parcels for that episode.

Damn young fools; we were evacuated westwards on 22 January 1945 and liberated in late April.'

'Do you remember their names?' asked Preston.

'Certainly. Never forget a name. Both were young, late teens I should think. Both were corporals. One was called Marais, the other was Brandt. Frikki Brandt. Both Afrikaners. Can't recall their units though. We were all so muffled up, wearing whatever we could. Hardly ever saw regimental flashes.'

They thanked him profusely and drove back to Pretoria, for another session at Visagie Street. Unfortunately, Brandt is a very common Dutch name, with its variation Brand which lacks the terminal 't' but is pronounced the same. There were hundreds of them.

By nightfall, with the aid of the Archive staff, they had culled six Corporal Frederik Brandts, all deceased. Two had died in action in North Africa, two in Italy and one in a capsized landing craft. They opened the sixth file.

Captain Viljoen stared wide-eyed at the open file. 'I don't believe it,' he said softly. 'Who could have done it?'

'Who knows?' Preston replied. 'But it was a long time ago.'

The file was completely empty.

'I'm sorry about that,' said Viljoen as he drove Preston back to the Burgerspark. 'But it looks like the end of the trail.'

Late that evening from his hotel room Preston called Colonel Roberts. 'Sorry to trouble you again, Colonel. Do you recall at all whether Corporal Brandt had any special mate or friend in that hut? My own experience in the army is that there is usually one close mate.'

'Quite right, there usually is. I can't recall offhand. Let me sleep on it. If I think of anything I'll call you in the morning.'

The helpful colonel called Preston over breakfast. The clipped voice came down the line as if he were making a battle sitrep to headquarters. 'Remember something,' he said. 'Those huts were built for about a hundred men. But we were jammed in there at the end like sardines. Over two hundred chaps to a hut. Some slept on the floor, others had to share a bunk. Nothing poofy, you know, just had to be done.'

'I understand,' said Preston. 'And Brandt?'

'Shared a bunk with another corporal. Name of Levinson. RDLI.'

'I beg your pardon?'

'Royal Durban Light Infantry. Levinson was.'

Visagie Street came up faster this time. Levinson was not nearly so common a name, and they had a regiment. The file was out in fifteen minutes. His name was Max Levinson and he had been born in Durban. He had quit the army at the end of the war, so there was no pension and no address. But they knew he was sixty-five years old.

Preston tried the Durban telephone directory while Viljoen had Durban police run the name through their files. Viljoen came up first. There were two parking tickets and an address. Max Levinson ran a small hotel on the seafront. Viljoen called and got Mrs Levinson. She confirmed her husband had been in Stalag 344. At the moment he was out fishing.

They twiddled their thumbs until he came back at nightfall, then Preston spoke to him. The cheerful hotelier boomed down the line from the east coast. 'Sure I remember Frikki. Silly bastard did a runner into the woods. Never did hear of him again. What about him?'

'Where did he come from?' asked Preston.

'East London,' said Levinson without hesitation.

'What was his background?'

'He never said much about it,' replied Levinson. 'Afrikaner, of course. Fluent Afrikaans, poor English. Working class. Oh, I remember, he said his dad was a shunter in the railway yards there.'

Preston made his goodbyes and turned to Viljoen. 'East London,' he said, 'can we drive there?'

Viljoen sighed. 'I wouldn't advise it,' he said. 'It's hundreds of miles. We're a very big country, Mr Preston.

If you really want, we'll go by plane tomorrow. I'll arrange a police car and driver to meet us.'

'Unmarked car, please,' said Preston. 'Driver in plain clothes.'

Although the headquarters of the KGB is at the 'Centre' at number 2 Dzerzhinsky Square in central Moscow, and though the building is not small, it is far too cramped to contain even a portion of one of the Chief Directorates, Directorates and Departments that make up this huge organization. So the sub-headquarters are scattered all over.

The First Chief Directorate is based at Yasyenevo on the outer ring road around Moscow, almost due south of the city. Almost all the FCD is housed in a modern aluminium and glass seven-storey edifice shaped in the form of a three-pointed star, rather like the logo of Mercedes cars.

It was built by the Finns on contract and was intended for the International Department of the Central Committee. But when it was finished, the ID people did not like it; they wanted to stay close to central Moscow, so it was given to the FCD. It suits the First Chief Directorate admirably, being well out of town and away from prying eyes.

Staffers of the FCD are officially 'under cover' even in their own country. As many of them will have to go abroad (or already have been) posing as diplomats, the last thing they need is to be seen coming out of FCD headquarters by a nosy tourist who might put them on candid camera.

But there is one Directorate within the FCD that is so secret it is not even based with the rest at Yasyenevo. If the FCD is secret, the 'S' or Illegals Directorate within it is top secret. Not only do its agents not meet their fellow FCD colleagues, they do not even meet each other. Their training and briefing are on a one-to-one basis, just the instructor and one pupil. They do not check in each morning to any office, since that way they would see each other.

The reason is simple in Soviet psychology: Russians are paranoid about secrecy and betrayal – there is nothing particularly Communist about this, it goes back to czarist days. The 'Illegals' are men and occasionally women who are rigorously trained to go into foreign countries and live under deep cover.

Yet 'Illegals' have been caught and have cooperated with their captors; others have defected and spilled all they knew. Therefore, the less they know the better. It is axiomatic in espionage that one cannot betray what or whom one does not know.

The 'Illegals' therefore are boarded out in scores of small flats in central Moscow, and report singly for training and briefing. In order to be close to his 'lads', the Director of the S Directorate still keeps his office at the Centre on Dzerzhinsky Square. It is on the sixth floor, three storeys above Chairman Chebrikov and two above his First Deputy Chairman, Generals Tsinev and Kryuchkov.

It was to this unpretentious sanctum that two men came on the afternoon of Wednesday, 18 March, while Preston was talking to Max Levinson, to confront the Director of the Illegals, a seamy old veteran who had been in clandestine espionage all his adult life. What they presented to him did not please him.

'There is only one man who fits this bill,' he grudgingly admitted. 'He is outstanding.'

One of the men from the Central Committee offered a small card. 'Then, Comrade Major-General, you will detach him from his duties forthwith and require him to report to this address.'

The Director nodded glumly. He knew the address. When the men had gone he recalled their authorization again. It was from the Central Committee all right, and though it did not say so in as many words, he had no doubt from whom it came with that kind of authority rating. He sighed resignedly. It was hard to lose one of the best men he had ever trained, a really exceptional agent, but there was no arguing with that particular order. He was a serving officer; it was not for him to question orders. He depressed a switch on his intercom.

'Tell Major Valeri Petrofsky to report to me,' he said.

The first plane out of Johannesburg for East London arrived on time at Ben Schoeman, the small, neat, blue and white airport which serves South Africa's fourth commercial port and city. The police driver was waiting in the concourse and led them to a plain Ford saloon in the parking lot.

'Where to, Captain?' he asked. Viljoen raised an eyebrow at Preston.

'The railway headquarters,' said Preston. 'More particularly, the administration building.'

The driver nodded and set off. East London's modern railway station is on Fleet Street, and directly opposite stands a rather shabby old complex of single-storey buildings in green and cream, the administration offices.

Inside, Viljoen's open-sesame identity card brought them quickly to the director of the finance department. He listened to Preston's query.

'Yes, we do pay pensions to all retired railway staff still living in this area,' he said. 'What was the name?'

'Brandt,' said Preston. 'I'm afraid I don't have a first name. But he was a shunter, many years ago.'

The director summoned an assistant and they all trooped down dingy corridors to the records office. The assistant burrowed for a while and came up with a pension slip.

'Here he is,' he said. 'The only one we have. Retired three years ago. Koos Brandt.'

'How old would he be?' asked Preston.

'Sixty-three,' said the assistant after a glance at the card. Preston shook his head. If Frikki Brandt had been the same age as Jan Marais, and his father about thirty years older, the old man would be over ninety.

'The man I seek would be about ninety by now,' he said.

The director and his assistant were adamant. There were no other retired Brandts.

'Then can you find me,' asked Preston, 'the three oldest pensioners still alive and in receipt of their weekly pension?'

'They're not listed by age,' protested the assistant. 'They're listed alphabetically.'

Viljoen drew the director aside and spoke urgently in his ear in Afrikaans. Whatever he said had its effect. The director looked impressed.

'Go ahead,' he told his assistant. 'One by one. Anyone born before 1910. We'll be in my office.'

It took an hour. The assistant produced three pension slips.

'There's one of ninety,' he said, 'but he was a porter at the passenger terminal. One of eighty, a former cleaner. This one is eighty-one. He's a former shunter from the marshalling yards.'

The man was called Fourie and his address was given as somewhere up in the Quigney.

Ten minutes later they were driving through the Quigney, the old quarter of East London, dating back fifty years and more. Some of its humble bungalows had been done up; others were shabby and run down, the homes of the poorer white working class. From behind Moore Street they could hear the clang of the railway workshops and the shunting yards, where the big trains are assembled to haul freight from the docks of East London up to the land-locked Transvaal via Bloemfontein. They found the house one block off Moore Street.

An old coloured woman answered the door, face like a pickled walnut and white hair drawn back in a bun. Viljoen spoke to her in Afrikaans. The old woman pointed towards the horizon and muttered something before firmly closing the door. Viljoen escorted Preston back to the car.

'She says he's up at the Institute,' Viljoen told the driver. 'Know what she means?'

'Yes, sir. The old Railway Institute. Now they call it Turnbull Park. Up Paterson Street. It's the social and recreation club for railway workers.'

It turned out to be a large, single-storey building set in a walled car park adjacent to its own three bowling greens. Through the doors they passed an array of snooker tables and TV lounges before arriving at a flourishing bar.

'Papa Fourie?' said the barman. 'Sure, he's out there watching the bowling.'

They found the old man by one of the greens, sitting in the warm autumn sunshine nursing a pint of beer. Preston put his question.

The old man stared at him for a while before nodding. 'Yes, I remember Joe Brandt. He's been dead these many years.'

'He had a son. Frederik, or Frikki.'

'That's right. Good heavens, young man, you're taking me back quite a bit. Nice kid. Used to come down to the yards sometimes after school. Joe used to let him ride the shunting locos with him. Quite a treat for a lad in those days.'

'That would be the mid to late 1930's?' asked Preston.

The old man nodded. 'About then. Just after Joe and his family came here.'

'Around 1943 the boy Frikki went away to the war,' said Preston.

Papa Fourie stared at him for a while from rheumy eyes that were trying to look backwards through more than fifty years of uneventful life. That's right,' he said. 'The boy never came back. They told Joe he had died somewhere in Germany. It broke Joe's heart. He doted on that boy, had great plans for him. He was never the same, not after that telegram arrived at the end of the war. He died in 1950, I always reckoned of a broken heart. His wife wasn't long after him, couple of years perhaps.'

'You said just now "just after Joe and his family came

here",' Viljoen reminded him. 'Which part of South Africa did they come from?'

Papa Fourie looked puzzled. 'They didn't come from South Africa,' he said.

'They were an Afrikaner family,' repeated Viljoen.

'Who told you that?'

'The Army,' said Viljoen.

The old man smiled. 'I suppose young Frikki would have passed himself off as an Afrikaner in the army,' he said. 'No, they came from Germany. Immigrants. About the middle of the thirties. Joe never spoke good Afrikaans to the day he died. Of course, the boy did. Learned at school.'

When they were back in the parked car Viljoen turned to Preston and asked, 'Well?'

'Where are the records of the Immigration people kept in South Africa?'

'In the basement at Union Building, along with the rest of the state archives,' said Viljoen.

'Could the archivists up there run a check for me while we wait here?' asked Preston.

'Sure. Let's go to the police station. We can phone better from there.'

The police station is also on Fleet Street, a three-floor yellow-brick fortress with opaque windows, right next to the drill hall of the Kaffrarian Rifles. They put in their request and lunched in the canteen, while up in Pretoria an archivist lost his lunch hour while he went through the files. Happily, they had all been computerized and the file number came up quickly. The archivist withdrew the file, typed up a resumé and put it on the telex.

In East London the telex was brought to Preston and Viljoen over coffee. Viljoen translated it word for word.

'Good God,' he said when he had finished it. 'Who would ever have thought it?'

Preston seemed pensive. He rose and crossed the canteen to speak to their driver who was at a separate table. 'Is there a synagogue in East London?'

'Yes, sir. In Park Avenue. Two minutes from here.'

The white-painted, black-domed synagogue, surmounted by the star of David, was empty on a Thursday afternoon, save for a coloured caretaker in an old army greatcoat and wool bonnet. He gave them the address of Rabbi Blum in the suburb of Salbourne. They knocked on his door just after three o'clock.

He opened it himself, a stalwart, bearded man in his mid-fifties with iron-grey hair. One glance was enough; he was too young.

Preston introduced himself. 'Can you tell me please, who was the rabbi here before yourself?'

'Certainly, Rabbi Shapiro.'

'Have you any idea if he is still alive and where I might find him?'

'You'd better come in,' said Rabbi Blum.

He led the way into his house, down a corridor and opened a door at the end. The room was a bedsitter, in which a very old man sat before a gas fire sipping a cup of black tea.

'Uncle Solomon, there's someone here to see you,' he said.

Preston left the house an hour later and rejoined Viljoen, who had returned to the car.

'The airport,' Preston told the driver, and to Viljoen, 'Could you arrange a meeting with General Pienaar tomorrow morning?'

That afternoon two more men were transferred from their posts in the Soviet armed forces to special assignment.

West of Moscow about a hundred miles, just off the road to Minsk and set in a large forest, is a complex of radio dish aerials and supporting buildings. It is one of the USSR's listening posts for radio signals coming in from Warsaw Pact military units and from abroad, but it can also listen in to messages between other parties far outside the Soviet borders. One section of the complex is screened off and is solely for KGB use.

One of the men was a warrant officer radio operator from his section.

'He's the best man I've got,' complained the commanding colonel to his deputy when the men from the Central Committee had left. 'Good? I'll say he's good. Given the equipment, he can pick up a cockroach scratching its arse in California.'

The other posted man was a colonel in the Soviet Army and if he were in uniform, which he seldom was, his flashes would indicate he was with the artillery. In fact he was more scientist than soldier, and worked in the Directorate of Ordnance, Research Division.

'So,' said General Pienaar when they were seated round the coffee table in the leather club chairs, 'our diplomat Jan Marais. Is he guilty or not?'

'Guilty,' said Preston, 'as hell.'

'I think I'd like to hear you prove that, Mr Preston. Where did he go wrong? Where was he turned?'

'He didn't and he wasn't,' said Preston. 'He never put a foot wrong. You have read his handwritten autobiography?'

'Yes, and, as Captain Viljoen may have pointed out, we too have checked everything in that man's career from birth to the present day. We can find not one discrepancy.'

'There aren't any,' said Preston. 'The story of his boyhood is absolutely accurate to the last detail. I believe he could even today describe that boyhood for five hours without repeating himself once and without being wrong in a single detail.'

'Then it's true. Everything that is checkable is true,' said the general.

'Everything that is checkable, yes. It is all true up to the point when those two young soldiers dropped from the tailboard of a German lorry in Silesia and started running. After that it's all lies. Let me explain by starting at the other end, the man who jumped with Jan Marais, the story of Frikki Brandt.

'In 1933 Adolf Hitler came to power in Germany. In 1935 a German railway worker called Josef Brandt went to the South African legation in Berlin and pleaded for an immigration visa on compassionate grounds: that he was in danger of persecution because he was a Jew. His appeal was heard and he was granted a visa to emigrate to South Africa with his young family. Your own archives confirm the application and the issue of the visa.'

'That's right,' nodded General Pienaar. 'There were many Jewish immigrants to South Africa during the Hitler period. South Africa has a good record on that issue, better than some.'

'In September 1935,' continued Preston, 'Josef Brandt, with his wife Ilse and his ten-year-old son Friedrich, boarded ship at Bremerhaven and six weeks later disembarked at East London. There was then a large German community and a small Jewish one there. He elected to stay and sought a job on the railways. A kindly Immigration official informed the local rabbi of the arrival of the new family.

'The rabbi, an energetic young man called Solomon Shapiro, visited the newcomers and tried to help by encouraging them to join in the Jewish community life. They refused, and he assumed they wished to try to assimilate into the Gentile community. He was disappointed but not yet suspicious.

'Then in 1938 the boy, now Afrikanerized into Frederik or Frikki, turned thirteen. It was time for his bar-mitzvah, the coming-of-age for a Jewish boy. However the Brandts might wish to assimilate, that is an important thing for a man with an only son. Although none of them had ever been to *schul*, Rabbi Shapiro visited the family to ask if they would like him to officiate. They gave him a flea in his ear, and his suspicions hardened into certainty.'

'What certainty?' asked the general, perplexed.

'The certainty that they were not Jewish,' said Preston. 'He told me last night. At a bar-mitzvah, the boy is blessed by the rabbi. First the rabbi must be convinced of the boy's Jewishness. The mother must produce a document, called a *ketubah*, confirming that her marriage was solemnized in a synagogue, according to the Jewish faith. Ilse Brandt had no *ketubah*. There could ne no bar-mitzvah.'

'So they entered South Africa on false pretences,' said General Pienaar. 'It was a hell of a long time ago.'

'More than that,' said Preston. 'I can't prove it, but I think I'm right. Josef Brandt was correct when he told your legation all those years ago that he was under threat from the Gestapo. But not as a Jew. As a militant, activist German Communist. He knew if he told your legation that, he'd never get a visa.'

'Go on,' said the general grimly.

'By the time he was eighteen, the son Frikki was completely imbued with his father's secret ideals, a dedicated Communist prepared to work for the Comintern.

'In 1943 two young men joined the South African Army and went to war; Jan Marais from Duiwelskloof to fight for South Africa and the British Commonwealth, and Frikki Brandt to fight for his ideological motherland, the Soviet Union.

'They never met in basic training, or on the troop convoy, or in Italy or at Moosberg. But they met at Stalag 344. I don't know whether Brandt had worked out his escape plans by then, but he picked for his companion a young man tall and blond like himself. I believe it was he, not Marais, who initiated that run into the forest when the truck broke down.'

'But what about the pneumonia?' asked Viljoen.

'There was no pneumonia,' said Preston, 'nor did they fall into the hands of Catholic Polish partisans. More likely they fell in with Communist partisans, to whom Brandt could talk in fluent German. They would have led them to the Red Army, and thence to the NKVD, with the trusting Marais tailing along.

'It was between March and August 1945 that the switch

took place. All that talk about freezing cells was rubbish. Marais would have been squeezed for every last detail of his childhood and education and Brandt would have memorized it, until, despite his poor written English, he could write that curriculum vitae with his eyes closed.

'They probably gave Brandt a crash course in English as well, changing his appearance a bit, putting Marais's dog tag round his neck, until finally they were ready. After that, with his usefulness served, Jan Marais was probably liquidated.

'They roughed Brandt up a bit, gave him a few chemicals to make him realistically ill, and handed him back at Potsdam. He spent time in a hospital at Bielefeld, and more outside Glasgow. By the winter of 1945 all South African soldiers would have gone home; he was unlikely to run across anyone from the Wits/De La Rey regiment. And in December he sailed for Cape Town, arriving in January 1946.

'There was one problem. He could not go to Duiwelskloof. He had no intention of going. Then someone at Defence HQ sent old Farmer Marais a cable to say his son was home at last, having been posted "missing, presumed dead". To Brandt's horror a cable arrived – I admit I am guessing here, but it makes sense – urging him to return home. He made himself ill again and went into Wynberg Military Hospital.

'The old father would not be put off. He cabled again, to say he was coming all the way to Cape Town. In desperation Brandt appealed to his friends in the Comintern, and the matter was arranged. They ran the old man down, on a lonely road in the Mootseki Valley, did half a wheel change on his car and made it look like a hit-and-run. After that it was plain sailing. The young man could not get home for the funeral, everyone at Duiwelskloof understood that, and lawyer Benson had no suspicion when he was asked to realize the estate and mail the proceeds to Cape Town.'

There was silence in the general's office, disturbed only

by the buzzing of a fly on the window pane. The general nodded several times.

'It makes sense,' he conceded at last. 'But there's no proof. We cannot prove the Brandts were not Jewish, let alone were Communists. Can you give me anything that puts it beyond doubt?'

Preston reached into his pocket and produced the photograph, which he laid on General Pienaar's desk. 'That is a picture, the last picture, of the real Jan Marais. As you see, he was a useful cricketer in his boyhood. He was a bowler. If you look you will see his fingers are gripping the ball in the manner of a spin bowler. You will also see he is left-handed.

'I have spent a week studying the Jan Marais in London; at close range, through binoculars. In driving, smoking, eating, drinking – he is right-handed. General, you can do many things to a man to change him; you can change his hair, his speech, his face, his mannerisms. But you cannot turn a left-handed spin bowler into a right-handed man.'

General Pienaar, who had played cricket for half of his life, stared down at the photograph. 'So what have we got up there in London, Mr Preston?'

'General, you have got a dedicated Communist agent who has worked inside the South African Foreign Service more than forty years for the Soviet Union.'

General Pienaar lifted his eyes from the desk and gazed out across the valley to the Voortrekker Monument. 'I'll break him,' he whispered, 'I'll break him into tiny pieces and stamp them into the bushveld.'

Preston coughed. 'Bearing in mind that we also have a problem because of this man, could I ask you to restrain your hand until you have talked personally to Sir Nigel Irvine?'

'Very well, Mr Preston,' General Pienaar nodded, 'I will talk to Sir Nigel first. Now, what are your plans?'

'There is a flight back to London this evening, sir. I would like to be on it.'

General Pienaar rose and held out his hand. 'Good day, Mr Preston. Captain Viljoen will see you on the plane. And thank you for your assistance.'

From the hotel, as he packed, Preston made a call to Dennis Grey who drove up from Johannesburg and took a message for coded transmission to London. He had his answer two hours later. Sir Bernard Hemmings would come into the office the next day, Saturday, to meet him.

Preston and Viljoen stood in the departure lounge just before 8 p.m. as the last calls for passengers on the South African Airways flight for London were made. Preston showed his boarding pass and Viljoen his all-purpose ID card. They went through to the cooler darkness of the tarmac.

'I'll say this for you, Englesman, you're a damned good *jagdhond*.'

'Thank you,' said Preston.

'Do you know what a *jagdhond* is?'

'I believe,' said Preston carefully, 'that the Cape hunting dog is slow, ungainly, but very tenacious.'

It was the first time that week that Captain Viljoen threw back his head and laughed. Then he grew serious. 'May I ask you something?'

'Yes.'

'Why did you put a flower on the old man's grave?'

Preston stared across at the waiting airliner, its cabin lights blazing in the semi-darkness twenty yards away. The last passengers were climbing the steps.

'They had taken away his son,' he said, 'and then they killed him to stop him finding out. It seemed the thing to do.'

Viljoen held out his hand. 'Goodbye, John, and good luck.'

'Goodbye, Andries.'

Ten minutes later the flying springbok on the fin of the jetliner tilted its straining nose towards the sky and lifted off for the north and Europe.

11

Sir Bernard Hemmings, with Brian Harcourt-Smith by his side, sat in silence and listened to Preston's report until he had finished.

'Good God,' he said heavily when Preston was silent, 'so it *was* Moscow after all. There'll be the devil to pay. The damage must have been huge. Brian, are both men still under surveillance?'

'Yes, Sir Bernard.'

'Keep it that way through the weekend. Make no move to close in until the Paragon Committee have had a chance to hear what we have. John, I know you must be tired, but can you have your report written up by Sunday night?'

'Yes, sir.'

'Then have it on my desk first thing Monday morning. I'll reach the various committee members at their homes and ask for an urgent meeting for Monday morning.'

When Major Valeri Petrofsky was shown into the sitting-room of the elegant dacha at Usovo, he was in a spirit of extreme trepidation. He had never met the General Secretary of the Communist Party of the Soviet Union, nor ever imagined he would do so.

He had had a confusing, even terrifying, three days. Since being seconded to special duties by his own director, he had been sequestered in a flat in central Moscow, guarded night and day by two men from the Ninth Directorate, the Kremlin Guards. Not unnaturally, he had feared the worst, without having the faintest idea what he was supposed to have done.

Then the abrupt order that Sunday evening to dress in his best suit of civilian clothes and follow the guards downstairs to a waiting Chaika; followed by the silent drive to Usovo. He did not even recognize the dacha to which he was brought.

It was only when Major Pavlov had told him: 'The Comrade General Secretary will see you now,' that he had realized where he was. His throat was dry as he stepped through the door in the sitting-room. He tried to compose himself, telling himself he would answer any accusations levelled at him respectfully and truthfully.

Inside the door he stood rigidly to attention. The old man in the wheelchair observed him silently for several minutes, then raised a hand and beckoned him forward. Petrofsky took four smart steps and stopped again, still to attention. But when the Soviet leader spoke, the whiplash of accusation in his voice was missing. He spoke quite softly. 'Major Petrofsky, you are not a tailor's dummy. Come forward into the light where I can see you. And sit down.'

Petrofsky was stunned. To be seated in the presence of the General Secretary was, for a young major, unheard-of. He did as he was told, perching on the edge of the indicated chair, back stiff, knees together.

'Have you any idea why I have sent for you?'

'No, Comrade General Secretary.'

'No, I suppose not. It was necessary that no-one know. Then I will tell you.

'There is a mission that has to be performed. Its outcome will be of quite incalculable importance to the Soviet Union and the victory of the Revolution. If it succeeds, the benefits to our country will be inestimable; if it fails, the damage to us will be catastrophic. I have personally chosen you, Valeri Alexeivitch, to accomplish that mission.'

Petrofsky's mind whirled. His original fear that he was destined to disgrace and exile was replaced by an almost uncontrollable jubilation. Ever since, as a brilliant scholar at Moscow University, he had been plucked from an intended career in the Foreign Ministry to become one of the First Chief Directorate's bright young men; ever since he had volunteered for and been accepted by the élite Illegals Directorate, he had dreamed of an important mission. But his wildest dreams had not encompassed anything like this. He allowed himself at last to look the General Secretary straight in the eye. 'Thank you, Comrade General Secretary.'

'Others will brief you as to the details,' the General Secretary continued. 'Time will be short, but you have already been trained to the peak of your abilities, and you will have all for the mission that you need.

'I have asked to see you personally for one reason. There is something that must be put to you and I have chosen to put it myself. If the mission succeeds, and I have no doubt it will, you will return here to promotion and honours beyond your imaginings. I will see to it.

'But if anything should go wrong, if the police and troops of the country to which you will be sent are seen to be closing in, you will have to take steps without hesitation to ensure that you are not taken alive. Do you understand, Valeri Alexeivitch?'

'Yes, I do, Comrade General Secretary.'

'To be taken alive, to be rigorously interrogated, to be broken – oh yes, it is possible nowadays, there are no reserves of courage that can resist the chemicals – to be paraded before an international press conference, all this would be a living hell anyway. But the damage of such a spectacle to the Soviet Union, to this your country, would be beyond estimation and beyond repair.'

Major Petrofsky took a deep breath.

'I will not fail,' he said. 'But if it comes to it, I will never be taken alive.'

The General Secretary pressed a buzzer beneath the table and the door opened. Major Pavlov stood there.

'Then go, young man. You will be told here in this house, by a man whom you may have seen before, what the misson involves. Then you will go to another place for intensive briefing. We will not meet again – until you return.'

When the door closed upon the two majors of the KGB the General Secretary stared for a while into the flickering flames of the log fire. Such a fine young man, he thought. Such a pity.

As Petrofsky followed the back of Major Pavlov down two long corridors to the guest wing, he felt as if his ribcage could hardly contain the emotions of expectation and pride within it.

Major Valeri Alexeivitch Petrofsky was a dyed-in-the-wool Russian soldier and patriot. Steeped in the English language, he had heard the phrase 'to die for God, King and country' and he understood its meaning. He had no God, but he had been personally entrusted by the leader of his country and he was determined, as he walked down that corridor at Usovo, that if the moment should ever come he would not shrink from what had to be done.

Major Pavlov stopped at a door, knocked and pushed it open. He stood aside to let Petrofsky enter. Then he closed the door and withdrew. A white-haired man rose from a chair by a table covered in notes and maps, and came forward.

'So you are Major Petrofsky,' he smiled, holding out his hand.

Petrofsky was surprised by the stutter. He knew the face, though they had never met. In the folklore of the FCD this man was, younger entrants were taught, one of the Five Stars, a man to be respected, a man who represented one of the great triumphs of Soviet ideology over capitalism.

'Yes, Comrade Colonel,' he said.

Philby had read the file until he knew it perfectly. Petrofsky was still only thirty-six and had been trained for a decade to pass for an Englishman. He had twice been in Britain on familiarization trips, each time living under deep cover, each time going nowhere near the Soviet Embassy, and neither time undertaking any mission at all.

These familiarization trips were simply to enable

illegals, before they went operational, to acclimatize themselves to everything they would one day see again: simple things, opening a bank account, having a scrape with another car driver and knowing what to do, using the London Underground, and always improving the use of modern slang phrases.

Philby knew the young man in front of him not only spoke perfect English, but was tone-perfect in four regional accents and had faultless command of Welsh and Irish. He dropped into English himself.

'Sit down,' he said. 'Now, I am simply going to describe to you the broad outlines of the misson. Others will give you all the details. Time will be short, desperately short, so you will have to absorb everything faster than ever in your life before.'

As they talked, Philby realized that after thirty years away from his native land, and despite reading every newspaper and magazine from Britain that he could lay hands on, it was he who was out of practice, whose phraseology was stilted and old-fashioned. The young Russian spoke like a modern Englishman of his age.

It took two hours for Philby to outline the plan called Aurora and what it involved. Petrofsky drank in the details. He was excited and amazed by the audacity of it.

'You will spend the next few days with a team of four men only. They will brief you on a whole range of names, places, dates, transmission times, rendezvous and back-up rendezvous. You will memorize them all. The only thing you will have to take in with you will be block of one-time pads. Well, that's it.'

Petrofsky sat nodding at what he had been told. 'I have told the Comrade General Secretary, I shall not fail,' he said. 'It will be done, as required and on time. If the components arrive, it will be done.'

Philby rose. 'Good, then I will have you driven back to Moscow to the place where you will spend the remaining time until your departure.'

As Philby crossed the room to the internal phone, Petrofsky was startled by a loud 'coo' from the corner. He looked to see a large cage in which a handsome pigeon with a splint on one leg was regarding them. Philby turned with an apologetic grin.

'I call him Hopalong,' he said as he dialled for Major Pavlov to return. 'Found him in the street last winter with a broken wing and leg. The wing has mended but the leg keeps giving trouble.'

Petrofsky crossed to the cage and scratched the bars with a fingernail. But the pigeon waddled away to the far side. The door opened to admit Major Pavlov. As usual he said nothing but gestured to Petrofsky to follow him.

'Until we meet again. Good luck,' said Philby.

The members of the Paragon Committee sat and read Preston's report until the last one had finished.

'So,' said Sir Anthony Plumb to open the discussion, 'now at least we know what, where, when and who. We still don't know why.'

'Nor how much,' interposed Sir Patrick Strickland. 'The damage assessment is still unattempted and we have simply got to inform our allies, even though nothing sensitive – save for one fictitious paper – has gone on its way to Moscow since January.'

'Agreed,' said Sir Anthony. 'All right, gentlemen, I think we must concur the time for further investigation is over. How do we handle this man? Any ideas? Brian?'

Brian Harcourt-Smith was without his Director-General, and represented MI5 alone. He chose his words carefully. 'We take the view that with Berenson, Marais and the cutout Benotti the ring is complete. It seems to the Security Service that it is unlikely there were more agents being run by this one ring. Berenson would have been so important it seems to us likely the entire ring was set up to handle him alone.'

There were nods of agreement round the table.

'And your recommendation?' asked Sir Anthony.

‘That we pick them all up, roll up the whole ring,’ said Harcourt-Smith.

‘There’s a foreign diplomat involved,’ objected Sir Hubert Villiers of the Home Office.

‘I think Pretoria may be prepared to waive immunity in this case,’ said Sir Patrick Strickland. ‘General Pienaar must have reported all this to Mr Botha by now. They’ll no doubt want Marais when we have had a chat to him.’

‘Well, that seems decisive enough,’ said Sir Anthony. ‘How about you, Nigel?’

Sir Nigel Irvine had been staring at the ceiling as if lost in thought. At the question he seemed to wake up. ‘I was just wondering,’ he said quietly. ‘We pick them up. Then what?’

‘Interrogation,’ said Harcourt-Smith. ‘We can begin damage assessment and inform our allies of the round-up of the entire ring to sweeten the pill a bit.’

‘Yes,’ said Sir Nigel, ‘it’s good. But what after that?’

He began to address the Secretaries of the three ministries and the Cabinet. ‘It seems to me we have four choices. We can pick up Berenson and formally charge him under the Official Secrets Act, which we’ll have to do if we arrest him. But do we actually have a case that will stand up in court? We know we are right, but can we prove it against a first-class legal defence? Apart from anything else, a formal arrest and charge would cause a major scandal, which would be certain to rebound against the government.’

Sir Martin Flannery, the Cabinet Secretary, took the point. Unlike anyone else in the room, he knew of the intention to hold a snap summer election, because the Prime Minister had told him in strictest confidence. A lifelong civil servant of the old school, Sir Martin offered his total loyalty to the present government, as he had to three previous governments, two of them Labour. He would offer that same loyalty to any democratically elected successor government. He pursed his lips.

‘Then,’ resumed Sir Nigel, ‘we could leave Berenson

and Marais in place, but seek to feed Berenson doctored documents to pass on to Moscow. But that wouldn't work for long. Berenson is too highly placed and knowledgeable to be fooled by that.'

Sir Peregrine Jones nodded. He knew that on that point Sir Nigel was right.

'Or we could pick Berenson up and try to get his complete cooperation in damage assessment by an immunity-from-prosecution deal. Personally, I hate immunity for traitors. You never know whether they have told you the whole truth or tricked you, as Blunt did. And it always gets out eventually, with an even worse scandal.'

Sir Hubert Villiers, whose ministry contained the Law Officers to the Crown, frowned in agreement. He too hated immunity deals and they all knew the Prime Minister felt the same.

'That seems to leave,' said the Chief of the SIS smoothly, 'the question of detention without trial and rigorous interrogation. In a word, third degree. I suppose I'm just old-fashioned, but I've never had much confidence in it. He might admit to fifty documents, but we'd none of us know to the day we died if there weren't another fifty.'

There was silence for a while.

'They're all pretty unpleasant,' agreed Sir Anthony Plumb, 'but it looks as if we'll have to go with Brian's suggestion if there aren't any others.'

'There might just be one,' said Sir Nigel gently. 'It could be, you know, that Berenson's reruitment was a genuine false-flag approach.'

Most of those present knew what a false-flag recruitment was, but Sir Hubert Villiers of the Home Office and Sir Martin Flannery of the Cabinet frowned in puzzlement.

Sir Nigel explained. 'It involves the recruitment of a source by men who pretend to be working for one country, with whom the subject is sympathetic, while in reality they are working for another. The Israeli Mossad are particular experts at this technique. Being able to produce agents who can pass for just about any nation under the sun, the Israelis have worked some remarkable 'stings' with false flags.

'For example: a loyal West German working in the Middle East is approached while on furlough in Germany by two fellow-Germans who, with impeccable supporting evidence, prove to him that they represent the BND, the West German intelligence arm. They spin him a tale to the effect that the French, working on the same project in Iraq, are passing on technology secrets that are patently forbidden by NATO. They are doing this to secure greater commercial orders. Would the German help his own country by reporting back what is going on? As a loyal German he agrees, and spends years working for Jerusalem. It has happened many times.

'It makes sense, you know,' pursued Sir Nigel. 'We've all been through Berenson's file until we are no doubt sick of it. But with what we now know, the false-flag technique could be the answer.'

There were several nods as they recalled the contents of Berenson's file. He had started his career in the Foreign Office, straight out of university. He had progressed quite well, serving abroad on three occasions and rising steadily if not spectacularly in the diplomatic corps.

In the mid-sixties he had married Lady Fiona Glen and shortly afterwards had been posted to Pretoria, accompanied by his wife. It was probably there, confronted by the traditional and almost limitless South Africa hospitality, that he had developed his deep sympathy and admiration for South Africa. With a Labour government in power in Britain and Rhodesia in rebellion, his increasingly outspoken admiration of Pretoria had not gone down very well.

On his return to Britain in 1969 word had apparently reached him that his next posting was likely to be somewhere less controversial – say, Bolivia. The men round the table could only surmise, but it was perfectly likely that Lady Fiona, while prepared to take Pretoria in her stride, had put her foot down flatly at the idea of leaving her beloved horses and social life to spend three years halfway up the Andes. Whatever had been the reason, George Berenson had applied for a transfer to Defence, regarded as going downmarket. But with his wife's fortune, he should care. With the constraints of the Foreign Office removed from him, he had become a member of several pro-South African friendship societies, usually the preserve of those politically of the Right wing.

Sir Peregrine Jones at least knew that Berenson's known and too overt Right-wing sympathies had made it impossible for him, Jones, to recommend Berenson for a knighthood, something he now realized might well have fuelled Berenson's resentment.

Since reading the report an hour earlier the senior civil servants had assumed Berenson's pro-South African sympathies to be the cover of a secret Soviet sympathizer. Now Sir Nigel Irvine's suggestion had put a different cast on things again.

'A false flag?' mused Sir Paddy Strickland. 'You mean he really thought he was passing secrets to South Africa?'

'I am seized by this enigma,' said 'C'. 'If he was a secret Soviet sympathizer or closet Communist all along, why didn't the Centre run him with a Soviet controller? I can think of five in their embassy who could have done the job equally well.'

'Well, I confess I don't know . . .' said Sir Arthur Plumb. At that moment he glanced up and looked down the table, catching Sir Nigel Irvine's eye. Irvine dropped one eyelid quickly down and then back up again. Sir Anthony Plumb forced his gaze back to the Berenson file in front of him.

You cunning bastard, Nigel, he thought, you're not speculating at all. You actually know.

In fact Andreyev had reported something two days earlier. It was not much, just canteen scuttlebutt from inside the Soviet Embassy. He had been drinking with the

Line N man and discussing tradecraft in general. He had mentioned the usefulness, on occasion, of false-flag recruitment; the Illegals Directorate representative had laughed, winked and tapped the side of his nose with a forefinger. Andreyev took the gesture to mean that there *was* a false-flag operation going on in London at that moment of which the Line N man knew something. Sir Nigel, when he heard, took the same view.

Another thought occurred to Sir Anthony. If you really do know, Nigel, it must be because you have a source right inside their *rezidentura*. You old fox. Then another thought occurred, and it was less pleasant. Why not say so outright? They were all completely reliable around that table, were they not? A cold worm of unease stirred inside him. He looked up.

'Well, I think we should seriously consider Nigel's suggestion. It does make sense. What have you in mind, Nigel?'

'The man's a traitor, no doubt about that,' said 'C'. 'If he's presented with the documents that were anonymously returned to us, I've no doubt he'll be pretty shaken. But if he's then given John Preston's South Africa file to read, and he *did* think he was working for Pretoria, I don't think he'll be able to mask his collapse. If he *was* a secret Communist all along, he'll know of Marais's ideology anyway, so it won't come as a surprise to him. I think a trained observer should be able to tell.'

'And if it *was* a false-flag approach?' asked Sir Perry Jones.

'Then I think we'll get his complete and unstinted cooperation in damage assessment. More, I think he could be persuaded to turn voluntarily, enabling us to mount a major disinformation operation against Moscow. Now *that* we could take to our allies as a big plus.'

Sir Paddy Strickland of the Foreign Office was won over. It was agreed to pursue Sir Nigel's tactic.

'One last thing, who goes to see him?' asked Sir Anthony. Sir Nigel Irvine coughed. 'Well, of course, it's really down to "Five",' he said. 'But a disinformation operation against the Centre would be for "Six" to handle. Then again, I happen to know the man. Actually, we were at school together.'

'Good Lord,' exclaimed Plumb. 'He's a bit younger than you, isn't he?'

'Five years, actually. He used to clean my boots.'

'All right. Are we agreed? Anyone against? You've got it, Nigel. You take him, he's yours. Tell us how you get on.'

On Tuesday, the 24th, a South African tourist arrived from Johannesburg at London's Heathrow airport where he passed through the formalities without difficulty.

As he emerged from the Customs hall carrying his own grip a young man moved forward and murmured a question in his ear. The burly South African nodded in confirmation. The younger man took his grip and led him outside to a waiting car.

Instead of heading towards London, the driver took the M25 ring road and then the M3 towards Hampshire. An hour later it drew up in front of the door of a handsome country house outside Basingstoke. The South African, relieved of his coat, was ushered into the library. From a seat by the fire an Englishman in country tweeds and of the same age rose to greet him.

'Henry Pienaar, how good to see you again. It's been too long. Welcome to England.'

'Nigel, how have you been keeping?'

The heads of the two intelligence services had an hour before lunch was called, so after the usual preliminaries they settled down to discuss the problem that had brought General Pienaar to the country house maintained by the SIS for the hospitality of notable but clandestine guests.

By evening Sir Nigel Irvine had secured the agreement he sought. The South Africans would agree to leave Jan Marais in place to give Irvine a chance to mount a major disinformation exercise through George Berenson, assuming he would play ball.

The British would keep Marais under total surveillance; it was their responsibility to ensure Marais had no chance to do a moonlight flit to Moscow, since the South Africans now had their own damage assessment to face – forty years' worth of it.

It was further agreed that when the disinformation exercise had run its course, Irvine would inform Pienaar that Marais was no longer needed. He would be called home, the British would 'house' him aboard the South African jet and Pienaar's men would make the arrest when the jet was airborne, i.e. on South African sovereign territory.

After dinner Sir Nigel excused himself; his car was waiting. Pienaar would spend the night, do some shopping in London's West End the next day, and take the evening flight home.

'Just don't let him go,' said General Pienaar as he saw Sir Nigel off at the door. 'I want that bastard back home by the end of the year.'

'You'll have him,' promised Sir Nigel. 'Just don't spook him in the meantime.'

While the head of the NIS was trying to find something in Bond Street for Mrs Pienaar, John Preston was at Charles Street for a meeting with Brian Harcourt-Smith. The Deputy Director-General was in his most eager-to-please mood.

'Well, John, I gather congratulations are in order. The committee was most impressed by your revelations from South Africa.'

'Thanks, Brian.'

'Yes, indeed. It'll all be handled by the committee from now on. Can't say exactly what's to be done, but Tony Plumb asked me to pass on his personal sentiments. Now . . .' he spread his hands flat and placed them on his blotter '. . . to the future.'

'The future?'

'You see, I'm in a bit of a dilemma. You've been on this case for eight weeks, some of the time out on the street with the Watchers, most of it in the basement at Cork, and now South Africa. During all this time young March, your number two, has been running C.1(A) and doing very well into the bargain.

'Now, I ask myself, what am I supposed to do with him? I don't think it would be quite fair to bang him back to the two slot – after all, he's been round all the ministries, made some extremely useful suggestions and a couple of very positive changes.'

He would, thought Preston. March was a young eager-beaver, very much one of Harcourt-Smith's protégés.

'Anyway, I know you've only been at C.1(A) for ten weeks, and that's pretty short, but seeing as you've covered yourself in glory, it might be a well-judged moment to move on. I've had a word with Personnel and as luck would have it Cranley at C.5(C) is taking early retirement at the end of the week. His wife, you know, has not been well for a long time, he wants to take her off to the Lake District. So he's taking his pension and leaving. I thought it would suit you.'

Preston pondered. C.5(C)?

'Ports and Airports?' he queried.

It was another liaison job. Immigration, Customs, Special Branch, Serious Crimes Squad, Narcotics Squad – they all monitored ports and airports checking on various kinds of unsavoury characters seeking to bring themselves or their illicit cargoes into the country. Preston suspected C.5(C) would have to try to pick up whatever did not fall into anyone else's category.

Harcourt-Smith raised an admonitory finger. 'It's important, John. The special responsibility, of course, is to keep a weather eye open for SovBloc illegals and couriers and so forth. It gets one out and about, the sort of thing you like.'

And away from head office while the struggle for the

succession goes on, thought Preston. He knew he was a Bernard Hemmings man, down the line, and was aware Harcourt-Smith would know it too. He thought of protesting, of demanding a meeting with Sir Bernard to put his case for staying where he was.

'Anyway, I want you to give it a try,' said Harcourt-Smith. 'It's still in Gordon, so you won't have to move house.'

Preston knew he was outmanoeuvred. Harcourt-Smith had spent half a lifetime working the head-office system. At least, Preston thought, he could be a field man again, even if it was what he termed another 'policeman's job'.

'I'll expect you to start on Monday morning then,' said Harcourt-Smith.

On the Friday Major Valeri Petrofsky slipped quietly into Britain.

He had flown from Moscow to Zürich with a Swedish identity, dropped the whole identity into a sealed envelope addressed to a KGB safe house in the city, and adopted the papers of a Swiss engineer that were waiting for him in another envelope deposited with the post office in the concourse. From Zürich he connected to Dublin.

On the same flight was his escort, who neither knew nor cared what his charge was doing. The escort was simply carrying out his orders. In a room at Dublin's International Airport Hotel the two men came together. Petrofsky stripped to the skin and handed back the European-style clothes. He put on what the escort had brought in his own handgrip – British clothes from top to toe, plus an overnight case filled with the usual medley of pyjamas, sponge bag, half-read novel and a change of clothes.

The escort had already plucked off the airport's messages board an envelope, prepared by the Line N man at the Dublin embassy and pinned to the notice board four hours earlier. It contained a ticket stub from the Eblana Theatre for the previous evening's performance, a receipt for an overnight stay at the New Jury's Hotel for the previous evening in the appropriate name, and the return half of a London-Dublin-London ticket on Aer Lingus.

Finally Petrofsky was handed his new passport. When he went back to the airport concourse and checked in, not an eyebrow was raised. He was an Englishman returning home from a one-day business trip to Dublin. There are no passport checks between Dublin and London; at the London end arriving passengers must produce their boarding pass or ticket stub as identification. They also pass two blank-eyed Special Branch men who affect to see nothing and miss very, very little. Neither had ever seen Petrofsky's face because he had never entered Britain by Heathrow Airport before. Had they asked, he could have produced a perfect British passport in the name of James Duncan Ross. It was a passport that could not have been faulted by the Passport Office itself, for the good and simple reason that the Passport Office had issued it.

Passing through Customs without a check, the Russian took a taxi to King's Cross Station. There he went to a left-luggage locker. He already had the key. The locker was one of several maintained permanently around the British capital by the Line N man in the embassy and the key had long been copied. From the locker the Russian produced a package, sealed exactly as it had arrived in the diplomatic bag at the embassy two days earlier. The Line N man had not seen its contents, nor wanted to. He never asked why the package had to be left in a locker in a main station either. It was not his job to.

The package Petrofsky slipped unopened into his grip. He could open it at leisure later. He already knew what it contained. From King's Cross he took another taxi across London to Liverpool Street Station and there boarded the early evening train for Ipswich in the county of Suffolk. Just in time for dinner he checked into the Great White Horse Hotel.

Had any curious policeman insisted on looking inside the package stowed in the handgrip of the young Englishman on the Ipswich train, he would have been amazed. In part it contained a Finnish Sako automatic pistol with a full magazine and the nose cone of each round carefully cut in the form of an X. The cuts had been filled with a mixture of gelatine and potassium cyanide concentrate. Not only would they expand on impact with the human body, but recovery from the venom would be out of the question.

The other part of the contents consisted of the rest of the 'legend' of James Duncan Ross.

A 'legend' in term-of-art parlance is the fictitious life story of a nonexistent man, supported by a host of perfectly real documents of every kind and description. Usually, the person on whom the legend is built did exist once, but died in circumstances that left no trace and caused no stir. The identity is then taken over and fleshed out, as the skeleton of the dead man can never be, by supportive documentation going backwards and forwards over the lifespan.

The real James Duncan Ross, or what little was left of him, had been rotting in the deep bush of the Zambezi River for years. He had been born in 1950, the son of Angus and Kirstie Ross of Kilbride, Scotland. In 1951 Angus Ross, tired of the cheerless rationing of postwar Britain, had emigrated with his wife and baby son to Southern Rhodesia as it was then called. An engineer, he had got a job in agricultural implements and machinery and by 1960 was able to found his own business.

He prospered, being able to send the young James to a good preparatory school and on to Michaelhouse. By 1971 the boy, with his National Service behind him, was able to join his father in the company. But this was Ian Smith's Rhodesia now, and the war against the guerrillas of Joshua Nkomo's ZIPRA and Robert Mugabe's ZANLA was getting more vicious.

Every able-bodied male was in the Reserve, and periods spent back in the army became longer and longer. In 1976, serving with the Rhodesian Light Infantry, James Ross was caught in a ZIPRA ambush in deep bush on the southern bank of the Zambezi and was killed. The ZIPRA guerrillas closed in, stripped the body and vanished back to their bases in Zambia.

He should not have been carrying any identification at all, but just before his patrol set off he had received a letter from his girlfriend and had stuffed it in his combat jacket pocket. It came back to Zambia and fell into the hands of the KGB.

A very senior KGB officer, Vassili Solodovnikov, was then ambassador to Lusaka, and he ran various networks across all Southern Africa. One of them picked up the letter addressed to James Ross, care of his parents' home. The first checks into the deceased young officer produced a bonus: British born, Angus Ross and his son James had never abandoned their British passports. So the KGB caused James Duncan Ross to live again.

When, after Rhodesia became independent as Zimbabwe, Angus and Kristie Ross quit for South Africa, James apparently decided to return to Britain. Unseen hands withdrew a copy of his birth certificate from Somerset House in London; other hands filled out and sent in the postal application for a new passport. Checks were made, and it was granted.

In the making of a good legend, scores of people and thousands of hours are expended. The KGB has never lacked the staff or the patience. Bank accounts are opened and closed; driving licences carefully renewed before expiry; cars are bought and sold so that the name shows up on the Vehicle Licensing Centre computer. Jobs are taken and promotions earned; references are prepared, company pension funds topped up. One of the chores of junior intelligence staff is to keep this mass of documentation up to date.

Other teams go back into the past. What was the child's nickname? Where did he go to school? What did the boys call the science teacher behind his back? What was the family dog called?

By the time the legend is complete, and it can take

years, and by the time it has been memorized by its new bearer, it would need weeks of investigation to crack it – if at all. This was what Petrofsky carried in his head and handgrip. He was, and could prove he was, James Ross, moving from the West Country to take over the East Anglian representation of a Swiss-based corporation marketing computer software. He had a handsome bank balance at Barclays Bank, Dorchester, Dorset, which he was about to transfer to Colchester. He had mastered the scrawled Ross signature to perfection.

Britain is a very private country. Almost alone in the world, the British do not have to carry any personal identification on their persons. If asked, the production of a letter addressed to oneself will usually do, as if that proves anything. A driving licence, even though British licences bear no photograph, is proof positive. A man is expected to be who he says he is.

Valeri Alexeivitch Petrofsky was perfectly confident as he dined that night in Ipswich, and rightly so, that no-one would doubt he was James Duncan Ross. After dinner he sought from the reception desk the Yellow Pages commercial directory and turned to the section for estate agents.

12

While Major Petrofsky was dining at the Great White Horse in Ipswich, the doorbell rang at an apartment on the eighth floor of Fontenoy House in Belgravia. It was opened by the owner, Mr George Berenson. For a second he stared in surprise at the figure in the corridor.

'Good Lord, Sir Nigel . . .'

They knew each other vaguely, not so much from shared schooldays many years before, but from having seen each other occasionally around the Whitehall circuit.

The Chief of the SIS nodded politely but formally. 'Evening, Berenson, mind if I come in?'

'Of course, of course, by all means . . .'

George Berenson was flustered though he had no idea of the purpose of the visit. The use by Sir Nigel of his surname without prefix indicated the tone of the visit was to be courteous but by no means chatty. There would be no 'George' and 'Nigel' informality.

'Is Lady Fiona in?'

'No, she's gone off to one of her committee meetings. We have the place to ourselves.'

Sir Nigel knew that anyway. He had sat in his car and watched Berenson's wife leave before making his approach.

Relieved of his coat but retaining his briefcase, Sir Nigel was shown to a chair in the sitting-room, not ten feet from the by-now-repaired wall safe behind the mirror. Berenson seated himself opposite. 'Well now, what can I do for you?'

Sir Nigel opened his case and carefully laid ten photocopies on the glass-topped coffee table. 'I think you might, with advantage, have a look at these.'

Berenson silently studied the top copy, lifted it to look

at the one underneath, and then the third. At the third sheet he stopped and put them down. He had gone very pale but was still in control of himself. He kept his eyes on the papers. 'I don't suppose there is anything I can say.'

'Not much,' said Sir Nigel calmly. 'They were returned to us, some time ago. We know how you came to lose them – rather bad luck from your point of view. After they were returned, we kept you under surveillance for some weeks, watched the abstraction of the Ascension Island paper, the passing of it to Benotti and thence to Marais. It's pretty well tied up, you know.'

A little of what he said was provable, but most was pure bluff; he had no wish to let Berenson know just how weak was the legal case against him. The Deputy Head of Defence Procurement straightened his back and raised his eyes. Now comes the defiance, thought Irvine, the attempt at self-justification. Funny how they all run to pattern. Berenson met his gaze. The defiance was there. 'Well, since you know it all, what are you going to do?'

'Ask a few questions,' said Sir Nigel. 'For example, how long has it been going on and why did you start?'

Despite his effort at self-control and defiance, Berenson was still confused enough not to have wondered at one very simple point: it was not the duty of the Chief of the SIS to have this sort of confrontation. Spies for foreign powers were picked up by counter-intelligence. But his desire to justify himself overcame his capacity for analysis. 'As to the first, just over two years.'

Could be worse, thought Sir Nigel. He knew Marais had been in Britain for almost three years, but Berenson might have been run by another South African pro-Soviet sleeper even before that. Apparently not.

'As to the second, I would have thought it was obvious.'

'Let's assume I'm a bit slow,' suggested Sir Nigel. 'So enlighten me. Why?'

Berenson drew a deep breath. Perhaps, like so many before him, he had prepared his defence inside his own head often enough, arguing before the courtroom of his own conscience, or what passed for one. 'I take the view, and have done for years, that the only struggle on this planet worth a light is the one against Communism and Soviet imperialism,' he began. 'In that struggle, South Africa forms one of the bastions. Probably the principal bastion, if not the only one, south of the Sahara. For a long time I have thought it futile and self-defeating for the Western powers, on dubious moral grounds, to treat South Africa as a leper, to deprive her of any share in our joint planning to respond to the Soviet threat on a global scale.

'I have believed for years that South Africa has been shabbily treated by the Western powers, that it was both wrong and stupid to exclude her from access to NATO's contingency planning.'

Sir Nigel nodded, as if the thought had never occurred to him. 'And you thought it right and proper to redress the balance?'

'Yes, I did. And, the Official Secrets Act notwithstanding, I still do.'

The vanity, thought Sir Nigel, always the vanity, the monumental self-esteem of inadequate men. Nunn May, Pontecorvo, Fuchs, Prime, the thread ran through them all; the self-arrogated right to play God, the conviction that the traitor alone is right and all his colleagues fools; coupled with the drug-like love of power derived from what he sees as the manipulation of policy, through the transfer of secrets, to the ends in which he believes and to the confusion of his supposed opponents in his own government, those who have passed him over for promotion or honours.

'Mmmm. Tell me, did you begin at your suggestion, or Marais's?'

Berenson thought for a while. 'Jan Marais is a diplomat, so he is beyond your power,' he said. 'There's no harm in my saying. It was at his suggestion. We never met when I was stationed in Pretoria. We met here, just after he had arrived. We found we had a lot in common. He persuaded me that if a time of conflict with the USSR ever came, South Africa would have to stand alone in the southern hemisphere, astride the vital routes from the Indian to the South Atlantic oceans, and probably with Soviet bases strung throughout black Africa. It seemed to us both that without some indication of how NATO would operate in these two spheres, she would be hamstrung, even though our staunchest ally in those parts.'

'Powerful argument,' nodded Sir Nigel regretfully. 'You know, when we traced Marais as your controller, I took a risk and put the name straight to General Pienaar. He denied Marais had ever worked for him.'

'Well, he would.'

'Yes, he would. But we sent a man down there to check out Pienaar's claim. Perhaps you ought to look at his report.'

He produced from his case the report Preston had brought back from Pretoria, the photograph of the boy Marais clipped to the top. With a shrug Berenson began to read the seven foolscap pages. At one point he sucked in his breath sharply, pushed his knuckles into his mouth and gnawed at one. When he had turned the last page he put both open hands up to cover his face and rocked slowly back and forth.

'Oh my God,' he breathed, 'what have I done?'

'A hell of a lot of damage, actually,' said Sir Nigel. He let Berenson absorb the full measure of his misery without interruption. He sat back and gazed at the destroyed mandarin without pity. For Sir Nigel, he was just another grubbly little traitor who could take a solemn oath to his queen and country, and for his own conceit betray them all. A man of the same degree, if not the scale, of Donald Maclean.

Berenson was no longer pale, he was ashen grey. When he took his hands from his face, he had aged by many years. 'Is there anything, anything at all, that I can do?'

Sir Nigel shrugged as if there was little enough that anyone could do. He decided to turn the knife a few more twists. 'There's a faction, of course, who want an early arrest. You and Marais. Pretoria has waived his immunity. You'd get a middle-class, middle-aged jury, the Crown counsel would see to that. Honest people, but not devious. They'd probably never believe in the false-flag recruitment at all. We're talking about life, and at your age that would mean *life*, in Parkhurst or Dartmoor.'

He let it sink in for several minutes.

'As it happens, I managed to keep the hard-line faction at bay for a while. There is another way . . .'

'Sir Nigel, I will do anything, I mean it. Anything . . .'

How true, thought the Chief, how very true. If only you knew.

'Three things, actually,' he said out loud. 'One, you continue going to the Ministry as if nothing had happened, maintain the usual façade, the usual routines, make not a ripple to disturb the surface of the water.

'Two, here in this apartment, after dark and if necessary through the night, you help us with the damage assessment. The only possible way to mitigate the damage already done is for us to know everything, every single thing, that went to Moscow. You withhold one dot or comma, and it'll be porridge and mailbags until you croak.'

'Yes, yes, of course. That I can do. I recall every single document that was passed over. Everything . . . Er, you said three things.'

'Yes,' said Sir Nigel studying his fingernails. 'The third is tricky. You maintain relations with Marais . . .'

'I . . . What?'

'You don't have to see him. I'd prefer you didn't. I don't think you're enough of an actor to keep up the pretence in his presence. Just the usual contact through coded phone calls when you want to make a delivery.'

Berenson was genuinely bewildered. 'A delivery of what?'

'Material that my people, in collaboration with others, will prepare for you. Disinformation, if you like. Apart from your work with the Defence people on damage assessment, I want you to colloborate with me. Do some real damage to the Soviets.'

Berenson grasped as a drowning man at a straw.

Five minutes later Sir Nigel rose. The damage assessment people would be round after the weekend. He let himself out. As he walked down the corridor to the lift, he was quietly satisfied. He thought of the broken and terrified man he had left behind. From now on, you bastard, you work for me, he thought.

The young girl in the front office at Oxborrow's looked up as the stranger entered. She took in his appearance with appreciation. Medium height, compact and fit-looking, with a ready smile, nut-brown hair and hazel eyes. She liked the hazel eyes.

'Can I help you?'

'I hope so. I'm new to the district, but I've been told you do lettings of furnished houses.'

'Oh, yes. You'll want to speak to Mr Knights. He handles houses for rent. What name shall I say?'

He smiled again. 'Ross,' he said, 'James Ross.'

She depressed a switch and spoke into the intercom. 'There's a Mr Ross in the office, Mr Knights. About a furnished house. Can you see him?'

Two minutes later James Ross was seated in the office of Mr Knights.

'I've just moved up from Dorset to take over East Anglia for my company,' he said easily. 'Ideally I'd like my wife and kids to come up and join me as soon as possible.'

'Perhaps you're looking to buy a house, then?'

'Not just yet. For one thing, I want to look around for the right house. Then, the details tend to take a bit of time. Secondly, I may only be here for a limited period. Depends on head office. You know.'

'Of course, of course.' Mr Knights understood completely. 'A short lease on a house would help you to get settled while waiting to see if you would be staying longer?'

'Exactly,' said Ross. 'In a nutshell.'

'Furnished or unfurnished?'

'Furnished, if you have such a thing.'

'Quite right,' said Mr Knights, reaching for a selection of folders. 'Unfurnished lettings are almost impossible to come by. You can't always get the people out at the end of the lease. Now, we've got four on the books at the moment.'

He offered Mr Ross the brochures. Two were evidently too large to be plausible for a commercial representative and needed a lot of upkeep. The other two were possibles. Mr Knights had an hour and drove him to see both. One was perfect, a small, neat brick house in a small, neat brick road in a small, neat brick private-sector housing estate off the Belstead Road.

'It belongs to a Mr Johnson I believe,' said Mr Knights as they came downstairs, 'an engineer working on contract in Saudi Arabia for a year. But there's only a six-month lease left to run.'

'That should do very well,' said Mr Ross.

It was number 12 Cherryhayes Close. All the surrounding streets had names ending in 'hayes' so that the whole complex was known as simply 'The Hayes'. There was Brackenhayes, Gorsehayes, Almondhayes and Heatherhayes all around. Number 12 Cherryhayes was separated from the pavement by a 6-foot strip of grass and there was no fence. A single lock-up garage was attached to one side – Petrofsky knew he would need a garage. The back garden was small and fenced, reached through a door from the tiny kitchen. The downstairs contained the glass-panelled front door which led into a narrow hall. Straight in line with the front door was the staircase to the upper landing. Under the stairs was a broom cupboard.

For the rest, there was the single sitting-room at the front and the kitchen down the passage between the stairs and the sitting-room door. Upstairs were two bedrooms, one front and one back, and the bathroom/toilet. It was inconspicuous and blended with all the other identical brick boxes down the street, themselves occupied by mainly young couples, he in commerce or industry, she coping with the house and one or two toddlers. The place a man waiting for his wife and children to join him from Dorset at the end of the school term would choose and not be noticed very much.

'I'll take it,' he said.

'If we can just go back to the office and sort out the details . . .' said Mr Knights.

Being a furnished letting, the details were easy. A two-sheet formal lease to be signed and witnessed, a month's deposit in advance and a month's rent on top. Mr Ross produced a reference from his employers in Geneva and asked Mr Knights to call his bank in Dorchester on Monday morning to clear the cheque which he wrote out there and then. Mr Knights felt he could have the paperwork sorted to everyone's satisfaction by Monday evening, if the cheque and the references were in order. Ross smiled. They would be, he knew.

Alan Fox was also in his office that Saturday morning, at the special request of his friend Sir Nigel Irvine, who had called to say he needed a meeting. The English knight was ushered up the stairs at the American Embassy shortly after ten o'clock.

Alan Fox was the local Head of Station for the American CIA and he went back a long way. He had known Nigel Irvine for twenty years.

'I'm afraid we seem to have come across a small problem,' said Sir Nigel when he was seated. 'One of our civil servants in the Defence Ministry turns out to have been a bad egg.'

'Oh, for Christ's sake, Nigel, not another leak,' expostulated Fox.

Irvine looked apologetic. 'I'm afraid that's what it has to be,' he admitted. 'Something rather like your Harper affair.'

Alan Fox winced. The blow had struck home. Back in 1983 the Americans had been badly hurt on discovering that an engineer working in Silicon Valley, California, had blown to the Poles (and thence to the Russians) a vast tract of secret information about the US Minuteman missile systems.

Along with the earlier Boyce spying case, the Harper affair had levelled the score somewhat. The British had long tolerated rib-tickling references from the Americans about Philby, Burgess and Maclean, not to mention Blake, Vassall, Blunt and Prime, and even after all those years the stigma still stuck. It had almost made the British feel a bit better when the Americans had two bad ones over Boyce and Harper. At least other people had traitors as well.

'Ouch,' said Fox, 'that's what I've always liked about you, Nigel. You can't see a belt without wanting to hit below it.'

Fox was known in London for his acerbic wit. He had made his mark at an early meeting of the Joint Intelligence Committee when Sir Anthony Plumb had been complaining that unlike all the others he had no nice little acronym to describe his job. He was just the Chairman of the JIC, or the Coordinator of Intelligence. Why could he not have a group of initials that made up a short word in themselves?

'How about,' drawled Fox from his end of the table, 'Supreme Head of Intelligence Targeting?'

Sir Anthony preferred not to be known as the SHIT of Whitehall and dropped the matter of the acronym.

'OK, so how bad is it?' Fox asked.

'Not as bad as it might be,' said Sir Nigel, and told Fox the story from beginning to end.

The American leaned forward with interest. 'You mean he's really been turned right around? He's going to pass over just what he's told?'

'It's either that or the rest of his life eating prison porridge. He'll be under surveillance all the time. Of course, he may have a warning code for Marais that he can slip into a phone call, but I think not. He really is of the extreme Right, and it *was* a false-flag recruitment.'

Fox pondered for a while. 'How high do you reckon the Centre rates this Berenson, Nigel?'

'We start damage assessment on Monday,' said Irvine, 'but I think in view of his eminence in the Ministry, he must be rated very high in Moscow. Maybe even a Director's Case.'

'Could we pass some of our disinformation down the same line?' asked Fox. His mind could already see some useful ploys that Langley would love to pass to Moscow.

'I don't want to overload the circuits,' said Nigel. 'The rhythm of the stuff passed over must be maintained, as well as the type of stuff. But, yes, we *could* cut you in on this one.'

'And you want me to persuade my people to go easy on London?'

Sir Nigel shrugged. 'The damage that has been done is done. It's very good for the ego to make a hell of a fuss. But nonproductive. I'd like us to rectify the damage and inflict some of our own.'

'OK, Nigel, you've got it. I'll tell our people to back off. We get the damage assessment right off the presses? And we'll prepare a couple of pieces about our nuclear subs in the Atlantic and Indian oceans that will make the Centre look the wrong way. I'll stay in touch.'

On Monday morning Petrofsky rented a small and modest family saloon from an agency in Colchester. He explained that he was from Dorchester and was house-hunting in Essex and Suffolk. His own car was with his wife and family in Dorset, which was why he did not wish to buy a car for such a short spell. His driving licence was in perfect order, with a Dorchester address. Insurance, of course, came with the rental. He wished for a long-term rental, possibly up to three months, and opted for the budget plan.

He paid a week's rental in cash, and left a cheque for the

month after that. The next problem was going to be harder and would need the services of an insurance broker. He located and visited such a broker in the same town and explained his position.

He had worked abroad for some years and prior to that he had always driven a company car. As such, he had no regular insurance company in Britain. Now he had decided to return home and start up on his own account. He would need to purchase a vehicle, and for that would need insurance cover. Could the broker assist him?

The broker would be delighted. He assured himself the new client had a spotless driving licence, an international driving licence, a solid and respectable appearance and a bank account which even that morning he had transferred from Dorchester to Colchester.

What sort of vehicle did he intend to buy? A motorcycle. Yes, indeed. So much easier in dense traffic. Of course, in the hands of teenagers these were difficult to insure. But a mature professional man – no problem. Comprehensive would be a bit difficult perhaps . . . ah, the client would settle for third party only? And the address? House-hunting at the moment. Quite understandable. But staying at the Great White Horse in Ipswich? Perfectly acceptable. Then if Mr Ross would inform him of the registration number of his motorcycle when he made the purchase, and any change of address, he was sure he could secure third-party insurance cover in one or two days.

Petrofsky returned in his rented car to Ipswich. It had been a busy day but he was satisfied he had raised no suspicions and yet left behind no pursuable trace of himself. The car-rental agency and the hotel had been given an address in Dorchester that did not exist. Oxborrow's, the estate agents, and the insurance broker had the hotel as a temporary address and Oxborrow's knew about number 12 Cherrhayes. Barclays Bank in Colchester also had the hotel as his address while he was 'house-hunting'.

He would retain the room at the hotel until he had secured his insurance cover from the broker, then leave. The idea that any of the parties would ever be able to get in touch with each other was remote in the extreme. Apart from Oxborrow's, the trail stopped at the hotel or at a nonexistent address in Dorchester. So long as payments were kept up on the house and the car, so long as the insurance broker got a valid cheque for one year's premium on the motorcycle, none of them would think anything of him. Barclays at Colchester had been told to send him statements once a quarter, but by the end of June he would be long gone.

He returned to the estate agents to sign the lease and complete the formalities.

That Monday evening the spearhead of the damage assessment team arrived at George Berenson's apartment in Belgravia to begin their work.

It was a small group of MI5 experts and Defence Ministry analysts. The first task was identification: of every single document that had passed to Moscow. They had with them copies of the Registry files, withdrawals and returns, in case Berenson's memory failed him.

Later other analysts, basing their studies on the list of documents passed, would try to assess and mitigate the damage done, proposing what could still be changed, what plans would have to be cancelled, which tactical and strategic dispositions would have to be annulled and which could stay in place. They worked through the night and were later able to report that Berenson had been cooperation itself. What they thought of him privately did not form part of their report since it was unprintable.

Another team, working deep inside the Ministry, began to prepare the next batch of classified documents that Berenson would pass to Jan Marais and his controllers somewhere inside the First Chief Directorate at Yasyenevo.

* * *

John Preston moved into his new office as head of C.5(C) on the Wednesday, bringing his personal files with him. Fortunately he was moving up only one floor, to the third at Gordon. As he sat at his desk his eye caught sight of the calendar on the wall. It was 1 April, April Fool's Day.

How very appropriate, he thought bitterly.

The only ray on his horizon was the knowledge that in just over a week his son Tommy would be home for the Easter vacation. They would have a full week together before Julia, back from skiing with her boyfriend at Verbier, would claim him for the rest of the holiday.

For a whole week his small Kensington flat would reverberate to the sound of twelve-year-old enthusiasms, to tales of prowess on the rugby field, jokes played upon the French master and the need for further supplies of jam and cake for illegal consumption after lights-out in the dormitory. He smiled at the prospect and resolved to take at least four days off. He had planned a few good father-and-son expeditions and hoped they would meet with Tommy's approval. He was interrupted by Jeff Bright, his Deputy Head of Section.

Bright, he knew, would have had his job except that his youth simply did not make it possible. He was another of Harcourt-Smith's protégés, happy and flattered to be invited regularly for a quiet drink by the Deputy Director-General and to report everything that went on in the section. He would go far under the forthcoming Director-Generalship of Harcourt-Smith.

'I thought you might like to see the list of the ports and airports we have to keep an eye on, John,' said Bright.

Preston studied the lists put before him. Were there really that number of airports with flights orginating or terminating outside the British Isles? And the list of ports able to receive commercial cargo vessels arriving from foreign ports went on for pages. He sighed and started to read.

The following day Petrofsky found what he was looking

for. Operating on a policy of making different purchases in different towns in the Suffolk/Essex area, he had gone to Stowmarket. The motorcycle was a BMW shaft-drive K100, not new but in excellent condition, a big, powerful machine, three years old but with only 22,000 miles on the clock. The same shop also stocked the accessories – black leather trousers and jacket, gauntlets, zip-sided jackboots and crash-helmets with dark slide-down visors. He bought a complete outfit.

A 20 per cent deposit secured him the motorcycle, but not to take away. He asked for panniers to be fitted outside the rear wheel, with a lockable fibreglass box on top of them, and was told he could collect the machine in two days.

From a phone booth he called the insurance broker in Colchester and gave him the registration number of the BMW. The broker was confident he could have his temporary thirty-day insurance cover note by the next day. He would mail it to the Great White Horse Hotel in Ipswich.

From Stowmarket Petrofsky motored north to Thetford, just over the county border in Norfolk. There was nothing particular about Thetford; it just lay approximately in the line he needed. He found what he wanted just after lunch. In Magdalen Street, between 13A and the Salvation Army hall, is a recessed rectangular yard containing thirty-one lock-up garages. One had a 'To Let' notice stuck on its door.

He traced the owner, who lived locally, rented the garage for three months – paying for it in cash and giving a fictitious name and address – and was given the key. The garage was small, but would serve his purpose admirably.

He hung up his motorcycle leathers, helmet and boots and during what remained of the afternoon bought two ten-gallon plastic drums from two different shops, filled them with petrol at two different garages, and stored them in his lock-up. At sundown he motored back to Ipswich, telling the hotel receptionist that he would check out the following morning.

Preston realized he was becoming bored to the point of distraction. He had only been in the job two days, and they had been spent reading files.

He sat over lunch in the canteen and seriously thought of taking early retirement. That presented two problems. It would not be easy for a man in his mid-forties to get good employment, the more so as his arcane qualifications were hardly the type that the big corporations would find of irresistible interest.

The second concern was his loyalty to Sir Bernard Hemmings. He had been in the service only six years, but the Old Man had been very good to him. He liked Sir Bernard and he knew the knives were out for the ailing Director-General.

The ultimate decision in the choice of the head of MI5 or the Chief of MI6 in Britain lies with the committee of the so-called 'Wise Men'. For MI5 these would normally be the Permanent Under-Secretary of the Home Office, the Ministry controlling MI5; plus the PUS at Defence; and the Cabinet Secretary and the chairman of the Joint Intelligence Commitee.

These would 'recommend' a favoured candidate to the Home Secretary and Prime Minister, the two senior politicians involved. It would be rare for the politicians to decline the recommendation of the Wise Men.

But before they would make a decision the mandarins would take soundings in their own inimitable way. There would be discreet lunches in clubs, drinks at bars, murmured discussions over coffee. In the case of the proposed Director-General of MI5, the Chief of the SIS would be consulted, but as in this case Sir Nigel Irvine was himself moving close to retirement, he would have to have a very good reason to advise against a leading candidate for the other intelligence service. After all, *he* would not have to work with the man.

Among the most influential of the sources sounded out by the Wise Men would be the outgoing DG of MI5 himself. Preston knew that an honourable man like Sir Bernard Hemmings would feel bound to take a straw poll of his own heads of section throughout the six branches of the service. That straw poll would weigh heavily with him, whatever his personal feelings might be. Not for nothing had Brian Harcourt-Smith used his increasing predominance in the day-to-day running of the service to place one of his protégés after another at the head of the numerous sections.

Preston was in no doubt Harcourt-Smith would like him to leave before the autumn, along with two or three others who had gone into civilian life over the past twelve months.

'Sod him,' he remarked to no-one in particular in a largely empty canteen. 'I'll stay.'

While Preston was at lunch Petrofsky left the hotel, his luggage by now increased by a large suitcase full of clothes that he had bought locally. He told the receptionist that he would be moving to the Norfolk area and that any mail arriving for him should be held pending collection.

He rang the insurance broker in Colchester, to learn that the temporary cover note for the motorcycle had been issued. The Russian asked the broker not to mail it; he would collect it himself.

This he did immediately, and late that afternoon moved into number 12 Cherryhayes. He spent part of the night working carefully with his one-time pads, preparing a coded message that no computer would break. Code-breaking, he knew, is based on patterns and repetitions, however sophisticated the computer used to crack the code. Using a one-time pad for each word of a short message leaves no patterns and no repetitions.

On the Saturday morning he drove to Thetford, garaged his car and took a local taxi to Stowmarket. Here, with a certified cheque, he paid the balance on the price of the

BMW, borrowed the toilet to change into his leathers and crash helmet, which he had brought in a canvas grip, stuffed the grip and his ordinary jacket, trousers and shoes into the panniers, and rode away.

It was a long ride and took him many hours. It was not until late evening that he arrived back at Thetford, changed clothes, exchanged motorcycle for family saloon and motored sedately back to Cherryhayes Close, Ipswich, arriving at midnight. He was not observed, but had he been it would have been as that nice young Mr Ross who had moved into number 12 on Friday.

On a Saturday evening United States Master Sergeant Averell Cook would have preferred to be dating his girlfriend in nearby Bedford. Or even playing pool with friends in the commissary. Instead he was taking the swing shift at the joint British–American listening station at Chicksands.

The head office of the British electronic monitoring and code-breaking complex is at the Government Communications HQ at Cheltenham, Gloucestershire, in the south of England. But GCHQ has outstations in various parts of the country, and one of them, Chicksands in Bedfordshire, is run jointly by GCHQ and the American National Security Agency.

The days when attentive men sat hunched into earphones trying to pick up and record the manual tapping of a Morse key operated by some German agent in Britain are long gone. In the business of listening, analysing, filtering the innocent from the not-so-innocent, recording the latter and decoding, computers have taken over.

Master Sergeant Cook was confident and rightly so that if any of the forest of aerials above him picked up an electronic whisper, it would pass that whisper to the banks of computers below. The scanning of the bands was automatic, the recording of any whisper in the ether that should not be there equally automatic.

If such a whisper occurred, the eternally watchful

computer would trigger its own 'hit' button deep inside its own multicoloured entrails, record the transmission, take an immediate bearing on its source, instruct other brother computers across the country to take a crossbearing, and alert him.

At 11.43 p.m. something caused the master computer to operate its own 'hit' button. Something or someone had transmitted what was not expected and out of the whirling kaleidoscope of electronic signals that fill the air of this planet twenty-four hours in every day, the computer had noticed and traced it. Master Sergeant Cook noted the warning signal and reached for a telephone.

What the computer had picked up was a 'squirt', a brief shriek of sound that lasted only a few seconds and would make no sense to the human ear.

A squirt is the end product of quite a laborious procedure in the sending of clandestine messages. First the message is written out 'in clear' and as brief as possible. Then it is encoded, but it still remains a list of letters or figures. The encoded message is tapped out on a Morse key, not to a listening world but to a tape machine. The tape is then speeded up to an extreme degree, so that the dots and dashes that make up the transmission are telescoped, to emerge as a single screech lasting only a few seconds. When the transmitter is ready to go, the operator simply sends that single screech, then packs up his set and moves sharply somewhere else.

Within ten minutes, that Saturday night, the triangulators had pinpointed the spot from which the screech had come. Other computers at Menwith Hill in Yorkshire and Brawdy in Wales had also caught the brief squirt transmission and taken a bearing. When the local police got there, the spot turned out to be a lay-by on a lonely road high in the Derbyshire Peak District. There was no-one there.

In due course the message went to Cheltenham and was slowed down to a pace at which the dots and dashes could be transcribed into letters. But after twenty-four hours going through the electronic brains called the code-breakers, the answer was still a big zero.

'It's a sleeper transmitter, probably somewhere in the Midlands and he's gone to "active",' the chief analyst reported to the Director-General of GCHQ. 'But our man seems to be using a fresh one-time pad for every word. Unless we can have a lot more of it, we won't break it.'

It was decided to keep a close watch on the channel the secret sender had used, though if he broadcast again he would almost certainly use a different channel.

A brief flimsy recording the incident went to the desks, among others, of Sir Bernard Hemmings and Sir Nigel Irvine.

The message had been received elsewhere, notably in Moscow. Decoded with a replica set of the one-time pads used in a quiet backwater of Ipswich, the message told those interested that the man on the ground had completed all his preliminary tasks ahead of schedule and was ready to receive his first courier.

13

The spring thaw would not be long in coming, but for the moment crusted snow hung on the branches of the birch and fir trees far below. From the spectacular double-glazed window on the seventh and top floor of the First Chief Directorate building at Yasyenevo the man gazing out at the landscape could make out, across the sea of winter trees, the tip of the western end of the lake where, in summer, the foreign diplomats from Moscow like to come and disport themselves.

That Sunday morning Lieutenant-General Yevgeni Sergeivitch Karpov would have preferred to be with his wife and teenage children at their dacha at Peredelkino, but even when one has risen as high in the service as Karpov, there are some things that have to be taken care of personally. The arrival of the bagman due home from Copenhagen was such a matter.

He glanced at his watch. It was nearly noon and the man was late. Turning from the window he sighed and threw himself into the easy swivel chair behind his desk.

At fifty-seven, Yevgeni Karpov was at the pinnacle of promotion and power achievable by a professional intelligence officer within the KGB, or at least within the First Chief Directorate. Fedorchuk had gone higher, right up to the chairmanship itself, and on to the MVD, but that had been on the General Secretary's coat-tails. Moreover, Fedorchuck had not been FCD; he had rarely left the Soviet Union; he had made his bones crushing internal dissident and nationalist movements.

But for a man who had spent years serving his country abroad – always a minus in terms of promotion to the highest offices in the Union – Karpov had done well. A lean, fit-looking man in a beautifully cut suit, one of the perks of being FCD, he was a full Lieutenant-General and First Deputy Head of the First Chief Directorate. As such, he was the highest-ranking professional IO in foreign intelligence, the equivalent of the Deputy Directors of Operations and Intelligence at the CIA, and of Sir Nigel Irvine at the British SIS.

Years earlier, on his accession to power, the General Secretary had plucked Fedorchuk out of the Chairmanship of the KGB to overlord the Interior Ministry, and General Chebrikov had gone up to replace him. It had left a slot vacant; Chebrikov had been one of the two First Deputy Chairmen.

The vacant post of First Deputy Chairman had been offered to Colonel-General Kryuchkov, who had jumped at it. The trouble was, Kryuchkov was then Head of the FCD and he did not want to relinquish that powerful post. He wanted to hold both posts together. Even Kryuchkov had realized – and Karpov privately thought the man as thick as two short planks – that he could not be in two places at once; he could not be in his First Deputy Chairman's office at the Centre on Dzerzhinsky Square and in the office of the Head of the FCD out at Yasyenevo at the same time.

What happened was that the post of First Deputy Head of the FCD, which had existed for years, increased substantially in importance. It had already been a job for an officer of considerable operational experience, indeed the highest in the FCD to which a career officer could aspire. With Kryuchkov no longer resident at 'the village' – KGB house jargon for Yasyenevo – the job of his First Deputy had become even more important.

When the incumbent, General B. S. Ivanov, retired, there were two possible candidates in line to succeed: Karpov, then a bit young but heading up the important Third Department in Room 6013, the department covering Britain, Australia, New Zealand and Scandinavia; and Vadim Vassilyevitch Kirpichenko, rather older, a bit senior and heading the 'S' or 'Illegals' Directorate. Kirpichenko had got the job.

As a sort of consolation prize Karpov had been promoted to be Head of the powerful 'Illegals' Directorate, a post he had held for two fascinating years.

Then in the early spring of 1985 Kirpichenko had done the decent thing: speeding down the Sadovaya Spasskaya ring road at close to a hundred, his car had clipped a pool of oil left by a leaking truck and had gone completely out of control. A week later there had been a quiet private ceremony at Novodevichii Cemetery, and a week after that Karpov had got the job, rising from Major-General to Lieutenant-General.

He had been happy to hand the 'Illegals' Directorate over to old Borisov, who had been number two there for so long few cared to remember just how many years it had been, and who deserved the job anyway.

The phone on his desk rang and he snatched it up.

'Comrade Major-General Borisov on the line for you.'

Speak of the devil, he thought. Then he frowned. He had a private line that did not pass through the switchboard and his old colleague had not used it. Must be phoning from outside. Telling his secretary to bring the bagman from Copenhagen to him the moment he arrived, he depressed the outside-line switch and took Borisov's call.

'Pavel Petrovitch, how are you this fine day?'

'I tried you at home, then at the dacha. Ludmilla said you were at work.'

'So I am. It's all right for some.'

Karpov was gently pulling the older man's leg. Borisov was a widower, lived alone and put in more working weekends than almost anyone else.

'Yevgeni Sergeivitch, I need to see you.'

'Of course. You don't need to ask. You want to come over here tomorrow or shall I come into town?'

'Could you make it today?'

Even odder, thought Karpov. Something must have

really got into the old boy. He sounded as though he might have been drinking.

'Have you been on the bottle, Pavel Petrovitch?'

'Maybe I have,' said the truculent voice down the line. 'Maybe a man needs a few drams now and again. Especially when he has problems.'

Karpov realized that, whatever it was, it was serious. He dropped the bantering tone. 'All right, *starets*,' he said soothingly, 'where are you?'

'You know my cottage?'

'Of course. You want me to come out there?'

'Yes, I'd be grateful,' said Borisov. 'When can you make it?'

'Say about six,' proposed Karpov.

'I'll have a bottle of pepper vodka ready,' said the voice, and Borisov hung up.

'Not on my account,' muttered Karpov. Unlike most Russians, Karpov hardly drank at all, and when he did he preferred a decent Armenian brandy or a Scotch single malt which came to him personally in the bag from London. Vodka he regarded as an abomination and pepper vodka even worse.

Bang goes my Sunday afternoon at Peredelkino, he thought, and rang to tell Ludmilla he could not make it. He made no mention of Borisov; just told her he could not get away and that he would see her at their central Moscow apartment about midnight.

Still, he was perturbed by Borisov's unusual truculence; they went back a long way together, too long for him to take offence, but it was odd in a man habitually so genial and phlegmatic.

That Sunday afternoon the regular Aeroflot service from Moscow came into London's Heathrow Airport just after five.

As with all Aeroflot crews there was one member who worked for two masters, the Soviet state airline and the KGB. First Officer Romanov was not a KGB staffer, just *agyent*, meaning an informer upon his colleagues and from time to time a runner of messages and errands.

The whole crew closed the aircraft down and left it in the hands of the ground staff for the night. They would fly it back to Moscow the next day. As usual, they went through the flight-crew entry procedures and Customs gave a cursory check of their shoulderbags and grips. Several had their own portable transistor radios, and no-one took any notice of Romanov's Sony model on its shoulder strap. Western luxury items were part of the perks of foreign travel for a Soviet citizen, everyone knew that, and although they had an extremely tight foreign-currency allowance, cassettes and players, along with radios and perfume for the wife back in Moscow, were among the top priorities.

After clearing Immigration and Customs formalities the whole crew boarded their minibus for the Green Park Hotel, where Aeroflot crews often stay. Whoever had given Romanov that transistor radio in Moscow just three hours before take-off must have known that Aeroflot crews are hardly ever shadowed at Heathrow. The British counter-intelligence people seem to accept that though they may constitute a risk, it must be a tolerable one compared to the mounting of a pretty major surveillance operation.

When he got to his bedroom Romanov could not help looking at the radio with curiosity. Then he shrugged, locked it in his case and went down to the bar to join the other officers in a drink. He knew exactly what to do with it after breakfast the next day. He would do it, then forget all about it. He did not know then that on his return to Moscow he would be going straight into quarantine.

Karpov's car crunched up the snow-clogged track just before six and he cursed Borisov's insistence on having his weekend cottage in such a forsaken place.

Everyone in the service knew Borisov was a one-off. In a society that regards all individualism or deviation from the norm, not to mention eccentricity, as extremely suspect, Borisov got away with it because he was unusually good at his job. He had been in clandestine intelligence since he was a boy and some of the coups he had mounted against the West were legendary in the training schools and the canteens where the junior men took their lunches.

After half a mile down the track Karpov could make out the lights of the log cabin, or *izba*, that Borisov favoured for his weekend retreat. Others were content, even eager, to site their weekend places in the approved zones according to their station in the pecking order, and those zones were all west of Moscow along the curve of the river across the Uspenskoye Bridge. Not Borisov. Well east of the capital, deep in the forests, he liked to retire at the weekends, or those when he could get away from his desk, to play rustic peasant in a traditional *izba*. The Chaika came to a halt in front of the timber door.

'Wait here,' Karpov told his driver.

'I'd better turn around and get some of those logs under the wheels or we'll stick solid,' grumbled Misha.

Karpov nodded his agreement and climbed out. He had not brought galoshes because he had not envisaged wading through snow up to the knees. He stumbled to the door and hammered on it. The door opened to reveal an oblong of yellow light, thrown apparently by paraffin lamps, and in the space stood Major-General Pavel Petrovitch Borisov dressed in a Siberian shirt, cord trousers and felt boots.

'You look like something out of a Tolstoy novel,' remarked Karpov as he was shown into the main sitting-room where a brick stove full of logs gave the cottage a womb-like warmth.

'Better than something out of a Bond Street window,' grumbled Borisov as he took Karpov's coat and hung it on a wooden peg. He uncorked a bottle of vodka so strong it poured like syrup and filled two shot glasses. The men seated themselves, a table between them.

'Bottoms up.' Karpov raised his glass, Russian style, between forefinger and thumb, pinkie extended.

'Up yours,' replied Borisov and they drained the first slug.

An old peasant woman shaped like a teacosy, blank face and grey hair in a tight bun, like an incarnation of Mother Russia, came in from the back, banged down a collation of black bread, onions, gherkins and cheese cubes, and left without a word.

'So what's the problem, *starets*?' asked Karpov.

Borisov was five years older than himself and not for the first time he was struck by the man's spitting image to the late Dwight Eisenhower. Karpov knew he was, unlike many in the service, much liked by his colleagues and adored by his young agents. They had long given him the affectionate nickname '*starets*', a word once meaning a Russian village headman but now more like 'the Old Man' or '*le patron*'.

Borisov stared at him moodily across the table. 'Yevgeni Sergeivitch, how long have we known each other?'

'More years than I care to remember,' said Karpov.

'And in that time, have I ever lied to you?'

'Not that I know of.' Karpov was pensive.

'And are you now going to lie to me?'

'Not if I can help it,' said Karpov carefully. What on earth had got into the old boy?

'Then what the hell are you doing to my department?' demanded Borisov loudly.

Karpov considered the question carefully. 'Why don't you tell me what is happening to your department?' he countered.

'It's being stripped, that's what,' snarled Borisov. 'You have to be behind it. Or aware of it. How the hell am I supposed to run the "S" operation when my best men, my best documents and my best facilities are being stripped from me? Bloody years of hard work . . . all confiscated within a matter of days.'

He had had his explosion, the thing that he had bottled up until now. Karpov sat back lost in thought while Borisov topped up the glasses. He had not risen as high as he had within the labyrinthine corridors of the KGB without developing a sixth sense for danger. Borisov was no alarmist; there had to be something behind what he said, but Karpov quite genuinely did not know what it was. He leaned forward.

'Pal Petrovitch,' he said, dropping into the very familiar diminutive of Pavel, 'as you say, we have been around for a good many years. Believe me, I don't know what you're talking about. Will you please stop shouting and tell me?'

Borisov was mollified, albeit puzzled by Karpov's assurance of ignorance. 'All right,' he said, as if explaining the obvious to a child. 'First, two goons arrive from the Central Committee and demand that I hand over to them my best illegal, a man I've spent years training personally and of whom I had the greatest hopes. They say he has to be detached for "special duties", whatever that may mean.

'OK, I give them my best man. I don't like it, but I do it. Two days later they are back. They want my best legend, a legend that took over ten years to put together. Not since that damn Iranian affair have I been treated like that. You remember the Iranian buisness? I'm still not recovered from that.'

Karpov nodded. He had not been with the Illegals Directorate then, but Borisov had told him about it all when they worked together during his two-year tenure of the directorship of the Illegals. In the last days of the Shah of Iran, the International Department of the Central Committee had decided it would be a nice idea to spirit the entire politburo of the Iranian Tudeh (Communist) Party out of Iran covertly.

They had raided Borisov's magpie-hoarded files and confiscated twenty-two perfect Iranian legends, cover stories Borisov had been saving to send people *into* Iran, not get them out.

'Stripped to the bone,' he had screamed at the time, 'just to get those flea-bitten wogs to safety.'

Later he had complained to Karpov, 'It didn't do them much good either. The Ayatollah's in charge, the Tudeh is still banned, and we can't even mount an operation in there any more.'

Karpov knew that affair still rankled, but the new business was more odd. For one thing, the demand should have come through him.

'Who did you give them?' he asked.

'Petrofsky,' said Borisov resignedly. 'I had to. They asked for the best, and he was way ahead of the others. Remember Petrofsky?'

Karpov nodded. He had only headed the Illegals for two years, but he recalled all their best names and on-going operations. In his present post he had total access anyway.

'Whose authority was on these indents?'

'Well, technically the Central Committee. But from the authority rating . . .' Borisov pointed a rigid finger at the ceiling and, by inference, the sky.

'God?' queried Karpov.

'Almost. Our beloved General Secretary. At least, that's my guess.'

'Anything else?'

'Yep. Just after the legend, the same clowns are back again. That time they took the receiver crystal of one of the covert transmitters you seeded into England four years ago. That was why I thought it was all down to you.'

Karpov's eyes narrowed. When he had been Director of the Illegals, the NATO countries had been deploying Pershing Two and Cruise missiles. Washington had been running around the world trying to re-enact the last reel of every John Wayne movie ever written and the politburo had been worried sick. He had received orders to upgrade the Illegals' contingency planning for massive behind-the-lines sabotage operations in Western Europe, for use in the event of any actual outbreak of hostilities.

To fulfil this order he had seeded a number of clandestine radio transmitters into Western Europe, including three into Britain. The men guarding the sets and trained to operate them were all sleepers ordered to lie low until activated by an agent with the proper identification codes.

The sets were ultra-modern, scrambling their messages as they were transmitted, and to unscramble the message the receiving set would need a programmed crystal. These were stored in a safe in the Illegals Directorate.

'Which transmitter?' he enquired.

'The one you always called Poplar.'

Karpov nodded. He knew all operations, agents and assets had official code names. But he had been a specialist in Britain for so long and knew London so well that he had private code names for his own operation, and they were based in London districts whose names had two syllables. The three transmitters he had caused to be placed in Britain were, for him, Hackney, Shoreditch and Poplar.

'Any more, Pal Petrovitch?'

'Sure. These guys are never satisfied. The last one they took was Igor Volkov.'

Major Volkov, formerly of the executive Action Department until the Politburo had decided straight hit jobs were becoming too embarrassing and the Bulgars and East Germans should be told to do the dirty work. Then Department V, or Executive Action, had gone in more for sabotage.

'What's his speciality?'

'Bringing clandestine packages through state borders, particularly in Western Europe.'

'Smuggling.'

'All right, smuggling. He's good. He knows more about the borders in that part of the world, the customs and immigration procedures, and how to get round them, than anyone else we've got. Well . . . had, I should say. They took him too.'

Karpov rose and leaned forward, placing both hands on the older man's shoulders.

'Look, *starets*, I give you my word, this is not my operation. I didn't even know about it. But we both know it has to be very big, and that means it's dangerous to start poking around. Stay cool, bite on the bullet, absorb your losses. I'll try and find out quietly what is going on and when you can have your assets back. For your part, stay buttoned up, tighter than a Georgian's purse, OK?'

Borisov raised both his hands, palms forward, in a gesture of innocence. 'You know me, Yevgeni Sergeivitch, I'm going to die the oldest man in Russia.'

Karpov laughed. He pulled on his coat and made for the door. Borisov followed to see him out.

'I think you will, too,' said Karpov.

When the door was closed behind him, Karpov tapped on his driver's window.

'Follow me until I want to get in,' he said. He started to walk down the snowy track, oblivious of the ice that clung to his town shoes and worsted trousers. The freezing night air was refreshing on the face, driving away some of the vodka fumes, and he needed a clear head to think. What he had learned had made him very angry indeed. Someone, and he had few doubts who it might be, was mounting a private operation in Britain. Apart from the massive snub to the First Deputy Head of the First Chief Directorate, he, Karpov, had spent so many years in Britain, or running agents within it, that he regarded it as his private preserve.

As General Karpov walked down the track lost in thought, a phone rang in a small flat in Highgate, London, not five hundred yards from the tomb of Karl Marx.

'Are you there, Barry?' a woman's voice called from the kitchen. From the sitting-room a male voice called back: 'Yes, I'll get it.'

The man walked to the hall and took the phone while his wife continued preparing their Sunday dinner.

'Barry?'

'Speaking.'

'Ah, sorry to disturb you on a Sunday evening. It's "C".'

'Oh, evening, sir.'

Barry Banks was surprised. It was not unheard of, but not frequent, that the Master called one of his people at home.

'Look, Barry, what time do you normally get into Charles Street in the morning?'

'About ten, sir.'

'Could you leave an hour earlier tomorrow and drop by Sentinel to have a word with me?'

'Yes. Of course.'

'Good. Then I'll see you about nine.'

Barry Banks was K.7 at the Charles Street headquarters of MI5, but he was actually an MI6 man whose job was to act as Sir Nigel Irvine's link with the Security Service. He wondered idly as he ate the supper his wife had prepared for him what Sir Nigel Irvine could want and why it had to be asked out of hours.

Yevgeni Karpov had not a shred of doubt that a secret operation had been mounted and was being carried out, and that it concerned Britain. Petrofsky, he knew, was an expert at passing for a Britisher right in the heart of that country; the legend that had been abstracted from Borisov's files fitted Petrofsky to a T; the Poplar transmitter was hidden away in the north Midlands of England. If Volkov had been transferred because of his speciality in bringing packages into Britian, there must be other transfers already made, but from different directorates outside Borisov's orbit.

All of which pointed unswervingly to the likelihood that Petrofsky would be going to Britain under deep cover, or had already gone. Nothing strange in that, it was what he had been trained for. What *was* strange was that the First Chief Directorate in the form of himself had been kept rigorously out of the operation. It made little sense, bearing in mind his own personal expertise in Britain and British affairs.

He went back twenty years in his connection with Britain, since that evening in September 1967 when he had been trawling in the bars of West Berlin frequented by off-duty British service personnel. As a keen and rising 'illegal', it was his assignment at the time.

His eye had fallen on a morose, sour-looking young man farther down the bar, whose civilian suit and haircut had said 'British armed forces'. He moved in on the lonely drinker and discovered he was a twenty-nine-year-old radio operator with a signals/intelligence (i.e. monitoring) unit, serving with the Royal Air Force at Gatow. He was also thoroughly discontented with his lot in life.

Between that September and January 1968 Karpov had worked on the RAF man, first pretending to be a German, as was his cover, and then admitting he was Russian. It was an easy pull, so easy it was almost suspect. But it was genuine, all right; the Englishman was flattered to be the subject of KGB attention, had the inadequate man's hatred of his own service and country, and agreed to work for Moscow. During the summer of 1968 Karpov trained him personally in East Berlin, getting to know and despise him more. The RAF man's tour in Berlin and his contract in the RAF was coming to a close, and he was due that September of 1968 to return to Britain and demobilization. It was suggested that on leaving the Air Force, he apply for a job at Government Communications HQ at Cheltenham. He agreed, and in September 1968 did precisely that. His name was Geoffrey Prime.

Karpov, to be able to continue to run Prime, was transferred under diplomatic cover to the Soviet Embassy in London, and continued to control Prime for three years until in 1971 he came back to Moscow and handed the control over to a successor. But the case had done his career a power of good, and he was promoted major, with a transfer back to the Third Department. From here he handled Prime's source material throughout the mid-seventies. It is axiomatic in any intelligence service that an operation producing excellent material will be noted and praised, and the officer controlling that operation is inseparable from the praise.

In 1977 Prime resigned from GCHQ; the British knew there was a leak there somewhere and the hounds were sniffing. In 1978 Karpov went back to London, this time as head of the entire *rezidentura* with the rank of colonel. Although out of GCHQ, Prime was still an agent, and Karpov sought to warn him to keep a very low profile indeed. There was, Karpov pointed out, not a shred of proof as to his pre-1977 activities, and Prime could only inculpate himself.

He'd be a free man today if he'd only been able to keep his dirty hands off little girls, thought Karpov savagely. For he had long known of Prime's inadequacy, and it was eventually a grubby indecent-assault charge that brought the police to his door, and to his confession. He got thirty-five years on seven charges of spying.

But London brought two bonuses to offset the reverse of the Prime affair. At a drinks party in 1980 he had been introduced to a civil servant from the British Defence Ministry. At first the man had not heard Karpov's name correctly and there were several minutes of polite conversation before the man realized Karpov was a Russian. When he did so, his attitude changed. Behind his abrupt and icy attitude, Karpov discerned a visceral loathing of himself, either as a Russian or as a Communist.

He was not upset, just intrigued. He learned the man's name was George Berenson, and further enquiries over the succeeding weeks revealed that the man was a dedicated anti-Communist and passionate admirer of South Africa. He privately tagged Berenson as a possible for a false-flag approach.

In May 1981 he had returned to Moscow to head the Third Department itself and asked around for a possible South African pro-Soviet sleeper. The Illegals Directorate mentioned that they had two men there, one an officer called Gerhardt in the South African navy, the other a diplomat called Marais. But Marais had just returned to Pretoria after three years in Bonn.

It was in the spring of 1983 that Karpov went up to Major-General and to the head of the Illegals Directorate, controlling Marais. He ordered the South African to ask for a London posting to terminate his long career, and in

1984 Marais got it. Karpov personally flew to Paris under deep cover and briefed Marais himself: Marais was to cultivate George Berenson and try to recruit him for South Africa.

In February 1985 after the death of Kirpichenko, Karpov succeeded to his present post and a month later, in March, Marais reported that Berenson was on the hook. That month the first batch of Berenson material came through; it was solid twenty-four-carat gold, the mother lode. Since then he had personally run the Berenson/Marais operation as a Director's Case, twice in two years meeting Marais in European cities to congratulate and debrief him. The bagman had that very lunch hour brought the latest batch of Berenson material, mailed by Marais to a KGB address in Copenhagen.

The London spell from 1978 to 1981 had brought a second benefit. As was his wont, he had given Prime and Berenson his personal code names: Prime had been Knightsbridge and Berenson was Hampstead. And then there was Chelsea . . .

He respected Chelsea, as he despised Prime and Berenson. Unlike the other two, Chelsea was not an agent, but a contact, a man high in his own country's establishment and a man who, like Karpov, was a pragmatist, a man wedded to the realities of his job, his country and the surrounding world. Karpov never ceased to be amazed at journalistic references in the West to intelligence officers living in a world of fantasy; for him, it was the politicians who lived in their dream world, seduced and bemused by their own propaganda.

Intelligence officers, he believed, might walk in shadowed streets, lie and deceive to carry out their mission, but if they ever wandered into the realm of fantasy, as the CIA's covert-action people had done so often, that was when they came badly unstuck.

Chelsea had twice dropped him hints that if the USSR continued on a certain course there would soon be a fearsome mess for them all to clear up; twice he had been right. Karpov, able to warn his own people of impending danger, had scored a mountain of credits when he turned out to be correct.

He stopped and forced his mind back to the present problem. Borisov was right: it was the General Secretary, mounting some kind of a personal and private operation right under his nose and inside Britain, but excluding the KGB from any part of it. He sensed danger; the old man was no professional intelligence officer despite his years at the head of the KGB. Karpov's own career might hang in the balance; yet it was vital to find out what on earth was going on. But carefully, very carefully.

He checked his watch. Half past eleven. He beckoned his car forward, climbed in and was driven home to Moscow.

Barry Banks arrived at the headquarters of the SIS at ten to nine that Monday morning. Sentinel House is a large, square and surprisingly tawdry-looking building on the South Bank, leased to a certain government ministry by the Greater London Council. Its lifts are erratic and around its lower floors a mosaic mural is for ever shedding its tiles like ceramic dandruff.

Banks identified himself at the front desk and went straight up. The Master received him at once, his usual bluff and genial self towards aspiring underlings.

'Do you know a chap called John Preston at "Five", by any chance?' asked 'C'.

'Yes, sir. Not well, but I've met him several times. Usually in the bar at Gordon, when I've been over there.'

'He heads C.1(A), doesn't he, Barry?'

'Not any more. He's been transferred to C.5(C). Last week.'

'Oh, really, that's rather sudden. I heard he'd done rather well at C.1(A).'

Sir Nigel felt no need to inform Banks that he had met Preston at the JIC meetings, or used him as his personal ferret in South Africa. Banks knew nothing of the

Berenson affair, nor did he need to know. For his part, Banks wondered what the Master had in mind. So far as he knew, Preston had nothing to do with 'Six'.

'Very sudden. In fact he was only at C.1(A) for a few weeks. Up till the New Year he was head of F.1(D). Then he must have done something that upset Sir Bernard, or more likely Brian Harcourt-Smith. He was booted out of there and into C.1(A). Then on April the first he was given the heave-ho again.'

Ah, thought Sir Nigel. Upset Harcourt-Smith, did he? Suspected as much. Wonder why. Aloud he said: 'Any idea what he could have done to upset Harcourt-Smith?'

'I did hear something, sir. From Preston. He wasn't talking to me, but close enough for me to hear. He was in the bar at Gordon at the time, about two weeks back. He seemed a bit upset himself. Apparently he spent years preparing a report and submitted it last Christmas. He thought it was worth attention, but Harcourt-Smith NFA-ed it.'

'Mmmmmm. F.1(D) . . . that's extreme-Left activities, isn't it? Look, Barry, I want you to do something for me. No need to make a song and dance about it. Just quietly. Find out the file number on that report and draw it from Registry, will you? Put it in the bag and send it over here, marked to me personally.'

Banks found himself back on the street and heading north towards Charles just before ten.

The Aeroflot crew had a leisurely breakfast and at 9.29 First Officer Romanov checked his watch and went to the men's toilets. He had been there before and ascertained the cubicle he was to take. It was the second from the end. The one at the end already had its door closed and locked. He went into the adjacent one and locked the door.

At 9.30 he placed a small card on which he had written the prescribed six figures on the floor next to the partition. A hand came under the partition, withdrew the card, wrote something on it and placed it back on the floor.

Romanov picked it up. On the reverse side were the six figures he had been expecting.

With identification established, he placed the transistor on the floor and the same hand drew it silently into the next-door cubicle. Outside, someone was using the urinal. Romanov flushed the pan, unlocked the door, washed his hands until the urinal-user had left, then followed him out. The minibus for Heathrow was at the door. None of the crew noticed his Sony was missing; they just thought it was in his grip. Courier One had delivered.

Barry Banks phoned Sir Nigel just before the hour of noon. It was an internal line and very secure.

'It's rather odd, Sir Nigel,' he said. 'I secured the file number of that report you wanted and went to Registry for it. I know the file clerk pretty well. He confirmed it's in the NFA section. But it's out.'

'Out?'

'Out. Withdrawn.'

'By whom?'

'A man called Swanton. I know him. The odd thing is he's in Finance. So I asked him if I could borrow it. That's the second odd thing. He refused, said he wasn't finished with it yet. According to Registry, he's had it three weeks. Before that it was out to someone else.'

'The lavatory attendant?' asked Sir Nigel.

'Almost. Someone in Admin.'

Sir Nigel thought for a while. The best way to keep a file permanently out of circulation was to keep it on permanent withdrawal to oneself or one's protégés. He had little doubt Swanton and the other man were Harcourt-Smith's young men.

'Barry, I want you to find out Preston's personal address. Then meet me here at five.'

General Karpov sat at his desk that afternoon at Yasyenevo and rubbed his stiff neck. It had not been a restful night. He had lain awake most of it, with Ludmilla sleeping by his side. By dawn he had come to a conclusion and further thought in the moments he could snatch from his daily work had not altered it.

It was the General Secretary who was behind the mysterious operation being mounted in Britain, but despite his pretensions to read and speak English, he had no knowledge of the country. He would have relied on the advice of someone who did. There were many – in the Foreign Ministry, the International Department of the Central Committee, the GRU and the KGB. But if he was avoiding the KGB, why not the others?

So, a personal adviser. And the more he thought, the more the name of his personal *béte noire* kept cropping up. Years ago, as a young man making his way in the service, he had admired Philby. They all had. But with the passing years he had risen while Philby had fallen. He had also watched the English renegade deteriorate into a drunken wreck. The fact was, Philby had not been near a British classified document (except those shown to him by the KGB) since 1951. He had quit Britain in 1955 for Beirut and had not even been in the West since his final defection in 1963. Twenty-four years. Karpov reckoned *he* knew Britain better than Philby by now.

There was more. He knew that when he was at the KGB the General Secretary had in some way become impressed by Philby, his old-world mannerisms and tastes, his affectation of the English gentleman, his dislike of the modern world with all its pop music, motorcycles and blue jeans – tastes that mirrored the General Secretary's own. Several times, to Karpov's certain knowledge, the General Secretary had had recourse to Philby's advice as a sort of backstop to the advice he received from the First Chief Directorate. Why not now?

Finally in Karpov's catalogue, there was the tip that once, just once, Philby had let something slip, something extremely interesting. He wanted to return home. For that, if for nothing else, Karpov did not trust him. Not one inch. He recalled the lined, smiling face across the table from him at Kryuchkov's dinner party before the New Year. What had he said about Britain then? Something about her political stability being overestimated by his department?

There were pieces, and they were beginning to slot together. He decided to check out Mr Harold Adrian Russell Philby. But he knew that even at his level things were noted; withdrawals from Registry, official requests for information, phone calls, memoranda. It had to be unofficial, personal and above all verbal. The General Secretary was a very dangerous man to antagonize.

John Preston had arrived in his own street and was a hundred yards from the entrance to his apartment block when he heard the hail. He turned to see Barry Banks crossing the road towards him.

'Hallo, Barry, small world. What are you doing here?'

He knew the man from K.7 lived up north in the Highgate area. Perhaps he was going to a concert at the nearby Albert Hall.

'Waiting for you, actually,' said Banks with a friendly grin. 'Look, a colleague of mine wants to meet you. Would you mind?'

Preston was intrigued but not suspicious. He knew Banks was from 'Six', but not who might want to meet him. He allowed Banks to guide him across the road and a hundred yards down. Banks stopped at a parked Ford Granada, opened the back door and gestured Preston to look inside. He did so.

'Good evening, John. Do you mind if we have a couple of words?'

In surprise Preston climbed in beside the seated figure in the greatcoat. Banks closed the door and wandered away.

'Look, I know it's an odd way to meet. But there we are. Don't want to cause any waves, do we? I just felt I had not had a decent opportunity to thank you for the work you did down in South Africa. It was a first-class job. Henry Pienaar was most impressed. So was I.'

'Thank you, Sir Nigel.' Now, what on earth did the wily old fox want? It certainly wasn't that. But 'C' seemed lost in thought.

'There *is* another matter,' he said at length, as if thinking aloud. 'Young Barry tells me it has come to his notice that last Christmas you put in a most interesting report about the extreme Left in this country. I could well be wrong, but there might have been a foreign dimension to some of the funding going on, if you see what I mean. The thing is, your report was not circulated to us in the Firm. Pity, that.'

'It was NFA-ed,' said Preston quickly.

'Yes, yes, so Barry tells me. Pity, really. I'd have liked to have a glance at it. No chance of getting hold of a copy?'

'It's in the Registry,' said Preston, puzzled. 'It may be NFA-ed but it's on file. Barry has only got to withdraw it and send it over in the bag.'

'Actually, no,' said Sir Nigel. 'It's already been withdrawn. By Swanton. And he hasn't finished with it. Won't pass it over.'

'But he's in Finance,' protested Preston.

'Yes,' murmured Sir Nigel regretfully, 'and before that it was out to someone in Admin. One might also think it was being kept out of sight.'

Preston sat there stunned. Through the windscreen he could see Banks dawdling up the street. 'There is another copy,' he said. 'My own. It's in my personal safe.'

Banks drove them. In the evening traffic it was a crawl from Kensington to Gordon Street. An hour later Preston leaned through the window of the Granada and handed his copy to Sir Nigel.

14

General Yevgeni Karpov climbed the last of the stairs to the third floor of the apartment block on Prospekt Mira and rang the buzzer. After several minutes the door opened. Philby's wife stood in the frame. From inside Karpov could hear the sound of small boys at their tea. He had chosen 6 p.m. on the hunch that they would be home from school by then.

'Hello, Erita.'

She tilted her head back in a small gesture of defiance. A very protective lady. Perhaps she knew Karpov was no admirer of her husband.

'Comrade General.'

'Is Kim at home?'

'No. He's away.'

Not, 'he's out' but 'he's away', thought Karpov. He affected surprise. 'Oh, I had hoped to catch him. Do you know when he'll be back?'

'No. He'll be back when he'll be back.'

'Any idea where I might contact him?'

'No.'

Karpov frowned. Something Philby had said at that Kryuchkov dinner . . . About not being allowed to drive since his stroke. He had already checked the basement car park. The Philby Volga was there.

'I thought you drove him around these days, Erita.'

She had a half-smile. Not the face of a woman whose husband has walked out on her. More the smile of a woman whose husband has obtained a promotion.

'Not any more. He has a driver.'

'I'm impressed. Well, sorry to have missed him. I'll try and catch him when he gets back.'

He descended the stairs deep in thought. Retired

colonels did not rate a personal driver. Back in his own flat two blocks behind the Ukraina Hotel he called the KGB motor pool and insisted on speaking to the chief clerk. When he identified himself the reaction was suitably deferential. He was bluff and jovial. 'I'm not in the habit of handing out bouquets of carnations, but I see no reason not to when good work has been done.'

'Thank you, Comrade General.'

'That chauffeur who has been driving for my friend Comrade Colonel Philby. He speaks extremely highly of him. A very fine driver, so he says. If my own man is ever sick I must ask for him personally.'

'Thank you again, Comrade General. I'll tell Driver Gregoriev myself.'

Karpov hung up. Driver Gregoriev. Never heard of him. But a quiet talk with the man might be useful.

The next morning, 8 April, the *Akademik Komarov* moved quietly past Greenock and into the Clyde, bound upriver for the port of Glasgow. She stopped briefly at Greenock to pick up the pilot and two Customs officers.

They had the usual glass in the captain's cabin and ascertained she was out of Leningrad and in ballast to pick up a cargo of heavy-duty pump accessories from Weir of Cathcart Limited. The Customs men checked the crew list but did not memorize any particular name. Later it would be established that Deckhand Konstantin Semyonov was on the list.

The habitual practice when Soviet illegals enter a country by ship is that they do *not* feature on the crew list. They arrive crouched in a tiny cubbyhole or oubliette, skilfully cut into the ship's structure and so well hidden that the most thorough rummage crew would not find it. Then, if the man for operational or accidental reasons fails to go out on the same ship, there is no discrepancy in the crew list. But this was a hurried operation. There had been no time for structural changes.

The extra crewman had arrived with the men from

Moscow only hours before the *Komarov* was due to leave Leningrad for Glasgow on a long-scheduled freight run, and the captain and his resident political officer had no choice but to put him in the crew list. His seaman's paybook was in order and he would be coming back, they were told.

Nevertheless, the man had taken over a cabin to himself, spent the whole voyage in it, and the two genuine deckhands whose cabin it was had become fed up with sleeping in bags on the wardroom floor. These bags were cleared away by the time the Scottish pilot came on board. Down in his cabin, tense for evident reasons, Courier Two was waiting for midnight.

While the Clyde pilot stood on the bridge of the *Komarov* and the fields of Strathclyde slid by as he munched his breakfast sandwiches, it was already noon in Moscow. Karpov called the KGB motor pool again. There was a new chief clerk on duty, as he knew there would be.

'My driver looks as if he's going down with flu,' he said. 'He'll see the day out, but I'm giving him tomorrow off.'

'I'll ensure that you get a replacement, Comrade General.'

'I'd prefer Driver Gregoriev. Is he available? I've heard the best reports of him.'

There was a rustle of paper as the clerk checked his files. 'Yes, indeed. He's been on secondment but he's back in the pool.'

'Good. Have him report to my Moscow flat at eight tomorrow morning. I'll have the keys, and the Chaika will be in the basement.'

Stranger and stranger, he thought as he put the phone down. Gregoriev had been ordered to drive Philby around for a while. Why? Because there was a great deal of driving to do, too much for Erita to cope with? Or so that Erita should not know where he was going? And now the man was back in the pool again. Meaning? Probably that Philby was now somewhere else and did not need a driver any more, at least not until the end of whatever operation he was involved in.

That evening Karpov told his grateful regular driver he could have the following day off and take his family out.

The same Wednesday evening Sir Nigel Irvine had a dinner date with a friend in Oxford.

One of the charming things about St Anthony's College, Oxford, like so many highly influential British institutions, is that so far as the general public is concerned it does not exist.

In fact it does exist, but is so small and so discreet that anyone who, surveying the groves of Academe in the British Isles, blinked would probably miss it. Its hall is small, elegant and tucked away out of sight; it offers no degree courses, educates no students, has no undergraduates and therefore no graduates, and awards no degrees. It has a few resident professors and fellows, who sometimes dine together in hall but live in rooms scattered around the city, and others who live elsewhere and simply visit. It occasionally invites outsiders to address the fellows – an extraordinary honour – and the professors and fellows occasionally submit papers to the higher echelons of the British establishment, where they are taken very seriously. Its funding is as private as the profile it maintains.

In fact it is a 'think tank' where assembled intellects, often with extensive nonacademic experience, pursue the study of one single discipline, current affairs.

That evening Sir Nigel dined in hall with his host, Professor Jeremy Sweeting, and after an excellent repast the professor took the Master back to his rooms, an agreeable house on the outskirts of Oxford, for port and coffee.

'Now, Nigel,' said Professor Sweeting when they had broached a vintage Taylor and were at ease before the fire in the study, 'what can I do for you?'

'Have you by any chance, Jeremy, heard of a thing called the MBR?'

Professor Sweeting held his port in midair. He stared at

it for a long while. 'You know, Nigel, you really do have a way of spoiling a chap's evening when you have a mind to. Where did you hear those letters?'

For answer Sir Nigel Irvine passed over the Preston Report. Professor Sweeting read it carefully and it took an hour. Irvine knew that, unlike John Preston, the professor was no legman. He did not get out on the ground. But he had an encyclopedic knowledge of Marxian theory and practice, of dialectical materialism and of the teachings of Lenin on the applicability of theory to the practice of the achievement of power. His pursuit and his absorption was to read, study, collate and analyse.

'Remarkable,' said Sweeting as he handed back the report. 'A different approach, a different attitude, of course, and a completely different methodology. But we've come up with the same answers.

'Care to tell me what answers you have come up with?' asked Sir Nigel gently.

'It's only theory, of course,' apologized Professor Sweeting. 'A thousand straws in the wind that may, or may not, make up a bale of hay. Anyway, this is what *I've* been on since June 1983 . . .'

He talked for two hours, and when Sir Nigel left to be driven back to London in the small hours he was a very pensive man.

The *Akademik Komarov* was tied up at the Finnieston Quay in the heart of Glasgow, so that the giant crane there could hoist the pumps aboard in the morning. There are no Customs or Immigration checks there; foreign seamen can simply walk off their ships, across the quay and into the streets of Glasgow.

At midnight, while Professor Sweeting was still talking, Deckhand Semyonov walked down the gangplank, followed the quay for a hundred yards, avoided Betty's Bar outside whose door a few drunken sailors were still protesting their right to just one more drink, and turned up Finnieston Street.

He was unremarkable, dressed in scuffed shoes, cord trousers, a rollneck sweater and anorak. Under one arm he clutched a canvas gunnysack held closed by a drawstring. Passing under the Clydeside Expressway, he reached Argyle Street, turned left and followed it to Partick Cross. He consulted no map but headed on into Hyndland Road. A mile farther on, he reached another major artery, the Great Western Road. He had memorized his route days before.

He checked his watch here; it told him he still had half an hour and the rendezvous could not be more than ten minutes' walk ahead. He turned left and proceeded in the direction of the Pond Hotel, next to the boating lake and a hundred yards past the BP service station whose lights he could see blazing in the distance. He was almost at the bus stop at the junction of the Great Western and Hughenden roads when he saw them. They were lounging about in the passenger shelter of the bus stop, it was half past one in the morning and there were five of them.

In some parts of Britain they call them skinheads, or punks, but in Glasgow they call them Neds. He thought of crossing the road but he was too late. One of them called out to him, and they spilled out of the bus shelter. He could speak some English, but their broad, drink-slurred Glaswegian dialect defeated him. They blocked the pavement, so he stepped into the road. One of them grabbed his arm and shouted at him. What the lout actually said was: 'Wha' ha' ya got in ya wee sack, then?'

But he could not understand, so he shook his head and tried to walk past. Then they were on him and he went down under a rain of blows. When he was in the gutter the kicking started. He dimly felt hands tearing at his gunny sack, so he clutched it to his belly with both hands and rolled over, taking the blows around the head and kidneys.

Devonshire Terrace overlooks the junction, a row of solid, four-storey, middle-class houses in buff and grey sandstone blocks. On the top floor of one, Mrs Sylvester, old, widowed, alone and riddled with arthritis, was unable to sleep. She heard the shouts from the street below and hobbled from her bed to the window. What she saw caused her to limp across the room to the telephone, where she dialled 999 and asked for the police. She told the police operator which road junction to send the car to, but hung up when asked for her name and address. Respectable people, and those of Devonshire Terrace are very respectable, do not like to get involved.

Police constables Alistair Craig and Hugh McBain were in their divisional patrol car a mile down the Great Western at the Hillhead end when the call came through. Traffic was nearly zero and they reached the bus stop in ninety seconds. The Neds saw them coming from the headlights and the siren, and they ceased trying to rip away the gunny sack, choosing to race away across the grass verge that separates Hughenden road from the Great Western, so the car could not follow them. By the time PC Craig could leap out of the patrol car they were disappearing shadows and pursuit was useless. In any case, the priority was the victim.

Craig bent over the man. He was huddled in the embryo position and unconscious.

'Ambulance, Hughie,' he called across to PC McBain and the driver was already on the radio. It came from the Western Infirmary six minutes later. Meanwhile the two officers left the injured man strictly alone, as per procedure, save that they covered him with a blanket.

The ambulance men eased the limp form on to a stretcher trolley and into the back of the vehicle. As they were tucking the blanket round him, Craig lifted the gunny sack and placed it in the rear of the ambulance.

'You go with him, I'll follow,' shouted McBain, so Craig climbed into the ambulance as well. They all arrived at casualty admissions in less than five minutes. The ambulance men quickly wheeled the injured man through the swing doors, down the corridor, round two corners and into the rear of the casualty ward. As it was an emergency admission there was no need to pass through the public waiting room, where the usual collection of small-hours-of-the-morning drunks nursed the cuts and bruises collected while in earlier contact with a number of unyielding objects.

Craig waited for McBain to park the patrol car and join him in the entrance.

'You handle the admission forms, Hughie, I'll go along and see if I can get you a name and address.'

McBain sighed. Admission forms went on for ever. Craig lifted the gunny sack from the ground and followed the trolley down the passage to casualty. This department at the Western Infirmary consists of a passage with swing doors at each end and twelve curtained examination rooms, six either side of the central corridor. Eleven of the rooms are used for examinations; the twelfth is the sister's office, and is nearest the rear entrance through which the trolleys come. The doors at the other end have one-way mirrors in their panels and give on to the public waiting room where the walking wounded are made to sit and wait their turn.

Leaving McBain at the porter's desk with a sheaf of admission forms to fill in, Craig went through the mirrored doors to see the unconscious man on his trolley parked at the other end. The ward sister gave him the usual once-over – he was alive at any rate – and ordered the porters to put the man on the bench in one of the examination rooms so the trolley could be returned to the ambulance. The one they chose was the room opposite the sister's cubicle.

The junior houseman, an Indian called Dr Mehta, was summoned. He had the porters strip the injured man to the waist – he could see no signs of blood leaking through the trousers – and made a lengthier examination, before ordering an X-ray exam. Then he left to attend to another emergency admission from a car crash.

The ward sister telephoned X-ray but it was occupied. They would let her know when they were free. She put on her kettle to make a cup of tea. PC Craig, having ascertained his anonymous charge was still unconscious on his back across the corridor, took the man's anorak, entered her office and placed both anorak and gunny sack on her table.

'Have you a spare cup of that brew?' he asked the sister in the jocular familiarity used by the people of the night who spend their duties cleaning up the mess of a major city.

'I might,' she said, 'but I don't see why I should waste it on the likes of you.'

Craig grinned. He felt through the pockets of the anorak and extracted a seaman's paybook. It bore the photograph of the man in the examination room across the way, and was in two languages, Russian and French. He understood neither. He could not read Cyrillic script, but the name was in Roman letters also, in the French language section.

'Who's Jimmy?' asked the ward sister, preparing two cups of tea.

'Looks like a seaman, and a Russian at that,' said Craig, perturbed. A citizen of Glasgow roughed up by a gang of Neds was one thing; a foreigner and a Russian at that could spell problems. To try to discover what ship the man could be off, Craig emptied the gunny sack.

It contained simply a rolled-up thick-knit jersey, wrapped around a circular screwtop tobacco tin. Inside the tin was not tobacco but cotton wool, shrouding two discs of aluminium with, between them, another 2-inch-diameter disc of a dull grey metal. Craig examined the three discs without interest, replaced them in their bed of cotton wool, screwed the tin shut again, and laid it on the table beside the pay book. What he did not know was that across the corridor the victim of the mugging attack had come to and was peering through the curtains at him. What he did know was that it was time to tell Division he had an injured Russian on his hands.

'Use your phone, pet?' he asked the sister, and reached out for it.

'Don't you "pet" me,' called back the sister, who was

somewhat older than twenty-four-year-old PC Craig. 'God, they get younger every day.'

PC Craig began to dial. Just what went through Konstantin Semyonov's mind will never be known. Dazed and confused, probably suffering concussion from the kicks to the head, he could see the unmistakable black uniform of a British policeman with his back to him across the corridor. He could see his own paybook and the consignment he had been told to bring to Britain and deliver to the agent at the boating lake sitting on the table by the policeman's hand. He had watched the officer examine the consignment – he personally had never dared open the tin – and now the man was phoning. Perhaps he had visions of endless third degree in some reeking cellar beneath Strathclyde police headquarters . . .

The first thing PC Craig knew, he was roughly elbowed aside, caught completely unawares. A bare arm pushed past him, reached for the tin and grabbed it. He responded fast, dropping the telephone and grasping the outstretched arm.

'What the hell, Jimmy . . .' he shouted: then, assuming the poor fellow was hallucinating, he grabbed the man and tried to restrain him. The tin was shaken from the Russian's hand and fell to the floor. For a moment Semyonov stared at the Scottish policeman, then panicked and ran. Still calling 'Hey, Jimmy, come back here . . .' PC Craig thundered down the corridor after him.

Shortie Patterson was a drunk. A lifetime dedicated to sampling the produce of Speyside had made him unemployed and unemployable. He was no ordinary drunk; he had elevated intoxication to an art form. The previous day he had drawn his benefit and made straight for the nearest boozer, and by midnight had been paralytic. In the small hours he took exception to the offensive attitude of a lamppost that refused to respond to his entreaties for the price of a dram, so he had hit the creature.

He had been in X-ray with his broken hand and was going back down the corridor to his booth when a man with a bare and battered torso and bruised and bloody face came running out of an adjacent cubicle pursued by a policeman. Shortie knew his duty to a fellow-sufferer. He had no love for policemen, who seemed to have nothing better to do than pluck him out of perfectly comfortable gutters and hand him over to people who made him bath. He let the running man pass him, then stuck out a foot.

'You stupid wee bugger,' shouted Craig as he crashed down. By the time he was up, he had lost ten yards on the Russian.

Semyonov came through the mirrored doors into the public waiting room, missed seeing the narrow door to the outside that lay to his left, and ran through the larger double doors to his right. This led him back into the trolley passage down which he had been wheeled thirty minutes earlier. He turned right again, to find a trolley approaching him surrounded by a doctor and two nurses holding up plasma bottles – Dr Mehta's road-accident victim. The trolley blocked the whole passage; behind him he heard running boots.

To his left was a square lobby containing two lift doors. One door was closing upon an empty elevator. He threw himself through the gap just as the door closed. As the lift rose, he heard the policeman banging impotently on it. He leaned back and closed his eyes in misery.

PC Craig made for the stairwell and ran up. At every level he checked the lights above the elevator doors. The lift was still climbing. At the top and tenth floor he was hot, angry and puffed out.

Semyonov had got out at the tenth. He looked into one door available to him, but it was a ward of sleeping patients. There was one other door, open and leading to stairs. He ran up to find himself in another corridor, but with only shower rooms, a pantry and stores leading off it. At the far end was the last door, and in the warm, humid night it stood open. It led to the flat roof of the block.

PC Craig had lost ground, but he made the final doorway eventually and stepped out into the night air.

Adjusting his eyes to the darkness, he made out the figure of a man by the north parapet. His annoyance died away. I'd probably panic if I woke up in a Moscow hospital, he thought. He started to walk towards the figure, hands held up to show they were empty.

'C'mon, Jimmy, or Ivan, or whatever your name is. You're all right. You got a bang on the head, tha's all. Come on away down wi' me.'

His eyes were accustomed now. He could see the Russian's face quite clearly in the glow from the city below. The man watched him approach until he was twenty feet away. Then he looked down, took a deep breath, closed his eyes, and jumped.

PC Craig could not believe it for several seconds, even after he heard the soggy smack of the body impacting a hundred feet down into the staff car park.

'Oh Christ,' he breathed, 'I'm in bother.'

With fumbling fingers he reached for his personal radio and called up Division.

A hundred yards after the BP service station, half a mile from the bus stop, lies the boating pond, in the shadow of the Pond Hotel. From the pavement, a set of stone steps leads down to the walkway round the pool and close to the bottom of the steps are two wooden benches.

The silent figure in black motorcycle leathers checked his watch. Three o'clock. The rendezvous had been for two. One hour's delay was all that was allowed. There was a second, back-up rendezvous; different place, twenty-four hours later. He would be there. If the contact failed to show up, he would have to use the radio again. He rose and left.

PC Hugh McBain had been away from the porter's desk when the chase ran straight through the casualty department waiting room. He was at his car checking exact times for the mugging attack and the logged appeal calls. The first thing he knew was when his 'neighbour' (Glasgow slang for partner) came down into the waiting room looking pale and shaken.

'Alistair, have you got that name and address yet?' he asked.

'He is . . . he was . . . a Russian seaman,' said Craig.

'Oh hell, that's all we need. How do you spell it?'

'Hughie, he's just . . . thrown himself off the roof.'

McBain put down his pen and stared in disbelief at his neighbour. Then the training took over. Any policeman knows, when things go wrong you cover your back, you follow the procedures right down the line, no cowboy tactics, no clever-clever initiatives.

'Have you called up Division?' he asked.

'Aye, someone's on their way over.'

'Let's get the doctor,' said McBain.

They found Dr Mehta, already worked to fatigue by the night's admissions. He followed them to the car park, spent no more than two minutes examining the gross and burst cadaver, pronounced it dead and no longer his concern, and returned to his duties. Two porters brought a blanket to cover it, and thirty minutes later an ambulance took the thing to the city mortuary in Jocelyn Square by the Salt Market. There other hands would strip off the rest of the clothing – shoes, socks, belt, trousers, underpants and wrist-watch – each to be bagged and tagged for collection.

Inside the hospital there were more forms to fill out – the admission forms were kept as evidence, although now useless for practical purposes – and the two police constables bagged and tagged the rest of the dead man's items. They were listed as: anorak 1, rollneck pullover 1, canvas gunny sack 1, thick-knit jersey (rolled) 1, and round tobacco tin 1.

Before they were finished, about fifteen minutes after Craig's first call, an inspector and a sergeant, both uniformed, arrived from Division and asked for an office. They were loaned an empty administrator's office and began to take statements from the two constables. After ten minutes the inspector sent the sergeant to his car to call in the duty chief superintendent. It was four o'clock on Thursday, 9 April, but in Moscow it was eight.

General Yevgeni Karpov waited until they were out of the main traffic of southern Moscow and on the open road to Yasyenevo before he started to converse with Driver Gregoriev. Apparently the thirty-year-old driver knew he had been singled out by the general and was eager to please.

'How do you like driving for us?'

'Very much, sir.'

'Well, it gets you out and about, I suppose. Better than a stuffy desk job.'

'Yes, sir.'

'Been driving for my friend Colonel Philby recently, I hear.'

A slight pause. Damn, he's been told not to mention it, thought Karpov.

'Er, yes sir.'

'Used to drive himself, until he had his stroke.'

'So he told me, sir.'

Better get on with it. 'Whereabouts did you drive him?'

A longer pause. Karpov could see the driver's face in the mirror. He was disturbed, in a quandary.

'Oh, just around Moscow, sir.'

'Anywhere specific around Moscow, Gregoriev?'

'No, sir. Just around.'

'Pull over, Gregoriev.'

The Chaika pulled out of the privileged centre lane, through the southbound traffic and into a lay-by.

Karpov leaned forward. 'You know who I am, Driver?'

'Yes, sir.'

'And you know my rank in the KGB?'

'Yes, sir. Lieutenant-General.'

'Then don't play games with me, young man. Where exactly did you drive him?'

Gregoriev swallowed. Karpov could see he was wrestling with himself. The question was: who had told him to stay silent as to where he had driven Philby? If it was Philby himself, Karpov outranked him. But if it was someone higher . . . In fact it had been Major Pavlov, and he had frightened Gregoriev badly. He was only a major, but to a Russian the people from the First Chief Directorate are an unknown quantity, whereas a major of the Kremlin Guards . . . . Still, a general was still a general.

'Mostly to a series of conferences, Comrade General. Some at central Moscow apartments, but I never went inside so I never saw which exact apartment he went to.'

'Some in central Moscow . . . And the others?'

'Mainly, no, sir, I think always at a dacha out at Zhukovka.'

Central Committee country, thought Karpov. 'Do you know whose?'

'No, sir. Honestly. He just gave me directions to it. Then I used to wait in the car.'

'Who else turned up at these conferences?'

'There was one occasion, sir, when two cars arrived together. I saw the man from the other car get out and enter the dacha . . .'

'And you recognized him?'

'Yes, sir. Before I joined the KGB motor pool, I was a driver in the Army. In 1985 I used to drive for a colonel of the GRU. We were based at Kandahar in Afghanistan. Once this officer was in the rear seat with my colonel. It was General Marchenko.'

Well, well, well, thought Karpov, my old friend Pyotr Marchenko, specialist in destabilization.

'Anyone else at these conferences?'

'Just one other car, sir. We drivers chatted a bit, what with the hours of waiting and that. But he was a surly devil. All I learned was that he drove for a member of the Academy of Sciences. Honestly, sir, that's all I know.'

'Drive on, Gregoriev.'

Karpov leaned back and watched the passing landscape

of trees. So, there were four of them, met to prepare something for the General Secretary. The host was Central Committee or Supreme Soviet, and the other three were Philby, Marchenko and an unnamed academician.

Tomorrow was Friday, when the *vlasti* finished as early as they could and went to their dachas. He knew Marchenko had his villa close to Peredelkino, not far from his own. He also knew Marchenko's weakness, and sighed. He had better take a lot of brandy with him. It would be a heavy session.

Chief Superintendent Charlie Forbes listened to PCs Craig and McBain carefully and quietly, interjecting a soft-spoken question now and again. He had no doubt they were telling the truth, but he had been long enough in the force to know the truth does not always save your neck.

It was a bad business. Technically, the Russian had been in police custody, even though under treatment at a hospital. There had been no-one else on that roof but PC Craig. There was no evident reason why the man should have jumped. He personally did not even care why, assuming like everyone else that the man had been severely concussed and in a state of panic due to temporary hallucination. His whole attention was on the possible perspectives for the Strathclyde police.

There would be the ship to trace, the captain to interview, formal identification of the body, the Soviet consul to be informed, and of course the press, the bloody press, some elements of whom would hint darkly at their usual hobby-horse, police brutality. The darn thing was, when they asked their pointed questions, he did not have any answers. Why should the silly man have jumped?

At half past four there was nothing more to do at the hospital. The machine would roll into action by dawn. He ordered them all back to divisional HQ.

By six o'clock the two PCs had finished their lengthy statements. Charlie Forbes was in his office coping with the demands of the procedural machine. A search, probably futile, was on for the lady who had dialled 999. Statements had been taken from the two ambulance men who had answered McBain's call via the divisional switchboard. At least there would be no doubt about the beating the Neds gave the man.

The casualty ward sister had told her version, the harassed Dr Mehta had made a statement, the casualty front-desk porter had testified to seeing the bare-chested man run through the waiting room pursued by Craig. After that no-one had seen either of them on the chase up to the roof.

Forbes had identified the only Soviet ship in port as the *Akademik Komarov* and dispatched a police car to ask the captain to identify the body; he had awoken the Soviet consul, who would be at his office at nine, protest at the ready no doubt. He had alerted his own Chief Constable, and the Procurator Fiscal, whose office in Scotland includes the duties of a coroner.

The dead man's personal effects, the 'productions', had all been bagged and were being taken to Partick police station (the mugging had been in Partick) to be retained under lock and key on the direction of the Procurator Fiscal, who had promised to authorize the post mortem for 10 a.m. Charlie Forbes stretched and called the canteen for coffee and rolls.

While Chief Superintendent Forbes at the Strathclyde HQ in Pitt Street sorted the paperwork, across at Division PCs Craig and McBain signed their statements and repaired to their canteen for breakfast. Both were worried men, and they shared their worries with a grizzled detective sergeant from the plain-clothes branch who shared their table. After breakfast they sought and received permission to go home and sleep.

Something they said caused the detective to go to the pay phone in the hall outside the canteen and make a call. The man he disturbed with a faceful of shaving foam was Detective Inspector Carmichael, who listened carefully, hung up and finished his shaving in pensive mood. DI Carmichael was from the Special Branch.

At half past seven Carmichael traced the chief inspector in the uniformed branch who would be attending the post mortem and asked if he might tag along. Be my guest, said the chief inspector. City morgue at ten.

At that same morgue at eight o'clock the captain of the *Akademik Komarov*, accompanied by his inseparable political officer, stared at a video screen on which the battered face of Deckhand Semyonov soon appeared. He nodded slowly and muttered in Russian.

'That is him,' said the political officer. 'We wish to see our consul.'

'He'll be at Pitt Street at nine o'clock,' said the uniformed sergeant who was accompanying them. Both Russians appeared shaken and subdued. It must be bad to lose a close shipmate, thought the sergeant.

At nine the Soviet consul was ushered into the Pitt Street office of Chief Superintendent Forbes. He spoke fluent English. Forbes asked him to be seated and launched into a narration of the night's events. Before he finished, the consul was coming back at him.

'This is outrage,' he began. 'I must contact the Soviet Embassy in London without delay . . .'

There was a knock on the door and the captain was shown in with his political officer. The uniformed sergeant was their escort, but another man was with them. He nodded to Forbes. 'Morning, sir. Mind if I sit in?'

'Help yourself, Carmichael. I think it's going to be a rough one.'

But no. The political officer from the ship had hardly been in the room ten seconds before he drew the consul aside and whispered furiously in his ear. The consul made his excuses and the two men withdrew to the corridor. Three minutes later they were back. The consul was formal and correct. He would of course have to communicate with his embassy. He was sure the Strathclyde police would do all in their power to apprehend the hooligans.

Would it be possible for the body of the seaman and all his effects to depart for Leningrad on the *Akademik Komarov*, which was due to sail this day?

Forbes was polite but adamant. Police inquiries to arrest the muggers would continue. In that period the body would have to remain at the morgue and all the dead man's effects would be retained under lock and key at Partick police station. The consul nodded. He too understood procedures. And with that they left.

At ten Carmichael entered the post-mortem room where Professor Harland was scrubbing up. The chatter as usual was about the weather, the golf prospects, the norms of everyday life. A few feet away on a slab above the drains lay the battered and pulped body of Semyonov.

'Mind if I have a look?' asked Carmichael. The police pathologist nodded.

Carmichael spent ten minutes looking over what was left of Semyonov. When he left, just as the professor started to cut, he went to his office at Pitt Street and made a call to Edinburgh, more precisely to the Scottish Home and Health Department, known as the Scottish Office, at Saint Andrew's House.

There he spoke to a retired assistant commissioner who was on the staff of the Scottish Office for one reason: liaison with MI5 in London.

At noon the phone rang in the office of C.4(C) in Gordon. Bright took it, listened for a moment and held it out to Preston.

'It's for you. They won't talk to anyone else.'

'Who is it?'

'The Scottish Office, Edinburgh.'

Preston took the phone, 'John Preston . . . Yes, good morning to you . . .'

He listened for several minutes, his brow furrowed. He noted the name Carmichael on a scratch pad.

'Yes, I think I'd better come up. Would you tell Inspector Carmichael I'll be on the three o'clock shuttle, and could he meet me at Glasgow Airport? Thank you.'

'Glasgow?' asked Bright. 'What have they been up to?'

'Oh some Russian seaman who took a tumble off a roof, and who may not have been all he should have been. I'll be back tomorrow. It's probably nothing. Still, anything to get out of the office.'

15

Glasgow Airport lies eight miles southwest of the city and is linked by the M8 motorway. Preston's flight landed just after half past four and with only a handgrip to carry he was in the concourse ten minutes later. He went to Airport Information and they paged 'Mr Carmichael'.

The detective inspector of Special Branch appeared and they introduced themselves. Five minutes later they were in the inspector's car and pulling on to the motorway towards the darkening city.

'Let's talk as we drive,' suggested Preston. 'Start from the beginning and tell me what happened.'

Carmichael was succinct and accurate. There were a lot of gaps he could not fill in, but he had had time to read the statements of the two police constables, especially that of PC Craig, so he could recount most of it. Preston heard him out in silence.

'So what caused you to phone the Scottish Office and ask for someone to come up from London?' he asked at length.

'I could be wrong, but there seems to me a possibility the man was not a merchant seaman,' said Carmichael.

'Go on.'

'It was something Craig said in the canteen at Division this morning,' said Carmichael. 'I wasn't there, but the remark was overheard by a CID man, who called me up. What Craig said McBain agreed with. But neither of them mentioned it in their official statements. As you know, statements are about the facts; this was the police officers' speculation. Still, it seemed worth checking out.'

'I'm listening.'

'They said when they found the seaman, he was huddled in the embryo position, his hands clasped round the gunny sack, which was pressed into his belly. The phrase Craig used was that he seemed to be protecting it like a baby.'

Preston could see the oddity. If a man is being kicked half to death, the instinct is to roll into a ball, like Semyonov, but to use the hands to protect the head. Why would man take the force of the kicks on an unprotected head in order to guard a worthless canvas bag?

'Then,' resumed Carmichael, 'I began to wonder about the time and place. Seamen in the port of Glasgow go to Betty's or the Stable Bar. This man was four miles from the docks, walking up a dual carriageway towards nowhere, long after closing hours, without a bar in sight. What the hell was he doing there at that hour?'

'Good question,' said Preston. 'What next?'

'At ten this morning I went to the post mortem. The body was pretty badly smashed by the fall, but the front of the face was all right, except for a couple of bruises. Most of the blows from the Neds were to the back of the head and the body. I've seen the faces of merchant navy deckhands before. They are weather-beaten, wind-burned, brown and lined. This man had a bland, pale face, the face of a man not accustomed to life on the foredeck.

'Then, his hands. They should have been brown on the backs, calloused on the palms. They were soft and white, like those of a desk worker. Lastly, the teeth. I'd expect a deckhand out of Leningrad to have basic dentistry, the fillings of amalgam and any false teeth of steel, Russian-style. This man had gold fillings and two gold caps.'

Preston nodded approvingly. Carmichael was sharp. They had arrived in the car park of the hotel where Carmichael had booked Preston for the night.

'One last thing. Small, but it may mean something,' said Carmichael. 'Before the post mortem the Soviet consul went to see our Chief Super at Pitt Street. I was there myself. It seemed he was on the verge of lodging a protest; then the captain of the ship arrived and his political officer was with him. The officer pulled the consul into the passage and they had a whispered conversation. When the consul returned, he was all civility and understanding. It was as if the political officer had told him something about the dead man. I got the impression they didn't want to make any waves at all until they had checked with the Embassy.'

'Have you told anyone in the uniformed branch that I'm here?' asked Preston.

'Not yet,' replied Carmichael. 'Do you want me to?'

Preston shook his head. 'Wait till the morning. We'll decide then. It may be nothing.'

'Anything else you want?'

'Copies of the various statements, the lot if you can get them. And the list of the man's effects. By the way, where are they?'

'Locked up at Partick police station. I'll get you the copies and drop them off here later.'

General Karpov called a friend in the GRU and spun a story to the effect that one of his bagmen had brought him a couple of bottles of French brandy from Paris. He personally never touched the stuff, but he owed Pyotr Marchenko a favour. He would drop the brandy over at Marchenko's dacha during the weekend. He just needed to know there would be someone to take it in. Did the colleague have Marchenko's country number at Peredelkino? The GRU man did indeed. He gave it to Karpov and thought no more about it.

Most of the dachas of the Soviet élite have a housekeeper or manservant in residence during the winter months to keep the fires alight so that the owners' weekends do not start freezing cold. It was Marchenko's housekeeper who answered. Yes, the general *was* expected the following day, Friday; he usually arrived about six in the evening. Karpov thanked her and hung up. He decided he would dismiss his chauffeur, drive himself, and surprise the GRU general at seven.

* * *

Preston lay awake in his bed thinking. Carmichael had brought him all the statements taken at the Western Infirmary and at Division. Like all police-recorded depositions, they were stilted and formal, quite unlike the way people actually narrate what they have seen and heard. The facts were there, of course, but not the impressions.

What Preston could not know, because Craig had not mentioned it and the ward sister had not seen it, was that before running off down the passage between the examination rooms, Semyonov had grabbed for the round tobacco tin. Craig had simply said the injured man 'pushed past me'.

Nor was the list of personal effects, the productions, much more helpful. It mentioned a round tobacco tin 'and contents', which could have been two ounces of shag tobacco.

Preston ran over the possibilities in his mind. One: Semyonov was an illegal being landed in Britain. Deduction: very unlikely. He was on the crew list of the ship and would be conspicuous by his absence when the vessel departed for Leningrad.

All right. So: he was to come into Glasgow with the ship, and leave with it that Thursday night. What was he doing in the small hours halfway up the Great Western road? Making a drop or keeping a rendezvous. Good. Or even *collecting* a package to bring back to Leningrad. Even better. But after that the options ran out.

If he had delivered what he came to deliver, why try to protect his gunny sack as if his life depended on it? It would have been empty of its cargo.

If he had come to pick something up, but had not yet done that, the same reasoning applied. If he had already made the pick-up, why was not something of considerable interest such as a packet of papers found on his person?

If what he had come to deliver or collect could be concealed about a human form, why bring a gunny sack at all? If there was something sewn into his anorak or trousers, or concealed in the heel of a shoe, why not let the

Neds take the sack, which was what they were after? He could have saved himself a beating, and got to his rendezvous or back to his ship (whichever direction he was heading) with a couple of bruises.

Preston threw a few more 'possibles' into the food-mixer. He had come as a courier to make a face-to-face rendezvous with a Soviet illegal already resident in Britain. To pass a verbal message? Unlikely, there were a score of better ways of passing coded information. To receive a verbal report? Same applied. To change places with a resident illegal, to replace the man? No, the photograph in his paybook was identifiably Semyonov. If he had been changing places with an illegal, Moscow would have given him a duplicate paybook with the appropriate photograph, so the man he was replacing could go out on the *Komarov* as Deckhand Semyonov. That paybook would have been on his person. Unless it was sewn into the lining . . . of what?

The lining of his jacket? Then why take a beating to protect the sack? The canvas base of the sack itself? Much more likely. It all seemed to come back to that damned sack.

Just before midnight he called Carmichael at his home. 'Can you pick me up at eight?' he asked. 'I want to go to Partick and have a look at the productions. Can you front me?'

Over breakfast on the Friday morning Yevgeni Karpov told his wife Ludmilla: 'Can you take the kids out to the dacha in the Volga this afternoon?'

'Of course. You'll join us straight from the office?'

He nodded absently. 'I'll be late. I've got to see someone from GRU.'

Ludmilla Karpova sighed inwardly. She knew he kept a partridge-plump little secretary in a small apartment in the Arbat district. She knew because wives will talk, and in a society as stratified as theirs most of her social friends were the wives of other officers of similar rank. She also knew he did not know she knew.

She was fifty and they had been married twenty-eight years. It had been a good marriage, considering the job he did, and she had been a good wife. Like others who had married officers of the FCD, she had long lost count of the evenings she had waited up, while he had been buried in the cipher room of an embassy on foreign soil. She had stuck it through the endless tedium of countless diplomatic cocktail parties, speaking no foreign language, while her husband made the rounds, elegant, affable, fluent in English, French and German, doing his job under embassy cover.

She had lost count of the weeks she had spent alone when the children were small and he was a junior officer, their home a tiny and cramped apartment without any daily help, and he away on a course, or an assignment, or standing in the shadows by the Berlin Wall waiting for a bagman to come home to the East.

She had known the panic and nameless fear that even the innocent feel when, on foreign station, one of the colleagues had gone over to the West, and the KR (counter-intelligence) people had grilled her for hours about anything the man or his wife might have said in her hearing. She had watched in pity as the defector's wife, a woman she might have known well but dared not now touch with a sterilized bargepole, was escorted out to the waiting Aeroflot plane. It went with the job, he had said as he comforted her.

That had been years before. Now her Zhenia was a general, the Moscow apartment was airy and spacious, she had made the dacha lovely in the way she knew he liked, with pine and rugs, comfortable but rustic. The two boys were a credit to them, both at university, one to be a doctor the other a physicist. There would be no more horrid embassy apartments, and in three years he could retire with honours and a good pension. So, if he had to have a bit of skirt one evening a week, he was no different from most of his contemporaries. Better perhaps the way it was than that he be a drunken brute, like some, or a passed-over major going nowhere but to one of the forsaken Asian republics to end his career. Still, she sighed inwardly.

Partick police station is not the most glamorous edifice in the fine city of Glasow and the productions from the previous night's mugging/suicide had simply slotted into the routine. The duty desk sergeant handed over to a constable and led Carmichael and Preston to the rear, where he unlocked a bare room stacked with filing cabinets. He accepted Carmichael's card without expression of surprise, and his explanation that he and his colleague had to check the productions in order to complete their own reports, the dead man being a foreign seaman and that. The sergeant knew all about reports; he spent half his life filling them in. But he declined to quit the room while they opened the bags and looked over the contents.

Preston started with the shoes, checking for false heels, detachable soles or cavity toecaps. Nothing. The socks took less time, as did the underpants. He had the back off the shattered wristwatch, but it was just a wristwatch. The trousers took longer; he felt all the seams and hems, looking for new stitching or a thickness that could not be accounted for by a double layer of the fabric. Nothing.

The rollneck jersey the man had been wearing was easy; there were no seams and no hidden papers or hard lumps. He spent much longer on the anorak, but it too yielded no fruit. By the time he got to the gunny sack he was more convinced than before that if the mysterious Comrade Semyonov had had something with him, the answer lay here.

He started with the rolled-up sweater that had been in it, more for elimination purposes than anything. It was clean. Then he began on the sack itself. It took half an hour before he was satisfied the base was just a double-stitched disc of canvas, the sides of single canvas, and the eyelets at the top were not miniature transmitters nor the cord a secret aerial.

That left the tobacco tin. It was of Russian origin, an ordinary screwtop tin and still smelt faintly of pungent tobacco. The cotton wool was cotton wool and that left three discs of metal; two shiny like aluminium, and light in weight, the other dull like lead and heavy. He sat staring at them for a while as they lay on the table; Carmichael looked at him, and the sergeant looked at the floor.

It was not what they were that puzzled him; it was what they were not. They were not anything. The aluminium discs had been above and below the heavy disc; the heavy one was 2 inches in diameter, the lighter ones 3 inches. He tried to imagine what purpose they could possible serve, in radio communications, coding and decoding, in photography. And the answer was – nothing. They were just metal discs. Still, he was more than ever convinced that a man had died rather than let them fall into the hands of the Neds, who would have thrown them in the gutter anyway, or than let himself be interrogated about them.

He rose and suggested lunch. The sergeant, who felt he had wasted a morning, put the productions back in their bags and relocked them in a filing cabinet. Then he showed them out.

During lunch at the Pond Hotel – Preston had suggested they drive past the spot of the mugging – he excused himself to make a telephone call. 'It may take a while,' he told Carmichael. 'Have a brandy on the Sassenachs.'

Carmichael grinned. 'I'll do that, and I'll toast Bannockburn.'

Out of sight of the dining-room, Preston left the hotel and walked over to the BP filling station where he made several small purchases from the rack of parts in the adjacent shop. Then he went back to the hotel and made his call to London, giving the number of Partick police station and telling his assistant Bright exactly when he wanted the callback.

Half an hour later they were back in the police station where a plainly disgruntled sergeant led them once again to the room where the productions were stored. Preston seated himself behind the table, facing the wall phone across the room. In front of him on the table he built up a rampart of clothing from the various bags. At three o'clock the phone rang: the switchboard was putting the London call through to the extension. The sergeant took it.

'It's for you, sir. London on the line,' he said to Preston.

'Would you mind taking it?' Preston asked Carmichael. 'Find out if it's urgent.'

Carmichael rose and crossed the room to where the sergeant held the phone. For a second both the Scottish officers were facing the wall.

Ten minutes later Preston was finished for the last time. Carmichael drove him back to the airport.

'I'll file a report, of course,' said Preston. 'But I can't see what the hell the Russian was so fussed about. How long will those productions spend locked up in Partick?'

'Oh, weeks yet. The Soviet consul's been told that. The search for the Neds is still on, but it's a long shot. We might pick up one of them on another charge and get a squeal. But I doubt it.'

Preston checked in. Boarding was immediate.

'You know, the stupid thing is,' said Carmichael as he saw him off, 'if that Russian had stayed cool, we'd have driven him back to his ship with our apologies, him and his wee toy with him.'

When the plane was airborne Preston went to the toilet for a bit of privacy and examined the three discs that he had wrapped in his handkerchief. They still meant nothing to him.

The three washers he had obtained from the garage shop and switched for the Russian's 'wee toys' would suffice for a while. In the meantime there was a man he wanted to look at the Russian discs. He worked outside London and Bright should have asked him to stay on that Friday evening until Preston arrived.

* * *

Karpov arrived at General Marchenko's dacha in darkness just after seven. The door was answered by the general's batman, a soldier, who showed him into the sitting-room. Marchenko was already on his feet and seemed both surprised and pleased to see his friend from the other, and bigger, intelligence service.

'Yevgeni Sergeivitch,' he boomed, 'what brings you to my humble cottage?'

Karpov had a carrier bag in his hand. He held it up and delved inside. 'One of my boys just got back from Turkey, via Armenia,' he said. 'A bright lad, he knows not to come empty-handed. Since there's bugger all in Anatolia, he stopped at Erevan and put these in his grip.'

He produced one of the four bottles the bag contained, the finest of all the Armenian brandies.

Marchenko's eyes lit up. 'Akhtamar,' he shouted, 'nothing but the best for the FCD.'

'Well,' continued Karpov easily, 'I was driving to my own place up the road and I thought: who will take a glass of Akhtamar to help me through it. And back came the answer: old Peter Marchenko. So I made a short detour. Shall we see what it tastes like?'

Marchenko roared with laughter. 'Sasha, glasses,' he shouted.

Preston landed just before five, collected his car from the short-term park and headed for the M4 motorway. Instead of turning east for London he took the west lane towards Berkshire. Thirty minutes brought him to his destination, an institution on the outskirts of the village of Aldermaston.

Known simply as 'Aldermaston', the Atomic Weapons Research Establishment, so beloved of peace marchers looking for a target, is in fact a multi-discipline unit. It does indeed design and build nuclear devices, but it also researches into chemistry, physics, conventional explosives, engineering, pure and applied mathematics, radio-biology, medicine, health and safety standards and electronics. By the by, it has a very fine metallurgy department.

Years earlier, one of the scientists based at Aldermaston had given a lecture to a group of intelligence officers in Ulster on the kinds of metals the IRA bomb-makers favoured for their devices. Preston had been one of those in the lecture hall and recalled the Welsh scientist's name.

Dr Dafydd Wynne-Evans was waiting for him in the hallway. Preston introduced himself and reminded Dr Wynne-Evans of his lecture many years before.

'Well, well, what a memory you've got,' he said in his lilting Welsh accent. 'All right, Mr Preston, what can I do for you?'

Preston dug into his pocket, produced the handkerchief and held it out to show the three discs it contained. 'These were taken off somebody in Glasgow,' he said. 'They defeat me. I'd like to know what they are and what they could be used for.'

The doctor looked at them closely. 'Nefarious purposes, you think?'

'Could be.'

'Difficult to say without tests,' said the metallurgist. 'Look, I've got a dinner tonight and my daughter's wedding tomorrow. Can I run them through some tests on Monday and call you?'

'Monday will do fine,' said Preston. 'I'm taking a few days off actually. I'll be at home. Can I give you my number in Kensington?'

Dr Wynne-Evans hurried upstairs, locked the discs in his safe for the night, bade goodbye to Preston and hurried to his dinner. Preston drove back to London.

While he was driving, the listening station at Menwith Hill in Yorkshire picked up a single squirt from a clandestine transmitter. Menwith got it first, but Brawdy in Wales and Chicksands in Bedfordshire also got a trace, and computed the cross-bearings. It was somewhere in the hills north of Sheffield.

When the Sheffield police got there the spot turned out to be a lay-by on a lonely road between Barnsley and Pontefract. There was no-one there.

Later that evening one of the duty officers at GCHQ Cheltenham accepted a drink in the office of the duty director.

'It's the same bugger,' he said. 'He's car-borne and he's got a good set. He only spent five seconds on the air, and it looks indecipherable. First, the Derbyshire Peak District, now the Yorkshire hills. It looks as if he's somewhere in the north Midlands.'

'Keep after him,' said the Director. 'We haven't had a sleeper transmitter go suddenly active in ages. I wonder what he's saying.'

What Major Valeri Petrofsky had been saying, although transmitted by his operator when he was long gone, was: Courier Two never showed. Inform soonest re arrival substitute.

The first bottle of Akhtamar stood empty on the table and the second was well broached. Marchenko was flushed, but he could be a two-bottle-a-day man when the mood took him and he was still well in control.

Karpov, although he seldom drank for pleasure and even more rarely alone, had seasoned his stomach for years on the diplomatic circuit. He had a good head when he needed it. Apart from that, he had forced half a pound of white butter down his throat before leaving Yasyenevo, and though he had nearly gagged on it, the fat was lining his stomach and retarding the onset of the alcohol's effect.

'What have you been up to these days, Peter?' he asked using the diminutive address-form.

Marchenko's eyes narrowed. 'Why do you ask?'

'Come on, Peter, we go back a long way. Remember when I saved your arse in Afghanistan three years back? You owe me a favour. What's going down?'

Marchenko remembered. He nodded solemnly. In 1984 he was heading a big GRU operation against the Moslem rebels up near the Khyber Pass. There was one particularly outstanding guerrilla leader who ran raids into Afghanistan, using as his bases the refugee camps inside Pakistan. Marchenko had rashly sent a snatch squad over the border to get him. They had run into bad trouble. The pro-Soviet Afghans had been unmasked by the Pathans and had died horribly. The single Russian accompanying them had been lucky to survive: the Pathans had handed him to the Pakistani authorities of the North West Frontier district, hoping for some arms in exchange.

Marchenko had been out on a limb. He had appealed to Karpov, then heading the Illegals Directorate and Karpov had endangered one of his best undercover Pakistani officers in Islamabad to get the Russian sprung and back over the border. A big international incident then could have broken Marchenko, and he would have joined the long list of Soviet officers whose careers had crashed in that miserable country.

'Yes, all right, I know I owe you, Zhenia, but don't ask what I've been on for the past few weeks. Special assignment, very close to the chest. Know what I mean, no names no pack drill.' He tapped the side of his nose with a sausage-like forefinger and nodded solemnly.

Karpov leaned forward and topped up the GRU general's glass from the third bottle. 'Sure, I know, sorry I asked,' he said reassuringly. 'Won't mention it again. Won't mention the operation again.'

Marchenko waved an admonitory finger. His eyes were bloodshot. He reminded Karpov of a wounded boar in a thicket, brain dimmed by alcohol instead of pain and blood loss, but still dangerous. 'Not operation, no operation, sodding thing cancelled. Sworn to secrecy . . . all of us. Very high up . . . higher than you could imagine. Don't mention it again, OK?'

'Wouldn't dream of it,' said Karpov, topping up the rummers again. He was taking advantage of Marchenko's drunkenness to fill the GRU man's glass fuller than his own, but he was still having to focus his gaze with an effort.

Two hours later the last Akhtamar was a third gone. Marchenko was slumped, chin on chest. Karpov raised his glass in another of the endless toasts. 'Here's to oblivion.'

'Oblivion?' Marchenko shook his head in bewilderment. 'I'm all right. Drink you FCD sods under the table any time. Not oblivious . . .'

'No,' corrected Karpov, 'oblivion of the Plan. We just forget it, right?'

'Aurora? Right, forget it. Bloody good idea though.'

They drank. Karpov topped them up. 'Sod 'em all,' he proposed, 'Screw Philby . . . and the academician.'

Marchenko nodded in agreement, the brandy that had missed his mouth dripping off his jowls.

'Krilov? Asshole. Forget 'em all.'

It was midnight when Karpov staggered to his car. He leaned against a tree, stuck two fingers down his throat and threw up what he could into the snow, sucking in gulps of the freezing night air. It helped, but the drive to his dacha was murder. He made it with a scraped fender and two nasty scares. Ludmilla was still up, in a housecoat, and she put him to bed, terrified that he had actually driven out from Moscow in that condition.

On the Saturday morning John Preston drove down to Tonbridge to pick up his son Tommy. As usual when his dad collected him from school, the boy was a torrent of words, memories of the term just past, projects for the term yet to come, plans for the holiday about to begin, praise for his best friends and their virtues, scorn for the infamies of those he disliked.

The trunk and tuck box were in the boot, and the drive back to London was, for John Preston, bliss. He mentioned the several things he had planned for their one week together and was happy they seemed to meet with approval. The lad's face only fell when he recalled he would be returned after a week to the smart, brittle and pricelessly expensive Mayfair apartment where Julia lived with her gown-manufacturer companion. The man was old enough to be his grandfather, and Preston suspected that any breakages in the flat would lead to a severe frost in the atmosphere.

'Dad,' said Tommy as they drove over Vauxhall Bridge, 'why can't I come and stay with you all the time?'

Preston sighed. It was not easy to explain the break-up of a marriage, or the cost of it, to a twelve-year-old.

'Because,' he said carefully, 'your Mummy and Archie aren't actually married. If I insisted to Mummy on a formal divorce, she could ask for and get an allowance from me called maintenance. Which, incidentally, I couldn't afford, not on my salary. At least, not enough to keep myself, you at school, and her. It just wouldn't go that far. And if I couldn't pay that allowance, the court might decide your best chances in life were with Mummy. So, we wouldn't get to see each other even as often as we do.'

'I didn't know it came down to money,' said the boy sadly.

'In the end most things come down to money. Sad but true. Years ago, if I had been able to afford a better kind of life for all three of us, Mummy and I might not have broken up. I was just an army officer, and even when I quit the Army to join the Home Office, the salary still wasn't enough.'

'Just what *do* you do in the Home Office?' asked the boy. He was dropping the subject of his parents' estrangement, the way the young will try to blank out something that hurts them.

'Oh, a sort of minor civil servant,' said Preston.

'Gosh, must be jolly dull.'

'Yes,' Preston conceded, 'I suppose it is, really.'

Yevgeni Karpov woke at noon with an imperial hangover that half a dozen aspirins were only just able to contain.

After lunch he felt somewhat better and decided to go for a stroll.

There was something at the back of his mind; a memory, a half-recollection that he had heard the name Krilov somewhere in the not too distant past. It bothered him. One of the restricted-list reference books he kept at the dacha gave him the details of Professor Krilov, Vladimir Ilich; historian, professor at Moscow University, lifelong member of the Party, member of the Academy of Sciences, member of the Supreme Soviet, etc., etc. All that he knew; but there was something else.

He ploughed through the snow, his head bowed, deep in thought. The boys had gone off on their skis to take advantage of the last of the good powder snow before the coming thaw spoiled it all. Ludmilla Karpova trailed along behind her husband. She knew his mood and refrained from interrupting.

The previous evening she had been surprised but quite happy at the state he had been in. She knew he hardly ever drank, and never that heavily, which counted out a visit to his girlfriend. Perhaps he really had been with a colleague from the GRU, one of the so-called 'neighbours'. Whatever, something had got on top of him, but it was not a partridge in the Arbat.

Just after three, whatever he had been racking his brains for came to him. He stopped several yards ahead of her, said 'Damn. Of course,' and perked up at once. He took her arm, all smiles, and they walked back to the dacha.

General Karpov knew he had some quiet reseach to do in his office the next morning, and that he would visit Professor Krilov in his Moscow apartment on the Monday evening.

16

The phone call on the Monday morning caught John Preston just as he was about to leave home with his son.

'Mr Preston? Dafydd Wynne-Evans here.'

For a moment the name meant nothing to him; then he recalled his request of the Friday evening.

'I've had a look at your little piece of metal. Very interesting. Can you come out here and have a chat with me?'

'Well, actually I'm taking a few days off,' said Preston. 'Would the end of the week suit?'

There was a pause from the Aldermaston end. 'I think it might be better before then, if you could spare the time.'

'Er, oh, well, could you give me the gist of it down the phone?'

'Much better we talk about it face to face,' said Dr Wynne-Evans.

Preston thought for a moment. He was taking Tommy to the Windsor Safari Park for the day. But that was also in Berkshire. 'Could I come by this afternoon, say, about five?' he asked.

'Five it is,' said the scientist. 'Ask for me at the desk. I'll have you shown up.'

Professor Krilov lived on the top floor of a block on Komsomolski Prospekt, with commanding views of the Moskva River and handy for the university on the southern side. General Karpov pressed the buzzer just after six and it was the academic himself who answered it. He surveyed his visitor without recognition.

'Comrade Professor Krilov?'

'Yes.'

'My name is General Karpov. I wonder if we might have a word or two?'

He held out his personal pass. Professor Krilov studied it, taking in the rank and the fact his visitor was from the First Chief Directorate of the KGB. Then he handed it back and gestured Karpov to enter. He led the way to a well-furnished sitting room, took his guest's coat and bade him be seated.

'To what do I owe the honour?' he asked when he had seated himself opposite Karpov. He was a man of distinction in his own right, not in any way awed by a general of the KGB.

Karpov realized the professor was different. Erita Philby he could trick into revealing the existence of the chauffeur; Driver Gregoriev he could browbeat by his intimidating rank: Marchenko was an old colleague and a too heavy drinker. Krilov was high in the Party, the Supreme Soviet, the Academy and the élite of the state. He decided to waste no time, but to play his cards fast and without mercy. It was the only way.

'Professor Krilov, in the interests of the state, I wish you to tell me something. I wish you to tell me what you know about Plan Aurora.'

Professor Krilov sat as if he had been slapped. Then he flushed angrily. 'General Karpov, you exceed yourself,' he snapped. 'I do not know what you are talking about.'

'I believe you do,' said Karpov evenly, 'and I believe you should tell me what this plan entails.'

In answer, Professor Krilov held out a peremptory hand. 'Your authority, please.'

'My authority is my rank and my service,' said Karpov.

'If you have no personal signed authority from the Comrade General Secretary, you have no authority at all,' said Krilov icily. He rose and made for the telephone. 'Indeed, I think it high time your line of questioning came to the attention of an authority far higher than yourself.' He picked up the receiver and prepared to dial.

'That might not be a very good idea,' said Karpov. 'Did you know that one of your fellow-consultants, retired colonel of the KGB Philby has already gone missing?'

Krilov stopped dialling. 'What do you mean – gone missing?' he asked. The first edge of hesitation had entered his hitherto completely assured bearing.

'Please sit down and hear me out,' said Karpov.

The academic did so. Farther into the apartment a door opened and closed. In the second of its opening a blare of Western jazz music could be heard, which muted when the door closed.

'I mean gone missing,' said Karpov. 'Missing from his apartment, driver dismissed, wife no idea where he is or when, if at all, he'll be back.'

It was a gamble, and a damnably high one. But an air of worry entered the professor's gaze. Then he reasserted himself. 'There can be no question of my discussing affairs of state with you, Comrade General. I think I must ask you to leave.

'It's not quite that easy,' said Karpov. 'Tell me, Professor, you have a son, Leonid, do you not?'

The sudden switch of topic genuinely dumbfounded the professor.

'Yes,' he conceded. 'I do. So what?'

'So let me explain,' suggested Karpov.

On the other side of Europe John Preston and his son were driving out of the Windsor Safari Park at the close of a warm spring day.

'I've just got one call to make before we go home,' said the father. 'It's not far and it shouldn't take long. Have you ever been to Aldermaston?'

The boy's eyes opened wide. 'The bomb factory?' he asked.

'It's not quite a bomb factory,' Preston corrected. 'It's a research establishment.'

'Gosh, no. Are we going there? Will they let us in?'

'Well, they'll let me in. You'll have to sit in the car in the park. But it won't take long.'

He turned north to cut into the M4 motorway.

'Your son returned nine weeks ago from a visit to Canada, where he had acted as one of the interpreters to a trade delegation,' said General Karpov quietly.

Krilov nodded. 'So?'

'While he was there my own KR people noted that an attractive young person was spending a deal of time – too much time, it was judged – trying to get into conversation with the members of our delegation, notably the younger members, secretaries, interpreters and so forth. The person concerned was photographed and finally identified as an entrapment agent. American not Canadian and almost certainly employed by the CIA.

'As a result, that young agent was put under surveillance and was observed to set up a rendezvous with your son Leonid in a hotel room. To put not too fine a point on it, the pair had a brief but torrid affair.'

Professor Krilov's face was mottled with rage. He seemed to have trouble enunciating his words. 'How dare you. How dare you have the impertinence to come here and seek to subject me, a member of the Academy of Sciences and the Supreme Soviet, to crude blackmail. The Party shall hear of this. You know the rule: only the Party can discipline the Party. You may be a general of the KGB, but you have overstepped your authority by a hundred miles, General Karpov.'

Yevgeni Karpov sat, as if humbled, staring at the table, as the professor went on. 'So, my son screwed a foreign girl while in Canada. That the girl turned out to be an American was certainly something of which he was completely unaware. Indiscreet, perhaps, but no more. Was he recruited by this CIA girl?'

'No,' admitted Karpov.

'Did he betray any state secrets?'

'No.'

'Then you have nothing, Comrade General, but a brief youthful indiscretion. He'll be rebuked. But the rebuke for your counter-intelligence people will be the greater. They should have warned him. As to the bedroom business, we are not so unworldly in the Soviet Union as you seem to think. Strong young men have been screwing girls since time began . . .'

Karpov had opened his attaché case and produced a large photograph, one of a sheaf that lay inside the case, and placed it on the table. Professor Krilov stared at it and his words died. The flush went out of his cheeks, draining away until his elderly face appeared grey in the lamplight. He shook his head several times.

'I am sorry,' said Karpov very gently, 'truly sorry. The surveillance was on the American boy, not your son. It was not intended that it should come to this.'

'I don't believe it,' croaked the professor.

'I have sons of my own,' murmured Karpov. 'I believe I can understand, or try to understand, how you feel.'

The academic sucked in his breath, rose, muttered, 'Excuse me,' and left the room. Karpov sighed and replaced the photograph in his case. From down the corridor he heard the blare of jazz as a door opened, the sudden ending of the music, and voices, two voices, raised in anger. One was the roar of the father, the other a higher-pitched voice as of a young man. The altercation ended with the sound of a slap. Seconds later Professor Krilov re-entered the room. He seated himself, eyes dull, shoulders sloping.

'What are you going to do?' he whispered.

Karpov sighed. 'My duty is very clear. As you said, only the Party may discipline the Party. I should by rights hand over the report and the photographs to the Central Committee.

'You know the law. You know what they do to "golden boys". It's five years, without remission and strict regime. I'm afraid, once in the camps, word gets around. After that, the young man becomes – how shall I put it? –

anybody's. A lad from a sheltered background would be hard put to survive that sort of thing.'

'But . . .' prompted the professor.

'But . . . I can decide that there is a chance the CIA will seek to pursue the matter. I have that right. I can decide the Americans could become impatient and send their agent into the Soviet Union to resume contact with Leonid. I have the right to decide the entrapment of your son could possibly be turned into an operation to trap a CIA agent. While waiting, I would be able to keep the file in my personal safe, and the waiting could take a very long time. I have that authority; in operational matters, yes, I have that authority.'

'And the price?'

'I think you know that.'

'What do you want to know about Plan Aurora?'

'Just start from the beginning.'

Preston swung into the main gate at Aldermaston, found a slot in the visitor's car park and got out.

'Sorry, Tommy, no farther. Just wait for me here. I hope I won't be long.'

He crossed in the dusk to the swing doors and presented himself to the two men on the desk. They examined his ID card and rang Dr Wynne-Evans, who sanctioned the visit to his office. It was three floors up. He was shown in and gestured to a seat facing the desk.

The scientist regarded him over his glasses. 'May I ask you where you got this little exhibit?' he enquired, pointing to the heavy, lead-like disc of metal which now sat in a sealed glass jar.

'It was taken off someone in Glasgow during the small hours of Thursday morning. What about the other two discs?'

'Oh, they're just ordinary aluminium, boyo. Nothing strange about them. Just used to keep this one safe and sound. This is the one that interests me.'

'Do you know what it is?' asked Preston.

Dr Wynne-Evans seemed startled by the naïvety of the question. 'Of course I know what it is,' he said. 'It's my job to know what it is. It's a disc of pure polonium.'

Preston frowned. He had never heard of such a metal.

'Well, it all started in early January with two memoranda submitted by Philby to the General Secretary. In these papers, Philby maintained there existed within the British Labour Party a Hard Left wing that had grown so strong it was in a position to take over complete control of the party machine more or less when it wished. That corresponds with my own view.'

'And mine,' murmured Karpov.

'Philby went further. He claimed there was within the Hard Left wing a group, an inner kernel, of dedicated Marxist–Leninists who had framed an intention to do just that; but not in the period before Britain's next general election. After it, in the very wake of a Labour electoral victory. In short, to await the victory at the polls of Mr Neil Kinnock and then to topple him from the Party leadership. His replacement would be Britain's first Marxist–Leninist Premier, who would institute a series of policies wholly in line with Soviet foreign and defence interests, most notably in the area of unilateral nuclear disarmament and the expulsion of all American forces.'

'Feasible,' nodded General Karpov. 'So a committee of four of you was called together to advise how this electoral victory could best be achieved?'

Professor Krilov looked up, surprised. 'Yes. There was Philby, General Marchenko, myself and Dr Rogov.'

'The Chess Grand Master?'

'And physicist,' added Krilov. 'What we came up with was Plan Aurora, which would have been an act of massive destabilization of the British electorate by pushing millions towards a mood of determined unilateralism.'

'You say . . . *would* have?'

'Yes. The plan was principally Rogov's idea. He

supported it strongly. Marchenko went along, with reservations. Philby, well, no-one could tell what Philby was really thinking. Just kept nodding and smiling, waiting to see which way the wind blew.'

'That's Philby,' agreed Karpov. 'And then you presented it?'

'Yes. On 12 March. I opposed the plan. The General Secretary agreed with me. He denounced it roundly, ordered all notes and files destroyed, and swore all four of us never to mention the issue again under any circumstances.'

'Tell me, why did you oppose it?'

'It seemed to me reckless and dangerous. Apart from anything, it was in complete contravention of the Fourth Protocol. If that protocol is ever breached, God knows where the world will end up.'

'The Fourth Protocol?'

'Yes. To the international Nuclear Non-Proliferation Treaty. You remember that, of course.'

'One has to remember so much,' said Karpov gently. 'Please remind me.'

I've never heard of polonium,' said Preston.

'No, well, you probably wouldn't have,' said Dr Wynne-Evans. 'I mean, you don't find it hanging about on your workbench. It's very rare.'

'And what are its uses, Doctor?'

'Well, it is occasionally – only very occasionally, mind – used in curative medicine. Was your man in Glasgow on his way to a medical conference or exhibition?'

'No,' said Preston firmly, 'he was in no way heading for a medical conference.'

'Well, that would have accounted for a ten per cent possibility of what it was intended for – before you relieved him of his burden. Since he wasn't going to a medical conference, I'm afraid that leaves the 90 per cent likelihood. Apart from these two functions, polonium has no known use on this planet.'

'And the other use?'

'Well, a disc of polonium this size will do nothing on its own. But in close juxtaposition with a disc of another metal called lithium, the two combine to form an initiator.'

'A what?'

'An initiator.'

'And what, pray, the hell is that?'

'On 1 July 1968,' said Professor Krilov, 'the Nuclear Non-Proliferation Treaty was signed between the three (then) nuclear powers of the world, the USA, Great Britain and the USSR.

'In the Treaty the three signatory nations pledged themselves not to impart the technology or the materiel capable of enabling the construction of a nuclear weapon to any nation not then in possession of such technology or materiel. Do you recall that?'

'Yes,' said Karpov, 'I remember that much.'

'Well, the signing ceremonies in Washington, London and Moscow were attended by huge and worldwide publicity. A complete absence of publicity surrounded the later signing of four secret protocols to that treaty.

'Each of the protocols foresaw the development of a possible future hazard, which was not then technically possible but which, it was then estimated, might one day become technically possible.

'Over the years the first three protocols passed into history, either because the hazard was established to be quite impossible or because an antidote was discovered as fast as the threat became reality. But by the early eighties the Fourth Protocol, the most secret of them all, had become a living nightmare.'

'What exactly did the Fourth Protocol envisage?' asked Karpov.

Professor Krilov sighed. 'We relied on Dr Rogov for this information. As you know, he is a nuclear physicist; that is his branch of science. The Fourth Protocol foresaw technological advances in the manufacture of nuclear bombs, mainly in the areas of miniaturization and simplification. This apparently is what has happened. In one area the weapons have become infinitely more powerful, but more complex to construct and large in size. Another branch of the science has gone the other way. The basic atomic bomb, which it once took a huge bomber to drop on Japan in 1945, can now be made small enough to go in a suitcase and simple enough to be assembled from a dozen prefabricated, milled and threaded components, like a child's construction kit.'

'And that is what the Fourth Protocol banned?'

Professor Krilov shook his head. 'It went further. It forbade any of the signatory nations to introduce on to the territory of any nation a device in assembled or unassembled form by covert means, for detonation in, say, a rented house or flat in the heart of a city.'

'No four-minute warning,' mused Karpov, 'no radar detection of an incoming missile, no counterstrike, no identification of the perpetrator. Just a megaton explosion from a basement bedsitter.'

'That's right,' nodded the professor. 'That's why I called it a living nightmare. The open societies of the West are more vulnerable, but we are none of us immune from smuggled artefacts. If the Fourth Protocol is ever breached, all those ranks of rockets and electronic countermeasures, indeed most of the arms/industrial complex, becomes irrelevant.'

'And that was what Plan Aurora had in mind.'

Krilov nodded. He seemed to clam up.

'But since,' pursued Karpov, 'it was all stopped and prohibited, the whole plan has become what, in the service, we call archival.'

Krilov seemed to grasp at the word. 'That's right. It's just archival now.'

'So tell me what it *would* have been,' Karpov pressed him.

'Well, Plan Aurora intended to infiltrate into Britain a top-class Soviet agent who would rent a provincial villa and become the Executive Officer of Aurora.

'To him, using a variety of couriers, would be smuggled the ten or so component parts of a small atomic bomb of about one and a half kiloton power.'

'So small? Hiroshima was ten kilotons.'

'It was not intended to cause huge damage. That would have cancelled the general election. It was intended to create a supposed nuclear accident and panic the ten per cent floating vote into unilateralism and support at the polls of the only party pledged to unilateralism, the Labour Party.'

'I'm sorry,' said Karpov, 'please go on.'

'The device would have been detonated six days before polling day,' said the professor. 'The place was vitally important. The one selected was the United States Air Force base at Bentwaters in Suffolk. Apparently F-5 strike planes are based there and they carry small tactical nuclear devices for use against our massed tank divisions in the event of our invading Western Europe.'

Karpov nodded. He knew Bentwaters and the information was correct.

'The Executive Officer,' went on Professor Krilov, 'would have been ordered to take the assembled device by car to the very perimeter wire of the base in the small hours of the morning. The whole base, it seems is in the heart of Rendlesham Forest. He would cause the explosion just before dawn.

'Because of the smallness of the device, damage would be limited to the airbase itself, which would be vaporized, Rendlesham Forest, three hamlets, a village, the foreshore and a bird sanctuary. The base being right next to the Suffolk coast, the cloud of radioactive dust thrown up would have drifted on the prevailing west wind out over the North Sea. By the time it reached the coast of Holland ninety-five per cent of it would have become inert or fallen into the sea. The intent was not to cause an ecological catastrophe, but fear and a violent wave of hatred of America.'

'They might not have believed it,' said Karpov. 'A lot of things could have gone wrong. The Executive Officer could have been caught alive.'

Professor Krilov shook his head. 'Rogov thought of all that. He worked it out like a chess game. The officer in question would have been told that after pressing the button he had two hours on the timer to drive as far as he could. In fact the timer would be a sealed unit, set for instant detonation.'

Poor Petrofsky, thought Karpov.

'And the credibility angle?' he asked.

'On the evening of the same day as the explosion,' said Krilov, 'a man who is apparently a covert Soviet agent would have flown to Prague and given an international press conference. An Israeli nuclear physicist called Dr Nahum Wisser. It seems he works for us.'

General Karpov kept a deadpan face. 'You amaze me,' he said. He knew the file of Dr Wisser. He had once had a son on whom he doted and the youth had been a soldier in the Israeli Army stationed in Beirut in 1982. When the Phalangists devasted the Palestinian refugee camps of Sabra and Shatila, the young Lieutenant Wisser had tried to intervene. He had been cut down by a bullet.

Carefully constructed evidence had been presented to the grieving father, already a committed opponent of the Likud Party, that it had been an Israeli bullet that killed his son. In his bitterness and rage Dr Wisser had swung a little farther left and agreed to work for Russia.

'Anyway, Dr Wisser would have claimed to the world that he had collaborated for years with the Americans while on exchange visits in the development of ultra-small nuclear warheads. This, it seems, is true. He would have gone on to say that he had repeatedly warned the Americans that these ultra-small warheads were not stable enough to permit deployment. But the Americans were impatient to deploy these new warheads so as to increase the range of their F-5s by being able to take on board extra fuel.

'It was calculated that these claims, appearing on the day following the explosion, the fifth before the polling date, would turn the wave of anti-Americanism in Britain into a gale that not even the Conservatives could hope to stem.'

Karpov nodded. 'Yes, I believe it would have done that. Anything more from the fertile brain of Dr Rogov?'

'Much more,' said Krilov glumly. 'He suggested the American reaction would be a histrionic and violent denial. Thus, on the fourth day before polling, the General Secretary would announce to the world that if the Americans intended to enter a period of insanity, that was their business. But he for his part had no alternative in the protection of the Soviet people but to put all our forces on Red Alert.

'That evening, one of our friends, very close to Mr Kinnock, would have urged the Labour leader to fly to Moscow, see the General Secretary personally and intervene for peace. Had there been any hesitation, our own ambassador would have invited him round to the Embassy for friendly discussions of the crisis. With the cameras on him, it was doubtful he would have resisted.

'Well, he would have been issued a visa within minutes, and flown on Aeroflot the next morning at dawn. The General Secretary would have received him before the cameras of the world's press, and a few hours later they would have parted, both looking extremely grave.'

'As no doubt he would have been given cause to look,' suggested Karpov.

'Precisely. But, while he was still airborne back to London in the evening, the General Secretary would have issued a statement to the world: wholly and solely as a result of the plea of the British Labour leader, he, the General Secretary, was standing all Soviet forces back to Green status. Mr Kinnock would have landed in London with the stature of global statesman.

'The day before polling he would have made a resounding speech to the British nation on the issue of a final renunciation of the nuclear madness once and for all. It was calculated in Plan Aurora that the events of the previous six days would have shattered the traditional alliance with America, isolated the USA from all European sympathy, and swung ten per cent, the vital ten per cent, of the British electorate to vote Labour into office. After that the Hard Left would have taken over. And that, General, was Plan Aurora.'

Karpov rose. 'You have been very kind, Professor. And very wise. Remain silent, and I shall also. As you say, it's all archival now. And your son's file will remain in my safe for a very long time. Goodbye. I do not think I shall be troubling you again.'

He leaned back against the cushions as the Chaika swept him away down Komsomolski Prospekt. Oh yes, it's brilliant, he thought, but is there time?

Like the General Secretary, he too knew of the forthcoming election in Britain, slated for that June, sixty days away. The information to the General Secretary had, after all, come through his *rezidentura* in their London embassy.

He ran the plan over and over in his mind, seeking the flaws. It's good, he thought at last, damn good. Just so long as it works . . . The alternative would be catastrophic.

'An initiator, my dear man, is a sort of detonator for a bomb,' said Dr Wynne-Evans.

'Oh,' said Preston. He felt somewhat deflated. There had been bombs before in Britain. Nasty but local. He had seen quite a few in Ireland. He had heard of detonators, primers, triggers, but never an initiator. Still, it looked as if the Russian Semyonov had been carrying in a component for a terrorist group somewhere in Scotland. Which group? Tartan Army, anarchists or an IRA active service unit? The Russian connection was odd; very much worth the trip to Glasgow.

'This, er, initiator of polonium and lithium, would it be used in an anti-personnel bomb?' he asked.

'Oh yes, you could say so, boyo,' replied the Welshman. 'An initiator, you see, is what sets off a nuke.'

Part Three

17

Brian Harcourt-Smith listened attentively, leaning back, eyes on the ceiling, fingers toying with a slim gold propelling pencil.

'That's it?' he asked when Preston had finished his verbal report.

'Yes,' said Preston.

'This Dr Wynne-Evans, is he prepared to put his deductions in written form?'

'Hardly deductions, Brian. It's a scientific analysis of the metal, coupled with its only two known uses. And, yes, he has agreed to put it in the form of a written report. I'll attach it to my own.'

'And your own deductions? Or should I say scientific analysis?'

Preston ignored the patronage. 'I think it inescapable that Deckhand Semyonov had arrived in Glasgow to deposit his tin and its contents in a dead drop, or hand it over personally to someone he was due to meet,' he said. 'Either way, that means there is an "Illegal" here, in on the ground. I think we could try to find him.'

'A charming idea. The trouble is, we haven't a clue where to start. Look, John, let me be frank. You leave me, as so often, in an extremely difficult position. I really do not see how I can take this matter higher unless you can provide me with a little more evidence than a single disc of rare metal taken from a lamentably dead Rusian seaman.'

'It's been identified as one half of the initiator of a nuclear device,' Preston pointed out. 'It's hardly just a bit of metal.'

'Very well. One half of what might be the trigger of what might be a device; which might have been destined for a Soviet illegal who might be resident in Britain.

Believe me, John, when you submit me your full report I shall as ever consider it with the greatest gravity.'

'And then NFA it?' asked Preston.

Harcourt-Smith's smile was unfaltering and dangerous. 'Not necessarily. Any report from you will be treated on its merits, like anyone else's. Now I suggest you try to find for me at least some corroborative evidence to support your evident predilection for the conspiracy theory. Make that your next priority.'

'All right,' said Preston as he rose. 'I'll get stuck into it.'

'You do that,' said Harcourt-Smith.

When Preston had gone the Deputy Director-General consulted a list of in-house numbers and called the head of Personnel.

On the following day, Wednesday, the 15th, a British Airways flight from Paris touched down about noon at Birmingham Airport. Among the passengers was a young man with a Danish passport.

The name on the passport was also Danish, and had anyone been so curious as to address him in Danish, he would have responded fluently. He had in fact had a Danish mother, from whom he had learned his basic grasp of the language, now honed to perfection in several language schools and on visits to Denmark.

His father had, however, been a German, and the young man, born well after the Second World War, originated from Erfurt where he had been raised. That made him an East German. He also happened to be a staff officer in the East German HVA intelligence service.

He had no idea of the significance of his mission in Britain, nor did he care to find out. His instructions were simple and he followed them to the letter. Passing without difficulty through Customs and Immigration, he hailed a cab and asked to be taken to the Midland Hotel in New Street. Throughout the journey, and during the check-in procedures, he was careful to favour his left arm which was encased in a plaster cast. He had been warned, if warning was necessary, under no circumstances to attempt to pick up his grip with the 'broken' arm.

Once in his room he locked the door and went to work on the plaster cast with the tough steel cutters tucked at the bottom of his sponge bag, carefully snipping down the inside of the forearm along the line of tiny indentations that marked the cutting path.

When the cut was complete he prised the cast open half an inch and withdrew his arm, wrist and hand. The empty cast he dropped into the plastic carrier bag he had brought with him.

He spent the entire afternoon in his room so that the day staff at reception should not see him with the cast off, and only left the hotel late at night when a different staff was on duty.

The newspaper kiosk at New Street Station was where they had said it would be, and at the appointed hour a figure in black leather motorcycle clothing approached him. The muttered exchange of identification took seconds, the plastic bag changed hands and the figure in leather was gone. Neither of them had attracted a passing glance.

At the hour of dawn, when the night staff at the hotel were still on duty, the Dane checked out, took the early train to Manchester and flew out from that airport, where no-one had ever seen him before, with or without a plaster cast. By sundown, via Hamburg, he was back in Berlin where he went through the Wall as a Dane at Checkpoint Charlie. His own people met him on the other side, heard his report and spirited him away. Courier Three had delivered.

John Preston was annoyed and not in the best of humours. The week he had arranged to take off work to be with Tommy was being ruined. Tuesday had been partly taken up with his verbal report to Harcourt-Smith and Tommy had had to spend the day reading or watching the television.

Preston had insisted on keeping their date to go to Madame Tussaud's waxwork museum that Wednesday morning, but had come into the office in the afternoon to finish his written report. The letter from Crichton in Personnel was on his desk. He read it with something close to disbelief.

It was couched as ever in the friendliest terms. A glance at the files had shown that Preston was owed four weeks' leave; he would be, of course, aware of the rules of the service; backlogging of leave was not encouraged for obvious reasons; necessity to keep all leave-taking up to date, blah, blah blah. In short, he would be required to take up his backlog of leave forthwith, i.e. as of the following morning.

'Bloody idiots,' he called to the office in general, 'some of them couldn't find their way to the can without a labrador.'

He called Personnel and insisted on speaking to Crichton personally. 'Tim, it's me, John Preston. Look, what's this letter doing on my desk? I can't take leave now; I'm on a case, right in the middle of it . . . yes, I know it's important not to backlog leave, but this case is also important, a damn sight more so, actually . . .'

He heard out the bureaucrat's explanation concerning the disruption caused to the system if staffers backlogged too much leave, then cut in. 'Look, Tim, let's keep it short. All you have to do is call Brian Harcourt-Smith. He'll vouch for the importance of the case I'm on. I can take the leave in the summer.'

'John,' said Tim Crichton gently, 'that letter was written at the express orders of Brian.'

Preston stared at the handset for several moments. 'I see,' he said finally, and put it down.

'Where are you going?' asked Bright as he headed for the door.

'To get a stiff drink,' said Preston.

It was well after lunch and the bar was almost empty. The late-lunch crowd had not yet been replaced by the early-evening thirst-quenchers. There was a couple over from Charles Street having a head-to-head in one corner, so he took a stool at the bar itself. He wanted to be alone.

'Whisky,' he said, 'large one.'

'Same for me,' said a voice at his elbow. 'And it's my round.'

He turned to see Barry Banks from K.7.

'Hello, John,' said Banks, 'saw you scooting down here as I was crossing the lobby. Just wanted to say I have something for you. The Master was most grateful.'

'Oh, yes, that. Not at all.'

'I'll bring it to your office tomorrow,' said Banks.

'Don't bother,' said Preston angrily. 'We are down here to celebrate my four weeks' leave. As of tomorrow. Enforced. Cheers.'

'Don't knock it,' said Banks gently. 'Most people can't wait to get away from the place.'

He had already noticed Preston was nursing a grudge of some kind, and intended to ease the reason for it from his MI5 colleague. What he was not able to tell Preston was that he had been asked by Sir Nigel Irvine to cultivate the black sheep of Mr Harcourt-Smith's books, and to report back on what he learned.

An hour and three whiskies later Preston was still sunk in gloom. 'I'm thinking of quitting,' he said suddenly.

Banks, a good listener who only interjected to extract information was concerned. 'Pretty drastic,' he said. 'Are things that bad?'

'Look, Barry, I don't mind free-falling from twenty thousand feet. I don't even mind people taking pot shots at me when the chute opens. But I get bloody annoyed when the flak's coming from my own side. Is that unreasonable?'

'Sounds perfectly justified to me,' said Banks. 'So who's shooting?'

'Whizzkid upstairs,' growled Preston. 'Just put in another report he didn't seem to like.'

'NFA-ed again?'

Preston shrugged. 'It will be.'

The door opened to admit a crowd from upstairs. Brian Harcourt-Smith was at the centre of it, several of his heads of section around him.

Preston drained his glass. 'Well, I must love you and leave you. Taking my boy to the pictures tonight.'

When he had gone Barry Banks finished his drink, avoided an invitation to join the group at the bar and went to his office. From there he made a long phone call to 'C' in his office in Sentinel House.

It was not until the small hours of the Thursday that Major Petrofsky arrived back at Cherryhayes Close. The black leathers and visored mask were with the BMW in their garage at Thetford. When he drove his little Ford quietly on to the hard pad in front of his garage and let himself into the house, he was in a sober suit and light raincoat. No-one noticed him or the plastic carrier bag in his hand.

With the door firmly locked behind him, he went upstairs and pulled open the bottom drawer of the clothes chest. Inside was a Sony transistor radio. Beside it he laid the empty plaster cast.

He did not interfere with either item. He did not know what they contained, nor did he wish to find out. That would be for the Assembler, who would not arrive to perform his task until the complete list of required components had been safely received.

Before sleeping he made himself a cup of tea. There were nine couriers in all. That meant nine first rendezvous and nine back-ups in case of a no-show at the first. He had memorized them all, plus another six which represented the three extra couriers to be used as replacements if necessary.

One of those would now have to be called on, as Courier Two had failed to show. Petrofsky had no idea why that courier had failed. Far away in Moscow, Major Volkov knew. Moscow had had a complete report from the Glasgow consul, who had assured his government that the dead seaman's effects were locked up in Partick police station and would remain there until further notice.

Petrofsky checked his mental list. Courier Four was due in four days, and the meet was in the West End of London. It was dawn of the 16th when he slept. As he drifted off, he could hear the whine of a milk float entering the close and the clatter of the day's first deliveries.

This time Banks was more open. He was waiting for Preston in the lobby of his own apartment block when the MI5 man drove up on the Friday afternoon with Tommy in the passenger seat.

The pair of them had been out at the Hendon Aircraft Museum where the boy, enthused by the fighter planes of bygone ages, had announced he intended to be a pilot when he grew up. His father knew he had decided on at least six careers in the past, and would change his mind again before the year was out. It had been a good afternoon.

Banks seemed surprised to see the boy; he had evidently not expected his presence. He nodded and smiled, and Preston introduced him as 'someone from the office'.

'What is it this time?' asked Preston.

'A colleague of mine wants another word with you,' said Banks carefully.

'Monday do?' asked Preston. On Sunday his week with Tommy would be over and he would drive the boy to Mayfair to hand him over to Julia.

'Actually, he's waiting for you now.'

'Back seat of a car again?' asked Preston.

'Er, no. Small flat we keep in Chelsea.'

Preston sighed. 'Give me the address. I'll go, while you take Tommy for an ice- cream up the road.'

'I'll have to check,' said Banks.

He went into a nearby phone booth and made a call. Preston and his son waited on the pavement.

Banks came back and nodded. 'It's all right,' he said, and gave Preston a piece of paper. Preston drove off while

Tommy showed Banks the directions to his favourite ice-cream parlour.

The flat was small and discreet, in a modern block off Chelsea Manor Street. Sir Nigel answered the door himself. He was as usual full of old-world courtesy.

'My dear John, how good of you to come.'

If someone had been brought to his presence trussed like a chicken and borne by four heavies, he would still have said: 'How good of you to come.'

When they were seated in the small sitting room the Master held out the original Preston Report. 'My sincere thanks. Extremely interesting.'

'But not apparently believable.'

Sir Nigel glanced at the younger man sharply but chose his words with care. 'I would not necessarily agree with that.' Then he smiled quickly and changed the subject. 'Now, please don't think ill of Barry, but I asked him to keep an eye on you. It appears you are not too happy in your work at present.'

'I'm not in work at present, sir. I'm on compulsory leave.'

'So I gather. Something that happened in Glasgow, was it?'

'You have not yet received a report on the Glasgow incident of last week? It concerned a Russian seaman, a man I believe to be a courier. Surely that involves "Six"?'

'Doubtless it will be on its way before long,' said Sir Nigel carefully. 'Would you be kind enough to tell me about it?'

Preston started at the beginning and told the tale through to the end, so far as he knew it. Sir Nigel sat as if lost in thought, which he was: taking in every word with part of his mind and calculating with the rest.

They would not really try it, would they? he was thinking. Not breach the Fourth Protocol? Or would they? Desperate men sometimes take desperate measures, and he had several reasons to know that in a number of areas – food production, the economy and Afghanistan –

the USSR was in desperate waters. He noted that Preston had stopped talking.

'Do forgive me,' he said. 'What do you deduce from it all?'

'I believe Semyonov was not a merchant navy deckhand but a courier. That seems to me unavoidable. I do not believe he would have gone to those lengths to protect what he was carrying, or end his life to avoid what he must have thought was interrogation by us, unless he had been instructed his mission was of crucial importance.'

'Fair enough,' conceded Sir Nigel. 'And so?'

'And so I believe there was an intended recipient of that disc of polonium, either directly through a rendezvous or by dead drop. That means he's here, on the ground. I think we should try to find him.'

Sir Nigel pursed his lips. 'If he's a top illegal, finding him would be a needle-in-a-haystack affair,' he murmured.

'Yes, I know that.'

'So if you had not been sent on compulsory leave, what would you have sought authority to do?'

'I think, Sir Nigel, that one disc of polonium is no use to anybody. Whatever the illegal is up to, there must be other components. Now, it seems whoever mounted the Semyonov incursion has taken a policy decision not to use the Soviet Embassy diplomatic bag. I don't know why, but it would have been much easier to ship a small, lead-lined package into Britain in the embassy bag and have one of their Line N people leave it at a dead drop for collection by the man on the ground. So I ask myself why they didn't just do that. And the short answer is I don't know.'

'Right,' conceded Sir Nigel, 'so?'

'So, if there has been one consignment, useless in itself, there must be others. Some may have already arrived. On the law of averages, there must be more yet to come. And apparently they are coming in via mules or couriers who pose as harmless seamen or God knows what else besides.'

'And you would want to do what?' asked Sir Nigel.

Preston took a deep breath. 'I would have wanted,' he stressed the conditional aspect, 'to check back on all entrants from the Soviet Union over the past forty, fifty, even a hundred days. One could not count on another mugging by hooligans, but there might have been some other incident. If not, I would want to tighten up controls on all entrants from the USSR, and even from the whole SovBloc, to see if we could intercept another component. As head of C.5(C) I could have done that.'

'And you think now that you won't get the chance?'

Preston shook his head. 'Even if I was allowed back to work tomorrow, I'm pretty certain I would be off the case. Apparently I'm an alarmist and I make waves.'

Sir Nigel nodded pensively. 'Poaching between the services is not regarded as terribly good form,' he said as if thinking aloud. 'When I asked you to go down to South Africa for me, it was Sir Bernard who sanctioned it. Later I learned the attachment, however temporary, had caused – how shall I put it? – some hostility in certain quarters at Charles Street.

'Now, I don't need an open quarrel with my sister service. On the other hand, I take a view, shared by yourself, that there might be more to this iceberg than the tip. In short, you have three weeks' leave. Would you be prepared to spend them working on this case?'

'For whom?' asked Preston, bewildered.

'For me,' said Sir Nigel. 'You couldn't come to Sentinel. You'd be seen. Word would get around.'

'Then work where?'

'Here,' said 'C'. 'It's small but comfortable. I have the authority to ask for exactly the same information as you, if you were at your desk. Any incident involving a Soviet or SovBloc arrival will have been recorded, either on paper or in a computer. Since you cannot be brought to the files or the computer, I can arrange for the files and the printout to be brought to you. What do you say?'

'If Charles Street finds out, I'm finished with "Five",' said Preston. He was thinking of his salary, of his pension, of the chances of getting another job at his age, of Tommy.

'How much longer do you think you have got at Charles under its present management?' asked Sir Nigel.

Preston laughed shortly. 'Not long,' he said. 'All right, sir, I'll do it. I want to stay on this case. There's something buried in there somewhere.'

Sir Nigel nodded approvingly. 'You're a tenacious man, John. I like tenacity. It usually yields results. Be here on Monday at nine. I'll have two of my own lads waiting for you. Ask them for what you want, and they'll get it.'

On the Monday morning as Preston started work in the Chelsea flat, an internationally famous Czech concert pianist arrived at Heathrow Airport from Prague, en route to his Wigmore Hall concert the following evening.

The airport authorities had been alerted and in deference to his venerability Customs and Immigration formalities were as little onerous as possible. The old musician was met after the Customs hall by a representative of the Victor Hochhauser Organization and, with his small retinue, whisked off to his suite at the Cumberland Hotel.

His retinue consisted of three; his dresser, who looked after his clothes and his other personal effects with dedicated devotion; a female secretary who handled his fan mail and correspondence; and his personal aide, a tall lugubrious man called Lichka who took care of negotiations with host organizations and finances, and seemed to live on a diet of antacid tablets.

That Monday Mr Lichka was working his way through an abnormally large amount of his pills. He had not wanted to do what was required of him, but the men from the StB had been extremely persuasive. No-one in their right mind deliberately affronted the men of the StB, Czechoslovakia's secret police and intelligence organization, or wished to be invited for further discussions at their headquarters, the dreaded Monastery. The men had made plain his grand-daughter's entry into university would be so much easier to arrange if he was prepared to help them, a polite way of saying the girl did not stand a chance of entering university if he failed them.

When they had given him his shoes back, he could find no trace of interference, and according to instructions had worn them on the flight and straight through Heathrow Airport.

That evening a man walked up to the reception desk and politely asked the number of Mr Lichka's room. Equally politely he was given it. Five minutes later, at the precise hour he had been briefed to expect, there was a soft knock on Lichka's door. A piece of paper was pushed under it. He checked the identification code, opened the door 5 inches and passed out a plastic bag containing his pair of shoes. Unseen hands took the bag and he closed the door. When he had flushed the scrap of paper down the toilet pan he sighed with relief. It had been easier than he had expected. Now, he thought, we can get on with the business of playing music.

Before midnight, in a backwater of Ipswich, the shoes joined the plaster cast and the radio in a bottom drawer. Courier Four had delivered.

Sir Nigel Irvine visited Preston at the Chelsea apartment on the Friday afternoon. The MI5 man was looking exhausted and the flat was awash with files and computer printout paper.

He had spent five days and had come up with nothing. He started with every entry into Britain from the USSR over the past forty days. There had been hundreds. Delegates, industrial buyers, journalists, trade-union stooges, a choir group from Georgia, a dance troupe of Cossacks, ten athletes and all their entourage, and a team of doctors for a medical conference in Manchester. And those were just the Russians.

Also entering from the Soviet Union were the returning tourists; the culture vultures who had been admiring the Hermitage Museum in Leningrad, through the school party which had been singing in Kiev to the 'peace' delegation which had been providing a rich fodder for the Soviet propaganda machine by condemning its own country in press conferences in Moscow and Kharkov.

Even that list did not include the Aeroflot crews who had been shuttling in and out as part of the normal air traffic, so First Officer Romanov hardly rated a mention.

There was, of course, no reference to a Dane coming into Birmingham from Paris and leaving through Manchester.

By the Wednesday Preston had had two options; stay with ex-USSR entrants but go back sixty days, or widen the net to take in *all* entrants from any SovBloc country. That meant thousands and thousands of arrivals. He had decided to stay with his forty-day timescale but to include the non-Soviet Communist states. The paperwork began to get waist high.

Customs had been most helpful. There had been some confiscations, but always for an excess of the duty-free allowance. Nothing of inexplicable character had been confiscated. Immigration had come up with no bent passports, but that was to be expected. The weird and wonderful bits of paperwork sometimes proffered at passport control by people from the Third World were never produced by people from the Communist world. Not even time-expired passports, the usual reason for an Immigration officer stopping a visitor from entry. In Communist countries the departing traveller's passport was so thoroughly checked before departure that there was little chance of a stop at the British end.

'And that,' said Preston gloomily, 'still leaves the uncheckables. The other merchant seamen, entering without controls at over twenty commercial ports; the crews off the fishing factory ships now riding off Scotland; the commercial aircrews who are hardly checked at all; and those with diplomatic cover.'

'As I thought,' said Sir Nigel. 'Not easy. Have you any idea what you are looking for?'

'Yes, sir. I had one of your lads spend Monday out at Aldermaston with the people in nuclear engineering. It seems that disc of polonium would be suitable for a device at once small, crude, basic in design, and not very powerful; if one can describe any atomic bomb as "not very powerful".' He handed Sir Nigel a list of items. 'Those are, at a guess, something like what we are looking for.'

'C' studied the list of artefacts. 'Is that all it takes?' he asked at length.

'In kit form, apparently yes. I'd no idea they could be made so basic. Apart from the fissionable core and the steel tamper, that stuff could be hidden almost anywhere and excite no attention.'

'All right, John, where do you go now?'

'I'm looking for a pattern, Sir Nigel. It's all I can look for. A pattern of entries and exits by the same passport number. If one or two couriers are being used, they would have to come in and out frequently, using different entry and exit points, probably different departure points abroad; but if a pattern shows up, we could put out an all-nation alert for a limited group of passport numbers. It's not much, but it's all I have.'

Sir Nigel rose. 'Keep at it, John. I'll get you access to anything you ask for. Let's just pray whoever we are dealing with slips up, just once, by using the same courier twice or three times.'

But Major Volkov was better than that. He did not slip up. He had no idea what the components were nor what use they were for. He simply knew he had been ordered to ensure their entry into Britain in time for a series of rendezvous inside the island, that each courier would have memorized his primary and back-up rendezvous, and that nothing was to pass through the KGB *rezidentura* in the London embassy.

He had nine cargoes to infiltrate and twelve prepared couriers. Some, he knew, were not professionals, but where their cover was impeccable and their journey arranged weeks or months earlier, as in the case of Lichka the Czech, he had homed in on them.

In order not to alert Major-General Borisov by stripping him of a further twelve 'illegals' and their legends, he had cast his net wider than the USSR by calling on three of the sister services; the StB of Czechoslovakia, the SB service of Poland and most of all the obedient and unquestioning Haupt Verwaltung Aufklärung (HVA) of East Germany.

The East Germans were particularly good. While there are Polish and Czech communities in West Germany, France and Britain, the East Germans had one great advantage. Because of the ethnic identity of East Germans and West Germans, and the fact that millions of former East Germans had already fled to West Germany, the HVA from their East Berlin base ran by far the greater number of in-place illegals in the West than any other East Bloc service.

Volkov had decided to use only two Russians, and they would be the first to go in. He had no way of knowing one would be mugged by street thugs, nor was he aware the false seaman's consignment was no longer locked up in a Glasgow police station. He just took treble precautions because that was his nature and his training.

For his remaining seven cargoes he was using one courier supplied by the Poles, two by the Czechs (including Lichka) and four by the East Germans. The tenth courier, replacing the dead Courier Two, would also come from the Poles. For the structural alterations that he needed to make to two motor vehicles, he was even using a garage and workshop run by the HVA in Brunswick, West Germany.

Only the two Russians and the Czech Lichka would have East Bloc depature points; plus, now, the tenth who would have to come from the Polish Airline, LOT.

Volkov was simply not allowing the appearance of any of the patterns Preston now sought in his sea of paperwork in Chelsea.

* * *

Sir Nigel Irvine, like so many who have to work in central London, tried to get away at the weekends for a breath of fresh air. He and Lady Irvine stayed in London during the week but kept a small and rustic cottage in southeast Dorset, on the Isle of Purbeck at a village called Langton Matravers.

That Sunday 'C' had donned a tweed coat and hat, taken a thick ash stick and walked down the lanes and tracks to the cliffs above Chapman's Pool at St Alban's Head. The sun was bright but the wind chill. It blew the silver tushes that escaped his hat over his ears like small wings. He took the cliff path and walked deep in thought, occasionally pausing to stare out over the tossed white-caps of the English Channel.

He was thinking of the conclusions of Preston's original report and of the remarkable concurrence of Sweeting in his Oxford reclusiveness. Coincidence? Straws in the wind? Grounds for conviction? Or just a lot of nonsense from a too imaginative civil servant and a fanciful academic?

And if it were all true, could there by any link with a small disc of polonium from Leningrad that had arrived uninvited in a Glasgow police station?

If the metal disc was what Wynne-Evans had said, what did that mean? Could it possibly mean that someone, far out over those tossing waves, was really trying to breach the Fourth Protocol?

And if it was true, who could that someone be? Chebrikov and Kryuchkov of the KGB? They would never dare act except under the orders of the General Secretary. And if the General Secretary, why?

And why not use the diplomatic bag? So much simpler, easier, safer. To the latter, he thought he could discern a reason. Using the embassy bag would mean using the KGB *rezidentura* inside the embassy. Better than Chebrikov, Kryuchkov or the General Secretary, he knew it was penetrated. He had his source Andreyev inside it.

That made sense. The General Secretary, he suspected, had good reason to be shaken by the recent spate of defections from the KGB. All the evidence coming across was that the disillusionment at every level in Russia had become so profound it was even affecting the élite of élite. Apart from the defections, starting in the late seventies and growing through the eighties, there had been mass expulsions of Soviet diplomats across the world, caused in part by their own desperation to recruit agents, but leading to even further desperation as the diplomatic controllers were expelled and the networks left in disarray. Even Third World countries which, a decade ago, danced to the Soviet tune, were now asserting themselves and expelling Soviet agents for grossly undiplomatic conduct.

Yes, a major operation conducted outside the auspices of the KGB made sense. He had heard on good authority that the General Secretary personally was becoming paranoid about the level of Western penetration of the KGB itself. For every traitor who runs over, went the adage in the intelligence community, you can bet there's another one still in place.

So, there was a man out there, running couriers and their cargoes into Britain; dangerous cargoes, bringing anarchy and chaos in a manner he could not yet discern but was ceasing to doubt, even as he walked. And that man worked for another man, very high, who had no love for this small island.

'But you won't find them, John,' he murmured to the unheeding wind. 'You're good, but they are better. And they hold the aces.'

Sir Nigel Irvine was one of the last of the old grandees, one of a passing breed, being replaced at every level of his society by new men of a different type, even at the highest stratum of the civil service where continuity of style and type was something of a household god.

So he gazed out at the Channel, as so many Englishmen had done before him, and made his decision. He was not convinced of the existence of a threat to the land of his forefathers; only of the possibility of the existence of a threat. But it was enough.

Farther along the coast, on the downs above the small Sussex port of Newhaven, another man gazed at the tossing waves of the English Channel.

He was dressed in black motorcycle leathers, his helmet on the seat of his parked BMW motorcycle. A few Sunday strollers with their children walked across the downs but they took no notice of him.

He was watching the approach of a ferry, well over the horizon and beating her way towards the shelter of the harbour mole. The *Cornouailles* would arrive from Dieppe in thirty minutes. Somewhere on board should be Courier Five.

In fact Courier Five was on the foredeck watching the approach of the English coast. He was one of those who had no car, but his ticket was for the boat train right through to London.

Anton Zelewski, his passport said, and it was perfectly accurate. A West German passport, the Immigration officer noted, but there was nothing odd in that. Hundreds of thousands of West Germans have Polish-sounding names. He was passed through.

Customs examined his suitcase and his bag with the duty-free allowance, bought on board the ship. His bottle of gin and his twenty-five cigars in an unopened box were within the permitted limit. The Customs officer nodded him through and turned his attention to someone else.

Zelewski had indeed bought a box of twenty-five good cigars in the duty-free shop on the *Cornouailles*. He had then retired to a lavatory, locked himself in and eased the identifying duty-free labels off the newly bought box, only to stick those labels on an identical box he had brought with him. The ones from the duty-free shop went overboard to a waiting sea.

In the train to London he sought out the first first-class carriage from the engine, selected the required window seat, and waited. Just before Lewes the door opened and a man in black leather stood there. A glance confirmed the compartment was empty except for the German.

'Does this train go straight to London?' he asked in unaccented English.

'I believe it also stops at Lewes,' Zelewski replied.

The man held out his hand. Zelewski passed him the flat box of cigars. The man stuffed it down his jacket front, zipped up, nodded and left. When the train started out of Lewes, Zelewski saw the man once again, on the down-line platform, going back to Newhaven.

Before midnight the cigars joined the radio, plaster cast, and shoes in Ipswich. Courier Five had delivered.

18

Sir Nigel was right. By Thursday, the last day of April, the reams of computer printout showed up no pattern at all of East Bloc citizens, from whatever point of departure, entering Britain on repeated occasions over the previous forty days. Nor was there a pattern of persons of whatever nationality entering the country from East Bloc countries over the same period.

A number of passports containing various irregularities had shown up, but that was par for the course. Each had been checked, its bearer strip-searched, and the answer was still a big zero. Three passports on the stop list had appeared; two were previous deportees seeking re-entry and one was an American underworld figure connected to gambling and narcotics. These three were also searched before being put on the next plane out, but there was not an iota of evidence that they had been couriers for Moscow.

If they're using West Bloc citizens, or in-place illegals with impeccable documentation as West Bloc citizens, I'll never find them, thought Preston.

Sir Nigel had again relied on his long friendship with Sir Bernard Hemmings to secure the cooperation of 'Five'.

'I have reason to believe the Centre is going to try to slip an important "illegal" into the country in the next few weeks,' he had said. 'The trouble is, Bernard, I don't have an identity, description or point of entry. Still, any help your contacts at the point of entry could give us would be highly appreciated.'

Sir Bernard had made the request a 'Five' operation, and the other arms of the state – Customs, Immigration, Special Branch and Docks Police – had agreed to keep more than the usual weather eye open either for a foreigner trying to slip past the controls or for an odd or unexplainable item being carried in as luggage.

The explanation was plausible enough and not even Brian Harcourt-Smith linked it to the report by John Preston on the polonium disc, still in his pending tray while he considered what to do with it.

The camper van arrived on May Day. It had West German registration and arrived on the ferry at Dover from Calais. The owner and driver, whose papers were in perfect order, was Helmut Dorn and he had with him his wife Lisa and their two small children, Uwe, a flaxen-haired boy of five, and Brigitte, their seven-year-old daughter.

When they passed Immigration the van rolled towards the nothing-to-declare Green Zone of Customs, but one of the waiting officers gestured it to stop. After re-examining the papers, the Customs officer asked to see in the back. Herr Dorn complied.

The two children were playing in the living area and stopped when the uniformed Customs man entered. He nodded and smiled at them; they giggled. He glanced around the neat and tidy interior, then began to look into the cupboards. If Herr Dorn was nervous he hid it well.

Most of the cupboards contained the usual bric-a-brac of a family on a camping holiday; clothes, cooking utensils, etc. The Customs man flicked up the bench seats beneath which lockers served as extra storage space. One of them was apparently the children's toy locker. It contained two dolls, a teddy bear and a collection of soft rubber balls, brightly painted with large gaudy discs in different colours.

The little girl, overcoming her shyness, delved into the locker and pulled out one of the dolls. She babbled excitedly at the Customs officer in German. He did not understand, but he nodded and smiled.

'Very nice, love,' he said. Then he turned to Herr Dorn and stepped out of the back door. 'Very well, sir. Enjoy your holiday.'

The camper van rolled with the rest of the column out of the sheds and on to the road towards the town of Dover and the highways towards the rest of Kent and to London.

'Gott sei dank,' breathed Dorn to his wife, *'wir sind durch.'*

She did the map-reading, but it was simple enough. The main M20 to London was so clearly marked no-one could miss it. Dorn checked his watch several times. He was a bit late, but his orders were under no circumstances to exceed the speed limit.

They found the village of Charing, lying to one side of the main road, without difficulty, and just to the north of it the Happy Eater cafeteria on the left. Dorn swung into the car park and stopped. Lisa Dorn took the children out of the rear and into the café for a snack. Dorn, according to orders, raised the engine cover and buried his head beneath it. Several seconds later he felt a presence beside him and looked up. A young Englishman in black motorcycle leathers stood there.

'Having a little trouble?' he asked.

'I think it must be the carburettor,' he said.

'No,' said the motorcyclist gravely, 'I suspect it comes from the distributor. Also, you are late.'

'I'm sorry, it was the ferry. Also Customs. I have the package in the back.'

Inside the van the motorcyclist produced a canvas bag from his jacket front, while Dorn, grunting and straining, lifted one of the children's play balls out of the toy locker.

It was only just 5 inches in diameter, but it weighed a mite over 20 kilogrammes or 44 pounds. Pure uranium 235 is, after all, twice as heavy as lead.

Carrying the canvas bag across the car park to his motorcycle, Valeri Petrofsky had to use his considerable strength to hold the bag one-handed as though it contained nothing of note. No-one noticed him anyway. Dorn closed his engine cover and joined his family in the café. The motorcycle, with its cargo in the box behind the pillion, roared away towards London, the Dartford tunnel and Suffolk. Courier Six had delivered.

By 4 May Preston realized he was up a blind alley. It had been nearly three weeks and he still had nothing to show for his ferreting than a single disc of polonium that had fallen into his hands by a pure fluke. He knew it was out of the question to ask for the strip-searching of every visitor entering Britain. All he could do was ask for increased surveillance on all East Bloc citizens coming in, plus an immediate alert to himself in the case of any suspect passport. There was one other, last, chance.

From what the experts in nuclear engineering at Aldermaston had reported, three of the items required even for the most basic nuclear bomb would have to be extremely heavy. One would be a block of pure uranium 235, one would be a tamper, cylindrical or globular in shape, made of high-tensile hardened steel 1 inch thick; the third would be a steel tube, also high-tensile and hardened, also of 1-inch-thick metal, about 18 inches long and weighing 30 pounds.

He estimated these three at least would have to be brought into the country in vehicles, and asked for an intensification of searches of foreign vehicles with an eye on cargoes resembling a ball, a globe and a tube of extreme heaviness.

He knew the catchment area was vast. There was a constant stream of motorcycles, cars, vans, trucks and juggernauts flowing in and out of the country every day of the year. The commercial traffic alone, if every truck were stopped and stripped, would almost bring the country to a halt. He was looking for the proverbial needle in the haystack, and he did not even have a magnet.

The strain was beginning to tell on George Berenson. His wife had left him and returned to her brother's stately home in Yorkshire. He had completed twelve sessions with the team from the Ministry and identified for them every single document he had ever passed to Jan Marais. He knew he was under surveillance and that did not help his nerves either.

Nor did the daily routine of going to the Ministry fully aware that his Permanent Under-Secretary, Sir Peregrine Jones, knew about his treachery. The final strain upon him was caused by the fact that he still had to pass occasional packages of apparently purloined documents from the Ministry to Marais, for sending on to Moscow. He had managed to avoid actually meeting Marais since he had learned the South African was a Soviet agent. But he was required to read the material he was passing to Moscow via Marais, just in case Marais called him for a clarification of something already sent.

Every time he read the papers he was to transmit, he was impressed by the skill of the forgers. Each document was based on a real paper that had passed across his desk, but with changes so subtle that no individual detail could arouse suspicion. Yet the cumulative effect was to give a quite false impression of Britain's and NATO's strength and preparedness.

On Wednesday, 6 May, he received and read a batch of seven papers referring to recent decisions, proposals, briefings and queries supposed to have reached his desk over the previous fortnight. All were marked either 'Top Secret' or 'Cosmic', and one of them caused him to raise his eyebrows. He passed them to the Benotti ice-cream parlour that evening and received his coded call of acknowledgement of safe receipt twenty-four hours later.

That Sunday, 10 May, in the seclusion of his bedroom at Cherryhayes Close, Valeri Petrofsky crouched over his powerful portable radio set and listened to the stream of signals in Morse coming over the Moscow Radio commercial band he had been allocated.

His set was not a transmitter: Moscow would never allow a valuable illegal to endanger himself by transmitting his own messages, not with British and American direction-finding counter-measures as good as they were. What he had was a huge Braun radio, purchasable in any good radio shop, that would pick up almost any channel in the world.

Petrofsky was tense. It had been a month since he had used the Poplar transmitter to alert Moscow that he had lost a courier and his cargo, and to ask for a replacement. Each second evening and on alternate mornings, whenever he was not out on his motorcycle making collections, he had listened for his reply. So far it had not come.

At ten past ten that evening he heard his own call sign coming over the air waves. He already had his pad and pencil ready. After a pause the message began. He jotted down the letters straight from Morse into English, a jumble of indecipherable figures. The Germans, British and Americans at least would be jotting down the same letters in their various listening posts.

When the transmission ended he switched off the set, sat at his dressing table, selected the appropriate one-time pad, and began to decipher. He had it in fifteen minutes: Firebird Ten replacing Two RVT. It was repeated three times.

He knew Rendezvous T. It was one of the spare rendezvous, to be used only if the occasion demanded, as indeed it now had. And it was in an airport hotel. He preferred wayside cafés or railway stations, but knew that although he was the kingpin of the operation, there were some couriers who for professional reasons only had a few hours in London and could not leave the city.

There was one other problem. They were slotting Courier Ten between two other meets, and perilously close to the meeting with Courier Seven.

Ten had to be met at the hour of breakfast in the Post House, Heathrow; Seven would be waiting in a hotel car park outside Colchester that same morning at eleven. It would mean hard riding, but he could do it.

* * *

Late in the evening of Tuesday, 12 May, the lights were still burning in Number 10 Downing Street, office and residence of the British Premier. Mrs Margaret Thatcher had called a strategy conference of her closest advisers and Inner Cabinet. The only issue on the agenda was that of the forthcoming general election; to formalize the decision and decide the timing.

As usual, she made her own view plain from the outset. She believed she would be right to go for a third administration, even though the constitution allowed her to govern until June 1988. There were several who at once doubted the wisdom of going to the country so soon though on previous evidence they doubted they would get very far. When the British Prime Minister had a gut feeling for something, it took some very powerful counter-arguments to dissuade her. On this issue statistics seemed to support her.

The Conservative Party chairman had all the public-opinion-poll findings at his fingertips. The Liberal/Social Democratic Alliance, he pointed out, still seemed to enjoy about 20 per cent of the support of the electorate.

That would mean that in Britain, which does not have run-off ballots like the French or proportional representation like the Irish, the winner-take-all method of decision would give the Alliance between fifteen and twenty seats. Of the seventeen from Northern Ireland twelve would probably go to various types of Unionists who would support the Conservatives in Parliament, and five to the Nationalist factions who would boycott London or vote Hard Left. That left 613 constituencies in which the outcome looked like the traditional fight between Conservative and Labour. For a clear majority Mrs Thatcher would need 325 of them.

The polls further showed, the Party chairman intoned, that Labour stood only 4 percentage points behind the Conservatives. Since June 1983, with its newfound image of unity, moderation and tolerance, the Labour Party had hauled itself back by a full 10 percentage points. The Hard

Left was almost mute, the crazy Left repudiated, the manifesto moderated and the public television appearances by members of the Shadow Cabinet had for a year been almost wholly confined to the Centrist wing. The British public had nigh completely regained its confidence in the Labour Party as an alternative party of government.

The chairman pointed out to his solemn colleagues that the Conservative lead was 2 points lower than six months earlier and 1 point lower than three months ago. The trend was clear. The same trend was being reported by the party organization in the constituencies.

The economic indicators showed that while for the moment the economy was buoyant, the weather fine, and seasonal factors were cutting the unemployment figure, they could expect public-sector strikes in the autumn in pursuit of wage claims. If these were bad, the Conservative popularity could fall suddenly in the winter and stay that way until the spring.

There was general agreement by midnight that it had to be the summer of 1987, or not until June 1988. No autumn or early spring elections. In the small hours the Prime Minister carried her Cabinet with her. Only on one point was there heated discussion – the length of the election campaign.

In Britain general elections are by tradition held on a Thursday after a four-week campaign. It is rare but not unconstitutional for a campaign to be cut to three weeks. The Prime Minister's instinct was for a three-week campaign, a snap election to catch the Opposition unprepared and unready.

Finally it was agreed; she would seek an audience with the Queen on Thursday, 28 May, and ask for a dissolution of Parliament. In accordance with tradition, she would return to make a public statement from Downing Street immediately afterwards. From that moment the election campaign would be on. Polling day: Thursday 18 June.

While the ministers still slept in the hour before dawn, the big BMW cruised towards London from the northeast. Petrofsky rode out to the Post House Hotel at Heathrow Airport, parked in the car lot, locked the machine and shut away his crash helmet in the box behind the pillion.

He eased off his black leather jacket and zip-sided trousers. Beneath the leather trousers he wore an ordinary pair of grey flannels, creased but passable. He dropped his jackboots into one of the panniers, from which he had taken a pair of shoes. The leathers went into the other pannier, from which came a nondescript tweed jacket and fawn raincoat. When he left the machine and walked into the hotel reception area, he was just an ordinary man in an ordinary mackintosh.

Karel Wosniak had not slept well. For one thing he had been given the shock of his life the previous evening. Normally the aircrews of the Polish LOT airlines on which he was a senior steward passed through Customs and Immigration almost as a formality. This time they had been searched, really searched. When the British officer attending to him had started to rummage through his sponge bag he had nearly been sick with worry. When the man extracted the electric razor the SB people had given him in Warsaw before take-off, he had thought he would faint. Fortunately it was not a battery-operated or rechargeable model. There had been no available electric plug to turn it on. The officer had put it back and completed his search, to no avail. Wosniak supposed that if someone *had* turned the shaver on it would not have worked. After all, there must be *something* in it apart from the usual motor. Why else should he be required to bring it to London?

At eight precisely he entered the public toilets just off the reception area on the ground floor of the Post House. A nondescript-looking man in a fawn raincoat was washing his hands. Damn, thought Wosniak, when the contact shows up we'll have to wait until this Englishman leaves. Then the man spoke to him, in English.

'Morning. Is that the Yugoslav airline uniform?'

Wosniak sighed with relief. 'No, I am from the Polish national airline.'

'Lovely country, Poland,' said the stranger, wiping his hands. He seemed completely at ease. Wosniak was new to this; first and last time, he had sworn to himself. He just stood on the tiled floor holding his razor. 'I have spent many happy times in your country.'

That's it, thought Wosniak. 'Many happy times' . . . the phrase for identification.

He held out the razor. The Englishman scowled and glanced at one of the booth doors. With a start Wosniak realized the door was closed; there was someone in there. The stranger nodded to the shelf above the washbasins. Wosniak put the razor on it. Then the Englishman nodded towards the urinals. Hastily Wosniak unzipped his fly and stood in front of one.

'Thank you,' he burbled, 'I too think it is beautiful.'

The man in the fawn coat pocketed the razor, held up five fingers to indicate Wosniak should stay there for five minutes, and left.

An hour later Petrofsky and his motorcycle were clearing the suburbs where northeast London borders the county of Essex. The A12 stretched out in front of him. It was nine o'clock.

At that hour the *Tor Britannia* ferry of the DFDS line from Gothenburg was easing herself alongside the Parkston Quay at Harwich, eighty miles away on the Essex coast. The passengers, when they came off, were the usual crowd of tourists, students and commercial visitors. Among the latter was Mr Stig Lundqvist driving his big Saab saloon car.

His papers said he was a Swedish businessman and they did not lie. He was indeed Swedish and had been all his life. The papers omitted to mention that he was also a long-time Communist agent and worked like Herr Helmut Dorn for the redoubtable General Marcus Wolf, the

Jewish head of Foreign Operations of the East German HVA intelligence service.

He was nevertheless asked to step out of his car and bring his suitcases to the examination bench. This he did with a courteous smile.

Another Customs officer lifted the engine cover and glanced inside. He was looking for a globe the size of a small football, or a rod-like tube, secreted within the compartment. There was nothing like that. He glanced under the frame of the car and finally into the empty boot. He sighed. These demands from London were a pain in the neck. The empty boot contained nothing but the usual toolkit, a wheeljack strapped to one side and the fire extinguisher banded to the other. The Swede stood by his side, his suitcases in his hand.

'Please,' said the Swede, 'iss all right?'

'Yes, thank you, sir. Enjoy your stay.'

An hour later, just before eleven, the Saab rolled into the car park of the Kings Ford Park Hotel in the village of Layer-de-la-Haye just south of Colchester. Mr Lundqvist got out and stretched. It was the hour of mid-morning coffee and there were several cars in the park, all unattended. He glanced at his watch; five minutes to rendezvous time. Close, but he knew he would have had the extra hour of waiting time had he been late, then a backup rendezvous somewhere else. He wondered if and when the contact would show. There was no-one else around, save for a young man tinkering with the engine of a BMW motorcycle. He had no idea what his contact would look like. He lit a cigarette, got back into his car and sat there.

At eleven there was a tap on the window. The motorcyclist stood outside. Lundqvist pressed the button and the window hissed down.

'Yes?'

'Does the S on your number plate stand for Sweden or Switzerland?' asked the Englishman.

Lundqvist smiled with relief. He had stopped on the

road and detached the fire extinguisher, which now reposed in a hessian bag on the passenger seat.

'It stands for Sweden,' he said. 'I have just arrived from Gothenberg.'

'Never been there,' said the man. Then without a change of inflection he added, 'Got something for me?'

'Yes,' said the Swede, 'it's in the bag beside me.'

'There are windows looking on to the car park,' said the motorcyclist. 'Drive round the car park, swing past the motorcycle and drop the bag to me out of the driver's window. Keep the car between me and the windows. Five minutes from now.'

He sauntered back to his machine and went on tinkering. Five minutes later the Saab swung past him and the bag slipped to the ground; he had picked it up and dropped it into his open pannier before the Saab cleared the hotel windows. He never saw the Saab again, nor did he want to.

One hour later he was in his lock-up garage in Thetford, exchanging motorcycle for family saloon and stowing his two cargoes in the car boot. He had no idea what they contained. That was not his job.

In the early afternoon he was home in Ipswich, the two consignments stored in his bedroom. Couriers Ten and Seven had delivered.

John Preston had been due back at work in Gordon Street on 13 May.

'I know it's frustrating, but I'd like you to stay on,' said Sir Nigel Irvine on one of his visits. 'You'll have to call in with a bad dose of flu. If you need a doctor's chit, let me know. I have a couple who'll oblige.'

By the 16th Preston knew he was up a blind alley. Without a major national alert, Customs and Immigration had done all they could. The sheer volume of human traffic prevented the intensive searching of every visitor. It was five weeks since the Russian seaman had been mugged in Glasgow, and he was convinced he had missed the rest of the couriers. Perhaps they had all been in the country before Semyonov, and the deckhand had been the last. Perhaps . . .

With growing desperation he realized he did not know if he had a deadline at all, or if he did, when it was.

On Thursday 21 May, the ferry from Ostend berthed at Folkestone and discharged its habitual contents of tourists on foot, others in cars, and the grunting stream of TIR juggernauts that haul the freight of the European Economic community from one end of Europe to the other.

Seven of the huge lorries were of German registration, Ostend being a favoured port on the Britain run of firms operating in north Germany. The big Hanomag articulated rig with its containerized cargo on the trailer behind was no different from all the others. The fat sheaf of paperwork that took an hour to clear was in good order and there was no reason to believe the driver worked for anyone other than the haulage contractors whose name was printed on the side of his cab. Nor was there any reason to think the rig contained anything other than its prescribed delivery of German coffee machines for the British breakfast table.

Behind the cab two big vertical exhaust pipes jutted up towards the sky, carrying the fumes from the diesel engine up and away from other road users. It was already evening, the day shift was drawing to a weary close, and the truck was waved forward on the road to Ashford and London.

No-one at Folkestone could be expected to know that one of those vertical exhaust tubes, belching dark fumes as it left the Customs shed, had a by-pass pipe inside it to to carry the fumes, or, amid the roar of starting engines, that the sound baffles had been removed to create extra space.

Long after dark, on the parking area of a wayside transport café near Lenham in Kent, the driver climbed to the top of his cab, unbolted that exhaust pipe and withdrew from it an 18-inch-long package wrapped in heat-proof cladding. He never opened it; he just handed it to a black-clothed motorcyclist who sped off into the darkness. Courier Eight had delivered.

'It's no good, Sir Nigel,' John Preston told the Chief of the SIS on the Friday evening. 'I don't know what the hell's going on. I fear the worst, but I can't prove it. I've tried to find one other, just one more, of those couriers I believe to have come into this country, and I've failed. I think I should go back to Gordon on Monday.'

'I know how you feel, John,' said Sir Nigel. 'I feel much the same. Please give me just one more week.'

'I can't see the point,' said Preston. 'What more can we do?'

'Pray, I suppose,' said 'C' gently.

'One break,' said Preston angrily, 'all I need is just one small break.'

19

John Preston got his break on the following Monday afternoon.

Just after four an airliner of Austrian Airlines came into Heathrow from Vienna. One of the travellers aboard, who presented himself at the passport desk for non-UK and non-EEC citizens, offered a perfectly authentic Austrian passport announcing its bearer to be one Franz Winkler.

The Immigration officer examined the familiar green plastic-covered Reisepass, fronted by the emblematic gold eagle, with the usual apparent indifference of his profession. It was of current issue, dotted with half a dozen other European entry and exit stamps, and had a valid UK visa.

Beneath his desk the officer's left hand tapped out the passport number, perforated through every page of the booklet. He glanced at the display screen, closed the passport and handed it back with a brief smile. 'Thank you, sir. And the next please.'

As Herr Winkler picked up his handgrip and moved through, the officer raised his eyes towards a small window facing him twenty feet away. At the same time his right foot pressed an 'alert' button near the floor. From the office window one of the resident Special Branch men caught his gaze. The Immigration man looked in the direction of Herr Winkler's back and nodded. The face of the Special Branch detective withdrew from the window and seconds later he and a colleague were slipping quietly after the Austrian. Another man was rustling up a car in front of the concourse.

Winkler had no heavy luggage so he ignored the carousels in the baggage hall and went straight through the Green channel of Customs. In the concourse he spent some time at the Midland Bank changing traveller's cheques into sterling currency, during which time one of the SB men got a good picture of him from an upper balcony.

When the Austrian took a cab from the rank in front of Number Two Building, the SB officers piled into their own unmarked saloon and were right behind him. The driver concentrated on following the taxi; the senior SB detective used the radio to inform Scotland Yard whence, according to procedure, the information went also to Charles Street. There was a standing order to the effect that 'Six' was also interested in any visitor carrying a bent passport, so the tip-off was passed by Charles Street to Sentinel House.

Winkler took his cab as far as Bayswater and paid it off at the junction of Edgware Road and Sussex Gardens. Then as he walked, grip in hand, down Sussex Gardens, one side of which is almost entirely taken up with modest bed-and-breakfast boarding houses of the type favoured by commercial travellers and late arrivals from nearby Paddington Station on modest budgets.

He seemed to the Special Branch officers across the road in their car to have no reservation, for he ambled down the street until he came to a boarding house with a 'Vacancies' notice in the window, and went in. He must have got a room because he did not emerge.

It was one hour after Winkler's cab had left Heathrow, and at that time the phone rang in Preston's Chelsea flat. His contact man at Sentinel, the one ordered by Sir Nigel to liaise with Preston, was on the line.

'There's a Joe just came in at Heathrow,' said the MI6 man. 'It may be nothing, but his passport number came up little red lights on the computer. Name of Franz Winkler, Austrian, off the Vienna flight.'

'They didn't pick him up, I hope?' said Preston. He was thinking; Austria is conventiently close to Czechoslovakia and Hungary. Being neutral, it is also a good jump-off point for SovBloc illegals.

'No,' said the man at Sentinel, 'according to our standing request they tailed him . . . Hold on . . .' He came back on the line a few seconds later. 'They've just housed him at a small B-and-B hotel in Paddington.'

'Can you pass me over to "C"?' asked Preston.

Sir Nigel was in conference, which he left to return to his private office.

'Yes, John.'

Preston related the basic facts to the Chief of the SIS – they had not reached him by then.

'Do you think he's the man you've been waiting for?'

'He could be a courier,' said Preston. 'He's as good as we've had in the past six weeks.'

'So what do you want, John?'

'I'd like "Six" to ask for the Watchers to take over. All reports reaching the Watchers' controller at Cork to be monitored by one of your people as and when they come in; same to be fed at once to Sentinel and then to me. If he makes a meet, I'd like both men tailed.'

'All right,' said Sir Nigel. 'I'll ask for the Watchers to take over. Barry Banks will sit in at the Cork radio room and pass the developments down the line as they come in.'

The Chief personally called up the Director of 'K' Branch and made his request. The head of 'K' contacted his colleagues at 'A' Branch and a standby team of Watchers started to head for Sussex Gardens in Paddington. They happened to be led by Harry Burkinshaw.

Preston paced his small apartment in a rage of frustration. He wanted to be out on the streets, or at least at the centre of the operation, not tucked away like a deep-cover man in his own country, the pawn in a power game being conducted at a level far above his head.

By seven that evening Harry Burkinshaw's men had moved in, taking over the watch from the Special Branch men who happily went off duty. It was a warm and pleasant evening; the four Watchers who formed the 'box' took up their unobtrusive stations around the hotel, one up the street, one down, one across and one in back. The two cars positioned themselves amid scores of others parked along Sussex Gardens, ready to move if Chummy took flight. All six men were in contact via their personal communicator sets and Burkinshaw with head office, the radio room in the basement at Cork.

Barry Banks was in Cork also, since this was an operation requested by 'Six', and they all waited for Winkler to make contact.

The trouble was, he did not. He did nothing. He just sat in his hotel room behind the net curtains and lay low. At 8.30 he came out, walked to a restaurant on Edgware Road, had a simple supper and went back again. He made no drop, picked up no instruction, left nothing at his table, spoke to no-one in the street.

But he did two things of interest. He stopped sharply in Edgware Road on his way to the restaurant, stared in a plateglass window for several seconds, then headed back the way he had come. It's one of the oldest tricks for trying to spot a tail, and not a very good one.

On leaving the restaurant he paused by the kerbside, waited for a gap in the surging traffic, then sprinted across. On the far side he paused again and scanned the street to see if anyone else had sprinted across after him. No-one had. All Winkler had done was join Burkinshaw's fourth Watcher, who had been across Edgware Road all the time. While Winkler scanned the traffic to see who might be risking life and limb to pursue him, the Watcher was a few feet away pretending to hail a cab.

'He's bent all right,' Burkinshaw told Cork. 'He's surveillance-conscious, and not very good.'

Burkinshaw's judgement reached Preston in his Chelsea hideout. He nodded in relief. It was beginning to look better.

After his gyrations on Edgware Road, Winkler returned to his boarding house and spent the rest of the night inside. Meanwhile another small operation was taking its inspired course in the basement at Sentinel House. The photos of Winkler taken by the Special Branch men in

Heathrow Airport, backed by others taken on the street in Bayswater, had been developed and placed reverentially before the gaze of the legendary Miss Blodwyn.

Identification of foreign agents, or foreigners who might possibly be agents, forms a major part of any intelligence organization. To assist in this task, hundreds of thousands of pictures are taken every year by all the agencies of people who may, or may not, be working for their rivals. Foreign diplomats, members of trade, scientific and cultural delegations – all are photographed as a matter of course, particularly but not always if they come from Communist or sympathizer countries.

The archives grow and grow. The portraits often include twenty shots of the same man or woman, taken at different times and in different places. They are never thrown away. What they are used for is to get a 'make'.

If a Russian with the name of Ivanov shows up accompanying a Soviet trade delegation to Canada, his photographed face will almost certainly be passed by the Royal Canadian Mounted Police to their colleagues in Washington, London and the other NATO allies. It may well be that the same face, calling itself Kozlov, was once snapped five years earlier as a visiting journalist at the independence celebrations of an African republic. If there is any question as to Mr Ivanov's real profession as he takes in the beauties of Ottawa, a make like that will dispel all doubts. It tags him as a full-time KGB hood.

The exchange of such photos among the allied intelligence arms, and they include the brilliant Israeli Mossad, is continuous and comprehensive. Very few SocBloc visitors to the West, or even the Third World, do not end up gazing from an album of photographs in at least twenty different democratic capitals. No-one entering the Soviet Union does not end up in the Centre's master gallery of happy snaps.

It is the almost hilarious case, but perfectly true, that while Britain's CIA 'cousins' use banks of computers stored with millions and millions of facial features to try to match up the incoming daily flow of photographs, Britain uses Blodwyn.

An elderly and often ill-used lady, forever harassed by her younger male colleagues for a quick make, Blodwyn has been in the job forty years and works underneath Sentinel House where she presides over the huge archive of pictures that make up MI6's 'mug book'. Not a book at all, it is in fact a cavernous vault where are stored rows and rows of volumes of photographs of which she alone possesses an encyclopedic knowledge.

Her mind is something like the CIA's computer bank, which she can occasionally defeat. In it are stored not the tiniest detail of the Thirty Years' War or even the Wall Street stock prices but faces. Shapes of noses, lines of jaws, casts of eyes; the sag of a cheek, the curve of a lip, the way a glass or cigarette is held; the glint of a capped tooth in a smile taken in an Australian pub and showing up years later in a London supermarket – all are grist to the mill of her remarkable memory.

That night, while Bayswater slept and Burkinshaw's men hugged the shadows, Blodwyn sat and stared at the face of Franz Winkler. Two silent younger men from 'Six' waited. After an hour she simply said, 'Far East,' and went off along the rows of her albums. She had her make in the small hours of Tuesday, 26 May.

It wasn't a good photograph and it was five years old. The hair was darker then, the waist slimmer. He was at a reception at the Indian Embassy, standing beside his own ambassador smiling deferentially.

One of the younger men stared at the two photographs doubtfully. 'Are you sure, Blodwyn?'

If looks could cripple he would have needed to invest in a wheelchair. He backed away hastily and made for a telephone.

'There's a make,' he said. 'He's a Czech. Five years ago he was a low-level gofer in the Czech Embassy in Tokyo. Name: Jiri Hayek.'

Preston was woken by the telephone at three in the

morning. He listened, thanked the caller and replaced the phone. He smiled happily.

'Gotcha,' he said.

At ten in the morning Winkler was still inside his hotel. Control of the operation at Cork Street had been taken over by Simon Margery, from K.2(B), the Soviet Satellites/Czechoslovakia (Operations) desk. After all, a Czech was their affair. Barry Banks, who had slept in the office, was with him, passing developments down the line to Sentinel House.

At the same hour John Preston made a personal call to the Legal Counsellor at the American Embassy, a personal contact. The Legal Counsellor at the US Embassy in Grosvenor Square is always the London representative of the FBI. Preston made his request and was told he would be called back as soon as the answer came from America, probably in five to six hours, bearing in mind the time difference.

At eleven Winkler emerged from the boarding house. He walked to Edgware Road again, hailed a cab and set off towards Park Lane. At Hyde Park Corner the cab, tailed by two cars containing the Watcher team, went down Piccadilly. Winkler dismissed it in Piccadilly, close to the Circus end, and tried another few basic manoeuvres to throw off a tail he had not even spotted.

'Here we go again,' Len Stewart muttered into his lapel. He had read Burkinshaw's log and expected something similar. Winkler shot suddenly down an arcade at a near run, emerged at the other end, scuttled down the pavement and turned to watch the entrance to the arcade from which he had just emerged. No-one came out. They did not need to. There was already a Watcher at the southern end of the arcade.

The Watchers know London better than any policeman or cab driver. They know how many exits every major building has, where the arcades and underpasses go, where the narrow passages are located and where they lead to. Wherever a Joe tries to scuttle, there will always be one man there ahead of him, one coming slowly behind, and two flankers. The box never shatters, and it is a very clever Joe who can spot it.

Satisfied he had no tail, Winkler entered the British Rail Travel Centre in Lower Regent Street. There he enquired the times of trains to Sheffield. The scarved Scottish football fan standing a few feet away and trying to get back to Motherwell was one of the Watchers. Winkler paid cash for a second-class return ticket to Sheffield, noted that the last train of the night was out of St Pancras Station at 9.25, thanked the rail clerk and left.

He had lunch at a café nearby, returned to Sussex Gardens and stayed there all afternoon.

Preston received the news about the train ticket to Sheffield just after one. He caught Sir Nigel Irvine just as 'C' was about to leave for lunch at his club.

'It may be a blind, but it looks as if he's going out of town,' he said. 'He may be heading for his rendezvous. It could be on the train, or in Sheffield. Maybe he's delayed so long because he was early. The point is, sir, if he leaves London we will need a field controller, going with the Watcher team. I want to be that controller.'

'Yes, see what you mean. Not easy. Still, I'll see what I can do.'

Sir Nigel sighed. Bang goes lunch, he thought. He summoned his personal aide. 'Cancel my lunch at White's. Get my car ready. And take a telegram. In that order.'

While the aide tackled the first two tasks, Sir Nigel called Sir Bernard Hemmings at his home number near Farnham in Surrey.

'Sorry to trouble you, Bernard. Something's cropped up that I'd like your advice on. No . . . better face to face. Would you mind if I came down? Lovely day, after all. Yes, right, about three then.'

'The cable?' said his aide.

'Yes.'

'To whom?'

'Myself.'

'Certainly. From?'

'Head of Station, Vienna.'

'Shall I alert him, sir?'

'No need to bother him. Just arrange with Cipher Room for me to receive his cable in three minutes.

'Of course. And the text?'

Sir Nigel dictated it. Sending himself an urgent message to justify what he wanted to do anyway was an old trick that he had picked up from his one-time mentor, the late Sir Maurice Oldfield. When the Cipher Room sent it back up in the form it would have been received from Vienna, the old mandarin put it in his pocket and went down to his car.

He found Sir Bernard in his garden at Tilford, enjoying the warm May sunshine, a blanket round his knees.

'Meant to come in today,' said the Director-General of 'Five' with well-feigned joviality. 'Be in tomorrow no doubt.'

'Of course, of course.'

'Now, how can I help?'

'Ticklish,' said Sir Nigel. 'Someone has just flown into London from Vienna. Apparent Austrian businessman. But he's a phoney. We got a make on him last night. Czech agent, one of the StB boys. Low Level, we think he's a courier.'

Sir Bernard nodded. 'Yes, I keep in touch, even from here. Heard all about it. My chaps are on top of him, aren't they?'

'Very much so. The thing is, it looks as if he may be leaving London tonight. For the north. "Five" will need a field controller to go with the Watcher team.'

'Of course. We'll have one. Brian can handle it.'

'Yes. It's your operation, of course. Still . . . you remember the Berenson affair? We never did discover two things. Does Marais communicate through the *rezidentura* here in London, or does he use couriers sent in from outside? And was Berenson the only man in the ring run by Marais or were there others?'

'I recall. We were going to put those questions on ice until we could get a few answers out of Marais.'

'That's right. Then today I got this cable from my Head of Station in Vienna.'

He proffered the cable. Sir Bernard read it and his eyebrows rose. 'Linked? Could they be?'

'Possible. Winkler, a.k.a. Hayek, seems to be a courier of some kind. Vienna confirms he's nominally StB, but actually working for the KGB itself. We know Marais was twice in Vienna in the past two years, while he was running Berenson. Each time on cultural jaunts, but . . .'

'The missing link?'

Sir Nigel shrugged. Never over sell.

'So what's he going to Sheffield for?'

'Who knows, Bernard? Is there another ring up there in Yorkshire? Could Winkler be a bagman for more than one ring?'

'So what do you want from "Five"? More Watchers?'

'No, John Preston. You'll recall he tracked down Berenson first, then Marais. I liked his style. He's been on leave for a while. Then he had a dose of flu, so they tell me. But he's due to return to work tomorrow. He's been off so long, he'll probably have no current cases anyway. Technically, he's Ports and Airports, C.5(C). But you know how the K boys are always worked off their feet. If he could just have a temporary attachment to K.2(B), you could designate him field controller for this one . . .'

'Well, I don't know, Nigel. This is really down to Brian . . .'

'I'd be awfully grateful, Bernard. Let's face it, Preston was on the Berenson hunt from the start. If Winkler is part of it all, he might even see a face he's seen before.'

'All right,' said Sir Bernard. 'You've got it. I'll issue the instruction from here.'

'I could take it back if you like,' said 'C'. 'Save you

the trouble. Send my driver up to Charles Street with the chit . . .'

He left Tilford with his chit, a written order from Sir Bernard Hemmings putting John Preston on temporary attachment to 'K' Branch and naming him field controller of the Winkler operation once it left the metropolis.

Sir Nigel had two copies made; one for himself and one for John Preston. The original went to Charles Street. Brian Harcourt-Smith was out of the office, so the order was left on his desk.

At seven that evening John Preston left the Chelsea apartment for the last time. He was out in the open again and loved it.

At Sussex Gardens he slipped up behind Harry Burkinshaw. 'Hello, Harry.'

'Good lord, John Preston. What are you doing here?'

'Taking a breath of air.'

'Well, don't make yourself visible. We've got a Joe holed up there across the road.'

'I know. I gather he's due to leave for Sheffield on the 9.25.'

'How did you know that?'

Preston produced his copy of Sir Bernard's instruction.

Burkinshaw studied it. 'Wow. From the DG himself. Join the party then. Just stay out of sight.'

'Got a spare lapel set?'

Burkinshaw nodded down the road. 'Round the corner in Radnor Place. Brown Cortina. There's a spare in the glove compartment.'

'I'll wait in the car,' said Preston.

Burkinshaw was puzzled. No-one had told him about Preston joining them as field controller. He did not even know Preston was in Czech Section. Still, the DG's signature carried a lot of weight. For his part he would just get on with his job. He shrugged, popped another mint, and went on watching.

At half past eight Winkler left the hotel. He was

carrying his grip. He hailed a passing cab and gave his instructions to the driver.

As he stepped out of the doorway, Burkinshaw called in his team and his two cars. He jumped in the first one and they were a hundred yards behind the cab across Edgware Road. Preston was in the second car. Ten minutes later they knew they were heading east towards the station. Burkinshaw reported this. Simon Margery's voice came back from Cork. 'OK, Harry, our field controller is on his way.'

'We've got a field controller,' said Burkinshaw. 'He's with us.'

This was news to Margery. He asked the controller's name. When he heard it he thought there had been a mistake. 'He's not even with K.2(B),' he protested.

'He is now,' said Burkinshaw, unfazed. 'I've seen the chit, signed by the DG.'

Margery from Cork Street called up Charles. As the cavalcade cruised east through the dusk, a flap ensued at Charles Street. The instruction from Sir Bernard was traced and confirmed. Margery threw up his hands in exasperation. 'Why can't the buggers up there in Charles ever make up their minds?' he asked an uncaring world. He called off the colleague he had designated to take over at St Pancras Station. Then he tried to trace Brian Harcourt-Smith to complain.

Winkler paid off his cab on the forecourt of the station, headed through the single brick archway into the vaulted dome of the Victorian railway station, and consulted the departure board. Around him the four Watchers and Preston vaporized into the throng of passengers in the brick and cast-iron concourse.

The 9.25 was at platform 2, calling at Leicester, Derby, Chesterfield and Sheffield. Having found his train, Winkler walked up the length of it; past the three first-class carriages, the buffet car, to the three blue-upholstered second-class carriages near the front end. He selected the middle one, hefted his grip on to the rack and sat quietly awaiting the departure.

It was an open-plan carriage and after a few minutes a young black man with earphones over his head and a Walkman music player clipped on to his belt came in and sat three rows away. Once seated, the man nodded his head in time to the apparent reggae blasting into his ears, closed his eyes and enjoyed his music. One of Burkinshaw's team was in place; the earphones were silent of reggae music but were picking up Harry's instruction on strength five.

One of Burkinshaw's team took the front carriage, Harry and John Preston the third, so that Winkler was boxed, and the fourth man took a first-class seat at the rear in case Winkler did a runner down the train to shake off what he thought was a tail.

At 9.25 on the dot the Inter-City 125 hissed out of St Pancras and headed north. At 9.30 Brian Harcourt-Smith was traced to the dining room of his club and called to the phone. It was Simon Margery. What he heard caused the Deputy DG of 'Five' to hasten outside, grab a taxi and race the two miles across the West End to Charles Street.

On his desk he found the order written out earlier that afternoon by Sir Bernard Hemmings. He went quite pale with rage.

He was a highly self-disciplined man, and after thinking the matter over for several minutes he picked up the phone and asked the operator in his usual courteous manner to get him the service's Legal Adviser at his home.

The Legal Adviser is the man who does most of the liaison between the service and the Special Branch. While the call was coming through he checked train times to Sheffied. The Legal Adviser was plucked from his seat in front of the television in Camberley and came on the line.

'I need Special Branch to make an arrest,' said Harcourt-Smith. 'I have reason to believe an illegal immigrant suspected of being a Soviet agent may escape surveillance. Name, Franz Winkler, supposed Austrian citizen. Holding charge: suspected false passport. He'll be arriving by train from London at Sheffield at 11.59. Yes, I know it's short notice. That's why it's urgent. Yes, please get on to the Commander Special Branch at the Yard and ask him to jack up his Sheffield operation to make the arrest when the train arrives at Sheffield.'

He put the phone down grimly. John Preston might have been sicked on him as field director of the surveillance team, but an arrest of a suspect was a policy matter, and that was his department.

The train was almost empty. Two carriages instead of six would have amply accommodated the sixty passengers on board. Barney, the Watcher in the front carriage, shared the space with ten others, all innocent passengers. He was facing aft so that he could see the top of Winkler's head through the inter-carriage door glass.

Ginger, the young black with the headphones who was with Winkler in the second carriage, had five others in there with him. There were a dozen sharing sixty seats with Preston and Burkinshaw in the third. For an hour and a quarter Winkler did nothing; he had no reading matter; he just stared out of the window at the dark countryside beyond.

At 10.45 the train slowed for Leicester and he moved. He took his grip off the rack, walked up the carriage, passed out to the toilet area and pulled down the window of the door giving on to the platform. Ginger informed the rest, who prepared to move at short notice if they had to.

Another passenger pushed past Winkler as the train stopped.

'Excuse, please, is this Sheffield?' Winkler asked.

'No, it's Leicester,' the man said and descended to the platform.

'Ah, so. Thank you,' said Winkler. He put down his grip, but stayed at the open window looking up and down the platform during the brief stopover. As the train pulled out, he returned to his seat and put his grip back on the rack.

At 11.12 he did it again at Derby. This time he asked a

porter on the platform of the cavernous concrete hall that forms Derby Station.

'Derby,' sang out the porter. 'Sheffield is the one after next.'

Again Winkler spent the stopover gazing out of the open window, then returned to his seat and tossed his grip on to the rack. Preston was watching him through the inter-carriage doors.

At 11.43 they rolled into Chesterfield, a Victorian station but beautifully maintained with bright paintwork and hanging baskets of flowers. This time Winkler left his grip where it was, but went to lean out of the window as two or three passengers quit the train and hurried through the ticket barrier. The platform was empty before the train began to roll. When it did, Winkler snapped open the door, jumped to the moving concrete and slammed the door closed with a backward movement of one arm.

Burkinshaw was very rarely caught off balance by a Joe, but he later admitted Winkler had got him cold. All four of the Watchers could easily have made the platform, but there was not an iota of cover on that strip of stone and they would have been about as unobtrusive as a sow in a synagogue. Winkler must have seen them and aborted his rendezvous, wherever it was. Preston and Burkinshaw ran forward to the boarding platform where they were joined by Ginger from the carriage in front. The window was still open. Preston stuck his head out and looked back. Winkler, satisfied at last that he had no tail, was striding briskly down the platform with his back to the train.

'Harry, get back here with the team by car,' shouted Preston. 'Get me on the radio when you're in range. Ginger, close the door after me.'

He shoved the door open, stepped to the running board, dropped into the paratrooper's 'land' position and jumped.

Paratroopers hit the deck at about eleven miles per hour; sideways speed depends on the wind. The train was doing thirty when Preston slammed into the embankment, praying he would not hit a concrete post or large stone. He was lucky; the thick May grass took some of the shock, then he was rolling, knees together, elbows in, head down. Harry told him later he couldn't watch. Ginger said he was bouncing like a toy, along the embankment and down towards the spinning wheels. When he finally stopped, he was lying in the gully between the grass and the permanent way. He hauled himself to his feet, turned and began to jog back towards the lights of the station.

When he appeared at the ticket barrier the guard was closing for the night. He looked at the grazed apparition in the torn coat with amazement.

'The last man through here,' said Preston, 'short, stocky, grey mackintosh. Where did he go?'

The guard nodded towards the forecourt and Preston ran. Too late the guard realized he had not collected the ticket. In the forecourt Preston saw the tail lights of a taxi sweeping out of the yard and towards the town. It was the last taxi. He could, he knew, get the local police to trace the taxi driver and ask where he took that client, but he had no doubt Winkler would dismiss the taxi short of his ultimate destination and walk the rest. A few feet away a railway porter was kick-starting his moped.

'I need to borrow your bike,' said Preston.

'Bog off,' said the porter.

There was no time for identification or argument; the lights of the taxi were passing under the new ring road and out of sight. So Preston hit him, just once, on the jaw. The porter crashed over. Preston caught the falling moped, jerked it free of the man's legs, straddled it and rode off.

He was lucky with the traffic lights. The taxi had gone up Corporation Street and Preston would never have caught it on his tiny-engined putt-putt except that the lights outside the central library were at red. When the taxi rolled down Holywell Street and into Saltergate, he was a hundred yards behind, and then he lost more ground as the bigger engine outpaced him for the straight half mile of that highway. If Winkler had been taken out into the countryside due west of Chesterfield, Preston could never have caught him.

Fortunately the taxi's brake lights flashed on when it was a speck in the distance. Winkler was paying it off where Saltergate becomes Ashgate Road. As Preston closed the gap, he could see Winkler beside the car, looking up and down. There was no other traffic; nothing for it but to keep going. He puttered past the halted taxi like a late home-goer about his business, swerved into Foljambe Road and stopped. Winkler crossed the top of the road on foot; Preston followed. Winkler never looked back again. He just strolled round the boundary wall of Chesterfield football ground and into Compton Street. Here he approached a house and knocked on the door. Moving between patches of shadow, Preston had reached the corner of the street and was hidden behind a bush in the garden of the corner house.

Up the street he saw lights come on in a darkened house and the door opened. There was a brief conversation on the doorstep, and Winkler went inside. Preston sighed, and settled behind his bush for a night-long vigil. He could not read the number of the house Winkler had entered, nor could he watch the rear of the place as well, but he could see the towering wall of the football ground behind the house, so perhaps there was no feasible exit on that side.

At two in the morning he heard the faint noise on his communicator as Burkinshaw came back into range. He identified himself and gave his position. At half past two he heard the soft pad of footsteps and hissed to give his location. Burkinshaw joined him in the shrubbery. 'You all right, John?'

'Yes. He's housed up there, second beyond the tree, with a light behind the curtain.'

'Got it. John, there was a reception party at Sheffield. Two Special Branch and three uniformed. Drummed up by London. Did you want an arrest?'

'Absolutely not. Winkler's a courier. I want the big fish.

He might be inside that house. What happened to the Sheffield party?'

Burkinshaw laughed. 'Thank God for the British police. Sheffield is Yorkshire, this is Derbyshire. They're going to have to sort it out between their Chief Constables in the morning. It gives you time.'

'Yeah. Where are the others?'

'Down the street. We came back by taxi, and dismissed it. John, we've got no wheels. Also, come the dawn, this street's got no cover.'

'Put two at the top end and two down here,' said Preston. 'I'm going back into the town centre to find the police station and ask for a bit of backup. If Chummy leaves, tell me. But shadow him with two of the team, keep two on that house.'

He left the garden and walked back into central Chesterfield looking for the police station which he found in Beetwell Street. As he walked, a phrase kept repeating itself in his head. There was something about Winkler's performance that did not make sense.

20

Superintendent Robin King was not pleased to be woken at three in the morning, but on hearing there was an officer of MI5 from London at his police station seeking assistance he agreed to come at once, and was there, unshaven and uncombed, twenty minutes later.

He listened attentively while Preston explained the gist of the story: that a foreigner believed to be a Soviet agent had been tailed from London, had jumped train at Chesterfield and been followed to a house in Compton Street, number as yet unknown.

'I do not yet know who lives in that house, or why our suspect has visited it. I intend to find out, but for the moment I do not want an arrest. I want to watch the house. Later this morning we can sort out a fuller authority through the Chief Constable for Derbyshire; for the moment the problem is more urgent. I have four men of our Watcher Service in that street, but come the daylight they'll stick out like sore thumbs. So I need some assistance now.'

'What exactly can I do for you, Mr Preston?' the senior police officer asked.

'Have you got an unmarked van, for instance?'

'No. Several police cars, unmarked, and a couple of vans, but with police insignia on the side.'

'Can we get hold of an unmarked van and park it in that street with my men inside, just as a temporary measure?'

The superintendent called the duty sergeant on the phone. He put the same question and listened for a while. 'Raise him on the phone and ask him to call me right now,' he said. To Preston: 'One of our men has a van. It's pretty battered, he's always having his leg pulled about it.'

Thirty minutes later the sleepy police constable had

made rendezvous with the Watcher team outside the football stadium main entrance. Burkinshaw and his men piled inside and the van was driven into Compton Street and parked opposite the suspect house. On instructions, the policeman climbed out, stretched and walked away down the road, for all the world like a man coming home from night shift.

From the rear windows Burkinshaw peered out and came on the radio to Preston. 'That's better,' he said, 'we've got a great view of the house across the road. By the way, it's number 59.'

'Hold on there for a while,' said Preston, 'I'm trying to fix something better. Meanwhile, if Winkler leaves on foot, tail him with two men and leave two to stay with the house. If he leaves by car, follow in the van.'

'Superintendent, we may have to stake out that house for a longer period. That means taking over the front upper room of a house across the road. Can we find anyone in Compton Street who might let us do that?'

The police chief was thoughtful. 'I do know someone who lives in Compton Street,' he said. 'We're both Masons, members of the same lodge. That's how I know him. A former chief petty officer in the Navy, retired now. He's at number 68. I don't know where it is in the street though.'

Burkinshaw confirmed that 68 was across the road and two houses up. The upper front window, almost certainly the main bedroom, would give perfect observation of the target. Superintendent King rang his friend from the station.

At Preston's suggestion he told the sleepy householder, a Mr Sam Royston, that this was a police operation; they wished to watch a possible suspect who had taken refuge across the road. When he had gathered his wits Mr Royston rose to the occasion. As a law-abiding citizen he would certainly allow the police to use his front room.

The van was quietly driven round the block into West Street; Burkinshaw and his team slipped between the houses there, over the garden fences and entered Mr Royston's house on Compton Street from the back garden. Just before the summer sun flooded the road the Watcher team settled down in the Roystons' unmade-up bedroom behind the lace curtains, through which they could see number 59 across the street.

Mr Royston, ramrod stiff in camel dressing gown and bristling with the self-importance of a patriot asked to assist the Queen's officers, glowered through the curtains at the house almost opposite.

'Bank robbers, are they? Drug traffickers?'

'Something like that,' assented Burkinshaw.

'Foreigners,' growled Royston. 'Never did like 'em. Should never have let 'em all into the country.'

Ginger, whose parents had come from Jamaica, stared stolidly through the curtains. Mungo, the Scot, was bringing a pair of chairs up from below. Mrs Royston emerged like a mouse from some secret hiding place, having removed her curlers and pins.

'Would anyone,' she enquired, 'like a nice cup of tea?'

Barney, who was young and handsome, flashed his most winning smile. 'That would be lovely, mum.'

It made her day. She began to prepare the first of what turned out to be an endless relay of cups of tea, a brew upon which she appeared to live without any visible recourse to solid foods.

At the police station the desk sergeant had also established the identity of the inhabitants of 59 Compton Street.

'Two Greek Cypriots, sir,' he reported to Superintendent King. 'Both bachelors and brothers. Andreas and Spiridon Stephanides. Been here about four years, according to the constable on that beat. Seems they run a doner kebab and Greek takeaway at Holywell Cross.'

Preston had spent half an hour on the phone to London. First he raised the duty officer at Sentinel, who put him through to Barry Banks.

'Barry, I want you to contact "C" wherever he is and ask him to call me back.'

Sir Nigel Irvine came on the line five minutes later, calm and lucid as if he had not been asleep at all. Preston informed him of the night's events.

'Sir, there was a reception party at Sheffield. Two SBs and three uniformed, authorized to make an arrest.'

'I don't think that was part of the arrangement, John.'

'Not as far as I was concerned.'

'All right, John, I'll handle it at this end. You've got the house. Are you going to move in now?'

'I've got *a* house,' corrected Preston. 'I don't want to move in because I don't think it's the end of the trail. One other thing, sir. If Winkler leaves and heads for home, I want him to be allowed to go in peace. If he is a courier, or message carrier, or just checking up, his people will be expecting him back in Vienna. If he fails to show, they'll switch off the cutouts from top to bottom.'

'Yes,' said Sir Nigel carefully. 'I'll have a word with Sir Bernard about that. Do you want to stay with the operation up there or come back to London?'

'I'd like to stay up here if possible.'

'All right. I'll make it a top-level request from "Six" that what you want is accorded to you. Now, cover your back and make your operational report to Charles Street.'

When he put the phone down, Sir Nigel called Sir Bernard Hemmings at his home. The Director-General of 'Five' agreed to meet him for breakfast at the Cavalry and Guards Club at eight.

'So you see, Bernard, it really may be the Centre is mounting quite a large operation inside this country at the moment,' said 'C' as he buttered his second piece of toast.

Sir Bernard Hemmings was deeply disturbed. He sat with his food untouched in front of him.

'Brian should have told me about the Glasgow incident,' he said. 'What the hell's that report still sitting on his desk for?'

'We all make errors of judgement from time to time. *Errare humanum est*, and all that,' murmured Sir Nigel. 'After all, my Vienna people thought Winkler was a bagman for a long-standing ring of agents, and I deduced Jan Marais might be one of that ring. Now it appears there could be two separate operations after all.'

He refrained from admitting he himself had written the Vienna telegram of the previous day in order to obtain what he wanted from his colleague – Preston's inclusion as field controller in the Winkler operation. For 'C' there was a time for candour and a time for discreet silence.

'And the second operation, the one linked to the intercept in Glasgow?' asked Sir Bernard.

Sir Nigel shrugged. 'I just don't know, Bernard. We're all feeling our way in the dark. Brian evidently does not believe it. He may be right. In which case I'm the one with egg all over his face. And yet, the Glasgow affair, the mysterious transmitter in the Midlands, the arrival of Winkler. That man Winkler was a lucky break, maybe the last we'll get.'

'Then what are your conclusions, Nigel?'

Sir Nigel smiled apologetically. It was the question he had been waiting for. 'No conclusions, Bernard. A few tentative deductions. If Winkler is a courier, I'd expect him to make his contact and hand over his package or pick up the package he came to collect, at some public place. A car park, river embankment, garden bench, seat by a pond.

'If there is a big operation going on here, there must be a top-level illegal in on the ground. The man running the show. If you were him, would you want the couriers turning up at your doorstep? Of course not. You'd have one cutout, maybe two. Do have some coffee.'

'All right, agreed.' Sir Bernard waited as his colleague poured him a cup.

'Therefore, Bernard, it occurs to me that Winkler cannot be the big fish. He's small potatoes, a bagman, a courier or something else. Same goes for the two Cypriots in a small house in Chesterfield. Sleepers, wouldn't you say?'

'Yes,' agreed Sir Bernard, 'low-level sleepers.'

'It begins to look, therefore, as if the Chesterfield house might be a depository for incoming packages, a mail box, a safe house, or maybe the home of the transmitter. After all, it's in the right area; the two squirts intercepted by GCHQ were from the Derbyshire Peak District and the hills north of Sheffield, an easy drive from Chesterfield.'

'And Winkler?'

'What can one think, Bernard? A technician sent in to repair the transmitter if it developed problems; a supervisor to check on progress? Either way, I think we should let him report back that everything is in order.'

'And the big fish, you think he might show up personally?'

Sir Nigel shrugged again. His personal fear was that Brian Harcourt-Smith, baulked of his intended arrest at Sheffield, would try to engineer the storming of the Chesterfield house. For Sir Nigel, this would be wholly premature.

'I should have thought there has to be a contact there somewhere. Either he comes to the Greeks or they go to him,' he said.

'You know something, Nigel, I think we should stake out that house in Chesterfield, at least for a while.'

The Chief of the SIS looked grave. 'Bernard, old friend, I happen to agree with you. But your young Brian seems very gung-ho to move in and make a few arrests. He tried last night at Sheffield. Of course, arrests look good for a while, but . . .'

'You leave Brian Harcourt-Smith to me, Nigel,' said Sir Bernard grimly. 'I may be pegging out, but there's a bark left in the old dog yet. You know, I'm going to take over the direction of this operation personally.'

Sir Nigel leaned forward and placed his hand over Sir Bernard's forearm. 'I really wish you would, Bernard.'

* * *

Winkler left the house in Compton Street at half past nine, on foot. Mungo and Barney slipped out of the rear of the Roystons' house, through the gardens, and picked up the Czech on the corner of Ashgate Road. He went back to the station, took the London train and was picked up at St Pancras by a fresh team. Mungo and Barney went back to Derbyshire.

Winkler never returned to his boarding house. Whatever he had left there he abandoned like the grip on the train with pyjamas and shirt, and went straight to Heathrow. He caught the afternoon flight out to Vienna. Irvine's head of station in Vienna later reported he was met by two men from the Soviet Embassy.

Preston spent the rest of the day closeted in the police station attending to the wealth of administrative detail involved in a stakeout in the provinces.

The bureaucratic machine ground into action: Charles Street jacked up the Home Office who authorized the Chief Constable of Derbyshire to instruct Superintendent King to afford Preston and his men every co-operation. Mr King was happy to do so anyway, but the paperwork had to be in order.

Len Stewart with a second team came up by car and were billeted in police bachelor quarters. Photos were taken with a long lens of both Greek brothers as they left Compton Street for their taverna at Holywell Cross just before noon, and dispatched by motorcycle to London. Other experts came in from Manchester, went into the local telephone exchange and put a tap on both the Greeks' phones, at the house and the taverna. A direction-finder bleeper was slipped into their car.

By late afternoon London had a make on the Greeks. They were not true Cypriots, but they were brothers. Veteran Greek Communists, once active in the ELAS movement, they had left mainland Greece for Cyprus twenty years earlier. Athens had therefore kindly informed London that their real name was Costapopoulos.

From Cyprus, according to Nicosia, they had vanished eight years earlier.

Immigration Records at Croydon informed that the Stephanides brothers had entered Britain five years before as legitimate Cypriot citizens and been permitted to stay.

Records in Chesterfield showed they had arrived there just three-and-a-half years earlier from London, taken a long lease on the kebab house and bought the small terrace residence in Compton Street. Since then they had lived as peaceful and law-abiding citizens. Six days a week they opened their taverna for the lunch trade, which was slack, and stayed open until late, when they did a thriving trade in takeaway suppers.

Nobody in the police station except Superintendent King was told the real reason for the stakeout, and only six were told at all. The others were informed it was part of a nationwide drugs-bust operation. London people were only being brought in because they knew the faces.

Just after sundown Preston cleared up at the police headquarters and went to join Burkinshaw and his team.

Before leaving the police station he thanked Superintendent King profusely for all the latter's assistance to him.

'Are you going to sit in during the stakeout?' asked the police chief.

'Yes, I'll be there,' said Preston. 'Why do you ask?'

Superintendent King smiled sadly. 'Half of last night we had a very aggrieved railway porter downstairs. Seems someone knocked him off his moped in the station yard and made off on it. We found the moped in Foljambe Road, quite undamaged. Still, he gave us a very clear description of his assailant. You won't be going out much, will you?'

'No, I shouldn't think so.'

'How very wise,' suggested Superintendent King.

At his house in Compton Street Mr Royston had been urged to continue his normal routine, visiting the shops in the morning and the bowling green in the afternoon. Extra food and drink would be brought in after dark, in case neighbours wondered at the Roystons' sudden and vastly increased appetite. A small television was brought in for what Mr Royston termed 'the lads upstairs' and they all settled down to wait and watch.

The Roystons had moved into the back bedroom, and the single bed from that room was brought to the front. It would be shared in shifts by the Watchers. Also brought in was a powerful set of binoculars on a tripod, plus a camera with a long lens for daylight shots and an infra-red lens for night photography. Two fuelled cars were parked close by, and Len Stewart's people were running the communications room at the police station, linking the Royston house with its hand-held sets and London.

When Preston arrived the four Watchers seemed to have made themselves quite at home. Barney and Mungo, back from London, were snoozing, one on the bed and the other on the floor. Ginger was sitting in an easy chair sipping a cup of fresh-brewed tea; Harry Burkinshaw was sitting like a buddha in an armchair behind the lace curtains gazing across at the empty house.

A man who had spent half his life standing in the rain, he was quiet content. He was warm, dry, had a large supply of mints and his shoes off. There were worse ways, as he well knew. The target house even backed on to a 15-foot concrete wall, the football ground, which meant no-one need spend the night crouched in the bushes. Preston took the spare chair beside him, behind the mounted camera, and accepted a cup of tea from Ginger.

'Are you bringing up the covert-entry team?' Harry asked. He meant the skilled burglars the Technical Services maintained for clandestine break-ins.

'No,' said Preston, 'for one thing, we don't even know there might not be someone in there as well. For another, there could be a range of warning devices to indicate if an entry has taken place, and we might not spot them all. Finally, what I'm waiting for is a Chummy to show up. When he does, we take the cars and tail him. Len can take over the house.'

They settled down in companionable silence. Barney woke up. 'Anything on the telly?' he asked. 'Not much,' said Ginger, 'The evening news. Usual rubbish.'

Twenty-four hours later, on the Thursday evening at the same hour, the news was quite interesting. On their small screen they saw the Prime Minister, standing on the steps of Number 10 Downing Street in a neat blue suit, facing a horde of press and television crews.

She announced she had returned from Buckingham Palace where she had asked for a dissolution of Parliament. In consequence, the country would prepare for a general election, to be held on 18 June next.

The rest of the evening was devoted to the sensation, with the leaders and luminaries of all the parties announcing their confident expectation of victory.

'Turn-up for the book,' Burkinshaw remarked to Preston. He could get no reply. Preston watched the screen lost in thought. At last he said: 'I think I've got it.'

'Well, don't use our loo,' said Mungo.

'What's that, John?' asked Harry when the laughter died down.

'My deadline,' said Preston, but he refused to elaborate.

By 1987 very few European-manufactured cars still retained the old-style large round headlights, but one that did was the evergreen Austin Mini. It was a vehicle of this type that was among the many cars to disembark on the evening of 2 June from the Cherbourg ferry arriving at Southampton.

The car had been bought in Austria four weeks earlier, driven to the clandestine garage in Germany, modified there, and driven back to Salzburg. The car had perfect Austrian papers, as did the tourist driving it, though he was in fact a Czech, the second and last of the contributions by the StB to Major Volkov's plan to import into Britain the components Valeri Petrofsky needed.

The Mini was searched at Customs and nothing amiss was discovered. Clearing Southampton docks, the driver followed the London directions until, in the northern suburbs of the port city, he pulled off the road into a large car park. It was quite dark already and at the rear of the park he was out of sight of those still speeding down the main highway. He descended and with a screw-driver began to work on the headlights.

First he removed the chrome ring covering the gap between the headlight unit and the surrounding metal of the car's wing. Using a larger screwdriver, he then undid the screws holding the headlight unit firmly inside the wing. When they came free he eased the entire headlight unit out of its socket, detatched the electric flexes running from the car's electrical system into the rear of the lamp bowl, and laid the unit, which appeared exceptionally heavy, in a canvas bag by his side.

It took almost an hour to extract both headlamp units. When he had finished the small car stared sightlessly ahead with empty sockets. In the morning, the agent knew, he would return with freshly purchased headlights from Southampton, fit them and drive away.

For the moment he hefted the heavy canvas bag, went back to the high road and walked three hundred yards back towards the port. The bus stop was where they had said it would be. He checked his watch: ten minutes to rendezvous.

Exactly ten minutes later a man in motorcycle leathers strolled up to the bus stop. There was no-one else there. The newcomer glanced down the road and remarked: 'It's always a long wait for the last bus of the night.'

The Czech sighed with relief. 'Yes,' he replied, 'but, thank God, I should be home by midnight.'

They waited in silence until the bus into Southampton arrived. The Czech left the grip on the ground and boarded the bus. As the tail lights disappeared towards the city, the motorcyclist lifted the grip and walked away, back up the road to the roadside housing estate where he had left his motorcycle.

By dawn, having ridden to Thetford to change and

switch vehicles, he arrived home in Cherryhayes Close, Ipswich, carrying the last of the scheduled list of components he had waited for these long weeks. Courier Nine had delivered.

Two days later the stakeout on the house in Compton Street, Chesterfield, was one week old and absolutely nothing to report.

The two Greek brothers lived lives of impeccable uneventfulness. They rose about nine, busied themselves about their house, where they appeared to do all their own cleaning and dusting, and left in their five-year-old saloon car for their restaurant just before midday. They stayed there until close to midnight, when they returned home to sleep. There were no visitors and few phone calls. What calls there were involved orders for meat and vegetables or other harmless sundries.

Down at the taverna at Holywell Cross, Len Stewart and his people reported much the same. The telephone was used more frequently, but again the talk was of orders for food, bookings for a table or deliveries of wine. It was not possible for a Watcher to dine there every night; the Greeks were apparently professionals who had spent years in the clandestine life and would have spotted a customer who came too frequently or loitered too long. But Stewart and his team did their best.

For the team in the Royston house the main problem was boredom. Even Mr and Mrs Royston were tiring of the incovenience caused by their presence after the initial excitement had worn off. Mr Royston had agreed to volunteer as a canvasser for the Conservative Party – he resolutely declined to assist anybody else – and the front windows of the house now bore posters in favour of the local Tory candidate.

This enabled more coming and going than usual, since anyone with a Conservative rosette seen leaving or entering the house would attract no attention from the neighbours. The ruse enabled Burkinshaw and his team, suitably rosetted, to take an occasional stroll while the Greeks were at their restaurant. It broke the monotony. The only one who seemed immune from boredom was Harry Burkinshaw himself.

For the rest, the principal distraction was the television, kept at low volume particularly when the Roystons were out, and the prime topic day and evening was the continuing election campaign. One week into the campaign three things were becoming clear.

The Liberal/Social Democrat Alliance had still failed to surge in the opinion polls and the issue seemed to be increasingly developing into the traditional race between the Conservatives and the Labour Party. The second factor was that all public-opinion polls indicated the two main parties were much closer than could have been foreseen four years earlier in 1983 when the Conservatives won their landslide; further, constituency-level polling indicated the outcome in the eighty most marginal constituencies would almost certainly decide the colour of the country's next government. In every poll it was the floating vote, varying between 10 and 20 per cent, that held the balance.

The third development was that despite all the economic and ideological issues involved, and despite the efforts of all parties to make the most of them, the campaign was becoming increasingly dominated by the much more emotive issue of unilateral nuclear disarmament. In more and more polls the nuclear arms race issue was showing as first or second priority of concern.

The pacifist movements, broadly Left and broadly united for once, were mounting what was in effect a parallel campaign of their own. Huge demonstrations took place on an almost daily basis, rewarded with equally copious coverage by press and TV. The movements, while demonstrating no noticeable fund-raising organization, seemed able from their combined resources to hire hundreds of coaches at commercial rates to transport their demonstrators hither and thither across the land.

Hard Left luminaries of the Labour Party, agnostics or atheists to a man, shared every public or TV platform with clerics of the trendier wing of the Anglican church, where the members of the two groups spent their allocated air time nodding in grave agreement with the points made by the other.

Inevitably, even though the Alliance was not unilateralist, the primary target of the disarmers was the Conservative Party, just as their primary ally became the Labour Party. The Labour Leader, supported by the National Executive, seeing which way the wind was blowing, publicly aligned himself and the party to every one of the unilateralists' demands.

Another theme that ran through the Left campaign was anti-Americanism. On a hundred platforms it rapidly became impossible for the interviewer or show host to extract a single condemnatory word from the disarmers' spokesmen against Soviet Russia; the constantly reiterated theme was of hatred of America, portrayed as the warmonger, the imperialist and the threat to peace.

On Tuesday, 4 June, the campaign was enlivened by the sudden Soviet offer to 'guarantee' the whole of Western Europe, neutrals and NATO nations alike, a nuclear-free zone in perpetuity if America would do the same.

An attempt by the British Defence Minister to explain that (a) the removal of European/US defences was verifiable while Soviet warhead detargeting was not, and (b) that the Warsaw Pact had a four-to-one conventional weapon superiority over NATO, was howled down twice before lunch and the Minister had to be removed from the grip of the pacifists by bodyguards.

'Anyone would think,' grumbled Harry Burkinshaw as he popped another mint, 'that this election was a national referendum on nuclear disarmament.'

'It is,' said Preston shortly.

Friday found Major Petrofsky shopping in Ipswich town centre. From a hardware store he bought a light, short-handled, two-wheeled trolley of the type used for shifting sacks, dustbins or heavy suitcases. A builders' merchant yielded two 10-foot planks.

In an office-equipment shop he acquired a small steel filing cabinet 30 inches tall, 18 wide and 12 deep, with a door that locked securely.

A timber store provided a variety of laths, batons and short joists, while a do-it-yourself shop sold him a complete tool box including a high-speed drill with a selection of bits for steel or timber, plus nails, bolts, nuts, screws and a pair of heavy-duty industrial gloves.

From a packaging warehouse he bought a quantity of foam insulation and he rounded off the morning in an electrical emporium with the purchase of four cubic 9-volt batteries and a selection of multicoloured single-flex wiring. It took two journeys in his hatchback saloon car to bring the loads back to Cherryhayes Close, where he stored them in the garage. After dark he brought most of the gear inside the house.

That night the radio told him in Morse the details of the arrival of the Assembler, the one even he had not been required to memorize. It would be Rendezvous X and the date Monday, the 8th. Tight, he thought, damn tight, but he would still be on target.

While Petrofsky was crouched over his one-time pad deciphering the message and the Greeks were serving moussaka and kebab to the queue of people who had just quit the nearby bars at closing time, Preston was in the police station on the phone to Sir Bernard Hemmings.

'The question is, John, how long we can keep going up there in Chesterfield without any results,' said Sir Bernard.

'It's only been a week, sir,' said Preston. 'Stakeouts have lasted a lot longer.'

'Yes, I well know that. The thing is, we usually have more to go on. There's a growing move here that advocates crashing in on the Greeks to see what it is they've got stashed away in that house, if anything. Why won't you agree a clandestine entry while they're at work?'

'Because I think they're top pros, and they'd spot they'd been done over. If that happened they probably have a fool-proof way of warning off their controller from ever visiting them again.'

'Yes, I suppose you're right. It's all very well you sitting over that house like a tethered goat in India waiting for the tiger to come, but supposing the tiger doesn't show?'

'I believe he will, sooner or later, Sir Bernard,' said Preston. 'Please, give me a bit more time.'

'All right,' conceded Hemmings after a pause for a consultation at the other end. 'A week, John. Next Friday I'll have to jack up the Special Branch lads to go in there and take the place apart. Let's face it, the man you're looking for could be inside there all the time.'

'I don't believe he is. Winkler would never have visited the lair of the tiger himself. I believe he's still out there somewhere, and that he'll come.'

'Very well. One week, John. Friday next it is.'

Sir Bernard hung up. Preston stared at the handset. The election was thirteen days away. He was beginning to feel dejected, that he could have been wrong all along. Nobody else, with the possible exception of Sir Nigel, believed in his hunch. A small disc of polonium and a low-level Czech bagman were not much to go on, and might not even be linked.

'All right, Sir Bernard,' he told the buzzing handset, 'one week. After that I'm jacking it in anyway.'

The Finnair jet from Helsinki arrived the following Monday afternoon on time as usual and its complement of passengers passed through Heathrow without undue problems. One of them was a tall, bearded man of middle age whose Finnish passport claimed him to be Urho Nuutila, and whose fluent command of the language could be partly explained by his Karelian parentage. He was in fact a Russian called Vassiliev and by profession a scientist in nuclear engineering attached to the Soviet Army Artillery, Ordnance Research Directorate. Like most Finns he spoke passable English.

Having cleared Customs he took the airport courtesy coach to the Heathrow Penta Hotel, walked in through the front, kept going right past reception and emerged at the rear door, giving on to the car park. He waited by that door in the late afternoon sunshine, unnoticed by anyone, until a small hatchback saloon drew abreast of him. The driver had his window open.

'Is this where the coaches from the airport drop the passengers?' he asked.

'No,' said the traveller. 'I think that is round the front.'

'Where are you from?' asked the young man.

'Finland, actually,' said the bearded one.

'It must be cold in Finland.'

'No, at this time of year it is very hot. The main problem is the mosquitoes.'

The young man nodded. Vassiliev walked around the car and climbed in. They drove off.

'Name?' asked Petrofsky.

'Vassiliev.'

'That'll do. Nothing more. I'm Ross.'

'Far to go?' asked Vassiliev.

'About two hours.'

They drove the rest of the way in silence. Petrofsky made three separate manoeuvres to detect a tail had there been one. There was not. They arrived at Cherryhayes Close by the last light of day. On the next-door patch of front lawn his neighbour Mr Armitage was mowing the grass.

'Company?' he said as Vassiliev descended from the car and walked to the front door.

Petrofsky took the man's single small case from the back and winked at Armitage. 'Head office,' he whispered. 'Best behaviour. Might get promotion.'

'Oh, I should think so then,' grinned Armitage. He nodded in encouragement and went on mowing.

Inside the sitting-room Petrofsky closed the curtains as he always did before putting on the light. Vassiliev stood motionless in the gloom.

'Right,' he said when the lights went on, 'to business. Have you got all the nine consignments that were sent to you?'

'Yes. All nine.'

'Let's confirm them. One child's playball, weighing about twenty kilogrammes.'

'Check.'

'One pair shoes, one box cigars, one plaster cast.'

'Check.'

'One transistor radio, one electric shaver, one steel tube, extremely heavy.'

'That must be this.' Petrofsky went to a cupboard and held up a short length of heavy metal in heat-resistant cladding.

'It is,' said Vassiliev. 'Finally, one hand-held fire extinguisher, unusually heavy, and one pair car head-lamps, also very heavy.'

'Check.'

'Well, that's it then. If you've got the rest of the innocent commercial purchases, I'll start assembling in the morning.'

'Why not now?'

'Look, young man, first, the sawing and drilling is hardly going to please the neighbours at this hour. Secondly, I'm tired. With this kind of toy you don't make mistakes. I'll start fresh tomorrow and be finished by sundown.'

Petrofsky nodded. 'Take the back bedroom. I'll run you to Heathrow on Wednesday in time for the morning flight.'

21

Vassiliev elected to work in the sitting-room, with the curtains closed and by electric light. First he asked for the nine consignments to be assembled.

'We'll need a garbage bag,' he said. Petrofsky fetched him one from the kitchen.

'Pass the consignments to me as I ask for them,' said the Assembler. 'First, the cigar box.'

He broke open the seals and opened the lid. The box had two levels of cigars, thirteen on the top and twelve below, each in an aluminium tube.

'It should be third from the left, bottom row.'

It was. He emptied the cigar from its tube and slit it open with a razor. From the sliced tobacco inside he withdrew a slim glass phial with a crimped end and two twisted wires sticking out. An electric detonator. The waste went into the bag.

'Plaster cast.'

The case had been made in two layers, the first allowed to harden before the second was applied. Between the two layers a sheet of grey, putty-like substance had been rolled flat, encased in polythene to prevent adhesion, and wrapped around the arm. Vassiliev prised the two layers of plaster of Paris apart, peeled the grey plasticine from its cavity, pulled away the polythene protector sheets and rolled it back into a ball. Half a pound of plastic explosive.

Given Mr Lichka's shoes, he cut away the heels of both. From one came a steel disc, 2 inches in diameter, 1 inch thick. Its rim was threaded to turn it into a broad, flat screw, and one surface had a deep cut to take a wide-headed screwdriver. From the other heel came a flatter 2-inch-wide disc of grey metal; it was of lithium, an inert metal that, when bonded during the explosion to the polonium, would form the initiator and cause the atomic reaction to reach its full force.

The complementary disc of polonium came from the electric shaver that had so worried Karel Wosniak, and replaced the one lost up in Glasgow. There were five of the smuggled consignments left.

The heat-resistant cladding from the Hanomag truck exhaust pipe was stripped away to reveal a steel tube weighing 20 kilogrammes. It had an internal diameter of 2 inches, external 4 inches, for the metal's thickness was 1 inch and it was of hardened steel. One end was flanged and threaded internally, the other capped in steel. The capping had a small hole in the centre, capable of allowing the electric detonator to be passed through it.

From First Officer Romanov's transistor radio Vassiliev extracted the timer device, a flat sealed steel box, the size of two cigarette packs end to end. It had two large round buttons on one face, red and yellow; from the other face protruded two coloured wires, negative and positive. Each corner had an ear-like lug with a hole, for bolting to the outside of the steel cabinet that would contain the bomb.

Taking the fire extinguisher from Mr Lundqvist's Saab, the Assembler unscrewed the base, which the preparation team had cut open, reassembled and repainted to hide the seam. Out of the interior came not fire-damper foam but wadding, and last of all a heavy rod of lead-like metal, 5 inches long and 2 inches in diameter. Small though it was, it still weighed 4½ kilogrammes. Vassiliev pulled on the heavy gloves to handle it. It was pure uranium 235.

'Isn't that stuff radioactive?' asked Petrofsky, who had watched in fascination.

'Yes, but not dangerously so. People think all radioactive materials are dangerous to the same level. Not so. Luminous watches are radioactive, but we wear them. Uranium is an alpha-emitter, low level. Now plutonium, that's really lethal. So is this stuff when it goes critical. It will just before detonation, but not yet.'

The pair of headlamps from the Mini took a lot of

stripping. Vassiliev took out the glass lamps, the filament inside and the inner reflector bowl. What he was left with was a pair of extremely heavy semi-spherical bowls, each of 1-inch-thick hardened steel. Each bowl had a flange around its rim, drilled with sixteen holes to take the nuts and bolts. Joined together, they would form a perfect globe.

One of the bowls had at its base a 2-inch-wide hole, threaded inside to accept the steel plug from Lichka's left shoe. The other had a short stump of tube sticking from its base, internally 2 inches wide and flanged and threaded on its outer side to screw into the steel 'gun' tube from the Hanomag's exhaust system.

The last item was the child's ball, brought in by the camper van. Vassiliev cut away the bright rubberized skin. A ball of metal gleamed in the light.

'That's lead wrapping,' he said. 'The ball of uranium, the fissionable core of the nuke, is inside. I'll get it out later. It's also radioactive, like that piece over there.'

Having satisfied himself he had his nine components, he started work on the steel filing cabinet. Turning it on its back, he lifted the lid and with the timber laths and batons prepared an inner frame in the form of a low cradle which rested on the floor of the chest. This he covered with a thick layer of shock-absorbent foam rubber.

'I'll pack more round the sides and over the top when the bomb's inside,' he explained.

Taking the four batteries he wired them up, terminal to terminal, then lashed them into a block with masking tape. Finally he bored four small holes in the lid of the cabinet and wired the block of batteries inside the lid. It was midday.

'Right,' he said, 'let's put the device together. By the way, have you ever seen a nuke?'

'No,' said Petrofsky hoarsely. He was an expert in unarmed combat, unafraid of fists, knives or guns. But the cold-blooded joviality of Vassiliev as he handled enough destructive power to flatten a town worried him. Like most people, he regarded nuclear science as an occult art.

'Once they were very complicated,' said the Assembler, 'very large, even the low-power ones, and could only be made under extremely complex laboratory conditions. Today the really sophisticated ones, the multimegaton hydrogen weapons, still are. But the basic atomic bomb today has been simplified to a point where it can be assembled on just about any workbench. Given the right parts, of course, and a bit of caution and knowhow.'

'Great,' said Petrofsky. Vassiliev was cutting away the thin lead sheeting round the ball of uranium 235. The lead had been wrapped around cold, like wrapping paper, and its seams blazed with a blow torch to seal them. It came apart quite easily. Inside was the inner ball, 5 inches in diameter, with a 2-inch-wide hole drilled straight through the middle.

'Want to know how it works?' asked Vassiliev.

'Sure.'

'This ball is uranium. Weight, fifteen and a half kilogrammes. Not enough mass to have reached criticality. Uranium goes critical as its mass increases beyond criticality point.'

'What is "critical"?'

'It starts to fizz. Not literally, like lemonade. I mean fizz in radioactive terms. It passes to the threshold of detonation. This ball is not yet at that stage. See that short rod over there?'

'Yes.'

It was the uranium rod from the hollow fire extinguisher.

'That rod will fit exactly into the two-inch hole in the centre of this ball. When it does, the whole mass will go critical. The steel tube over there is like a gun barrel, with the uranium rod as the bullet. In detonation the plastic explosive will blast the rod down the tube and into the heart of this ball.'

'And it goes bang.'

'Not quite. You need the initiator. Left to itself the

uranium would fizz into extinction, create a hell of a lot of radioactivity but no explosion. To get the bang you have to bombard the critical uranium with a blizzard of neutrons. Those two discs, the lithium and the polonium, form the initiator. Left apart they are harmless; the polonium is a mild alpha-emitter, the lithium is inert. Smash them together and they do something odd. They start a reaction; they emit that blizzard of neutrons we need. Subjected to this, the uranium tears itself apart in a gigantic release of energy; the destruction of matter. It takes one hundred millionth of a second. The steel tamper is to hold it all together for that tiny period.'

'Who drops in the initiator?' asked Petrofsky in an attempt at gallows humour.

Vassiliev grinned. 'No-one. The two discs are in there already, but held apart. We put the polonium at one end of the hole in the uranium ball, and the other on the nose of the incoming uranium projectile. The bullet comes down the tube, into the heat of the ball and the lithium on its nose is slammed into the polonium waiting at the other end of the tunnel. That's it.'

Vassiliev used a drop of superglue to stick the polonium disc to one face of the flat steel plug from Lichka's shoe heel. Then he screwed the plug into the hole at the base of one of the tamper bowls. Taking the uranium ball, he lowered it into the bowl. The interior of that bowl had four nodules, which slotted into four indentations cast in the uranium. When they met and engaged, the ball was held in place. Vassiliev took a pencil torch and peered down the hole through the core of the uranium ball.

'There it is,' he said, 'waiting at the bottom of the hole.'

Then he placed the second bowl over the top, to form a perfect globe, and spent an hour tightening the sixteen bolts round the flange to hold the two halves together.

'Now, the gun,' he remarked. He pushed the plastic explosive down the 18-inch-long steel tube, tamping it firmly but gently with a broom handle from the kitchen, until it was packed tight. Through the small hole in the base of the tube, Petrofsky could make out the plastic explosive bulging up. With the same superglue, Vassiliev attached the lithium disc to the flat nose of the uranium rod, wrapped it in a tissue to ensure it could not slip back down the tube from vibration, and rammed the rod down on to the explosive at the bottom. Then he screwed the tube into the globe. It looked like a grey, 7-inch diameter melon with an 18-inch handle sticking out from one end; a sort of oversized stick grenade.

'Nearly done,' said Vassiliev. 'The rest is conventional bomb-making.'

He took the detonator, separated the wires from its end and insulated each with tape. If they touched each other, there could be premature detonation. A length of 5-amp flex was twisted on to each wire from the detonator. Then he pressed the detonator through the hole in the far end of the tube until it was embedded in the plastic explosive.

He lowered the bomb like a baby on to its foam cradle, packing more foam all round its sides, and yet more over the top, as if it were going to bed. Only the two wires were kept free. One of these was attached to the positive terminal of the battery block.

A third wire went from the negative terminal on the batteries, so Vassiliev still had one of each in his hands. He insulated each exposed end.

'Just in case they touched each other,' he grinned. 'Now that *would* be bad news.'

The single unused component was the timer box. Vassiliev used the drill to bore five holes in the side of the steel filing cabinet near the top. The centre hole was for the wires out of the back of the timer, which he fed through. The other four were for thin bolts with which he fixed the timer to the exterior of the cabinet. This done, he linked the wires from the batteries and detonator to those from the timer, according to their colour coding. Petrofsky held his breath.

'Don't worry,' said Vassiliev, who had noticed him.

'This timer was repeatedly tested back home. The cutout, or circuit-breaker, is inside, and it works.'

He stowed the last of the wires, insulated the joins heavily, and lowered the lid of the cabinet, locking it securely and tossing the key to Petrofsky.

'So, Comrade Ross, there it is. You can wheel it on the trolley into the rear of the hatchback, and it will not damage it. You can drive where you wish – the vibration will not disturb it. One last thing. The yellow button here will, if pushed firmly start the timer but not complete the electrical circuit. The timer will do that two hours later. Press this yellow one and you have two hours to get the hell out.

'The red one is a manual override. Press that and you get instant detonation.'

He did not know he was wrong. He really believed what he had been told. Only four men in Moscow knew both buttons were set for instant detonation.

It was evening. 'Now, friend Ross, I want to eat, drink a little, sleep well and go home tomorrow morning. If that is all right with you.'

'Sure,' said Petrofsky. 'Let's get the cabinet into the corner here, between the sideboard and the drinks table. Help yourself to a whisky. I'll rustle up some supper.'

They set off for Heathrow at ten in Petrofsky's small car. At a lay-by southwest of Colchester where the dense woods come close to the road, Petrofsky got out to relieve himself. Seconds later Vassiliev heard his sharp cries of alarm and ran to investigate. He ended his life with an expertly broken neck behind a screen of trees. The body, stripped of all identification, was laid in a shallow ditch and covered with fresh branches. It would probably be discovered in a day or so, maybe more. Police inquiries would eventually involve a photograph in the local papers, which his neighbour Armitage might or might not see, and might or might not recognize. It would be too late anyway. Petrofsky drove back to Ipswich.

He had no qualms. His orders had been quite clear on the matter of the Assembler. How Vassiliev had ever thought he was going home he could not imagine. In any case, he had other problems. Everything was ready, but time was short. He had visited Rendlesham Forest and picked his spot; in dense cover but hardly a hundred yards from the perimeter wire of USAF Base Bentwaters. There would be no-one there at four in the morning when he pressed the yellow button to initiate detonation at six. Fresh branches would cover the cabinet while the minutes ticked away and while he drove hard towards London.

The only thing he did not know was which morning. The signal to go operational would, he knew, come on the Radio Moscow English-language service news at 10 p.m. the previous evening. It would be in the form of a deliberate word fluff by the newsreader in the first news item. But since Vassiliev could not tell them, Moscow still had to be informed that all was in place. It meant the last message by radio. After that the Greeks would be dispensable. In the dusk of a warm June evening he left Cherryhayes Close and drove sedately north towards Thetford and his motorcycle. At nine he began to ride northwest into the British Midlands.

The boredom of an ordinary evening for the Watchers in the upper front room of the Royston house was broken just after ten when Len Stewart came on the air from the police station.

'John, one of my lads was eating in the taverna just now. The phone rang twice, then the caller rang off. It rang again twice, then he rang off again. Then he did it a third time. The listeners confirm it.'

'Did the Greeks try to answer it?'

'They didn't reach it in time the first occasion it rang. After that they didn't reach for it. Just went on serving . . . Hold on . . . John, are you there?'

'Yes, of course.'

'My people outside report one of the Greeks is leaving. Through the back. He's going for his car.'

'Two cars and four men to follow,' said Preston. 'Remaining two to stay with the taverna. The runner may be leaving town.'

But he was not. Andreas Stephanides drove back to Compton Street, parked the car and let himself in. Lights went on behind the curtains. Nothing else happened. At 11.20, earlier than usual, Spiridon closed the taverna and walked home, arriving at quarter to twelve.

Preston's tiger came just before the hour of midnight. The street was very quiet. Almost all the lights were doused. Preston had scattered his four cars and their crews far and wide, and nobody saw him come. The first they knew, there was a mutter from one of Stewart's men.

'There's a man at the top end of Compton Street, junction of Cross Street.'

'Doing?' asked Preston.

'Nothing. Standing motionless in the shadows.'

'Wait.'

It was pitch dark in the Roystons' upper front room. The curtains were back, the men standing away from the window. Mungo crouched behind the camera which was wearing its infra-red lens. Preston held his small radio close to one ear. Stewart's team of six, and his own two drivers with their cars, were out there somewhere, all linked by radio. A door opened down the street as someone put a cat out. It closed again.

'He's moving,' the radio muttered. 'Down towards you. Slowly.'

'Got him,' hissed Ginger who was at one of the side windows of the bay. 'Medium height and build, dark long raincoat.'

'Mungo, can you get him under that street light, just before the Greeks' house?' asked Burkinshaw.

Mungo turned the lens a fraction. 'I'm focused on the pool of light,' he said.

'He's ten yards short,' said Ginger.

Without a sound the figure in the raincoat entered the glimmer cast by the street lamp. Mungo's camera threw off five fast exposures. The man passed out of the light and arrived at the gate of the Stephanides' house. He went up the short path and tapped, instead of ringing, at the door. It opened at once. There was no light in the hall. The dark raincoat passed inside. The door closed.

Across the street the tension broke. 'Mungo, get that film out of there and over to the police lab. I want it developed and passed straight to Scotland Yard. Immediate on-pass to Charles and Sentinel. I'll tell them to be ready to try and get a make.'

Something was bothering Preston. Something about the way the man walked. It was a warm night, why a raincoat? To keep dry? The sun had shone all day. To cover something? Pale clothing, distinctive clothing?

'Mungo, what was he wearing? You saw him in close-up.'

Mungo was halfway out the door. 'A raincoat,' he said. 'Dark. Long.'

'Under that.'

Ginger whistled. 'Boots. Remember them now. Ten inches of jackboot.'

'Shit, he's on a motorcycle,' said Preston. He spoke into the radio. 'Everyone out on the streets. On foot only. No car engine. Every street in the district except Compton Street. We're looking for a motorcycle with a warm engine block.'

The problem is, he thought, I don't know how long he's going to be in there. Five minutes, ten, sixty?

He called up Len Stewart, 'Len, John here. If we get that motorcycle I want a DF bleeper in it somewhere. Meanwhile call up Superintendent King. He'll have to mount the operation. When Chummy leaves we'll be after him. Harry's team and me. I want you to stay with your boys on the Greeks. When we are all one hour clear, the police can take the house and the Greeks.'

Len Stewart, inside the police station, assented and

started to phone Superintendent King at home.

It was twenty minutes before one of the roving team found the motorcycle. He reported to Preston, still at the Royston House.

'There's a big BMW, top end of Queen Street. Carrier box behind the pillion, locked. Two panniers either side of the rear wheel, unlocked. Engine and exhaust still warm.'

'Registration number?'

The number was given him. He passed it to Len Stewart at the police station. Stewart asked for an immediate make on it. It turned out to be a Suffolk number, registered to a Mr James Duncan Ross of Dorchester.

'It's either a stolen vehicle, false plate, or blind address,' muttered Preston.

Hours later the Dorchester police established it was the last of the three.

The man who had found the motorcycle was ordered to plant the bleeper in one of the panniers, switch it on and get well away from the vehicle. The man, Joe, was one of Burkinshaw's two drivers. He went back to his car, effaced himself behind the steering wheel and confirmed the direction-finder was functioning.

'OK,' said Preston, 'we're doing a changeover. All drivers back to their cars. Len Stewart's three, move towards the West Street rear entrance to our observation post and relieve us. One by one, quietly and now.'

To the men around him in the room he said: 'Harry, pack up. You go first. Take the lead car, I'll join you. Barney, Ginger, take the backup car. If Mungo can join us, he'll ride with me.'

One by one Stewart's team arrived through the back to replace Burkinshaw's men. Preston prayed the agent across the road would not move out while the changeover was taking place. He was the last to leave, putting his head round the door of the Roystons' bedroom to thank them for their help and assure them it would all be over by dawn. The whispers that came back were more than a little worried.

Preston slipped through the gardens into West Street and five minutes later joined Burkinshaw and Joe the driver in their lead car, parked down Foljambe Road. Ginger and Barney reported in from the second car, at the top end of Marsden Street off Saltergate.

'Of course,' said Burkinshaw gloomily, 'if it's not the motorcycle, we're up shit creek without a paddle.'

Preston was in the back. Beside the driver Burkinshaw watched the display panel of the console in front of him. Like a small radar screen, it showed a flashing pulse of light at rhythmic intervals, glowing on a quadrant that gave its direction from the end-to-end axis of the car in which they were sitting, and approximate distance – half a mile. The second car carried the same device, enabling the two operators to get a cross-bearing if they wished.

'It's got to be the motorcycle,' said Preston desperately. 'We'd never tail him in these streets anyway. They're too empty and he's too good.'

'He's leaving.'

The sudden bark from the radio cut off further talk. Stewart's men in the Royston house reported the man in the raincoat had left the door across the street. They confirmed he walked up Compton Street towards Cross Street and in the direction of the BMW. Then he passed out of sight. Two minutes later one of Stewart's drivers, behind his windscreen in St Margaret's Drive, reported the agent had crossed the top of that street, still walking towards Queen Street. Then nothing. Five minutes went by. Preston prayed.

'He's moving.'

Burkinshaw was jumping up and down in the front seat in excitement, most unusual for this phlegmatic Watcher. The flashing blip was slowly cruising across the screen as the motorcycle changed the angle between itself and the car.

'Target on the move,' the second car confirmed.

'Give him a mile, then take off,' said Preston. 'Start engines now.'

The blip moved south and east through the centre of Chesterfield. When it was close to the Lordsmill roundabout the cars began to follow. When they reached the roundabout there was no doubt. The signal from the motorcycle was steady and strong, straight down the A617 to Mansfield and Newark. Range: just over a mile. Even their lights would be out of sight of the motorcyclist ahead. Joe grinned.

'Try and shake us now, you bastard,' he remarked.

Preston would have been happier if the man ahead were in a car. Motorcycles were brutes to follow. Fast and manoeuvrable, they could weave between dense traffic that blocked a tailing car, dive down narrow alleys or between bollards that no car could enter. Even out in the country they could leave the road and ride over grassland where a car would be hard put to follow. The essence was to keep the man ahead unaware they were following.

The motorcyclist up ahead was good. He stayed within the speed limit, but seldom came below it, taking the bends without slackening speed. He kept to the A617 beneath the sweep of the M1 motorway, through Mansfield asleep in the small hours of the morning and on towards Newark. Derbyshire gave way to the fat, rich farmland of Nottinghamshire and he never slackened pace.

Just before Newark he stopped.

'Range closing fast,' said Joe suddenly.

'Dowse lights, pull over,' snapped Preston.

In fact Petrofsky had swerved into a side road, killed his engine and lights, and now sat at the junction staring back the way he had come. A big truck thundered past him and vanished towards Newark. Nothing else. A mile up the road the two Watcher cars held station by the roadside. Petrofsky stayed still for five minutes, then gunned his engine and went off down the road to the southeast. When they saw the flashing light on the console move away, the Watchers followed, always keeping at least a mile distance.

The chase ran over the River Trent, where the lights of

the huge sugar refinery glowed away to their right, then into Newark itself. It was just short of three o'clock. Inside the town the signal wavered wildly as the pursuer car swerved through the streets. The blip seemed to settle on the A46 towards Lincoln and the cars were half a mile up the road before Joe slammed on the brakes.

'He's away to our right,' he said. 'Distance increasing.'

'Turn back,' said Preston. They found the turn-off inside Newark; the target had gone down the A17 southeast again towards Sleaford.

In Chesterfield the police operation moved on the Stephanides' house at 2.55. There were ten uniformed officers fronted by two Special Branch men in plain clothes. Ten minutes earlier and they would have had the two Soviet agents cold. It was just bad luck. At the moment the SB men approached the door, it opened.

The Greek brothers were apparently preparing to leave in their car with their radio to make the transmission that was encoded and recorded inside the transmitter. Andreas Stephanides was coming out to start their car when he saw the policemen. Spiridon was behind him carrying the transmitter. Andreas gave a single yell of alarm, stepped back and slammed the door. The police charged, shoulders first.

When the door came down Andreas was behind and under it. He came up fighting like an animal in the narrow hallway and it took two officers to flatten him again.

The Special Branch men stepped over the mêlée, had a quick glance through the ground-floor rooms, called to the two men in the back garden who had seen no-one emerge, and ran up the stairs. The bedrooms were empty. They found Spiridon in the tiny loft beneath the eaves. The transmitter was on the floor; a flex from it was plugged into a wall socket and a small red light on the console glowed. He came quietly.

At Menwith Hill GCHQ listening post intercepted a single

squirt from the covert transmitter and logged it at 02.58 on the morning of Tuesday, 11 June. Triangulation was immediate and pointed to a spot in the western end of the town of Chesterfield. The police station there was alerted at once and the call was patched through to the car being used by Superintendent Robin King. He took the call and told Menwith Hill 'I know. We've got them.'

In Moscow the warrant officer radio operator removed his headphones and nodded towards the teleprinter. 'Faint but clear,' he said.

The printer began to chatter, sending out a screed of paper covered in a jumble of meaningless letters. When it fell silent the officer beside the radio tore off the sheet and fed it through the decoder, already set to the formula of the agreed one-time pad. The decoder absorbed the sheet, its computer ran through the permutations, and it delivered the message in clear. The officer read the text and smiled. He telephoned a number, identified himself, checked the identity of the man he was addressing and said: 'Aurora is "go".'

After Newark the countryside flattened and the wind increased. The pursuit entered the gently rolling wolds of Lincolnshire and the arrow-straight roads that lead into the Fen country. The flashing blip was steady and strong, leading Preston's two cars down the A17 past Sleaford towards the Wash and the county of Norfolk.

Southeast of Sleaford Petrofsky stopped again, scanning the dark horizon behind him for lights. There were none. A mile behind him the pursuers waited in darkened silence. When the blip began to move up the oscilloscope screen, they followed again.

At the village of Sutterton there was another moment of confusion. Two roads led out of the far side of the sleeping township: the A16 due south for Spalding and the A17 southeast for Long Sutton and King's Lynn across the border in Norfolk. It took two minutes to discern that the flashing blip was moving definitely down the A17 towards Norfolk. The gap had increased to three miles.

'Close up,' ordered Preston, and Joe kept the speedometer needle on the figure of 90 until the gap was back to a mile and a half.

South of King's Lynn they crossed the spread of the River Ouse and seconds later the blip took the road due south from the by-pass towards Downham Market and Thetford.

'Where the hell's he going?' grumbled Joe.

'He's got a base down there somewhere,' said Preston from behind him. 'Just keep tracking.'

To their left a flush of pink dusted the eastern horizon and the silhouettes of the passing trees became clearer. Joe went from headlamps to side lights.

Far to the south the lights were also dimmed on the columns of coaches as they growled on choked roads through the Suffolk market town of Bury St Edmunds. There were two hundred of them, converging from a variety of different directions across the country, packed to the windows with the marchers. Other demonstrators came in cars, motorcycles, bicycles and on foot. The slow cavalcade, hung with its banners and placards, moved out of the town and up the A143 to come to rest at Ixworth junction. Down the narrow lanes the coaches could go no farther. They stopped on the verge of the main road close to the junction and discharged their yawning cargoes on to the brightening dawn of the Suffolk countryside. The marshals then began to urge and cajole the throng into some semblance of a column while the Suffolk police sat astride their motorcycles and watched.

In London the lights were still burning. Sir Bernard Hemmings had been driven from his home, alerted as he had requested when the Watcher teams in Chesterfield began to follow their man. He was in the basement radio room at Cork Street with Brian Harcourt-Smith beside him.

Across the city Sir Nigel Irvine was in his office at Sentinel House, also roused at his own request. Beneath him in the basement, Blodwyn had sat for half the night and stared at the face of a man beneath a street lamp in a small Derbyshire town. She had been driven from her Camden Town home in the small hours and had only agreed to come on the personal request of Sir Nigel himself. He had greeted her personally with flowers; for him she would walk over broken glass, but for no-one else.

'He's never been here before,' she had said as soon as she set eyes on the photograph, 'and yet . . .'

After an hour it was to the Middle East that she turned her attention, and at four she had him. It was a contribution, from the Israeli Mossad, six years old, a bit blurred and just the one picture. Even the Mossad had not been sure; the accompanying text made plain it was only a suspicion.

One of their men had taken it on the streets of Damascus. The man had been Timothy Donnelly then, salesman for Waterford Crystal. On a hunch the Mossad had snapped him and checked with their people in Dublin. Timothy Donnelly existed, but he was not in Damascus. By the time this was learned, the man in the picture had vanished. He had never surfaced again.

'That's him,' she said. 'The ears prove it. He should have worn a hat.'

Sir Nigel called the basement in Cork Street. 'We think we have a make, Bernard,' he said. 'We can run you off a print and send it over.'

They almost lost him six miles south of King's Lynn. The pursuit cars were heading south to Downham Market when the blip began to drift, imperceptibly at first, then more definitely, towards the east. Preston consulted his road map.

'He turned off back there on to the A134,' he said. 'Heading for Thetford. Take a left here.'

They got on the trail again at Stradsett, and then it was a

straight run through the thickening forests of beech, oak and pine to Thetford. They had reached the top of Gallows Hill and could see the ancient market town spread out ahead of them in the dim light of dawn when Joe slewed to a halt.

'He's stopped again.'

Another check for a tail? He had always done that in open countryside before.

'Where is he?'

Joe studied the range indicator and pointed ahead. 'Right in the heart of the town, John.'

Preston conned the road map. Apart from the road they were on, there were five others leading out of Thetford. It was like a star. The daylight was growing. It was five o'clock. Preston yawned. 'We'll give him ten.'

The blip never moved for ten minutes, nor another five. Preston sent his second car round the ring road. From four points the second car triangulated with the first; the blip was right in the centre of Thetford. Preston picked up the hand mike. 'OK, I think we have his base. We're moving in.'

The two cars closed on the centre of town. They converged on Magdalen Street and at 5.25 found the hollow square of lock-up garages. Joe manoeuvred the nose of the car until it pointed unswervingly at one of the doors. The tension among the men began to mount.

'He's in there,' said Joe.

Preston climbed out. He was joined by Barney and Ginger from the other car.

'Ginger, can you lose that door handle?'

For answer Ginger took a sparkplug spanner from the toolkit in one of the cars, slipped it over the garage door handle and jerked it sharply. There was a crack inside the lock. He looked at Preston, who nodded. Ginger swept the up-and-over garage door open and stood hastily back.

The men in the yard just stared. The motor cycle occupied the centre of the garage on its stand. From a hook hung a set of black leathers and a crash helmet. A pair of jack boots stood near the wall. In the dust and oil on the floor were the tracks of a pair of small motorcar tyres.

'Oh Jesus,' said Harry Burkinshaw, 'it's a switchover.'

Joe leaned out of his window. 'Cork just came on the police network. They say they have a full-face picture. Where do you want it sent?'

'Thetford police station,' said Preston. He gazed up at the clear blue sky above him. 'But it's too late,' he whispered.

22

Just after five the marchers were finally in a column seven men abreast and over a mile long. The head of the column began to move up the narrow road from Ixworth junction called the A1088, their destination the village of Little Fakenham and thence down the even narrower lane to the Royal Air Force base at Honington.

It was a bright, sunny morning and they were all in good spirits despite the early hour, which had been decreed by the organizers so as to catch the first arrival of the American Galaxy transports bringing in the Cruise missiles. As the head of the column began to surge between the hedgerows flanking the road, the body of the crowd started the ritual chant: 'No to Cruise – Yanks out.'

Years earlier RAF Honington had been a base for Tornado strike bombers and had attracted no attention from the nation as a whole. It was left to the villagers of Little Fakenham, Honington and Sapiston to tolerate the howling of the Tornadoes over their heads. The decision to create at Honington Britain's third Cruise missile base had changed all that.

The Tornadoes had gone to Scotland but in their place the peace of the rustic neighbourhood had been shattered by protesters, mainly female and possessed of the strangest personal habits, who had infested the fields and set up shanty camps on patches of common land. That had been going on for two years.

There had been marcher demonstrations before, but this was to be the biggest. Press and television were in heavy atttendance, the cameramen running backwards up the road to film the dignitaries in the front rank. These included three members of the Shadow Cabinet, two bishops, a monsignor, various luminaries of the reformed churches, five trade-union leaders and two noted academics.

Behind them came the column of pacifists, conscientious objectors, clerics, Quakers, students, pro-Soviet Marxist–Leninists, anti-Soviet Trotskyites, lecturers and Labour activists, with an admixture of unemployed, punks, gays and bearded ecologists. There were also hundreds of equally concerned housewives, working men, teachers and school-children.

Up the two sides of the road were scattered the resident female protesters, most sporting placards and banners, some in anoraks and crewcuts, who held hands with their younger lady friends or clapped the approaching marchers. The whole column was preceded by two police motorcycle outriders.

By 5.15 Valeri Petrofsky was clear of Thetford and as usual was motoring sedately south down the A1088 to pick up the main road to Ipswich and home. He had been up all night and was tired. But he knew his message must have been sent by 3.30 and Moscow would know he had not let them down.

He crossed the border into Suffolk near Euston Hall and noted a police motorcyclist stationary by the side of the road astride his machine. It was the wrong road and the wrong hour; he had motored this road many times over the previous months and he had never seen a police patrolman on it.

A mile later at Little Fakenham all his animal senses went to full alert. Two white Rover police cars were parked on the northern side of the village. Beside them a group of senior officers were in consultation with two more motorcycle patrolmen. They glanced up at him as he drove by, but made no move to stop him.

The move came later at Ixworth Thorpe. He had just cleared the village itself and was approaching its church on the right hand side when he saw the police motorcycle leaning against the hedge and the figure of the patrolman in the centre of the road, arm raised to stop him. He began to slow, his right hand dropping to the map pocket inside the door panel where, under a rolled woollen sweater, lay the Finnish automatic.

If it was a trap, he was boxed from behind. But the policeman seemed alone. There was no-one else nearby, radio held to mouth. He slowed to a halt. The towering figure in black Vinyl strolled to his driver's window and bent down. Petrofsky found himself confronting a ruddy Suffolk face with no hint of guile in it.

'Could I ask you to pull over to the side of the road, please, sir? Just there in front of the church. Then you'll come to no 'arm.'

So it *was* a trap. The threat was thinly veiled. But why was there no-one else about?

'What seems to be the trouble, officer?'

''Fraid the road's blocked a bit farther down, sir. We'll have it clear directly.'

Truth or trick? There *might* be an overturned tractor down there. He decided not to shoot the policeman and make a dash for it. Not yet. He nodded, let in the clutch and pulled the car on to the lay-by in front of the church. Then he waited. In his mirror he could see the policeman taking no more notice of him, but signalling another saloon into the same lay-by. This could be it, he thought. Counter-intelligence. But there was only one man in the other car. It stopped behind him. The man climbed out.

'What's going on?' he called to the policeman. Petrofsky could hear them through his open window.

'Ain't you 'eard, sir? It's the demonstration. Been in all the papers. And the telly.'

'Oh hell,' said the other driver, 'I didn't realize it was this road. Or at this hour.'

'They won't take long to pass,' said the policeman comfortingly. 'No more 'n an hour.'

At that moment the head of the column came into sight round the bend. Petrofsky gazed at the banners in the distance and heard the faint shouts with disgust and contempt. He climbed out to watch.

* * *

The hollow square of tarmac off Magdalen Street with its thirty lock-up garages was becoming crowded. Minutes after the discovery of the abandoned garage, Preston had sent Barney and the second car racing up Grove Lane to the police station to ask for help. There had been a duty constable in the front office at that hour, and a sergeant having tea in the back.

Simultaneously Preston had called up London on the police network and even though it was an open circuit and he would normally have used the cover parlance of a car-hire company, he threw caution to the winds and spoke in clear to Sir Bernard himself.

'I need backup from the police forces of Norfolk and Suffolk,' he said. 'Also a chopper, sir. Very fast. Or it's all over.' He had spent the waiting twenty minutes studying the large-scale road map of East Anglia, spread on the bonnet of Joe's car.

After five minutes a Thetford motorcycle patrolman, raised by his station sergeant, drifted into the yard, shut off his engine and parked his bike. He walked over to Preston, easing off his helmet as he did so.

'You the gentlemen from London?' he asked. 'Anything I can do to help?'

'Not unless you're a magician,' sighed Preston.

Barney arrived back from the police station. 'Here's the photograph, John. Came through while I was talking to the DS.'

Preston studied the handsome young face taken on a Damascus street.

'You bastard,' he muttered. His words were drowned, so no-one else heard. Two American F-111 strike bombers raced across the town in tight formation, low, heading east. The howl of their engines broke the calm of the waking borough. The policeman did not glance up. Barney, standing beside Preston, followed their progress out of sight. 'Noisy sods,' he said.

'Ah, they always be coming over Thetford,' said the

local copper. ‘Hardly notice them after a while. Come from Lakenheath.’

‘London Airport’s bad enough,’ said Barney who lived at Hounslow, ‘but at least the airliners don’t fly that low. Don’t think I could live with that for long.’

‘Don’t mind ’em, just so long as they stay up in the air,’ said the policeman, unwrapping a chocolate bar. ‘Wouldn’t like one to crash, though. They carry atomic bombs, they do. Small, mind.’

Preston turned slowly round. ‘What did you say?’ he asked.

Out of Cork Street MI5 had been working fast. Dispensing with the usual liaison from the Legal Adviser, Sir Bernard Hemmings had personally called both the Assistant Chief Constables (Crime) for the counties of Norfolk and Suffolk. The officer in Norwich was still abed, but in Ipswich his opposite number was already in his office because of the demonstration that was tying up half the Suffolk force.

The ACC for Norfolk was reached at the same time as the call to him from Thetford police station came through. He authorized complete cooperation; the paperwork could follow later.

Brian Harcourt-Smith was chasing up a helicopter. Britain’s two intelligence agencies have call on a Special Flight of so-called ‘dedicated’ helicopters, held at Northolt outside London. It is possible to call one up in a hurry, but normally advance arrangements are made. The Deputy Director-General’s urgent inquiry brought the answer that a chopper could be airborne in forty minutes and at Thetford forty after that. Harcourt-Smith asked Northolt to hold on.

‘Eighty minutes,’ he said to Sir Bernard.

The DG happened to be talking to the ACC of Suffolk in his Ipswich office. ‘Would you have a police helicopter available? Right now?’ he asked the Suffolk officer.

There was a pause while the ACC consulted his

colleague in Traffic Control on an internal line. 'We have one in the air over Bury St Edmunds,' he said.

'Please get it to Thetford and take aboard one of our officers,' said Sir Bernard. 'It's a matter of national security, I assure you.'

'I'll give the order now,' said the ACC of Suffolk.

Preston beckoned the Thetford policeman across to his car.

'Point out to me the American airbases around here,' he said.

The patrolman put a thick finger on the map.

'Well, they're a bit all over, sir. There's Sculthorpe up here in north Norfolk, Lakenheath and Mildenhall out here to the west, Chicksands in Bedfordshire, though I do believe they don't fly out of there any more. And then there's Bentwaters, here on the Suffolk coast near Woodbridge.'

It was six o'clock. The marchers swirled around the two parked cars on the lay-by in front of the church of All Saints, a tiny but beautiful building, old as the village, thatched with Norfolk reed and without electric light, so that evensong is still held by candlelight.

Petrofsky stood by his car watching them amble by, arms crossed, his face bland. His private thoughts were venomous. Across the fields behind him a Traffic Control helicopter clattered north, but he failed to hear it for the chanting of the marchers.

The other car driver, who turned out to be a biscuit salesman returning home from a seminar on the sales appeal of butter osbornes, walked over to him. He nodded towards the marchers.

'Arseholes,' he muttered above the chant of 'No to Cruise – Yanks out'. The Russian smiled and nodded. Getting no further reaction, the salesman wandered back to his own car, climbed in and began to read his stack of promotional literature.

If Valeri Petrofsky had had a more developed sense of humour he might have smiled at his situation. He was standing in front of the church of a god in whom he did not believe, in a country he was seeking to destroy, giving passage to people he heartily despised. And yet if his mission was successful, all the marchers' demands would be fulfilled.

He sighed as he thought of the speedy way his own country's MVD troops would deal with this march before handing over the ringleaders to the lads in the Fifth Chief Directorate for an extended question-and-answer session down at Lefortovo.

Preston stared down at the map on which he had ringed the five American airbases. If I were an illegal, living in a foreign country under deep cover and on a mission, he thought, I would want to hide myself in a large town or city.

In Norfolk there were King's Lynn, Norwich and Yarmouth. In Suffolk Lowestoft, Bury St Edmunds, and Ipswich. To get back to King's Lynn, close to USAF Sculthorpe, the man he was chasing would have driven back past him on Gallows Hill. No-one had. That left four bases, three away to the west and one in the south.

He considered the line of the ride that had brought his quarry from Chesterfield to Thetford. Due southeast, all the way. It would be logical to site the switchover point from motorcycle to car somewhere along the line of travel. From Lakenheath and Mildenhall to the transmitter house at Chesterfield, it would have been more logical to rent a lock-up garage in Ely or Peterborough, en route for the Midlands.

He took the line southeast from the Midlands to Thetford and extended it farther southeast. It pointed directly at Ipswich. Twelve miles from Ipswich, in a dense forest and close to the shore, was Bentwaters. He recalled from somewhere that they flew F-5s out of there, modern strike bombers with tactical nukes, designed to halt an onslaught by 29,000 massed tanks.

Behind him the policeman's radio set crackled into life. The man walked over and answered the call. 'There's a helicopter coming up from the south,' he said.

'It's for me,' said Preston.

'Oh, ah, where do you want it to land?'

'Is there a flat area nearby?' asked Preston.

'Place we call The Meadows,' said the patrolman. 'Down Castle Street by the roundabout. Should be dry enough.'

'Tell him to go down there,' said Preston. 'I'll join him.'

He called to his team, some of whom were dozing in the cars. 'Everybody in. We're going down to The Meadows.'

As they piled into the two cars he took his map over to the patrolman. 'Tell me, if you were here in Thetford and driving to Ipswich, which way would you go?'

Without hesitation the police motorcyclist pointed to a spot on the map. 'I'd take the A1088, straight down to Ixworth, over the junction and on down to cut into the A45 main road to Ipswich here at Elmswell village.'

Preston nodded. 'So would I. Let's hope Chummy thinks the same. I want you to stay here and try to trace any other garage tenant who might have seen the missing man's car. I need that registration number.'

The light Bell helicopter was waiting in the meadow by the roundabout. Preston climbed out, taking his personal radio with him.

'Stay here,' he told Harry Burkinshaw. 'It's a long shot. He's probably miles away. He's got at least a fifty-minute start. I'll go as far as Ipswich and see if I can spot anything. If not, it's down to that registration number. Someone may have seen it. If Thetford police trace anyone who did, I'll be up there.'

He ducked under the whirling rotors and climbed into the narrow cabin, produced his ID card to the pilot and nodded to the traffic controller who had squeezed into the back.

'That was fast,' he shouted to the pilot.

'I was airborne already,' the pilot shouted back.

The helicopter lifted off and climbed away from Thetford.

'Where do you want to go?'

'Down the A1088.'

'Want to see the demo, eh?'

'What demo?'

The pilot looked at him as if he had just arrived from Mars. The chopper, nose down, whirled southeast with the line of the A1088 to starboard so that Preston could see it.

'The RAF Honington demo,' the pilot said. 'It's been in all the papers. And on TV.'

Of course he had seen the news coverage of the projected demonstration against the base. He had spent two weeks watching television in Chesterfield. He had just not realized the base lay down the A1088 between Thetford and Ixworth. In thirty seconds he could see the real thing.

Away to his right the morning sun glinted on the runways of the airbase. A giant American Galaxy transport was taxiing round the perimeter after landing. Outside the base's several gates were the black lines of Suffolk policemen, hundreds of them, standing back to the wire, facing the demonstrators.

From the swelling crowd in front of the police cordon, a dark line of marchers, banners flapping and waving above their heads, ran back down the access lane to the A1088, debouched on to that road and ran southeast towards Ixworth junction.

Straight below him he could look down at Little Fakenham village, with Honington village swimming into view. He could make out the barns of Honington Hall and the red brick of Malting Row across the road. Here the marchers were at their thickest as they swirled around the entrance to the narrow lane leading to the base. His heart gave a thump.

Up the road from Honington village centre there was a

line of cars tail-backed for half a mile; all drivers who had not realized that road would be blocked for part of the early morning, or who had hoped to get through in time. There were over a hundred vehicles.

Farther down, right in the heart of the marching column, he could see the glint of two or three car roofs, evidently drivers who had been allowed through just before the road was closed but who had not made Ixworth junction in time to avoid being trapped. There were some in Ixworth Thorpe village centre and a couple parked near a small church farther on.

'I wonder,' he whispered.

Valeri Petrofsky saw the policeman who had originally stopped him strolling in his direction. The column had thinned a bit; it was the tail end that was passing.

'Sorry it's taken so long, sir. Seems there were more of them than foreseen.'

Petrofsky shrugged amiably. 'Can't be helped, officer. I was a fool to try it. Thought I'd get through in time.'

'Ah, there's quite a few motorists been caught by it all. Won't be long now. About ten minutes for the marchers, then there's a few big outside-broadcast vans bringing up the tail. Soon as they're past, we'll open the road again.'

Across the fields in front of them a police helicopter went past in a wide circle. In its open doorway Petrofsky could see the traffic controller talking into his handset.

'Harry, can you hear me? Come in Harry, it's John.'

Preston was sitting in the doorway of the chopper over Ixworth Thorpe trying to raise Burkinshaw.

The Watcher's voice came back, scratchy and tinny, from Thetford. 'Harry here. Read you, John.'

'Harry, there's an anti-Cruise demo going on down here. There's a chance, just a chance, that Chummy got caught up in it. Hold on.'

He turned to the pilot. 'How long's that been going on?'

‘’Bout an hour.’

‘When did they close the road at Ixworth down there?’

From the rear the traffic officer leaned forward. ‘Five twenty,’ he said. Preston glanced at his watch. Six twenty-five.

‘Harry, get the hell down the A134 to Bury St Edmunds, pick up the A45 and meet me at the junction of the 1088 and the 45 at Elmswell. Use the copper up at the garages as an outrider. And Harry, tell Joe to drive like never in his life.’

He tapped the pilot on the shoulder. ‘Take me down to Elmswell and set me down in a field near the road junction.’

By air it was only five minutes. As they passed over Ixworth junction across the A143 Preston could see the long, snaking column of parked coaches on the verge, the ones that had brought the bulk of the marchers to this picturesque and sylvan part of the countryside. Two minutes later he could make out the big dual-carriageway A45 running from Bury St Edmunds to Ipswich.

The pilot banked into a turn, looking for a landing spot. There were meadows near the point where the narrow lane-like A1088 debouched into the sweep of the A45.

‘They could be water meadows,’ shouted the pilot. ‘I’ll hover. You can jump from a couple of feet.’

Preston nodded. He turned to the traffic controller who was in uniform. ‘Grab your cap. You’re coming with me.’

‘That’s not my job,’ protested the sergeant. ‘I’m Traffic Control.’

‘That’s what I want you for. Come on, let’s go.’

He jumped the two feet from the step of the Bell into thick long grass. The police sergeant, holding his flat cap against the draught of the rotors, followed him. The pilot lifted away and turned towards Ipswich and his base.

With Preston in the lead, the pair plodded across the meadow, climbed the fence and dropped on to the A1088. A hundred yards away it joined the A45. Across the junction they could see the unending stream of traffic heading towards Ipswich.

'Now what?' asked the police sergeant.

'Now, you stand here in the road and stop cars coming south down this road. Ask the drivers if they have been on the road from as far north as Honington. If they joined this road south of Ixworth junction, or at it, let 'em go. Tell me when you get the first one to have come through the demo.'

He walked down to the A45 and looked right towards Bury St Edmunds. 'Come on, Harry. Come on.'

The cars coming south stopped for the police uniform in their path, but all averred they had joined the road south of the anti-nuclear demonstration. Twenty minutes later Preston saw the Thetford patrolman, siren wailing to clear a path, racing towards him, followed by the two Watcher cars. They all screeched to a halt at the entrance to the A1088.

The policeman raised his visor. 'I hope you know what you're doing, sir. I don't reckon that journey's ever been done faster. There's going to be questions.'

Preston thanked him and ordered both his cars a few yards up the narrow secondary road. He pointed to a grassy bank. 'Joe, ram it.'

'Do what?'

'Ram it. Not hard enough to wreck the car. Just make it look good.'

The two Suffolk policemen stared in amazement as Joe rammed his car into the bank by the road. His rear end stuck out, blocking half the freeway. Preston pointed the other car fifteen yards farther up.

'Out,' he ordered the driver. 'Come on lads, all together now. On its side.'

It took seven shoves before the MI5 car rolled on to its side. Taking a rock from the hedgerow Preston smashed a side window on Joe's car, scooping handfuls of the crystalline fragments and scattering them across the road.

'Ginger, lie on the road, here, near Joe's car, Barney, get a blanket from the boot and put it over him. Right over. Face and all,' said Preston. 'OK, the rest of you, over the hedge and stay out of sight.'

Preston beckoned the two policemen to him. 'Sergeant, there's been a nasty pile-up. I want you to stand by the body and direct the traffic past it. Officer, park your bike, walk up the road and slow down oncoming traffic as it approaches.

The two policemen had had orders from Ipswich and Norwich respectively. Cooperate with the men from London. Even if they were maniacs.

Preston sat at the base of the bank, a handkerchief pressed to his face as if to staunch blood from a broken nose.

There is nothing like a body by the roadside to slow down drivers, or cause them to stare through the side window as they crawl past. Preston had made sure Ginger's 'body' was on the driver's side for cars coming south down the A1088.

Major Valeri Petrofsky was in the seventeenth car. Like the others before it, the modest family hatchback saloon slowed to the patrolman's flapping hand, then crawled past the crash scene. On the grassy bank, eyes half closed, the memory of the photo in his pocket imprinted on the mind, Preston looked across at the Russian twelve feet away as the saloon swerved slowly between the two cars that almost blocked the road.

From the side of his eye he saw the little saloon turn left into the A45, pause for a break in the traffic, and pull into the Ipswich-bound stream. Then he was up and running. The two drivers and two Watchers came back over the fence at his call. An amazed motorist who was just slowing down saw the body leap off the ground and help others to pull a crashed car back on to its four wheels, where it fell with a crunch.

Joe climbed behind the wheel of his own car and backed it out of the bank. Barney wiped mud and grass off its headlights before climbing in. Harry Burkinshaw took not one but three strong mints and popped the lot. Preston approached the motorcycle patrolman.

'You'd better get back to Thetford, and many, many thanks for all your help.'

To the sergeant on foot he said: 'I'm afraid I'll have to leave you here. Your uniform's too noticeable to come with us. But many thanks for your help.'

The two MI5 cars swept away towards the A45 and turned left to Ipswich. The uninvolved motorist who had seen it all asked the abandoned sergeant: 'Are they making a film for the telly?'

'I shouldn't be at all bloody surprised,' said the sergeant. 'By the way, sir, can you give me a lift into Ipswich?'

The industrial and commuter traffic into Ipswich was dense, and became thicker as they approached the town. It provided good cover for the two Watcher cars, who constantly shifted position so they could alternately keep the Ford hatchback in view.

They came into town past Whitton, but short of the town centre the small saloon up ahead took a right into Chevallier Street and round the ring to the Handford Bridge where it crossed the River Orwell. South of the river the quarry followed the Ranelagh Road and then took another right.

'He's heading out of town again,' said Joe, holding station five cars behind the quarry. They were entering Belstead Road, which leaves Ipswich heading south.

Quite suddenly the hatchback pulled to the left and entered a small private housing estate.

'Steady,' Preston warned Joe, 'he mustn't see us now.'

He told the second car to stay at the junction of the access road and Belstead, in case the quarry came round in a circle and back out again. Joe cruised slowly into the complex of seven culs-de-sac that make up The Hayes. They went past the entrance to Cherryhayes Close just in time to see the man they were tailing parked on the hardpad in front of a small house halfway up the close. The man was climbing out of his car. Preston ordered Joe to keep going until out of sight and stop.

'Harry, give me your hat and see if there's a Conservative rosette in the glove pocket.'

There was; left over from the two weeks when the team had used it to enter and leave the Royston house by the front door without arousing suspicion. Preston pinned it to his jacket, stripped off the raincoat he had worn by the roadside where he had first seen Petrofsky face to face, donned Harry's porkpie hat, and climbed out.

He walked into Cherryhayes Close and strolled up the side opposite the house of the Soviet agent. Directly facing number 12 was number 9. It had a Social Democratic party poster in the window. He walked to the front door and knocked.

It was opened by a pretty young woman. From inside Preston could hear a child's voice, then that of a man. It was eight o'clock; the family was at breakfast.

Preston raised his hat. 'Good morning, madam.'

Seeing his rosette, the woman said: 'Oh, I'm sorry, you're really wasting your time here. We vote SDP.'

'I perfectly understand, ma'am. But I have a piece of promotional literature which I would be most grateful if you would show to your husband.'

He handed her his plastic card, identifying him as an officer of MI5. She did not look at it, but sighed. 'Oh, very well. But I'm sure it won't change anything.'

She left him standing on the doorstep, withdrew into the house and seconds later Preston heard a whispered conversation from the kitchen in the back. A man came out and walked down the hall, holding the card. A young business executive in dark trousers, white shirt, club tie. No jacket; that would come when he left for work. He held Preston's card and was frowning. 'What on earth's this?' he asked.

'What it seems to be, sir. It's the identification card of an officer of MI5.'

'It's not a joke?'

'No, it's perfectly genuine.'

'I see. Well, what do you want?'

'Would you let me come in and close the door?'

The young man paused for a moment, then nodded. Preston doffed his hat again and stepped over the threshold. He closed the door behind him.

Across the street Valeri Petrofsky was in his sitting-room behind the opaque net curtains. He was tired, his muscles ached from the riding, and he helped himself to a whisky.

Glancing through the curtains he could see one of the seemingly endless political canvassers talking to the people at number 9. He had had three himself over the past ten days, and another wad of party literature had been on his doormat when he arrived. He watched the householder allow the man into his hallway. Another convert, he thought. Fat lot of good it will do them.

Preston sighed with relief. The young man watched him doubtfully. From behind, his wife stared from the kitchen door. The face of a small girl of about three appeared round the doorframe by her mother's knee.

'Are you really from MI5?' asked the man.

'Yes. We don't have two heads and green ears, you know.'

For the first time the younger man smiled. 'No. Of course not. It's just a surprise. But what do you want with us?'

'Nothing, of course,' grinned Preston. 'I don't even know who you are. My colleagues and I have tailed a man we believe to be a foreign agent, and he has gone into the house across the road. I would like to borrow your phone and perhaps allow a couple of men to observe the house from your upper bedroom window.'

'Number 12?' asked the man. 'Jim Ross? He's not a foreigner.'

'We think he may be. Could I use the phone?'

'Well, yes. I suppose so.' He turned towards his family. 'Come on, all back in the kitchen.'

Preston rang Charles Street and was put through to Sir Bernard Hemmings who was still in Cork. Burkinshaw had already used the police radio net to inform Cork in guarded language that the 'client' was at his home in Ipswich and that the 'taxis' were in the neighbourhood and on call.

'Preston?' said the Director-General down the line. 'John? Where are you exactly?'

'A small residential cul-de-sac called Cherryhayes Close in Ipswich,' said Preston. 'We've run Chummy to earth. I'm certain this time it's his base.'

'Do you think it's time we moved in?'

'Yes, sir. I do. I fear he may be armed. I think you know what I mean. I don't think it's one for the Special Branch or the local force.'

He told his DG what he wanted, then replaced the receiver and put in a private call to Sir Nigel in Sentinel House.

'Yes, John, I agree,' said 'C' when he had been given the same information. 'If he's got with him what we think, it had better be as you ask. The SAS.'

23

To call in the Special Air Service, Britain's élite and multi-role regiment of experts in deep penetration, observation and (occasionally) urban assault, is not as easy as the more adventurous television dramas might suggest.

The SAS never operates on its own initiative. Under the constitution it can, like any part of the armed forces, only operate inside the United Kingdom in support of the civil authority, that is, the police. Thus ostensibly the local police remain in overall command of the operation. In reality, once the SAS men have been given the 'go' order, the local police are well advised to step smartly backwards.

Under the law, it is the Chief Constable of a county in which an emergency has arisen, that the local police are deemed not to be able to handle unassisted, who must make a formal request to the Home Office for the SAS to be brought in. It may be the Chief Constable is 'advised' to make the request, and he would be a bold man to refuse to do so if the advice came from high enough.

When the Chief Constable has made his formal request to the Permanent Under-Secretary at the Home Office, the latter will pass the request to his opposite number in Defence, who in turn will apprise the Director of Military Operations of the request, and the DMO will alert the SAS at their Hereford base camp.

That the procedure can work within minutes is due in part to the fact that it has been rehearsed and honed to a fine art over and over again; and partly to the fact that the British establishment, when required to move fast, contains enough interpersonal relationships to permit a great deal of procedure to be kept at verbal level, with the inevitable paperwork left to catch up later. British bureaucracy may appear slow and cumbersome to the

British, but it is greased lightning compared with its European and American counterparts.

Most British Chief Constables have in any case been to Hereford to meet the unit known simply as 'the Regiment' and to be shown exactly what kinds of assistance could be put at their disposal if requested. Few have emerged unimpressed.

That morning the Chief Constable of Suffolk was told from London of the crisis that had been visited on him in the form of a suspected foreign agent, believed to be armed and perhaps with a bomb, holed up in Cherryhayes Close, Ipswich. He contacted Sir Hubert Villiers in Whitehall, where his call was expected. Sir Hubert briefed his Minister and his colleague, the Cabinet Secretary, who informed the Prime Minister. Downing Street's assent having been obtained, Sir Hubert passed the by now politically cleared request to Sir Peregrine Jones at Defence, who knew it all anyway because he had had a chat with Sir Martin Flannery. Within sixty minutes of the first contact between the Home Office and the head of the Suffolk Constabulary, the Director of Military Operations was talking on a scrambled line to the commanding officer of the SAS at Hereford.

The fighting arm of the SAS is based on a module of four. Four men make up a patrol, four patrols a troop and four troops a squadron. They rotate through the various SAS commitments: Northern Ireland, the Middle East, Jungle Training and Special Projects, apart from the continuing NATO tasks and the maintenance of one squadron on stand-by at Hereford.

The commitments tend to last from six to nine months, and that month it was 'B' Squadron that was based at Hereford. As usual there was one troop on half-hour standby and another on two-hour readiness. The four troops in each squadron are always the Air Troop (free-fallers), Boat Troop (marine trained in canoes and subaqua expertise), Mountain Troop (climbers) and Mobile Troop (armed Land Rovers).

When Brigadier Jeremy Cripps finished his call from London it was to Seven Troop, the free-fall parachute men of 'B' Squadron, that the task fell of going to Ipswich.

'What is your normal routine at this hour?' asked Preston of the householder, whose name was Mr Adrian. The young executive had just finished a conversation with the Assistant Chief Constable (Crime) down at his office in Ipswich police headquarters on the corner of Civic Drive and Elm Street. If there had been any lingering doubt in Mr Adrian's mind as to the authenticity of his unexpected guest of half an hour earlier, it had been dispelled. Preston had suggested Adrian make the call himself, and he was rightly convinced the Suffolk police was backing the MI5 officer in his sitting-room.

He had also been told the man across the street might be armed and dangerous, and that an arrest would have to be made later in the day.

'Well, I drive to work at about quarter to nine, that's in ten minutes. About ten my wife Lucinda takes Samantha to playschool. She usually does her shopping, picks up Samantha at midday and returns home. On foot. I get back from work around six thirty, by car of course.'

'I'd like you to take a day off work,' said Preston. 'Ring your office now and say you are not well. But leave the house at the usual time. You will be met at the top of the road, where Belstead Road joins the access to The Hayes, by a police car.'

'What about my wife and child?'

'I'd like Mrs Adrian to wait here until the usual hour, then leave with Samantha and shopping basket, walk up there and join you. Is there anywhere you can go for the day?'

'There's my mother at Felixstowe,' said Mrs Adrian nervously.

'Could you spend the day with her? Perhaps even tonight?'

'What about our house?'

'I assure you, Mr Adrian, nothing will happen to it,' said Preston optimistically. He might have added it would either be unharmed, or vaporized if things went wrong. 'I must ask you to let me and my colleagues use it as an observation post for the man across the way. We will come and go via the back. We will do absolutely no damage.'

'What do you think, darling?' Mr Adrian asked his wife.

She nodded. 'I just want to get Samantha out of here,' she said.

'In one hour, I promise you,' said Preston. 'Mr Ross across there has been up all night because we have been tailing him. He's probably asleep and in any case no police move against the house will take place before the afternoon, maybe the early evening.'

'All right,' said Adrian, 'we'll do it.'

He made his call to the office to excuse himself for the day, and drove off at fifteen minutes to nine o'clock. From his upper bedroom window Valeri Petrofsky saw him go. The Russian was preparing to catch a few hours' sleep. There was nothing unusual going on in the road. Adrian always left for work at this hour.

Preston noted there was waste ground behind number 9. He called up Harry Burkinshaw and Barney who came in through the back, nodded to an embarrassed Mrs Adrian and went up to the front bedroom to adopt again their profession in life – watching. Ginger had found a patch of high ground a quarter of a mile away from which he could see both the estuary of the Orwell and the docks by its side, and the small housing estate spread out below. With glasses he could monitor the rear of number 12 Cherryhayes Close.

'It backs on to the rear garden of another house in Brackenhayes,' he told Preston on his radio. 'No sign of movement in house or garden. All windows closed; that's odd in this weather.'

'Keep watching,' said Preston. 'I'll be here. If I have to go, Harry will take over.'

An hour later Mrs Adrian and her child walked calmly out of the house and away.

In the town itself another operation was moving up through the gears. The Chief Constable, who had risen through the uniformed branch, had handed the details of the pending operation to the ACC (Crime), Chief Superintendent Peter Low.

Low had two detectives at the Town Hall, who elicited from the rating department that the target house was owned by a certain Mr Johnson but that rating bills were to be sent to Oxborrow's, the estate agents. A call to the agents explained that Mr Johnson was away in Saudi Arabia and the house was let to a Mr James Duncan Ross. A second picture of Ross, alias Timothy Donnelly of the streets of Damascus, was telexed up to Ipswich and shown to Oxborrow's, who identified the tenant.

The Town Hall housing department also came up with the architects who had designed the estate called The Hayes, and from this partnership detailed floor plans were obtained for the property called number 12. They were even more helpful; other houses, identical in design to the last detail, had been built elsewhere in Ipswich, and one was found to be still standing empty. It would be useful for the SAS assault team; they would know the exact geography of the house when they went in.

The other part of Peter Low's duties was to find a 'holding area' for the SAS men when they arrived. A holding area has to be private, covered and quickly available, with access for vehicles and telephone communication. An empty warehouse down on Eagle Wharf was traced and the owner agreed to let the police borrow it for 'a training exercise'.

It had big sliding doors which could open to admit the vehicle convoy and close to keep out prying eyes, a floor area ample enough to construct a replica of the house in The Hayes out of lumber and sacking screen walls, and a small glass-sided office to use as an ops room.

Just before noon an army Scout helicopter swished into the far side of Ipswich municipal airport and disgorged three men. One was the CO of the SAS Regiment, Brigadier Cripps, one was the ops officer, a staff major with the Regiment, and the third was the team commander, Captain Julian Lyndhurst. They were all in plain clothes, carried grips with their uniforms inside, and were met by an unmarked police car which took them straight to the holding area, where the police were establishing their operational centre.

Chief Superintendent Low briefed the three officers to the limit of his ability, which was to the limit of what he had been told by London. He had talked on the telephone to John Preston, but not yet met him.

'There's a John Preston, I understand,' said Brigadier Cripps, 'who is the field controller from MI5. Is he about?'

'I believe he's still up at the observation post,' said Low, 'the house he has taken over opposite the target dwelling. I can call him and ask him to leave by the back and come to join us.'

'I wonder, sir,' said Captain Lyndhurst to his CO, 'whether I might not go up there right away. Give me a chance to have a first look at the "stronghold" and I could come back with this Preston chap.'

'All right, since a car has to go up anyway,' said the CO.

The police pointed out the rear door of number 9 to the captain fifteen minutes later up on the hillside across the estuary from Eagle Wharf. Still in civilian clothes, the twenty-nine-year-old captain walked across the rough ground, hopped over the garden fence and in through the back door. He met Barney in the kitchen where he was brewing a cup of tea on Mrs Adrian's stove.

'Lyndhurst,' said the officer, 'from the Regiment. Is Mr Preston here?'

'John,' Barney called up the stairs in a hoarse whisper, as the house was supposed to be empty, 'brown job here to see you.'

Lyndhurst mounted to the front bedroom where he

found John Preston and introduced himself. Harry Burkinshaw muttered something about a cup of tea and left. The captain stared across the road at number 12.

'There still seem to be some gaps in our information,' drawled Lyndhurst. 'Who exactly do you think is in there?'

'I believe it's a Soviet agent,' said Preston, 'an illegal, living here under the cover of James Duncan Ross. Mid-thirties, medium height and build, probably very fit, a top pro.'

He handed Lyndhurst the photograph taken on the Damascus street. The captain studied it with interest. 'Anyone else in there?'

'Possibly. We don't know. Ross himself certainly. He might have a helper. We can't talk to the neighbours. In this kind of area we could never stop them gawping. The people who live here said before they left they were sure he was living alone. But we can't prove that.'

'And according to our briefing, you think he's armed, maybe dangerous. Bit too much for the local lads, even with handguns, mmmm?'

'Yes, we believe he has a bomb in there with him. He would have to be stopped before he can get to it.'

'Bomb, eh?' said Lyndhurst with apparent lack of interest. He had done two tours in Northern Ireland. 'Big enough to make a mess of the house, or the entire street?'

'A bit bigger than that,' said Preston. 'If we're right, it's a small nuke.'

The tall officer turned his entire gaze from the house across the street and his pale blue eyes held Preston's. 'Bloody hell,' he said, 'I'm impressed.'

'Well, that's a plus,' said Preston, 'By the way, I want him, and I want him alive.'

'Let's go back to the docks and talk to the CO,' said Lyndhurst.

While Lyndhurst had been at Cherryhayes Close, two other helicopters had arrived at the airport from Hereford, a Puma and a Chinook. The first bore the assault team, the second their numerous and arcane pieces of equipment.

The team was under the temporary leadership of the Deputy Team Commander, a veteran staff sergeant called Steve Bilbow. He was short, dark and wiry, tough as old boot leather, with bright black-button eyes and a ready grin. Like all the senior NCOs in the Regiment, he had been with them a long time, in his case fifteen years.

The SAS is unusual in this sense also: the officers are almost all on temporary attachment from their 'parent' regiments, staying usually two to three years before returning to their parent units. Only the other ranks stay with the SAS, and not all of them, just the best. Even the Commanding Officer, though he will probably have served with the Regiment before in his career, serves a short term as CO. Very few officers are long-stay men, and they are all in Logistics/Supply/Technical posts in SAS Group HQ.

Steve Bilbow had entered as a trooper from the Parachute Regiment, done his tour, been selected on merit for extension of attachment and had risen to staff sergeant. He had done two fighting tours in Dhofar, sweated through the jungles of Belize, frozen through the countless nights in ambush in South Armagh and relaxed in the Cameron Highlands of Malaya. He had helped train the West German GSG-9 teams and worked with Charlie Beckwith's Delta group in America.

In his time he had known the boredom of the endless repetitiveness of the training that brought the men of the SAS to the ultimate peak of fitness and preparation, and the high-adrenaline operations: racing under rebel fire for the shelter of a sangar in the hills of Oman, running a covert snatch squad against Republican gunmen in East Belfast, and doing five hundred parachute jumps, most of them HALO jobs – high altitude, low opening.

To his chagrin, he had been one of the stand-by team when colleagues stormed the Iranian Embassy in London in 1980 and he had not been called on.

The rest of the team comprised one photographer, three intelligence collators, eight snipers and nine assaulters. Steve hoped and prayed he would lead the assault team. Several unmarked police vans had met them at the airport and brought them to the holding area. When Preston and Lyndhurst arrived back at the warehouse the team had arrived and were spreading their gear over the floor before the bemused gaze of several Ipswich policemen.

'Hello, Steve,' said Captain Lyndhurst. 'Everything OK?'

'Hello, boss. Yes, fine. Just getting sorted.'

'I've seen the stronghold. It's a small private house. One occupant known, maybe two. And a bomb. It'll be a small assault, no room for more. I'd like you first in.'

'Try and stop me, boss,' Bilbow grinned.

The accent in the SAS is on self-discipline rather than the externally applied kind. Any man who cannot produce the self-discipline needed to go through what the SAS men must do will not be there for long anyway. Those who can do not need rigid formality in personal relationships, such as are proper in a line regiment.

Thus officers habitually address those they command, apart from each other, by first names. Other ranks tend to address their commissioned officers as 'boss', although the CO gets a 'sir'. Between each other, SAS troopers refer to an officer as 'a Rupert'.

Staff Sergeant Bilbow caught sight of Preston, and his face lit up in a delighted grin. 'Major Preston . . . Good heavens, it's been a long time.'

Preston stuck out a hand and smiled back.

The last time he had seen Steve Bilbow was when, in the aftermath of the shootout in the Bogside, he had taken refuge in a safe house where four SAS men under Bilbow's command had been running a covert snatch squad. Apart from that, they were both ex-paras, which always forms a bond.

'I'm with "Five" now,' said Preston, 'field controller for this op, at least from "Five's" end.'

'What have you got for us?' asked Steve.

'Russian. KGB agent. Top pro. Probably done the *spetsnaz* course, so he'll be good, fast and probably armed.'

'Lovely. *Spetsnaz*, eh? We'll see how good they really are.'

All three present knew of the *spetsnaz* troops, the crack Russian élite saboteurs, Soviet equivalent of the SAS.

'Sorry to break up the party, but let's get the briefing under way,' said Lyndhurst.

He and Preston mounted the stairs to the upper office where they met Brigadier Cripps, the ops major, the ACC (Crime) Chief Superintendent Low and the SAS intelligence collators. Preston spent an hour giving as thorough a briefing as he could, and the atmosphere grew extremely grave.

'Have you any proof there's a nuclear device in there?' asked the ACC at length.

'No sir. We intercepted a component in Glasgow destined for delivery to someone working under cover in this country. The backroom boys say it could have no other use in this world. We know the man in that house is a Soviet illegal – he was made on the streets of Damascus by the Mossad. His association with the secret transmitter in Chesterfield confirms what he is. So I am left with deductions.

'Unless the component taken in Glasgow was for the construction of a small device inside Britain, then what the hell was it for? On that, I come up with no other feasible explanation. As to Ross, unless there are two major covert operations being mounted in Britain by the KGB, that component was destined for him. QED.'

'Yes,' said Brigadier Cripps, 'I think we have to go with it. We have to assume it's there. If it's not, we'll have to talk to friend Ross rather earnestly.'

Chief Superintendent Low was having a private nightmare. He had to accept there was no other way but storming the house; what he was trying to envisage was the state of Ipswich if the device went off.

'Couldn't we evacuate?' he asked with little hope.

'He'd notice,' said Preston flatly. 'I think if he knows he's ruined, he'll take us all with him.'

The soldiers nodded. They knew that, deep inside Soviet Russia, they would have to do the same.

The lunch hour was gone and no-one had noticed. Food would have been superfluous. The afternoon was spent in reconnaissance and preparation.

Steve Bilbow went back to the airport with the photographer and a policeman. The three took the Scout in one single run down the estuary of the Orwell, well away from the estate known as The Hayes, but on a track from which they could keep it in vision. The policeman pointed out the house; the photographer ran off fifty stills while Steve took a long pan shot on video for screening in the holding area.

The entire assualt team, still in civilian clothes, went with the police to see the replica house built by the same architects to the same plans. By the time they got back to the holding area, they could see the stronghold on video and in close-up still pictures.

They spent the rest of the afternoon inside the warehouse, practising with the replica that the policemen had helped build under SAS supervision on the floor. It was only timber beams and sacking, but its dimensions were perfect and showed up one overriding factor: space inside the house was very limited. A narrow front door, narrow hall, cramped stairway and small rooms.

Captain Lyndhurst decided to use only six assaulters, to the eternal grief of the four who were left out. There would also be three snipers; two in the Adrians' upper front bedroom and one on the hill overlooking the back garden.

The back of number 12 Cherryhayes Close would be covered by two of Lyndhurst's six assaulters. They would be in full gear but their combat suits would be covered by civilian mackintoshes. They would be driven in an unmarked police car to Brackenhayes Close. Here they would disembark and, without asking permission of the householder, would walk through the front garden of the house backing on to the stronghold, down the side passage between house and garage and into the back garden.

Here they would strip off the raincoats, hop over the garden fence and take up position in the back garden of the stronghold.

'There may be a trip wire of fishing line across the garden,' warned Lyndhurst. 'But probably close to the rear of the house itself. Stand well back. On the signal, I want one stun grenade straight through the window of the rear bedroom and another through the kitchen window. Then unclip the HK's and hold position. Do not fire into the house; Steve and the lads will be coming up front.'

The 'rear-access' men nodded. Captain Lyndhurst knew that he would not be in the assault. Formerly a lieutenant in the Queen's Dragoon Guards, he was on his first tour with the SAS and had captain's rank because the SAS have no officers under that rank. He would revert to lieutenant on return to his parent regiment in a year, though he hoped to come back to the SAS later as a squadron commander.

He also knew the tradition of the SAS, which is at variance with the convention for the rest of the Army: officers participate in combat in desert or jungle but never in an urban environment. Only NCOs and troopers carry out assaults.

The main attack, Lyndhurst had agreed with his CO and the ops officer, would be via the front. A van would draw up quietly and four assaulters would step out. Two would take the front door: one with the Wingmaster, the other with the 7-pound sledgehammer and/or bolt cutters if necessary.

The instant the door came down, the assault front rank would go in, Steve Bilbow and a corporal. The door squad would drop their Wingmaster and hammer, rip their HKs off their chests and enter the hallway as backup to the first pair.

On entering the hallway, Steve would step straight past the stairs to the door of the sitting-room on his left. The corporal would race up the stairs to take the front bedroom. Of the backup men (ex-door squad), one would follow the corporal up the stairs in case Chummy was in the bathroom, the other would follow Steve into the sitting-room.

The signal for the two men in the back garden to hurl their stun grenades into the two rear rooms, kitchen and back bedroom, would be the crash of the Wingmaster at the front. By the time entry had been made, therefore, anyone in the kitchen or back bedroom should be reeling around wondering what had hit him.

Preston, who had volunteered to return to the observation post, was allowed to listen to the details of the assault.

He already knew that the SAS was the only regiment in the British Army allowed to choose its weaponry from a worldwide menu. For close assault they had chosen the German Heckler and Koch short-barrelled 9-millimetre rapid-fire sub-machine gun, light, easy to handle and very reliable, with an up-and-over folding stock.

The HK they habitually wore slantwise across the chest, held in place by two springclips, loaded and cocked. This left their arms free for door-opening, entering through windows or throwing stun grenades. Once that was done, a single jerk brought the HK off the chest and into operation in less than half a second.

For the taking of doors, practice had shown it was faster to blast off both hinges rather than take the lock. For this they favoured the Remington Wingmaster pump-action repeater shotgun, but with solid heads in the cartridges rather than buckshot.

Apart from these playthings, one of the door squad would need a hammer and bolt cutters in case the door, having lost its hinges, was held at the other side by several bolts and a chain. They also carried stun grenades, designed to blind temporarily by their flash and deafen by their crack, but not to kill. Lastly, each man would have his thirteen-shot 9-millimetre Browning automatic on his hip.

In the assault, Lyndhurst stressed, timing was of the essence. For the hour of the attack he had chosen 9.45 p.m., when dusk would be deep in the Close and therefore confusing, but not yet darkest night.

He himself would be in the Adrians' house across the road, watching the target house and in contact with the approaching van bearing his assaulters by radio. If there was any pedestrian moving down the Close at 9.44 he could tell the van driver to hold until they had cleared the door of the stronghold to be assaulted. Thus he could monitor the approach of the team. The police car bringing the two rear-garden men to position would also be on that wavelength, and would drop those two men ninety seconds before the front door came down.

He had one last refinement. As the van cruised up the Close, he would ring Ross from the Adrians' phone across the road. He already knew the telephone in all these houses was on a small table in the hallway. The ploy was to distance the Soviet agent from his bomb, wherever it was, and to give the assaulters the chance of a fast shot.

Firing as usual would be the formula of two fast bursts of two shots each. Although the HK can empty its thirty-round magazine in a couple of seconds, the SAS are accurate enough even in the confused conditions of a terrorist-hostage situation to limit their firing to two-shot bursts, with one repeat. Anyone stopping those four rounds will speedily feel very unwell. Such economy also keeps the hostage alive.

Immediately after the operation the police would move into the Close in strength to calm down the inevitable crowd that would come pouring out of the adjacent houses. A police cordon would be thrown right round the front of the house, while the assaulters left through the rear to cross the gardens and board their van, by then waiting in Brackenhayes Close. As for the interior of the stronghold, the civil authority would take over there as well. A team of six from Aldermaston was due in Ipswich that evening by teatime.

At six Preston left the holding area and returned to the observation post, the Adrians' house, which he entered by the rear unobserved.

'Lights have just come on,' said Harry Burkinshaw, when Preston joined him in the front bedroom. Preston could see the sitting-room curtains of the house opposite were drawn, but there was a glow behind them and a reflected glow through the panels of the front door.

'I think I saw movement behind the net curtains in the upstairs bedroom just after you left,' said Barney. 'But he didn't put the light on; well, he wouldn't. It was just after lunch. Anyway, he hasn't come out.'

Preston called up Ginger on his hillside, but the story was the same. No movement at the back either.

'It'll start getting dusk in a couple of hours,' Ginger told him over the radio. 'Vision will deteriorate after that.'

Valeri Petrofsky had slept fitfully and not well. Just before one o'clock he awoke fully, propped himself up and stared across his bedroom, through the net curtains at the house across the way. After ten minutes he hauled himself off the bed, went to the bathroom and showered.

He made a snack lunch in the kitchen at two and ate it at the kitchen table, occasionally glancing into the back garden where a fine and invisible fishing line ran across the garden from side to side, round a small pulley attached by night to the garden fence and his back door. It was fixed round the bottom of a column of empty tin cans. He slackened the tension when he was out of the house and tightened it when he was at home. No-one had yet brought the tins clattering down.

The afternoon wore on. Not unnaturally, considering

what sat, armed and primed, in his sitting-room, he was tense, all his senses at full alert. He tried to read, but could not concentrate. Moscow must have had his message for twelve hours by now. He listened to some radio music, then at six settled in the sitting-room. Although he could see the bright summer evening on the faces of the houses opposite, his own house faced east so it was now in shadow. The dark would deepen in his sitting-room from now on. He drew the curtains as ever before putting on the reading lamps, then, for want of anything better to do, switched on the television. As usual it was dominated by the election campaign.

In the holding area warehouse the tension was mounting. Last preparations were being made to the assaulters' van, a plain grey Volkswagen with sliding side door. Two unused assaulters in plain clothes would be in the front, one driving and the other on the radio to Captain Lyndhurst. They checked those radios over and over again, as with every other piece of equipment.

The van would be led to the entrance to The Hayes by a plain police car; the driver of the van had memorized the layout of The Hayes and knew where to find Cherryhayes Close. As they entered The Hayes, they would come under radio control of the captain in his window seat. The rear of the van had been lined with polystyrene foam sheeting to prevent the clink of metal on metal.

The assault team was dressing and 'tooling up'. Each man, over his underwear, pulled on the standard one-piece black boiler suit of fire-resistant fabric. At the last moment this would be complemented by a treated black fabric Balaclava hood. After that came the body armour, lightweight knitted Kevlar by Bristol Armour, designed to absorb a bullet's impact by spreading it outwards and sideways from the point of penetration. Behind the Kevlar the men stuffed the ceramic 'trauma pads' to complete the job of blunting the onrushing projectile even further.

Over all this went the harness to hold the assault

weapon, the HK, and the grenades and handgun. On their feet they wore the traditional desert boots, ankle high with thick rubber soles, known as 'boots des.' and whose colour can only be described as 'dirty'.

Captain Lyndhurst had a last word with each man and the longest with his number two, Steve Bilbow. There was, of course, no mention of good luck; anything else, but never 'Good luck'. Then the commander left for the observation post.

He entered the Adrians' house just after eight. Preston could feel the tension emanating from the man. At 8.30 the phone rang. Barney was in the hall so he took it. There had been several that day. Preston had decided it would be fruitless not to answer; someone might come round to the house. Each time the caller had been told the Adrians were at her mother's for the day and that the speaker was one of the team of painters redoing the sitting-room. No caller had refused to accept this explanation. When Barney lifted the receiver Captain Lyndhurst was coming out of the kitchen with a cup of tea.

'It's for you,' he said and went back upstairs.

From nine onwards the tension rose steadily. Lyndhurst spent much time on the radio to the holding area, from which at 9.15 the grey van and its police car shepherd left for The Hayes. At 9.33 the two vehicles had reached the access on Belstead Road, two hundred yards from the target. They had to pause and wait. At 9.41 Mr Armitage came out to leave four bottles for the milkman. Infuriatingly, he paused to inspect in the gathering gloom his stone bowl of flowers in the centre of his front lawn. Then he greeted a neighbour across the road.

'Go back in, you old fool,' whispered Lyndhurst, standing in the sitting-room and gazing across the road at the lights behind the curtains of the stronghold. At 9.42 the plain police car with the two rear-garden men was in position in Brackenhayes and waiting. Ten seconds later Mr Armitage called good night to his neighbour and went back inside.

At 9.43 the grey van entered the close called Gorsehayes, the access road to the whole complex. Standing in the hall by the telephone, Preston could hear the chitchat between the van driver and Lyndhurst. The van was cruising slowly and quietly towards the entrance to Cherryhayes.

There was still no pedestrian on the road. Lyndhurst ordered the two rear-garden men to quit their police car and start moving.

'Entering Cherryhayes fifteen seconds,' muttered the van's co-driver.

'Slow down, thirty seconds to go,' replied Lyndhurst. Twenty seconds later he said, 'Enter the Close now.'

Round the corner came the van, quite slowly, on side lights. 'Eight seconds,' murmured Lyndhurst into the receiver, then a savage whisper to Preston: 'Dial now.'

The van cruised up the Close, passed the door of number 12 and stopped in front of Mr Armitage's bowl of flowers. It was deliberate; the assaulters wanted to approach the stronghold slantwise. The oiled side door slid back and into the gloom four men in black stepped in complete silence. There was no running, no pounding of feet or hoarse cries. In rehearsed order they walked calmly across Mr Armitage's lawn, round the parked hatchback of Mr Ross and up to the front door of number 12. The man with the Wingmaster knew which side the hinges would be. Before he had finished walking his gun was at the shoulder. He made out the hinge positions and took careful aim. Beside him another figure waited with a sledgehammer swung back. Behind them were Steve and the corporal, HK's ready . . .

In his sitting-room Major Valeri Petrofsky was unquiet. He could not concentrate on the television; his senses picked up too much – the clatter of a man putting out milk bottles, the miaow of a cat, the snarl of a motorcycle engine far away, the hoot of a freighter entering the estuary of the Orwell across the valley.

Nine-thirty had produced another current affairs programme with yet more interviews with ministers and hopeful ministers-to-be. In exasperation he flicked over to BBC 2, only to find a documentary about birds. He sighed. It was better than politics.

It had hardly been on ten minutes when he heard Armitage next door putting out his empty milk bottles. Always the same number and always the same time of night, he thought. Then the old fool was calling to someone across the street. Something on the television caught his eye and he stared in amazement. The interviewer was talking to a lanky man in a flat cap about his passion, which appeared to be pigeons. He was holding one up in front of the camera, a sleek creature with a distinctive cast to its beak and head.

Petrofsky sat bolt upright, concentrating on the bird with almost all of his attention, listening to the interview with the rest. He was sure the bird was identical to one he had seen somewhere before.

'Is this lovely bird for showing in competition?' the girl interviewer was asking. She was new, a bit too bright, trying to squeeze more from the interview than it merited.

'Good Lord, no,' said the flat-cap man. 'This isn't a fancy. It's a Westcott.'

In a bright flash of recall, Petrofsky saw again the room in the guest suite at the General Secretary's dacha at Usovo. 'Found him in the street last winter . . .' the wizened old Englishman had said, and the bird had gazed out of its cage with bright clever eyes.

'Well, it's not the sort we would see about the town . . .' suggested the girl on the television. She was floundering. At that moment the telephone in Petrofsky's hallway rang . . .

Normally he would have gone to answer it, in case it was a neighbour. To pretend to be out would have been suspicious, with the house lights on. And he would not have taken his handgun to the hall. But he stayed and stared at the screen. The phone rang on, insistently. With the television, it drowned the soft pad of rubber-soled feet on the pavement.

'I should hope not,' replied the flat-cap man cheerfully. 'A Westcott ain't a "streetie" neither. It's probably one of the finest strains of racer there is. This little beauty will always speed back to the loft where it was raised. That's why they're more commonly known as homers.'

Petrofsky came out of his chair with a snarl of rage. The big, precision-made Sako target pistol that he had kept close to him since he had entered Britain came up with him from its place down the side of the seat cushion. He uttered one short word in Russian. No-one heard him, but the word was 'traitor'.

At that moment there was a roar, then another, so close together they were almost one. With them came the shatter of glass from his front door, two huge bangs from the rear of the house, and the thud of feet in the hall. Petrofsky spun towards the sitting-room door and fired three times. His Sako Triace, made to take three interchangeable barrels, had the heaviest calibre of the three fitted. It also packed five rounds in its magazine. He kept to three; he might need the other two for himself. But the three he fired slammed through the flimsy woodwork of the closed door into the hall beyond . . .

The citizens of Cherryhayes Close will describe that night for the rest of their lives, but none will ever get it quite right.

The roar of the Wingmaster catapulted them all out of their chairs as it tore the twin hinges off the door. The moment he had fired, the gunman stepped sideways and back to give room to his mate. One swing of the sledge and the lock, bolt and chain at the other side flew in all directions. Then he too stepped sideways and back. Both men dropped their weapons and flicked their HKs forward and out.

Steve and the corporal had already gone through the gap. The corporal took three bounds to get up the stairs, the sledgehammer man on his heels. Steve ran past the ringing telephone, reached the sitting-room, turned to face it and was lifted off his feet. The three slugs that ripped across the hallway hit him with an audible 'whap' and blew him against the stairs. The Wingmaster man simply leaned across the still closed door and fired two two-round bursts. Then he kicked the door open and went in on the roll, coming to his feet at the crouch well inside the room.

When the shotgun fired, Captain Lyndhurst opened the front door across the road and watched, Preston behind him. In the lighted hallway the captain saw his deputy team commander approach the sitting-room door, only to be thrown aside like a rag doll. Lyndhurst started to walk forward, Preston behind him.

As the trooper who had fired the two bursts came to his feet and surveyed the inert figure on the carpet, Captain Lyndhurst appeared in the doorway. He took in the scene at a glance, despite the drifting plume of cordite smoke.

'Go and help Steve in the hall,' he said crisply. The trooper did not argue. The man on the floor began to move. Lyndhurst drew his Browning from beneath his jacket.

The trooper had been good. Petrofsky had taken one slug in the left knee, one in the lower stomach and one in the right shoulder. His pistol had been flung across the room. Despite the distortion caused by the woodwork, the trooper had connected with three out of the four slugs. Petrofsky was in hideous pain, but he was alive. He began to crawl. Twelve feet away he could see the grey steel, the flat box on its side, the two buttons, one yellow and one red. Captain Lyndhurst took careful aim and fired once.

John Preston ran past him so fast he jostled the officer's hip as he ran. He went on his knees beside the body on the floor. It was on its side, half the back of the head blown away, the mouth still working like a fish on a slab. Preston bent his head to the dying face. Lyndhurst still had his gun at the aim, but the MI5 man was between him and the Russian. He stepped to one side to get a clearer shot, then lowered the Browning.

Preston was rising. There was no need for a second shot.

'We'd better get the wallahs from Aldermaston to have a look at *that*,' said Lyndhurst, gesturing at the steel cabinet in the corner.

'I wanted him alive,' said Preston.

'Sorry, old boy. Couldn't be done,' said the captain.

At that moment both men jumped at the sound of a loud click, and a voice speaking to them from the sideboard. They saw the sound came from a large radio set, which had switched itself on with a timer device. The voice said: 'Good evening. This is Radio Moscow, the English-language service, and here is the ten o'clock news.

'In Terry . . . I'm sorry, I'll say that again. In Teheran today the government stated . . .'

Captain Lyndhurst stepped over and switched the machine off. The man on the floor stared at the moquette carpet with sightless eyes, immune to the coded message meant for him alone.

24

The lunch invitation was for one o'clock on Friday, 19 June, at Brooks's Club in St James's. Preston entered the portals at that hour but even before he could announce himself to the club porter in the booth to his right, Sir Nigel was striding down the marbled hall to meet him.

'My dear John, how kind of you to come.'

They adjourned to the bar for a pre-lunch drink, where the conversation was informal. Preston was able to tell the Chief that he had just returned from Hereford where he had visited Steve Bilbow in hospital. The staff sergeant had had a lucky escape. Only when the flattened slugs from the Russian's gun were removed from his body armour did one of the doctors notice a sticky smear and have it analysed. The cyanide compound had failed to enter the bloodstream; the SAS man had been saved by the trauma pads. Otherwise he was heavily bruised, slightly dented but in good shape.

'Excellent,' said Sir Nigel with genuine enthusiasm, 'one does so hate to lose a good man.'

For the rest, most of the bar was discussing the election result and many of those present had been up half the night waiting for the last results in the close-fought contest to come in from the provinces.

At half past the hour they went in to lunch. Sir Nigel had a corner table where they could talk in privacy. On the way in they passed the Cabinet Secretary, Sir Martin Flannery, coming the other way. Although they all knew each other, Sir Martin saw at once that his colleague was 'in conference'. The mandarins acknowledged each other's presence with an imperceptible inclination of the head, sufficient for two scholars of Oxford. Backslapping is best left to foreigners.

'I really asked you here, John,' said 'C' as he spread his linen napkin over his knees, 'to offer you my thanks and my congratulations. A remarkable operation and an excellent result. I suggest the rack of lamb, quite delicious at this time of year.'

'As to the congratulations, sir, I fear I can hardly accept them,' said Preston quietly.

Sir Nigel studied the menu through his halfmoon glasses. 'Indeed? Are you being admirably modest or not so admirably discourteous? Ah! Beans, carrots and perhaps a roast potato, my dear.'

'Simply realistic, I hope,' said Preston when the waitress departed. 'Might we discuss the man we knew as Franz Winkler?'

'Whom you so brilliantly tailed to Chesterfield.'

'Permit me to be frank, Sir Nigel. Winkler could not have shaken off a headache with a box of aspirins. He was an incompetent and a fool.'

'I believe he almost lost you all at Chesterfield railway station.'

'A fluke,' said Preston. 'With a bigger Watcher operation, we'd have had men at each stop along the line. The point is, his manoeuvres were clumsy; they told us he was a pro, and a bad one at that, yet failed to shake us.'

'I see. What else about Winkler? Ah, the lamb, and cooked to perfection.'

They waited until they were served and the waitress was gone. Preston picked at his food, troubled. Sir Nigel ate with enjoyment.

'Franz Winkler came into Heathrow with a genuine Austrian passport containing a valid British visa.'

'So he did, to be sure.'

'And we both know, as did the Immigration officer, that Austrian citizens do not need a visa to enter Britain. Any consular officer of ours in Vienna would have told Winkler that. It was the visa that prompted the passport control officer at Heathrow to run the passport number through the computer. And it turned out to be false.'

'We all make mistakes,' murmured Sir Nigel.

'The KGB does not make that kind of mistake, sir. Their documentation is accurate to the point of brilliant.'

'Don't overestimate them, John. All large organizations occasionally make a balls-up. More carrots? No? Then, if I may . . .'

'The point is, sir, there were two flaws in that passport. The reason the number of it caused red lights to flick on was that three years ago another supposed Austrian bearing a passport with the same number was arrested in California by the FBI and is now serving time in Soledad.'

'Really? Good Lord, not very clever of the Soviets after all.'

'I called up the FBI man here in London and asked what the charge had been. It appears the other agent was trying to blackmail an executive of the Intel Corporation in Silicon Valley into selling him secrets of technology.'

'Very naughty.'

'Nuclear technology.'

'Which gave you the impression . . . ?'

'That Franz Winkler came into this country lit up like a neon sign. And the sign was a message – a message on two legs.'

Sir Nigel's face was still wreathed in good humour, but some of the twinkle had faded from his eyes. 'And what did this remarkable message say, John?'

'I think it said: I cannot give you the executive illegal agent because I do not know where he is. But follow this man; he will lead you to the transmitter. And he did. So I staked out the transmitter and the agent came to it at last.'

'What exactly are you trying to say?' Sir Nigel replaced his knife and fork on the empty plate and dabbed his mouth with his napkin.

'I believe, sir, that the operation was blown. It seems to me unavoidable to conclude that someone on the other side deliberately blew it away.'

'What an extraordinary suggestion. Let me recommend the strawberry flan. Had some last week. Different batch, of course: Yes? Two, my dear, if you please. Yes, a little fresh cream.'

'May I ask a question?' said Preston when the plates had been cleared.

'I'm sure you will anyway,' smiled Sir Nigel.

'Why did the Russian have to die?'

'As I understand, he was crawling towards a nuclear bomb with every apparent intention of detonating it.'

'I was there,' said Preston as the strawberry flan arrived. They waited until the cream had been poured. 'The man was wounded in the thigh, stomach and shoulder. Captain Lyndhurst could have stopped him with a kick. There was no need to blow his head off.'

'I'm sure the good captain wished to make absolutely sure,' suggested the Master.

'With the Russian alive, Sir Nigel, we would have had the Soviet Union bang to rights, caught in the act. Without him, we have nothing that cannot be convincingly denied. In other words, the whole thing now has to be suppressed for ever.'

'How true,' nodded the spymaster, masticating thoughtfully on a mouthful of shortcake pastry and strawberries.

'Captain Lyndhurst happens to be the son of Lord Frinton.'

'Indeed. Frinton? Does one know him?'

'Apparently. You were at school together.'

'Really? There were so many. Hard to recall.'

'And I believe Julian Lyndhurst is your godson.'

'My dear John, you *do* check up on things, don't you now?'

Sir Nigel had finished his dessert. He steepled his hands, placed his chin on his knuckles and regarded the MI5 investigator steadily. The courtesy remained; the good humour was draining away. 'Anything else?'

Preston nodded gravely. 'An hour before the assault on the house went in, Captain Lyndhurst took a call in the hallway of the house across the road. I checked with my colleague who first took the phone. The caller was ringing from a call box.'

'No doubt one of his colleagues.'

'No, sir. They were using radios. And no-one outside that operation knew we were inside the house. None, that is, but a very few in London.'

'May I ask what you are suggesting?'

'Just one more detail, Sir Nigel. Before he died, that Russian whispered one word. He seemed very determined to get that single word out before he went. I had my ear close to his mouth at the time. What he said was: Philby.'

'Philby? Good heavens. I wonder what he could have meant by that.'

'I think I know. I think he thought Harold Philby had betrayed him, and I believe he was right.'

'I see. And may I be privileged to know of your deductions?' The Chief's voice was soft, but his tone was devoid of all his earlier bonhomie.

Preston took a deep breath. 'I deduce that Philby the traitor was a party to this operation, possibly from the outset. If he was, he would have been in a no-lose situation. Like others, I have heard it whispered that he wants to return home, here to England, to spend his last days.

'If the plan had worked, he could probably have earned his release from his Soviet masters and his entry from a Hard Left government in London. Perhaps a year from now. Or he could tell London the general outline of the plan, then betray it.'

'And which of these two remarkable choices do you suspect he made?'

'The second one, Sir Nigel.'

'To what end, pray?'

'To buy his ticket home. From this end. A trade.'

'And you think I would be a party to that trade?'

'I don't know what to think, Sir Nigel. I don't know what *else* to think. There has been talk . . . about his old colleagues, the magic circle, the solidarity of the establishment of which he was once a member . . . that sort of thing.' Preston studied his plate, with its half-eaten strawberries.

Sir Nigel gazed at the ceiling for a long time, before letting out a profound sigh. 'You're a remarkable man, John. Tell me, what are you doing this day week?'

'Nothing, I believe.'

'Then please meet me at the door of Sentinel House at eight of the morning. Bring your passport. And now, if you'll forgive me, I suggest we forego coffee in the library . . .'

The man in the upper window of the safe house in the Geneva back street stood and watched the departure of his visitor. The head and shoulders of the guest appeared below him; the man walked down the short path to the front gate and stepped into the road where his car waited.

The car's driver stepped out, came round the vehicle and opened the door for the senior man. Then he walked back to the driver's door.

Before he climbed back in, Preston raised his gaze to the figure behind the glass in the upper window. When he was behind the steering wheel he asked: 'That's him? That's really him? The man from Moscow?'

'Yes, that's him. And now, the airport, if you please,' replied Sir Nigel from the rear seat. They drove away.

'Well, John, I promised you an explanation,' said Sir Nigel a few moments later. 'Ask your questions.'

Preston could see the face of the Chief in his mirror. The older man was gazing out at the passing countryside. 'The operation?'

'You were quite right. It was mounted personally by the General Secretary with the advice and assistance of Philby. It seems it was called Plan Aurora. It *was* betrayed, but not by Philby.'

'Why was it blown away?'

Sir Nigel thought for several minutes. 'From quite an early stage I believed that you could be right. Both in your tentative conclusions in what is now called the Preston

Report of last December, and in your deductions after the intercept in Glasgow. Even though Harcourt-Smith declined to believe in either. I was not certain the two were linked, but I was not prepared to discount it. The more I looked at it, the more I became convinced that Plan Aurora was not a true KGB operation. It had not the hallmarks, the painstaking care. It looked like a hasty operation, mounted by a man or a group who distrusted the KGB. Yet there was little hope of your finding the agent in time.'

'I was floundering in the dark, Sir Nigel. And I knew it. There were no patterns of Soviet couriers showing up on any of our immigration controls. Without Winkler I'd never have got to Ipswich in time.'

They drove for several minutes in silence. Preston waited for the Master to resume in his own time.

'So, I sent a message to Moscow,' said Sir Nigel eventually.

'From yourself?'

'Good Lord, no. That would never have done. Much too obvious. Through another source, one I hoped would be believed. It was not a very truthful message, I'm afraid. Sometimes one must tell untruths in our business. But it went through a channel I hoped would be believed.'

'And it was?'

'Thankfully, yes. When Winkler arrived I was sure the message had been received, understood and, above all, believed as true.'

'Winkler was the reply?' asked Preston.

'Yes. Poor man. He believed he was on a routine mission to check on the Greeks and their transmitter. By the by, he was found drowned in Prague two weeks ago. Knew too much, I suppose.'

'And the Russian in Ipswich?'

'His name, I have just learned, was Petrofsky. A first-class professional, and a patriot.'

'But he too had to die?'

'John, it was a terrible decision. But unavoidable. The

arrival of Winkler was an offer, a proposal for a trade-off. No formal agreement, of course. Just a tacit understanding. The man Petrofsky could not be taken alive and interrogated. I had to go along with the unwritten and unspoken trade with the man in the window back there at the safe house.'

'If we had got Petrofsky alive, we'd have had the Soviet Union over a barrel.'

'Yes, John, indeed we would. We could have subjected them to a huge international humiliation. And to what end? The USSR could not have taken it lying down. They'd have had to reply, somewhere else in the world. What would you have wished? A return to the worst aspects of the Cold War?'

'It seems a pity to lose an opportunity to screw them, sir.'

'John, they're big and armed and dangerous. The USSR is going to be there tomorrow and next week and next year. Somehow we have to share this planet with them. Better they be ruled by pragmatic and realistic men than hot-heads and zealots.'

'And that merits a trade with men like the one in the window, Sir Nigel?'

'Sometimes it has to be done. I'm a professional, so is he. There are journalists and writers who would have it that we in our profession live in a dream world. In reality it's the reverse. It is the politicians who dream their dreams, sometimes dangerous dreams, like the General Secretary's dream of changing the face of Europe as his personal monument.

'A top intelligence officer has to be harder-headed than the toughest businessman. One has to trim to the reality, John. When the dreams take command one ends up with the Bay of Pigs. The first break in the Cuba missiles impasse was suggested by the KGB *rezident* in New York. It was Khrushchev, not the professionals, who had gone over the top.'

'So what happens next, sir?'

The old spymaster sighed. 'We leave it to them. There will be some changes made. They will make them in their own inimitable way. The man back there in the house will set them in train. His career will be advanced, that of others broken.'

'And Philby?' asked Preston.

'What about Philby?'

'Is he trying to come home?'

Sir Nigel shrugged impatiently. 'For years past,' he said. 'And, yes, he's in touch from time to time, covertly, with my people in our embassy over there. We breed pigeons . . .'

'Pigeons . . . ?'

'Very old-fashioned, I know. And simple. But still surprisingly efficient. That's how he communicates. But *not* about Plan Aurora. And even if he had . . . so far as I am concerned . . .'

'So far as you are concerned . . . ?'

'He can rot in hell,' said Sir Nigel softly.

They drove for a while in silence.

'What about you, John? Will you stay with "Five" now?'

'I don't think so, sir. I've had a good run. The DG retires on 1 September, but he'll take final leave next month. I don't fancy my chances under his successor.'

'Can't take you into "Six". You know that. We don't take late entrants. Thought of returning to Civvy Street?'

'Not the best time for a man of forty-six with no known skills to get a job nowadays,' said Preston.

'I have some friends,' mused the Master. 'They're in asset protection. They might be able to use a good man. I could have a word.'

'Asset protection?'

'Oil wells, mines, deposits, race horses. Things people want kept safe from theft or destruction. Even themselves. It would pay well. Enable you to take full care of that son of yours.'

'It seems I'm not the only one who checks up on things,' grinned Preston.

The older man was staring out of the window, as if at something far away and long ago. 'Had a son myself once,' he said quietly. 'Just the one. Fine lad. Killed in the Falklands. Know how you feel.'

With surprise Preston glanced at the man in the mirror. It had never occurred to him that this urbane and wily spymaster had once played horse-and-rider with a small boy on a sitting-room carpet.

'I'm sorry. Perhaps I'll take you up on that.'

They arrived at the airport, checked in the rented car and flew back to London, as anonymous as they had come.

The man in the window of the safe house watched the Britisher's car drive away. His own would not be there for an hour. He turned back to the room and sat down at the desk to study again the folder he had been brought and which he still held in his hands. He was pleased; it had been a good meeting and the documents he had would secure his future.

As a professional Lieutenant-General Yevgeni Karpov was sorry about Plan Aurora. It had been good: subtle, low-profile and effective. But also as a professional he knew that once an operation was well and truly burned there was nothing for it but to cancel and repudiate the whole thing before it was too late. To delay would have been utterly disastrous.

He recalled clearly the batch of documents that his bagman had brought from Jan Marais in London, the product of his agent Hampstead. Six had been the usual stuff, top-rate intelligence material such as only a man of the eminence of George Berenson could have acquired. The seventh had caused him to sit transfixed.

It was a personal memorandum from Berenson to Marais, for on-passing to Pretoria. In it the Defence Ministry official had told how, as Deputy Director of

Procurement, with special responsibility for nuclear devices, he had been present at a very restricted briefing by the Director-General of MI5, Sir Bernard Hemmings.

The counter-intelligence chief had told the small group that his agency had uncovered the existence and most of the details of a Soviet conspiracy to import in kit form, assemble and detonate a small atomic device inside Britain. The sting was in the tail: MI5 was closing fast upon the Russian 'illegal' in command of the operation in Britain, and was confident of catching him with all the necessary evidence upon him.

Entirely because of its source, General Karpov had believed the report completely. There was an immediate temptation to let the British go ahead; but second thoughts showed this to be disastrous. If the British succeeded alone and unaided, there would be no obligation to suppress the horrendous scandal. To create that obligation, he needed to send a message, and to a man who would understand what had to be done, someone he could deal with across the great divide.

Then there was the question of his personal self-advancement . . . It was after a long lonely walk in the spring-green forests of Peredelkino that he had decided to take the most dangerous gamble of his life. He had decided to pay his discreet visit to the private office of Nubar Gevorkovitch Vartanyan.

He had chosen his man with care. The Politburo member from Armenia was believed to be the man who headed the covert faction inside the Politburo that privately thought it was time for a change at the top.

Vartanyan had listened to him without saying a word, secure that he was far too highly placed for his office to be bugged. He just stared at the KGB general with his black lizard's eyes as he listened. When Karpov had finished, he had asked: 'You are certain your information is correct, Comrade General?'

'I have the full narrative from Professor Krilov on tape,'

said Karpov. 'The machine was in my briefcase at the time.'

'And the information from London?'

'Its source is impeccable. I have run the man personally for nearly three years.'

The Armenian power broker stared at him for a long time as if reflecting on many things, not least how this information could be used to advantage.

'If what you say is true, there has been recklessness and adventurism at the highest level in our country. If such could be proved, but one would need the proof, there might have to be changes at the top. Good day to you.'

Karpov had understood. When the man on the pinnacle in Soviet Russia fell, all his placemen fell with him. If there were changes at the top, there would be a vacant slot as Chairman of the KGB, a slot that Karpov felt would suit him admirably. But to cobble together his alliance of Party forces, Vartanyan would need proof, more proof, solid, irrefutable, documentary proof, that the act of recklessness had almost brought disaster. No-one had ever forgotten that Mikhail Suslov had toppled Khrushchev in 1964 on charges of adventurism over the 1962 Cuban missile crisis.

Shortly after the meeting Karpov had sent in Winkler, the most bumbling agent his files could unearth. His message had been read and understood. Now he held in his hands the proof his Armenian patron had needed. He looked through the documents again.

The report of the mythical interrogation and the confession of Major Valeri Petrofsky to the British would need some amendment, but he had people out at Yasyenevo who could accomplish that. The interrogation report forms were absolutely authentic, that was the main thing. Even Mr Preston's reports on his progress, suitably amended to exclude any mention of Winkler, were photocopies of the originals.

The General Secretary personally would not be able or willing to save the traitor Philby, nor, later, would he be able to save himself. Vartanyan would see to that, and he could not be ungrateful.

Karpov's car came to take him to Zürich and the Moscow plane. He rose. It had been a good meeting. And as always it had been rewarding to negotiate with Chelsea.

Epilogue

Sir Bernard Hemmings formally retired on 1 September 1987, although he had been on leave since mid-July. He died in November that year, his pension rights assured to the benefit of his wife and step-daughter.

Brian Harcourt-Smith did not succeed him as Director-General. The Wise Men took their soundings and though it was agreed there was nothing in the least sinister in Harcourt-Smith's attempts to pass the Preston Report no farther, or to discount the significance of the Glasgow intercept, it could not be avoided that these constituted two serious errors of judgement. There being no other discernible successor inside 'Five', a man was brought in from outside as Director-General. Mr Harcourt-Smith resigned some months later and joined the board of a merchant bank in the City.

John Preston retired in early September and joined the staff of the asset-protection people. His salary was more than doubled, enabling him to seek his divorce and make a strong case for the custody of his son Tommy, whose welfare and education he could now guarantee. Julia abruptly withdrew her objection and the custody was granted.

Sir Nigel Irvine retired, as scheduled, on the last day of the year, departing his office in time for Christmas. He went to live at his cottage at Langton Matravers where he joined fully in the life of the village and told anyone who asked that, prior to retirement, he had done 'something boring in Whitehall'.

Jan Marais was summoned to Pretoria in early December for consultations. As the Boeing 747 of South African Airlines lifted off from Heathrow, two burly NIS agents emerged from the flight-crew rest area and put handcuffs on him. He did not enjoy his retirement, the whole of which was spent several feet below ground level assisting teams of large gentlemen with their enquiries.

The arrest of Marais having taken place in public, news of it soon leaked out, which alerted General Karpov that his sleeper had been burned. He was confident Marais, alias Frikki Brandt, would not long resist the interrogators, and waited for the arrest of George Berenson and the consequent dismay in the Western Alliance.

In mid-December Berenson took early retirement from the Ministry, but there was no arrest. After the personal intervention of Sir Nigel Irvine, the man was allowed to retire to the British Virgin Islands on a small but adequate pension from his wife.

The news told General Karpov that his top agent had not only been blown, but turned as well. What he did not know was just *when* Berenson had been turned to the service of the British. Then, from inside his own *rezidentura* in London, KGB agent Andreyev reported he had heard a rumour to the effect Berenson had turned to MI5 from the very first approach Jan Marais had ever made to him.

Within a week the analysts at Yasyenevo had to accept that three years of what was actually perfectly good intelligence would have to be junked as suspect from the start.

It was the Master's last stroke.

THE END